THE BURDENS OF HEIRS

The Burdens of Heirs

Pembrook - Act I

Anais & Alexis

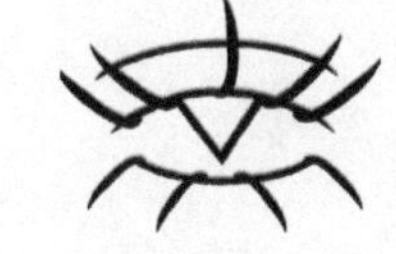

The Norns' Visions

The Burdens of Heirs
Pembrook – Act I

Published by The Norns' Visions

Hardcover Edition
ISBN: 979-8-9931379-2-6

Content Warning:

This series contains mature themes, including emotional, psychological, and interpersonal challenges. While handled with care, realism, and respect, certain moments may be intense for some readers.

A detailed list of content warnings, including chapter numbers for intimate scenes, can be found at the back of the book.

Language Note:

This book uses British English (e.g., *armour/colour/realise*) for immersion and to reflect the time and setting of the story.

In this world, Old Norse is often spoken between characters.
We render it phonetically (e.g., *kom thoo meth*) to reflect its sound
and use minimal special characters to ensure readability.

These lines will not be explained in the text unless a character within the story understands them.

In cases where Old Norse is understood, the lines may appear in italicized English—sometimes phonetically, sometimes fully translated—depending on what best serves the scene.
This is done to create a sense of language barrier and enhance immersion.

Important story information is never hidden exclusively within the Old Norse text;
translations or context will always be provide when necessary.

We do not speak Old Norse fluently, but have done our best to ensure that the translations are as accurate as possible.

The Old Norse used here follows *The Vikings of Bjornstad: Old Norse Dictionary* for vocabulary and orthography, with additional context taken from the *Poetic Edda*, one of the most important surviving sources of Old Norse myth and language. At times, wording may be adapted or made more poetic to suit narrative tone or clarity.

Our goal is to honor the spirit of the language and the culture it comes from to the best of our ability.

To the heart that refused its cage.

To the hearts that will never rest.

The Story's Weave

***Passage III:** Hjarta í Myrkri*

Heirs Hall

Voices of Worthyn

Power-wrought and sword-bred

—Ezekiel (eh-zeh-kee-el), The Iron Monarch, Lord Father
Ruler of Worthyn. Father of Vincent and Elias. Known for his brutality in the Perdyr—Worthyn War.

—Lilli (*li-lee*), The Absent Light, Deceased Queen
Mother of Vincent and Elias. Revered for her kindness and duty to the crown.

—Elias, The Devoted
Son of Lilli and Ezekiel. First Prince of Worthyn. Trained in the Northern War Camps.

—Vincent, The Fallen Heir
Son of Lilli and Ezekiel. Second Prince of Worthyn. Trained in the Northern War Camps.

—Nimble, The Jester, The Laughing Watcher

Voices of Pembrook

Faith-draped and peace-kept

—Mark "Phillip", The Reluctant Ruler
Honest King. Father of Adalja. Loving husband.

—Natja (*naht-yuh),* The Silent Fury
Wife of Mark. Known for her rigidity and firm hand.

—Adalja (*uh-dahl-yuh),* The One Born Watching
Princess of Pembrook. Poised and practised. Daughter of Mark and Natja.

—Brahms (*br-aw-mz*), The Cockwatcher, The Broken Shield
Loyal knight. Raised in service to Adalja. Mocked early for guarding chickens.

Voices of Ragnarvik
Salt-stained and rune-led

—Dagrun (*dag-roon)*, The Drowned Flame
Jarl of Ragnarvik. Proud father of Olivja. Loving husband, drunken mind.

—Solvig (*soul-veeg)*, The Grieving Flame
Highwife Völva. Mother of Olivja. Wife to Dagrun.

—Olivja (*oh-leev-yah)*, The Flame Bearer
Dottir of Ragnarvik. Proud Pagan. Mother of Loki.

MIDHELM

"A curse by any other name is still love."

Passage I: Ljósbringa

[Where the Heart Opens]

Thread I

ᚦᛖ ᛒᚢᚱᛞᛖᚾᛋ ᛟᚠ ᚺᛖᛁᚱᛋ ᚦᛖ ᛒᚢᚱᛞᛖᚾᛋ ᛟᚠ ᚺᛖᛁᚱᛋ ᚦᛖ ᛒᚢᚱᛞᛖᚾᛋ

ᚨᛞᚨᛚᛃᚨ

A flash of white tore through Pembrook's polished stone halls—a streak against the candle-lit dark. Banners snapped overhead in the wind that poured through arched windows, their silken blues and whites rippling like waves.

Her nightgown clung where sweat dampened it and fluttered loose elsewhere—a white-and-blue whisper of defiance. Boot-laces bit into her ankles with every pounding step, but she didn't slow.

"Stop!"
The shout cracked through the air.
She didn't stop—didn't turn to look. She couldn't afford to.

"Princess Adalja!"
The voice grew closer.

She risked a glance over her shoulder; firelight flashed in her pale eyes as she glared at three knights thundering after her. Their armour rattled and groaned, torchlight flickering gold and silver across polished steel—shadows chased her heels.

Facing forward again, she fisted the hem of her nightgown, hiking it higher despite how it bared her legs and fluttered indecently. Her breath came hot and ragged; her chest ached from the sprint, deep-blue cloak snapping like a sail behind her. Dark curls streamed like a banner of rebellion, wild in the corridor wind. Her blue eyes burned sharp and unblinking—desperate.

The garden doors loomed ahead, carved oak framed by stone archways etched with faded prayers. She slammed into them and burst through.
Night hit her like a slap.

Cold air knifed through the thin cotton, chilling sweat on her skin. Dew-slick grass bowed beneath her boots. The castle gardens sprawled, moon-washed and ghostly, statues of saints standing watch.

She didn't stop to marvel. It was nothing special.

"Helga!" Her voice cracked. "Come!"

A shrill whinny pierced the silence, followed by a flicker of motion at the stables—then a blur of grey. Her mare.

Helga thundered from the shadows, feathered hooves tearing the earth, blue eyes bright with recognition. Her dark mane whipped as she searched for her rider.

Adalja ran to meet her.

Helga bore no saddle. No bridle. It was the middle of the gods-damned night. But it didn't matter.

She grabbed the mane and jumped—missed.

"Princess!"

The knights were close enough now to see the panic in their faces.

Gods, please—

She jumped again, every muscle straining, and landed hard against Helga's back. She clung tight, heart thundering against the mare's spine, then laughed—breathless and wild.

"Go, Helga! Go!"

And they were gone.

The wind howled past her ears. Her cloak streamed behind her like a torn flag. The rhythm of hooves was the only sound she trusted.

Behind her, the courtyard exploded in motion—scrambling knights, whinnying horses, doors slamming open.

But they were too late.

She disappeared into the night.

They tore through the castle gates, then down the winding paths of Pembrook's lower town. Cobblestones blurred beneath them, rooftops vanished behind. Moonlight clung to the narrow streets, silvering every shuttered window and ivy-laced wall.

Adalja leaned forward, her fingers tangled in Helga's mane, the sting of tears barely held back against the cold wind.

She knew exactly what waited in Fairtide.

And she couldn't wait any longer to find it.

SHE SLOWED HELGA TO A QUIET TROT as they neared the southern gates—tall stone guardians looming over the trade town. Adalja drew her hood low, letting shadow cloak her features. The gate guards barely lifted their heads as she passed, eyes glazed with boredom or drink.

After stabling Helga, she slipped into the night, hugging the cold walls like a drifting wraith.

Tonight, the trade port was alive again.

Far from what it used to be and even further from what it had become.

It was wild. Loud. Joyous. *United.*

Before the war, Fairtide was a living thing—bustling with voices, bartering hands, music, and sea wind. But that life had withered.

War hollowed it, leaving a ghost town where merchants desperately clung to life and empty stalls haunted the marketplace. Its role as the lifeblood of Midhelm's commerce, destroyed.

But not tonight.

Tonight was different.

The Harvest Moon hung high, full and amber, bathing the town in gold. Every corner of Fairtide came alive. All of Midhelm gathered here. They filled the streets with laughter and dancing, masks and cloaks swirling through the shadows.

Painted faces grinned under lantern light, their features twisting with joy or menace—depending on how the firelight struck.

The cobblestone streets, damp with the ocean's kiss, glistened under ropes of lanterns strung between rooftops and wooden posts. Turnips carved into ghoulish faces glowed with flickering fire from within, perched on windowsills, barrels, and crooked fence posts.

Down by the harbor, drakkars rocked in rhythm with the tide, their carved prows glinting like beasts under moonlight. The docks pulsed with music—drums thumping, lutes plucking, voices singing in languages she didn't know but yearned to understand. The sea wind was sharp, but the heat of bodies, fires, and ale staved off the chill.

Vendors hawked roasted nuts, game, sugared fruit, and fresh loaves. Children in fox masks shrieked and chased each other with wooden swords.

Royals, farmers, warriors, whores, wanderers—all were welcomed.

That meant the *Pagans were here*, too.

That was why she had come.

For them. For their day.

Skuggadagr, they called it. The Day of Shadows.

She'd heard the name whispered by knights in the Pembrook halls, always with a measure of disdain or unease. But Adalja had only ever been intrigued.

She was enchanted by the Norse—by their freedom, their fearlessness, the way they lived and died without apology. She often dreamt of them: blurred, wild things full of ritual, gods, and ale. A life so warm, so familiar, it felt like both memory and prophecy.

Norse life was nothing like court life—no endless rituals, no stifling religion, no rules or responsibilities pressed into her shoulders like stone.

So tonight, she would taste something different. Not as Princess Adalja of Pembrook.

Tonight, she would be a shadow in Fairtide.

Because her family owned the port, Pembrook banners—the winged broadsword in proud white and blue—fluttered from every rooftop and tower like a silent watcher, judging her every move.

She stuck to the alleys—ducking behind barrels, crawling over puddles of mead, creeping past old carts—all while hiding her silks beneath the folds of a commoner's cloak.

"Skal!" — "Skal, yeg kepee vith thig ath botneenum!"

Adalja peeked over the edge of a sticky ale barrel; fingertips slick with the drink.

At the end of the alley, two Norsemen leaned together, tankards raised, laughter booming. They tossed back the last of their ale, gasping and howling with satisfaction before turning back towards the barrel she leaned against.

She yelped softly and ducked down beneath the rim.

"They say Ragnarvik agreed to marriage—"

*"Feefl...*poor whelp. They hope she'll kill from within, aye?"

The barrel jolted as they roared with laughter.

Adalja barely heard the words, her heart hammering in her chest so loud it drowned out the rest. She crouched lower, breath shallow. And yet—

Gods, she was smiling.

She peeked back over the edge, blue eyes wide with wonder.

What was it about them that pulled her so fiercely?

Her family had forbidden her from visiting the Ragnarvik lands, forbade her from even setting foot in Fairtide without an escort. No number of lectures or refusals had shaken the hunger from her bones. She had tasted this place many times as a child; now it was all she could think about.

She wanted it. All of it. She wanted *to be* one of them.

The coast cleared.

She crept out from behind the barrel, ready to dart to a new hiding place, limbs light with excitement. She leaned forward—

YANK.

A gloved hand clamped over her mouth and dragged her behind the barrels. She screamed, or tried to. The leather glove muffled her entirely.

Gods, no. They found me!

She kicked. She thrashed. She bit down on the middle finger of the glove.

"Damn you, Adalja!"

She froze. The hand yanked away, and she whirled around.

Brahms slumped back against the wall, armoured knees spread, dark curls plastered with sweat. He yanked his glove away, inspecting his hand with a scowl. Head tilted, he gazed up through his lashes.

"You bit me...like a *cursed* rat—"

Before he could finish, she lunged forward. The princess leaned between his legs, hand clamped over his mouth.

"Would you be quiet?" she hissed.

Their eyes locked.

His skin gleamed like polished copper in the firelight—his dark eyes, furious—but she saw the worry beneath them. For a fleeting moment, she nearly felt sorry.

Nearly.

He was her knight. Though not like any sworn knight—he was hers, and hers alone.

They were raised together, though he was two years older. Brahms knew her since before she could read, back when she still clung to her nursemaid's skirts and cried at thunderstorms. He was meant to protect her. Sworn to it. Shaped for it.

And yet, more often than not, he was chasing her, not guarding her.

He pulled her hand from his mouth. "You must return to Pembrook—"

"*Gods*, Brahms, don't start."

"Gods?" He scoffed. "You spend two breaths in Fairtide and start speaking in tongues?" His voice was low as he peeked around the barrel.

"Oh, I wish for more than to speak their language," she smirked, teeth tugging her lip, eyes alight. "Join me or trot home...empty-handed...*again*."

His mouth dropped open. *The audacity*.

But then—*why was he surprised*?

Before he could respond, Adalja slipped around the barrels, disappearing into the crowd, music, and firelight.

"ADDY—!" he whisper-shouted after her, but she was gone.

Gone into Fairtide. Gone into Skuggadagr.

And Brahms, as always, gave chase.

She smiled to herself as she took it all in, spinning through the revelry, desperate to not miss a thing. Not the topless ladies, or the toppling drunkards, or the tapping dancers.

Laughter rang like bells above the deeper notes of lutes and drums. Smoke, spice, sea-salt thickened the air. Lantern flames caught on gold bangles, sweat-slicked brows, the rims of raised horns.

Heavens, was this what it felt like to live? To truly live?

At the centre of the trade town, a building older than the rest loomed through the lantern light—a hulking wooden tavern with sagging beams and iron-bound doors. Moss climbed its stones like ivy, and its thatched roof dipped low, heavy with age and storm.

Adalja's grin widened as she caught sight of its swinging sign: **Odin's Horn**—runes carved deep beneath the name, glowing faintly from the torch set just above it.

It was a stubborn relic of Fairtide's fleeting glory, a tavern worn but unyielding amidst the wreckage of war. And it was full—lit from within like a hearth.

She stepped up the wooden steps, barely dodging a drunk woman pushing through the door, the lively sounds spilling into the space until the door shut on its own.

Adalja glanced back, chuckling at Brahms as he struggled to get through the crowd.

The princess pushed open the heavy door, the wood creaking loud enough to draw a few heads.

Inside the tavern pulsed—Norse folk pressed shoulder to shoulder, tankards clashing, songs shouted more than sung. Men and women alike danced between the tables, some standing on them, some passed out under them. A group in the corner played a fast, furious tune on bone flutes and hide-drums, the rhythm primal and infectious.

Furs lined the benches. Spears and axes hung on the walls like decorations. The fire pit in the centre roared high, surrounded by a ring of half-naked warriors playing some drunken game involving knives and empty mugs. Someone had painted a crude god on the ceiling in ash and wine.

Adalja's eyes shone.

"This," she said, breath stolen, "is glorious!"

Brahms grunted beside her, hand never far from his hilt.

They pushed their way to a small table near the back, half-shadowed beneath an iron sconce dripping with wax. Adalja sat first, peeling back her hood, sweat curling her hair against her cheeks.

Brahms remained standing a moment longer, scanning the room, jaw tight. Then he sat beside her with a resigned sigh.

Before they could speak, a shadow blocked the firelight.

A tall figure approached their table—a woman, towering and broad-shouldered, clothed in a bright tunic and patchworked furs that hung heavy with the scent of fire and wind.

Her arms were thick with muscle, inked in faint runes and old scars—a silver ring pierced her brow, catching the torchlight as she moved.

"Well, well," she drawled, voice deep, amused, thick with the Norse accent. "An honour to host a princess."

Adalja froze; Brahms tensed.

The woman leaned down slightly, her grin wolfish. "You're a long way from home, dove."

Dove, she grimaced. She never liked being called that.

Brahms straightened beside her, shoulders stiffening, his hand drifting low towards the hilt at his belt.

The woman's dark eyes slid to him, glinting with amusement.
"Easy, metal-bones. The Pembrooks are guests here."

Adalja blinked. Her name had not been uttered beyond her kingdom's walls in years. Yet this woman saw her—knew her.

"We...we are?" she asked.

"Of course." The woman's smile remained, though her gaze turned curious. "Though it's been many moons since one of your kind graced our floors. I didn't expect you to come slinking in like some half-starved warrior lookin' for mead...or maybe a kiss."

The fire behind them cracked, throwing gold across the wood.

Adalja glanced down at her ale-stained hands, then raised her chin with a dangerous little smile.

"Perhaps I'm here for...*both*?"

"Adalja!" Brahms gasped.

The woman barked out a laugh and brought her hand down hard on Adalja's shoulder. The strike nearly sent her forward into the table.

"I like this one!" the woman announced, loud enough for the entire tavern to hear. Then she turned towards the ale-sellers, shouting something in throaty Norse as she strode away, her laugh trailing behind her like smoke.

Adalja bit her lip, electric with thrill, and looked at Brahms, whose face had gone pale.

"Your mother...is going to have my head," he said.

Two brimming tankards thudded onto their table moments later.

Adalja ignored Brahms' ever-present worry, sliding the mug towards him with a knowing smile, a single brow raised.

"Not if we drown in drink first," she cooed, waiting for that hidden, mischievous spark in Brahms to catch fire. It always did, eventually.

They locked eyes.

Five heartbeats. That's all it took. Then his hand moved, fast, grasping the mug like a challenge.

The tavern swallowed them whole.

Ales spilled like tides over beaten tables, soaking wood and boots alike. Roaring laughter and music clashed in the rafters. Adalja—cheeks flushed and curls untamed—surrendered herself to the pulse of the night. Her dress, once delicate, was now a tapestry of spilled drink and reckless joy; it swayed around her knees as she twirled and spun.

Brahms had long since surrendered to the chaos, one hand locked with a laughing woman, the other held by a bearded man stomping in rhythm beside him. He spun, stumbled, and bellowed with laughter, and Adalja nearly fell over from the sight.

No one seemed to care who they were.

Maybe, in this moment, they weren't out of place at all.

Eventually, the Norsewoman returned—not with more drink, but with a smirk sharp as a dagger.

She stopped at their table and tilted her head, eyes gleaming.

"Your knight seems far more at home than you," she said, arms crossed, voice low and bemused. "Or is that the mead speaking to him?"

She sat across from Adalja, fingers drumming on the ale-stained wood. Her muscles tensed and rippled.

Adalja didn't answer.

Her gaze was locked on Brahms, drunk and dancing, laughter in his throat. She was too busy watching the way the firelight caught in his curls, too enchanted by the sight of him—of them all—so free.

"Why are you here, Heir of Pembrook?" the woman asked, more pointedly now. "You sneak around like a thief, yet all you steal are glances..."

Adalja turned at last, blue eyes distant.

"It is...a strange warmth," she murmured. "To glimpse a life that will never be mine."

Her fingers fidgeted under the table, clenching and unclenching in her lap.

The barkeep's gaze narrowed.

"*Ah*...it wounds me, truly," she said, rising from the bench with a grunt, the wood groaning under her strength. "To see someone, so young, convinced the world's carved in stone."

She dusted her lap and tilted her head at Adalja.

"We are not so different, Shield-folk and Faith-borns. Men drew lines in the sand and called them kingdoms—named some holy, noble—named others dirty, uncivilised. But the sea? She does not obey such lines. She devours them, reclaims them...*changes* them. Why not you?"

Adalja blinked.

"Do not let your title bind you," the woman went on, voice softer now, almost reverent. "Do not let silk and scripture chain your soul. You are not thread in your mother's loom. You are not bound by banners."

She leaned forward slightly, eyes fierce.

"You are no line in the sand, Princess Adalja."
Her voice lowered to a whisper, as if casting a spell:

"Be the oceans. *Be the waves.*"

And with that, the barkeep was gone, vanishing into the firelight and shadow, swallowed by the song of the night.

Adalja sat for a long moment, the words echoing in her bones, in the beat of her pulse. The air smelled of salt and sweat and fire. Somewhere, Brahms shouted her name with joy, calling her back to the dance.

And for the first time in her life...

She thought she might belong somewhere other than Pembrook.

The hours blurred. Laughter gave way to low murmurs, music to softer songs. The fire in the hearth burned low, casting long shadows across empty mugs and weary shoulders.

Eventually, Brahms returned to her, cheeks flushed, curls damp with sweat, his grin softened by exhaustion. He dropped into the seat beside her with a grunt, groaning like an old man as he leaned back, arm draping around Adalja's shoulders.

"Me thinks I've been kissed by half the tavern," he muttered, though there wasn't a shred of exasperation, only happiness.

Adalja smiled, then stood. "Come on then...before I have to fight a barbarian for you..."

They slipped from Odin's Horn with the tide of the night, stepping out into the cold Fairtide air. The celebration hummed in distant corners, but the streets near the tavern had quieted.

Side by side, beneath fluttering lanterns and the hush of the sea wind, the princess and her knight walked back towards the city stables.

Not as nobility. Not as shield-folk.

Just two souls who had tasted something freer than they were meant to.

THREAD II

ᚦᛖ ᛒᚢᚱᛞᛖᚾᛋ ᛟᚠ ᚺᛖᛁᚱᛋ ᚦᛖ ᛒᚢᚱᛞᛖᚾᛋ ᛟᚠ ᚺᛖᛁᚱᛋ ᚦᛖ ᛒᚢᚱᛞᛖᚾᛋ

ᛟᛚᛁᚡᛃᚨ

THE AMBER-EYED HEIRESS gazed downwards at the leatherbound diary resting atop her wooden desk. Her name, Olivja, was carved across the front in runes.

Her tanned fingers brushed the cover with care, hesitating.
To open it meant risking the tide of feeling that would spill out through her quill.

Her feelings were too vast—too magnificently strong—to release half-heartedly.

Writing was not typical for warriors. Nor was drawing. Those were "noble pastimes"; Eastern and Western things.

But the Ragnarviks were far more than just warriors.

Settled decades ago in the southern parts of Midhelm, many had traded their sea-faring gear for pitchforks and ploughs, fishing nets and hammers. They were a peaceful, honourable folk, known for their quiet strength and resilience.

No longer did they set out hoping for land or villages to conquer. Instead, they settled—choosing freedom and rest.

Olivja, however, was the Dottir of Ragnarvik, the Jarl's daughter, Dagrun and Solvig's wild heir—and therefore, she had no rest.

There were moments when she envied the simple life—free of title, free of burden. Though daughter to the Jarl and heir to the high seat of Ragnarvik, most days she was alone.

The hirdmen passed her in the halls like drifting ghosts, and her dire-wolf shadow was often the only soul that stayed close.

And with her father either drunk on mead or lost in old songs, shoulders heavy with the pressures of ruling.

She answered the villagers' pleas. Balanced ledgers. Sent aid where it was needed. Wrote treaties. Filed taxes. Oversaw grain shipments.

And worst of all—she wove.

Tapestries. Banners. Blankets.

Gods. So. Much. Weaving.

Yet no amount of thread could untangle the knots her family had frayed into.

The Jarl's loyalty to a northern ally's ten-year war had drained them of everything—silver, horses, warriors, *patience.*

What began as an oath of brotherhood had become a pit with no bottom. And still, her father refused to pull back, refused to see what the kingdom had become.

Ragnarvik's people were proud, but pride did not fill bellies.

They were the strongest warriors of Midhelm, but even warriors bled.

And now, they bled hungry, tired, and aimless.

Olivja had warned him, argued, *begged*.

But her father had built his rule on crumbling stone, and now it was caving in. Though the crown had not yet touched her brow, she walked with fate coiled at her heels.

She pressed her palm to the rune-carved cover and exhaled.

Something shifted in the air. A decision had been made behind closed doors again—one she wouldn't like.

So...she'd write later.

A gentle knock at her wooden door pulled her attention away from her thinking.

Loki, her wolf, slowly lifted his head from where he lay on the bed, giving a few shakes that sent puffs of grey fur drifting through the room.

He whined in response to her standing, and she clicked her tongue to quiet him. Two maids entered her room, and Olivja's posture relaxed in the presence of familiar faces.

She never had to put on a show for her caretakers the way she did for others. The white-haired maid, Edith, her Amma—grandmother—slowly entered the room, confusion painting her wrinkled face.

"Lady Olivja?" She called to the heiress, her voice raspy with time. "Have you not begun your preparations?"

Her eyes narrowed and shifted to the younger maid, who went straight for the wardrobe. Olivja's hip-length hair whipped around as she turned, the woven braids, meticulously weaved throughout, hit her sides and biceps in the process.

Her hair was thick and unruly, a true testament to her Norse heritage, always braided in some way, but left to fall freely down her back like a warrior's mane.

"Preparations...? For bed?" Olivja asked, equally confused. She stepped closer to the eldest caretaker, "...speak plain, *Amma*?"

Even though she was painfully responsible for so much, she was not yet the Jarl. Olivja was often left playing catch up to plans made without her knowing.

Naturally, her tone heightened with suspicion as the other maid began grabbing things left and right from her wardrobe.

"W-what is the meaning of this!?" Olivja's tone hardened, and in turn, her wolf nervously shifted, sensing the shift in her demeanor.

A heavy sigh left her Amma's lips as she took deliberate steps towards the oak bed, resting her aged frame for a moment.

Given the long pause and her effort to get comfortable before continuing, Olivja braced for the worst.

"Highborne, the Jarl has come upon a...*convenient* solution to aid our allies and free our jarldom of debt." Edith began, hardly able to make eye contact with Olivja as she spoke honestly, "Forgive us. We assumed he told you."

"You've lived long enough to know not to assume such foolishness," Olivja uttered. Her voice carried a melodic cadence, though oftentimes a hint of her father's hard, guttural accent slipped through, giving her speech a unique, almost musical quality.

"Your father has arranged your marriage," Edith's words floated in the air like an evil spirit, filling the room with a dark weight.

"With one of the Worthyn Heirs."

There it is.

Olivja closed her eyes while her sweating fingers clutched the fabric of her tunic-dress, beige with red accents.

Worthyn; the royal kingdom responsible for the war. Of course it boiled down to *this*.

The woman's anger was growing, and she knew better than to take it out on the messenger.

"Where is he?" She asked, not needing to hear any more. Her father would tell her all.

"His study." Edith replied gently, her hand patting Loki's scruff.

Donning her robe, Olivja stormed from her quarters, stomping barefoot down the pelt covered halls.

Over thirty winters had passed since the Ragnarvik first landed in Midhelm—long enough for wood to rot and stone to rise in its place. What was once a wooden longhouse had become a sprawling keep. At twenty-one, Olivja had grown with the keep, and she took pride in that fact.

Red banners with the brown Ragnarvik crest, the Ragnarvik rune, fluttered with her movement. The nearer to her father's study, the more hirdmen—the Ragnarvik guards—lined the walls.

His study was nothing more than a dusted room full of scrolls, trashed with empty barrels and chalices, mappings of the seas and stars, and carvings of the old gods. Her hands pushed open the large wooden doors and sleeping near the arched open window was Jarl Ragnarvik.

The dark haired, tan-skinned, darkly tattooed, majesty slouched over his oak desk, flask in hand, snoring atop a stack of relevant decrees and poetry.

"*Pabbi*," she called to him gently at first, keeping her distance.

He didn't respond, so she came closer.

"Dagrun!...*Fodir!*"
She yelled a few more times, and finally—her father sat up quickly, gasping sharply.

"Wha-...what..?" he grumbled, sitting back in his chair, sniffling as his thick dark braid swayed in turn.

When his dark eyes fell on his dottir, he sighed and brought the flask to his lips once more, his lip ring softly clinked against the lip.

"What've I told ye about comin' in here, *eh*?" His voice was slurred, heavy and thick with an accent that struck the air like Thor's hammer, rumbling deep in his chest, the power of the ancients fuelling his words.

But all that power was as *wasted* as he was.

She ignored his drowsy warning, moving on with her line of questioning. "Share with me what you *have not* told me, fodir. What have you done?"

"Please, Liv, *verdum ver ber-yast svona snema?*" The Jarl tossed back another swig of mead, grumbling in their tongue. He said *Liv* like *leave*, the "i" long and sharp. *Must we fight so early?*

The question made her scoff.

The man was too drunk to even realise what time it was.

"The sun set hours ago!" Olivja shouted, breathing quickly, anger boiling.

There was a brief silence as her father glanced out the window, the harvest moon was out and beaming through the window, illuminating the room in a soft glow. The Jarl slowly looked back to his daughter and set down the flask—*for once.*

Standing from his chair, he leaned his tall, thick frame up against the desk, looking down to the papers he was sleeping on. "King Worthyn and I have been discussing the finalization of our alliance—"

"No..." She whimpered.
He continued.

"He'll be sending a carriage for you and I...We'll plan the wedding details upon'rarrival," he sighed, slurring his words. His tattooed hands weakly wiped his eyes, clearing his throat as though preparing for his daughter's inevitable anger.

He was right to prepare.

"No! I refuse!" she shouted.

As her hands shakily held her robe at her chest, she searched his eyes for any receptiveness. There was none.

"It is carved in stone, Olivja," he said.

Perhaps if she wasn't so angry, she would have been able to acknowledge the tinge of remorse that hung on his words.

"But—" she had nothing to say. If he was being truthful, then there was nothing she *could* say.

Her tearful eyes, be it by willpower or shock, kept from overflowing throughout the conversation.

Her father was gazing down at the documents on his desk, not able to look her in her warm eyes. Without looking, she knew what he was reading; the agreement between the kings. A shaky sigh left her lips.

She felt betrayed. Olivja had done everything she could to help her jarldom, and in the end her father would still resort to giving her away.

No...not her *father*.
She trusted him...her father knew how she felt about marriage, about *the Worthyns*. This decision was not solely on his shoulders.

"*Hvar er Mama*?" Olivja quickly demanded, asking where her mother was, releasing her shawl as her hands fell in fists at her sides.

"Do not bother her with this, child—"

"Then I'll go to her myself!" she said, turning swiftly out of the study, leaving her father to drunkenly grieve over the choice he had agreed to.

Stupid. That's what she was for going to her father instead of her mother. He was clueless...The Highwife was not.

When she arrived at the Jarl's Quarters, a hird was positioned directly in front of the bronze plated doors. He stood solid, cloaked in a bright red tunic and a dark woollen cape, firmly gripping a spear with a deadly iron tip. Every scar, every mark on his armour, spoke of loyalty and battle, bound to protect the Ragnarvik Jarldom.

"By all means, keep standing there," Olivja grumbled at him, breathing heavily after walking so quickly across the keep.

All of the Ragnarvik hirdmen respected the heiress deeply—even in her worsts. They understood her struggles and often witnessed them firsthand.

Her mother and father never laid a hand on her, only severely chastised. Apart from her moments fighting against injustices, Olivja was a good daughter, pagan, and heir.

"The Highwife Völva wishes to be alone, Highborne," the hird casually warned her, using the proper title for her mother.

Völva, a witch of the Norse ways, was a role everyone respected highly. Though her duties as a seeress were reduced in the jarldom, the Highwife was a powerful woman with widespread influence, enough to scare even the bravest of shield-folk, including Olivja.

However...despite the warning, he stepped aside from the door, chuckling, as if he knew he couldn't stop her from entering—or perhaps he didn't want to try.

"Don't say I didn't warn you, *Jarl's Dottir,*" he said beneath his breath, crossing his spear across his chest.

She stepped past and upon entering her mother's room, the Jarl's Dottir immediately understood why her mother was so adamant on alone time.

Sitting on the side of her bed, feet flat on the floor, was the ginger haired highwife in nothing but an open, lace robe. Standing directly in front of the Ragnarvik highwife was a blonde maid, her gown resting on the floor at her ankles.

Olivja practically choked at the sight, freezing in place at the door. The maid gasped, making eye contact with the heiress, quickly trying to cover her naked frame

"Ah-ah-ah, eyes on me," the highwife cooed in Norse, grabbing the maid's chin. She angled the woman's face back towards her and smiled, *"Your gaze is mine."*

The dottir looked away from the scene, down to her fists as she tried her best to ignore the wet-smacking sounds that floated from the bed.

Olivja had walked in on her mother's affairs before—too many times, always by accident. Highwife Solvig never tried to hide her interest in women. If anything, she flaunted it.

Olivja figured that was why Dagrun drank. However, it was still clear to *everyone* that her mother loved her father...*in some strange way*...Liv never dared ask for the details.

"AHEM. I'd like a word, Highwife," Olivja interrupted, her hands clenching and unclenching at her sides, "*Alone.*"

Her voice deepened, turned sharper when she spoke their tongue...*and she loved it.*

The kissing stopped and a heavy sigh left the highwife's lips. "W*e'll continue this later...go seek my husband."* She sighed to the maid and Olivja slowly lifted her eyes.

She watched as the young woman scrambled to get her dress back over her shoulders. The maid's blush brightened her cheeks as she swiftly bolted from the room, shutting the heir and the highwife together.

Solvig stood from the bed and walked to her wooden vanity, her long wavy red hair covering her backside from being exposed through her sheer robe. Her mother sighed repetitively, making it known that Olivja had disappointed her. That, or she was mentally preparing for her daughter's tirade.

Olivja got right to the point. *"A marriage. Mama, how could you?"*

Despite her confidence, she was anxious confronting her mother—*everyone was.*

"Olivja, you knew this would happen one day...please. I can't handle your anger," Her mother spoke softly, gazing into her reflection in a polished bronze plate.

Her green eyes were sunken, dark circles edged them, but she was as beautiful as ever. The highwife cleaned the smeared liptint across her lips and the coal beneath her eyes.

Her nonchalant behaviour was enraging...but she was always this way. Nothing ever upset her mother.

"I have every right to be furious..." the heiress said beneath her breath, crossing her arms.

"Oh? Your Pabbi wishes to bring an end to the war and you are furious?" Solvig continued, her tone dark.

"I wish for the end as well—but mother, to the Worthyns!? To damn faith-borns!? This is CRUEL!" Olivja's volume peaked, appalled that her mother was willing to give her up, it didn't matter if it was to a friend or not.

"Cruel..." the highwife repeated with a scoff, in disbelief. *"Olivja...you should be grateful."*

Solvig shot her a glance over her shoulder, an all-knowing glance.

"You and I both know you'll never be content with marriage," she said. *"This isn't about your wishes—it's about our people, about keeping peace. Your father chose wisely."*

"But, this is not being done by his hands...YOU fed him this solution!" Olivja shouted, shaking with anger. *"Mama, I swear it—I can make this right without a man's name tied to mine—"*

"You cannot, Olivja. Not this," her mother replied quietly.

She finally turned to face her daughter, with a displeased, saddened gaze.

"Should we have given you the false hope of choice, I regret it," Solvig spoke, crossing her arms. *"But understand—you hold no power in these things...not without a man at your side."*

Olivja hated hearing that. Her fists trembled with restraint—any tighter, and she'd scar herself.

"You let me bear the weight of the jarldom, yet deny me the right to choose my own mate?" Her responses were increasingly passive, irritation growing.

"That is enough, Olivja..." Her mother sighed again, running her hands through her long hair, *"The decision for you to marry a Worthyn boy has been set in stone for many moons."*

The highwife stepped closer, words echoing, *"Your hand is bound to the peace of our kingdoms. Refusal will stain your conscience with innocent blood. Is that what you wish to bear?"*

Olivja had a hard time processing those words.

The thought that she was nothing more than a bartering tool was so cruel and yet, the heiress knew they were true, so she said nothing.

If her marriage truly meant the end of the war...how *could* she refuse?

"You shall marry. And when your hand is given to Vincent, and the war lies behind us, then perhaps freedom will be yours to taste."

The heiress shuddered.

"Vincent...?" She repeated the name with a tearful scoff, remembering the name of the Worthyn boy she had spent far too much time with. Her closest thing to a friend apart from her wolf.

Heavy tears poured down her cheeks. Trembling, Olivja's hands clenched the sides of her nightgown.

"But...He...he wants no part of me—Mama, I—"

Her mother walked back to her bed, sighing as she rubbed her temples with two fingers.

"If not this, then what, Olivja? Say it. Tell me," Solvig hissed, running her hands down across her face, *"If you hold the key to ease our people's hunger and fatigue, speak."*

She gripped the edge of her mattress, closing her eyes tightly. *"Soon our people will be looking for answers, the same as you—they know not why we fight alongside Worthyn. They've lost sight of the meaning of it, of their struggles, of this battle."*

Solvig paused, opening her eyes to stare down at the fur rug at her toes. *"Without this marriage, we will not only lose the war but our peoples' support...all that we have fought for will crumble. They question your father's hold on his Jarlship—would you have him fall for your want of freedom?"*

Olivja went quiet again, apart from the heavier cries that left her quivering lips.

"No...gods, no," Olivja cried, finally releasing her dress. Her hands came up to her face and she wiped desperately at her tears, a poor attempt at composing herself.

The highwife watched the young woman sob at the door and for a split moment, Solvig's face filled with pity. Slowly, she silently stalked towards her whimpering daughter. Without another word she pulled Olivja into her arms, weakly hugging her with a sigh.

"*My little valk...*" Her mother's tone was soft now, as it always was when speaking to her in their native tongue. Nostalgia bloomed in her chest—warm and aching.

She gently stroked the top of her head while Olivja clung to her chest, *"The world shows no mercy to women like us. The sooner you bow to this truth, the sooner peace will find you."*

But Olivja couldn't accept it.

"You do this not for yourself, nor solely for your father," the highwife mumbled, sharp and collected, *"This marriage will turn the tide of battle."*

Olivja's eyes watered against her mother's warmth, but she nodded, understanding every word.

"You will become their guiding flame—for the nobles, for the clans, for the warriors and knights."

Her chin was directed up to her mother's face.

To her surprise, the highwife did not have a gentle expression like her words, she looked pained, heartbroken.

"Our lands united will bring peace to the broken," she said. Solvig's chilled gaze pierced through her daughter's vulnerable frame.

She continued with a whisper, now in common tongue: "Your hand belongs to Vincent, to Worthyn...Do not forget it."

As the heiress looked into the highwife's face, a cold chill ran down her back.

She was naive to come to her mother and expect any change. Olivja was left feeling worse than before, tucking her tail between her legs.

"Yes, Modir." Olivja said, no longer crying.

"Good." Her mother dropped her chin, turning to return to her nightly routine.
"Now be gone—and dry your eyes before they break your father's heart."

Olivja said nothing more.

She walked out with her mother's perfume still clinging to her skin—and the weight of a Ragnarvik's legacy rotting on her shoulders.

THREAD III

ᚨᛞᚨᛚᛃᚨ

"LADY ADALJA." Sapphire's voice was soft—almost cautious—as she shook her shoulder.

Adalja groaned and curled tighter beneath the covers. *Gods,* her head throbbed.
"What time is it?" she muttered, her throat scratchy.

"'Tis nearly half till midday—"

"*What?*" Adalja jolted upright, her wide, glassy eyes stinging at the sudden light.

She rubbed at her tangled curls, wincing as her gaze found Sapphire standing dutifully by the bed. Afternoon sunlight streamed through the arched window, catching on the red strands of her maid's hair.

"She's livid, isn't she?" Adalja rasped. It wasn't really a question—more an exhausted acknowledgment of the truth.
She's always angry, she thought, stifling a yawn.

Last night had been a mistake. A reckless sacrifice of sleep for freedom. She'd abandoned every expectation placed on her—every discussion about the kingdom's future—just to feel alive for a few hours. And now she'd pay for it.

Sapphire grimaced, offering the faintest nod.

"Queen Pembrook requests your presence in the dining hall of the East Wing."

Sapphire's gaze flicked nervously about the dim chamber, taking in the thick stone walls, the familiar clutter of Adalja's belongings strewn carelessly in corners, clinging to the walls and crevices of her dresser.

"I believe she's aware of last night's...activities."

Adalja groaned and buried her face in her hands, her fingers pressing against her throbbing temples. For a moment, she stayed there, willing herself not to exist.

But Sapphire waited, silent and still, and Adalja sighed.

She dragged herself upright, stretching her aching limbs as her feet slid to the floor. The chill of the stone sent a shiver up her spine. The bed creaked as she pushed away from its weight, its carved oak frame adorned with angels and lilies staring back at her like silent judges.

The night before had left its mark. Her body ached from the wine, the dancing, the running. Her legs still protested with every movement, but beneath the soft nausea there lingered a quiet sense of victory—bittersweet, carved deep into her skin and spirit alike.

Adalja tugged the deep blue nightdress tighter around her sore frame and moved for the door. Sapphire fell into step behind her as they shuffled into the vast corridors beyond.

The castle walls rose high on either side, cavernous and cold, the sound of their footsteps swallowed by stone.

Adalja crossed her arms tight against her body, her eyes flicking to the gilded portraits lining the hall—saints and martyrs painted in holy light, their serene faces following her like silent sentinels.

Above, chandeliers gleamed with soft candlelight, their glow reflecting faintly off the polished floors. Yet even that warmth felt cold, swallowed in the enormity of the space. The grandeur pressed in around her, beautiful and suffocating all at once.

As they neared the East Wing, faint murmurs reached them—the low voices of staff, the distant hum of a hymn drifting from the chapel.

The doors to the dining hall loomed ahead, flanked by carved pillars draped in Pembrook banners. The aged blue linen hung still, frayed slightly at the edges, its embroidered angel wings held together by the blade of a sword.

Holy. Heavy. But no one had ever shared the story behind it—not her mother, not even her father.

Adalja inhaled deeply, raking her fingers through her dark hair in an effort to tame it, before pushing open the heavy oak doors.

The dining hall stretched out before her like a testament to the kingdom's wealth and faith. A long wooden table, polished to a near-mirror sheen, dominated the room. Its surface was set with gilded goblets, engraved silverware, and intricately embroidered tablecloths featuring the kingdom's crest. A massive stone hearth roared at one end, its warmth failing to penetrate the icy tension of the room.

At the head of the table sat Queen Pembrook, regal and severe. Her dress was a deep blue velvet, embroidered with white thread in patterns of celestial stars. Blue and white; the Pembrook colours.

A modest silver crown rested atop her loosely braided hair, and her piercing gaze locked onto Adalja the moment she entered.

"Hello, Mother," Adalja said quickly, her voice steady despite the queen's inevitable scrutiny.

She moved to take her place at the table, her steps purposeful yet laden with a quiet defiance.

"Adalja...*late as ever.*"

The princess stayed quiet, clearing her throat as she tucked herself into her chair.

"What are these whispers," the queen began, her voice low and venomous, "that the Princess of Pembrook was drinking and dancing with *Norsemen*?" Her tone curled around the words like a whip, setting her chalice down with a resounding thud that echoed in the vast chamber.

"Hm?" she pressed, her gaze cutting into Adalja like a blade.

Adalja's fingers brushed her knuckles beneath the table—a poor attempt at self-soothing.

Her eyes flicked towards the guard standing silently in the corner, who'd witnessed the entire scene. Then quickly, she looked back.

"It was—I..."

"What in all of heaven do you think this looks like for our family?" her mother snapped, cutting her off before she could speak.

"*I—*"

"That the noble Pembrook heir is frolicking with Midhelm's enemy? In a godforsaken tavern—do you not see the hypocrisy?" the Queen asked, anger barely restrained. "We are a family of peace—yet you drank among *heathens—*"

"They are not h—"

"And above it all, you risked yourself without protection. *In the midst of war.*"

Adalja bit the inside of her cheek, waiting for the smallest pause to wedge in a reply.

"Mother," she said softly, "I...I only wished for a night away. It wasn't simply Norsefolk—our own kind were celebrating as well."

She rubbed one foot against the other beneath the table, grounding herself as flashes of the previous night surged through her.

"*Our kind?*" the queen scoffed, chuckling.

"Adalja, You are the *sole* princess of Midhelm. There are noble daughters, wealthy Pembrians, and yes—plenty of pretty, *foolish* girls like yourself. But none of them bear the crown's blood. You stand alone in that. You have *no kind.*"

Adalja shuddered at that—the cruelty, the brutality, the isolation.
She bowed and nodded, nails curling in her skin because she knew her mother was wrong.

She knew of the Daughter in Ragnarvik...maybe not entirely a *princess*, but royal-blooded all the same.

"Enough of this...Let us both hope that this news doesn't reach the Worthyns," Queen Natja shook her head, hands going up to rub the tiredness from her glossy eyes.

"Let not a single thing undo the marriage that awaits."

The remark came and went too fast—Adalja's face tightened, caught between confusion and anger.

"I beg your pardon...?"
It was the only thing Adalja could manage to say without choking up completely at the sudden drop of news. "Mother, please—if this is a way to punish me, I—"

"This is no punishment," Natja said, tilting her head across the table. "You are the *Princess,*" her tone sharpened with warning, "and you will learn to accept the roles of a Queen."

"Mother, *please,*" Adalja stood, chair scraping against polished stone, hugging herself tightly around her chest, "I'm not ready."

But the queen paid her no mind. Natja cleared her throat, her sharp eyes snapping towards the guard who lingered near the door.

"We'll be leaving for their kingdom shortly," she exhaled, waving towards the knight stationed at the corner. "Sir Brahms—"

The knight stepped forward, bowing his head in a smooth, practised motion.
"At your service, My Lady Natja," Brahms said hastily, a shy smile flickering across his face as he stood at attention.

"Please, darling, escort my daughter to her chambers," Natja ordered, dismissing the conversation with a wave of her hand.

Her gaze shifted to Adalja, whose stunned silence spoke louder than any protest. Disappointment flickered across the young princess' face, but her glare burned with quiet rebellion.

Adalja hesitated, her hands clawing at her arms as she hugged them to her chest.

For a moment, she locked eyes with her mother, her deep-seated rage simmering beneath the surface. Finally, with a huff, she spun on her heel and strode towards the door she had entered, her nightgown flowing behind her like a shadow.

"PRINCESS PEMBROOK, WAIT!" Brahms called after her, his brow furrowed with concern.
But Adalja didn't stop.

She turned sharply towards the inner pleasure gardens, her bare feet pattering softly over the stone floors. Angelic tapestries blurred past as she picked up speed, ignoring Brahms' repeated calls.

"*Adalja!*"

She threw open a pair of double doors and stepped into the sanctuary of the garden.

The air shifted at once—warm and fragrant, thick with the scent of blooming flowers and damp earth. Dark green vines wove along the walls, their tendrils climbing towards the stained-glass dome overhead. Sunlight streamed through colored panes, casting a kaleidoscope of hues across the lush greenery below.

It was a place made for whispers, for wine, for lovers who dared speak truth beneath heaven's gaze.
But not for her.
Not now.

This was the only place that had ever wrapped her in safety. And right now, she needed just that.

"*Gods...I refuse it...*" Adalja whimpered, her voice fading as she strode towards her familiar corner.

Nestled there, in a cradle of ferns and ivy, was her harp. Its polished frame caught the dappled light, gleaming as if it had been waiting for her.

She sank onto the well-worn blanket spread across the ground, arms curling around her knees as she hugged them to her chest.

She curled into herself, silent, ignoring the footsteps behind her.

Brahms stepped cautiously into the garden, his eyes scanning the vibrant sanctuary. A shaky breath escaped him when he spotted her, and he approached with care.

"Don't come any closer!" she called, clutching herself tighter. "You will not command me to my chambers like some child..." Adalja added, not looking at him. Her voice was soft, her eyes glassy with tears.

A pause.
Then:

"Twas never my intention..." Brahms said carefully, his gaze flickering between her and the harp. He cleared his throat. "Adalja...I apologise on behalf of your parents—"

"Brahms." Her tone was firmer now, finally glancing up at him, eyes begging. "You've offered those words before. They never change how I feel."

He sighed almost immediately, reading the quiet desperation in her voice.

Without another word, he unbuckled the straps of his armour. Metal pieces clinked gently as he set them aside.

Beneath the plating, he wore a simple dark blue shirt and trousers—plain, unremarkable, a contrast to the armour she always saw.

"Forgive me," he murmured, settling across from her. "I'm not the best at comfort."

His voice held a thread of reluctant amusement, softened by something else—something closer to care.

They sat in silence for a while, both of them at war with the coming news.

Adalja had always known this day would come...though she'd hoped for more time. She was twenty-one, well past marrying age, after all—she shouldn't have been so surprised.

Deep down, she always hoped she would have been given the option to choose, as her mother did. But maybe they were forcing this on her because they knew her well enough—knew that Adalja would marry a Pagan if it were up to her.

Adalja eventually pulled her small harp into her lap, carelessly plucking at the strings, her melody laced with unease.

And Brahms listened...*he always listened.*

"I overheard something in Fairtide last night," she said, her voice barely audible above the soft notes.

Brahms leaned back on his palms, casting a wary glance around the empty gardens. "That so? I was plastered," he grinned. "Whatever it was, I'm sure it was simple alehouse whispers."

Adalja's fingers struck a discordant note, her jaw tightening. "No. They spoke of *Ragnarvik*..." she continued, her tone edged with unease. "It seems...they are making plans for marriage as well."

"Did they say to whom?" Brahms asked casually.

Before she could answer, he sighed heavily, running a hand through his disheveled curls as he looked up at the leaves dangling overhead.

"God," he scoffed, almost laughing. "Can't imagine *that* girl slung on some nobleman's arm. Must be some Chieftain shield-brute from her land," he added with a chuckle.

Adalja hummed thoughtfully, her melody resuming. "That's what *I thought,*" she snickered with a growing smirk, her voice barely above the music.

The garden fell quiet, the soft notes of the harp filling the space. After a moment, Adalja spoke again, her tone tentative.

"I was a fool for thinking I could have the marriage of my dreams," she began, her words measured, "But it was always just a tool, wasn't it? Was never something I was *meant* to want..."

Brahms froze, his face drooping, dark eyes lowering to her hands. "Not a fool for wanting it," he murmured, shrugging his shoulders. "Just a fool in general—"

Adalja cut him off by pinching his bicep, hard enough to cut him off with a squeal. "I am in pain and you would mock me?"

"*Agh—I yield—I yield!*" Brahms yelped, yanking his bicep away so he could rub out his arm with a hissed exhale.

The noblewoman wished she could have more fun with him, happier expressions, but she couldn't. Not now...not knowing these were likely her last moments in this very sanctuary.

Her fingers stilled on the strings, her dread apparent. Slowly, she lay down flat on the blanket, looking up at the glass ceiling.

She knew better than to try to argue with the King and Queen about this. She was brave enough to rebel in secret, but to their face, she was as obedient as she had to be.

"Maybe I should have run away last night..." she whispered, her voice weaker now, her throat tight with the grief of it all. Above her, a few birds fluttered near the ceiling.

She couldn't watch. She closed her eyes and sighed shakily, not wanting to cry. Gods, her mother always made her cry like this.

Her bottom lip quivered as a tear raced to each temple.

"Running away wouldn't solve anything, Addy, you're smart enough to know that." Brahms said with a sigh, shuffling a bit closer to her.

He lay back as well, keeping himself propped on his side. A gloved hand reached out and caught a tear. His scent hit her then, cedarwood and leather...a comforting smell that always meant help was there.

"This could be the start of something good...at least now, you'll be away from Pembrook, from your mother..." Brahms shrugged, his expression softening. "And you'll still have your *handsome knight.*"

Adalja chuckled sadly, a partial cry as she let her head fall towards Brahms, looking up at him, "You'll intimidate my suitor for me, then?"

"As long as he isn't more handsome." Brahms grinned playfully, his voice low as his gaze locked onto hers.

Adalja's cheeks flushed faintly, her expression a mixture of admiration and gratitude.

"That's impossible," Adalja said finally, her smile carrying a teasing edge. Her eyes rolled as she turned away from him and sat back on her knees.

She looked down at him then, tilting her head, curls falling over her shoulders, "I had fun with you last night...I'm quite happy you found me."

Brahms smirked at her, catching a loose curl and brushing it gently behind her ear. "We've never once lacked for amusement, you and I...perhaps Worthyn won't prove so dreadful after all."

Adalja nibbled her bottom lip. She wasn't so sure she trusted him on that. But did she really have a choice?

"We should probably head to my chambers before I disgrace my family any further..." She rolled her eyes with a playful sigh and rose slowly, casting one last, lingering glance around the garden.

She wasn't ready for change.
But then...would she ever be?

Brahms fell into step beside her as they left the garden behind, walking in silence—comfortable, quiet, and heavy with all the unknowns that waited ahead.

THREAD IV

ᚦᛖ ᛒᚢᚱᛞᛖᚾᛋ ᛟᚠ ᚺᛖᛁᚱᛋ ᚦᛖ ᛒᚢᚱᛞᛖᚾᛋ ᛟᚠ ᚺᛖᛁᚱᛋ ᚦᛖ ᛒᚢᚱᛞᛖᚾᛋ

ᛟᛚᛁᚠᛃᚨ

Against the Highwife's orders, Olivja's tears poured for the remainder of the night into Loki's fur.

She hoped Freyja would hear her weeping and grant her a different fate. Hoped the crying might make her uglier. She wanted to take that chance; perhaps a puffy face would be enough to keep Vincent Worthyn away for good.

Edith and a few other women returned to Olivja's room early in the morning to begin her daily regimen. Typically, it only involved a warm bath, getting her hair done and being put into a tunic but, because the heiress was meeting her suitor, this time was considerably more *invasive.*

"Forgive me, my lady," the younger maid grunted, yanking at the ribbons of the heiress' beige corset, pulling her waist into something utterly unnatural.

Olivja had never worn one before.
She wouldn't—*couldn't*—do it again.

"Nearly done," the maid huffed, breathless.
Contorting another woman's ribs and organs was no easy task.

In that moment, she found a newfound respect for the noble faith-born ladies. They were warriors of their own kind—their battles fought in how they dressed.

She remained silent, unmoving.
The corset's bite was a welcome distraction, but even pain couldn't stop her thoughts from wandering.

She thought of how much the gown must have cost her family—that she'd need to look presentable, or risk wasting silver with a single wrong word from her mouth.

Then again, the war-hungry Worthyns were rich beyond anything the Ragnarviks could imagine. This dress was likely nothing to them—a trinket among their endless extravagance.

Nothing like what her people wore. Nothing like what they could afford.

The Norse relied on one another to survive, not gowns or crowns. They made their own weapons, their own food, their own homes. Self-sustaining.

But the war had stolen much—miners, fathers, farmers. Ragnarvik still offered iron ore and warhorses, trained and ferocious, but with each passing battle, both mines and mounts waned. And yet Worthyn wanted *more.*

Olivja's hand in marriage would bind Ragnarvik blades to Worthyn banners. Her people would be forced to fight in the war under her name...

Norse and noble—side by side in battle. A once-in-a-lifetime alliance, within sight.

Her mother's words echoed through her like a curse: Marriage...or failure.
There was no choice.

"Finished, highborne."

Olivja felt the maid pull away and she looked at herself in the polished plate. Her bosom was nearly spilling from the top of her poised corset, a garment meant for *princesses*, not shield-folk.
But, at least, it was a symbol of her people in colour.

The light brown of her bodice contrasted against the cascading red fabric of her lace trimmed gown—the Ragnarvik colours. Her hair fell down her back with random braids scattered throughout. Her honey-toned face was bare save for lined eyes, and a small vine-shaped crown was woven into the braids of her hair.

Olivja felt beautiful. She *always did.* But, this new version of noble beauty wasn't for *her* to love...She wasn't meant to feel beautiful, she was meant to feel sculpted.

Staring at the beautiful, strange, heiress in the reflection, her eyes watered. She visualised other fates where she may have once enjoyed being sculpted for someone else, someone she loved.

Olivja had never dreamt of marriage. To her, such fantasies belonged outside the bounds of reality—unnecessary for survival.
How wrong she had been.

Her fox-fur cloak was placed around her bare shoulders and she slipped her arms beneath the clasp.

"The carriage is arriving, child," Edith said gently, her hands lingering on her shoulders, squeezing them gently.

It struck her then—this might be the last time she would ever stand in her jarldom. And as the thought passed, the tears she'd been holding slipped quietly down her cheeks.

"Oh, my brave one," her Amma sighed and turned Olivja around, wiping her face to preserve the makeup. "Vincent's become a strong man, no doubt. Midgard still breathes light—*hold fast to it.*"

It was such a cruel thing to ask of her. Crueler still—was knowing that she was going to marry someone she once called a friend.

Once. That friendship had sailed long ago, pushed out to sea by *him* himself.

She shook her head, fists tightening at her sides as silent curses against their future burned in her thoughts.

"Light..." she repeated.
Yet I am forever cast in shadows.

She didn't say it out loud. Didn't wish to spoil her Amma's hope with more pessimism.

Amber eyes fell to the bottom of her gown.
She couldn't handle looking or speaking to anyone any longer.
What was the point?

A final squeeze alerted Olivja that she had run out of time for sulking. A few other hand maids said their tearful goodbyes before she was escorted out. Her mother didn't come to say goodbye, likely too ashamed of what she was doing to her own daughter.

Keeping her head down, she moved through the building for the last time. She didn't want to believe it would be forever, so she refused to act like it.

Not having a last look might bring regret, but she pushed the thought away. Deep down, she was certain she would return home. Someday.

Her brown, fur boots tapped softly against the steps as she walked into the main room where her father waited. Her eyes hit him and her stomach dropped.

He was dressed so cleanly, in a dark red tunic, snug beneath his brown jerkin. His long hair was braided in the same fashion that his beard and mustache were. His lip and eyebrow ring glistening in the low light.

He looked handsome, *kingly*. Though, despite being well dressed, the dark circles beneath his sad eyes were elevated by the brightly coloured red.

"Highlord." Edith bowed shallowly, due to her old age, and he addressed her with a simple nod.

"Fodir," she spoke casually despite her inner struggles, trying to avoid any final words that brewed inside the Jarl.

"Oli—"

"Is the carriage nearly here?" she interrupted, avoiding eye contact as she moved towards the oak doors, her back to him.

She looked up at the Ragnarvik rune burned into the wood.
Freyja, give me strength.

She could feel the tension rising between them...but she had nothing good to say. Her head stayed pinned forward.

"Aye, the carriage *is* here," her father confirmed but continued, grabbing her hand in his large, warm paw. "But, dottir, if I may—"

"No, fodir! You may not!" The Jarl's Dottir cried out in the tongue of their ancestors, her words rough and fiery with emotion.

She turned to face him, ripping her hand free. Tears threatened to spill, so she squeezed her eyes shut, desperate to hold herself together. But she was terrible at it—never able to hide what she felt, no matter how much she wanted to.

Hirdmen turned away at the shout. Even Edith kept her head down. Usually, she would chastise Olivja for speaking in such a tone—but not today.

Everyone in the room silently knew that this would be the heiress' last outburst in Ragnarvik.

Her father's eyes were tearful. She couldn't tell if he was drunk or of sound-mind, but it didn't matter; he acted the samc no matter what.

He stood there in shock, clenching his jaw, his weathered hands curling behind his back as he shifted his stance. His silence spoke volumes, heavy with unspoken regret or stubborn pride—it was hard to tell which.

Without another word, he stepped past her and pushed open the heavy double doors, their iron hinges groaning from overuse.

A shaky breath escaped her lips, forming a thin mist in the cool morning air. She stood frozen within the keep's shadow as she caught sight of Worthyn's horse-drawn carriage, waiting at the end of the wide stone staircase.

The courtyard was massive, a sprawling circle of stone and gravel that acted as the heart of Ragnarvik's keep. It was alive with activity—blacksmiths hammering steel on anvils, the clang ringing through the air warriors sparring in distant corners.

Beyond those walls, the territory stretched vast and wild—a growing jarldom of turf-roofed homes and stone communities, patchwork of farmland and villages that seemed to roll endlessly until it reached the base of the distant mountains.

Those mountains loomed tall and ancient, their snow-dusted peaks standing as silent witnesses to the moment unfolding in the courtyard below. Behind the keep, the ocean roared and churned, the cliffs dropping to white pebbled shores and restless waters.

A harsh wind swept through, carrying the salty tang of the ocean waves crashing against the shore below, mingling with the scent of leather, fire, and sage.

Her father took a few steps ahead of her, before he turned and offered her a reassuring expression, though sadness weighed down his brows. When she finally stepped out, his burly arm was extended towards her.

Duty—and duty alone—pressed her forward.

Reaching out, she gently rested her hand on his forearm, her fingers barely gripping him. Together, they descended the wide stone steps, their matching boots tapping against the damp surface, the sound swallowed by the bustling noise of the courtyard.

It wasn't until they neared the gates that the sound of shattering whines and yelps echoed through the open enclosure.

Olivja froze.
Her breath hitched in her throat as she turned, her tearful eyes locking onto the source.

There, near the farthest edge of the courtyard where the wood and stone walls curved to meet the towering gates, stood her wolf—restrained by thick chains gripped tightly in the hands of two struggling handlers.

The world narrowed to him. Nothing else mattered.
Just her wolf. Her child. The last tether to the life she was about to leave behind.

He growled low and guttural, sharp teeth flashing as he snapped at the restraints. His golden eyes locked onto Olivja, wide with desperation. He pulled against the chains with every ounce of strength, as if he understood what was happening—that his mother, his master, was leaving him.

Olivja's chest caved.
She sprinted across the courtyard, stumbling once over the uneven ground but never stopping.

A soft sob escaped her lips as she dropped to her knees before him.

The wolf's posture shifted at once. Growls gave way to whimpers. His paws stamped the earth, head twisting with hope that she had come to free him. His tongue flicked out to lick her face—warm, rough, and rank with the scent of blood and bone. Both a comfort and a cruelty.

She buried her fingers in his thick fur, tears soaking into his coat as she whispered apologies into his ear—words meant for him alone.

Behind her, the handlers exchanged uneasy glances, their grips tightening on the chains.

"Loki, *stothva...*" Olivja sadly commanded him to stop as he licked her salty tears, a final treat from her to him, "You'll cost me time..."

The heiress ruffled his ears, placing kisses on his snout, and then between his ears, his head as large as her torso.

"Be good, boy...Protect mama..." she cried to him, a few tears dripping onto his fur.

He whined in response, allowing her to hold him for a moment longer before she carefully stepped back, wiping her eyes with the back of her hand.

A voice broke through the moment—sharp and impatient.

"Jarl's Dottir," her father called, his tone commanding, though it wavered slightly. "The carriage waits."

"Goodbye, my son..." she whimpered, but she could hardly keep it together. She forced herself away, covering her mouth to stifle a sob.

As the handlers began to pull the wolf back, his claws scraped against the gravel, resisting every step. Olivja's heart shattered with each whimper that reached her ears.

The Worthyn coachman waited patiently for her to descend before opening the wooden carriage door for them. The heiress was assisted into the carriage, then Edith, and finally the Jarl.

Granting herself the kindness, she lifted her head as the carriage pulled off and gazed behind her. Her eyes stayed trained on her shrinking home as they rode north.

When their jarldom was no longer in sight, the sense of abandonment finally settled in. Her head fell into her palms and the repressed tears broke free.

THE RHYTHMIC CLOPPING of the two horses filled the silent cabin that held the Ragnarviks. Olivja's cries had quieted over the duration of the ride, and as they drew nearer, her expression became numb and vacant. The sun was beginning to set, casting a golden glow into the carriage.

"We'll be arriving shortly..." Edith's raspy voice cut through the depressive cloud that hovered between them, "My Jarl...?"

Her Amma then realised the man was sleeping.

"*Dagrun*!"

With a quick snort, the dark haired gentleman sat up straight.

Olivja watched him with a straight face, betrayed by his actions, longing for the man he used to be.

After wiping some drool from his beard, he cleared his throat.
"Apologies, Maiden," he grumbled a genuine apology, glancing out the carriage window to gauge the remaining distance.

"Not far now. Best speak what still needs sayin' to your dottir."

As he contemplated the comment there was a brief pause, then:
"Worthyn is set on this union, so...be ready. You'll have little resting time once we arrive..."

"*Well, isn't that a feast of joy...*" Olivja said beneath her breath.
"I don't see why he's so keen on *me*—" she added, a bit louder, "of all the cursed women in Midhelm, he picks the one cursed *most*."

She shifted her weight angrily, crossing her arms.
"You've stripped our people bare to please the cross-bearers—and now you offer me, too, *like coin*." The heiress could no longer hide the betrayal in her voice, nor the tears pooling at her waterline.

Her father sighed, pausing to collect his answers—answers they all knew wouldn't be good enough for Olivja.

"Without our people, Worthyn will fall," he finally said. "This war is all that stands between us and ruin...I'll give all I have...even if it breaks me."

Jarl Ragnarvik's words were riddled with pain. Olivja was all he had left. His last coin to pay. And he was giving it to King Worthyn.

After his defeated comment, the rest of the ride was silent. Olivja shied away from further conversing.
She wouldn't make it worse.

The carriage slowed and then jolted to a stop.

A cold chill ran up her exposed arms, raising the hairs on the back of her neck. Her father cleared his throat and, once the carriage door opened, he stepped out.

The heiress kept her head straight as Edith was assisted out of the carriage by the Jarl.

Olivja didn't want to exit. The carriage was the last object tying her to her childhood. Once she stepped foot onto the Worthyn grounds, it would become her new home...She didn't want that.

But they were waiting...

She manoeuvred awkwardly in her elaborate attire, having to scoot and slide across the seat to reach the door. Edith and her father's steady hands kept her from stumbling, guiding her out of the carriage.

A sense of disappointment settled within her. The Worthyn Castle was far from the Ragnarvik keep, in every sense. Despite supposedly having more wealth than the Ragnarviks, their building was bare and regimented.

The front courtyard was lined with armoured knights, standing post with their spears. The castle loomed with a dark, military grandeur that sharply contrasted Ragnarvik's rustic jarldom. The absence of foliage and the unadorned walls lacked the warmth and welcome feel she was accustomed to.

She had visited the Worthyn grounds all throughout her childhood, and it was fitting that the scenery was darker and more barren than ever before.

Smacked in the middle of the courtyard sat a large fountain, once sprouting with sparkling water, was now completely dried out, mirroring the emptiness hollowing the heiress from within.

A few feet in front of her were the Worthyn Princes, dressed in black and silver cords, a spitting image of discipline and power.

The twin brothers stood side by side, both with the same black cowls and masks covering their faces.

She exhaled sharply at the sight of things. *Still? After all these years?*

Both of their waterlines were darkened by a thick line of coal, a common touch of makeup for men. As they came closer—movements almost rehearsed—both removed their hoods and tugged away their coverings, revealing their matured faces and the sharp, cat-like eyes of emerald green that watched her with quiet precision.

Olivja was speechless.

A sudden contrast to the dark attire, their striking snow-white hair shimmered in the sun. They were the picture-perfect example of royal men: chiseled faces, tall, well-built frames, the expensive, tailored attire.

Prince Vincent on the left, with shoulder-length locks, tilted his head at the heiress, gazing with an indiscernible expression. But she could hardly look at him...not with all the rage between them.

But, even if only looking for a second, she noticed that Vincent was wider than his brother now, taller and more muscular too.

His brother, Elias, sported shorter hair and was smiling softly, his eyes gentle and unknowing of the tension between them.

Taking her by her arm, the Jarl walked his daughter forward, closer to the two men.

"Gentlemen," her father initiated, clearing his throat, "King Ezekiel—"

"—Had *other* matters to attend to," the taller son spoke up, slightly bowing to her father. "Forgive his absence, My Lord, but I can assure you his presence is far from necessary."

Olivja could hardly watch.

She missed them. That much was true.
She imagined another universe where instead of scowling, she ran up to him.

She could see it clearly, a hopeful, happy reunion full of deep hugs and laughter...

But it had been far too long. Far too much distance. And she was angry.

The time put between them had done more than enough to dampen their once strong connection. The longer she stood before the grown boys, the less familiar they became.

Even at her respectable height, Olivja had to tilt her chin to look the princes in the eye, her eyes level with his chin. Vincent loomed over her, like a mountain over a hill, his imposing stature only adding to the tension of being in his presence once again.

"*Hah.* Scrubbed the mud off, did you? You almost look like proper men," her father chuckled lightly. "When will your father be joining us?"

"Please address us properly, King Ragnarvik," he corrected and then continued as if it were nothing. "Though...I will admit, it *is* good to see you. Pleased to see you haven't changed in the *slightest.*"

Olivja heard the slight, and it caused her jaw to clench. Ever so slightly, her eyes raised, glaring.

"Our father won't return for a while, likely until after our weddings," Elias, the slightly shorter one, interjected kindly.

"Oh...very well." The Jarl cleared his throat and turned his body slightly towards the heiress.

"Olivja..." he cleared his throat a second time, urging her to greet them.

She raised her head slowly, glancing at her father, and then finally making eye contact with her suitor for longer than a glance.

Their families were close for over a decade...
She wondered, for a moment, if it was all an elaborate marriage ploy. If they were never friends at all.

Not that it mattered, this wasn't the same prince she grew up with, that much was evident.

"My Lords..." she cleared her throat.
"Been some time," Olivja said, slightly bowing her head, taking no steps closer.

She lingered in her father's shadow, clinging to the fragile sense of safety it offered.

"Far too long, Lady Olivja." Vincent returned, eyes crinkling softly at the edges, taking another step closer as he extended his hand to her, "The kingdom is brighter with your grace, once again."

The prince's expressions held a distant expression, one she was unsure how to dissect.

Hesitantly, she looked down at Vincent's extended hand.

Her father took it upon himself to escort her hand from his arm, gently tugging Olivja until her hand fell into the prince's warm palm.

At the touch, Olivja shuddered. His once boyish hands were now rough and calloused—*but so were hers.*

Gone were the soft surfaces of their childhood.

She kept her eyes angled at their connected hands, his thumb dancing across her skin. He raised her hand and with it her eyes.

And then he placed a firm kiss between her knuckles, catching her indifferent gaze before closing his eyes.

She could see the way his eyebrows twitched. After a moment, one far too long for comfort, he slowly lifted his head.

"Has she grown timid?" Vincent chuckled after clearing his throat and lowered her hand, but not after brushing his thumb over her knuckles, a final time.

"Ah...you'll find the truth runs the other way, Your Grace," her father said with a nervous laugh. "You'd think the years would tame her. But no—still my wild little fire."

She blinked, unsure whether to laugh or flinch. The words stung—but gods, they weren't wrong.

"I'll take your word for it, Ragnarvik...I'd prefer not to start over with her."

Vince laughed alongside Dagrun, tugging the heiress away from her father as he swung himself between the two of them.

He escorted them away from the carriage and towards the blinding castle, tucking her hand onto the corner of his arm as he continued.

"Am I wrong to assume you're still gorging your spirits, Dag?" Vincent asked. "You'll be impressed by our new barrels..."

The prince began charming Olivja's father in the one way everyone knew how; with mead. Already, Dagrun's words slurred; the thought of imported mead *alone* intoxicated him.

As the two men droned on, the sound of another carriage arriving in the distance caught her attention.

She glanced back, pausing in her steps.

Vincent tugged on her hand, attempting to pull her up the stairs, as her feet had slowed. When he noticed her refusal, he turned and paused.

"Oh? You thought only I had the *pleasure* of marrying, Liv?" he asked, a hint of resentment in his voice as he released her hand.

"You'll have to excuse me...*You there,* escort them inside," he called to the nearest guard, releasing her so he could quickly jog down the steps towards where his brother stood.

Olivja lingered, standing tall at the top of the stairs.
And what an unexpected mistake that was.

For, as the new arrivals poured out of the carriage, Olivja caught the eyes of someone she knew.

Hands shaking, eyes watering, her heart skipped a beat and failed all at once.

"*Adalja,*" she said beneath her breath, her lungs unsure of whether to stop breathing or pick up pace.

As Olivja's eyes found Adalja's blue ones, an entire decade of longing flashed before her. Her hands gripped her gown, hiking it upwards as she contemplated running down the steps to the Pembrook Princess.

At that point, her father had also turned.
Even more so than the Worthyns, the Ragnarviks had a *deep* history with the Pembrooks. Dagrun recognised them instantly, and it led to his hands immediately wrapping around Olivja's tensed biceps, gripping her—*holding her*—still.

"Dottir, *no*—" he hesitantly began, but was interrupted by a guard.

"This way," a knight's voice boomed, stepping directly in front of Olivja, blocking her view of the courtyard.

Olivja coiled her fists, ready to strike, to push her way through if it meant seeing Adalja again.

Edith rushed to her side, shrouding her in her arms, tugging her away from the armoured chest in front of her.

"Come. Now, Olivja...please," she whispered to her, the Norse words spilling off her tongue like a spell.

But it didn't work.

The unforgiving memory of their last goodbye struck her, freezing her in place.

THREAD V

ᚦᛖ ᛒᚢᚱᛞᛖᚾᛋ ᛟᚠ ᚺᛖᛁᚱᛋ ᚦᛖ ᛒᚢᚱᛞᛖᚾᛋ ᛟᚠ ᚺᛖᛁᚱᛋ ᚦᛖ ᛒᚢᚱᛞᛖᚾᛋ

ᛟᛚᛁᚹᛃᚨ

SMALL BARE FEET PITTER-PATTERED down the halls of the Ragnarvik castle. Quick, short breaths escaped ten-year-old Olivja as she fled from her two handmaidens, who were desperately trying to keep her in her room.

"*Little Heir*! *Please*!" the two women called, inciting a giggle from young Olivja, her laughter echoing softly against the wooden walls.

It was raining—and the entire keep knew what that meant: Olivja would want to be beneath it.

She bolted through Ragnarvik halls, searching for *Adalja's room.*

Back then, the Pembrooks lived in the same halls.
Back then, everything was better.

"I *must* hurry!" she giggled to herself, tying her tattered skirts in knots at her hips to keep them from dragging.

Eventually, she stopped in front of Adalja's room, gasping for breath as she raised her hand to bang on the oak door.

"Dali!" Olivja shouted at the top of her lungs, giggling as she pounded on the door, "Dali! Dali! Dali!" She was being annoying and persistent—but that was tradition.

Whenever it rained, the girls from the two families would play together, regardless of their parents' hesitation or the biting weather.

Olivja had no reason to think that this day would have been any different.

"HALLO!?"

No answer.

Olivja paused a moment, giving herself time to catch her breath, swallowing the dryness in her throat.

"A-Adalja?" she called, softer this time, and pushed open the door on her own, her voice barely audible over the patter of rain on the roof.

She peered inside...All of Adalja's things were gone. All that remained was a bare mattress and a small linen towel hanging near the bed.

On the bed sat a small, curly-headed Adalja. She lifted her head with a soft sniffle.

"Olivja?" The girl whimpered, slipping off the too-tall bed. She hit the ground, hands fidgeting at her stomach as she approached, eyes wide and glistening, her cloak draped around her shoulders.

The heiress smiled.
"I-it's raining! Let's go play!" Olivja's voice was full of excitement, but she was hesitant given the look she was receiving.

Adalja looked...*angry at her.*
She never looked angry.

"No," the little princess said, barely audible over the storm outside, "I *hate* the rain." Her gaze stayed fixated on the ground between them, her fingers tightly gripping the delicate fabric of her cloak.

A flicker of confusion crossed Olivja's face, chased quickly by a quiet ache. "N...no, you *love* the rain! That's dumb talk!"

Adalja's voice cracked with emotion, tears welling in her eyes. "But—"

Olivja wasn't taking no for an answer.

Her small hand found Adalja's and she tugged her out of her room and down the Ragnarvik halls.

Ignoring further protests, Olivja burst through the double doors, yanking the princess down the steps with her into the pouring rain.

She gasped with glee. The entire kingdom was bathed in a dense fog and shower, the cool raindrops decorating their hair in drops of glistening dew.

"See!? The gods shower us!" Olivja exclaimed, dropping Adalja's hand to twirl beneath the cool drizzle. Her laughter echoed in the courtyard as her wide smile lit up her face, the raindrops clinging to her hair like tiny jewels.

"Adalja!"

The shrill voice sliced through the moment, freezing Olivja mid-spin. Her smile faltered, then fell completely as she turned towards the source.

Standing beyond a carriage piled high with chests and bags were the Pembrooks. Natja's stern expression was a tempest in its own right.

Adalja stiffened beside her, the remaining light in her eyes fading. Olivja's heart sank as tension rolled over them like a wave—the rain suddenly colder, heavier.

Natja's boots splashed against the rain-slicked gravel as she approached, her outstretched hand commanding.

"We are leaving. *Now.* Get in the carriage," the queen said, her tone as unyielding as steel.

Liv gasped, stomach dropping.
"L—Leaving?" the heiress asked with a tremble and quickly jumped in front of Adalja.

"Where? W-why?" Olivja's voice cracked, a mixture of confusion and dread. Her mind raced as she turned to Adalja, whose tears had quietly returned, carving thin rivers down her pale cheeks.

She wouldn't stand for the princess' tears.

Liv grabbed her hand tightly, desperate to keep her close.
"You don't need to go! Let's run!" Her words were frantic, but Adalja didn't move, her small shoulders slumping in fear of the inevitable.

Natja wasted no time.
She seized Adalja's arm, pulling her away from Olivja's grasp with a force that sent the Norsegirl stumbling.

Liv fell to the gravel, the rough wet stones biting into her cheeks. The cold, soaked ground seeped through her skirts, but the pain inside her chest eclipsed it all.

"Adalja!" she cried, her voice barely rising above the rain.
It pelted her face, mixing with her tears. Soaked hair and sediment clung to her cheeks, but she didn't care.
She couldn't care.

King Pembrook stepped forward, taking Adalja into his arms with a tenderness that felt like a betrayal. His sad eyes briefly met Olivja's, but no words passed between them.

Then,
Thunk—

Natja glanced down sharply, her mouth a thin line of disapproval.
A rock landed with a pathetic tumble at her feet.

She looked up to meet Olivja's furious glare. The little girl's fists were clenched around a second rock, her fingers white from the pressure.

"Olivja," Natja said, her voice colder than the sky, "we are leaving Ragnarvik. No stone, nor tantrum, will stop it. You can ask your father why."

"DON'T speak of my Pabbi!" she screamed, her voice raw and breaking.

Her hands trembled as she hurled the second rock. It struck Natja's leg, but the woman didn't flinch—the rock was no bigger than a coin.

"Enough!" the queen's voice boomed like thunder, her patience snapping. "Get inside, Olivja, before sickness finds you!"

But Olivja wouldn't listen.

She scrambled to her feet, her wet skirt clinging to her legs and tangling her steps as she lunged forward—only to fall to the ground again.

"NO! DON'T GO! PLEASE!" Her cries echoed through the courtyard, mingling with the relentless drumming of rain on the cobblestones.

Natja didn't look back. Her damp, white cloak swirled behind her as she guided Phillip and Adalja towards the carriage.

Olivja pushed up and ran after them, her small feet splashing through the cold puddles, her breaths coming in sharp, ragged gasps. She reached the carriage as Phillip was climbing inside, settling Adalja onto the bench beside him.

Adalja pressed her little hands against the fogged glass window, her tearful face barely visible through the condensation.

"Oli!" Adalja's call was faint but piercing, her pain mirrored in her wide, wet eyes.

"Addy!" Olivja cried, her voice breaking, her chest heaving.
"Why are you leaving!?" Olivja sobbed, her cries raw and unrelenting.

She reached for the carriage—

Strong arms wrapped around her from behind, lifting her off the ground. She kicked and thrashed against them, her little hands clawing at the air as she screamed.

"No! NO! PLEASE! *Freyja! Freyja, bring her back!!*" Olivja screamed, hoping the gods would hear her.

"Stop this, Olivja!"

It was Brahms.

His voice was firm but pained, his grip unyielding as he held her struggling body. The storm whipped around them, rain soaking them both as Olivja's cries grew weaker, her energy waning.

"LET ME GO!!" Olivja's words were raw, pleading, but they were drowned by the storm.

And Brahms was too strong to break free from, even at only twelve.

He held her tightly, his grip firm as she fought, her heart racing faster than her body could move.

His face was close, his brow furrowed with concern as he struggled to keep hold of her, his voice full of pity. "Highborne, please—You'll make this harder for everyone!"

The words hit like a slap. She wasn't making it harder—she was trying to save her friend. Her oldest friend.
She couldn't let them take her.

"Brahms!" Olivja begged, her voice cracking as she pushed against Brahms. "They're taking her away!" Her words didn't come out right, broken and jumbled, but her meaning was clear.

However, it became clear that Brahms was already well aware of everything.

"Liv!" her Amma called through the fog and chaos, approaching the screaming heiress. "Olivja—what have you done?!" Edith yelled, panting.

Brahms, with a grunt of effort, hauled the scrambling heiress towards the keep doors, her sobs growing heavier.

"Why is this happening!? No—I need to speak to them! *Please*!" Her defiance wore on, but eventually Brahms passed her into Edith's firmer grip.

The young boy locked eyes with the heiress a final time before running back towards the carriage.

Something broke inside her—loud, invisible, irreparable.

With a final attempt, she looked up to her Amma in tears.

"Natja pushed me! And they're stealing Adalja! Please, *Amma*—you—you must help her!" Choking on snot and rain, she buried her damp face into her chest, clinging to her like a wounded animal.

"We have to go now! They're leaving, Amma!"
But her cries fell on deaf ears.

The little heir received no response. No sympathy.

Edith was there for one reason and one reason alone; to return her to her room. She grabbed a strong hold of her wrist and without another word, tugged her back inside.

Olivja made a scene the entire way—crying and yanking at her wrists, slipping on the stone flooring.

But Edith kept her head perfectly straight, appearing completely unphased by her pleas and begs.

By the time they reached the safety and warmth of her room, Olivja had finally given up. Her sobs had quieted into gentle whimpers and hiccups as she defeatedly waddled in her wet skirts.

“Keep her in her room...” The tired woman sighed as she passed her off to two hirdmen at her bedroom door.

That was the last time she played in the rain.
And the last time she saw her friend.

THREAD VI

ᚦᛖ ᛒᚢᚱᛞᛖᚾᛊ ᛟᚠ ᚺᛖᛁᚱᛊ ᚦᛖ ᛒᚢᚱᛞᛖᚾᛊ ᛟᚠ ᚺᛖᛁᚱᛊ ᚦᛖ ᛒᚢᚱᛞᛖᚾᛊ

ᚨᛞᚨᛚᛃᚨ

THE IRON GATES GROANED OPEN, their ancient weight creaking against the late afternoon chill—a chill that had settled in Adalja's bones. The Worthyn knights stood stoically, their armour gleaming under the muted light, unmoved by the bustle of the arriving carriages. Inside the royal carriage, anticipation hung thick.

Adalja glanced down, her nerves worsening with each moment of silence. The gown she wore fit snugly, accentuating her curves, embellished with pearls that mirrored raindrops.

She knew the dress was perfect, she knew *she* looked perfect, but no matter how flawless of a princess she appeared to be, she didn't feel right. She tugged her dark blue cloak around herself, her hands fidgeting.

As though he could sense her fears, Brahms leaned towards Adalja, his voice low and soothing, breaking the tension that hung between them.

"So, Adalja," he said gently, his dark eyes searching her face. "Are you looking forward to meeting your prince?"

Adalja glanced out the window, watching as the guards exchanged sharp salutes and signaled for their approach. She let out a quiet sigh, her fingers brushing the embroidered hem of her gown.

"Of course," she muttered, her voice soft, though her tone bartered no particular excitement.

The carriage lurched forward, jostling them both as it made the final stretch up the stone-paved road before halting abruptly. The doors swung open with purpose, revealing two towering Worthyn guards standing like statues, their spears planted firmly in the ground. Their stern expressions betrayed no warmth as they awaited the royal party's descent.

Brahms, ever the optimist, stepped out first, the crunch of his boots against the ground was the only sound breaking the tension.
"Well met, friend! A fair afternoon it is!" he greeted warmly, extending a hand.

His cheerful disposition met an impenetrable wall of indifference as the guards didn't so much as blink in acknowledgment. He hesitated for only a moment before turning to assist Adalja with an awkward clear of his throat.

The faint scuff of boots and muffled clinking of armour filled the silence as her mother followed, her regal presence commanding attention. Adalja straightened instinctively at the sight of her mother's gaze.

Brahms stepped in close behind her, mimicking the Worthyn guards' rigid stance. He leaned close, his tone light despite the stiff formality surrounding them.

"Some tough men, eh?" he whispered.
Adalja's lips twitched into a faint, reluctant smile.
"Should I ask one of them to a duel?" he pressed with a grin.

She shot him a warning glance over her shoulder, her amusement fleeting but genuine. Before she could reply, a commanding voice boomed across the courtyard, drawing every eye towards the grand stone staircase leading into the castle.

"Welcome!"

Approaching were two men of striking similarity. Both were tall, their faces sharp and angular, with sharp green eyes and hair as pale as fresh snow.

The shorter-haired man reached them first, his expression warm and practised as he dipped into a small bow.

"Greetings, Noble Pembrooks," he said, his voice carrying the charm of diplomacy. "You must be Princess Adalja. I am Prince Elias, and this—" he gestured to the man beside him.

The broader prince cut in with a gentle grin, his voice deeper, *darker*.
"Prince Vincent. The pleasure is all mine," he interjected, his eyes briefly

flicking over her with a playful intensity. "Your presence here has been long awaited."

Adalja's practised smile slipped into place. She curtsied gracefully, her head lowered with care to avoid tipping her crown—a delicate piece of silver. It was set with soft pearls, deep lapis, and moonstone—their cool hues reflecting the heraldry of Pembrook.

"Pleasure to meet you, Princes of Worthyn," she said with measured politeness, eyes peeking through her lashes to meet his gaze.

Elias' smile widened as a faint blush crept onto his pale cheeks. He extended a hand towards her, his fingers calloused yet inviting.

Steeling herself, she placed her hand in his, allowing him to guide her the final step forward into her new reality.

His green eyes seemed sharper with the coal lining them, a dark contrast that seemed to pull her in. A blush crept onto her cheeks as he placed a soft kiss on the back of her palm.

Their hands lingered just a moment too long before he let go.

"Tell me, has the Jarl of Ragnarvik arrived?" King Mark of Pembrook asked, suddenly—and with an odd note of excitement

Adalja's eyes wandered nervously as she stood in the bustling courtyard of Worthyn Castle. Servants hurried past carrying trunks, the clinking of armour from patrolling knights filled the air.

She tried to ground herself, smoothing her trembling hands over the soft fabric of her skirt, but her breath hitched when her gaze drifted upwards.

At the top of the grand staircase stood a figure she recognised instantly—though the years had changed her.

Adalja froze, her heart skipping painfully as her fingers gripped the folds of her gown.

Olivja Ragnarvik.

Even from a distance, she could see the way Olivja's features had sharpened with age, her youthful softness replaced by the daring confidence of a Norsewoman.

Her thick hair rested over one shoulder and her piercing amber eyes scanned the courtyard below.

For a fleeting moment, their gazes met, and the world seemed to still.

Adalja felt the weight of something unspoken in Olivja's golden eyes—steady, burning, impossible to look away from.

Just as Adalja parted her lips, a Worthyn knight stepped in front of the Ragnarvik heir, *shattering* the moment.

The knight spoke quietly to Olivja, gesturing towards the castle doors. Olivja hesitated, her eyes flitting over the knight's shoulder as though she desperately searched for Adalja one last time. But the knight ushered her inside, leaving Adalja breathless.

"Princess?" Elias' smooth, confident voice startled her back to the present. He was suddenly at her side, his sharp green eyes studying her with a mix of amusement and concern.

"Y-Yes?" She managed, her voice unsteady as she turned to face him, forcing a smile that didn't quite reach her eyes.

He offered his arm with a slight bow, his grin both charming and reassuring. "Allow me to escort you to your chambers. It seems the excitement of Worthyn Castle has already begun to overwhelm."

Adalja blinked at him, trying to steady herself, and let out a soft, breathy laugh.

"Yes, th-thank you, My Lord," she said, her voice regaining some of its composure.

Tentatively, she rested her hand on his arm, and he led her away from the courtyard towards the coolness of Worthyn's interior.

Elias glanced at her as they ascended the first steps, his voice low and inviting. "I trust Worthyn Castle hasn't entirely frightened you off. Though I'll admit, the place does have a way of imposing itself."

She shook her head with a faint smile, her thoughts ever clouded by the sight of Olivja. "*Ahem*—Not at all. I daresay...it's...*beautiful*," she replied, though her tone revealed her distraction.

Elias didn't press further, though his curious gaze lingered on her as they climbed the grand staircase.

The air inside was cool and carried the faint scent of polished stone and ancient wood. Sunlight streamed through high arched windows. Her gaze drifted, lingering on the carvings lining the walls—each one a tale of battle, triumph, and sanctity.

Elias walked with an easy confidence, his footsteps steady and sure against the stone. "You're quite...quiet," he remarked, his voice smooth and gentle, meant to coax her from whatever thoughts had taken hold.

Adalja managed a small laugh, though her fingers briefly tightened on his arm. "One hardly knows where to begin," she said softly. "Your home...it's like nothing I've ever known."

He chuckled lightly, his smile warm. "It carries a presence one can't quite ignore...Though, if I may, it pales in comparison to its newest guest."

Her cheeks flushed faintly and she glanced at him out of the corner of her eye. "You're far too kind, My Lord," she replied, a polite deflection.

They turned down another corridor, this one darker, lit by sconces that cast flickering golden light across tapestries depicting Worthyn's noble history.

Elias slowed his pace, giving her time to take it all in.

"This wing is quieter," he explained, his tone conversational. "Reserved for distinguished guests. I hope you'll find it to your liking."

"It's...lovely," she said, though her voice was breathy and distracted—distant, even to her own ears.

Elias glanced down at her, his brow furrowing slightly.

"You seem far away, Princess. I do hope I haven't bored you already," he teased, though there was a note of genuine concern beneath his words.

"No! Not at all," she replied quickly. "Forgive me. It's been an eventful evening...My heart's ahead of my head...*I think*..." Adalja said, trailing off.

"I see," he replied with a nod, his smile softening. "Should you require anything, you need only ask, Princess."

They reached a tall oak door adorned with intricate metalwork, and Elias paused, resting his free hand on the latch.

"Here we are," he announced with a small smile. "Your chambers. Though, I'll warn you, the view from the nook has been known to enrapture all who witness it."

Adalja chuckled softly, letting go of his arm as he pushed the door open. The room was both grand and inviting, with a large canopy bed draped in pristine grey and white linens, a roaring hearth, and, as promised, a window nook overlooking the sprawling Worthyn forests.

Elias stepped aside, allowing her to enter first. "I trust you'll find everything to your liking. If not, I'll personally see to it that it's remedied."

She turned to him, her smile growing a touch more genuine as she held her hands behind her.

"Thank you, My Lord. You've been most kind."

He inclined his head slightly, his green eyes lingering on her blues. "You're quite deserving of such, Princess. Rest well. I'll find you at supper."

With that, he stepped back into the corridor, offering one last charming grin before closing the door softly behind him.

The quiet pressed in as she stared at the wood grain. Her heart was torn—still warm from Elias' kindness, yet chilled by the ghost Olivja had become in her thoughts.

The princess turned slowly, moving towards the window. Rain tapped lightly against the glass.

She wasn't sure which feeling frightened her more:
The ease of falling into Elias—
Or the ache that never left when Olivja returned.

Thread VII

ᚦᛖ ᛒᚢᚱᛞᛖᚾᛋ ᛟᚠ ᚺᛖᛁᚱᛋ ᚦᛖ ᛒᚢᚱᛞᛖᚾᛋ ᛟᚠ ᚺᛖᛁᚱᛋ ᚦᛖ ᛒᚢᚱᛞᛖᚾᛋ

ᛟᛚᛁᚠᛃᚨ

Edith had successfully pulled Olivja inside, a sudden memory of past bonds rendered her unable to resist.

Numbly, she followed the guard and her Amma up the stairs and into her new room, her father nowhere to be found.

The small room bore signs of wealth. The canopy bed, draped with white and grey mesh, sat upon grey stone flooring. Fur rugs softened the stark stone floor. But Olivja couldn't care less for the way the room looked.

The moment the knight left them, Olivja's mask shattered. Her eyes welled with tears as she raised her head, searching Edith's face for an answer.

"Explain this." Her voice trembled, as fractured as her thoughts, hands clutching where her heart ached to break free.

"Did you know?" A gentle whisper left her, far from accusatory.

"I did not, highborn, on my life I swear it," Edith stepped close, trying to calm the fury rising like thunder within the Norsewoman.
But this storm had brewed before—for Adalja.

Amma's wrinkled hands reached up, gently cupping Olivja's cheeks, grounding her the best she could.

"*Breath, child, we'll figure this out.*"
But no words, not even from their native tongue, could reach her now.

She was already drowning in the depths of a sunken, broken heart.

"Amma...I—"

The door opened.
Her father entered, eyes low, heavy with remorse.

Olivja's tears froze the moment they met his gaze. Her face, once grieving, turned to stone.
The betrayal from her parents never ended.

There was silence. A true, suffocating calm before the storm—
Then she broke.

She screamed. A ragged cry that ripped from her chest as she lunged, but Edith caught her just in time.

"*THOO* knew!" she sobbed, her grief echoing off the walls. "You *knew* she'd be here! *Hvee gairthee thoo* do this—Why did you do this, pabbi?!"

Her hair whipped wildly around her like fire as she fought against the arms that held her back, her voice collapsing between Norse and English, rage and despair.

Carelessly, the young woman shouted at her father, weakly prying at the arms that kept her from attacking him.

"Olivja, control your anger! They'll hear you!" Edith hissed, trying to keep her grounded.

But her father's response was enough.

"How could I!?" Dagrun barked, suddenly switching into their native tongue—thick with fury, sharp with grief. "*Olivja*! *Have you not yearned for Adalja's return*!?"

He stepped forward, towering and unrelenting, his words rolling like thunder. "*Is being near her not enough*!?" he shouted. "*You would curse me for reuniting us all*?"

He had never shouted like this. Not at her. Not in their language. Not in anger.

That's how she knew—it was no cruel scheme. Even if it felt like betrayal.

His voice struck the room like an axe splitting timber—commanding, real. And for the first time in a long time, she heard her father again.
The *powerful* Jarl of Ragnarvik.
Not the drunk.

It sent a chill through her chest, freezing her in place, silencing her.

She clung to Edith's arms, chest heaving, glare fixed on her father.

"Is that what you think of me, dottir? That your own father plots against you?" His voice thundered, hands cutting sharply through the air. With a growl, he dragged both hands down his face, then back across his braid in frustration.

Olivja crumbled to the floor with a growl of her own, her chest heaving. Edith's grip still held firm—but now, it felt more like a hug than restraint.

"You speak as if free of guilt, *pabbi...*" she cried. "But you kept this from me. Is that not plotting?"

Dagrun faltered, staring into his daughter's tear-stained face. His fury slipped. His eyes dropped to the floor. And with a sigh, the weak, helpless drunk reappeared in his eyes.

"Olivja...If you had known your Adalja was to be wed," he murmured, "you would not have come."

Her expression dropped—eyes softening beneath the chilling assumption.
And yet...he was still wrong.

Because Olivja *would* have come—not a soul, nor god, could stop her.
But she wouldn't have come to bless the marriage.
No. *Only* to steal her princess away.

And maybe she still would.

With her gaze fixed on the floor, she whispered, fragile as glass, "Leave me."

Without hesitation, her Amma pulled away. She placed a soft kiss to Olivja's head before shuffling to the door. She left without another word.

But Dagrun lingered, regret carved into the lines of his face.
"Liv—*Valk*...My rose, please understand..."
He tried, stammering around the names that once soothed her. He took a step back, uncertain.

"Please understand...I need to be alone."
Her voice trembled.
Though the words couldn't be further from the truth.

The door opened once more. Then shut.
And Olivja was alone, writhing in her sorrow.

Tears returned. Her hands clawed at the bodice, frantic for relief—for air. Frustrated cries tore from her as she ripped away the jewels and crown, flinging them onto the cold stone.

She was not *this*.
She would *never* become *this*.

When the corset fell, she kicked off her fur-lined boots towards the corner. The dress slipped from her shoulders—she threw it like it burned her. Growling and stomping, the frantic heir paced in nothing but her sheer underdress, grabbing fistfuls of her hair, pulling—aching.

What could be done?

She had waited ten years for this. To see her Adalja again. Ten years spent nursing a flame she never dared let die.

Even after the Pembrooks abandoned the Ragnarviks and vanished inland, Olivja never stopped writing, never stopped begging, never stopped *hoping* she'd see the princess.

And now the gods had twisted her *one wish* into punishment—a cruel joke.

Not only was she being forced to marry...But she had to stand by, helpless, as the woman she loved was forced to marry too.

No matter how deeply she searched, there was no solution. No justification that calmed her seas.
And so she fell.

Knees to stone—hands grasping the silken folds of her discarded gown. She pulled it to her face and *screamed*.

If anything, the dress was a decent silencer.

Muffled, sobs born of frustration and despair tore through her throat as she buried herself in the fabric, drenching it in tears until her voice gave out. Until the pulsing anger faded into a tired numbness.

Her pounding head was the first sign she'd fully exhausted herself, temples aching with the remnants of her tantrum.

She slumped beside the bed, resting her temple against its edge, closing her eyes—half-hoping they'd never open again.

"Princess Ragnarvik...?"

A gentle voice stirred her from sleep. Olivja kept her eyes shut, unwilling to return to the world.

The door creaked open and wary footsteps approached. And through the fog of her grief, she heard the soft patter of rain beating against the windows—like something sacred had heard her.

Or perhaps the gods were crying with her.

Her eyes fluttered open.

A young woman stood above her. Familiar. She was one of the many Worthyn assistants, raised to serve like all others.

"Princess...?" she asked again, cautious. "Prince Vincent ordered that we prepare you for supper."

Olivja slowly lifted her head, tears sitting on her cheeks and lashes.

The dark-haired maid stuttered, her hands clenching her grey apron tightly. "Apologies for disrupting your rest, My Grace."

Using the bed, the heiress pushed herself to her feet.

The woman hesitated, uncertain whether to help or pull back—but before she could decide, Olivja was already seated on the mattress.

"Y-your Highness has selected an evening gown for you, Princess Ragnarvik," the maid stammered. "Supper will be ready shortly."

She eyed the silver gown in her arms—frilled, ribbon-bound, cinched tight. Ridiculous.

Outside, thunder cracked across the sky, lightning lighting the walls in a brief flash.

I see.
The Gods are not crying—They are shedding tears of laughter at my expense.

She cleared her throat, "I do not need dressing, *thank you.*"

"B-but, you see, the ribbons are particularly tricky, Princess O—"

"I'll see to my own clothes." Olivja said quickly with no room to budge. "You may go."

The maid bowed her head and stepped out, and the door latched shut behind her.

Olivja stood.

The storm rumbled low in the distance as she crossed the room, opened her chamber door, and dragged in one of the old wooden chests left just outside.

Inside lay a folded linen dress—simple, a bit rough at the seams, dyed an ashy wood-brown and laced down the front with fraying red cord. She dug deeper, fingers brushing familiar textures until she found her old belt—its tarnished bronze buckle scratched from years of wear, its hanging fur and satchel pieces swaying as she lifted it.

One by one, she laid the pieces out before her. Not *princess* things.
Not *noble-supper* things.
Her things.

She dressed quickly and slipped into worn fur-lined boots, the leather molding like a second skin. Her attire held the kind of comfort that had nothing to do with softness, and everything to do with familiarity.

Then, with a steady breath, she reached for the bronze, vine-inspired crown. It was the only thing she allowed. The only piece she'd keep on her terms.

Once finished, she glanced in the polished mirror and smirked.

Hopefully, the unpolished Ragnarvik attire would be enough to distract from the puffiness of her eyes. At the very least, she looked herself again.

Then, the door clicked open again.

Olivja gazed back and her breath caught.

A finely dressed Vincent stalked into her room, his hood and mask shielding his head once again, leaving only his eyes, brows and bridge of his nose exposed.

She felt more comfortable with the mask off, it was reminiscent of the Vincent she once knew. Back then, he never had to hide his face with her.

They paused, staring at each other across the room—the bridge of all unsaid stretched too wide to cross.

He spoke first after the silence proved too heavy to bear.

"Olivja," he said, his green eyes analyzing every curve and trim, "you've grown."

He took a single step closer and Olivja retreated with a mirrored step of her own.

"*Hardly*."
Already exasperated, the heiress turned away from him, wanting no conversation with the prince.

Seeing him again stirred something in her.
Not relief—just bitter nostalgia. And abandonment.

She hadn't seen Vincent in nearly four years. When she turned sixteen, he and Elias were sent away on a training mission by their father. They promised they'd return in two years and, at first, she believed them.

Vincent had written to her a few times, brief letters that never said enough—but then, right around the time they were meant to come home, the letters stopped.
No warning. No explanation. Only silence.

She had waited. She had wondered.
And then, slowly, she learned to resent him for it.

Now, after all these years, after the absence and the unanswered questions, after the anger that had festered beneath her ribs like an open wound—now was the moment she saw him again.

Not because he had come back for her. Not because he owed her an apology.
But because she had been sent to marry him.
She had no words for it.

"Come now, Livvy. It's—it's *good* to see you again. I..." Vincent sighed quietly, a note of nostalgia curling through his voice. "...I never thought I'd see you in a crown." His tone carried a smirk she knew was there, even if she couldn't see it.

Between them, it had always been bickering, pushing, testing. But four years had turned playful jabs into something sharper.

Olivja exhaled through her nose, sharp and short. Her head tilted slightly, a sharp glare cutting at him over her shoulder.

"*Ahem*—You look...*well*," he said, burying the tease in a compliment, but the damage was done.

Wrapping her arms around herself tightly was an attempt to shield herself from any more hurt that day.

A breath escaped him, this one unsteady.
He was rambling, desperate.
"Forgive me. Please—just a moment of your time. I swear it shall be worth it."

"A moment of *my* time..." Olivja scoffed. "And what, *Vincent*, makes you think you deserve even that?"

"Liv—"

"Speak plain!" she snapped, turning in a whirl of fury.
Her hands clenched at her sides, her voice cutting through the air like a blade.
"Four summers. Four winters, Vincent!?"

The silence between them thickened, neither one willing to look away.
Then, with a heavy sigh, Vincent relented.

"Life...became difficult once we returned, Olivja," he admitted, his voice steady but guarded.

She stared at him, unblinking, waiting—daring him to give her something real.
When he hesitated, she scoffed again.

"Is that all? You left me behind, and *that* is your excuse? When have we ever walked a path without thorns?"

Vincent exhaled sharply through his nose.
"Everything here was falling apart. The war, the chaos." His words were clipped, controlled. "It was easier to keep you away."

"Aye," her voice dripped with bitter amusement as she turned her back to him once more, shoulders shrugging. "Because it's the easiest thing *for all*—to turn their backs and leave me behind, *isn't it?*"

"It wasn't like that," he said, his tone laced with frustration. "Liv, I wish you'd trust me."

"Perhaps I did—*four summers ago.*" The words came out quiet, nearly lost to the tension crackling between them.

But then she straightened, forcing steel into her spine.

It didn't matter. None of it did.
Even if they'd stayed the best of friends, it wouldn't have changed a thing.

Because there was no world in which she would accept this marriage—not out of hatred for Vincent, but out of hatred for the faith-borns' warped notion of love and duty.

Before she could take another breath, a sudden touch against her wrist sent a jolt through her.

She gasped, spinning around—only to find herself trapped beneath his stare.

He was close. Too close. Towering over her in a way that made her stomach twist with something that felt like anger, but was laced with something she didn't want to name.

"Don't turn away from me, Olivja. Please," Vincent said, his fingers firm yet careful against her skin.

"I'm not the boy you once knew. I'm a different man now. And...our childish feud? It's over. I can assure you—"

Olivja cut in, "What an easy claim to make when all I knew was the boy who left."

There was salt in her words—bitter and raw—but there was honesty too. "Truth be told...I liked the fire between us," she muttered, looking away.

Vincent's lips curled into something close to amusement, if not for the lingering edge of something deeper—something darker.

His hand moved before she could stop it, tilting her chin upwards, his calloused thumb sweeping across her cheek where dampness lingered. Her breath caught.

"I did as well, Liv," Vincent whispered, his voice barely above a breath. "That's why this is so difficult...But...if you simply grant me some time, I'm hopeful it will all work out the way I desire and—when it's all done—things can return to the way they were...just as you wish."

Her amber eyes widened, both at his words and at the way his touch was impossibly gentle. She swallowed hard, contemplating his words for only a moment before she became overwhelmed by their closeness.

Stepping back, her hands pressed against his firm chest, releasing herself from his grasp with a heavy breath.

It would take a lot more than a simple conversation and touch for her to welcome Vincent as her future husband. She was stubborn...because she didn't want things to change between them, not like this...*not ever*.

"Vincent, I...I only long for my home. I have no need for your excuses or reassurances," she said, saying whatever she could to steer the conversation away from her heartbreak.

Olivja had been reminded of more than one failed friendship today...and it all weighed down on her like a horse.

He straightened, sighing.

"*Princess,*" he pinched the bridge of his nose, "you act as though our kingdom has never treated you well." His attempts at reassurance fell short.

"I'd say your kingdom has given me nothing but torment—"

"*Don't* play the fool, Liv," he interrupted, a hint of annoyance in his tone, "You enjoyed your time here with us, I know it—you said it yourself."

Olivja stayed quiet, keeping her gaze to the wooden floors. Vincent knew her better than she cared to admit. The Worthyn's held a special place in her heart, but that place was now tainted by plans of marriage.

"I didn't come here to argue with you...I came here to—"

"I require a moment alone, Vincent."

Silence followed briefly, then he sighed again and footsteps echoed.

Slowly, he backed towards the door. She looked up as he turned to leave. His green eyes met hers a final time.

He shut the door.

And despite the weight of the entire day, the only thought she was left with was: perhaps, regardless if it was for better or worse, *he had changed after all*.

THREAD VIII

"I SAID GIVE IT BACK, VINCENT!!"

The sounds of the young heiress Olivja echoed through the stone dungeons beneath the Worthyn castle nine years ago.

Barefooted, the girl bolted after a slightly older Vincent, who had torn away her smokkr overdress, leaving her running about in just her pale linen shirt and breeches.

"If you want to act like a boy, you can dress like one!"

Ahead of her, the fourteen-year-old Vincent flailed the apron over his head, howling with laughter as she failed to catch up to him.

His hood slipped back, white hair catching the wind. He bounded up the stairs leading them to the main floor of the castle; a risk considering their parents were somewhere above.

"VINCENT!" Olivja gasped for breath, shouting for him once more as he rounded the steps above her and left her in the dust.

As she reached the tops of the stairs, Vincent was waiting, smiling like he enjoyed watching her struggle to catch him.

With a battle cry, Olivja dove from the top stair, missing him by a few inches before he ran off again.

"DAMN you!" the girl growled, dropping to all fours before pushing herself into a sprint again.

"C'mon, Heiress! You run like a noble-girl!" Vincent chortled, clearly thrilled by their chaos.

This was the farthest he had gone with his pranks. Usually, he would steal a shoe or shove her into a puddle, but having her sprint through the castle in her boy-ish breeches was utterly humiliating for her. Insulting her speed only fuelled her fire further.

They barreled down the carpeted halls as knights and maids gasped, scrambling to avoid the blur of adolescent chaos.

One maid in particular carried a large tub of water...Vincent, in a moment of cruel humor, swerved to narrowly avoid her—leaving her squarely in Olivja's path.

Unfortunately, Olivja had her sights set on reaching her rival and wasted no time plowing through her, drenching the both of them in dirty bath water. An explosion of water cascaded onto the carpets, but Olivja continued sprinting past, wiping her eyes with the backs of her hands.

"Sorry, Madame!!" Olivja cried out, looking back to see the soaked woman being helped by a few knights.

She knew she'd hear about that later.

Turning her head forward, she growled as Vincent looked back at her, laughing harder than before now that the water had drenched her pale pants, rendering them nearly transparent.

Olivja, now red in the face, had murderous intent.

"Liv's a lady after all!" he laughed again, turning back to round the corner to the main foyer.

They flew down the stairs, and this time Olivja knew she had him.
As his feet hit the last step of the stone stairs, Olivja put full faith in her jump, launching herself off of the step she was on, willing to injure herself if it meant catching Vincent.

He turned—too late.
She was already upon him.

The young heiress crashed into him, sending them both sprawling onto the flatstone of the lobby. He hit his back, knocking the wind out of his lungs as all of her weight pressed into his diaphragm. But, his inability to breathe didn't stop her from raining down slaps.

"Do I HIT like a noble-girl!?" Olivja laughed.
He grappled with her, trying to pin her hands above him.

Other footsteps quickly followed down the steps, Elias had been slowly catching up to the two of them with the girl's robe, desperate to help her become less exposed.

"Olivja!"
Eli's shout stole her attention just long enough for Vincent to take advantage of it.

A hard slap sent Olivja to the ground, leaving her groaning as she held her cheek.

Vincent rolled onto all fours, wheezing as he struggled to catch his breath. Elias went to Olivja, whose eyes stung with tears.

He had never hit her so hard before, and now she was angrier than ever.

She pushed Elias away from covering her and dove for Vincent again, this time not holding back at all. They went back and forth, scratching and hitting.

She mounted his chest, raising a heavy fist—only to freeze as a booming voice thundered through the hall.
"*CHILDREN!*"

King Ezekiel's voice shot fear into all three of them.

Olivja and Vincent however were too focussed on their childish feud to care about the consequences. Both of them continued hammering into each other until Ezekiel's thundering footsteps forced them to look up in terror.

Standing as tall as a door, King Worthyn, in all his horrible grace, towered. His long, straight black hair fell over his shoulders like rivers of ink, framing his sharply carved, pallid face.

Behind him trailed his jester—a thin thing, moving more like a demonic snake than a man.

The king's stature was similar to Olivja's father's—though Dagrun was burlier, and, as Olivja would say, carried 'a lot more love.'

Ezekiel's low catlike eyes shot to Vincent, hardly paying attention to the Ragnarvik girl at all.

"Get. Up."
Ezekiel's voice was low, clipped, and heavy with command.

Vincent didn't hesitate, shoving Olivja off his lap and scrambling to his feet as Ezekiel yanked the back of his neck with an iron grip.

"*Oi*!" Olivja shouted, glaring up at the Worthyn king as he manhandled Vincent.

Despite her anger with her friend...she disliked Ezekiel more.

"Let him go!" she barked, already halfway to launching herself at Ezekiel the same way she had at Vincent.

However, more footsteps echoed in the hallway and Olivja turned her head, her stomach dropping as she saw Madame Gothel, soaked in water, following closely behind an exasperated Jarl Ragnarvik, his hand pressed to his temple.

She slowly stood, forgetting that her entire lower half was practically exposed to the families. Her eyes were fixed on Vincent, who hung his head in shame as his father's grip held him fast.

"What is the meaning of this?" Ezekiel growled, his voice sharp and laced with cold fury as he shook Vincent like a ragdoll.

"We were playing a game, Your Grace!" Olivja interjected, breathing heavily, her hands balled in small fists at her sides as she demanded the king's attention.

Ezekiel finally looked at her and, with a deep chuckle, he released Vincent, bringing a hand to his own mouth in shocked amusement.

"My darling Olivja, what on earth—"
Ezekiel's laugh was dark and dry, almost bitter as he took in the drenched, disheveled princess, the soaked maid, the ruined apron, and the bruises marring tender skin.

His gaze sharpened. Slowly, he dropped his hand to his hips, his dark presence filling the room like smoke.

"A game involving a lack of clothing?" Ezekiel's laugh was cold and cutting. He shot a pointed glance at Vincent.

"A bit young for consummation, isn't it?" he asked, glancing towards Dagrun, who shook his head in shamed disbelief. The jester tossed her head with a wide smile, the bells on her braided hair jingling in place of laughter.

Back then, she had no idea what deeper meaning those words held.

"Did my son expose you? Is that why you hound him?" Ezekiel's voice dropped into a hard edge, amusement draining completely. "He knows better than to act a *child*—"

"HE IS a child!" Olivja interrupted, but in the corner of her eye she noticed her father shamefully covering his eyes in his palm. She quickly tried to recover her respect. "*M-My Lord*...but no. I did it myself. I hit him because...I was embarrassed."

She knew Ezekiel's punishments ran far harsher than her father's. Getting in trouble meant nothing to her, but by the way Vincent was unable to look his father in the eyes; she knew it meant worse for him.

"You drenched *yourself* and stripped off your dress of your *own accord*, Princess Ragnarvik?" he asked. Ezekiel's eyebrow arched in a cold scoff, his eyes narrowing as if daring her to lie again.

Immediately, her palms grew clammy, and she struggled to meet his eyes, swallowing hard as she prepared to double down—wet hair dripping around her in scattered puddles.

"I..."

"Yes, Lord Father...she did. It was a dare. I was trying to bring Liv her cloak when Vincent threatened to tell Dagrun and she got angry." Elias fibbed from behind with a trembling voice.

The foyer went quiet as Ezekiel's suspicion grew. His sharp eyes narrowed, the motion small, but sharp with intent. He crossed his arms over his massive chest, tilting his head at the three youngins.

"Princess Olivja, you should know better than to expose yourself so carelessly," the man said, tutting the roof of his mouth.

"You'll belong to a man one day. What shame he'll carry, knowing half the keep saw what should've been his alone. You must be mindful of your *virtue*—it is your true worth."

As Ezekiel lectured her, the heiress hung her head in feigned shame—though, in truth, she was rolling her eyes beneath her dripping hair.

She heard his footsteps. Her head shot up, eyes wide.

As Ezekiel approached he snatched the discarded smokkr from the floor. Behind him, Olivja caught sight of Vincent watching nervously—every trace of his earlier anger gone.

The king held out the skirt. Olivja snatched it and stepped into it hastily, tying it at her lower back with frantic fingers.

But before she could step away, a firm hand gripped her cheeks, forcing her still, gaze upturned. Ezekiel's inky-black stare met hers. His pupils were bottomless voids, pulling her in, paralyzing her.

He didn't blink. Every second dragged. His stillness peeled away her defenses, one by one.

"Olivja, heed my words carefully..."
His tone was soft, almost gentle—but laced with steel.

Her eyes darted towards Dagrun, who was stepping closer now, unease tightening his jaw at the sight of another king reprimanding his daughter.

Ezekiel lowered his voice to a whisper, his smile chilling.
"Your recklessness is beneath the crown we wear, child. One misstep—one foolish display—and you'll no longer be the jewel of this land. Your presence holds power. Guard it. Be prudent. Or it will be taken from you."

Olivja's eyes burned.
It was rare for Ezekiel to scold her—rarer still in front of her father. And Elias. And worst of all, Vincent.

She swallowed hard. Her hands trembled as they fidgeted with the damp ties at her back. Perhaps she was afraid, but fear made her reckless.
She cleared her throat.

"Jewels don't break easy..." She bared her teeth in a cocky grin.
"They crack skulls—"

"Your Highness!"
Dagrun stepped forward, interrupting with a sharp clearing of his throat. "Kiel...*ahem,* we should finish our discussion. My daughter's rest draws near, and we've a long ride home."

Ezekiel's black eyes narrowed. His smirk deepened and his grip tightened on her jaw, her face like an apple in his palm. Goosebumps flared along her wet shoulders.
Then he let go.

She staggered back, nearly falling into Elias.

"Stay the night then, friend," Ezekiel said with a chuckle, draping an arm around Dagrun. "We have far more to discuss now."

The two kings walked off, jester trailing, Dagrun muttering something low and tired that sent Ezekiel into loud, deep laughter.

Olivja stood frozen, watching them disappear, her breathing shaky as if Ezekiel were still looming over her. She shook her head, bewildered that her father could so easily laugh with that man.

She looked down at the flatstone floor—but more footsteps pulled her eyes upwards again.

Vincent was already on the stairs, brooding, flipping his hood and mask back over his head. Olivja sighed, knowing he was angry—at her, likely, but also at his father.

"We'll be punished later for that," Elias said quietly, placing a cloak gently over her soaked frame. He walked a step ahead, the two of them following Vincent in silence.

Olivja kept her head low, her thoughts spiralling. She winced, guilt gnawing at her.

"I...*ugh.* Forgive me." Her voice was hoarse, anger still smouldering beneath her apology. She hugged the cloak tighter to her chest, trembling from the cold and the adrenaline. "I can't help myself around him."

"Vince didn't mean—"

"I'm talking about *your father,*" she snapped. "Vincent can handle me."

They said nothing more as they reached Vincent's study—a warm, cluttered room of shelves and ink-stained desks, parchment and scribbled drafts. Vincent, ever the dramatist, ruled the room like it was a stage.

He slumped into his large wooden chair, turning it towards the door with a heavy thud. Legs spread wide, arms on the rests, one hand supporting his head as he stared off into space. His hair fell like a curtain over his sullen face.

The room was quiet.

Elias entered first. Olivja followed more slowly, shutting the door behind them. She drifted towards a shelf, her fingers brushing across Vincent's scrawled pages.

"Don't drip on my literature, princess," Vincent muttered from his chair, not looking at her. "You've already got me in a *world* of trouble."

"This isn't *literature,*" she said dryly. "It's a heap of horse-dung."

"That's rich, coming from *you.*"
He finally looked up. Their eyes locked.
Vincent scoffed and looked away, his voice cutting:
"Tch. A jewel? More like a hunk of iron."

Silence.

Then Elias snorted. A chuckle escaped him, followed by a fit of laughter. Olivja cracked a reluctant smile.

"She *is* like iron, isn't she?" Elias laughed, tossing back his cowl, shoulders shaking.

"I am not!" Olivja protested, half-grinning as her hair dripped in puddles on the floor.

"Indeed you are!" Vincent joined in, covering his face with his palm. "Olivja Ragnarvik—the *densest* princess in the realm!"

She crossed her arms and smirked sourly, hugging her cloak tighter as her teeth began to chatter. "You t-two are impossible."

The three of them remained huddled in Vincent's study, hiding from Ezekiel. When Vincent brought out a secret stash of his father's stolen wine, the night ended with the three of them passing out at the dim fireplace.

That was the majority of their evenings with each other; bickering and goofing, drinking and exploring. Once the boys turned eighteen, they were sent to train for the war and Olivja no longer saw them.

Perhaps there was a time where the Ragnarvik heiress felt welcomed at the Worthyn's, possibly even loved...
But that feeling died the moment war wedged itself between them—
Ugly and unrelenting.

THREAD IX

ᚦᛖ ᛒᚢᚱᛞᛖᚾᛊ ᛟᚠ ᚺᛖᛁᚱᛊ ᚦᛖ ᛒᚢᚱᛞᛖᚾᛊ ᛟᚠ ᚺᛖᛁᚱᛊ ᚦᛖ ᛒᚢᚱᛞᛖᚾᛊ

ᚨᛞᚨᛚᛃᚨ

ADALJA TOOK A STEADY BREATH, her eyes trailing the reflection in the tall, gold-framed mirror. The room was beautiful—spacious and stately—but hollow. Aside from her newly arrived belongings, it felt empty. Foreign.

The golden light of dusk poured in through the tall windows, draping the room in soft warmth, casting long shadows that stretched across the floor like reaching arms. But despite the glow, her chest tightened.

This was her home now. *It didn't feel like it.*

A quiet throat-clear pulled her back.

"All will be well, Adalja—truly," Brahms said gently from behind. "And...Prince Elias? He seems a good sort."

"*Oh, you know* the reason why my heart won't settle," she murmured.

Her voice was thin. Dry. She looked down, fingers picking at the edge of her pale blue dress, her eyes tracing her figure in the mirror again.
She couldn't stop looking.

The dress felt wrong—too delicate, too fitted, too...much. The colour clung to her skin like uncertainty... And in the back of her mind, all she could think was: *Would Olivja like it?*

She turned towards her knight, nibbling her bottom lip. "Is it too much?" she asked, voice quiet as a mouse.

He stood near the door, arms crossed, expression unreadable. "You're asking the wrong man."

"Please. I trust your judgment," she pressed, not letting it go this time. "How do I look?"

Brahms blinked slowly, his gaze trailing over the dress once...then twice. "Far too much," he said, blunt as ever.

Panic flickered behind her blue eyes. She whipped back to the mirror, searching for whatever flaw he'd seen. And then—in the corner of the reflection—she caught it: the smirk tugging at his lips.

"I kid, Princess," he laughed. But his gaze lingered—longer this time—and there was something in the way he looked at her. Something heavier. Warmer.

He cleared his throat, brushing it off. "You look *well*."

Three loud knocks rattled the door, startling them both.

"Your Prince is waiting, Adalja!" her mother shouted from the hallway.

"Y-Yes, Mother! Coming!" Adalja called back, shooting a sideways glance at Brahms, who had covered his mouth—either in shock, or to stifle a laugh.

Silence settled over her chambers until the sound of her mother's retreating footsteps assured them they were alone once more.

Adalja inhaled sharply and swallowed the sting of frustration. She smoothed her damp palms down the front of her bodice, then offered Brahms a tight, reluctant smile.

"Best we get through this quickly."

As the princess was escorted into the dining hall, her eyes flew to the ceilings.

Its high, vaulted ceilings seemed to stretch into the heavens, while the long table at the centre was surrounded by candlelight and the glint of polished silverware.

Maids stood posted around the walls like silent watchers, knights filtered between them. The hall itself was grand, but paled in comparison to the opulence of Pembrook.

Her gaze landed on the table last—on the noble and Norse heads seated in every chair. She swallowed, the weight of it all catching in her throat.

Ten years.

A decade had passed since the Ragnarviks, Pembrooks, and Worthyns last stood in the same room. The air thrummed—alive, watching, waiting. As if the room itself remembered.

Adalja certainly did. She remembered the day in perfect, painful clarity—the wake of Queen Worthyn. The day the Pembrooks named as "the moment Ragnarvik showed its true face." The day grief and fury split the kingdoms like fault lines.

She hadn't known, then, that one of the two white-haired boys weeping at their mother's coffin would one day become her husband.

"Your seat, Princess, is beside Prince Elias," Queen Natja called over, breaking the silence. She gestured towards the far end of the table.

It was on the same side as Heiress Olivja.

Adalja swallowed hard, forcing a soft smile as she stepped forward.

At the sight of her, Prince Elias shot up from his place at the table and was beside her in a blink, offering his arm.

"Allow me, Princess," he said gently, moving quickly to pull out her chair.

Gods, she could feel everyone's eyes on her. *Especially Olivja*.

Adalja's heart raced as she sat in front of her father, carefully flattening her gown beneath her.

The room fell into a tense hush, save for the soft hum of servants gliding in and out with trays of food and wine.

Across the table, her mother watched her like a hawk—eyes sharp, expression daring her to misstep.

But the princess hardly noticed...
Her mind swam with noise—the maids, the scent of roasted meats and wine, the strain of reunion, and the Ragnarvik Heiress' unreadable silence somewhere beside her.

The current kings and queen raised their goblets, a small ceremonial toast to mark the beginning of the meal. The beginning of their uneasy reunion.

Though truthfully, it felt more like a funeral feast.

Until the jester arrived.

A thin beast dressed in tight, form-fitting black and silver attire that exposed its ribs, stalked into the dining hall. It walked as though rehearsing steps from a dance, bells—woven through two tight, long braids—jingled with each movement. A lute was strapped to its back, a black satchel at their hip. But its eyes, piercing blue and hollow, were trained elsewhere.

No one turned to look. Adalja quickly averted her gaze from the demonic creature. No one spoke.

Well—except for her father, who never could contain himself around her mother. He leaned in close, murmuring soft things that made her face light up, her laugh flickering to life like flame to kindling.

Adalja glanced around while her mother was distracted, taking in the table's offerings—warm, fresh breads, glistening fruits, and pitchers of wine, early indulgences before the main course.

Opposite of Olivja was an empty chair, tucked neatly under the table. Beside it was Jarl Dagrun—refilling his tankard with wine—who sat across from Vincent. The Jarl's eyes were already glassy, rimmed red with drink or weariness. Or both.

Adalja's lips curled into a thin line. Gods...he looked so different. So *worn*.

A servant leaned in beside her, carefully plating her food: steamed cabbage and onions, thick slices of beef roasted with herbs and butter, soft carrots glistening with oil. Her eyes widened as her stomach gave a thunderous growl.

If nothing else, at least she would be well fed here.

As the others began to eat, Vincent's voice cut through the quiet like a blade. He cleared his throat, the sound echoing through the hall, drawing every gaze as he began discussing the future wedding plans.

Adalja barely listened—her focus glued to Elias.

Those piercing green eyes. The snow-white hair. The way his presence seemed untouched by the heaviness of the room.

He wasn't eating. He wasn't drinking. He sat with perfect posture, one hand resting lightly on the stem of his goblet, the other folded in his lap. It told her everything.

He was here for duty and formality. Not for a meal.
For her.

And her fingers wrapped tightly around her linen at the thought.

She studied him, the delicate eyelashes, the curve of his jaw—painfully enchanted despite herself. And just as her eyes trailed up the bridge of his nose—

He glanced sideways.

Their eyes locked.

Her heart slammed against her chest.

She looked across the table quickly, straightening her back, pretending to focus on the carved roast. She scooped a spoonful of cabbage as if she hadn't been admiring him like art on a cathedral nave.

She felt utterly foolish to have been caught staring.

The tension in the room only made everything feel worse. Every emotion—sharper, every heartbeat—louder, every stolen glance—more daring.

And just as she thought she could no longer bear it—she heard her.

Olivja's sarcastic, warm, sharp voice cut through the silence, like a slap you'd somehow beg for more of.

"*Tch*—A ball *before* the marriage? Why not the funerals too, while we're at it?"

Just like that, the tension had momentarily fallen away, Olivja's scoff cutting through it like a knife to butter.

Adalja fought the urge to snort. The heiress had the gall to say what everyone else was already thinking. Trying to hide her amusement, the princess shoved a warm carrot into her mouth.

Olivja sounded as brash as she always did when they were children...she loved it. She wanted more of it. More of anything that would make this dinner easier to swallow.

Vincent cooed, clearing his throat. "Liv...the only funeral to be mourned will be *yours*. You've barely touched your plate—starvation will be your undoing."

"So be it," the heiress said, for though she spurned her plate, her strength and health shone brighter than any at the table.

The prince disguised his irritation with a gentle chuckle, raising his goblet with a wink and a sip.

"It's a pity Solvig couldn't attend," Elias suddenly remarked with a deep exhale, his comment seeming to perk up Dagrun, who seized the excuse to mention his missing wife.

"Oh, my Sol," the Jarl cooed. "I extend her deepest shame," he said, taking a long drink from his mug. "My lovely wife is tending to our jarldom."

Natja's bitter laugh broke the soft moment as she laid down her utensils, dabbing at her mouth with her linen. "Ah, Solvig...*always* too occupied in Ragnarvik, isn't she?" Her tone was sharp, calculated, and it made Adalja's skin crawl.

Dagrun's expression twisted at the response. But the Jarl didn't turn to face her. His glare remained fixed straight ahead—past the candles, past the table, past the noise—eyes glassed with something darker than anger. Grief, perhaps. *Or memory.*

In his defense, Olivja slammed her hands onto the table, rattling goblets and pewter. She leaned forward, and Adalja finally caught a clearer view of her—a view that made her gasp more than any words could.

"If there's a point to your blabbering, Natja," the heiress snapped, "speak it true!"

The room fell silent, save for Dagrun's harsh cough as he choked on his drink, sputtering it back into his tankard before clearing his throat.

"Prince Elias!" Adalja's father cut in before anything worsened. "Will you be off to war after the marriage?"

Adalja shifted in her seat, her eyes flickering to Elias as she awaited his response. His gaze met hers once, then returned to her father across the table.

"Not quite the place for our bonding moon," the prince answered, a hint of amusement in his voice—surely there was a smile beneath that mask.

Brahms, stationed quietly in the corner of the dining hall, snorted to himself—his chuckle marked by the soft clink of armor. At the same moment, Olivja slammed her silverware against her plate, the sharp clang drowning out Brahms' laughter—a blessing in disguise.

No one else seemed to care about her anger.
It wasn't the first time Olivja had lashed out at the table. Surely it wouldn't be the last.

Dagrun suddenly stood, excusing himself from the table. The drunk Jarl turned and stumbled on his own feet, falling forward onto the stone with a heavy *thud.*

Adalja gasped, neck craning as she watched the mountain of a man topple over, like the sea of mead had finally washed him away.

Olivja flew to his rescue, chair scraping stone. "Pabbi!" she cried out.

Adalja leaned forward to watch the heiress tend to her unravelling father. Mark stood from the table as well, but Natja rested a firm hand on her husband's arm, forcing him to return to his seat.

They all watched in silence as Olivja struggled to carry her father—cursing at any knight who dared to offer help—as she dragged him out of the room.

The princess' hands clenched tight beneath the table, carving pale crescents into her skin like the marks of chains she couldn't see until now. Chains that kept her restrained to passivity.

Suddenly, ringing filled the space as the jester twirled forward, body arching and flipping like the sight of a fallen Jarl had enlivened it.

When it reached the space where Dagrun had fallen, the jester tumbled to the floor with an eruption of jingles. Its painted smile was a mockery of the Jarl as it crawled and twisted, rolling around the floor in a dramatic manner.

Both Vincent and Natja grinned at the sight, shaking their head in disbelief at the blatant disrespect from the lowly jester.
Mark and Adalja could barely watch.

And then—the pale, painted face popped into view across the table, rising slowly from the edge like a lurking sea creature breaching the surface. Its wide, unblinking eyes stared straight at the princess.

Adalja gasped and sank back into her chair, breath caught in her chest as the jester—yes, the jester—clambered up and into the seat across Vincent, the one that belonged to Highwife Solvig.

It didn't sit like a normal man.
No, it slouched sideways, bare feet swinging lazily over the armrest, its painted smile frozen and unmoving as it plucked casually at the strings of a battered lute.

A soft, odd little tune poured from the instrument—offbeat, aimless...clearly meant for the whole table.

Her hands worked anxiously at the linen in her lap, twisting it into knots. The conversation around her blurred, muted by the echo of someone else's absence.

Her gaze drifted to the doors. Somewhere beyond was the Norsewoman—no longer a wisp in half-remembered dreams, no longer a phantom on the edge of memory. She was real now. And Adalja felt the pull like a tide, desperate and unrelenting, aching to rise and chase it.

"So, Princess, have you travelled much before this?" Elias' smooth voice broke through, drawing Adalja's thoughts and gaze back to him.

Her hands quit their fidgeting. She was taken aback by his sudden question, painfully aware of the dryness in her throat.

"N-No, I...I have not, Your Grace," she stammered quietly, "the furthest I've been is to the Ragnarvik jarldom, but...that was when I was a child."

Elias seemed pleased by the answer, eyes squinting in a hidden smile. He leaned closer, closing the distance between them.

Adalja froze, hyper-aware of his proximity as he tugged his mask down slightly. Her breath hitched in her throat as she was reminded of his handsome features.

"Then, shall we slip away?" Elias asked quietly—words meant for her ears alone.

For a brief second, the world around them seemed to fade, focussing solely on her quick, beating heart.

Without thinking, she nodded.

And as soon as she did, Elias released his mask, hiding his face once more under the dark fabric. His strong, warm hand found hers beneath the table—fingers brushing over her clenched palm. He lifted her hand gently, and her stomach tumbled.

Without a word, he rose—pulling her with him, quietly severing her from the table, from the weight, from everything that kept her still.

Queen Natja and King Mark watched closely as Elias addressed the table, his voice loud and commanding: "Please excuse us, Majesties."

Adalja offered a polite smile to her parents, Vincent, and Brahms—who, as always, remained silent in his corner. Every eye in the room trailed her as Elias led her out of the dining hall, guiding her through the large doors.

He paused once they were in the hallway, letting the doors close behind them. There, he released her, stepping back to give her space.

"If anyone inquires...tell them I was burdened with matters of taxation," he said with a wink that left her watching with wide eyes. All she could do was nod to confirm she had heard him.

With an added chuckle, he bowed his head. "Have a good rest of your night, Princess Adalja," he said.

His eyes briefly flashing up through his white lashes, never once looking away from her. She found herself wishing he wouldn't stop.

"M-many thanks, Prince Elias," she sputtered quickly.

"The pleasure is mine," he replied, his voice soft.

With a polite smile, she turned on her heel and walked away with urgency, eager to find the stranger who wasn't so much a stranger after all.

She moved through the corridor, anticipation pushing her forward towards the bedchambers.

Then—suddenly—she stopped.

The sound of raindrops pattering against the stone walls caught her attention. Familiar. Haunting. It stirred memories of the two of them.

She moved without thinking, drawn to the gardens by the pull of her heart alone. At the doors, she paused. Two knights standing guard opened them without a word.

The cold wind struck her face, whipping curls past her shoulders with a draft that stole the breath from her lungs. The rain was heavy, cold, and relentless. It fell in dense sheets, the rhythm of droplets against cobblestones forming an enchantment in the air. The garden was alive with the sound of water trickling over leaves and pooling into puddles.

She knew the heiress was out there.

Without hesitation, she tied the hem of her gown into knots at her thighs and stepped forward. The cold hit her instantly.

She gasped as the rain soaked through the fabric, chilling her skin like needles of ice. Her arms wrapped around herself, clutching at her biceps.

Gods, if she isn't out there...

Shivering, she pressed onward, head on a swivel, searching the rain-dark garden for the only one she hoped to find.

Past the heart of the grounds, the rain fell harder, drenching the leaves and the stone paths in its relentless cadence.

Ahead of her, a solitary figure stood beneath an ancient tree, her back to Adalja, her hair darkened by the rain, falling in heavy, soaked strands.

It was Olivja.

Her breath caught as she surged forward. Her heart ran to close the distance her feet could not.

The heiress' posture was stiff, shoulders taut as if she carried the weight of the rain—or something far heavier. She seemed carved from stone, unyielding beneath the weather's onslaught, her stillness at odds with the storm that swirled around her.

"Olivja?" The name left her lips in a whisper, more prayer than call.
The sound was swallowed by thc rain, but there was a faint hitch in Olivja's shoulders—the only sign she'd been heard.

Still, the Norsewoman did not turn.

Adalja took a tentative step closer, her boots sinking into the sodden earth. The wet silk of her gown clung to her legs. The rain was cold, yes, but her heart burned hotter, fuelled by a surge of relief and happiness at the sight of *her.*

"Olivja...I can't believe you're here." Her voice faltered, the words dissolving on her tongue.

She was so close now she could see the rain tracing paths down Olivja's neck, disappearing into the soaked fabric of her tunic-dress. Adalja's chest ached—a deep, hollow yearning she couldn't name.

Finally, Olivja spoke, her voice soft but sharp, like the edge of a blade dulled by time but still capable of cutting. "I thought you *hated* the rain, Adalja."

The familiarity of her name on her tongue sent a shiver through her. It was both a gift and a wound, a reminder of the countless times they'd spoken to each other, back when their friendship was all that mattered to them.

"I..." Adalja paused. She swallowed a growing lump in her throat. "I didn't mean that, Olivja...please understand." Her lips shivering as the coldness between them seeped far deeper than the rain. "I-I had to sp-speak with you."

The Norsewoman turned then, slowly, as if the motion itself cost her something.

When their eyes met, the princess felt the years collapse into a single moment, her breath stolen.

Olivja's amber gaze was as vivid as she remembered, though shadowed now, clouded by a sadness she didn't know how to ease.

The rain clung to Olivja's lashes, dripping down her cheeks like tears, though her expression was inscrutable. Her beauty, the strength in her form, the elegance of her posture...it was like something of legends. *Of dreams.*

"You *had* to, Princess?" Olivja repeated, her tone weak but tinged with an edge that made Adalja flinch.

Neither stepped closer. But the heiress' presence did enough to fill the space between them—heavy, impossible to ignore.

"Yes...Of course. I-I wished to see you...t-to see if you were well," Adalja quickly corrected herself, the words stuttering with sincerity.

It was the truth, but something about it felt inadequate. A mere drop of rain against the fire that raged within the Ragnarvik woman.

"If I were well?" Olivja laughed—hollow, bitter. "And what would that look like, Adalja?" she asked, but gave her no time to respond. "Certainly I'm not well if I'm standing *here*, letting rain run down my spine like a *blade* as I relive our last moments...*again and again.*"

The princess shifted uncomfortably, hands—though numb—tightening on her biceps. She had imagined a warm reunion between them, against all odds. Now, all she felt was frost, and a chasm neither of them knew how to cross.

"Olivja," she managed, her voice trembling, shattered by time. "Forgive me."

There was a short pause where the two women simply stared at each other through the downpour.

And then Olivja stepped forward, closing the fragile distance between them with a speed that had the princess faltering backwards, just a step. Soon the heiress was entirely upon her, their bodies an arm's width apart.

Adalja gasped, frozen to the spot as her hands pressed against Olivja's stomach.

"Liv—!" The princess yelped. Her hands splayed, fingers curling into the soaked tunic-dress, torn between pulling her closer and pushing her away. It was then that she had noticed how much taller Olivja had gotten over the years, she towered a whole head above her now.

Olivja's cold hands flew up to Adalja's face, cupping her rain-slicked cheeks with a firmness that sent a jolt through her body.

"Look into my eyes," Liv demanded, her words a whisper against the deluge, her amber eyes boring down into Adalja's.

Her breath hitched as their gazes locked—and for a moment, the rain, the cold, the years between them vanished.

She was engulfed in those burning hues, her body igniting like kindling beneath their heat; Liv's eyes were the spark.

"I...*I am*," Adalja breathed, barely audible, her body trembling from far more than the cold.

"I should curse you for seeking me. *But I can't...*" Olivja's voice cracked, her words raw with emotion.

Her thumbs brushed against the princess' cheekbones, and the subtle tenderness of the gesture was a blade slicing through her resolve. The Norsewoman's touch was soft, reverent—like Adalja was a dream come to life.

"Tell me why you came," the heiress stepped closer, her body a shield against the relentless rain, their foreheads nearly touching. "Not here to this wretched kingdom—*here*, to the rain, with *me.*"

Adalja whimpered at the closeness, chest heaving, the heat of Olivja's body seeping through the damp chill between them. Her pulse thundered in her ears.

What was happening?
This was all so sudden. So *unexpected*.
She knew Norsefolk were forward, but *this?* This felt calculated, planned, deeply sought.

Olivja's desperation unfurled in the space between their lips, her voice softening into something achingly vulnerable. "Say there's a reason you stand before me. *Gods, say this is not a trick.*"

Her heart clenched, the intensity of Olivja's words weaving through her like fire. Her breath hit Adalja's parted lips, like a spirit's kiss.

"O-of course I'm here, Olivja, b-but..." Her words refused to come, trapped behind the wall of emotions rising inside her.

The Norsewoman leaned closer, her lips parting as if to speak again, but only her breath came, mingling with Adalja's. The closeness was so intimate it suffocated her, stole her composure, her *strength.*

Adalja's fingers tightened into the tunic, her brows furrowing as a flicker of heat—foreign and undeniable—spread through her, pooling low in her stomach.

Her eyes darted back to the castle.
Was someone watching? Her mother? Her suitor? Brahms? She couldn't be seen like this. Her wide eyes searched the heiress' matured yet familiar face, her chest heaving.

"W-what is the meaning of this, Olivja?" she whispered, her breath catching in the cold. "I—I don't understand why you..."

Her words were cut off by the heiress' fragile scoff

"Why I act this way?" Olivja's asked. "Because Adalja, I cannot contain what burns inside me *any longer*!" Her hands tightened on her cheeks, eyes shimmering—not from the rain alone but from a raw emotion she could not hide.

"Why did you come to me...?" she asked again, her voice lower as if it would coax an answer...it didn't.

The princess stood dumbfounded, staring up at the woman she once called a childhood friend—looming over her like some fated lover.

Her mind swirled, desperate to fit pieces together that *did not match.* Where was this intensity coming from? Why did it feel so strong...so right?

But when Adalja's silence proved too much, the grip on her cheeks shifted. Liv's fingers twitched before falling away like a tether snapping under strain.

The absence of her touch sent a hollow ache spiralling through Adalja.

The Norsewoman stepped back, shaking her head as if trying to rid herself of the moment entirely.

"I see...You're here because you think a handful of words in the rain will mend the hurt you put me through."

Adalja's hands hovered in the air where Olivja had been only moments before, face dropping. Guilt washed over her like the rain.

"I...I never wished to leave—to *hurt you,*" she whispered, her voice breaking. "They *took* me. I-I had no choice, Olivja. I—"

"The problem is not that you left, *Princess,*" the heiress interrupted, her voice teetering between fury and despair. "It's that you *stayed* away." The words cracked, the pain etched across her face.

"Olivja..." Adalja stepped forward, her voice pleading, but Olivja raised a hand, stopping her in her tracks.

"No," she said, the force startling Adalja. "Don't dare look at me with all that sorrow in your eyes. You don't get to feel sorry now. Not when you left me to bear this *alone.*"

Whatever words Adalja might have found vanished at the sound of a voice cutting through the storm—Vincent.

"Princess!"

Both women jolted, instinctively stepping further apart as if caught in a forbidden act. Adalja wrapped her arms tightly around herself again, weighed down curls clinging to her sad face.

Vincent jogged towards them, his green eyes blazing with a mix of worry and frustration. "What in the heavens are you two doing out here!?" he called, his voice echoing over the pattering rain.

Olivja tilted her head, a smirk tugging at her lips despite the storm that was raging through her just moments ago.

"Oh, truly, I was giving your voice a wide berth," she quipped, her words laced with biting sarcasm.

Vincent's jaw tightened, his patience clearly worn thin. Without hesitation, he grabbed Olivja's arm, his grip firm but not cruel.

"You're both soaked," he muttered, his tone exasperated. "You'll freeze out here for no good reason."

Olivja shot him a glare, but Vincent's hold didn't falter.

"*Inside*," he commanded, his voice brooking no argument.

Then, his sharp gaze shifted to Adalja, tone kinder and baring none of the irritation he pointed towards the Norsewoman. "Princess, I suggest you retreat from this rain before you catch your death."

Adalja opened her mouth, an objection forming on her lips, but Vincent turned back to the woman in his grasp.

"You stormed out in the middle of court dinner," he said, voice low and gruff as he dragged her towards the castle doors. "You're going to return with some dignity."

Olivja huffed, her defiance flickering in the curl of her lips, but she allowed herself to be guided away.

Adalja remained frozen in place, the rain soaking through her to the bone as she watched them disappear into the castle. Her hands trembled at her sides, her heart aching with a strange mixture of longing, guilt, and regret.

Eventually, she moved, her legs heavy as chains as she trudged to her chambers. The castle's cold stone floors deepened the chill in her bones, each step trailing water behind her.

She reached her door in silence—teeth chattering, heart leaden—the echo of Olivja's words still clinging to her like the wet on her skin.

Thread X

"Told you once—I have no hunger, Vince!" Olivja mumbled a bit louder as Vincent's strong hand pinched her bicep, dragging her through the castle to the dining hall.

Small drops of rain dripped from her dress and hair, soaking the smooth flooring wherever they went.

"The day has been long, Olivja," he said, breath hissing beneath his mask. "Dine with me. It is the least I ask."

Once through the doors, he shoved her arm away, pushing her towards the table. She reached out with both hands, steadying herself against the chair frame while swiftly turning to look at him. Irritation burned in her eyes, wanting nothing to do with him at this moment.

Liv was impatient to make it back to her chambers, where she could finally sit with the emptiness gnawing inside her. Her eyes kept flicking back to the hall, debating her escape. Her heart, thumping from seeing Adalja so close, raced faster as she gazed at Vincent.

Adalja's beautiful, matured image was burned into the back of her mind. There was so much she wanted to say, but she cursed herself for being too blinded by her resentment and hurt to do so.

That moment—stolen from them by Vincent—was ruined.

"Hopefully your food hasn't run cold," he said, coming closer, gripping the chair she was holding. He carefully removed her hands, sliding the chair backwards so she could sit. Then, he did the same for himself.

"The sooner you eat, the quicker we can get you out of that wet gown." His tone was calm, expecting no further resistance from her.

"I will not," Olivja said, crossing her shivering arms beneath her breasts. "I am not someone you can command, you should know that."

His new title as her suitor didn't change their history or dynamic. He was still the boy she knew as a child, and she was determined to keep it that way.

"Olivja, I suggest you—"

"I suggest *you* hold your tongue...lest you embarrass yourself *further,*" she said with a cocky smirk.

Vincent's eyes narrowed, his head tilting slightly to the left, as it always did when he grew irritated. Unsurprisingly, he chuckled, and for a moment, relief softened her chest.

Though truthfully, she was yearning for a fight that would resemble their younger days. Something to get her mind off the Pembrooks...he was good at that.

"Olivja..." he hummed, voice soft, a sign that he was *already* close to breaking. "Sit. *Down*."

But she stood her ground, unwavering and firm in her resistance. With a shake of her head, she smiled up at him, admiring the way his eyebrows curved in anger.

Some things never change.

"Hmm...no. The furs call to me, Vincent. Farewell."
She turned away completely, stepping towards the dining doors.

Suddenly, her body jolted backward as Vincent gripped her wrist, yanking her back until they were eye to eye again.

"I am the one who will excuse you—do not walk away from me," he hissed, his other hand catching her hips, knowing full well she wouldn't go down without a fight.

Olivja's stomach dropped.
Even amidst their playful banter and childhood romping, Vincent had never touched her with such *force.*

Now, with his rage-contorted face before her, something in her own expression twisted—an unfamiliar mix of shock and defiance. Her head throbbed, drowning beneath a crushing tide of fury.

She looked down at the tight grip on her wrist—
and her blood ran cold.

If Vincent was going to be her husband, one thing was certain:
He would not lay his hands on her vindictively.

In a final act of defiance, she thrust both hands into his chest, forcing him back a step. Pain shot through her palms on impact, her wrists buckling against his unyielding firmness. *Gods*, he was harder now than he ever used to be—like stone.

But she didn't waver. She stood tall, jaw set, curling her stinging hands into fists.

"You will not touch me in anger, Vincent!" Her breath quickened, her wrist still throbbing from his hold. The air between them crackled with tension. "Who do you think you are!?"

A heavy silence followed. She prayed he would hear the seriousness in her voice and retreat.

But he didn't.

With a sudden, violent bang, he shoved the chair back into place at the table. The impact sent several silver chalices rattling, spilling red mead across the wood in blooming puddles.

Olivja had no time to brace herself. He stepped forward.
And the next sound was sharper.
Louder.
Meaner.

The back of his stern hand struck her cheek with a force that echoed through the room.

Shock drowned out everything else.
Adrenaline surged in her veins as she fell into the edge of the table—a second blow.

She went down with the chalices, a grunt leaving her lips as she clung to the wood like a woman tossed overboard. Her cheek burned, the pain radiating down her neck, and though she fought it—tears welled at her waterline.

It became clear what kind of *changes* Vincent had undergone. He was no longer the boy she knew, but a man *craving control.*
And yet, she refused to believe it.

"You've hit me?" she whispered, stunned—more to herself than to him.

"Yes, Olivja. And I will do it again, if I must," Vincent hissed through clenched teeth, his nose rising in a snarl.

She looked up at her assailant, one hand still clutching her cheek. His hood had fallen. Strands of disheveled white hair clung to his face, damp with sweat or rain—she couldn't tell.

Those green eyes—sharp and venomous like a reptile's—were now bloodshot at the corners, raw with rage.

The Vincent she knew would never have harmed her...not like this.
Tears fell faster, her heart fracturing piece by piece—until it grew sharp enough to shield itself.

"Let that smack serve as a minuscule example of what happens when you refuse a king," he snapped beneath his breath. "Need I continue...?"

Her shock burned into anger.

"A king?" she spat. "You're no king, Vincent! And without me, you'll never be!" She pushed herself to her feet, voice rising. "Strike me again, and I swear—you'll know my wrath!"

But against her warning, his hand flew towards her—not in a slap, but a brutal grip. He seized the back of her head, fingers tangled in her hair. His other hand gripped her face, thumb digging into her jaw as he shoved her down to the ground.

He loomed over her like a predator, breath heavy, body taut with rage. His hands bruised where they held her, her tears soaking into the pads of his fingers.

"Get off me!" she screamed through squashed cheeks, finally striking back—her hands punching the hard wall of his chest. "I'll tell our fathers!"

"You'd be wise to keep your defiance from *my* father, Olivja," he said, unbothered by her fists, voice low and venomous. He jerked her head back against the ground, forcing a sharp wince from her lips.

"...My hands are a mere whisper compared to the might of my father's," the prince added, breath heavy. "So unless you wish to witness *his* hands...let this be the last time you disobey. Do. You. Understand?"

It took only a breath for her to bite back.

"I fear no Worthyn," she grunted. But her voice betrayed her—quivering as she stared up at the man she once trusted, her nose scrunching in disgust.

Her past was a shattered memory.
Her future loomed above her, cold and merciless.

Vincent's gaze darkened. With a frustrated snarl, he shoved off her, slamming her head against the floor in the same motion. The world rang in Olivja's ears, her eyes squeezing shut as pain flared through her skull. Dazed, she barely felt his fingers slip away before he straightened, chest heaving.

"Get her to bed," the prince ordered, flicking his hands at his sides. He uncoiled his fingers with a crack, rolled his neck—whether from relief or guilt, she couldn't tell. He ran both hands through his wild hair, combing it back with swollen fingers, then reached for his mask to settle it back in place.

The taste of blood coated her tongue—a broken lip, likely from the first slap.

If not for the pounding in her head, she might have kept fighting.
Perhaps she had a death wish.
Perhaps she just wanted her friend back.

Her spiralling thoughts scattered the moment her body lifted from the stone floor. Gravity tugged at her limbs, and a sharp, involuntary whimper escaped as pain throbbed through her skull.

The guard said nothing.
He simply turned and carried her back to her chambers—
And behind them, the echoes of her heartbreak deepened in the silence that followed her pain.

THREAD XI

ᚦᛖ ᛒᚢᚱᛞᛖᚾᛊ ᛟᚠ ᚺᛖᛁᚱᛊ ᚦᛖ ᛒᚢᚱᛞᛖᚾᛊ ᛟᚠ ᚺᛖᛁᚱᛊ ᚦᛖ ᛒᚢᚱᛞᛖᚾᛊ

ᛒᚱᚨᚺᛗᛊ

BRAHMS WATCHED ADALJA SLINK AWAY into the room the way she always did, the way her mother always made her. Small, quiet and humbled with her head low.

Prince Elias followed behind her in silence, towering over her effortlessly. The prince glanced over making eye contact for a passing second with Brahms before shutting the door softly.

The knight huffed to himself as he pulled his heavy helmet off, taking a deep breath to comfort his thoughts as the silence of the halls enveloped him once more. He didn't like to see Adalja seemingly falling into old habits of getting into mischief with the troubled heiress.

Alone...in the rain...with a pagan like her? He forced himself not to picture what might have happened if no one had intervened.

He shook himself from his thoughts as the quiet prince emerged from Adalja's room once more. His eyes fell to Brahms' as soon as the door clicked shut.

"Your Highness," Brahms greeted with a tight nod at the tall prince. "How...How is the Princess?" As he asked the question, his head tilted, peeking back at Adalja's quarters.

"I've seen to it that she shall get changed and I advised her to get some rest," Prince Elias noted, adjusting his dark mask while glancing back towards the room. "Please see to it that the Princess stays in bed...we are all well past our curfews," he added in a gentle yet formal tone. Then, those cat-like, green eyes turned to the knight with a certain intensity that sent a shiver through him.

"Ah, we do creep on witching hours," Brahms said with a smirk. His tone was lighthearted, hoping to cease any more of the tension that was building in the quiet hallway.

And it worked.

A small snort left the prince—though he tried to cover it up by shifting his body.

"Be seeing you, Sir Brahms," Elias exhaled, walking off towards his own chambers. Brahms watched him go.

Once alone—with a quiet groan—he rubbed his hands over his face, trying to shake off the stress of the day, the dinner, the presence of Worthyns.

But he couldn't relax just yet. Faint murmurs reached him from down the hall. A voice he knew *all too well.*

"Spare the help!! I'm not broken!" An angry shout came bouncing off the stone walls.

Olivja Ragnarvik.

She appeared, rounding the corner with two guards at her sides. Her jaw was set, shoulders rigid, yanking and pulling from their gloved hands as they tried to guide her. The guards' grim expressions mirrored hers but remained civil—steel-clad tempests held back by chains of discipline, and discipline alone.

"Evening, Princess Ragnarvik," Brahms called, his curiosity piqued by the brooding knights and her disheveled appearance. His eyes narrowed at the sight of a split lip.

"Is...all well?" he asked, taking a small step towards her, ready to defend if it called for it.

Sensing his defensive aura, one of the knights jutted out in front of her, shielding the heiress from his view. His hand tightened around his spear.

"*Oh—Now* you play protector? After all your *silence*?!" Olivja snapped, her voice laced with venom. "You're all knights in name only!"

A brutal jab, one that Brahms knew stung.

Her words hit their mark, and the men visibly stiffened, but they held their ground. Olivja shoved against their armoured chests, her forceful movements almost sending one of them off balance.

She stepped away, glaring at them until they reluctantly cleared their throats and retreated. Chest rising and falling, Olivja stood firm until they disappeared around the corner.

Brahms watched in silence, his mind wandering to the last time he had seen Olivja. He had always viewed her as a troublemaker, someone who only added complications to their lives.

Seeing Olivja in front of him again—bloodied and throwing a fit—proved that to him. But he couldn't suppress the wave of nostalgia that hit him. She looked just as wild and untamed as she did when she was younger. Her eyes met his, and for a moment, everything else faded.

"Brahms," Olivja greeted him coldly, but her gaze softened, only enough for him to catch the flicker of something deeper. Without missing a beat, she shifted her weight, crossing her arms. "You look worse."

He rolled his eyes, a knowing smile tugging at his lips. "This coming from a washed up *viking*...did you just crawl out the sea?" he asked, motioning to her dripping dress.

"Do you have the stones to call me that again?" she asked, tone dropping like a sudden drop in pressure. Olivja's eyes narrowed, and the corner of her lips twitched into a frown. He grimaced—he likely took that a *step* too far.

"S-sorry..." He cleared his throat. "Been a while, hasn't it?"

"On the contrary, *Bramble*," she replied with a sharp tone, the childhood nickname soaked in disdain. "Feels like only yesterday you *turned on me* and tore my whole world to shreds."

His smirk faltered.
"You're still seething over that, *Heiress Olivja*?" he asked with an eyeroll, though deep down, he knew the burdens of the past were not so easily forgotten.

"*Aye.* Though I *may* bend my anger," she said, her voice shifting, now more serious. "If you let me speak to Adalja."

Brahms' chest tightened. Of course, that was why she was here. He should have known. The momentary warmth of seeing her gave way to a familiar coldness as he glanced once at Adalja's door. "She's resting," he uttered—unconvincingly.

"You owe me this," Olivja responded *immediately*, her tone flat yet commanding.

Brahms laughed, crossing his arms over his spear. "I owe you nothing. My only debt is to the Pembrooks," he reminded, voice tinged with caution. "And they have *very* strong feelings about your family."

"You're shocked that I'm bitter," Olivja scoffed, her open palm gesturing down the hall towards where the king and queen lay. "Yet they've spat my name without consequence for years?"

"It is forbidden for me to judge My Lord and Lady," Brahms replied, his tone defensive, his loyalty still unwavering.

"But you would judge me?" Her voice faltered slightly. "After all this time?"

Guilt struck him like a sudden spear. And so, he hesitated, sighing under the heiress' persistence.

"Brahms, it's been *ten* turns of the sun," her voice was quiet but sincere. "Am I to be chained to my past *forever*? I only want to see her. Have I no right to redemption?"

The words caught him off guard, his grip faltering ever-so-slightly.
She appeased his sense of justice and impartiality—manipulating him into believing that she was deserving of another chance. Perhaps she was. Brahms wasn't sure if he was barring her due to old grudges or protectiveness over Adalja. So in his uncertainty, he stepped aside, exhaling slowly.

"One hour," he grumbled.

Instantly, Olivja's shoulders sagged in relief and her hands uncrossed. She swallowed, fingers nervously fidgeting at her hips, cheeks flushing with an emotion Brahms could only call nervousness.

"Thank you," she exhaled, her voice genuine—for the first time in their exchange—no, *in his life*.

She slipped through the door, which closed behind her with a soft click.

Brahms stood motionless for a moment, letting the silence settle over him.

The girls' reunion seemed too intimate, too personal, for him to intrude, even if he was curious. He placed his helmet back on and stepped away from the door, a small smirk on his lips as muffled voices spilled out from behind the closed door.

ᚨᛞᚨᛚᛃᚨ

ADALJA LAY QUIETLY ON HER BED, her eyes staring up at the ceiling. She couldn't sleep, not after hearing the faintest wisps of Olivja's voice outside her room.

Her hands lay beside her, gripping her mattress covers as she frustratedly recalled their conversation. Repeatedly, the scene replayed across her vision, filling her mind with an angry, disappointed Olivja.

Her lips quivered as a knot swelled in her throat. The thin, cotton nightgown she changed into did little to chase away the coldness in her chest.

The voices quieted.
And then the door to her room opened with a *creak*.

Adalja shut her eyes, feigning sleep.

The door creaked closed.

She opened her eyes and glanced over.

Olivja was standing at the door, illuminated by cool moonlight, still dripping with rainwater. Her expression was soft and wide-eyed.

Even from her bed, she could make out the split lip that wasn't there when she had approached her in the rain merely an hour ago. She grew sick at the first thought that came to her mind; *Vincent did this.*

Sitting up, Adalja flung the blankets off her legs, overrun with deep worry at the sight of her injury.

"Olivja, what happened—"

"Why did you follow me out there?" Olivja interrupted her with the same question from before.

Adalja's expression swiftly softened into confusion.

"What?" the princess mumbled, slowly sliding her legs over the side of the bed.

She realised quickly that if she hadn't followed Olivja out, that perhaps she would have never gotten hurt. A pang of guilt shot through her chest.

"Forgive me—It's my fault you were hurt."

"No. Not *this* time," Olivja whispered. "...but I'm not here to blame you, no. I—" Liv paused, and the princess stayed quiet.

"Adalja—where have you *been*?" she asked, her lips quivering in a frown.
She was wounded—in every sense of the word.

Though, the wounds Adalja gave her weren't as easily mended as the ones Vincent gave.

"In all those years...did I ever once cross your mind?" Olivja pressed, her ragged breaths mirroring her trembling composure.

The question seemed preposterous to the Pembrook princess.

Ever since she lost her friend, it was as though a part of her heart had been sealed off, rotting at the idea that she may never see her again. The princess' face scrunched, her hands nervously went to her sheets, desperately grasping them.

"*Of course* I thought about you...I was a child—I never *wanted* to leave you, Olivja."

"Your silence spoke louder than any *thought* you claim to have had," the heiress sounded angrier now, her voice cracking. "If I was truly on your mind...how can you prove it?"

Adalja went silent, unsure of both herself *and* the answer.

For the first several years, she didn't have a choice under the strict regime of her mother and father...but once she became more independent, perhaps it could have been possible.

Perhaps instead of drinking in Fairtide, she could have used her rebellion to see Olivja...But she didn't. The thought never once crossed her mind.

"My mother..." she swallowed, "she wouldn't have allowed it." Adalja said louder, her hands gripping the edge of the mattress tighter.

"Yet you follow me *now*, after a decade of silence? With your parents just around the bend?" The Norsewoman shook her head, throwing her hands up in defeat. "Call me a fool; I never once believed you'd pull away on your own."

Those words cut deeper than either of them could have anticipated. They *had* drifted apart...and it was absolutely in Adalja's hands.

Olivja's arms went around her torso and she squeezed defensively, holding herself together the only way she knew how.

"Ten winters, and not once did you write. I waited. *Gods, how I waited.*" The woman laughed like it was amusing. It *wasn't.*

"I...I wrote to you *every* full moon. For ten turns, Adalja. My damn fodir forced me to make my own parchment—*I used so much trying to reach you.*"

Adalja's facial expression softened...But as she comprehended Olivja's words, her brows twitched with frustration.

"...You think I forgot you—and *willingly*?" Adalja asked with parted lips and flowing tears, "Those letters were lost to me. I know not what you speak of!"

"Well...they were never *returned*," she scoffed, shrugging her shoulders. "What does that tell you?"

"Olivja—I received not a single letter from you—nor from Ragnarvik," she repeated, standing from the bed.

"You lie. I sent *hundreds*. The raven returned empty each time." Liv paused, chest heaving, eyes darting around like the room held answers....or perhaps the lost letters. "Are...are you speaking the truth?" she asked.

The princess confirmed it with a short nod.

She could hardly speak. Her eyes glistened. The thought of all those lost words—forgotten fragments of unrequited love—made her stomach ache.

Olivja's eyes drooped, her eyebrows lowering. She swallowed a lump so big, Adalja heard her gulp from her bed.

Then, with a nod of her own, the Norsewoman turned towards the door—like she was about to leave—and it spurred the princess into action.

"Liv! Wait!" She moved.

When she reached Olivja, her hands carefully gripped her wrists, holding her captive—the touch warming more than just skin.

"Listen to me...Th-they're of no importance. You've been with me—in my thoughts, *always.* I-I never needed words to recall you," the princess said, voice soft, eyes shimmering.

Adalja wanted to reassure her, despite the sharp urge to know what was written—despite the ache in her chest at the thought of Olivja searching for her through all their time apart. She couldn't believe it...she didn't want to.

Her gentle words succeeded in lifting Olivja's eyes, locking them with her own.

The two exchanged a much more meaningful look, mutually apologetic—mutually unguarded.

And then, Olivja tilted her head down at her, a few strands of damp hair falling in front of her face.

The princess bit her cheek at the sight of those amber eyes gazing down at her so...so *lovingly.*

The Norsewoman forced a handsome smirk, cutting through the tension with ease—building a *new* kind of tension, deep in Adalja's core. She couldn't look away.

"I figured *Brahms* was enough for you, princess," she uttered, trying to lighten the mood with a breathless tone.

"Is...is that a jest?" Adalja asked, tears spilling onto her cheeks.

Liv grinned a bit wider. "No...at least you *had* him. All I had was ink and parchment...and memories."

Their fingers touched for the shortest moment before the heiress brought a strong hand to Adalja's left cheek, swiping at her tears with a shaking thumb.

"No weeping, Addy. I—I'm sorry," she whispered, her own tears flowing silently—hypocritical yet unstoppable.

"I can't help it," the princess whimpered.

"I never thought our paths would cross again, Liv," she sobbed, choking on the truth of it. "It was easier to believe such...And I never thought you'd wish to see me. Even if I could, I...feared the weight of it."

Though she meant what she said, a shadow of falsehood lingered in her heart. She struggled with what this relationship now meant to her...What these *feelings* meant.

And yet, she couldn't help but weakly lean into Olivja's warm, strong, *familiar* touch.

"You speak of fear? *Gods,* I've been living in it," Olivja said. "Look at me—do I look untouched by it?"

Adalja took another look at Olivja's injuries and grimaced, hating the sight more than anything. She had dreamt of this reunion a hundred ways—but never soaked in rain, staring at a split lip.

"I'll speak to your father of his actions—he won't harm you again, if I—"

"No. You'll say nothing. I fear no man—least of all Vincent, I—" Olivja whispered, bringing her other hand up to Adalja's cheeks, framing her face with calloused palms. "...I fear only the thought of losing you, princess."

Adalja's cheeks burned brightly, and she was thankful with how dark it was in the room.

Who was this woman...?
The Olivja she once knew would've never admitted fear. But that girl was long gone. This one—this new Olivja—was stronger, more intense, and devastatingly beautiful.

She didn't know how to feel, and yet her body continued to react on its own, burning and tingling at every touch.

"I was a fool to think my letters ever reached you...I told myself you knew the truth and turned from me despite it," she paused, her hands trembling against her cheeks.

"But now...now I wonder if I lost you not by will, but by silence." Olivja's tone broke the more she spoke, her voice raspy from the cold and the tears. "They would have told you everything, Dali. *Everything.*"

"Olivja, no...never. You could never lose me," Adalja whispered, her blue eyes stunningly analyzing every inch of her long-lost companion.

"You will always be my—"
She paused and, for the shortest of moments, *faltered.*
"...my dearest friend."

Olivja took a shaky breath, not saying more, an indiscernible look in her eyes.

The princess closed the gap between them, ignoring whatever Olivja's expression might have said, and drew her into their first true embrace in a decade—both women holding each other tightly.

The Norsewoman's strong hands pushed back into her curly, semi-damp locks, and it was then that Adalja noticed the pervasive trembling between the both of them. Was it fear? The cold? Or something more...?

Adalja's arms tightened as she fell into her chest, eyes tightly shut.

"*Every* part of me waited for you..." Liv shuddered, breathing her in. "Gods. Missing you wasn't soft—it was *dread,* Adalja. *Dread.*"

She held her tighter, and Adalja whimpered, taken aback by the strength of her arms—*and her words.* The both of them sank to the ground while remaining in a deep embrace, thighs pressing between each other's to maintain the closeness.

Finally pulling away from her grasp, Adalja took a look at the tearful face of her old friend, their hands connecting in their laps as though it was muscle memory for them.

"The years should have hardened me...Yet here I am, unable to hold my ground..." Olivja's voice was airy and soft, tapering as her gaze dropped to Addy's lips, holding them captive.

The pagan's hands slowly, *gently,* closed around the princess' fingers. Adalja's cheeks flushed at the touch, but she quickly looked down, swallowing thickly.

"Well...that is welcome news..." she forced out with a shaking exhale. The princess carefully pried her hands from Olivja's, brushing her sweaty palms against her nightgown.

"Now..." Adalja cleared her throat, "we have much to speak of...I long to know *everything.*"

THREAD XII

ᚦᛖ ᛒᚢᚱᛞᛖᚾᛋ ᛟᚠ ᚺᛖᛁᚱᛋ ᚦᛖ ᛒᚢᚱᛞᛖᚾᛋ ᛟᚠ ᚺᛖᛁᚱᛋ ᚦᛖ ᛒᚢᚱᛞᛖᚾᛋ

ᛒᚱᚨᚺᛗᛋ

BRAHMS WOULDN'T DENY THE WAY HIS EAR CURVED TOWARDS THE CLOSED DOOR for the remainder of the night, eavesdropping on the princesses' shared laughter. The three of them were finally reunited, and it made his chest tighten with a familiar warmth.

The responsibility of watching the two women made him far too protective—he refused to give his duties to another knight for the evening. Even once their conversations quieted to heavy, sleeping breaths, he remained standing at the door, fist tightly clenched around his spear.

His dark eyes drooped as they slid around the hallways, memorizing the patterns of the walls—the carpets—the tapestries. *Anything* to keep him awake.

Each time he lost control of his posture amidst the exhaustion, he forced himself to pace in a circle, using his spear more like a cane than a weapon.

As the halls began filling with the golden light of the sunrise, Brahms groaned. He did it. He stayed awake all night.

He slumped back against the door with a sigh, closing his eyes in *brief* reward for his struggles...

"You stayed here 'till sunrise, *cockwatcher*?" A booming voice laughed, jolting Brahms into his upright position with a soft snort.

To his left, two Worthyn knights approached, tauntingly tilting their heads at him.

The shorter one was hooded, clad in blackened armour—tight leather that clung to his form, layered with chainmail—unlike any Worthyn knight he'd ever seen.

Brahms clenched his jaw.

*How wonderful...*the horrendous name had made its rounds of the castle already.

Slightly turning his body to face them, he tilted his own head, sucking at his teeth.

"*Aye*...unlike you, I'm not bound by a *bedtime,*" Brahms yawned, too tired to care. Too sleepy to anticipate the aggression that would come next.

With a force that woke him right up, they pushed him to the wall beside the Princess' door. The tallest, in common silver armour, put both hands on Brahms' chest, knocking both their spears to the ground with a clatter.

"But you *are* bound by *oath,*" the tall one growled. "Surely you know the rules of decorum? Laughing at our Prince is a punishable offense."

For a moment, he couldn't recall what they were angry over.
And then he remembered his lapse of judgement at supper—the snort that wasn't entirely covered by Olivja's outburst.

"Uhh...he made a jest, sir. Are you saying you do not find your prince amusing?" Brahms scoffed, unafraid—*maybe he should have been.*

The silvered knight's fists found the leather straps of Brahms' chestplate and jolted him roughly against the stone walls.

"You're the only jester *here*, cockwatcher, slouching while your princess sleeps. *Leave*. The true knights'll handle this," he said with a low rasp, brown eyes dragging across Brahms' smaller frame.

Reaching forward, Brahms took a firm hold of his wrists, ready to flip him onto his back if they pushed him further. Perhaps Brahms was shorter, but he was confident in his abilities.

"Call me that again, tin-man...and I'll *gladly* step away from the door," he said, voice calm—but god, his nerves were *itching*.

"*Sir Jori, Sir Kai*. Stand guard."

Brahms turned his head to the right side of the hall, clenching his jaw as he was left staring at a newly dressed, well-rested Prince Elias in his black-ruffled long sleeve and white pantaloons.

The Worthyn dogs exchanged looks to each other before slowly stepping back, casually grabbing their spears so they could right their posture on the opposite side of the hall.

"You're dismissed," the prince ordered and the knights turned on their heels, retreating down the hall to find another task.

Brahms glanced back at Adalja's room, nervous to leave them to be discovered by Elias. He cleared his throat, slowly inching his body towards the left to follow the other knights, but he was stopped almost instantly.

"Not you." Elias called and Brahms' hands ran cold.
"I'd like to have a word."

He wasn't sure what was worse; letting Adalja be discovered, or having to talk with her suitor.

After swallowing, Brahms turned to face the green-eyed prince, floored by his stature as he stood there tall, strong, and composed.

"My Lord, I meant no disrespect—"

"So you find me amusing?" Elias interrupted and his eyebrow arched. Perhaps there was even a hidden smile behind that mask, but there was no way to know for sure.

Brahms was unsure of how to respond. It was entirely possible the Worthyn prince would take offence at being called funny. But, he might just as easily be offended if Brahms called him unamusing.

"*Ah*—" He opened his mouth to speak but hesitated, caught between words. For a moment, it hung open—only deepening his embarrassment.

"Y-you have a way with words, Your Highness," Brahms dodged cleverly, his eyes darting nervously to the left before settling on Elias' again, his head dipping in a slight bow.

"*Hm.*" Elias hummed, which was a better response than he anticipated. "Speaking of words...Care to share why my Knights were calling you that?" The prince took another step closer, his hands clasped in front of his waist—far too neatly. Like it was rehearsed.

Brahms stood steadfast, clutching his spear tighter, cheeks burning at the question. *Naturally*—the prince arrived just in time to hear the god-awful name.

"Calling me *what*?" he asked with a sharp exhale but was met with a blank stare. Brahms bit his cheek, stifling the disappointment. "Oh...*Cockwatcher*? That old name..."

Shaking his head, the knight let out a long exhale through his nose, trying to make light of a very potent memory for him.

"I was plucked by Queen Pembrook when I was quite young. I was too small to begin Knight training when we returned to Pembrook, so I...guarded their chickens for quite some time." His voice trailed off, the words sounding more ridiculous the longer he spoke.

Saying it aloud only made it worse—it made him feel less like a knight, and more like a fool. Elias' expression remained unchanged, which somehow made Brahms even more anxious.

He rushed to explain himself, stumbling over his own thoughts. "B-But, eventually I proved myself. They made me Adalja's *personal* knight. I can assure you, Prince Elias, I *am* a good knight—"

"I never doubted your skills, Sir Brahms," Elias spoke gently, calming the worried winds in an instant. "In fact, you've already proven your dedication; what with staying posted here all night."

Shocked by his subtle compliment, Brahms straightened, lifting his eyebrows in surprise. It was made known very early by the other knights that his skills were below par in comparison to Worthyn men.

It was strange—being flattered by the prince. Unreal, almost.

"Y-yes, Your Grace. As I said before, My Lady Adalja is my *only* priority," Brahms said, clearing his throat.

The knight wondered if Prince Elias was planning on going into the room, and if he was, he wondered how he'd try to stop him. His fingers slipped on the shaft of the spear, damp with sweat. He tightened his grip anyway, eyes darting for anything—any excuse to look away.

"Well, if you wouldn't mind waking her, both ladies have an early appointment with our advisor," Elias kindly ordered him, much differently than the way he ordered his own knights. "And after, please rest. Sleep is a necessary evil."

"Yes, Your Grace...Of course." Brahms quickly agreed to the terms, whatever he had to do in order to keep the prince from barging in on Olivja and Adalja.

Elias glanced between him and the door. The knight held his breath, eyes darting around guiltily—the lies hiding poorly on his face.

"I can escort you to the Keep, if you'd like," the prince offered sweetly.

Brahms' throat tightened.
He wishes to walk me to my chambers...?
Every part of him ached to accept. But behind the door, the women he'd sworn to protect sat vulnerable. If someone came now...if they were caught...

A small chuckle came from behind the Prince's mask, breaking the knight's scattered focus. "That was another jest, Brahms. You were meant to laugh."

Brahms immediately forced a nervous laugh.

His eyebrow twitched as he swapped his spear to his other hand, his grip loosening with the amount of sweat that poured from his palm.

"H—hilarious, My Lord."

One more brief pause—a pause filled with far too much—ended their exchange.

"Rest well."
Elias' final words were fragile before he stepped down the hall, likely towards the morning meal.

The thought of food—or perhaps the prince—made his stomach curl. He watched Elias stride off for a few more moments until the desperate need for food and rest overcame him.

Now that he'd been excused—and given new orders—he was eager to act on them. He turned and gave a gentle knock on the door, a light warning to the women inside. Ensuring no one was watching, Brahms opened it himself and stepped in quietly.

At the foot of the bed, the two women sat fast asleep, their heads resting against one another. Books and scattered drawings lay draped across their laps—memories from the years they'd spent apart.

Brahms paused in the doorway, stilled by a wave of nostalgia at the sight of the princesses together again.

As they slept, their faces looked softer—youthful, even—as though time had rewound and none of them had ever been separated.

He almost regretted having to wake them. Somehow he knew their friendship would be tested by every moment spent under the Worthyns' watch.

Still, he closed the door behind him and cleared his throat—just enough to stir Olivja awake. Her eyes fluttered open. Her head had been resting on Adalja's, and even as she sat up, Adalja remained fast asleep against Liv's shoulder.

"Forgive my intrusion, Prince Elias summoned you. The both of you have a meeting with the Worthyn advisors." Brahms said exactly what Elias had asked him to, not wanting to risk upsetting Adalja's perfect suitor.

"*What joy*," Olivja grumbled with a quiet whisper, keeping still as though she didn't want to disturb Adalja.

But the princess stirred and shot upright quickly, gasping in fear that they had been caught resting together. Olivja flinched at how quickly Adalja pulled away, desperate not to be seen with her. Even Brahms cringed at it, and it had nothing to do with him.

As Adalja made eye contact with Brahms, she relaxed, sighing softly. "Thank goodness, it's you." She rubbed her sleepy eyes, missing the way Olivja's gaze darkened. Brahms caught it though.

"*Ahem.* Good morning, Princess." Brahms chuckled, crossing his arms around his spear as he taunted the two with his knowing gaze. "Sleep well?"

"Why, yes. Better than I expected," Adalja said, a pink blush sporting her cheeks.

And at that, the two women exchanged a *meaningful* gaze that had Brahms felt obligated to interrupt.

"*Ahem*—How nice. Now, let's not make this a custom. I cannot watch your door through the night again—it'll kill me," Brahms grumbled, too exhausted to maintain civility.

Olivja rose, brushing the wrinkles from her linen dress—matted from the rain and sleeping on the floor. "Aye...I'll be more careful," she mumbled.

Then, as she moved towards the door, she added with a wry sigh:
"Best not be seen with the likes of me, *hm?*"

Brahms slightly stepped aside, her words causing him to uneasily clench his jaw. She paused at the door and turned around, gazing at Adalja who still sat sleepily on the ground.

"I'll be seeing you, princess," Olivja bid her a charming farewell, letting her smooth words linger in the air for a moment before opening the door on her own to leave.

Brahms watched her closely as she stepped out, and once she was gone, his narrowed eyes slowly shifted back to Adalja, a look of skepticism darkening his gaze.

"Couldn't help yourself, could you, Addy?"

Adalja scoffed while pushing herself up onto the edge of her mattress, crossing her arms at his assumptions. "*You're the one* who let her in, Brahms...what was I supposed to do? Ignore her? Kick her out?"

"Surely either of those would have been better than *sleeping* with her." Brahms knew that he was pushing it, but his exhaustion and protectiveness clouded his sense of boundaries.

"You see it wrongly, Brahms," she said and looked away from him, her hands tightening around her biceps.

"All we did was speak...of all things. We drifted to sleep in our conversation..." she trailed off while selecting a small paper from the ground, bringing it up to the bed.

"It's been ten years—*ten years,* and I never once reached out to her—I suppose I simply didn't realise how quickly the time went by."

"The Queen kept you busy, that's all...do not be harsh on yourself, Princess." Brahms leaned against the closed door, eyes shifting tiredly around the mess.

"Doves fly both ways," he yawned, "...she could have written *too.*"

The comment made her freeze. She stared at him for a few long seconds before she looked down at the paper in her hands.

"Indeed...that would have made a difference, would it not have?" Her voice was fragile, holding the weight of feelings unknown to him.

He had no more to say. His exhaustion gnawed at his sense of duty, smudging the lines between care and jealousy.

"I bid you farewell, My Lady...Another knight will escort you to the meeting."

Brahms opened the door and slipped out before she could answer—before he could say something he'd regret.

Thread XIII

A knock pulled Adalja to her feet. Sapphire had finished lacing her boots just in time. A Worthyn knight pushed the wooden door wide enough for Adalja to glimpse Olivja in the hall, aloof, her eyes wandering elsewhere.

"Your Highness, the hour has come for your meeting with our advisor," he said, voice deep and polished, the refinement of his training evident in every word.

"Very well, thank you." Adalja stepped forward, clenching her dress the nearer she grew to Olivja.

Even outside the room, the Norsewoman averted her gaze. They began down the hall in silence.

The act of walking silently beside Olivja—marching towards a lecture with an authority figure—brought fond memories rushing back. She imagined the last time they were chastised for running in the halls or messing around in the kitchens.

Olivja always took the blame for whatever antics they got into, even when Adalja refused. Glancing over at her friend, her heart skipped a beat.

Ten years later, Olivja still wore that same pout when having to endure important duties. It was endearing to witness and Adalja, as always, wished she could express herself as freely. She was inspired by her, while others found her insufferable.

Olivja turned her head, sensing that Adalja was watching her.

Their eyes connected, so the princess nervously offered her a smile. Olivja gave a faint smile in return, though her gaze quickly shifted as the knight's clinking armour came to a stop.

An arched wooden door opened and the two women waited as the knight briefly stuck his head in the door.

"Pardon the intrusion, Madame Gothel, the princesses are ready for you," he said lowly, dipping back out of the room to stand at attention beside the door.

Slow footsteps revealed a small, older woman, with short white hair that curled softly at her ears and gathered at the nape of her neck. Her hunched frame made her no taller than a broom handle, but despite her disheveled age, she was dressed in extravagant grey robes that shrouded the shape of her body.

At her height, she looked like a bundle of moving laundry, and as she made eye contact with the princesses, she gave a dull smile.

"Good day, Your Highnesses," Gothel mumbled, giving an additional glance to Olivja, "Princess Olivja, how fare you?"

"Heiress," Olivja corrected, clearing her throat. "And go on—take a guess on how you *think* I fare, Gothel? I am to marry *Vincent*." Olivja quickly said, unable to look the advisor in her face.

Adalja's eyes widened. *Speaking to an elder of such high title like that!?*

The princess overlooked the fact that Olivja had a deeper relationship with the Worthyns than she did. She noticed the tension between the two, the way Gothel downheartedly looked away and the way Olivja's calmness merged into a numb vacancy.

"Marriage is not easy for anyone, child...in fact, many years ago, Queen Worthyn was *also* inspired to wed," the older woman turned down the hall and began meandering while rambling on about the history of Worthyn. The Princesses loosely followed.

"Marriage binds kingdoms, not people. And when those bonds break...well, wars follow, don't they? Who could've guessed the Perdyr jarldom would stir such *violence*...Our kingdom is strong, always has been, you know...Ezekiel, he's a mighty ruler, though a bit brash, if you ask me. Raised his boys the same way—oh, I tried to stop him, really I did...such good boys, they are."

Adalja paid close attention, but the longer they walked, the more disorganised the woman spoke and the harder it became to follow her train of thought. She was left squinting and repeating phrases to herself to try to understand them.

"They treat me so kindly. Indeed, they treat all with such grace, don't they? But war...it doth change folk, oh yes. Ever since the Queen's passing, things have shifted so greatly—surely thou hast noticed—ah, how the families have come undone. It is so very sad, truly..."

"Lilli was a wonderful mother...troubled, of course, same as all Norsewomen—ah, there she is now." The elder pointed with a curled hand at the wall.

They paused briefly at a large painted portrait of the Worthyn family.

A short, curvy woman with long white hair and light brown skin stood behind two boys—young Vincent and Elias, the spitting image of their mother. All three shared the same bright green eyes and snowy hair.

It was clear the greatest thing the boys had inherited from their father was the ghost-pale tone of their skin. That, and *the crown*.

Unmasked and smiling, Vincent and Elias each clutched the hem of Lilli's dress in their small fists.

They looked happy.

Adalja's gaze lingered on their smiles. Her fingers brushed the frame, then fell away, curling into the fabric of her gown.

"What happened to her?" Adalja uttered, tilting her head as she took a longer look at the portrait.

"Her own family would rather see her dead than wed to King Ezekiel...Perhaps there was jealousy, or maybe she wronged someone...No, no that's not it. Our dear Queen was a *flower* among thorns—so lovely, so bright—She crafted the most wonderful loaves of—"

"Madame Gothel," the heiress interrupted softly, clearing her throat, "You knew her well, tell us, what was she like in her youth when she was forced to marry—was she like us?"

The Norsewoman wore a silly grin. When their eyes met, Olivja winked at her.

Adalja's cheeks flushed. Her stomach stirred—like the woman had tossed a stone into a nest of bees. She hid the breath that caught in her throat with a cough, quickly turning away from the flirtatious Ragnarvik.

"Well no—my dear, because she was not *forced* to marry; she loved Ezekiel until her last breath, I'm certain. Ah, but young Lilli...she was like thee—" she pointed to Olivja, "Well, no, she was like thee, Princess Pembrook—gentle and so beautiful," the older woman continued slowly down the hall, and Adalja pushed onwards behind her as she rambled on.

"The Perdyr jarldom was quite poor, and so was Lilli, thus her unpolished demeanor, much like yours, dear Olivja—how did Ezekiel come to find her? I can't quite recall why he chose her, in truth—"

Suddenly, Adalja was pulled sharply to the left, swept from the hallway and into a dimly lit room. Olivja's hand curled tightly around her wrist, dragging her close before the door clicked shut behind them—latch sliding silently into place.

Heat surged through Adalja's veins as Olivja raised a finger to her lips, pressing it there gently—commanding silence.

With her other hand, Olivja caged her in, palm flat beside Adalja's head on the wall, taller and impossibly close. Their bodies pressed together, skin barely inches apart, breath mingling in the narrow, dark space between them.

Adalja's breath hitched, caught in a shriek she couldn't let out—her senses screaming. The faint pulse of Olivja's heartbeat, the warm brush of her breath, the subtle scent of earth and fire curling into her lungs...It devoured her nerves like a spark to wool.

A fragile breath escaped her lips—a sound she fought desperately to swallow—her teeth digging into the soft flesh of her cheek to still the tremor.

Outside, Gothel's voice faded into the distance, the corridor's dull murmur swallowed by thick, heavy quiet.

Adalja's fingers twitched to reach out, but Olivja's stare held her fast—captured and undone all at once. Then, with a slow, deliberate turn, she stepped back, breaking the contact but leaving behind a silence taut as string, thrumming with possibility.

The library they had snuck into was a dimly lit chamber filled with towering wooden shelves, their surfaces dusted with age. Ancient tomes, bound in leather and string lined the walls, their spines cracked and worn. A large, heavy table sat in the centre, strewn with scrolls and parchment, while the scent of old paper filled the air, bringing a soft smile to Adalja's lips.

A single window, arched and narrow, let in a sliver of the day's light, barely enough to read, but enough to stay hidden.

The heiress sighed.
"Why hear the biased, *disheveled* history from the senile right-hand when you can read it for yourself..." Olivja murmured, running her fingertips along the wooden shelves, dust piling at her touch and trickling to the floor like snow.

Adalja stood still at the door, eyes wide as she contemplated returning to the hall with Gothel, or staying with Olivja.

A sense of nostalgia washed over her; this wasn't the first time she had to make a choice between doing what she was supposed to, and doing what she wanted. She shook her head.

"They won't be pleased that we left such a lecture—"

"Tell me—have they *ever* been pleased with me?" Olivja asked, fully facing a shelf as her fingers danced across history, rarely taking a look back towards the door.

The princess was in disbelief, and yet she couldn't wipe the smile from her face as she stepped deeper into the library, hiking her dress up on both ends.

"I...cannot believe you still do things like this," Adalja playfully chastised, moving to the opposite side of the bookshelf.

The women exchanged glances through the small spaces between shelves, Olivja sporting a blended gaze of intrigue and allure that Adalja couldn't keep her eyes off of. The glance heated the space between them as though a fire had been lit—*dangerous for a library.*

She swallowed a small lump in her throat.

"Unlike most people—I'll never be worn down by the *expectations* nobles have of me." Olivja maintained eye contact as she murmured and her hand fell on a rolled up piece of paper. "*Aye,* here we are..."

The daring woman pulled it from the shelf and their eyes disconnected as Liv looked down at it, granting Adalja a moment of peace free from the heiress' intensity.

She marveled at how, even after all these years, her companion could still so effortlessly unnerve her. And on top of it, how a person could remain so unchanged, so certain, in a world so pressuring.

Adalja envied her—envied that steadiness, that strength. She wished she could be more like her.

Her gaze drifted to the stack of books before her, though none held her interest. Her thoughts were elsewhere—unravelling, questioning.

Who was she, truly? Was her personality her own...or merely a construct shaped by the expectations of others?

Olivja's footsteps moved to the middle of the room, so Adalja stepped around the shelf, her eyes falling on the wild woman, unfurling the scroll onto the table, shoving aside quills and parchment to make space. The heels of Adalja's boots quietly tapped on the floor as she approached.

"Olivja?"

"Look."

Her eyes trailed down to the map Liv had found.

A detailed drawing of the three kingdoms, and everything between them, was done in ink and perfectly preserved. Adalja stepped closer to Olivja, wanting to see more—perhaps also wanting to be nearer. She leaned one hand onto the table.

"The Perdyr name was burned from the maps after their betrayal. This one must be from before the war..." Olivja said, trailing her two fingers up a drawn path towards the forgotten territory.

On the north side of the map, another coastal jarldom was adorned with little drawn ships and houses...similar to the Ragnarvik jarldom in the south.

"Another Norse territory?" Adalja asked in shock, lowering her eyebrows, "I can't believe I've never seen it before."

"Thanks to our *noble sire*, we never will." Olivja grumbled, eyes narrowing in disapproval of King Ezekiel's harsh war engagements. It made sense for Olivja to be against the war if Perdyr was a Norse jarldom like hers.

Her parents rarely spoke of the Perdyr–Worthyn war, let alone the kingdom itself. She knew it existed but had no other knowledge. To see an entire realm on paper for the first time was unbelievable.

To herself, she wondered if murdering a Queen truly warranted an entire jarldom being wiped from existence...

Adalja gradually raised her gaze from the map, letting her eyes wander over the Norsewoman's face while she focussed on something else.

The Ragnarvik woman was beautiful—even more so in her anger. The dim light of the library cast perfect shadows across Olivja's intrigued expression...the thick furrowed brows, the swell of her lips, pursed in frustration.

Adalja's jaw clenched, and her stomach fluttered at the sight. She attributed the butterflies to the swarming feelings of nostalgia that always came whenever she was with her old friend.

But as Olivja lifted her amber eyes to meet Adalja's, her breath caught in her throat.

"Keep your eyes on the parchment, Princess...we're meant to be *learning*," Olivja smirked, a chuckle escaping her lips as she caught Adalja in the act of staring once again.

A warm blush flooded the shy princess' cheeks, and only then did she notice how close their faces were—barely a book's width apart.

"Perhaps I *am* learning...not only about the Worthyns," Adalja mumbled, her eyebrows lowering as she looked back at the paper. "Olivja...do you believe I've changed?"

The taller woman's gaze stayed fixed on her, and Adalja could feel the strength of her even in her peripherals. It made her nervous.

There was a short pause before Olivja scoffed.

"Why ask me? It's been ten winters since I last laid eyes on you, Adalja," Olivja said, eyes sharp as she edged closer—fingertips barely grazing atop the table.

Adalja flinched, a sudden burn igniting through her fingers, her stomach twisting into a tight, restless knot.

She glanced down, catching their twitching fingers—both aching to close the fragile gap. The flickering candlelight masked the heat spreading across her face, but she couldn't hide the tight gulp and forced shrug that barely concealed the storm inside.

"Y-you knew me better than anyone," she sighed, strained by the heaviness of their connection. "I thought...maybe *you* could tell me."

"*Do I* know you?" Olivja quietly countered, her golden eyes burning.

The Norsewoman's eyes dropped briefly to the space between their hands—so close they nearly brushed—then rose again to meet Adalja's. One corner of her mouth tugged upwards, just slightly, as if amused by something only she understood.

"I hope so...otherwise, I'm completely lost," Adalja said with a small, nervous chuckle. The words betrayed the deep uncertainty she felt inside.

Olivja hummed softly, smirk growing.
"I should warn you...to find what we're after, we'll need time. Just you, me, and the gods..." Her voice dropped slightly, playful but weighted with intent.

Adalja nodded quickly, her breath coming in unevenly.
Gods, how could she refuse this woman?

"I promise to tell you all my findings in exchange, *dove...*" Olivja grinned, leaning in closer as her voice lowered to a whisper. "Do you accept this quest?"

Dove—slang for the Pembrooks. Usually, the word made her bristle...but when Olivja said it, she loved it.

Adalja's fingers curled slightly on the table, knuckles white against the grain. The library was suffocating. Her gaze lingered on Olivja's face, then fell to the space between their hands. A breath caught in her throat, silent and shaking.

Olivja chuckled, catching her flustered state. With practised ease, she hooked her index finger under Adalja's chin, gently lifting her face to meet her gaze.

"My eyes are up here, Addy," she cooed, her voice smooth, the tease playing on her lips.

"O-of course—I...I know that," Adalja stammered, her nervous laugh doing little to mask her emotions.

"*And*?" Olivja leaned in just slightly, her head tilting the other way like a cat toying with its prey.

"Yes, I'll...I'll do whatever it takes." Adalja's voice wavered, but her words were firm.

Olivja's smirk softened into something more sincere. Her golden fingers moved, slow and deliberate. When they brushed against Adalja's, the spark of contact made the princess flinch—then freeze.

Olivja's hand slid forward, threading their fingers together with a coaxing ease.

"*Hversuh hlythin*," the heiress whispered—foreign words brushing against Adalja's skin like a spell.

Her wide eyes rose, waiting, silent, needing to understand.

The pause between them was heavy—thick with want and something unnamed. Olivja said nothing. She simply kept playing with her hand, sliding their fingers apart, then together again—slow, sure, maddening.

Adalja's chest ached. She couldn't look away. Her breath turned shallow.

Finally, Olivja murmured: *"How obedient."*

And then—
The door to the library swung open.

She sprang back as though burned, straightening in an instant. Their hands disentangled just in time, a flash of fear washing over her like she was a child again.

Olivja lingered for a moment, still leaning forward, her head turning slowly towards the intruders. A sigh escaped her lips as she pulled back.

"Adalja!"

Natja's sharp voice filled the room as she stormed towards the table, Prince Elias quietly following, the door to the library slamming shut behind them. Her eyes flicked to the open map before narrowing on Adalja, her expression painted with fury.

"What are you *doing*?" her mother demanded, her voice tight with anger.

Adalja's lips parted, but no sound came.
"I—" She glanced at Olivja, who remained relaxed, her golden eyes glinting with defiance.

"She's not here to play house, Natja—she's preparing to rule. You'd do well to remember that," Olivja snapped, ready to defend Adalja like they had never parted.

Her stomach buzzed with butterflies...or perhaps adrenaline.

"Your suitor and advisor are waiting, *Princess,*" Natja spoke through clenched teeth, keeping her hazel glare up at Olivja the entire time.

Heiress Ragnarvik had grown over the years, taking after her massive father, and now was a few inches taller than Queen Natja. The sight tugged at the corners of Adalja's mouth.

But, without another word or glance, Adalja ducked towards the door, avoiding her mother's gaze, and Elias' as well. Though the prince jogged to reach the door before Adalja did. His hand pulled the door open, and Olivja's final remark blasted in the room.

"I see the gods have begun reclaiming your hair, My Queen!" Olivja laughed and involuntarily pulled a small giggle out of Adalja.

The door shut heavily behind them and in an instant, her bicep was firmly gripped and yanked by her mother.

"You've fooled around with Olivja for the last time—"

"Your Grace," Elias firmly interrupted, slipping his hand around Adalja's hip. "I'll handle any reprimands for your daughter. Your heavy hand is unwelcomed here."

Natja's hand fell to her side in a fist, eyes softening. "A-adalja has *always* required heavy correction," the queen nervously began.

"Any hand laid on her is a hand laid on me...do you wish to correct *me* heavily as well, My Lady?" Elias said from behind his mask, guiding Adalja until her body was flush against his side, sending a warming protectiveness through her.

Adalja quickly looked away, the flush Olivja had left on her face still burning bright—easily mistaken as a reaction to Elias.

With a slow, heavy breath, Natja gave a small nod of apology.

"Forgive me, My Lord, I was unaware of your *perspective*...I'll be more careful with my actions." She folded her hands in front of herself, straightening her shoulders.

"Wonderful, please enjoy the remainder of your day before the rehearsal...you deserve it, Your Highness," Elias urged kindly as he subtly tugged Adalja to turn away with him.

Silently, they walked down the corridor, away from the library and back towards the main foyer. Adalja noticed, with some surprise, that they weren't heading directly towards her chambers.

She held her tongue, the tension from earlier still lingering in her chest. Being caught with Olivja had filled her with unease, and she worried it might have left a poor impression on Elias.

As they walked, she glanced up at him from beneath her lashes, her gaze flitting nervously over his profile. His expression was calm, his jaw set, though his silence only added to her growing nervousness.

When they exited the castle and stepped into the open air, his hand fell from her waist. His long strides carried him forward with purpose, and Adalja found herself trailing slightly behind until he stopped beneath a large stone archway leading to the gardens.

Tugging his mask below his chin, Elias—ever charming—leaned against the wall, watching her slowly catch up.

The silver embroidery along the edges of his black shirt shimmered faintly in the dim light of the overcast sky, perfectly reflecting the austere elegance of the Worthyn kingdom.

Adalja slowed as she approached him, her eyes flicking over his lean frame. From the dark leather boots to the intricate cuffs of his sleeves, every detail seemed impossibly refined yet effortlessly commanding. Her gaze lingered a moment longer on the relaxed confidence in his stance before nervously shifting upwards to meet his eyes.

"How was the lesson? I assume you grew bored of Gothel?" he asked lightheartedly, tilting his head at her and flashing his perfect teeth. She smiled with him, leaning against the wall opposite.

"W-well..." she began with a soft chuckle, recalling the rambling woman. "It was informative, but I still have many curiosities."

"She is difficult to comprehend, I apologise," he responded with a soft laugh, eyeing her expression. "Go on then, ask your questions, Fair One." He extended his palm towards her, playfully urging her to share her thoughts.

Adalja cleared her throat, nervous to ask a prince about his family history in the way he desired—especially after being called such a sweet nickname.

"Don't be coy, My Lady."

Adalja scoffed gently before a smile crept onto her lips. "Very well, very well...the Perdyr jarldom. Have you been there?"

Elias' eyebrows lowered then lifted, surprised by the question. "Perdyr? I'm surprised by your interest. Did Gothel speak much of them?"

"No...not Gothel..."

"*Ah*...the old map," Elias said, putting two and two together, nodding. He continued: "Yes, Princess, I have—granted, it wasn't a pleasant visit. I've seen the battlefields, trained on them. And...that's it. After our marriages, Perdyr will be no more."

"But...it was your mother's jarldom..." Adalja couldn't help but press further, intrigued by the idea that the Worthyns were razing the very land their queen once called home.

She hated the thought of war on behalf of all the innocents caught in the crossfire of royal ego. Realising she might have overstepped, she hurried to clarify.

"I—I only mean that...nearly a decade of loss? When will it be enough? Forgive me, I—"

"Don't apologise, Princess," Elias interrupted smoothly, raising his hand to stop her anxious rambling. "I concur with you. We may be a family enriched by violence, but I am not. I do not condone it...ever."

Adalja's chest swelled with admiration as his eyes dropped to his fidgeting hands, his mind plainly displaying the way it was swirling.

She enjoyed hearing that Elias was unlike his brother...it felt good knowing he was so much like her. She recognised that his dislike of violence must have played a role in his protection from her mother. But she was curious how this aversion would play while his family was in active war.

"Then...once we're married, are you going to leave for war?" she asked with quiet kindness.

"We'll do what we must..." Elias shrugged his shoulders quickly and Adalja nodded along with him. "Now," he hummed, "what other curiosities have bore into your beautiful mind?"

Adalja bit her bottom lip, curious how far she could push Elias for information before he refused her. "Your mother...she was beautiful—"

"I do not speak of my mother, dearest," he said firmly, but still with kindness...and a pensive sadness that she knew better than to disrespect.

"Of course."
She swallowed, freezing in her spot at the suddenness before nodding.
"Perhaps it's best that neither of us speak of our mothers," Adalja awkwardly said.

Elias stayed silent after her comment and a wave of anxiety filled her as she believed to have crossed the line.

"I apologise if I overstepped—"

"You have not," he assured, slowly looking into her eyes once again. "I have no more information on my mother than Gothel does...I wish I could curb your curiosity."

"Forgive me. Perhaps I shouldn't have become so distracted—"

"By Olivja?" Elias asked, chuckling once more, his head tilted with an all-knowing gaze.

Adalja's cheeks burned brighter and she immediately sighed. She was curious what Elias saw that made him ask about her, "I—um—"

"Pray...do not take this as me reprimanding you, sweetling. Olivja is known to be quite the distraction, I do not blame you." Elias laughed, running a loose hand through his hair, combing it back and in the process pushed down his hood.

"A distraction?" Adalja's interest piqued, and it showed in the way she pushed herself upright against the wall.

"What...can you tell me about your time with her?" she asked gently, her eyes lighting up with captivation.

"Well, how much time do we have...?" Elias laughed, his cat-like eyes shining with eagerness, his smile spreading.

He took her hand and brought it to his lips in a gentle kiss before redirecting her towards the garden.

With her hand still in his, Adalja followed—heart thrumming, breath caught—into the gardens, into his tender memories of the wild Ragnarvik woman.

THREAD XIV

THROUGH A HALLWAY WINDOW, Olivja watched in silence as Adalja and her suitor strolled into the gardens.

She'd stayed behind, regret simmering after a tiff with the queen.

Marriage traditions bored her—but the thought of Adalja alone with Elias made her stomach sick. She turned away from the view as footsteps approached from behind her.

"Meeting over?" Vincent asked, striding up the stone steps with arrogant flair. His hood was down, but the mask still shrouded the lower half of his face. "Or did you drive them mad already, Liv?"

As always, he found her at the worst time.
He slowed as he neared, chuckling low, arms crossing in mock disappointment. Both of them wore the same expression—exasperated and unamused.

"There's nothing left to learn about your bloodline. I know it all," Olivja said, mirroring his body language as she tucked her arms beneath her breasts. "Better for all of you that I'm not there when Princess Adalja hears your family's tale...I'm no kind judge."

After the previous evening, what had once been a shallow childhood rivalry was beginning to harden into something far more mature—resentment, and anger. She couldn't believe he had touched her like that. It felt like betrayal.

Now he stood tall before her, strong and glaring, irritation sharp in his eyes. Her fingertips buzzed with adrenaline, bracing for a violence she wasn't sure *wouldn't* come.

Somewhere in the back of her mind, she was bracing for him to retaliate with violence. Fear was no stranger to her. Neither was defiance. Her mother had once called it imprudence.
Still, she refused to let it silence her.

She stubbornly clung to the idea that she and Vincent could remain on friendly terms—but that felt impossible now, with him wearing the ego of a king.

"Always so quick-witted...I admired it before," Vincent sighed, cracking his neck to one side before slowly continuing

"Thankfully, Olivja, the depths of my family's history are far beyond your knowing," Vincent said, stepping closer—close enough to force her to choose: lift her chin to meet his gaze or look away.

She stepped back, spine meeting cold glass, refusing to tilt her chin. Their eyes locked—his low and dark, heavy with a familiar intensity that crawled beneath her skin.

"Yes? Well, I'd like to keep it that way," Olivja muttered, though her voice caught slightly as he continued closing the distance.

When he reached her, his hands came to rest on either side of the window frame, caging her in. His body loomed in front of hers, and only then did she finally avert her eyes, searching for anything to look at besides him.

"As would I," he said, his voice low, almost gentle—dangerously so. "Yet alas, you are woven into my tale. I have had no say. I never have."

The words hit like a dagger to the heart—sharp, merciless—confirming what she'd feared all along: their bond had been doomed from the start. Her face twisted, not in pain, but in pure resentment.

"Then forgive me," Olivja snapped, "for being the burden you and *everyone else* must drag behind." The bitterness crept into her throat, thick and cold.

Even friendship felt like another lie.
Every bond she touched seemed to rot in her hands.

Jaw clenched, she stared at his chest—anywhere but his eyes—as numbness crept over her like a rising tide. If she didn't feel it, it couldn't drown her.

"Do not let it wound you so deeply, Liv...You know well that is not the truth." His raspy tone lifted with a tease. The warmth of his breath grazed her ear, and a chill ran down her neck.

"Our fates were always meant to tangle this way. We were cast for our parts long before we could protest. And I won't have you ruin all I've done with your *reckless* tongue."

Olivja scoffed, tongue slipping over her bottom lip, a simmering rage pressing at her ribs like a blade she couldn't unsheathe.

She exhaled shakily, forcing calm into her voice. "As tempting as it is to take credit for your ruin, Vincent...you'll manage just fine without my help."

He stepped closer, his chest pressing against hers, his breath hot with frustration. "Princess, this anger of yours..." Vincent sighed, voice dropping—edged with warning.

His cat-like eyes burned with a fury that no longer felt like his own. It was a perfect reflection of the rest of his masked face. "You will learn to hold your tongue in the presence of a king—"

"You're n—"

A hand flew to her jaw, seizing her, forcing her gaze back to his with a painful snap.

"*I will be.* Olivja, I will be." His fingers dug into her cheeks, silencing her. His voice cracked like a whip through the space between them. "But what do you think will happen to you until then, hm? If you, a *Norsewoman,* spoke to a king this way?"

Their eyes locked, sharp as clashing swords. Olivja's breath came in short, angry bursts, her pulse hammering in her ears. She never imagined growing up would make their fights crueler.

Yet, even as this version of Vincent loomed over her—this cold, cruel imitation of a king—she could still see flickers of the boy she once knew. The boy who used to shove her into the mud just to pull her out laughing. The boy who once swore to protect her.

But that boy was gone—buried beneath the weight of his father's shadow.

"What, you'll kill me? Is that what you claim, Vincent?" she snapped, her voice thick with defiance, though she winced as his grip reopened the fresh scab on her lip.

"Not *ME, you simple girl*—Ezekiel! Or any goddamn noble in these walls!" He jolted her head, a growl ripping from his throat as he spat his father's name. But beneath the anger, there was something else. *Fear.*

"Then hold your tongue! Have you grown soft!?" Olivja snarled, twisting against his grip, hands shoving at his wrist.

Disobeying Ezekiel had been their only unspoken pact—the one thing they'd always shared.

"You think I'm the only one reporting to him?! *Hm?!*" His grip tightened, and a small, unwilling whimper of pain escaped her lips. "Don't be stupid, Olivja—"

And then, before he could finish, her voice came, raw and fraying at its edges.

"I am not *stupid,* Vincent! But you," she paused, trying to hide the tremble in her tone, "you vowed to mend things, but you only broke more!"

Her fingers curled around his forearm—not to fight, but to reach. A silent plea.

"We were friends before." Her breath hitched, her voice wounded, almost small. "What storm stole the fierce heart I once knew? You cared not for this before..."

It was a question she hadn't meant to ask. Saying it aloud made the distance real—an unbridgeable chasm, carved deeper with every year. She had already lost too much. Adalja, her home, her freedom. But this felt like the final betrayal.

For a fraction of a moment, his hand loosened. His eyes softened, just barely. And there was her Vincent, buried deep beneath the mask.

"We stopped being friends the night I left," he muttered. His voice was lower now, reluctant. His fingers still held her face, but not with force. Just enough to stay close. His thumb ghosted over the wound he gave her.

"Don't pretend this can be salvaged..." he said as he shook his head, a scoff slipping beneath his breath. "I know you *despise* me just as much as I despise myself."

She stilled. His honesty landed hard, wilting her expression.

"But no *storm* has ever drowned the truth of it—I still feel for you, Liv."

Olivja froze, just for a breath, before pride rose like armour across her face.

"If," she swallowed, "if you feel anything at all...you'd release me."

And she yanked her head away, desperate to break free—from the weight of his touch, his words, and the ghost of everything they used to be.

He opened his mouth, as if to say something, but the sound of footsteps cut through the tension like a blade.

Their moment shattered.
And yet, the damage was already done.

Vincent turned his head, unbothered to be seen holding her in such a way. If it were his knights, she knew—they wouldn't intervene.
When she saw Phillip Pembrook step into the hall, she felt no less hopeless.

As Vincent made eye contact with the King, he pulled away from her. But Phillip had seen the way he was holding her...

"We'll continue this later," he told her blandly, letting both of his hands fall to his sides as he turned to his left, walking away from the direction of King Pembrook after flipping the hood back over his head.

Olivja's breath came fast, her eyes locked on Vincent as he walked away.

She wanted to believe that Vincent cared about her...but there was something different about him now, something she couldn't quite place. She glanced down the hallway and sighed.

As if a split lip wasn't enough, the father of the woman she loved had to interrupt her marital discourse.

Phillip was standing frozen; Olivja interpreted that as him wanting to speak with her.

She glanced towards where Vincent had gone, silently weighing which path would hurt more...

She ultimately decided she would take the chance at having to speak to Phillip over dealing with the heartbreak of Vincent again. Clenching her fists at her sides, she walked to her right, facing Phillip, hoping she could pass without being forced to interact with another man she despised.

He remained still as she approached, which was a bad sign.

As she reached him, she held her breath.

In a short burst of movement, his arm shot out from his side, stopping her in her tracks. She clenched her jaw, feeling like an idiot for expecting silence—for expecting *peace.*

"...Does your father know he's violent with you?" His voice was stern, protective as he tried to help.

However, Olivja only saw him as yet another man with power who abandoned her, one who was completely unaware of her feelings and the reality of the situation she was being forced into.

She took a step back, ready to glare at more royalty. Finally meeting his older face, her heart twisted and clenched.

The last time she saw him, he left without even saying goodbye, and now he dared try to act protective over her? Not to mention, he spoke of her father, who was already a sore spot for her.

"And what would you do if he didn't?" Olivja asked, raising her palms in defeat, her shoulders sagging—words heavy even for herself.

Her voice cut—bitter and sharp. "Let it be. He stands with the Worthyns, and I'm not the reason he'd stray."

She tried to step forward, but Phillip's arm remained firm. His hand rested lightly against the cold stone wall, the other at his side, clenched in a loose fist as if unsure whether to hold his ground or let her pass.

"Olivja. A word," he said firmly, his voice gentle yet resolute.

She halted but didn't look at him. Her eyes dropped to the floor, where shadows danced against the flagstones from the flickering torches lining the hallway. There was a tension in the air, like the moment before a wave broke, and the sound of her sharp breath seemed to echo against the stone walls.

A brief silence passed as Olivja stole a glance at Phillip, taking in his demeanor. He stood tall, though his posture was softer than she remembered, as if the years had worn him down.

He was older now, his face powdered with age and wrinkled by time, his blue-Adalja-eyes framed by faint lines that deepened with his expression. Yet there was still strength in the set of his jaw, the broadness of his shoulders—he looked like a king. A handsome, tired king.

And as her gaze travelled across his face, something stirred inside her.

She saw kindness there, a tenderness she hadn't seen in so long—not even before their last meeting. But that only made it worse. She couldn't bear it. The image of him stood in stark contrast to the drunken slob her father had become, slouched on his throne and reeking of ale. All because of *this King.*

"We both know that isn't how your father feels," Phillip said quietly, his tone shifting to something softer. His piercing eyes watched her with concern—a glare twisted with care.

Olivja let out a bitter laugh, her lips curling into a sneer. "You know nothing, *Mark of Pembrook.*"

When the Pembrooks had left her family's land, he'd taken on a new name—one she'd never known him by. As if a name could scrub away the past, as if the bad blood between them could be washed clean.

The king took a small step closer, his voice lowering. "I *know* that your father may be bound by his duties, but he does care for you—"

"Oh—" she cut him off sharply, her voice rising as she snapped her head back towards him, "You speak of *caring*? You've done more harm to the Ragnarviks than ANY storm ever could!" Her golden eyes burned with fury, her words trembling with years of pent-up resentment.

Phillip flinched at her tone but held firm, his arm still barring her path. His jaw tightened for a moment, but then his expression softened and his hand relaxed slightly against the wall.

"I have *always* cared," he said, his voice low and steady, though his blue eyes betrayed the quiet sadness beneath his words. They bore into hers with an intensity that made her heart twist painfully. "My love for the Ragnarviks has been prevalent for longer than you know, little one."

"Well your *love* left bruises—not only on our skin," she exhaled, nails curling into her palms.

"I can't deny that." His hand lowered with a sigh, no longer confining her to the conversation. "...I must say I am proud of how you've matured, Dottir of Ragnarvik. I only wish I had been there to see more of your growth."

If not for the words he used, Olivja would have walked away the moment his hand lowered but, the last thing she ever expected to hear was an attempt of flattery from the King and she wasn't going to let it go unnoticed.

"Matured..." she mimicked and then scoffed. "Because I don't shout and swing like a child anymore? Don't be fooled—I'm still the *same* storm."

"Not that, Olivja—"

"Does your wife know you praise me?"

He faltered, blood rising to his cheeks. "N-no...Natja is unaware—"

"Then tell me—why waste your breath on a dirty *heathen* like me?" Olivja interrupted him once more, her anger being a result of a decade's worth of resentment towards the Pembrooks.

"You are no heathen," he said, voice tight with pain. "I've no peace with how we left things...I seek your forgiveness. Now that you're older, I thought—"

"Aye, My Lord, I am older. But I'm no more tamed than I was. And no less hurt."

Olivja could no longer keep in what had long burned in her chest. She glanced around the hall—quick, cautious—ensuring they were alone before she went on.

"I've missed you, Phillip," she said, biting her cheek. "But so long as I love her, there can be no honour between us. I'll ruin the alliance with Worthyn if I must—I won't let her marry him. I care not what it does to any of us."

She stepped forward, her breath catching.
"*You must know that.*"

The king looked deeply into Olivja's eyes, but there was no hesitation. His face was still soft and relaxed. There was no glimmer of fear or anger—as if he didn't hear her threat.

"I know," he murmured, his voice low, steady. Yet his face cracked, his brows drew together, as though the words physically hurt. "You must know I harbor no hatred for you, Olivja—"

"Aye? Then let the hatred be mine alone," she cut in, voice wavering. Her lips trembled, and tears burned in her golden eyes—threatening to spill.

"You'll die before I forgive you. But I'll love your daughter long after you're gone. Rest happily knowing that," she said, the words bitter with finality, her throat tightening as if they had stolen her last breath.

She straightened her spine, chin high, even as her hands clenched at her sides to keep from shaking.

Phillip's expression faltered, his mouth opening slightly as if he wanted to protest but couldn't find the words. A shadow of guilt crossed his face.

"I...never meant to root your life in anger, child," he said softly, his tone almost pleading.

Hot tears streamed down her cheeks—furious, unforgiving. She wanted to scream that he was wrong—that her life was rooted in *love,* not anger.

But, she couldn't stand to argue with him any longer.

Every second longer pulled her closer to crumbling—and forgiving him. Just like when she was younger—their fights always ended with her crying, wrapped around his legs in sorrow.

The hall was no longer the place for her. Swiftly she turned, knowing if she stayed, she'd lose what little restraint she had left.

As soon as she was out of sight, Olivja found the nearest room, slammed the door behind her, and sank to the floor—weeping into her knees like a child again.

It was all too much.
She was surrounded—suffocated—by her past. Close enough to haunt her, yet forever out of reach.

Thread XV

ᚦᛖ ᛒᚢᚱᛞᛖᚾᛊ ᛟᚠ ᚺᛖᛁᚱᛊ ᚦᛖ ᛒᚢᚱᛞᛖᚾᛊ ᛟᚠ ᚺᛖᛁᚱᛊ ᚦᛖ ᛒᚢᚱᛞᛖᚾᛊ

ᚨᛞᚨᛚᛃᚨ

Before supper, the families gathered to rehearse the Noble Knot, a traditional dance symbolizing the unity of nobles through marriage. Adalja had practised the steps countless times; her mother's insistence on perfection left little room for error.

Yet despite the stressing event, an odd calmness washed over Adalja as she awaited the dance.

She ran her nimble fingers over the folds of her dress, her eyes darting around the echoing room, scanning the potential partners. One in particular made her heart skip as their gazes locked.

Olivja stood near her father on the opposite side of the room, her arms crossed tightly over her chest, her face fixed in a familiar scowl. But as her golden eyes met Adalja's, her sharp expression softened a fraction. A ghost of a smile flickered at the corner of her lips, only to vanish as quickly as it had appeared.

A woman from the serving staff, carefully manoeuvred through the royals while carrying two heavy chairs.

"Oh, here, allow me," Adalja offered kindly, stepping forward to gently take one of the chairs from the struggling woman.

As she took a step back, her good deed was short-lived.

She bumped into something solid—an immovable force that sent her slightly off balance. The sudden movement caused her to drop the chair. It clattered against the stone floor, echoing through the hall.

Two large hands steadied her.

"Careful, Princess," a velvety voice rose from behind her, sending a chill down her spine. "If you keep dropping things, I may have to come to your rescue more often."

Adalja stiffened at the comment, her stomach twisting in discomfort as she looked up and saw Vincent's eyes beaming down at her, his amusement partially hidden beneath the mask.

"Until we meet again, Princess."

Before she could form a response, her father stepped up to her, a smile on his face, his hand extended towards her. She grasped it, offering a soft, nervous laugh as she turned to glance at Vincent who was already finding his position and dance partner—his brother.

Her father led her to the dance floor as the first harp notes wove through the air. The sound was gentle and familiar, lifting the mood of the room.

As the tempo of the melody picked up, Adalja focussed, following her father's lead through the first steps of the Noble Knot. Her mind surrendered to the rhythm. With quiet determination, she took over the lead, her movements fluid and precise.

"You're quite well rehearsed," Mark said with an exultant tone as he looked down at her, partially allowing her to guide their step. The shining greys of his clean and short kept facial hair sculpted his ageing face—he was a very comforting presence to Adalja.

As they moved along to the music, weaving amongst everyone and their partners, Adalja listened to her father mumble beneath the music.

"You've grown into such a beautiful woman," her father added in a whispered tone towards her, his conversation going unheard by the others beneath the soft music.

Adalja smiled up at him, shoulders tight, appreciating his compliment as though it were a great accomplishment.

"When I tried to dance with your mother...I was ill at ease, but she," he chuckled, a distant smile in his eyes and on lips at the fond memory. "She leads with *great* pride, just as you are now."

Adalja's hand gripped her father's.
"And I will continue to carry forth my mother's strength" she said at last, "...and my fathers."

She looked her father in his matching blue eyes with a hopeful glimmer, love and confidence surging in her chest.

"Indeed, you shall, my bluebird."

As they stepped to the music, Mark prepared to pass Adalja on, his hands releasing hers as he spun her towards her next partner.

BRAHMS

As the music swelled to a crescendo, the atmosphere grew thicker, charged with a palpable intensity. Natja's smirk deepened, her eyes glittering with something unreadable—perhaps approval, perhaps mischief.

"You've paid attention to her lessons," she chuckled beneath her breath, a tone of fondness spilling between them. Her voice was a soft murmur meant for Brahms alone, even as the music roared louder with each note.

"Always, My Queen," Brahms breathed, his voice laced with the faintest of smirks, though under his fingerless gloves, his hands trembled slightly.

The grip of his gloves felt tighter than usual, the sweat of his palms dampening the leather. It wasn't fear, but something else—something stirring beneath the surface.

He had never expected to become Natja's dance partner. They had asked him on a whim, to take the place of the absent Highwife Solvig. He had left his clunky armour in a corner of the room, left only in his loosely tied trousers, cinched at his knees, his armoured boots and a wrinkly tunic.

Who would have thought that a lowly knight like him would be given such an honour?

Natja's smile softened, a knowing glint in her eyes as she moved gracefully around him, the music lifting her in a fluid dance that seemed to float effortlessly.

She was the picture of poise, a queen in every sense, but there was a warmth in her presence that made Brahms feel less like a knight, and more like someone cherished.

"You would have been wise to inspire her to do the same," she teased, stepping into a more fluid rhythm, waiting for the cue to swap hands.

Brahms grinned, a familiar fire flickering within him. "If I did, you wouldn't have noticed how great *I am*," he replied, his tone more teasing than serious, though there was truth beneath the jest.

Natja laughed softly, the sound almost intimate despite the clamour of the ball around them. "I'll always notice your greatness, Brahms," she proclaimed, her words soft and genuine. "You would have made a wonderful prince."

The words caught him off guard, swirling through him like a gust of wind. He hadn't expected her to speak that way—not to him, and not in the midst of this dance. His heart skipped a beat, the compliment blooming warmth in his chest, before settling into an unfamiliar flutter.

For a moment, everything around them faded, and it was only him and the queen. Then, as the music dimmed, Natja spun him, sending him into a new rhythm.

Brahms faltered, his confidence momentarily shaken by the sincerity of her words. He had always known his place—beneath the throne, beside the king, and never in the limelight of royalty.

But now, as he spun into the next step, a faint blush crept onto his golden cheeks, his movements uncharacteristically awkward. His heavy foot caught on the other, and he stumbled slightly as he aimed to meet Prince Vincent—his new partner—halfway.

Before he could regain his footing, another set of hands caught his—strong and steady, with a grip that didn't hesitate. His heart skipped again—though this time it was something else entirely.

As his gaze lifted, he met the emerald, black-lined gaze of Elias. Those cat-like, penetrating eyes that never seemed to miss a thing. Elias was staring down at him, a veil of curiosity passing over his face.

"Careful," Elias murmured, his voice low and tinged with an almost playful warning, though Brahms could have sworn he saw something else in his eyes. "It's unlucky to fall here."

Brahms' heart raced, his pulse hammering in his ears as Elias' hand slid along the small of his back, pulling him close, guiding him through the steps they now shared. The knight's breath caught in his throat from the proximity to the prince.

He felt exposed in a way he had never experienced before with the heat of Elias' body pressing against his front. His mind, usually sharp and controlled, scattered under the prince's touch, each movement magnified, as though every step demanded perfection.

He glanced around, his gaze flicking nervously to the faces around him. This was a royal dance—a display for all to see. And yet, no one seemed to bat an eye at the unusual pairings tonight.

Jarl Ragnarvik danced with King Pembrook, and they shared a tender ease that calmed Brahms' anxious heart. No one seemed to care about the quiet intimacy that hung between himself and Elias.

A wave of relief washed over him, though the stirring in his chest only grew louder.

As Elias guided him through the dance, Brahms' own steps grew less certain. The music surged again, rising in intensity, and he found himself struggling to keep up.

His focus wavered as Elias' steady lead drew him in further, making it impossible to ignore the prince's presence.

With each spin, with each subtle pull and release of their hands, Brahms was drawn deeper into the rhythm of the dance—and the rhythm of Elias' body.

"Let me lead you, *darling knight,*" Elias' voice broke through the haze of his thoughts, rich with a chuckle that sent a shiver down Brahms' spine.

He realised—with some embarrassment—that they were mimicking each other's moves, both caught in the same pattern, neither taking control.

Elias, with his usual grace, smoothly took charge of the moment, his hands steady as they guided Brahms through the next sequence.

"Trust me," Elias whispered, his eyes locking onto Brahms with an intensity that left no room for argument. His gaze was unwavering, his voice like silk, weaving around Brahms until he could do nothing but surrender.

It was wrong, in a sense—inappropriate even.
A knight in the arms of a prince in such a dance. It was a strange, almost forbidden sensation—one that both thrilled and unsettled Brahms.

Yet, he could not pull away.

Something in the quiet trust Elias had offered—so unwavering, so steady—drew him in. The prince's presence seemed to dim the world around them.

As the music quieted once more and the final notes rang through the hall, Elias' voice brushed across Brahms' ear like a gentle breeze.

"It's been a pleasure, Brahms," he uttered, his warm words carrying a hint of finality, though the weight of the moment lingered in the air.

Brahms nodded, swallowing the lump that had formed in his throat.
The pleasure had been all his—and yet, it left him unsteady, craving more.

And as they separated, his heart still raced, the taste of Elias' closeness lingering like the final notes of a song.

As Olivja's father led her to the floor, she kept her eyes angled away from his face. She could smell the sweet wine that lingered on his mustache, and it only made her more upset.

She recalled the conversation she had with Phillip, where he tried to make an excuse for her father...Despite how disheveled her parents were, she would never think poorly of them.

She was disappointed that, when it came down to it, her father would sell her to a kingdom. And yet he held her closely and stayed silent as he guided her in the dance, respecting her choice not to make conversation.

Olivja took notice of how well he was doing in the dance and questioned how sound he was.

With a sudden turn, Dagrun fumbled and stumbled over her foot. With a short grumble, his tainted wine breath filled the space between them.

"Your mother was always the better dancer..." he said gently in their language, succeeding in bringing his daughter's eyes to his as he regained his step.

"Seems I backed the wrong teacher," she returned, a little nervous to speak Norse-tongue in front of all these nobles.

"Trust me, my rose," Dagrun chuckled deeply, his brown eyes twinkling with sorrow despite a happy smile on his lips. *"You've taken more than enough from your mother's blood."*

Seeing him with genuine happiness in his expression brought her deep sadness. He always had the same look in his eye when talking about her mother.

"You miss her?" Olivja asked beneath her breath, only enough for his ears to catch it.

"Like the moon does the sun, with every breath I take," he mumbled sweetly, awkwardly continuing the dance. Yet as he spoke of Highwife Solvig, his focus was unquestionable. *"The gods know it, and you should too—we love you, Valk, fiercely and without end."*

Her throat tightened, her eyes darting from the swirling space around her up to her father's matching eyes.

"I know it." She cleared her throat to distract from any rising emotion. *"Just a wee bit cross, that's all..."* her voice tapered off and his grip on her palm tightened for only a second.

"I know, Dottir."

She lowered her gaze and finished the dance, her father's warm hand slipping from hers as they passed partners. She caught a glimpse of him dancing into Phillip.

The pain of catching Phillip's eye for a second was completely washed away with the sweet image of the graceful Princess Adalja moving into her space.

The brave heiress instantly took Adalja's gentle hand into her own, a tight grip on one hand while the other quickly moved to cup her waist. Adalja looked up into Olivja's eyes with flushed cheeks as the Norsewoman took the role of the male counterpart of the dance with pride.

Olivja's excitement surged; sharing a dance of commitment—in such an intimate and public way—drove her all but mad.

For a moment, the quiet music lowered, heightening the shared silence between the two women. As they spun together in a slow tenderness, Adalja wore a small confident smirk.

"You truly wish to lead such a noble dance?" Adalja questioned, slowly lifting her chin to lock eyes with her. "My neck aches from your height now."

Being the first to break the two's silence spurred on the fire of excitement burning inside the pit of Olivja's stomach.

"I've waited ten long turns of the sun for this moment, wildflower..." Olivja responded with a quickness that only pulled at the already curving corners of the princess' lips. "Without a doubt, I am."

Though, against her confidence, Olivja's stomach twisted with knots as she took Adalja for steps far away from what was custom.

She never cared to learn this foolish dance—and she was making it known. Though her heart fluttered wildly—both at the closeness and the risk.

For the short moments that they danced together, everything was perfect.

She imagined a world where the two of them could blissfully partake in public engagements together, a world where their love wasn't pried away by petty alliances.

Unbeknownst to everyone else in the room, the Noble Knot was a perfect disguise for her feelings.

The tension in Olivja's fingers daringly tightened on Adalja's hand and drew her closer by the hip, savoring the warmth of their bodies pressed together. She moved with purpose, each step confident, leading the princess without hesitation.

"What dance is this, Lady Olivja?" Adalja asked, flustered. Her gaze remained locked on their feet, unable to follow the unfamiliar rhythm the Norsewoman commanded. "I can hardly focus."

Olivja watched her for a beat—Adalja's cheeks flushed, her lashes low, her voice nearly swallowed by the music.

"A courting one," she murmured at last, dipping her mouth to Adalja's temple. Her lips brushed softly against her hair—light enough to question if it happened at all. "Am I such a distraction to the noble lady?"

Adalja swallowed. Her breath caught. A slow smile curved across Olivja's face—first tender, then wicked, flashing teeth with a boldness that stole the air from Adalja's lungs.

"O-Olivja—!" she gasped, lifting her chin to meet her eyes at last, as if she'd been trying not to.

But that didn't stop her.

"Let my mouth make amends," Olivja exhaled, her voice a silken tease.

She laughed quietly under her breath, then pressed a careful, fleeting kiss to Adalja's hairline—bold, yet delicate.

The moment was swallowed by the dance, hidden beneath the turn of bodies and swirling gowns, as Olivja—reluctantly—passed the princess to her next partner.

The smile that Adalja had left her with quickly vanished as she caught Vincent's gleaming expression eagerly taking the princess' hand.

Olivja's movements grew unsteady and jerky as she stumbled into the other prince, eyes momentarily snapping up to meet Elias' gaze.

The Ragnarvik heiress had been avoiding the calmer brother since she arrived.

Unlike Vincent, Olivja had no problem with Elias; rather, the two of them were good friends. Under different circumstances, she would have enjoyed dancing with Elias and reminiscing, but all of their fond memories were tainted by his new engagement to Adalja.

She clenched her jaw as he supported her, bringing her upright as his hand fell to her hip.

"*Heiress Olivja*," Elias cooed, a gleam in his eye as he seemed pleased to finally have a chance to speak with her. "I'm *hurt* it's taken this long to be in your company once more."

She could tell he was smiling at her under there, and guilt struck her heart...she knew her anger towards him was unwarranted—born only of jealous feelings.

"...as am I, Elias," Olivja weakly returned as she held onto him lightly; jealousy made it difficult to touch him, no matter how neutral she tried to act. She looked away from his eyes, a knot forming in her throat.

"...is something the matter, Heiress?" Elias inquired, his eyebrows lowering in concern as the music crescendoed once more.

As much as she was trying to hide the way she was feeling about Elias, he read her with ease.

"Your *brother* is the matter...*always*," she answered with a weak whisper, knowing Elias would understand that Vincent was an upsetting individual, and hopefully wouldn't push the matter further.

She briefly glanced up at him despite her quarrels, but a flash of movement pulled both of their attention away to their left.

Adalja was up in the air as Vincent hoisted her by her hips, spinning together in an unchoreographed move.

The unusual pairing chuckled with each other, a bright blush donning Adalja's cheeks as she gazed down at a cheerful-eyed Vincent. To the sound of the music, she was carefully lowered back to the ground where Vincent swiftly continued the proper steps as though nothing happened.

Elias and Olivja had frozen in place despite the music's rapid progression. They both watched with similar expressions, deeply bothered by what they had witnessed.

"*Ah*..." Elias cleared his throat, witnessing the issue that *was* his brother. "Vince has always been one to turn things into a competition, hasn't he..." Elias tried to comfort with a nervous chuckle, whispering kindly above the music, desperate to calm the winds that swirled in her.

Olivja had to look away from Adalja, her stomach churning with nausea, rage—*jealousy*.

Elias tugged on her hand, trying to urge her to continue, but she felt hopeless.

The dance would go on, with or without her, their families would twirl around her no matter how she felt.
She was the eye of a raging, unjust hurricane.

With a final tug, Elias succeeded in unbalancing her so he could spin her towards the final pairings. In a few seconds, her hands were placed in that of Vincent's but, as quickly as she fell against him, she stepped back, no longer complacent in the Noble tradition.

"Get off me—" she grumbled under her breath, shoving at his chest.

Vincent grappled with her hip momentarily, trying to keep her still, but it was no use after the betrayal that had ignited her anger.

She spun on her heel and stormed towards the wooden doors, flinging them open with a dramatic flourish that turned heads in the ballroom.

As VINCENT SPUN ADALJA into the arms of Elias—arms she found far more pleasing—her gaze drifted in search of Olivja. She wondered what the heiress made of the exchange, or if it had flustered her as much as it had Adalja. Surely it had.

Her eyes hurriedly scanned the hall, and she found the Norsewoman storming out with the other prince close behind, everyone else dispersing from the dance as intended.

Now, only Adalja and Elias remained on the floor, their final dance.

Adalja swallowed a wave of shyness, knowing her mother would never allow her to end the dance early. She had no choice but to finish it with the same grace she had promised herself when first learning the steps.

The choreography was etched into her mind, but Vincent's abrupt behaviour had thrown her off balance. Still, Elias pulled her back into step, taking the lead with ease.

"My brother does have a flair for theatrics...are you well, Princess?" Elias asked, his voice smooth but edged with something that drew her gaze upwards.

His eyes locked onto hers with an intensity that made her heart race, the coal lining them sharpening the green.

"I am better now," she replied softly, though her voice was barely above a whisper.

A quiet chuckle rumbled through his chest as he spun her around, pulling her back into his embrace.

"Is that so?" he asked, his eyes glinting with amusement.

"Yes..." Adalja shifted uncomfortably as she responded. "Though I don't understand why Vincent acts so..." she trailed off, trying to find the right words. Her hand twitched around his, as if trying to add weight to her admission. "Why he acts chivalrous with me and not...*his* Princess. I'm not much to ponder."

Elias' grip on her tightened slightly, his eyes narrowing as he looked down at her.

"Even amongst others, your beauty shines the brightest, Princess," he said, his voice low and sincere.

"And Olivja? Well...she doesn't take well to chivalry," he chuckled and bowed his head, his hands steady as they continued their dance, the music winding down around them.

Adalja gave a small, self-conscious laugh.
"Then that warrants his unsolicited affections towards *me*?"

Elias squeezed her hip gently, his shoulders tense in a way that stilled her words.

"If my brother flusters you again, I will have a word with him," he spoke softly to her.

Her stomach twisted with a mixture of anxiety and something else. But Elias' steady hand on her hip comforted her in a way she hadn't expected.

"Though, tell me..." Elias' voice trailed off, soft but curious. "Is Vincent the only one to charm you, My Lady?" Elias asked, his voice playful yet quiet as he broke the flow of their steps.

The sudden movement startled Adalja, but in a way that momentarily distracted her from her worries about Olivja.

His hand traced from her hip to the small of her back, the gentle glide sending heat through her as he drew her closer. She blushed, not sure how to respond, until he spun her around, the speed of the motion making her laugh.

Her stomach fluttered, the sensation of being in his arms more electric than she had anticipated.

He stopped them both, pulling her against his chest so he could dip her, low and steady.

Adalja's laughter stopped instantly, her breath caught in her throat as she held onto him. He hovered over her, their faces inches apart, separated only by the thin fabric of his mask.

"*Elias.*" She breathed his name, unable to keep the tremor from her voice.

"Have I finally captured your attention back from my brother, My Fair Lady?" Elias asked, his tone both teasing and sincere.

They were suspended in the moment, their breaths mingling in the quiet. The music had faded, and everything else seemed to blur. For a few fleeting seconds, they were alone in the world, caught between the finish of the dance and something unspoken.

Their eyes stayed together, flickering, almost uncertain in this tension, but never straying.

Suddenly, clapping broke the silence, pulling them back into the present. The prince and princess' eyes broke away.

Elias gently pulled her back upright, their eyes meeting once more before she looked away, flustered. The applause of the families and servants echoed in the background, but Adalja remained focussed on Elias as he loosened his hold on her.

"The Pembrooks are a graceful bunch," he said, though there was a glint of something deeper.

Adalja managed a polite smile, her heart still racing. The intimacy of the dance lingered with her, but there was no time to process it.

She needed air. The adrenaline of the moment—mixed with the emotions swirling inside her—was almost too much.

Excusing herself from the floor, she passed by her father, eyes downcast, her mind far from the room.

ᛟᛚᛁᚠᛃᚨ

BEHIND HER, Olivja could hear Vincent's footsteps pounding the ground as he chased after her.

The door to the ballroom slammed shut a second time, echoing down the halls.

"Princess!" Vincent called, urgency creeping into his voice. "*Olivja*!" he added a chuckle, clearly enjoying her reaction, which only fuelled her fire.

Olivja stomped furiously down the carpeted halls, enraged—and as green-eyed as Vincent.

Before she could round a corner, Vincent caught up to her, yanking her wrist with enough force to make her growl in frustration.

He pulled her back towards him, tossing his cowl off his head to reveal an amused grin that only infuriated her more. Like a wild animal refusing to be tamed, Olivja fought against his grip, yanking herself in the opposite direction.

His grip seared her skin, though it wasn't pain that stole her breath—it was the thought of him touching Adalja the same way.

"*Princess*—calm thyself!" Vincent's laughter echoed through the corridor as he tugged on her, his playful demeanor suggesting he thought it all a game.

With his free hand, he gestured towards the ceiling in mock confusion. "Where are you running off to? Surely our little dance didn't upset you *this* much—"

"Don't play the fool, Vincent!" Olivja shouted, frustration lacing her voice. "You dare chastise me for disgrace, while you make a spectacle of yourself with *her*? Release me!"

Vincent scoffed at her, holding her completely still without even breaking a sweat, while Olivja was breathing heavily, trying—and failing—to pull away.

"Olivja, *please*, could you blame me? You can't expect a man to control himself in front of a woman like *that*—"

She stopped resisting him at his comment, a spark lighting beneath her feet. With a final tug of her wrist, Olivja stepped forward and delivered a hard slap with her free hand to Vincent's face.

He reeled from the force as she yanked her wrist free, palm vibrating like a bell from the impact.

"*Alas*! It seems I cannot control myself *either*! Could you blame me?" Olivja hissed like a cat. The thought of Vincent lusting over Adalja was enough to kill, she felt enough rage to do far more than slap.

She expected physical retaliation from him and perhaps she desired it after what she witnessed in the ballroom. She braced herself, huffing like a raging bull.

Vincent's head stayed still in the direction of the hit as though he was deciding how he wanted to continue.

Eventually, Vincent cleared his throat and rolled his head back to face Olivja, still smirking despite the growing redness on his cheek.

"*My Olivja*, I never took you for the jealous type," he mused, rubbing the burning handprint as though impressed by her strength. "Here I was thinking you had no interest in me this way...Perhaps I was mistaken."

She realised too late how her reaction must have looked to him, her mouth falling agape.

He saw jealousy, but not the kind that truly gripped her. The last thing she wanted was for Vincent to suspect the truth—that her anger had nothing to do with him and everything to do with Adalja.

But perhaps, letting him believe otherwise would serve her better.

Olivja swallowed hard, forcing herself to meet his gaze. If he suspected the truth, it would destroy her. It would destroy Adalja. She had no choice but to play along.

She *was* jealous—over whom? That did not matter.

"Well…I am to *marry* you, am I not?"
She forced the words out, swallowing her pride, willing herself to keep her expression unreadable. She wouldn't confirm that she wanted him—because it wasn't true. But she wouldn't deny it either.

Vincent's smirk faltered before stretching into a toothy grin.

"You tell *me*, love," he said, his voice laced with amusement. "Because unfortunately for you, I'll happily steal Princess Pembrook from my brother if she puts up less of a fight."

The blood drained from Olivja's face.

He didn't understand the power his words held, but they struck her like a blade. If he was implying that her defiance might drive him towards Adalja…then he was succeeding in forcing her hand. Her expression weakened.

"Was this your plan to subdue me? To make me behave by threatening to marry another?" She asked, her voice quieter now.

Her nails dug into her arms as she held his piercing stare. It wasn't jealousy over Vincent that tightened her throat—it was defeat.
He could have any woman in the world…She'd rather die than let him take Adalja over her.

Vincent laughed deeply and stepped forward, placing a hand on the wall beside her. He leaned in, eyes flickering with intrigue. His fingers found her chin, tilting it up towards him.

"I did not think my plan would fare so well, Liv," he said, his voice dropping, rich with mockery. "Who could have known you harbored such *strong* emotion towards me...?"

"I—"

The denial caught in her throat.

How she responded now would dictate the course of their fragile civility. If she rejected him outright, he might start questioning what had really provoked her outburst. And if he dug too deep, if he put the pieces together...

That was far more dangerous than letting him believe she wanted him.

Gulping, Olivja swallowed her sharpness—it cut like glass on the way down. She parted her lips and shrugged sweetly, as if the realisation had only just dawned on her.

"...Neither did I, Vincent," she uttered, as though saying it softly would make it less real. Her gaze dropped from his eyes to his ever-present smirk.

A thunderous applause erupted from the ballroom, pulling her back to reality. Whatever display had unfolded in their absence must have been spectacular.

"In that case, I'll take better care of your heart," Vincent teased, lowering his head as though savoring his victory. "You poor thing, this reveal must be awful for you."

"*Finally, you understand,*" she bit out, pressing a hand to his chest to create space between them. She cleared her throat, slipping free of his grasp. "Now, if you don't mind, I need a moment to gather what's left of my pride..."

Vincent looked at her with narrowed eyes. He sighed and leaned his body against the stone wall beside them, wiping his mouth on his palm before tugging his mask back over his nose.

"As you wish, Olivja."

Standing from the wall he reached forward a final time, swooping up her hand so he could kiss the backs of her knuckles through the fabric of his mask.

She stayed quiet and still, watching him with flushed cheeks until he dropped her hand again. He stepped back towards the ballroom, allowing her to finally breathe normally.

Despite how terrible he was, he was sweet enough to grant her the kindness of solitude, and that was more than enough to get in her good graces...at least temporarily.

She was sure this would backfire...but if pretending to like Vincent would keep his sights off of Adalja, so be it.

THREAD XVI

ᚦᛖ ᛒᚢᚱᛞᛖᚾᛋ ᛟᚠ ᚺᛖᛁᚱᛋ ᚦᛖ ᛒᚢᚱᛞᛖᚾᛋ ᛟᚠ ᚺᛖᛁᚱᛋ ᚦᛖ ᛒᚢᚱᛞᛖᚾᛋ

ᚨᛞᚨᛚᛃᚨ

ADALJA EXHALED as soon as she shoved through the heavy doors of the ballroom, tugging at her corset as if trying to free her ribcage from the tight bindings.

As if *that* was the reason she could not catch a breath.

The heavy stone floors echoed, her boot heels clicking on the cold floor as she walked away. Each step was a reminder of how far she'd strayed from her own peace, the ballroom now a distant memory behind her.

Adalja made her way down the stone corridors, the torchlight flickering against her shadow.

The floor beneath her gleamed, polished to a shine. Tapestries lined the passage; scenes of kings, war, and saints woven in black and white thread. They shimmered with a ghostly sheen as she passed. A faint trace of incense lingered in the air—sage and lavender—drifting from the rooms around her.

She turned a corner. And stopped cold.

Hanging upside down from the rafters above her was the jester—tall, bone-thin, almost inhumanly so. A woman—no, a man—no, something in-between.

Its face was smooth as porcelain, painted white and cracked in places like an old doll. A thick black smile had been painted across its mouth. Its limbs were long, unnaturally long, and its clothes—tattered silks and gauze—barely concealed the rest of its painted body, thin as twig and just as fragile.

Black hair was braided high and tight atop its head into two impossibly long plaits that hung straight down, almost to the stone floor. The braids swayed as they dangled, the bells woven into the pleats jingling with each movement. And then—

It dropped.

Adalja flinched, a helping hand flying forward instinctively—but it landed with a jingle, not with a thud, on its hands. Perfectly still.

It hand-walked towards her with the same grace as a dancer, legs bent grotesquely backward, joints jutting where they shouldn't. Then, without a word, it turned sharply and crept—still upside down—into the open room on her left. The braids dragged behind it, whispering along the stone.

Gone.

Adalja stared after it, frozen. A moment passed. Then another.

She'd never seen a jester before arriving in Worthyn. Her family had never kept them.

There was something about it—its silence, its smile, the way it looked right through her without having eyes for her at all. She couldn't name the feeling. Only that it felt like being watched from the inside out.

She shook herself and moved on, unsettled but not entirely disturbed. The encounter lingered in her mind, strange and weightless, like a dream she'd forgotten the meaning of.

But she pressed forward, more determined than before to find the gardens.

The pleasure garden she sought was the quiet heart of any royal castle—a hidden sanctuary like the one from her home—she simply needed to find it.

Its entrance lay behind a heavy stone archway, nearly devoured by thick vines. Few were ever permitted inside—only those closest to the crown.

As she stepped through, her thoughts drifted—briefly—back to home. To simpler flowers, gentler statues. Her father used to find her curled beneath a tree in their garden, asleep with a book on her chest and the sounds of flowing fountains trickling in her ears.

Worthyn's inner garden was a marvel of architecture unlike Pembrook's, but less pristine.

A glass conservatory rose before her, dark iron framing thick panes that soared towards the ceiling of drab glass. Inside bloomed an array of curated hedges and meticulously carved ancestors, carefully placed in a way that felt both haunting and regimented. Perfect, but cold.

"At last," Adalja breathed, as she stepped into the inner sanctuary.

She inhaled sharply, the soft smell of foliage mingling with the last warmth of the sun's rays. As she let the breath out slowly, her shoulders, which had been pulled taut, relaxed, dropping with the exhale.

The sun's golden light, softened by the roof above, cast a gentle glow on the garden below. Adalja stretched her arms out, tilting her face up to the rays as if they could melt away the pressure building inside her.

Adalja took her time, stepping softly on carefully placed stones leading to a three-tiered birdbath. Chirping filled the air—not wild birds, but imported species prized in the castle's garden.

Her footsteps were quiet in the peaceful solitude, allowing her mind to clear.

The dance with Olivja—with *everyone*—had heated her insides, stirring her thoughts like some stew of emotions. Olivja was the burning wood beneath the cauldron, Vincent the spice, Elias the ladle. And Adalja was the jumbled broth, spinning and bubbling and spilling over helplessly.

But, at least *here,* she could have a moment to simmer. To *cool.*

Just as she allowed herself to settle into the calm, the sound of the footsteps snapped her back to reality. She didn't need to turn around to know who it was.

Vincent.

The tension that had eased moments ago snapped tight again in her chest as his presence pressed close behind her. His shadow stretched across the cobblestone path, and she waited, breath held, wondering how he would approach her now.

"Pardon me."

Slowly she turned on her heel, facing him.

As Vincent made his way to the middle of the garden, his lined eyes fell to Adalja who stood beside the bird bath, flowing freely down all three tiers.

"Princess, I hope you don't mind my intrusion..." Vincent spoke again from behind his mask, a gentler tone now. His pointed green eyes scanned Adalja over once as he slowly approached—his towering frame crowding her quickly.

"Prince Vincent," Adalja greeted, swallowing the dryness in her throat as she adjusted herself, taking a deep breath. She hesitantly smiled, providing a graceful pleasantness.

"All alone?" Vincent asked, curiosity laced in his voice with a glint of mischief in his eyes. His step was calculated, inching closer to Adalja.

She adjusted uncomfortably, placing a hand on the bird bath beside her, steadying herself. The question seemed loaded for no reason, which left Adalja feeling more off-centered.

"Alone? No I...I'm here with the birds," she chuckled, swallowing a lump in her throat. "Forgive me, I was in desperate need of some peace after that show."

Adalja glanced up from the bird bath, hearing the soft chirpings of two birds overhead. The two beings fluttered beside each other near the roof of the garden. She only looked away from the birds once Vincent spoke again.

"Peace? Does something trouble your mind, Princess Adalja?" he asked, eyes narrowing down at her slightly, crinkling at the corners, studying her expressions with a quiet intensity.

"The rehearsal proved to be...far more than I anticipated..." Adalja quietly spoke, vaguely regarding the way everyone had stepped out of the choreography with her.

"That happens to be precisely why I'm here..." He cleared his throat, slowly pulling his mask beneath his chin. The Worthyn prince tilted his head ever so slightly. "But go on, Princess."

Adalja contemplated how to respond.
Vincent was a handsome man, in different ways than his brother.
She'd be lying if she denied any excited feelings he gave her during his flourish.

Gods, she couldn't believe this was how the dance had gone.
Not one admirer, but *three.*

She had to—at least—curb one.

After several moments of silence, using her hands to distract herself from looking up at him, she cleared her throat. "What were you seeking to accomplish during the rehearsal?"

Vincent responded quicker than she imagined he would.

"Accomplish? Did my improvised flourish fluster you, Madame?" His tone was amused and confident, which made the confusing stew within Adalja bubble up even worse.

Adalja clenched her jaw at his words, tilting her head. "Was that the intention of said *improvised flourish*?"

"Perhaps, yes. You're well-sized for certain amusements. Or...perhaps it was my intention to fluster *someone else*..." Vincent shrugged, stepping closer to Adalja. "What answer do you prefer, Mistress?"

Adalja's temper simmered, ready to boil over at Vincent's words—but one thing was certain: she wouldn't let his flirt go unchecked.

"My Lord..." Adalja began, her voice soft, almost shy. "I daresay...the Heir of Ragnarvik would not take kindly to such commentary. Flirtations like these are not without consequence..."

A fleeting expression twitched in his eyes—though quickly vanished.
"You're quite right about that. I've already paid dearly...though, Olivja has never taken kindly to *any* of my commentary," he chuckled softly, rubbing his cheek once.

Adalja's brows furrowed at his response, and she sighed. Nervously, her eyes flickered up towards the two fluttering birds.

"With both of our impending unions...you, to Heiress Olivja, and I, to your brother..." She trailed off, lost in thought, before shaking her head. "...Our loyalties, Your Grace. They lie with—"

"Please don't lecture me about loyalties, Princess," Vincent's voice lowered and he closed the space between them. "I came to apologise for my display...as precious as you are, darling, my eyes are *only* for her." Without warning, he reached forward, tucking a dark curl behind her ear.

The unexpected touch made her stiffen, retreating as her gaze snapped to his.

Only for her. Why did that make her stomach curl?

In the heat of his closeness, or perhaps a budding jealousy, she lost her balance, the weight of her body thrown off. Before she could regain her footing, the birdbath beside her, already unsteady from her leaning against it, teetered dangerously.

Adalja's heart jumped in her chest as she realised what was happening—but too late. She instinctively reached out, her fingers grazing the stone edge in a frantic attempt to catch it, but it was falling too quickly.

The heavy stone slipped further, and despite her best efforts to stop it, her feet slid on the cobblestones. The birdbath, now tipping wildly, dragged her with it, pulling her forward. Her arms strained as she fought against the heavy carved boulder, but her slender form couldn't prevent the inevitable.

With a sharp gasp, Adalja's feet finally gave way beneath her, sending her spiralling towards the ground. Before the fall could claim her, Vincent's strong arms swept around her, lifting her effortlessly.

His broad frame caught her, pulling her into his embrace and preventing her from hitting the cobblestones.

The stone bath crashed to the ground with a loud shattering sound, fragments scattering across the path.

Adalja gasped, hands flat against his broad chest—eyes wide, chest heaving. She looked at the crumbled stone, then up at Elias' charming brother.

The soup started to bubble again.

"Here I was believing you didn't wish to be in my arms." Vincent's chuckle rumbled low, the teasing edge evident in his words. "Shall we pretend I rescued you from something far more dangerous?"

His face dipped low, his proximity too close for comfort. Adalja's breath caught in her throat, her lips parted as she wrestled with the proper response: *Thank you! No we shall not! I do not wish to be in your arms!*

"Vincent—" Her voice was breathless, a wave of heat spreading through her.

His fingers curled into her hip, his other hand slipping between her shoulder-blades, tapping her spine as though impatiently waiting for her response.

Adalja cleared her throat, ready to say something through her heavy breaths until the sound of a voice she wasn't expecting spoke up from the further end of the garden, coming closer.

"Princess?"

She was called upon once again, and a moment later, Elias stepped up to the two of them with a quick jog—he had been looking for her.

Sharply, his eyes took it all in, from the embracing pair to the shattered bird bath at their feet. For a fleeting moment, both Vincent and Adalja shared the same look of shock—embarrassment—before Vincent's broke into a resolve-melting laugh, hands tugging her closer to his chest.

"How rude of you to interrupt us, brother," Vincent called with a lightness that *Adalja* knew to be a jest—*not Elias*.

A knot of anxiety tightened in Adalja's stomach as the situation unfolded unpredictably before her.

What had started as a simple escape into the garden—her last hope for a moment of peace and solitude—had quickly turned into another tangled mess.

All she'd longed for since her arrival was a brief respite, a chance to breathe and collect her thoughts. But now, it seemed her search for tranquility was slipping further out of reach with every passing moment.

The pot had officially been tipped over. There was no recovering her any longer.

"Interrupting?" Elias' voice cut through the tension, his tone measured and strategic as he narrowed his gaze between them. "Is all well, my love?"

Adalja cleared her throat, pushing at Vincent to quickly step away. She straightened her dress like some whore caught with a king, cheeks burning, eyes watering.

"Not *interrupting*—All is well—I assure you," Adalja replied, forcing a smile despite the rapid flutter of her heart.

She glanced from Elias to Vincent, whose eyes sparkled with mirth and something far deeper than what she was willing to figure out at the moment. "I apologise for the mess I've made, My Lords."

"What mess?" Prince Vincent asked with a casual shrug, slyly stepping in front of the ruined bird bath, tugging his mask back over his nose. He was trying to act as if the incident had never happened, and Adalja had a feeling it was more a jest than a shield.

Their eyes met—Vincent and Elias—locked in a silent exchange that spoke volumes, a conversation only they seemed to fully comprehend beneath the veils of their identical masks.

The air thickened, charged with an unspoken understanding, and Adalja, caught between them, shifted uncomfortably. She glanced quickly from one brother to the other, unsure where to focus her attention.

The tension weighed on her chest, thick and airless. In the glass dome above, the birds no longer fluttered—they fought, wings striking the barrier like the clash brewing between the two princes.

She took the chance to step toward Elias, careful not to give the impression she was unsure who to side with. She stepped close to him, close enough to catch his scent—minty and piney. Her eyes, bearing an apologetic flair, glanced back to Vincent.

Elias hooked his arm around her waist without asking—a possessive gesture that drew Vincent's quick, assessing gaze. Right as her thoughts began to wander, Elias' voice cut through the silence.

"There's no need for you to apologise, My Lady," Elias said, his tone now firm and tight, still fixated on Vincent. A thick tension settled over the garden as Elias finally turned his gaze down to the princess.

"Shall we?" His charming, gentle tone returned, his eyes trailing slowly down her frame before returning to meet her gaze.

The attention was overwhelming—far more than she was accustomed to—and it was suffocating.

Adalja nodded weakly, her voice a whisper as she gave a soft farewell to Vincent, who responded with a swift: "Have a good evening, Princess."

Without another word, she allowed herself to be guided away, her steps steady as she left the garden—and Vincent's presence—behind. As she followed Elias down the hallway, the encounter's intensity still pressed heavily on her chest.

She focussed on slow, deliberate breaths, trying to steady herself—but her heartbeat raced ahead, betraying the calm she fought to claim.

"I see my brother's...*enthusiasm* is not easily restrained. Though I trust it's nothing you've encouraged, Princess. He does have a way of...making his intentions known." His voice held a soft cadence as he escorted her to her room—his words too casual for what he had just witnessed.

"I...believe he means well." Adalja hesitated, glancing up at Elias, his hand firm against her lower back. Her voice was a little shakier than she intended as she continued: "Vincent can be...a tad forward, but his heart holds no malice."

"You're honourable to see it that way, but I apologise nonetheless," Elias said with a tinge of amusement before releasing her. "I hope you find peace in your room, dearest. I eagerly await the next time we meet."

With that, she was left alone in the hallway with only a fleeting glimpse of the prince as she entered her room. The door closed softly behind her, shutting out the tension of the day, but not the confusion that echoed within her.

And yet...a smile crept in, delicate and fleeting, as her hands brushed over her gown.

She did not attend supper that evening, her appetite lost to the intensity of what had transpired.

She had enough stewing for one day.

THREAD XVII

ᚦᛖ ᛒᚢᚱᛞᛖᚾᛊ ᛟᚠ ᚺᛖᛁᚱᛊ ᚦᛖ ᛒᚢᚱᛞᛖᚾᛊ ᛟᚠ ᚺᛖᛁᚱᛊ ᚦᛖ ᛒᚢᚱᛞᛖᚾᛊ

ᛟᛚᛁᚠᛃᚨ

THE JARL'S DOTTIR'S CHAMBER HUMMED with the soft rustle of fabric and the faint scent of lavender, as Edith tied the final lace of her corset with steady, practised hands.

Olivja's gaze drifted to the mirror, taking in the black gown that hugged her frame and fell to the floor in graceful folds. The long sleeves were delicate but confining, lined with tiny silver trimmings, and the corset, also silver, pressed against her ribs.

Her auburn hair fell loose around her shoulders, a few thin braids threaded with silver ribbon, their beads catching candlelight in the dim room. She felt beautiful...

If Freyja saw me now...she would smile.

No matter how much her culture prized grit and strength, she felt like a radiant goddess. Still, she'd insisted on wearing her dirt-caked, matted fur boots beneath the gown.

"You look divine, my dear child," Edith said softly, her tone warm and encouraging.

Olivja gave a small, half-hearted smile, her eyes shadowed with frustration—and resignation. She dreaded the celebration ahead—a ball thrown in honour of their marriages, a union she'd long resented.

It had only been two days since their rehearsal, and she was far from confident in the Noble Knot. She and Vincent had yet to dance together, and now they were expected to perform before the courts.

To everyone else, it was an evening of joy, laughter, and peace on the horizon. To Olivja, it was doom dressed in finery.

With a final sigh, she took Edith's arm, steadying herself before stepping into the corridor.

Together, they began the long walk to the grand ballroom. Olivja's heart was heavy with what lay ahead, softened only by her Amma's presence at her side.

The nearer they got, the louder the hallway became.

Muffled sounds of bustling conversations and laughter swarmed her ears as they reached the final stretch of hallway. There were two entryways to the ballroom, one that came from the Gardens—where the visitors shuffled in—and one from within the castle.

Near the doors stood the suitors—Adalja, Elias, Vincent—with Brahms and Sapphire stationed just behind them.

She glanced at Adalja—wearing the same design in inverted colors: a black corset where Olivja's was silver, a silver gown where hers was black.

At the sight, her legs grew heavy like bags of rocks, as though every step was carrying the full weight of her disappointment. She paused where she stood, half turning towards Edith with an expression that said, '*Please help me get out of this.*'

Her Amma gave her hand a reassuring squeeze, then nudged her gently towards the others.

Vincent stepped forward, clad in a brown jerkin over a red undershirt—the colours of Ragnarvik. She scoffed at the sight, the corners of her lips breaking into a smile...she liked seeing him in them.

Both brothers wore a new version of their infamous masks, Vincent's was red, and Elias' blue, to match his blue and white outfit—the Pembrook colours. Their white hair stood out as an accessory tonight, something they hardly showed so pridefully.

Vincent extended his elbow to her, his eyes loosely trailing over her frame for a moment before he murmured, "Is that Olivja? For a moment, I nearly mistook you for a real Worthyn princess." He tugged his mask down just long enough to press a kiss to the top of her head.

Her eyes went wide and she glared up at him, but he was already looking away, his mask returned as though the kiss never happened.

He was acting playful...though she wasn't in the mood for him.
Granted...it was a cunning slight.

"*Hm.* I shall do my best not to spoil the illusion, Your Highness...or should I say, *Norseman*," Olivja responded with an eye roll, glancing between him and Adalja whose eyes were also taking in her appearance. "Though, I wouldn't want to give you false hope...so keep your wits about you."

She played the part well—but it wouldn't hold for long. She ignored Vincent's elbow, stepping past him towards the doors which were opening for the couples.

A grand entrance for a grand occasion.

Olivja's eyes were rolling again.

This wasn't her first ball at the Worthyns.
And no matter how she tried to deny it, being here like this was nostalgic...and *painful*.

The last time she had seen Vincent and Elias was at a ball four years ago...she glanced up at Vincent for a moment. She wondered if he was thinking about that night too?

For the briefest second, his eyes darted down at her and locked onto hers.

He must have been.

Her mind wandered back to when they were younger—before everything became so tangled and tainted.

She already knew—this night would be nothing like that one. But...some part of her still hoped.

Fanfare filled the ballroom as the wooden doors opened to reveal them. Elias and Adalja entered first, hand in hand, with Vincent and Olivja following close behind.

Vincent had managed to snatch her hand mid-step, mirroring the other pair's posture. She held him—tentatively.

The troubadours paused as they were announced. To Olivja's relief, the Lords and Ladies barely glanced their way—once the music resumed, the crowd returned to dancing and drinking.

The Pembrook royals were crammed at a long table, sipping from chalices and chatting with other nobles. Her father, of course, was nowhere to be found. Vincent led her deeper into the ballroom, away from the others, towards the far end of the ballroom near two grand statues.

The prince let go of her hand and grabbed two flutes of wine. He turned, offering her one, while a tilt of his chin loosed his mask to fall to his neck. Her fingers hesitated before reluctantly pinching the flute's slender neck.

"I do not drink, Vincent," Olivja quickly announced, her eyes flashing to the intoxicating liquid before they looked back up, catching him in the act of downing his entire cup. She watched quietly: the long line of his neck, the subtle bob of his throat, the stray trickle of wine at his lips...

With a satisfied breath, he lowered the cup. "*Don't drink*...but you're a Pagan, Liv?" he scoffed, wiping wine from his mouth with the back of his hand.

"Or what...do you save yourself for the night of our union?" he chuckled, setting his cup on the base of his father's statue. "Surely I'm already worth drinking over."

Olivja shot him a glare. Gods, if anything made her want to drink—it was him.

Without a word, she brought the wine to her lips.

"Bravely done, my girl," Vincent laughed, cocking an eyebrow as she tossed back the wine in the same fashion as he. "And now, the illusion has been *tainted*."

He gestured at her with an open palm as wine dripped from the corner of her mouth. She set the cup down with a glare, wiping her mouth with the back of her hand.

"Spirits for the two *wildest* spirits," he declared over the music, grabbing a pewter pitcher to refill their flutes.

She stayed silent, watching him through lowered lashes as the burn in her stomach intensified. She could tell their last conversation had shifted something in him. He was being kind, attempting to charm her with his wit.

Unfortunately, Olivja's eyes weren't set on him the way he thought they were.

He turned back with the flutes, his smile dimmed as he placed hers into her hand.

"Care to dance, Olivja?" he asked, peering over the rim of his cup. "*You owe me one...*"

"You know my answer to that," Olivja said swiftly, gripping her silver flute tightly at the thought of Vincent's hands on her. "But...perhaps ask me again after my tenth cup."

Vincent took a sip, then chuckled, licking the excess from his lips.
"I will hold you to it this time, Your Highness."

This time?
Olivja rolled her eyes.

His swooning had her debating whether she liked him better violent than infatuated. She took another drink, eyes scanning the room as she lingered near Vincent. Annoying as he was, she felt safer with him than among a crowd of strangers.

"Nervous?" His voice snapped her back to him—just as a distracted nobleman bumped into her, hard. She stumbled forward, her entire flute of wine spilling onto both their chests—more on hers than his.

"*DAMN your eyes*!" she barked, slamming her cup down and whipping around towards the offender.

Vincent reached out before she could vengefully leave him, holding her still by the biceps.

"My wayward jewel! Calm thyself," he chuckled. "Hush now, let me see what they've done to my girl."

Olivja burned hot enough to evaporate the dampness on her chest. She spun towards him, her cheeks flushed with equal heat.

His gaze dropped to the spill on her corset, a red splash blooming across her chest, stark against the silver. She looked down and sighed. Even when she tried to look the part, something always got in the way.

Vincent now wore a matching stain across his chest...The two were a pair indeed.

"I'm...*Gods,* forgive me, Vincent," Olivja grumbled, wanting him to know that this wasn't some elaborate plan to humiliate them both.

But when she looked up, she caught something hollow in his eyes as he stared at her chest. It wasn't desire she saw, but disappointment. And pain.

Her brows drew together as she stepped closer to him—only for him to step back, raising a hand to stop her.

"You'll...have to excuse me while I clean up, princess...*Forgive me,*" he said darkly, his entire demeanor changing at the sight of their ruined clothes.

"I'll find who's to blame for ruining your gown, do not linger on my account. I will return for you shortly."

He stepped away without another word, lifting his red mask back over his face in the process. She stood there, wide-eyed and confused, wilder than she ever meant to look. And now—alone.

She sighed, watching as Vincent slipped through the crowd towards the exit, feeling like she ruined things, even if it was accidental. He seemed *truly* upset that he had to step away...

Her gaze drifted across the ballroom, then her stomach clenched. There was her father.

A small smile tugged at her lips as she saw his joy, dancing among lesser royals.

Dagrun—rarely in his right mind—was enjoying every moment, every drunken conversation the night had to offer. For the first time in his middle-aged life he was being celebrated and treated like a true *royal* king.

Best of all, everyone else was drunk, so no one judged him for being utterly inebriated. They saw not a *viking*, but a man committed to their way of life. She watched him mingle and hug strangers, laughing and dancing with nobles who gave the southern man their endless support and glee...

Norse people...they weren't particularly welcomed in noble courts and ballrooms. Not like this. For once, Olivja saw no prejudice—no hatred. No disgust.

It felt like they were finally welcoming her people as their own. And all because of her...and Vincent.

But the bliss soured quickly. Her smirk vanished as she considered what she was really seeing. The mere idea of an upcoming marriage was enough to bring so much peace...so much bliss.

Her family's burden settled heavily on her shoulders.

And then she saw the Worthyn jester, Nimble, pillared in the midst of nobles, a flickering centrepiece of spectacle.

A woman painted beautifully for laughs, yet in the firelight, she looked barely human. Her braids were tattered, swaying like tentacles or smoke, dragging on the stone floor like tendrils grasping for balance, bells jingling like they were playing for her.

Her mouth was painted in its usual grotesque grin—coal smeared too wide, lips dark and warped like a wound trying to smile. Her bright eyes gleamed, not at the crowd, but upwards, as if she could not bear to witness the rich watching her.

She balanced on one foot, the other pointed like a blade, arched and aloft. Her whole body trembled on the pivot beneath her toes...like she was waiting to shatter.

Her act was flawless, but made of nothing—*triviality dressed in mockery.* She juggled two porcelain vases and a pair of daggers, their sharp dance close enough to draw gasps.

And then—she caught one by the blade.
A slip. *A slice.* A trickle of blood on the polished floor.

Olivja gasped, watching from across the ballroom.

The jester's fingers jerked, but she kept going, her smile fixed, a painted promise of delight. Blood beaded on her palm—and still she tossed the next vase. The nobles howled with laughter. Her pain was a delight to those without souls.

She wobbled, balance faltering like a marionette on a frayed string—catching the next dagger by the blade again. Steel flashed with blood, slicing her again and again, like that was the point.

And the show went on. It *always* went on.

Olivja stood still, lips parted.

She was a ghost from Olivja's childhood, a half-seen myth, always flitting at the edge of memory.

But tonight, she looked like something else entirely:
A wound with feet. A silence wrapped in bells.

And then her eyes slid back to her father, surrounded by laughing nobles, in almost the same fashion as the jester.

Perhaps that's all they were—momentary jests. Beings made to bleed for their praise.

But unlike the jester, her father did not know the truth: the way their eyes truly fell on him. Not in welcome, but in mockery disguised as comradery. Control masked as partnership.

They laughed with him, yes, but only loud enough to cover the sound of their intentions.

Her father—an honourable Jarl, a ruler in name—was little more to them than a fool dancing for their amusement. For their comfort. And he didn't even know it.

Unable to bear the sight of her father, or the jester's bleeding act, her eyes found another man. One only *slightly* less disappointing.

Brahms.

For the first time, dressed in full *Worthyn* armour. Polished steel gleamed: curved breastplates, broad pauldrons, articulated leg and arm pieces shaped to his form.

Rivets bound the plates together, topped by a full helmet. The only reason she knew it was Brahms—*his height*. All the other knights stood taller.

Olivja poured herself another full cup of wine, tilted her head back, and downed it in one motion. She grimaced. Gods, it tasted awful. She couldn't imagine being her father...Surely it got better the more you drank.

She was determined to find out before the night was over.

The heiress skirted the edge of the ballroom, and space opened around her as she passed. Everyone knew her. The wild child of Jarl Ragnarvik.

She never intended for her defiance to leave such lasting impressions, but it turned out to be a blessing in disguise. No one dared approach her to offer congratulations. Perhaps it was the blood-like stain on her chest or the fire in her eye.

She thought briefly of Vincent and of the wandering eyes that reported to his father. A wave of guilt and fear washed over her.

She silently wished for Vincent to return before she accidentally made a fool of herself.

Eventually, she reached her knight-friend. His eyes were elsewhere. He didn't notice her until she cleared her throat.

"Is there a boy hiding somewhere beneath all that steel? May he come out?" Olivja taunted playfully, finding a sort of familiarity within her old pal.

Brahms turned his steel-covered head towards her, his eyes meeting hers through the carved metal holes that exposed his nose and mouth.

"Don't you have a suitor to displease?" he asked, matching her mock. They held a silent stare, the same unspoken challenge they'd always shared.

"Already handled. Try to keep up." Olivja sighed, guilt still twinging beneath her boldness for upsetting Vincent.

A servant passed with a tray of full chalices. She snatched one without hesitation.

"Aye, like father, like daughter? You two look in *very* high spirits." Brahms smirked as she sipped, laughing at her grimace.

"Well, if I must endure this against my will, I may as well indulge in my wine and forget it all by tomorrow...*you,* on the contrary, look like you're hating every second of *this.*" She motioned to his stiff armour with her cup, giggling at how utterly miserable he looked. "Don't tell me...Natja *finally* forced civility on you?"

She was having a blast—the wine tainting her mind with boldness. And she was already quite bold to begin with. Brahms' expression soured as he yanked off his helmet, sweat-slick curls bouncing against his copper skin.

"Trust I look better than *you*." He nodded towards her dress with an exaggerated scoff, tucking the helmet under one arm.

His comment reminded her of the mess. She glanced down—just as his gloved finger slid up from her chest to her chin, redirecting her gaze with a trickster's swipe.

And she fell for it completely. Her cheeks darkened as she caught his sly grin.

"*Ah*—still a hopeless fool, I see," he teased, snorting as he bit back a deeper laugh.

She lunged, shoving him just enough to make him stumble—his back hitting the wall behind him. As he straightened, she raised her cup and took another long drink.

Brahms, grinning, decided to retaliate one last time.

He flicked the bottom of her cup, forcing wine to spill past her lips, trailing down her neck and chest.

She coughed into her cup, choking on the burn. Then hurled it at his chest—*KLANG*. It bounced off the armour with satisfying impact.

"Damn porridge-brain!" she sputtered, wiping her mouth with her sleeve since it was already stained with dark reddish-purple hues.

Brahms finally cracked, his booming laugh joining hers as she gasped through the giggles. She grabbed another cup, still giggling like a child as she raised it to her lips.

Unfortunately, their enjoyment was cut short.

"Your father is a terrible influence on you." Natja's voice boomed from behind.

Olivja sighed, tossing Brahms an apologetic look before spinning to face her.

"Natja? Now I know I heard her, but she is nowhere to be found," Olivja muttered, arms crossing as she lifted her chin defiantly.

Then she glanced down, her grin spreading.
"*Ah—there she is.* He is, isn't he? Seems your husband agrees."

She looked past the short, fuming queen towards the floor, where Jarl Dagrun and King Phillip staggered with arms slung around each other.

Natja turned to look. Her hand clenched at the sight of her husband reveling like a joyous fool. When she turned back, Olivja was smirking—head tilted, gaze daring.

The queen's eyes narrowed. She glanced down at Liv's cup—temptation.

"Perhaps you could learn something from us *foolish vikings*...indulge a little? Lift your spirits? After all, you've far more reason to drink than I do..." Olivja chuckled, licking wine from her lips.

"As does your *daughter.*" The heiress' voice darkened at the mention of Adalja. "For once she's wed, she'll finally be free of *your grasp*. And to that—" she lifted her cup, "—I raise my drink."

She tipped the cup high and drank deeply, uncaring of the stares.

Let them think she was a drunk like her father. They already believed the worst of her and her family. She drained the wine and her stomach churned. She'd lost count of the cups by now. She tossed it to the floor, breath ragged, humming like a madwoman.

"For her sake, I hope you ease your ways, *Queen Natja*."

THREAD XVIII

ᚦᛖ ᛒᚢᚱᛞᛖᚾᛋ ᛟᚠ ᚺᛖᛁᚱᛋ ᚦᛖ ᛒᚢᚱᛞᛖᚾᛋ ᛟᚠ ᚺᛖᛁᚱᛋ ᚦᛖ ᛒᚢᚱᛞᛖᚾᛋ

ᚨᛞᚨᛚᛃᚨ

"OH, MY DEAR BLUEBIRD," Mark murmured warmly as Adalja approached her parents, draped in the finest silks and jewels that Pembrook's nobility could offer. His eyes roamed over her with wide, glistening wonder, hands lifting slightly as if to frame her before the world.

"You look..." His words failed him.

"*Exquisite*," Natja finished for him, her voice soft but full of pride. She stepped forward, arms already open, a glowing smile on her painted lips.

Adalja stood frozen. It was a punch to the gut, seeing her mother so radiant. So proud. *Was this a dream?*

Only a second passed before she moved, falling into the embrace like a child starved of warmth.
She was.

How pathetic it felt to know that, *her entire young adulthood,* she had been yearning for one thing from her mother—love. And how good it felt to finally get that—even if it was only a result of some marriage.

Her mother's arms wrapped tightly around her, drawing her close into velvet and perfume and the quiet hum of praise. Adalja bit the inside of her cheek to keep her composure, her breath catching as their love landed.

Natja hugged her as if she meant every bit of it—as if Adalja was the most precious thing she possessed. She pressed her face further into the crook of her mother's neck, eyes closed tightly against the emotion.

"You've made me proud beyond words, my dear," the queen murmured into her daughter's curls, drawing her a little closer. "A queen the realm shall honour, *truly.*"

And that was enough to undo her.

The tears came, soft and unwelcome, spilling despite her best efforts.
The words struck deep inside her, soothing and slicing all at once.

Of course her mother was proud. Her daughter finally stood beside a prince, lauded among Midhelm's finest nobility. Everything she had ever wished for her had come to pass.

So Adalja held her for as long as she could, arms wrapped tightly around her waist. When Natja finally pulled away, it left her both emptied and aching.

"Thank you..." Adalja murmured, her voice tight with emotion. She blinked hard, willing the rest of her tears away.

"Come sit with us soon, my dear," Mark said softly, his brows creased with bittersweet affection. He cupped her face in his broad hands, the touch warm and familiar. "Enjoy yourself first."

He nodded once, as though giving her permission to breathe—to live—and the simple tenderness of it squeezed her heart tight.

"Oh, my dearest," Natja laughed, giving his arm a playful tug. "Do not grow sentimental just yet...I shall keep you company until our daughter sees fit to join us—after she's had her fill."

Mark turned towards her mother, eyes crinkling with delight. "Might I have the honour of escorting you to the gardens, My Queen?" He was already bowing to press a kiss to Natja's temple.

Adalja flushed. "I'll leave you to it, then."
Her eyes flicked between them with quiet affection.

She didn't care if their kindness only came because she was finally doing what her mother had always wanted. It still felt good—achingly good—to be wanted at all.

She wanted to hold onto it forever. That warmth. That safety.
That rare, fleeting softness of parental love she hadn't realised she'd been

starving for. Even if it meant continuing to live the life her mother had chosen for her.

"Excuse us," Natja said with a knowing smile, glancing from her husband to her daughter. "We'll allow you some...*privacy*, for when your prince returns."

Adalja's face flushed a deeper red. Frustration and nerves tangled in her chest.

She watched them stroll towards the garden, hand in hand, like two lovers untouched by time. They vanished into the dark, but Adalja's gaze lingered far longer than she intended.

She longed for a love like that; one that endured, grew stronger with time, and never left. If her mother, of all people, had found it...Why not her?
Why not with *Elias*?

Adalja lingered near her parents' table, alone now, her skirts brushing softly against the stone as she stood still. She waited quietly, heart fluttering, eyes sweeping the hall in hope.

Elias would return soon. And when he did...she hoped that warmth might return with him.

The ballroom glittered all for her—black and silver silks draped from the beams, torches flickering between the towering columns, and music weaving through every breath.

And yet, Adalja had never felt more distant.

She looked down at her gown, deep silver threads shimmering beneath a tightly laced black corset. She never wore colours like these. She usually stood wrapped in soft cream, white and blues, like a proper princess of Pembrook. But tonight, draped in shadow and shine, she felt...different.

Dark. Mysterious. *Other.*

Yet it wasn't only the gown.

Her thoughts snagged on the moment she'd seen Vincent and Olivja together near the far wall of the ballroom—tucked behind the great statues of the two Kings of Worthyn.

She remembered the closeness between them, the way they leaned into one another, whispered teases meant for no one else. His smile, softer than she had ever known it to be. The kiss he placed on Olivja's head before they slipped into the ballroom.

Adalja's jaw tensed. Her fingers curled into the folds of her gown, fabric wrinkling beneath her palms. She stood still as a statue, breath caught tight in her chest, though she wasn't sure why. Not truly.

"You've no knight tonight. That makes this easier."

The voice slithered from behind—low, smooth, with a cadence that chilled the skin. Her head snapped up.

A man towered before her, tall, broad-shouldered, wrapped in robes of beige and gold that shimmered in the firelight. His hair, long and dark, was pulled into a neat warrior's tail at the base of his skull, and every bit of him radiated calculation. Precision. Control.

Except his eyes.
They were hungry.

Adalja's heart seized. She stepped back shakily until the table pressed against her backside, anchoring her in place. Her eyes flicked across the ballroom—left, right—but the laughter and music dulled everything. There was no one close. No familiar face. No knights.

"I-I beg your pardon," she said, voice delicate, a breath barely strong enough to part the space between them. "Will make...*what* simpler?"

The man smiled, a dangerous stretch of teeth that never touched his eyes.
"My attempt at stealing you away."

The words struck like a ice, chilling the air around her. He stepped closer, his shadow swallowing her whole. She wilted inward, hands gripping the table edge.

"Come with me, will you? Why waste your life in a Worthyn's war, when you could be *my* beautiful wife?"

His hand rose slowly. She watched it as one might watch a viper, frozen by the hypnotic sway of danger. Fingers, thick and calloused, lifted to pinch her chin with chilling ease. He tilted her face up until she was forced to meet the intensity of his stare.

There was no softness in his touch. No invitation. Only claim.

She felt the heat of him—the reek of wine and sweat clashing with fragrant oils. Her throat tightened. How could something so wrong unfold in a room full of people? How could danger feel so loud, while the world stayed deaf..?

But moments like this were too common.
Because Adalja was a prize to be won. To be *stolen*.
And it was no one's responsibility but Elias's to keep her from other men.

And she knew men like this. Men who spoke with authority as if it were a divine right. Men who desired not love, not partnership, but ownership. *Possession.*

"I-I-I," Adalja stammered. Her words tangled in her throat, barely audible over the thrum of her pulse. "I thank you, but...I've no wish to leave this spot."

The man tilted his head, studying her with detached curiosity, like a hawk appraising a cowering rabbit. That grin widened, and then—

She saw it.

A silver cross glinting at the hollow of his throat.

He was a holy man.

"You tempt me to act without mercy, little dove," he groaned, stroking the pad of his thumb along her bottom lip. "*Come now*, and save us both from committing sin. A pure thing like you deserves to be kept in my holy halls."

She flinched. As she tried to step away, his hand only tightened, sliding higher along her cheek, into the curls at the nape of her neck. His fingers closed around her skull like a shackle.

"I am sworn to Prince Elias," she managed, shaking her head with as much defiance as her trembling limbs could muster.

He leaned in close. Close enough that his breath warmed her skin, soured with wine and desire.

"There is no ring," he breathed. "Pretty wives deserve more than war-torn lands. I will give you peace. I will give you riches. *Heaven.*"

Adalja clenched her jaw. Her spine stiffened, even as her fear was swallowing her whole.

"Our *god* desires such a union as this." He chuckled darkly against her temple. "It would be sinful to refuse me."

Then came the pull.

His hand yanked her forward, steering her from the table and towards the ballroom's edge. The crowd spun in colour and song, blind to the horror unfurling at its fringe.

Her boots skidded across the stone as he dragged her through the hall, his hand like a collar around the back of her neck. Her limbs were weak, her voice buried. A muffled plea rang in her mind, but her lips wouldn't form it.

Her stomach turned to ice. Her lungs refused to fill. Each step away from the crowd felt like a descent into a pit she might never return from.

When they neared the grand doors that led into the dark castle corridors, she faltered. Once beyond those doors, she would be alone with him—there would be no saving her then.

Her knees buckled. Her steps faltered, snagging on the edge of her skirt. She dug her heels into the polished stone, her hands out against his side.

"*Please,*" she breathed, barely audible. "Let go of me! I do not wish for this!!"

His grip only tightened, pinching her veins.

But then—

The pressure vanished.

A grunt of pain cracked the air, followed by boot-scrapes and the taut snap of a fight beginning before a weapon was drawn.

Adalja stumbled back and spun, her hands flying to her throat.

There, between her and the man, stood Elias.

Mask forgotten. Shoulders squared. Eyes darker—green fallen to fury.

The Worthyn prince held the holy man's wrist in a crushing grip, his fingers coiled with the strength of a trained warrior.

Veins stood like cords along his forearm. His jaw, locked tight, trembled not with fear—but with fury. He was panting, like he ran across the entire ballroom just to reach her in time.

But he did. *He had reached her.*

The nobleman choked, eyes wide, lips parted in stunned silence. He didn't speak. He couldn't.

Elias had not raised his voice. He didn't need to.

"You'd be wise," the prince said, his voice low and cold, every syllable honed to a sharpened edge, "to treat my wife with the proper respect."

The shadows clung to him like a mantle, and even the firelight seemed wary of approaching too close.

Adalja could breathe again. And with that breath came the crashing weight of what had nearly been.

The man scoffed, a sneer crawling up his face. "*Wife*? She belongs to no man—not *yet*!"

Elias' gaze didn't flinch. Didn't blink. His stance alone carried the authority of a man who had already decided what would happen next.

"Adalja is mine. Set in stone," Elias said, voice like thunder rolling beneath the surface, "*long before tonight*."

Then, with the barest movement—subtle, but backed by the force of his training and fury—he twisted the man's wrist and shoved him back. The force sent the larger man stumbling a step.

Adalja watched as the stranger staggered, caught himself, then froze. There was a flicker of humiliation and rage, but he didn't dare strike back.

Not in the Worthyn halls. Not with Elias looking at him like that.

It was a gaze forged on the battlefield, one that had stared down death and emerged the victor. A gaze not of warning, but of judgment. A gaze not just of a man who knew how to kill—but of one who had done it before.

Then a knight stepped into view, as if summoned by Elias' look alone. Silver armour gleamed, the Worthyn crest bright upon his chest. With one heavy hand, he grasped the intruder's shoulder.

"You'll be escorted to the outer gates," the knight announced, "Speak a word, and it'll be to our god."

The holy man opened his mouth, perhaps to protest, perhaps to regain some shred of power—but the knight twisted his arm sharply. Not enough to break. Just enough to threaten.

The man's breath hissed through clenched teeth. He cast one last glance at Adalja, something dark and ugly behind his eyes, before being dragged into the dark halls of Worthyn.

The doors boomed closed.

Elias stayed frozen, staring after him with slow, measured breaths. Only after several heartbeats did he move—rolling his wrist once, as if to shake the memory of the man's filth from his skin.

Adalja exhaled and stepped forward, leaving the cold stone pillar behind her. She tried to compose herself, to become once more the princess expected of her. Her hand hovered at her neck, brushing the sensitive skin where the stranger's fingers had dug into her.

Elias turned, catching the movement—and that was all it took.

In a few long strides, boots tapping sharply against the stone, he reached her. He didn't speak. His strong, bony hands found her face, cupping her cheeks with a gentleness that broke something inside her. His thumbs skimmed beneath her eyes, brushing away tears before they could fall.

He stepped forward, bringing her around one of the largest columns, where the shadows pooled deeper and only torchlight flickered across the smooth walls. He shielded her, his body shrouding her from onlookers, from any further danger.

His brows furrowed deeply. The rage had not vanished—it had simply been displaced. Swallowed by concern.

"Where did he touch you?" he asked, voice still heavy with tension. "Did he strike you? Threaten you?"

"I'm well," she interrupted, a soft laugh escaping her, but it cracked halfway through. She blinked quickly, tears still fighting to surface. "I'm well. Forgive me, I-I should have done more. I should have shouted—"

"No," Elias shushed. "Do not apologise. Not to me. *Not to anyone.*"

His hands slipped down to her shoulders, steadying her, as if trying to tether her to the earth. Then, after a pause, he leaned in, lowering his head until his words were theirs alone.

"You were terrified, and still you spoke. That is more than most could do. That man should lose more than his pride for what he tried."

She swallowed, her throat tight. But she nodded, just once.

The ballroom noise swelled again—music, voices, a clatter of goblets—but it felt distant. Irrelevant.

"Show me where he hurt you," he murmured, voice softer now. His touch was cautious now, reverent even. He carefully lifted her chin.

Adalja's breath hitched, but she listened. *She trusted him*. She guided his hand beneath her jaw, to the sides of her neck, where the skin still ached.

A heavy, shared silence passed between them.
She kept her eyes on his as he studied the red imprints left by another man's desire.

He shuddered, his jaw clenching.
Gods, he looked at the handprint like his eyes alone could heal her.
Maybe they could...

Then, carefully, Elias mumbled:
"Look at me, Adalja."

He looked up, ready to catch her gaze—

But she was already looking. *Already lost in him.*

Their eyes locked, and she saw the way his throat worked. Then he leaned forward. His forehead touched hers, their skin warm, practically feverish. Her breath caught.

His lips parted, and with a soft breath, he murmured, "I would not have forgiven myself if I'd been even one second later, Dearest Princess..."

Her eyes closed, her stomach boiling with heat—*with infatuation*. She couldn't deny the strength in his words, nor the certainty in his tone. He meant every word.

"You are safe with me, I assure you. You walk this world beneath my watch now." Elias' voice was warm as it fanned her face.

She opened her eyes again, catching his as they glanced down at her parted lips.

"I will not let anything happen to you, Adalja," he promised, softer than before. The words hung between them, his gaze locking onto her blues—holding her captive.

No—she was happily taken by him.

"...I knew you'd come," she whispered to him, even if—for a moment—she doubted it. But she wouldn't doubt him again. *Never again.*

He closed the space between them and pulled her head against his chest. In that moment, the fear drained from her, replaced by something else. Not safety. Not love.

Comfort. Warmth.

She clung to the feeling as tightly as she clung to him. Her breath came easier there, wrapped in the quiet rhythm of his body.

She let herself listen to the beat of his heart—louder than the music, steadier than her own. It drowned out the memory of that man's breath, his hand, his hunger. For now, this was all she needed.

A sigh escaped her lips, soft against the fabric of his chest. Her eyes fluttered shut, the warmth of Elias' arms and the weight of his protection settling over her like a cloak.

Never had she felt so relieved—so confident—to be sworn to Elias.

"Come," he spoke into her hair, a gentle smile in his voice. "Let us return to the ballroom. I am eager for the world to see you by my side, and mine alone. *Hm?*"

Adalja's cheeks warmed. Her hands gripped the folds of his blue linen shirt, holding him a moment longer. She nodded once, then twice, heart beating wildly...no longer from fear.

"May I—" she cleared her throat, nibbling her bottom lip before continuing, "may I request a cup of wine first, My Lord?" Her voice was slightly muffled against the front of his jerkin.

His chest twitched with a low laugh. He leaned down and kissed the crown of her head—just once, firm and fond.

"You may," Elias replied. "*You've earned the entire vineyard, My Lady.*"

He guided her away from the shadowed space near the pillar, his arm around her waist, his fingers secure beneath her ribs.

The table sat waiting for them, two full flutes of wine lingering at the edge, placed in a rush.

"Now, let's hope our drinks have not spoiled," Elias cooed against her temple, releasing her so he could jog to the table before her.

He plucked the wine from the table and turned. Now that they'd stepped from the shadows, she finally took in his handsome attire.

He bowed before her, holding the flutes of wine level. Then the prince straightened, tall and calm in a blue tunic and white jerkin, his matching blue mask hanging at his neck. His laced boots tapped softly as he held out a flute for his lady, a soft smile on his lips.

"You look lovely in those colours," she said, eyes wandering over his frame and back up, slowly to take in the complete change of style.

He was in Pembrook colours, likely for the first time in his life. It gave her butterflies to imagine him as king of her land.

She knew Olivja would never wear such a thing.
Why she thought such a thing, she could not say.

A confident smirk curved his lips.
"And here I was, assuming I had no place in white...typically that's reserved for *pretty brides*," Elias teased, his voice lighter now, as though he hadn't nearly broken a man's hand only moments ago.

But she was thankful for it...It was easier to feel relaxed knowing he was as well.

He let the tease linger as their flutes clinked softly, and they drank in unison. A small bit of peace among the chaos.

The wine was sweet with grape and honey, clinging to her lips. She hummed her approval. His eyes glinted with satisfaction. Adalja didn't look away—never wanted to tear her gaze away.

After a breath, he spoke again.

"Shall we make my claim on you known to all these pitiful guests?" Elias offered, extending his elbow for her to take.

With a soft breath, she nodded, trying to ignore the way the pit of her stomach curled tight at his words. Or perhaps it was the wine...

He walked her around—mask off only for a sip of his drink, shortly returning each time—entertaining her and biding time while they awaited the Noble Knot.

But, every step Elias took was watchful. Every glance that lingered on Adalja for too long was met with his own glare.

And though the crowd had not seen what had happened earlier—they would feel it. The shift. The quiet claim of the prince on his princess. A warning in the shape of a man, and it made her feel freer—*safer*.

His hand never left hers. No matter the turn, no matter who approached, his grip only shifted, readjusted, ensuring she never strayed from his orbit. Even as he spoke to guests, even as nobles tugged him into conversations, his nimble hand remained with hers, steadfast. And her stomach flipped each time she realised it, her fingers clinging back with an equal stubbornness that said, *don't let me go*. And he listened.

As Elias engaged in a small conversation with a noblewoman—offering her congratulations—Adalja happily surveyed the ballroom.

And be it fate or coincidence, her eyes landed on the Ragnarvik heiress.

Olivja slipped through the crowd, weaving past patrons who barely cared to glance her way. She plucked pastries off trays and tables, chewing and spinning away before anyone even noticed—like some ballroom spirit.

She couldn't understand how no one else was as entranced as she...How no one else noticed her the way she did...

But just as quickly as she was lured in, Elias reeled her attention away.

After making a full round of the grand room, they slowed to a stop near the troubadours. The music echoed beautifully through the hall, floating along vaulted ceilings and intricate wooden beams.

Once they settled together, Elias grabbed another drink for them both from the wandering stewards.

Adalja could tell the wine was already affecting her; the first cup, drunk quickly on an empty stomach, had left her warm and light. But tonight, she was no stranger to spirits, especially when they soothed her.

"Do you still tremble? How fare you *now*, princess?" Elias asked, handing her another flute.

Their fingers brushed together as he passed it to her, sending a chill dancing up her fingertips. He hummed softly, coaxing her to answer as he sipped his own drink, his eyes flickering over her well-dressed frame with quiet appreciation.

"Are you certain you wish to hear it, Prince Elias?" Adalja asked before taking a large gulp of her wine. Her gaze trailed the dancers who spun and swayed with practised elegance. A small smile touched her lips even as she drank.

"You'd be surprised at how patient I can be when it comes to matters of the heart." Elias' voice carried a hum of understanding, layered with something deeper.

Adalja wondered if he meant their shared predicament—the looming marriage—but something in his tone suggested otherwise.

For a moment, she glanced towards her mother, laughing too easily beside her father, both of them surrounded by smiling nobles and grinning allies. Jarl Dagrun stood not far from them, drinking and nodding along to some tale she couldn't hear.

Adalja froze. Her mother's face was warm and inviting, a rare sight. The image of her parents' glee brought a bittersweet pang to her heart.

"I feel rather uncomfortable in the spotlight," she admitted with a sigh. "And yet, I would endure it all again if it brought my mother and father even a moment more of this peace."

She finished her drink, indulging like everyone else. Though, she truly meant what she said.

"My father...elicits the same emotions in me," Elias responded softly, a reluctant edge to his voice. But as he continued, his tone grew more confident. "At some point, though, it becomes our burden to bear—to continue their legacy. Their hands no longer burn from the torch they're passing."

She looked through her lashes to find his cat-like greens, his coal-lined gaze sharpened by the flickering candlelight. She nodded, turning his words over in her mind as her gaze drifted back to the lively crowd.

"Join me?" the charming prince asked, his eyes following her line of sight to the middle of the ballroom.

"*Where*?" Adalja tilted her head slightly, her blue eyes darting from the bustling dance floor to his eager expression. A beat passed. "Certainly not to dance, Your Grace." She laughed, though her cheeks burned under his gaze.

"If you're about to run, Lady Adalja, do give me a head start—I'd wish to catch you properly." Elias chuckled deeply, finishing his wine with a few short sips.

"Come—entertain me." He stepped closer, his grin widening.

"Bring me a song worthy of a dance...then ask me again," she snorted, the warming buzz emboldening her words. A nervous smile crept across her lips, threaded with anticipation.

"As you command, Princess." Elias smirked triumphantly, taking her up on the challenge. "Stay where you are." His voice purred low as he leaned in, plucking her empty glass before stepping away.

Bashful under his forward charm, she exhaled heavily as he disappeared into the crowd. She stood, rolling her taut shoulders to ease the ache as her thoughts whirled.

Her gaze returned to the ballroom, scanning the crowd.

There, in the centre of the revelry, stood the Worthyn jester. The strange creature juggled with eerie precision, delighting a cluster of intoxicated nobles whose laughter spilled like wine into the music. But it wasn't the painted fool who held Adalja's focus.

Just beyond, her eyes found Olivja.

They always did—as if a thread stitched between their souls tugged tight each time she looked away. It was instinctual now, reflexive. Olivja stole her focus before she even meant to.

The shieldwoman spun with wild, unlearned grace—her joy boundless, free in a way Adalja would never be. Every turn, every carefree twirl, struck something deep inside the princess.

What was it about Olivja that made her feel so...*covetous*?

Adalja's eyes narrowed, darkening with something fierce. She watched, unmoving.

The free-spirited heiress slowed her dance to take the hand of a petite blonde noblewoman. Olivja bent low, her lips brushing the woman's hand in a kiss that lingered longer than courtesy allowed.

The thread coiled in her chest.

It began as a twinge—a pulse of jealousy—but struck with startling clarity.

That should be me, she thought, tugging at one of her dark curls as though she could anchor herself in reality—in duty. As if it could unwind that same thread between them, to ease it.

Her mouth pursed, a delicate pout curving downwards into a scowl.

Still, she didn't look away. Couldn't.

She watched how Olivja's eyes drank in the blonde woman, lips lingering shamelessly too long. And then, without a word, Liv turned her head, eyes locking in an instant.

Adalja drew a sharp breath.

Liv smirked and moved—a ghost among gowns and laughter—towards the arched doors leading to the garden.

Beckoning.

Adalja's chest tightened.

She glanced where Elias had vanished, promising to return with wine—and, he hoped, a dance. But he had not yet returned...

Her gaze darted towards her parents, still deep in cheerful conversation, their flutes raised in celebration. Brahms was nowhere in sight, likely caught in his own tide of duty and watch.

She bit her cheek.

She knew she should wait.

But her feet were already moving.

First one step, then another, her laced boots barely whispering across the floor. Lit by nerves—and wine—her breath quickened as she slipped through the shifting bodies of the ballroom. Her cheeks flushed, her eyes glossy, her thoughts tangled.

She didn't care.
Because she was heading for the doors.
For *her*.
For Olivja.

She would follow her anywhere.
Even into the cold, dark night of Worthyn's gardens.

Thread XIX

ᚦᛖ ᛒᚢᚱᛞᛖᚾᛋ ᛟᚠ ᚺᛖᛁᚱᛋ ᚦᛖ ᛒᚢᚱᛞᛖᚾᛋ ᛟᚠ ᚺᛖᛁᚱᛋ ᚦᛖ ᛒᚢᚱᛞᛖᚾᛋ

ᛒᚱᚨᚺᛗᛋ

Brahms spent the beginning of the ball meandering quietly on the outskirts, away from most people, watching the perimeter closely and silently, as instructed.

Though, his focus was split—half on the patrons, half on the uncomfortable pinching of his newly polished, *borrowed* armour. With each step he took, the metal clinked and nipped at every joint. And he didn't appreciate the helmet's limited visibility.

Armour like the Worthyn's had always struck him as foolish for such occasions. He was glad the Pembrooks had little taste for parading their men like dressed-up warhorses.

How was he supposed to protect them in such restricting armour?
Well—that was the point, he was only meant to stand in it. He was nothing but a statue of perceived safety.

After his conversation with the Ragnarvik woman, he felt even more ridiculous. But he didn't have much of a choice *but* to stand pretty.

Spear in hand, Brahms rolled his plated shoulders, his sharp gaze grazing the edges of the ballroom, though he knew deep down there was no true threat to be found here.

Still, the weight of the metal at his shoulders grounded him. It gave him purpose. Watch. Guard. Endure.

He tilted his head ever so slightly for better vision through the narrow visor, letting his eyes sweep the length of the grand hall.

"Sir Brahms."

The familiar, silken voice rang unexpectedly in his ear. Brahms jolted, spinning on his heel, spear lifting instinctively.

"Oh dear *heavens*, child—"

Queen Natja flinched with a gasp, taking a step back as the tip of his spear nearly knocked a flute of wine clean from her hand. Her eyes were wide with surprise, but a laugh quickly followed, warm and melodic.

King Mark, close beside her, gave a knowing glance and chuckled as well, the sound unfamiliar yet strangely comforting to Brahms. The air between the royals tonight was light, almost childish in its affection.

"You'll find me for a dance?" the King asked gently, already stepping away as though the answer was a certainty. His hand lingered in Natja's, fingers reluctant to part.

"Always," she returned with a wink, her blush deepening. Their hands slipped apart fingertip by fingertip before she turned her attention back to the knight.

"My Lady—I apolog—"

"Easy," she cut him off with a wave of her hand, grinning as she glanced down at her flutes of wine in hand. "I did not know I was in such peril from drinking."

Brahms straightened, mouth opening again.

"My Queen—"

But again, she silenced him with a simple shake of her head. It wasn't commanding—it was maternal.

"Tonight, we can forgo the formality. It is a celebration, after all, my boy."

Something cracked open in Brahms' chest. Warmth seeped in, slow and unfamiliar. He had always held reverence for Natja—but beneath it, there had been something else. A connection he dared not name. One deeper than loyalty. Deeper than duty.

"Yes, of course, your Majesty," he agreed timidly, though a smile tugged unbidden at his lips. "It must be quite the celebration if I am dressed like some polished silverware." He dared a jest, teeth flashing beneath the metal helm.

He, though not as much as the King, always could make her smile.

A small laugh left her lips, nose scrunching in delight. She set the two flutes down on a nearby oak table, reaching up to adjust the shoulder plates of his armour with the ease of a mother straightening her child's cloak. Brahms stood there, still as stone, heart thudding under layers of steel.

He'd never known his mother. Never known any blood kin. And this moment, this gesture, scraped something raw in him. It was gentle. *Unspoken.*

She looked up at him with affection so soft, it nearly undid him. He laughed, breathless and nervous, trying to lighten the moment, but it only made it heavier.

"You have always been so honourable and good to this family..." Natja's voice trailed off as her gaze drifted to the crowd. Brahms followed it.

His eyes caught on King Mark standing tall in the centre of the dance floor, his hand clasped firmly around Jarl Ragnarvik's.

The King was leading the large Norseman in a slow, deliberate dance. Their steps were unhurried, almost graceful despite Dagrun's broad frame and drunken sway.

The air between them thrummed like a drawn bowstring, laughter spilling easily from their lips. But it wasn't the laughter of jesting men—it was warmer, deeper, the kind shared by two souls bound in ways they'd never voice aloud.

Their gazes never strayed.
Not once.

Not even with the gawking nobles standing by, allowing the space for two kings to move so fluidly together, like they were reliving a dream...or a memory of some kind.

Mark's fingers brushed along Dagrun's side in a guiding motion, and the Jarl allowed it, his grin wide and unrestrained, like a man unafraid to be led—even here, even now.

Brahms felt his chest tighten with a strange feeling.

"See—*that* is whose drink you should impale with your weapon," she said with a soft huff, amusement in her tone, shaking her head.

But even as she laughed, Brahms caught the shift. Her face betrayed her. Something wistful, aching, lingered in her expression. Her eyes weren't just looking. They were remembering.

He shifted his spear. "Are you well, My Lady?"

Queen Pembrook hummed softly, her eyes never straying from the Jarl and King dancing together. "A pair of kings playing at boyhood...They always return to it, don't they?"

"Pardon me, Miss Natja?"

She looked back to him, slowly—deliberately. A smile paired with glistening brown eyes shown up at him.

"How about mother—just this once, Brahms?"

His heart stopped.

"You've always been a son to me in all but blood," Natja continued, her meaning clear. "I believe it would suit us."

Brahms could hardly breathe. His throat tightened as he turned to face her fully. This time, not as a knight, but as something else. Something more.

"Are...are you certain, My Queen?" He cleared his throat, trying to pull himself together. His posture straightened out of habit, armour clicking quietly with the movement.

"You've always kept to your decorum when it mattered," Natja said with a chuckle. "Protecting Adalja, even if she never made it easy for you. And still you stood. Still you cared. I think tonight, we've all earned a moment to simply be ourselves. Don't you?"

"Yes, of course—Thank you...Que—mother," he said, and the word landed in the space between them like a vow. "Forgive me, I am speechless."

She shook her head, a kind smile touching her lips. The Queen stepped forward, raising the backs of her nimble fingers to his cheek, brushing faintly.

The action pressed into him like something warm carving its way in, nestling and making a home out of empty space.

Natja hummed, head tilting to eye him, but then her hand fell away, leaving a yearning clawing its way out of that space she'd made. "Say nothing. Enjoy yourself. Leave that foolish armour after the Noble Knot and come sit with us, hm?"

Brahms nodded without hesitation, a lump still in his throat. She smiled wider before plucking the drinks up once more, steps light as she went to her husband and the Ragnarvik man who were still dancing.

Mother.

Such a foreign word. Such a sacred one.
One he'd happily call her again.

He exhaled slowly, a small laugh escaping him as his armour clattered softly with his shaking shoulders. The first person he wanted to tell...

Was her daughter.

Brahms, after composing himself, searched the large hall, scanning each person around him for his princess. But as he caught sight of her, she was slipping away into the gardens. And in that space, Prince Elias appeared—making his way through the crowd, wine in each hand, his brows drawn in mild confusion.

His green eyes flickered over the courtly chaos, darting to familiar faces, uncertain and maybe—just maybe—a little concerned. Until his gaze caught on the knight.

Brahms' heart fluttered as Elias met his gaze. A slow, crooked smile curved the prince's lips as he adjusted his step, now with a newfound confidence, weaving easily through the crowd.

"Brahms? Tell me that is not you buried under all that metal," Elias laughed lightly, his tone teasing as he stepped in close.

The knight's composure faltered, caught off guard by the prince's charm. And for once, he was grateful for the obscuring cover of his dramatic helmet.

Words like that coming from Elias—gentle and familiar—made him far more nervous than any drunken slights Olivja had ever thrown his way.

“I fear it is so,” Brahms replied, his tone light and a touch breathless, bowing his head in greeting.

His eyes swept over the prince’s striking figure—the Pembrook colours, the way it matched the white of his hair. Brahms noted his smirk, the mask at his throat rather than hiding his face.

It was unfair, really—how effortlessly beautiful he was.

“Have you seen our sneaky Princess anywhere?” Elias asked, his voice casual, though the crease in his brow betrayed a deeper worry. “I went to ask the bard for a better tune, and now I’ve come up short.”

Brahms eased his worries, answering swiftly. “I watched her slip into the gardens...perhaps for a breath.” His head tilted towards the garden's entrance.

His shoulders eased, glancing towards the gardens. “Well...” Elias stepped forward, aligning himself beside the knight, their shoulders nearly brushing. Brahms could almost feel the faint warmth radiating from him.

The prince stole a glance his way.

“You must be weary beneath all that steel...Share a drink with me?”

His voice had changed—less princely, more intimate. The offer came with an easy smile as he extended the cup.

“Though I’m flattered, I cannot. My duty—”

“There are more than enough of my knights here tonight,” Elias interrupted, trying to leave no space for refusal.

Brahms cleared his throat, turning slightly, hesitant. “I am not to be without my armour at this time, Your Grace...but I thank you for the offer.”

Elias chuckled, shaking his head with mock disapproval. “Come now, do not sour my wine...” He nudged the cup towards Brahms with gentle insistence. “Set aside that foolish helm and take a sip. I swear it is worth the trouble.”

Brahms hesitated. His breath was shallow, his throat dry. He didn't want to seem too eager—but God, he was. The air between them felt charged, urging him to agree.

Finally, with a soft sigh of surrender, he removed the helmet in one smooth motion. His dark curls tumbled free, glinting faintly with sweat.

"I suppose any excuse is a good one to be free of this cursed shell," Brahms teased, trying to seem more collected than he was. He took the drink carefully, his fingers brushing Elias'.

The contact lingered. Intentionally ignored.

Brahms raised the cup to his lips, but paused when Elias gave a low *tsk* and shook his head.

"Is...this not proper enough?" Brahms asked, his brow cocked, the beginnings of a laugh forming. He was unsure what the prince was after.

Elias smiled again—wry, boyish. "Give me a toast first. Something grand, if you can manage—or amusing, if that is easier."

The knight let out a soft chuckle, mirroring the prince's raised cup. He didn't understand the game, but he wasn't about to walk away.

"To the Prince," Brahms declared with mock grandeur, clinking their drinks gently. "Brave in battle, charming in every room...May your enemies fall as easily as everyone else."

He met Elias' eyes, uncertain, watching for a reaction. For a beat, the prince seemed stunned—then amused—then something else entirely. A flush crept onto his cheeks.

"Well..." Elias cleared his throat, the toast clearly affecting him more than expected. "Cheers."

They drank together in silence. And when the wine was gone, neither of them moved to speak first. The music carried on around them, but the noise of the ballroom seemed seas away.

Brahms turned slightly towards him again, lips parted as if to speak, but found no words worth saying.

So he said nothing.

Yet Elias looked at him like he'd heard everything anyway.

And though it was brief, the warmth that lingered between them was something Brahms hadn't known he craved—something more than duty or allegiance. Something that made him feel, for once, *seen.*

In the quiet shared between them, his eyes wandered the dance hall, waiting for his princess' return. And then it finally dawned on him who else was missing amongst the crowd.

Olivja Ragnarvik.

Brahms grew tense, clenching his jaw. He knew in the back of his mind that Princess Pembrook was lingering elsewhere for one reason alone—and it was, without a doubt, the Reckless Ragnarvik.

He cleared his throat, flashing a nervous smile at Elias. "Thank you for the drink...I should go find our princess."

Elias looked almost disappointed, though he quickly masked it with a nod.

"Yes, I will have a place kept for her beside me at the table. My thanks to you, Brahms." Prince Elias spoke in a more formal tone, taking back the empty drink from the knight with a smile, his eyes flickering with something Brahms couldn't quite place.

Swiftly, Brahms made a beeline for the exit, scouring for the silver dress he knew his princess to be in, desperate to find her before the Noble Knot began.

Queen Natja was in too good of a mood to spoil it with Ragnarvik drama, so he made haste to find her as quickly as he could—before her mother realised she was missing.

Thread XX

As much as she enjoyed the twirling and spinning, Olivja quickly realised that her intoxication would keep the room spinning long after the dance had ended.

With a final bow to the blushing, giggling noblewomen, Olivja took her leave—pressing a parting kiss to the hand of the blonde she'd swept into her arms moments before.

These faith-borns...far too easy, she thought, rolling her eyes as she stumbled.

Lifting her head, she felt the tension of more eyes on her than before. Her gaze locked with a pair of icy hues across the room.

A sly smile curved Olivja's lips as she caught sight of Adalja—green-eyed and envious. She could read her stare across seas if she had to; their proximity only made it easier.

Even after years apart, Adalja wore the same expressions she always did when upset...it was comforting. Releasing the hand of her dance partner, Olivja took a step back, her gaze still fixed on the princess, daring her to follow if she so wished.

"Return to us soon, *Viking*!" a drunken girl called, tumbling into her gaggle of laughing friends.

Olivja didn't spare them a glance.
Her attention had already moved on—to a *different* noblewoman.

She decided not to tempt herself further by lingering within sight of her desires, and made her way slowly out to the garden.

Outside, the heat of the castle melted into the icy chill of the garden. Winter was upon them...a weight pressed down on her at the thought; autumn was her favourite time.

The flatstone clicked softly beneath her wine-splattered fur boots as she descended the steps into the gardens. The sounds of celebration dimmed the farther she walked, offering a moment of peace amid her hazy thoughts.

She wondered where Vincent was—not because she desired him, but to be sure he wasn't still upset with her.

She wondered what had gone through Adalja's mind when their eyes met. A blush crept to her cheeks—whether from the cold or her thoughts, she couldn't say. Glancing down at her ruined gown, she sighed, her steps faltering occasionally on the uneven stone of the garden path.

The outer gardens were lacklustre compared to the Ragnarvik lands. Statues, birdbaths, pillars—it reminded her of home...if all the life had been replaced by stone. The only green came from sparse evergreen bushes and pines; even the grass had begun to die.

She stepped into an aisle of stone *figures*.
Liv wasn't about to call them *Gods.*

Her fingertips trailed the stone, lingering on the cracks and bumps. The statues were hardly taken care of, cracked and crumbling, crawling with dead vines and cobwebs.

Glancing up, she ran her fingers across Ares and Hades on the left, Zeus and Athena on the right. She knew the stories...but to a Norsewoman, that was all they were.

She smirked to herself.
Oh, Tyr...you'd make cowards of them all.

The Norse gods didn't quarrel with children or strut like peacocks. The Greek gods feared death and sought immortality; the Norse embraced it—faced it with pride. The Norse gained worth through deeds and strength; the Greeks, through beauty and perfection.

Like her people, the Norse gods lived through honour and duty, and Olivja was proud of that. Her gods were *real.* Alive in *everything*.

Now the Worthyn and Pembrook folk had abandoned their Greek gods for some *new* one without even a face or name.

New God—same filth, she scoffed.

The nobles still ruled with wounded pride, just like their new god. Just like the Greeks before them.

Her eyes drifted forward, landing on another statue at the aisle's end—*Persephone.*

She was different from the others—more recent, more finely sculpted, adorned with finer details. She stepped closer, her expression softer. Her approach was gentler, one brow lifting in curiosity.

Of all the gods Ezekiel could have chosen to place during his reign...
Olivja's eyes narrowed.

"Why aren't you with your husband, *Persephone*?" Olivja asked the stone woman, looking back at the Hades statue on the opposite end of the pathway before returning to Persephone.

She was pleased to see the woman away from Hades, the man who had taken her. She appeared as her own being—free from the queenly chains of the underworld.

That's how it should have been...a woman free to choose her own path—no need for bargaining, violation, or negotiation. She deserved happiness in her own world, in her own glory...

Mark the day—Worthyn's made a wise choice, she thought, rolling her eyes.

"Would you prefer she go to him?" a gentler voice asked from behind, turning Olivja around in an instant.

Her smile grew at the sight of Adalja in a silver gown, glistening like diamonds in the moonlight, hands nervously tucked behind her back. The princess, however, wore a far less pleased expression.

"I'd sooner face Fenrir," Olivja said, emboldened by wine as she stepped towards the angry woman. "Let the goddess stay free. It suits her better—*beside me*."

Adalja scoffed, crossing her arms over her chest. "Where is your prince? Shouldn't *he* be beside *you*?" Her tone was thick with jealousy, which only thrilled Olivja further. "Or perhaps one of the *fair ladies* you danced with."

Yes. Be jealous of me. Olivja's thoughts darted like a startled cat, struck by a sudden burst of energy.

"I suppose I could ask them to join me instead...would you be a dear and fetch the blonde one for me?" Olivja teased, throwing her own words back at her as she advanced.

"So be it, then!" Adalja huffed, a pout forming as she stepped back from the encroaching Norsewoman.

But before she could turn, before she could take even a second step back, Liv was upon her. She seized both of Adalja's arms and, with a sharp tug, their hands tangled—Olivja yanking the princess deeper into the garden.

"Olivja!" Adalja gasped, her breath hitching as her hand was seized, but she didn't pull away. Not truly.

The tug had caught her off guard, yes. But there was something thrilling in it. Something that made Adalja's breath come faster.

Olivja laughed softly, wickedly, a sound that seemed to curl at the edge of the wind like smoke.

"So I was right, Princess *Persephone*..." she said with a grin that smouldered. "You *crave* this—to be led into the dark!" Her voice was sweet and sharp, like honey drizzled over a blade.

Adalja didn't answer. She didn't have to.

Hand in hand, Olivja led her beyond the hedged garden, past the stone fountains and flickering lanterns—out where the ground sloped gently down to the fields.

The long, wild hill rolled out before them like a darkened sea, stables in the distance, the scent of pine and hay riding the breeze. Beyond it all, the forest waited like a blackened wall, tall and still and watching.

The world had quieted around them.

And still—*Adalja didn't let go.*

The pair stumbled, still flushed from drink. As they made their way down the steep hill, Olivja's ankle twisted on the frosty grass, and she tumbled, yanking Adalja into the fall with a sharp shout.

They fell together, slipping on the frosted grass, their hair catching flecks of ice. The tumble ended with Adalja hovering just above Olivja, the two wearing opposite expressions: the heiress intrigued, the princess afraid.

"*Pardon me, madame...*" Olivja teased, eyes drifting across every beautiful part of the princess. "That's quite the charming way to land."

"*Oh,* Olivja!" She sighed with exasperation, slapping a hand to her chest. "I was finally not stumbling about, and yet you pull me to the ground?" Adalja smiled at last, playfully pushing herself up to brush frost from her gown.

The Norsewoman remained lying there a moment longer, gazing up at her in awe. Her world was spinning like a top, and Adalja was the centre, standing tall and graceful.

"Forgive me...I cannot help but fall before beautiful goddesses!" she laughed, shrugging as though her words hadn't just brought a blush to Adalja's cheeks.

"You stop that this instant." Adalja rolled her eyes, brushing off the compliment as she reached down to pull Olivja to her feet.

Their hands clasped—and once again, Olivja yanked the princess back down, tumbling her into the cold grass.

This time, Olivja swung herself over, pinning Adalja between her arms. She took a long look, moonlight slipping through the strands of her hair, lighting a sliver of her face. But Olivja wasn't the only one admiring. Adalja's gaze wandered too, sending butterflies through her stomach.

"Oh, *princess*...if I could stop falling for you, don't you think I would have done so *long ago*?" Olivja murmured, tilting her head with a cheeky grin.

Adalja blinked slowly, lashes fluttering from the wine before her eyes rolled in faint annoyance.

"Take it from the most *ungraceful* princess there is..."
She shoved Olivja back into the grass, then clambered unsteadily to her feet.
"Nothing good comes from falling."

Olivja decided to hold her tongue, despite having more to say.

She felt far too brave to keep quiet, and now was the perfect time, *wasn't it?*

Before the Noble Knot dance. Before the noble courts saw them with their suitors. Perhaps drinking was an awful idea...or exactly what she needed.

Adalja smirked, towering over her just a moment before turning back towards the castle.

The heiress wasn't finished yet.

She jumped to her feet, catching up with Adalja before her courage dissolved.

"Wait!" Olivja grabbed the princess's cold fingers, squeezing them in both hands as though pleading. "Come with me..." she asked softly.

Adalja was easy to persuade. Her face flickered with suspicion for just a second—but still, she let Olivja tug her the rest of the way down the hill to the stables.

"Surely you don't think a horse ride is a good idea!" Adalja laughed, still holding her hand like it was second nature...*like nothing about it was wrong.*

The gods knew it was right.

When Olivja noticed, her throat tightened. She gave Adalja's hand a gentle squeeze—a silent reminder of their choice to stay connected.

"You think I'd bother taming a nobleman's horse?" she laughed. "The only time I'll ride is with you slung over my shoulder like stolen silver." Olivja hummed, slurred but intentional.

She led them to the farthest edge of the stone stables, where the wall kissed the forest line. Quieter here. More secure. Olivja needed the stillness before she could speak her truth.

"Then why lead me this far?" Adalja asked, hesitant, her flustered face bathed in moonlight. "It can't be safe so far from our watchers—"

"Adalja," Olivja interrupted with a wide grin, releasing her hand so she could take a few steps back, her heart beating wildly, palms out to the sky.

"I want to be as far from the nobles as the winds can take me...I've never felt clearer...sharper. Like Thor *cracked* open the skies just for us. All of Midgard, bare beneath me. And I—"

"That's the wine talking, Liv! Hold your tongue!" Adalja giggled, leaning against the stable wall, twirling a curl as she marvelled at the Ragnarvik woman.

The sight of her like this set her heart throbbing, her stomach flipping and twisting. Being a drunk adult was a new experience; it brought back the same giddy feelings as when they were younger—only now, it came with risk. And Olivja loved it. Perhaps too much.

Stepping closer, she hugged herself beneath her breasts.

"Is it?" Olivja wondered, taking another glance at the stain over her heart. She lifted her gaze to Adalja, stepped closer, and murmured:
"If that's true...then do you wish to hear how the wine speaks to me?"

"Let your *spirits* ring!" Adalja giggled, a smile permanently on her pretty head.

"Well..." Olivja took a breath to steady herself, her voice soft as she recited one of the many letters she'd written for the Pembrook princess. "It speaks of how you shine brighter than the stars...and how your spirit flows like the river gods—steady, wild, and winding round me."

Her hands trembled—whether from nerves or the evening chill—as her low lidded eyes lingered on Adalja, full of quiet admiration.

Adalja gasped quietly, her amusement fading in an instant.

Olivja stepped closer, unbothered, the words spilling from her like a rush of wind: "Even in the blackest night, on the cruelest sea, you are the fire that keeps the dark from swallowing me."

Adalja's chest heaved with shock—and perhaps confusion—but she stayed silent.

"It tells me the gods carved you from something kinder than this world, Adalja...That you are the spark in my chest—the flame the gods lit in me. And *I'd burn for you. Gladly.*"

"Olivja—" Adalja's expression faltered, her eyes going wide and flustered as Olivja pressed on.

"Adalja, from the first glance, my heart was yours. I might not have known the gods' truth then, but I know it now." Olivja stopped her with a firm tone, stepping in close, bracing a hand on either side of her head.

"No distance could weaken it, nor could any measure of mead make me forget it...No stretch of time could *ever* undo what the gods have forged in me."

By the end of her confession, her chest ached, her hands were burning as they vibrated in the cold. Perhaps it was the wine, but for the first time she couldn't read Adalja's expression—and it made her nervous.

She braced for the cruelest awakening—one that would silence every feeling—as Adalja parted her soft lips.

"We shouldn't speak like this, Olivja," Adalja whispered to her, her cold breath turning to soft white clouds between them, "...we're both completely lost to our drink."

"Then let us be done speaking," Olivja returned her whisper, her voice low and thick with longing as she inched forward, closer—so close the tips of their cold noses brushed. Their breaths tangled, warm and unsteady in the chilled night air.

Olivja gave her pause. A heartbeat. An offering.

The last thing she wanted was to force something sacred, especially their first kiss. Not when she'd spent a lifetime imagining it.

Her left hand moved slowly, reverently, to Adalja's cheek. Her thumb brushed just beneath the eye, quivering with restraint. She held herself there, frozen between temptation and reverence.

But Adalja didn't pull away.

She stayed.

Wide-eyed, breathless, and entirely still—except for the slight lean forward. She didn't say anything, didn't need to. Her gaze spoke for her, eyes clinging to Olivja's like prayer. Perhaps even begging. Begging for what only Olivja could give her.

The fire in Olivja's chest flared to life.
Ten years of aching. Of wondering. Of devotion. Of yearning from a distance.

This was her reward. The gods had finally answered.

She moved in fast, surrendering to the pull of it. Her lips crashed against Adalja's with years of caged hunger, years of hope wrapped into one explosive moment.

Her fingers curled tight against the back of Adalja's neck, her other hand sliding to the curve of her waist, pulling her in.

What startled her most wasn't the sweetness of Adalja's lips—like wine and something impossibly delicate—but the way she kissed back: urgent, unafraid.

Adalja returned it with equal desperation, frantic—as if she'd been starving for this moment all her life too. Their hands tangled in each other's hair, wild and eager, grasping at roots.

Olivja's fingers trembled where they fisted in silk; dragging her in, deeper, closer—until their hearts pressed tight between them.

The kiss grew, deepened—tongues brushing, breath stolen. Adalja whimpered into her mouth, fingers clawing at the fabric over Olivja's hips as if trying to tear through to skin.

She was unmade, as if her soul had unravelled and tied itself back together inside Adalja's mouth. She could've cried from the relief, the joy, the sheer *rightness* of it.

Never—not in all her quiet, aching dreams—had it felt like this. So real. So right.

Her hands slipped down Adalja's back, splaying across her hips with a strength that betrayed just how desperate she was to keep her. *To love her.*

The press of their mouths turned frantic, messy, a clash of teeth and wine-laced breath. Still, she didn't stop. She couldn't.

She was dizzy. Drunk on everything—on her, on love, on years of silent longing finally in bloom.

Adalja trembled, one leg slipping between Olivja's—thighs tangled, arms woven in a lover's loom. She moaned softly into the kiss, and Olivja swore it nearly broke her.

Gods.

It was all real. It was happening. And it was *mutual.*

That kiss told her everything she'd needed to know. That maybe—just maybe—Adalja had always felt it too.

Olivja had waited *so long* for this. And still, even in the bliss of it, she pulled back. Even if only a breath's width away.

It hurt like Hel to stop.

But she needed to see her.

Their noses brushed. Her forehead pressed softly to Adalja's. She held the princess like a treasure—a sacred gift from the gods.

Their breaths came fast and shallow, chests heaving in sync, lips slick and swollen, stunned in the aftermath.

They didn't speak. Not yet.

Olivja gazed down into her moonlit eyes, searching for everything—answers, confessions, truth.

Everything felt right. *Everything.*

The way Adalja fit against her. The way her body melted into her arms. The way she looked at her—like Olivja had placed the stars in her palms and asked nothing in return.

This wasn't just a kiss. It was a promise.

A beginning.

Olivja leaned back slightly, loosening her grip to give Adalja room to breathe, to speak—to say *anything*. Because she needed to hear it.

After a kiss like that, there *had* to be something.

And Adalja—still breathless, still vibrating with anticipation—did not look away.

"Olivja," she breathed against her lips, voice broken and full of want. Her dainty hands slid to Olivja's sides, clutching the fabric of her gown with desperate fingers, pulling her closer again.

It took all of Olivja's strength to remain still, not to devour her mouth again. She pressed closer—just as the woman had silently begged her to—forearm flat against the stable wall, hand curled at Adalja's hip.

The only space between them was the fragile breath that left the princess' parted lips.

She waited.

Adalja opened her lips. Her voice shook.

"I—"

The sound of quick, incoming footsteps urged both women apart, their skin burning maroon as they fixed tangled hair and ruffled gowns.

"Princess Adalja?" Thankfully—though unthankfully—it was Brahms who approached the stable. He came around the side with a worried shout, panting as his wide eyes landed on the young women.

"We need to go b—"

He froze when he saw Olivja, not expecting the Ragnarvik and Pembrook heirs to be alone together at a time like this. He breathed heavily, eyebrows lowering with suspicion.

"...The Noble Knot is starting soon," he finished, clearing his throat at both of them.

The women could hardly look at each other, nor could they look at Brahms. Still blushing, still breathing hard, they kept their eyes on the frost-laced lawn—overwhelmed, as if the cold might quiet the heat curling in their core.

Olivja spoke first, still protecting Adalja—even in a moment as quiet as this.

"She'll go..." Olivja said calmly, gazing up at Brahms—who swiftly raised a brow in suspicion. "Go warm yourself, dove—I'll come find you soon."

She placed a firm hand on the small of Adalja's back, knowing there was so much more to say—and yet, absolutely nothing else could have been said.

Her hand slipped away, falling slowly to her side as Adalja stepped forward, one footfall at a time, ascending the hill beside her knight. Back towards duty. Towards the castle. Towards the world that did not know what had just bloomed in the shadows.

They shared one final glance.

Over her shoulder, Adalja looked back—a gaze soft with wonder, bashful and bright. There was something in it that sang of longing. Of a secret kept in the cradle of her ribs.

Olivja's smile curled like candle flame. She braced herself against the stable wall, fingers curling into the stone as she watched her disappear—step by step—until the last fold of her gown slipped beyond sight.

She didn't follow.

She couldn't risk it—not now.

Instead, she remained behind in the quiet, heart full and aching, replaying it all like ritual. She imagined what might've happened, if only they'd had more time. If only the Norns had granted them one more kiss. One more moment.

But she was not selfish. She was *grateful.*

And there, in the hush of the Worthyn night, Olivja stood smiling—ALIVE WITH DEVOTION AND THE MEMORY OF HER GIFT.

Passage II: Hjartaslitr

[The Tearing of Hearts]

THREAD XXI

ᚦᛖ ᛒᚢᚱᛞᛖᚾᛊ ᛟᚠ ᚺᛖᛁᚱᛊ ᚦᛖ ᛒᚢᚱᛞᛖᚾᛊ ᛟᚠ ᚺᛖᛁᚱᛊ ᚦᛖ ᛒᚢᚱᛞᛖᚾᛊ

ᛟᛚᛁᚠᛃᚨ

EVENTUALLY, OLIVJA DRIFTED OUT OF THE STABLES, her steps unhurried, unsteady.

She lingered beneath the stars, gaze tilted skyward, replaying every word she and Adalja had shared—every breath of their kiss.

"You've heard me all those years, haven't you, Freyja?" she shouted with a laugh to the sky, her Norse tongue slurred with mead. *"I'll never curse you again!"*

At last, her boots struck the flat-stone path that led back to the castle. Voices and footsteps spilled from open windows and the garden entrance—tense, hurried. The music had stopped.

A cold unease gripped her. Had their absence caused alarm?

Or perhaps...she'd lingered too long. Perhaps they were all waiting for her.

Gods, the dance!

She straightened, as best she could through the haze of drink, gathered her gown, and bolted through the double doors. The ballroom was chaos—nobles in silks and finery stumbling through the halls, panic etched into every face.

They rushed for the exits, hands over mouths, expressions tight with fear and confusion.

Something had happened.

Olivja scanned the room until her eyes landed on Vincent, weaving through the crowd towards her.

He'd changed back into his usual dark vest and black cowl, every trace of festivity stripped away. He reached her, seized her hands, and pulled her into a tight embrace—blocking her view of the room entirely.

"Olivja!" he breathed, gripping her shoulders, his voice muffled against the crown of her head. She didn't push him away, stunned by the suddenness, and the fear twisting in her gut.

"What...?" she asked, pulling back, struggling for space and clarity beneath his smothering grip.

His hands shifted to her face, cupping her cheeks as he stared into her eyes. Worry and confusion lived there, and it deepened her dread. She tried to turn—tried to see the chaos beyond him—but his grip held her fast.

"Come," he said suddenly. "I'll explain once you're safe." His volume was just loud enough to be heard over the noise.

But that only made her pulse spike faster.

"Safe?" she echoed, pushing at his hands and stepping back, needing—desperate—to see for herself.
"Vincent, what happened? *Where is Adalja*? *Elias*?!"

Frustrated by his silence, she peered around his tall frame into the ballroom.

Firstly, her eyes fell on Adalja, standing frozen and vacant-eyed. Beside her, Brahms looked stricken—horrified. Her father knelt, head buried in his hands, shoulders trembling with silent sobs. Several Worthyn guards circled two collapsed figures, ushering guests away with urgent movements. Before she could make sense of it, Vincent seized her shoulders and forced her back into the corridor.

"No! You tell me now, Vince!" she shouted, digging in her heels. "Speak, or I'll plant myself here 'til the gods drag me off!"

Even with nobles watching, she didn't care. Frustration burned through her—this silence, this secrecy—it was maddening.

Vincent, humiliated by the scene she was making, gripped the back of her neck and hauled her close again. He pinned her to the wall, blocking her from view—pressing so tightly, it stole her breath.

To the nobles, it looked like a lover's embrace. Reassurance in the wake of tragedy...but to Olivja, it was a cage.

"Be still," he hissed, yanking his mask below his chin, breath ragged, pride stinging.

She glared up at him, chest heaving.
Then, his lips found her ear, and he rasped the truth—the thing she'd missed while chasing stolen kisses.

"The Pembrooks are dead."

The words struck her still.

Her drunken haze vanished, but the world only spun faster.

And in the silence that followed, she swore she could hear the gods laughing: *Do you still wish to never curse us?*

Vincent slowly pulled back, eyes locked on her stunned face. He exhaled, voice low. "Now come."

Olivja walked in stunned silence beside Vincent, her thoughts a storm as he led her towards her bedroom. Adalja's trembling silhouette burned behind her eyes, a loop she couldn't escape.

"*How...?*" she asked, quiet as a mouse, folding her arms beneath her chest.

His hand applied steady pressure at the small of her back, fingers absently fidgeting with the ribbons of her corset as they walked.

"Poison, we presume. Perdyr," he muttered, green eyes sweeping the hall. "Our very public plan to wed during wartime hasn't been well received."

"No. That's...not possible," Liv whispered, her voice faint, slurred.

A chill crept in.
Her father wouldn't think twice before downing a poisoned drink, so long as it smelled of mead. But then—why had he survived? He, too, had handed his daughter to Worthyn. And gods knew, he drank enough to drown a man.

"Well, I imagine it was easy—after all...I sent every knight to find *you.*" His tone, clipped and sharp, landed like blame.

Olivja froze in place.

Her jaw tensed. There was no use in arguing—not yet, not without anything worth saying. Because what could she possibly say?

If the knights left the Pembrooks unguarded to search for her...
Then it was her love that had doomed them.

A lot of good your feelings do, Olivja.

A shaky breath left her lips. Guilt curled hot in her chest.

"F-forgive me, I drank too much," Olivja mumbled. "I...needed to breathe before I painted the ballroom..." Her voice withered with every word. Her vision blurred. She cleared her throat, gaze cast down, hands buzzing with shame. She clasped them tightly, trying to still the tremble.

"I'm not the one for your excuses. Walk." He pressed her forward, firm hand guiding her in silence.

But grief hit like a stone, weighing down her limbs. Her steps faltered, feet dragging. She stumbled forward until Vincent caught her arm to steady her.

He looked back, brow furrowed.
"Olivja?" His voice barely reached her—like muffled by seashells.

She looked up...and instantly regretted it.

His face blurred into the hallway, smeared and warping. His eyes were glowing, shining, like sun-lit emeralds—streaking through the spinning hallway like bolts of green lightning.

The flickering torches weren't just burning—they were *moving*, stretching out in long, wobbly lines, like they were as drunk as she was.

Every time she blinked, the glow smeared across the room, fading and then coming back like it couldn't make up its mind. The whole room was spinning slowly, even with her hands desperately clinging to him.

She couldn't tell if it was her swaying—or the world. The wine had claimed her, utterly.

Stress. Guilt. The kiss. The exhaustion. Whatever the reason, Olivja could no longer hide how drunk she was.

Everything slowed as if the Norns held their breath.
She glanced left as they passed a mirror—and there, in the glass, stood a child's reflection. Herself. Staring. Smiling. Waving.

A vision? A sign? Just the wine? Liv was far too drunk to give any meaning to it.

She drew a slow breath, her mouth watering as nausea crept higher.
"*Hmn...*" she whimpered, her head dipping sideways as she staggered another step.

He must have seen it coming—*whatever it was.* She was too drunk to tell.

Her ankle rolled, and suddenly, the floor disappeared.

Vincent had scooped her into his arms.

The sudden lift jerked her stomach. She slapped a hand over her mouth—this time, not to stop her words. Her head dropped limply to his chest as her vision steadied.

"I...don't need—*hic*—your help," she groaned. But her slow, ragged breaths told the truth.

"You're in no shape to argue, Olivja." His voice rumbled in his chest—low and steady—and her eyes fluttered shut.

"...then move, *lowly steed*," she muttered behind her hand. "Before I stain your chest red again."

He chuckled, chest jolting beneath her cheek. She glanced up—just in time to catch his eyes before he looked away.

"*God help me*, you're charming tonight," he murmured. "But it's time to quiet. Hearts mourn all around us."

Olivja went quiet immediately, her already flushed cheeks deepening as the Pembrook murders replayed in her mind—deaths she had, in one way or another, caused. The thought made nausea rise in her throat, hot and sudden.

She swallowed hard and turned away, blinking fast against the heat behind her eyes.

They walked in silence, her head swaying gently with each step like a pendulum out of sync. She closed her eyes. Each step rocking her like a sailboat on quiet seas.

THE COLD BITE OF STONE beneath her feet snapped her eyes open.

In front of her was a large wooden tub, warmly steaming in the centre of a bathing room. She squinted as strong hands steadied her hips—equally curious and irritated.

Then came the soft *thwip* of her corset ribbons loosening behind her. On instinct, she slammed her elbow backward, striking something solid.

"*Curses, woman!*" Vincent groaned, tightening his grip on her hip. "Be still! Lest you wish to bathe in your cage!" He gave her a rough jolt, as if trying to shake the drunkenness out of her, then returned to the laces.

The jolt blurred her vision, a groan slipping out as the pounding in her head swelled. She let herself sag against him, too tired—too drunk—to protest.

Once the ribbons fell, so did her bodice. Vincent tossed it aside with a sigh and turned her to face him.

She expected him to loom above her—but instead, he knelt, face level with her ribs, lip curled in frustration. Her elbow had split his lip; blood bloomed dark along his mouth.

Her expression softened in drunken amusement.

Sweet revenge.

"*Hm*," she smirked, voice thick with wine. "*—Hic—*the fault isss-yours." She gave him a wobbly grin and leaned on his shoulder for balance.

His tired gaze crawled slowly up her body, blood blooming across his lower lip. His stare lingered—far too long—before reaching her eyes with a look sharp enough to slice the last of her clothing clean off.

She had just bloodied him...yet it was not anger in his eyes. She swallowed hard. Her stomach twisted—not with nausea, but with something far more *irritating.*

His fingers traced down her sides, stopping only when they reached her ankles. "Are you going to hit me again if I help you out of this?" Vincent asked, his voice gentle—not flirtatious, not exasperated, just honest.

"...Only the gods s-know..." she retorted, though her jaw clenched as she stumbled back. His hands caught her hips again, steadying her once more.

He held her gaze a moment before sighing, bunching her dress at the hips until the bottom half was gathered at her waist. Still gripping the fabric, he rose to his feet, keeping their gaze locked as he pulled the dress up and over her head. As the dark blur of fabric cleared, she tilted her head slightly, keeping his gaze.

Vincent tossed the dress aside, and she saw his jaw clench. She was bare now...yet his green eyes remained fixed on her face.

Nudity, in her homeland, wasn't cause for shame—bathing halls were shared, and practical matters outweighed modesty. To be exposed wasn't unusual...But to have *someone else* strip you bare could be taken as an insult—a power play, a stripping of dignity.

Yet she didn't feel insulted. She didn't even feel small or uncomfortable. She felt valued—*cared for,* even. Maybe it was because she trusted him. Maybe it was the wine. The thought made her eyebrows lower—she shrugged it off with a scoff.

"This was no accident. You aimed to get me drunk," she grumbled, smacking his chest with enough force to stumble back herself.

"That's fine, *princess*...I'll take *all* the blame for getting you so thoroughly in your cups—after all, you were drinking for me, weren't you?"

He tugged her waist closer, his left hand lifting her chin, steadying her gaze as her eyes fluttered. Her bare form pressed against his chest, hiding her from his view. A shiver laced down her spine. Being naked hadn't unsettled her—until now. Until he touched her like that.

Gods, don't push me, Vincent, she thought, jaw clenching as her breath grew shallow.

Still, his eyes never left her face as he continued quietly:
"What was I thinking...assuming little Liv could carry her father's *legacy*," he cooed, cocking an eyebrow as he tested her limits.

"I...hate...chyou," she mumbled, her words slurring, eyes rolling as she struggled to focus on his. The way her head lolled must've shown her dizziness. His expression softened, concern flickering beneath the teasing.

"You'll find new reasons to hate me yet, Liv," Vincent muttered with a dry smile, rolling his sleeves to the elbows.

Without hesitation, he swept her into his arms again. The shift in gravity made her reel, her head spinning like the world had tipped over. He moved with a confidence that both steadied and unsettled her as he stepped towards the tub. The steam curled upwards like ghostly tendrils, the heat promising relief but also stirring her growing sense of vulnerability.

Vincent knelt beside the tub, his strong arms cradling her, wine-sweet breath brushing his jaw. He lowered her with deliberate care, keeping her steady until the water took her weight. Olivja closed her eyes, sinking into the rare sensation of being untethered from her drunken haze.

His hands lingered beneath the water long enough to ensure her balance before retreating, droplets trickling from his skin and echoing softly against the surface.

Despite his calculated movements, she sensed an undercurrent of tension, as though a war waged behind his steady green gaze. When her amber eyes fluttered open, she found him watching her intently, his focus unwavering.

"There," he said softly, his voice a low rumble that somehow settled the noise inside her. He straightened, giving her space but lingering close enough to intervene if needed. "Now, clean yourself. I'll wait outside."

Vincent stood and turned, his steps purposeful as though his resolve might crack if he stayed a moment longer. But as he reached for the door, a surge of panic overtook her. Her hands shot out of the water, gripping the edges of the tub with a gasp.

"Vince!" Her voice cracked, hoarse and raw from too much wine.

He froze, his back still turned.

"You...you'll let me drown in here?!" she sputtered, the words tumbling faster than she could think. "I can't—"

"Tempting offer," he cut in, his tone dry. He glanced back, a single green eye catching hers over his shoulder. "What are you asking for, princess?"

Her mouth opened, then closed again as her pride warred with her desperation. Finally, she sighed, her fingers gripping the wood until her knuckles turned white. "Nothing. Forget it. I'd rather drown," she muttered, sinking lower into the water, still clutching the sides.

For a moment, Vincent didn't move.

Her heart stuttered, wondering if this was the moment he would finally let her fend for herself. But then he exhaled heavily, the sound steeped in exasperation.

"You're making me work for this, Olivja," he muttered, dragging a wooden stool beside the tub before settling onto it.

She loosened her grip, though her hands still clung to the tub as her gaze followed him leaning for a nearby bucket.

"I'm not scrubbing you like some servant," he scoffed, but his hands were already working at the silver beads tangled in her hair.

The silence that followed was punctuated only by the soft splash of water and the gentle tug of his fingers. He worked with surprising tenderness, unwinding ribbons and easing out the braids.

A shiver ran down her spine as the brush grazed her scalp, the sensation at odds with the warm water pooling around her shoulders. For once, she had no energy for a biting comment—her exhaustion, guilt, and swirling thoughts pressed down on her like a weighted blanket.

She took a rag he'd dropped into the tub and began to wash, though her mind drifted elsewhere—*to the Pembrooks.* The news settled cold in her chest, untouched by the warmth of the bath. No matter how hard she scrubbed, she couldn't wash the guilt from her skin.

"*Stop*," Vincent said abruptly, his voice firm but not unkind. He gently tilted her head back, his fingers firm in her damp hair. "You're safe."

The words startled her, a soft gasp escaping as she flinched in the water. His other hand cupped her cheek, thumb brushing the corner of her mouth as he steadied her. The tenderness caught her off guard—her jaw slackened, lips parting as she looked up at him.

Safe. The concept felt foreign—distant.
But not so much beside him.

AT THE END OF HER BATH, he carried her to her chambers.

There, he nudged the door open with his shoulder, and the familiar scent of sage and faint wood smoke welcomed them. He set her gently on her feet at the edge of the bed, his hands steady on her shoulders as she swayed.

"*Stay*," he instructed—like you would a dog—his voice low but commanding.

Her amber eyes fluttered open, unfocussed and heavy-lidded. She made a weak attempt to protest. But Vincent ignored her, stepping away only long enough to rummage through her nearby chest.

He pulled out a simple sleeping gown, its soft fabric catching the light of the single candle flickering on the nightstand. When he returned, Olivja leaned unsteadily to the side, her knees ready to give out. Vincent caught her easily, steadying her by the hip.

"Liv," he muttered, exasperation mingling with a faint trace of amusement. "You're not making this easy."

Her head tipped back, lips parting in what might've been a retort—but no words came. Instead, she blinked up at him, her expression a muddled mix of defiance and vulnerability.

This wasn't the first time Vincent had taken care of her…though the last time had been long ago. And she barely remembered it. Her heart fluttered, nostalgia hitting hard enough to leave her wide-eyed—if only for a moment. Though, she couldn't be sure as to why.

"Arms up," he instructed, shaking the gown lightly in one hand.

She swallowed and obeyed, her movements sluggish and clumsy. Vincent slipped the gown over her head, his fingers brushing against her skin as he worked carefully to guide her arms through the sleeves. She shivered, and he hesitated for the briefest of moments before continuing.

"There," he said quietly, tugging the fabric into place and smoothing it over her shoulders.

"Look at that…you're halfway decent again, princess," he chuckled. She slowly blinked up at him, her glare sharp beneath heavy lids.

"Strange, I don't recall askin'," Olivja scoffed, hands moving to push him away. Though she wouldn't dare—she knew it'd do more harm than good.
"You look…*far* worse."

"And yet," Vincent sighed, his fingers trailing gently from her sides up to her cheek, guiding her face. He pulled her firm against his strong chest. "You're all over me, Ragnarvik…*tsk-tsk-tsk.*"

"Leave—*hic*—my room," she said, voice faltering as intoxication claimed her, eyes fluttering shut.

The bath hadn't done much to calm the restless spirits coursing through her. If anything, the heat of the bath made it worse. Both hands weakly rose, attempting to push him away. Before she could manage, he moved gently, taking her right hand in his and extending it to her side.

"I will…once you fulfil your end of our bargain," he murmured with a chuckle, tugging her closer, his waist pressing into hers. "One dance won't kill you—no more than the wine or the bath would."

Olivja blinked again, the world spinning in disorienting circles. She chose to focus on the veins in his neck, level with her eyes. The words she tried to speak danced just beyond her reach, slipping through the fog in her mind like smoke.

"Truly, it would..." she finally murmured, voice slow and soft, annoyance lacing each syllable. Her body felt like it was drifting, weightless, floating and falling all at once—each sensation exaggerated by the haze clouding her thoughts.

His other hand tightened on her hip, unyielding yet gentle, pulling her closer as he rocked from side to side. The movement was slow, purposeful, like a lullaby that barely stirred the air, and for a moment she couldn't remember why it irked her.

She swallowed against the bile rising in her throat, trying to hold onto her pride, but it slipped away like sand through her fingers. The rhythmic motion was oddly soothing—oddly nauseating—the tension in her body unwinding despite her best efforts to stay alert.

The room was bathed in the soft glow of a single candle, flickering shadows dancing across the walls. Moonlight filtered through the window, its silver rays delicate and serene.

It was a strange calm, at odds with the crash of thoughts swirling within her, but there was a comfort to it, like a soft, warm blanket wrapping around her fragile consciousness.

Olivja's breath slowed, and her eyes fluttered closed at the pressure of his lips against her forehead.

It was a prince's apology—silent, solemn, and full of ache. She wasn't sure if she was ready to accept it...but she would enjoy it—silently.

She succumbed to the gentle swaying, her body sinking into the rhythm, letting herself be carried along by the quiet, comforting motion.

The anger and frustration that had been building inside her slowly dissolved, replaced by a strange, unwelcome sense of calm. She didn't know how much longer she could fight it, nor if she wanted to.

Never would she have thought that she would be dancing with Vincent again, the last time was when they were much younger, and always around a campfire, and never alone. It was nice to feel it again.

His genuine kindness was rare, yet familiar. Perhaps it was the wine lowering her walls that brought the smile to her lips.

Her free hand slowly slid up his chest. She took notice of his calm, beating heart. It made her miss their childhood; it made her miss her father. Somehow, being in Vincent's arms felt like the safest place in the world.

Then his hand fell to temptation.
It slid downwards, settling on her backside, and her eyes opened.

Her expression withered. She yanked her hands from him and pressed them hard against his chest, destabilising herself—only herself. He came to her aid, gripping her hips with narrowed eyes, steadying her to keep her from falling.

"R'lease me! Clearly, yer hands want more than a dance!" Olivja shouted, feeling betrayed by his creeping curiosity. "You—you would take advantage of me at a time like this?!"

"Olivja—WHAT?! I-Iwas not—" His cheeks burned with blush, still holding her since she could hardly stand.

"No—no! Le' me go! I long for my bed!" She growled, pressing at his chest while taking weak steps backward. "You weasel!"

Vincent scoffed. Before she could muster another snarky remark, his hands gripped her hips harder—and she was suddenly thrown backward.

The world spun wildly as she landed, her head sinking into the furs. Her vision swayed, the room tilting and swirling around her. She blinked hard, trying to steady herself, but the haze deepened, leaving her lightheaded and helpless to the dizzying pull of the drink coursing through her.

Groaning, her head lolled to one side, then back towards the ceiling. She thought she wanted to go to bed—but quickly realised lying down was far worse than standing.

As she drifted back to reality, she felt the bed shift—first near her legs, then her hips, then her chest—until Vincent's face hovered above hers.

He braced one hand beside her head, his legs straddling her thighs, a slow, seductive smile curling across his face as their eyes met.

"You know, princess," Vincent breathed, his breath warm against her cheek as he leaned in. "If I meant to take advantage of you, I wouldn't have troubled myself with tending to you so carefully..." He paused.

"Besides, I'll take far more pleasure in bedding you when you're your usual, sharp self." His smirk faded, his gaze hardening: "Frankly, I dislike you like this."

She turned over his words. Her vision blurred, tears welling large in her eyes.

She'd been drinking, and look what it had become. What a mess.
There was no comfort in it. Only shame.
She thought of how people looked at her drunken father—with pity, with contempt. And now, she was no different.

Olivja drew in a sharp breath.
"*Aye*..." she exhaled, her voice ragged from the night's unravelling. "You're not alone in that."

Her stomach twisted. Her drunkenness had helped orchestrate the death of her lover's parents—her father's oldest friend. "It's all my fault...*everything*." Her voice trembled as much as her shoulders.

The wine dulled her will, and the tears came. She blinked hard, refusing to look at him.

Adalja had been pulled from her parents because of her. The knights had been sent away because of her.

She had an awful habit of ruining things.

He watched her in silence. Then, with a quiet sigh, his expression softened. He moved beside her, slow and quiet, his presence steady and warm. His arm slid across her abdomen, his hand settling on her hip.

With a gentle tug, he turned her onto her side. Her face found his chest—the dark fabric of his vest warm against her cheek. He held her close, steady and unyielding.

"Your pride is vast, pagan," he said, voice low. His hand tightened around her. His heart beat wildly beneath her cheek, betraying the calm in his voice. "No matter how easy it is to blame you...their deaths had *nothing* to do with you."

"But, Vince—"

"*No*," he uttered, his left hand threading into her damp hair. He pulled gently, forcing her head up to meet his eyes. "Were you the one who poisoned their drink? The one who made the final toast?"

She shook her head and he released her, letting her fall back into his chest.

"You are no killer, Olivja...just a reckless, drunken wench. Now sleep."

His hand stayed at her hip, respectful and still. He didn't move, allowing her to hide in his chest.

It helped more than she expected, grounding her as his words echoed in her head.

He was right—she had no part in the deaths of Adalja's family. She mourned them deeply, but grief had twisted into guilt. She had cared for them, and hated them, too. Her final moments with Natja and Phillip would haunt her forever.

For now, at least, she was with someone who didn't blame her. And in her storm, that felt like momentary peace.

Then, another drunken thought surfaced.
Why *was* he being her peace?

Her eyes fluttered open. She looked up at him, and he groaned.

"Why are you acting like this?" she whispered.

"Like *what*, Olivja? You're the one who's bloody drunk." His voice was breathy, fully exasperated, completely done with her by this point, but she didn't care. Vincent looked down at her, glaring.

"Not long 'go, you raised yer hand to me. Now you'd wash my skin with it? What's next—*kiss* the wounds you gave?"

"Have I not proven myself tonight? And still you dwell on that?" Vincent sighed, pulling a hand away to tiredly scrub his face. "I regret that. I do. Forgive me," the prince mumbled behind his palm, voice low and haunted. "But you think I'd strike you without cause?"

"Yes."

Silence settled thick between them.

"...You *know* you earned a slap for what you said," he murmured, resting his chin atop her head. "Do you believe I enjoyed it?" His question was barely audible, yet it carried a weight that made her stomach churn.

Her throat tightened, but she refused to cry in front of him again, not after everything. "Then why did you...?"

"You forced my hand, Liv...I didn't know what else to do in front of my father's men," he said, voice hoarse like it hurt to speak. "You infuriate me. You always have. But it's not hate—it has *never* been hate."

His breath hitched, barely audible. "But if correction is to be dealt...know that it shall be by my hand alone. No one else lays claim to you. Not in discipline. Not in affection. Not in *anything*."

She had no words for that. She wouldn't thank him for it, wouldn't offer him reassurance or forgiveness. His voice clashed with memory—anger, care, presence. Her jaw tensed, hands curled into his linen.

As if sensing her turmoil, Vincent shifted again, his hand brushing against her temple to push damp strands of hair from her face.

"I'll never touch you in anger again, I promise. Now, *please*...for the love of all that's holy, I beg thee, go to sleep," he murmured, the promise laced with something almost...*tender*.

Her eyes fluttered shut, not only from trust but from the sheer intensity of the evening.

She wanted to believe him, to find solace in his words, but she knew it wouldn't last. His words never did.

She breathed in his scent—amber and rosemary. The same as always. Familiar. The wine, his warmth, his presence...they pulled her into sleep.

THREAD XXII

ᚦᛖ ᛒᚢᚱᛞᛖᚾᛊ ᛟᚠ ᚺᛖᛁᚱᛊ ᚦᛖ ᛒᚢᚱᛞᛖᚾᛊ ᛟᚠ ᚺᛖᛁᚱᛊ ᚦᛖ ᛒᚢᚱᛞᛖᚾᛊ

ᛟᛚᛁᚡᛃᚨ

OLIVJA MIGHT'VE SLEPT THROUGH THE NIGHT—if not for the sudden jolt of nausea that wrenched her upright.

Clutching her mouth, she staggered to the window, flinging the shutters open just in time to vomit.

She groaned, wiped her mouth with the back of her hand, and slumped against the stone sill. The chill prickled her skin.

Eyes closed, she caught her breath, her body still shivering—from cold, from shock. Then she remembered how she'd fallen asleep. Her eyes flew open. She turned to the bed...but Vincent was gone.

Relief came first. Then the dread—how long had she been asleep?

Adalja!
She'd been sleeping—peacefully—while Adalja suffered and mourned.

With the Pembrook rulers dead, Adalja was the only heir. And selfishly—shamefully—Olivja thought of the pressure this would put on *them* to go through with the marriage.

Adalja couldn't go back to her Kingdom without a husband...but even with her parents alive, the same could be said for Olivja.

She didn't know the hour. It hardly mattered. She had to find her.

The door eased shut behind her with a soft click—her hand lingering on the handle.

Footsteps. Too light for a Worthyn knight. Olivja froze.

Brahms rounded the corner, helmet tucked beneath one arm. Adalja trailed just behind, head bowed low. As the heiress approached, Brahms stopped short—positioning himself between them, his armoured frame shielding Adalja.

"Brahms," she breathed, relieved—until she saw the look on his face. His eyebrows were low and his expression, while sad, held a firmness that was rare for him.

"You shouldn't be out of your room, Heiress," Brahms muttered, not meeting her eyes.

Her jaw tightened. Surely he didn't mean that.
"Now, now Bramble, calm thyself. I only wish to speak to her—"

"Talking to you is the last thing she needs," he snapped. "It's the last thing they would've wanted."

The anger towards Olivja was evident, but unwarranted, she thought. And bringing up the obvious disdain that the newly deceased Pembrook's held for her was uncalled for. Shaking her head, she took a step closer.

"Bit late to start caring now, isn't it? Already let me speak to her once." Olivja's voice cut clean—low, cold, and steady. "What's crawled into you?"

"*Crawled into me,*" he scoffed. "I'll tell you what, Olivja—every damned time we get involved with *you*—"

"Brahms." Adalja cut in, desperate to stop him before it worsened. But he barreled on, ignoring her.

"No! You know it's true! *Every time* she's near without fail, something happens!" He shouted to the both of them now, which pissed Olivja off for a number of reasons.

She didn't appreciate yelling, especially when anyone could hear them. The last thing Adalja needed was a fight between the three of them, and on top of it, he was essentially blaming everything on her, which was unfair.

"You hold *me* at fault?" she asked, giving him one last chance to pull back. The fire in her chest flared hotter.

Brahms, like Vincent before him, turned the knife. But where Vincent had softened—regretted—Brahms stood firm, unyielding. Hearing it from him cut deeper.

She stepped forward, jaw set, ready to fight if that's what it took to break whatever wall had formed between them.

"We've kept peace for *ten years*! You make me leave my post *once*—so *you* can talk to her—and now our parents are—"

"Brahms!" Adalja's louder voice stopped the both of them in their tracks, and thank goodness.

Olivja struggled to keep calm when angered, and Brahms was sparking every fire. It was no surprise that Adalja silenced them both instantly—this wasn't their first fight. But this time felt different.

For once, Olivja truly felt responsible...and perhaps it was the first time the cause was something that actually mattered. Vincent had sent *every* knight after her—including Brahms, their personal guard. And it was worse than Brahms knew.

Stepping from around him, Adalja's red face came into view. She rested a hand on his forearm. "You're relieved for the night." Her voice, soft and frayed, offered him mercy.

"But Adalja—"

"Thank you, Brahms." She cut him off—gentle, but firm—grasping at peace before it slipped away.

Brahms glanced at Adalja, concern softening his brow. She offered a quiet nod—reassurance, or something close to it. He sighed, jaw tight, and turned back to Olivja—his gaze now sharpened to steel.

Had it not been for Adalja, Olivja would have torn into the root of Brahms' sudden bitterness. But as always, her concern lay with the princess. It always did. There'd be time to argue with Brahms later.

He strode past them, fists clenched, jaw set—leaving the women in silence.

"Olivja—" Adalja began, voice low. But she knew better than to speak here—not after the shouting.

One glance from the wrong person, and the moment would vanish.

The heiress reached out, lacing their fingers together with practised ease.

"Come," she whispered, already guiding her down the hall—towards Adalja's chambers, where silence still held.

She eased the handle, slipping them inside. The door clicked shut behind them—barely a whisper. Olivja turned and found Adalja staring anywhere but at her.

Growing up together had been both a blessing and a curse—comfort between them came easily, even in silence. As children, all Olivja had ever wanted was for Adalja to feel joy. That hadn't changed. Only the hope had—the wild, impossible hope that once lit their world.

The dim lanterns bathed Adalja's pale skin in gold. The low light only made her look paler—ghostlike, hollowed. The princess stood near the door, gaze fixed on their joined hands. Her face was unreadable.

"Oh, Addy." Olivja sighed, tugging gently at her hand.

She pulled her into a tight hug, trembling hand sliding to the back of Adalja's head, tucking her into the crook of her neck.

"Shh. I'm here," she whispered, voice catching as the years pressed in all at once. She inhaled deeply, her senses swamped entirely by Adalja and the warm, heavy breaths against her collarbone.

After a pause, Adalja's arms slipped around her waist and tightened. Like when they were girls, the walls came down together.

"They're...both..." the words broke apart into sobs as she clung to Olivja—a momentary tether to this world.

For once, Olivja was quiet, left without comfort or answers. These weren't childhood wounds anymore. No amount of hugging or playing in the rain could chase this grief away.

"I know..." Olivja breathed, tears threatening. "Forgive me," she added, though she knew the blame wasn't hers. Still, Brahms' words lingered like splinters.

Who could say how differently the night might've gone—if Olivja hadn't pulled Adalja, Brahms, and every knight away from the Pembrooks.

She deeply mourned Phillip and Natja. But in truth—they'd been gone to her for years. The day they left, she'd begun grieving the King and Queen who once loved her.

Now they were truly gone.

Olivja's trembling mirrored Adalja's. Together, they took a breath and let grief give way to something colder: relief.

She held her close, grateful for the quiet. There were no words left, none that could mend what the night had taken.

At last, Adalja's sobs faded to quiet shudders.

Slowly, Adalja pulled away from the crook of Olivja's neck, her breath hitching as she tried to steady it. Olivja gently brushed the tears from Adalja's cheeks, cupping her face to search for whatever emotion still lingered there.

"Liv," Adalja murmured, eyes downcast. "I *must* marry him."

The words, barely a whisper, struck like a stone between them.

Olivja's hands, already still, went rigid. Her fingertips turned to ice as fear surged through her chest.

Why now? *Why say that now?* In any other moment, she might've taken it as a cruel joke.

She shook her head, scoffing through a pained breath, unwilling to let go.

"What? N-No, princess—what are you saying?" Olivja stammered. "Leave that worry for another day—we'll find another way. We always do."

"No." Adalja wrapped her fingers around Olivja's, pressing their joined hands to her cheek. They both trembled. "Olivja...this is the only way."

At last, their eyes met. But now, the roles had reversed—Adalja's gaze dry and resigned, Olivja's glassy and brimming. Still, despite the certainty in Adalja's voice, Olivja didn't move. She kept her hands on her face, her breathing unsteady.

"Only way?" Olivja hissed. "This is but a bandage for Ezekiel's foolish war! Adalja, *princess,* the gods did not carve this fate for us."

"I care not for the gods." Adalja drew Olivja's hands down, holding them between their chests. "I-I must do right by *them*...by my parents."

The words struck her harder than she expected. Olivja staggered back a step, a heavy breath escaping her lips.

"Adalja, I—" *Just admitted I love you.*

She wanted to remind her. To say it again. But what more could she say that would change anything? She'd finally said the words—on the very night Adalja lost everything. *Of course it would end like this.*

And, despite it all, she couldn't back down. Not after ten years. Not *yet.*

"They're gone, Adalja..." Olivja whispered, her tone soft. "They won't force you anymore." She clung to her hands, as if they were the only thing tethering them to hope. "I promise. We'll find another way—together—if only—"

"Olivja. I beg you," Adalja cut her off with a trembling whisper. "I won't forsake them. Nor my kingdom...No matter how much I may want—" She faltered, eyes falling to their joined hands.

Olivja felt everything at once—rage, shame, betrayal, heartbreak, grief. She kept her shattered gaze fixed on Adalja's distant eyes.

In that moment, Olivja was ready to burn Worthyn Castle to the ground. To take Adalja and flee to the farthest mountain cave where no one could follow. She wanted to scream—beg her to see, to choose her, to let her love her. She wanted to collapse. But when she spoke again, she did none of it.

"I understand," she lied, jaw tight as she pulled her hands free.

But she didn't understand. Could *never* understand.

If the roles were reversed, Olivja would never marry. Not for peace. Not for a throne. Not for anything other than Adalja's hand.

Throughout her entire life, her love for Adalja remained. Her love had been silent. Innocent. Expectationless.

But not anymore.

Adalja knew her heart. There was no doubt. Olivja had bared it all. But *still* she was turned away. And this time, there was no cruel parent forcing their hand. It was *Adalja's choice*—and that made it worse.

How could she marry Elias? How could she settle for anyone—if she truly loved me?

The only way Olivja could solve this mess in her mind was to come to the conclusion that Adalja did *not* love her.

The thought shattered her.

The Pembrooks were gone—there should be nothing left in their way. Olivja took another step backwards, preparing to leave the room.

"Olivja..." Adalja's voice broke the silence, trembling again. "Out of respect, the funeral will be private—"

"I understand," Olivja whispered before she could say it. She couldn't bear to hear it aloud.

"I won't set foot in their wake. I swear...I'll leave you be," she said. The promise was mumbled beneath her breath, more to herself than to Adalja.

"No—please wait," Adalja said quickly. "I cannot bear to lose you now, Olivja...i-it may be more complicated, b-but..." the princess trailed off.

Olivja let out a bitter breath, scoffing in disbelief. Her eyes fell, emptied of their fire.

"Adalja...you tear me in two and still...I remain *yours*," she exhaled. Olivja's voice was soft, though darkness clung to every word. "Break me. Bleed me. You will never be rid of me." *Even if it guts me. Even if it burns me to ash. What's another moon of longing?*

She stepped back—slow and final—until she reached the door. Eyes downcast, she pulled open the door and cleared her throat.

"Put no mind to my words at the stables. I'll carry them alone."

She turned to the cracked door. Hidden from Adalja's eyes, her tears finally fell—in streams like fire. She clutched the front of her nightgown, grounding herself as she stepped through the doorway.

"Sleep well, princess," she whispered—*and was gone.*

Thread XXIII

ᚦᛖ ᛒᚢᚱᛞᛖᚾᛋ ᛟᚠ ᚺᛖᛁᚱᛋ ᚦᛖ ᛒᚢᚱᛞᛖᚾᛋ ᛟᚠ ᚺᛖᛁᚱᛋ ᚦᛖ ᛒᚢᚱᛞᛖᚾᛋ

ᛒᚱᚨᚺᛗᛋ

She knows I'm right.

Brahms clenched his jaw, his thoughts a whirl of irritation and grief.

Of course Olivja had stopped him—she always did. She always found a way to insert herself, to challenge him, and she never failed to believe she knew better. Ever since they were children, she'd been the troublemaker, the reckless one who never seemed to face the consequences of her actions.

And yet, he cursed himself for believing she'd changed.

As soon as he was out of sight, Brahms allowed his carefully composed demeanor to crack. His frustration burned hotter with every step. He wiped the sweat from his brow, the air stifling despite the cool stone halls around him. He let out a low growl, the sound echoing through the empty corridor.

If I hadn't gone looking for her...

The thought repeated in his mind, each repetition sharper than the last. He envisioned alternate outcomes, imagining how things could have unfolded differently. He could've stopped the Pembrooks' deaths. He could've caught whoever poisoned them.

He was the best at being a knight. He'd been raised for it. It was all he knew.

But Olivja's interference had cost him everything.

Because of her, the two royals he had sworn to protect were gone. *Gone*, while he was left to pick up the pieces of his shattered duty, questioning himself in ways he never had before. And he hated it—he hated *her* for it.

His angry thoughts churned with no outlet, his fists curling at his sides as he stomped through the castle's winding halls. He knew Olivja would come to confront him eventually—she always did—but this time, he wasn't planning to back down.

"You know not what is best for her," he muttered aloud, mocking her voice. His lips twisted into a bitter smirk as he imagined their inevitable argument. "You think yourself better than I, simply for being some barbaric heir?"

The words tumbled out in a low grumble, growing sharper as his resentment fuelled his one-sided conversation.

"Not this time, Olivja. Not this time, blasted harlot," he scoffed, the insult barely audible under his breath, though the sound gave him a grim satisfaction.

Brahms' anger had begun to simmer, slowly replaced by a small, vindictive sense of victory as he replayed his imagined triumph over her.

His eyes wandered aimlessly—tracing the warped stonework, the uneven pattern of the stone—until they landed on something that didn't belong.

Something—no, *someone*—was stretched across a bench in the far corner of the hall, lounging like a corpse arranged for viewing. For a moment he wasn't sure if it was real or imagined. A trick of light, or something older and stranger.

It sprawled, limbs draped over the edges like a creature too long for its shell. Its legs dangled, lean and loose like a spider's, and its braids hung low, circling the bench almost, impossibly long.

He froze, head tilting to watch it more closely.

A sound met him then—faint and splintered. The high, off-tune whine of a lute—strings frayed and tuneless, yet somehow still playing. The melody rose in flickers, like dying candlelight: hesitant, warbling, *sad*. It was not a song so much as a whisper that had forgotten the words.

The thing on the bench plucked another string, then another, without looking up. Its head tilted to the side, a dark coal smudge of a smile on its lips. And he realised, it was the jester.

It cradled the warped lute like a lover, while flicking gently at its strings with fingers too pale, too long.

It did not look at him. It simply played. And the sound that came was not joyful, not even truly a song—just a threadbare melody, worn to the bone, as if someone had tried to hum grief itself and faltered halfway through.

A lullaby for something that had already died.

Brahms swallowed, shifting on his feet, his eyes never leaving the thing. But the fragile eerie calm shattered at the sudden clang of metal against stone.

His eyes flickered for the sound, but when he looked back at the bench, his breath caught. It now sat upright, lute beside it, watching him with wide, unblinking blue eyes. It made Brahms shiver, but the clang of metal tore him away from the haunt.

His instincts took over in an instant, his hand flying to the hilt of his sword as he turned towards the noise. His heart hammered in his chest, the hope of revenge lighting a dangerous spark within him.

Whoever did this—whoever killed my king and queen—I'll cut them down myself.

Without hesitation, Brahms strode towards the sound, his boots echoing sharply against the stone floor. His grip tightened on the hilt of his sword as he descended the steps, every muscle in his body coiled for a fight.

He emerged into a moonlit courtyard, the faint glow casting long shadows across the pillared pathway. The scent of straw and worn leather filled the air, the familiar signs of a training yard: dummies tied to wooden posts, weapons scattered across the ground, practice armour hanging from iron hooks.

It was a space meant for release, for discipline and focus. For a moment, Brahms thought it might be the perfect place to vent his rage. But the courtyard was already occupied.

Illuminated by silvery moonlight, Prince Elias crouched to retrieve a fallen broadsword. His muscular back glistened with sweat.

Brahms stopped short, his frustration momentarily forgotten as he watched the prince straighten, the sword gleaming in his hand. His dark, ruffled trousers sat low on his hips, exposing far more than would be considered appropriate for a prince.

Have mercy.

Brahms, initially in awe of the toned prince, quickly realised that he wasn't where he was supposed to be. Not only because he was Adalja's guard and should remain by her side, but also because the lack of clothing and other knights told Brahms that Prince Elias was in need of solitude.

With a soft grunt, Elias rolled his shoulders, muscles flexing. Brahms took this as his opportunity to leave quietly and quickly. He stepped backwards—

KLANG, CLANK.

Brahms' heavy foot struck a loose piece of armour, and amidst the stumble he dropped his own metal helmet and it rolled out into the courtyard, causing an explosion of noise.

Brahms quickly looked up at the courtyard, his eyes painted in shock and embarrassment. Startled by the sound, Elias defensively raised his sword and pointed it in Brahms' direction. His green eyes glared, coal slightly smeared.

"I—my—who put *that* there?" Brahms chuckled nervously, waiting to be scolded. "Pardon me, My Prince. I'll just be going—"

But Elias sighed in relief and lowered his sword, flexing his biceps in the process.

"Please avoid denting the steel, Sir Brahms," he commented while turning back towards his dummy. "Heading to your chambers already?...How is she?" Elias then asked with dull interest, sighing a second time.

"She? Oh—Adalja, right...Um...She's—" Brahms sighed as well, clenching his jaw as he remembered that Adalja was likely still with Olivja. Distracted by his returning rage, he forgot to finish responding, "*Ahem*—uh, Addy's resting."

Elias turned his gaze back towards Brahms, narrowing his eyes. The knight had never been a good liar.

"Hm. And you?" Elias' words softened but only for a moment. Soon after, his arms quickly brought up his sword to deliver a fatal blow to the straw-man. With a loud grunt, the dummy was sliced in two.

God.

Brahms swallowed hard, taken aback by the question—and the impressive show of strength.

"Me?" he questioned, crossing his arms beneath his armoured chest, unaware it made him look defensive. "I'm...*well*."

Nice one. He grumbled to himself, knowing that sounded far from convincing.

Elias turned back towards him fully—now that his dummy was destroyed—and took a few steps closer, approaching a second dummy that was nearer to the pillared pathway. The Prince's toned, pale chest glowed effortlessly beneath the starry sky, and for a moment, he questioned how Elias had gone unmarried for so long.

It was then, as Brahms' blatant stare trailed up to the prince's face, that he noticed the fresh wound that adorned Elias' lip.

Initially, he became protective; after all, one royal had already been attacked in his presence, and he was determined not to let it happen again.

However, it wasn't his place to inquire and he wanted to avoid offending Elias. Brahms took a small step forward, out into the moonlight as well, anchoring his hands to his hips.

"And *you*?" Brahms returned the same question with a chuckle, quickly using this as an opportunity to pull the attention off of his own afflicted demeanor. "What has befallen you, Your Highness?"

"Sparring..." Elias flashed him a quick look of ambivalence before turning back towards his dummy. "My wound will heal—" He swiftly stabbed the dummy through what would typically be a man's heart—Brahms' chest tightened—and grunted once more. "Will yours?"

Another scoff was pulled out of Brahms, his arms returning to their defensive position across his ribs. He leaned against the pillar to his right, which was unexpected of him. Posture played a big role as a royal guard, but it was the end of a long, tiring night; he hoped Elias would understand. Though somehow, he knew he wouldn't mind.

"I'm not *wounded*," Brahms said sourly, biting his cheek as he tried hard to control his very obviously wounded expression.

"You spoke of being raised alongside the Princess...Leading me to believe the Pembrooks meant a great deal to you," Elias recalled, slowly removing the sword from the dummy. "Then you are either a disloyal knight or a false one...which is it?"

Elias' white hair shone in the courtyard as he easily saw through the knight. He had a darker demeanor than at the ball...something weighed on him, he knew it.

Brahms cursed at himself once more for opening up so quickly to Adalja's suitor. He promised himself he wouldn't become fond of him, for her sake. He looked away from Elias, trying to think of an excuse but failing.

It was clear that Elias was on to him.

Shaking his head with another sigh, he glared at his helmet that still remained on the floor.

"'Tis my fault they're dead," Brahms admitted, and he hated it.

As much as he wanted to blame Olivja, he was mature enough to know he left his post by his own volition. "I left my post to find Adalja and now they're both...If I was there, I could have seen it."

"No," Elias spoke quickly and firmly.

Brahms flinched as he though maybe he was in trouble for admitting he left his post, but Elias continued in a softer tone. "Whoever did this could have poisoned you as well if you were there...Be glad you left."

Despite the fact that Elias had no idea the true reason Brahms was away, his words still held weight.

The idea that leaving his post stopped him from being poisoned hadn't crossed his mind. He grew angrier as he stood there because he now considered himself indebted to Olivja and her defiance.

Brahms' mouth opened, but no words came out. He didn't know what to say to that. His gaze slowly returned to the prince as he adjusted the leather bindings of his broadsword.

"I will be aiding in the funeral rites...Should you wish it, I can grant you a place beside Adalja and me—as a *guest*." Elias turned his back to him, tilting his sweat-damp head to one side.

Brahms was at a loss for words as he heard the gift he was offered. "A guest? Surely, you do not mean—"

"I do," Elias confirmed before taking a deep breath and slicing the head of a dummy clean off its hay shoulders. With another loud grunt and a pant, he tossed his sword to the ground.

"A loyal guard is a spoiled guard...Besides, plenty of knights will be patrolling that evening. You deserve to mourn with your family...Wouldn't you agree?"

Brahms blinked, taken aback.

He pushed himself off the pillar and straightened, suddenly aware of how little he deserved such kindness, having done so little. To be able to go to the Pembrook funeral as family, rather than as a knight, would be incredibly healing and freeing.

"Yes...My Lord," he agreed with a nod of his head, his throat suddenly becoming dry.

Elias, having cut down the last dummy, was breathing heavily while moving to his white nightshirt he had thrown to the ground during his training and tossed it around his neck.

"Very well," Elias confirmed with a heavy breath and looked over his shoulder to Brahms, their eyes connecting. "I shall have the seamstress prepare funeral attire for you...You cannot sit clad in armour."

Brahms, still stunned, nodded hesitantly. If Olivja wasn't with Adalja, he would have run right to her room to tell her the good news.

"Thank you," Brahms muttered as Elias walked closer. Suddenly, the knight's cheeks grew red and his breath caught in his chest.

Still resting on the floor between the two men was the shining helmet Brahms had ungracefully dropped. It was too late to go for it, for Elias was already bending to retrieve it. Brahms looked away, biting his bottom lip bashfully, ashamed that a Prince was picking up for him.

Elias' footsteps neared and Brahms' gaze snapped up.

Now, only a few feet in front of him—and standing a bit taller—the straight-faced Prince held out the helmet. He got a better look at Elias' stunning eyes...and his own lingered for a second too long.

"Try not to lose your head before then, Brahms." Elias' tone was somber and dark, despite how playful and teasing his words were.

"Aye...m-my thanks, Your Grace." Brahms quickly returned, swallowing sheepishly. It was hard to focus on anything apart from the closeness of the sweaty prince.

A slight smirk lifted the corner of Elias' mouth, but as quickly as it came, it vanished. Without another word, so did he.

For a short moment, Brahms lingered in the courtyard, still stunned by the conversation. Eventually he left, and while meandering to his chambers, Brahms glanced down at the helmet in his hands.

For the first time that night, he felt like himself—relieved, understood, and no longer alone.

THREAD XXIV

ᚦᛖ ᛒᚢᚱᛞᛖᚾᛋ ᛟᚠ ᚺᛖᛁᚱᛋ ᚦᛖ ᛒᚢᚱᛞᛖᚾᛋ ᛟᚠ ᚺᛖᛁᚱᛋ ᚦᛖ ᛒᚢᚱᛞᛖᚾᛋ

ᚨᛞᚨᛚᛃᚨ

IT HAD BEEN TWO DAYS SINCE THEY FOUND HER PARENTS POISONED. Two days since the castle had fallen into a suffocating silence—death and the unknown settling eerily in the halls.

For Adalja, those days felt like an eternity—each moment dragging on in slow, agonizing torment, as if time itself had turned cruel. And today felt frozen. Still. As if the world dared not move forward.

The Funeral.

She sat curled in the nook of her bedroom window, knees tucked tightly to her chest, gaze distant and fractured as she watched snow drift lazily to the ground below.

The soft white flakes fell like feathers, beautiful and indifferent, their serenity almost cruel in contrast to the devastation they blanketed.

Her usually immaculate curls tumbled in wild disarray, haphazardly pinned by Sapphire earlier, though Adalja hadn't cared enough to fix them. She hadn't cared to do much of anything.

Still dressed in her rumpled sleeping gown, she hadn't eaten, hadn't spoken, hadn't moved except to press herself tighter into the corner of the window.

Sapphire had tried for nearly an hour to rouse her—to coax her to dress, to speak...to do *anything*. But Adalja remained silent, her mind too hollow, too consumed by the aching grief clawing at her ribs.

Her eyes flicked briefly to the corner of her room, where the mourning gown hung like a shadow against the privacy screen. Its dark lace and heavy embroidery loomed, a cruel monument to what awaited her. The sight turned her stomach. Nausea swelled in her throat, rising and falling like a tide refusing to retreat.

She tugged absently at the loose sleeves of her gown, the deep blue fabric damp and clinging to her skin. Grief soaked through her, quiet and constant. Her tear-streaked cheeks—raw and flushed—were a testament to the maelstrom inside.

She thought of her father—of the calm strength that had once been her anchor—and for a moment, she could almost hear his voice.

Her vision blurred as she stared too long at the snow-covered trees beyond the castle walls. Then, a shift. A sound.

"Adalja—*sweetheart.*"

She blinked slowly, the voice tugging her from the haze.
"Eli..." Her voice cracked, a fragile whisper as she turned towards him, her bottom lip wavering.

The prince stood near her closed door, his posture cautious, his hood down but his mask still drawn over the bridge of his nose. He seemed to have been there for some time.

Elias adjusted his sleeves with a careful grace as he stepped forward, his voice a gentle hush. "Princess..." His green eyes drifted towards the dark gown hanging nearby. "It is time."

Adalja's hand pressed to her chest, but it did nothing to stop the ache hollowing her from the inside out. Her breath hitched. It was as if something had been scooped from beneath her ribs, leaving only silence and space.

She followed his gaze to the dress and slowly shook her head, lips parted but voiceless.

He stepped closer, his towering frame casting a quiet shield between her and the rest of the world. Reluctantly, he sat at her feet, and she shifted enough to make room on the cushion.

"Would you like my assistance?" His tone was soft and hesitant, the kind spoken only when words felt dangerous. His hand hovered above her knee, gloved but fingerless, the bare skin of his fingertips exposed, reaching—not demanding—but offering. Waiting.

Adalja didn't argue. She had no energy to do so.

Her mother would've wanted this—would've wanted Adalja to have Elias. It had always been their hope for her. Their plan. And now...now, Adalja couldn't bear to disobey. Not anymore. Not when this marriage was all she had left of them.

"I understand...how you're feeling," Elias began, his eyes still downcast, watching his hand as it finally rested gently on her knee. He squeezed lightly. "The grief of losing a parent," he finished, voice heavy with something unspoken.

Adalja brushed a curl behind her ear and turned to him fully, eyes searching for anything to anchor her.

"Your mother..." she croaked, sitting up a little straighter.

They held each other's gaze, grief speaking where words could not. Then with a shaky exhale, she mumbled: "The funeral is for them—for their lives. But all I feel is death, Elias. I am too weak to carry it."

His thumb moved against her knee in a slow, comforting motion before he rose to his feet again. Raising his hood, he extended a hand to her.

"Use my strength," Elias said, the firmness in his voice gentle but unshakable. "You can lean on me, Princess. I promised your father that."

Adalja stared at his outstretched hand, her breath catching as she slid her fingers into his. He pulled her up with care, guiding her to her feet like something precious.

"I'll be ready shortly," she said, a lump forming in her throat.

He nodded, releasing her hand slowly. "And I'll be right outside." Then, with one last glance, he turned and left, the door closing softly behind him.

The dress still waited. A ghost in the corner of the room. An omen of death. She stared at it in silence. Putting it on would make all of this *real. She didn't want that.*

If it were up to her, she would've stayed hidden in the castle. *With Olivja.*

But it wasn't up to her. Nothing had been, not for a long time.

The mourning gown was deep black, crafted from thick wool that scratched her skin but fell with grave elegance. The long sleeves flared at the wrists in solemn detail, and the layered skirt swept heavily against the stone floor, making her feel like a shadow made flesh. A wide black leather belt cinched the dress at her waist, the sharp folds cascading downwards in stark, funereal geometry.

Delicate lace trimmed the neckline and cuffs—almost invisible in the dim light—and silver thread stitched a faint Pembrook emblem across the bodice. The Pembrook name had not yet died...
But it would once she married Elias.

Her veil draped from a simple silver circlet atop her head, flowing behind her like a river of mourning. It veiled her face, obscuring her expression, its sheer linen both a shield and a burden. Beneath it, her pale skin looked almost grey, her half-pinned curls tucked tightly under its weight.

A knock at the door.

Her heart skipped.

Opening it, she was greeted by both Elias and Brahms, dressed in shades of dark mourning. Brahms looked particularly solemn, the delicate tailoring of a new coat accentuating his height and quiet strength.

"Brahms..." she whispered, voice catching at the sight of him. "You look...Mother would be proud."

He smiled softly and opened his arms. She stepped into him, wrapping her arms tightly around his torso, burying into the familiarity of him. The hug was long and lingering, a touch of warmth in a day made entirely of cold.

For a moment, her heart stirred—something almost like relief. Something that reminded her of life. Of her *childhood.*

When she finally opened her tear-filled eyes, she caught Elias watching them. His expression was soft, bittersweet, his gaze not filled with jealousy but something heavier. A quiet yearning. And when she offered him a look of gratitude, he nodded in recognition.

He had always respected Brahms. Treated him like an equal. And this—this meant everything to Adalja.

Elias stepped forward then, bending slightly to whisper beside her ear, his breath warm through the fabric of her veil. "The carriage awaits us for the abbey."

Adalja pulled gently away from Brahms and gave him one last look before they stepped out together. All three in silence.

She kept the veil drawn across her face as they descended the steps and crossed the courtyard. All of Worthyn and Pembrook would be there, watching her, awaiting her transformation. From daughter to ruler. From grief to duty.

THE CARRIAGE WHEELS ROLLED slowly over the cobblestones as they pulled away from the castle. Adalja sat between the two men, staring blankly out the window.

Her heart twisted. She watched the castle windows as they passed, her eyes searching—hoping—for a glimpse of Olivja's silhouette. But the windows only stared back, empty.

She bit down on her bottom lip, choking down the regret. She had banned her. She had made that choice. To protect the memory of her mother. Of her family. But it didn't mean it hurt any less.

She needed a shoulder. And not Brahms'. Not Elias'. Someone who knew her like her own reflection. Someone who knew how to carry her pain...*her heart.*

Now, with Worthyn's dark Mausoleum Chapel in sight, the reality settled deep into her bones.

Today, she would see her parents for the last time—and become a queen.

The horses neighed and stomped at the crypt's entrance, breath curling into the cold as the carriage slowed to a mournful halt.

Adalja did not move. Not yet. She was a statue today.
Cold, vacant, silent.

She simply breathed, fingers pressed to the veil across her lips, trying to summon the strength to step into a life she never asked for. One she never wanted.

"We have arrived, My Lady," Elias said, his voice softening her stone exterior.

A Worthyn knight opened the carriage door. Elias stepped out and extended his hand. Adalja gazed at it like it stung, brows furrowed under the veil.

She didn't want to do this. *Gods, Elias take me back.*

But the veil hid everything. Even from Elias. And even if he could see, it wouldn't matter.

This was her life now. Her duty.

She drew a sharp breath and took his hand, stepping out. Brahms followed close behind.

The courtyard beyond the chapel was already swelling with black-clad mourners. Dozens upon dozens of faces blurred together, a sea of veiled heads and furrowed brows, all turning as one towards her. Her steps faltered as she descended the carriage stairs, swallowed whole by the hush that overtook the crowd. Whispers stirred like wind over a grave, curling around her and the two men who flanked her.

She was grateful, suddenly, for the veil.

The thick black linen fell like a curtain, shielding her from stares that sliced like blades. As hidden as one could be without vanishing—tucked behind a mask of mourning.

"*But a Ghost of the court—*"
"*She's to be leading our people? Can't even show her face.*"
"*With a Worthyn man at her side, she'll be unstoppable...*"

But one whisper rang louder than the rest, its venom coiling into her ribs:
"*Poor thing...Mayhap now she will earn her crown.*"

The words carved deep in her chest, burrowing into her ribs. Adalja gripped Elias' arm tightly, her knuckles pale beneath her gloves. The three of them moved as if caught in a slow tide, entering through the heavy wooden doors into the circular heart of the building.

The moment the great doors closed behind them, the low murmur of the crowd died. Silence fell like snow.

The round chamber was packed with people, nobles and townsfolk alike standing shoulder to shoulder. Candles lit every alcove and niche, flickering like spirits in mourning. The crowd parted, reverent and hushed, forming a path straight to the centre where two polished coffins stood beneath the arched ceiling.

Draped in their finest silks and adorned with jeweled circlets, the King and Queen lay side by side—still regal, still revered.

Adalja stopped abruptly, her breath catching in her throat. Her stomach dropped like a stone, nausea creeping into her mouth. The sight of them—together, even in death—shattered something inside her.

Her gaze fled upwards to Elias, then to Brahms on her opposite side, both of whom had stepped closer, bracing her like walls against the weight. She couldn't look directly at her parents. Not yet.

Elias' hand remained hooked around hers, firm but gentle, his fingers flexing slightly against her own as though reminding her he was there. Their hands locked like a tether. She trembled beside him, but found quiet comfort in his grip.

In the back of her mind, a vow stirred—quiet but cold. Whatever she did from this day forward, she would do for them. In their name. For her people.

"My child," came the priest's voice, thick with sorrow. The aged man stepped forward, his wrinkled hand scooping Adalja's free one.

"Today we stand at the threshold of both grief and divine mystery, for you lay to rest not only your beloved parents, but also an era of your life that has now passed..." His tired eyes peered through her veil, then lifted to Elias with a small, respectful nod. His words hung heavy, but they were warm, an attempt to soften the unbearable.

"In this moment, you are called not only as a daughter, but as a sovereign, and I know this is a heavy mantle for any heart to bear. But take comfort, for in this sorrow, there is also a great responsibility—and with it, a divine calling to guide those who remain, Princess of Pembrook."

"Your Reverence..." Adalja croaked, her voice raw. Her hand slipped from Elias' at last and wrapped around the priest's fingers with both of her own, searching for something solid amid the wave crashing through her.

"Follow me, dear," the priest said gently. "Let us celebrate the beginning of a new life...and the passing of another under God."

She nodded once, almost imperceptibly, then allowed herself to be guided forward. Her feet moved on instinct alone.

At the centre of the room, her parents lay beneath a halo of candlelight. Adalja stopped short, her spine rigid, hands limp at her sides.

Her father's skin, once so warm and lively, looked ashen beneath the crown he still wore. The corners of his mouth were downturned, the familiar smile erased by the hush of death.

Her mother's expression, too, had softened—but in a way that unnerved her. The rigid lines of a queen had faded, leaving behind only the ghost of the woman beneath.

The priest turned towards the assembly.

"Children of God," he began, his voice commanding, solemn. The gathered mourners quieted fully now, hanging onto every word. "Together, with the beloved heir of Pembrook, we mourn the loss of the King and Queen. Yet hope endures. Their legacy lives on in their daughter, Princess Adalja, who will now lead us as our Queen—alongside her betrothed."

Each word landed like a weight in Adalja's chest. Her breath stilled. Her knees weakened. The pressure of every gaze became unbearable, pressing into her like the cold iron of a crown that had yet to be placed upon her head.

The murmurs began again, softer now—approval, curiosity, worry—but it was all noise in her ears. The priest's voice faded into a drone, overtaken by the roar inside her own mind. She couldn't breathe. Couldn't think.

"Hold steady, Addy," Brahms said softly. His voice came from behind her like a quiet tide pulling her back to shore.

But she didn't look at him—couldn't. His gaze was warm, steady. Hers was frozen, like winter behind her eyes.

The moment shifted. The priest stepped aside and signaled for condolences.

One by one, the mourners came forward, each with a gift or a murmured word of sympathy. Adalja remained motionless, held upright by the weight of duty alone. Elias stepped in, speaking gently to each guest in her stead—deflecting what he could, his words a barrier to her grief.

Eventually, the tide of people parted. The time had come to pay respects.

She froze.

The caskets stood before her, draped in royal silks and crowned with white lilies. The scent was overwhelming—cloying, thick, clinging to the roof of her mouth like perfume curled into poison.

Her feet refused to move. Brahms and Elias flanked her again, their presence silent but sure. Finally, Adalja stepped forward, her movements painfully slow, as if each step cost her something she'd never get back.

She knelt between the coffins. Her shaking hands lifted, brushing the edge of her father's pedestal.

A breath caught in her throat.

Memories surged—his laughter echoing across the courtyard, his hand warm on her shoulder, the way he'd call her *'my little bird'* with a pride that made her feel like the moon. She wanted to say so many things. To beg his forgiveness. To tell him she was sorry she didn't return sooner. But her voice failed her.

She turned to her mother. The ache in her chest twisted. The years of cold words and colder silences formed a knot in her throat. Still, she whispered the only thing she could manage: "May your soul find peace, Mother." The words tasted bitter. Heavy with truths left unsaid.

Beside her, Brahms lingered at Natja's casket. His hand touched hers, fingers brushing the stillness with reverence.

"Thank you...for being my mother," he murmured. His voice cracked like ice breaking beneath a footstep. For a breath, Adalja saw the boy he once was—hopeful, tender, untouched by politics.

And she ached. Ached for a warmth she had never known from that same woman.

Then, a final toll rang from the far wall—an old brass bell struck once by a servant—and the priest raised his voice again, calling into the stillness:
"Let us now hear from our Princess."

Adalja's body became rigid. The world tilted. She turned her head sharply to Elias, her eyes wide and pleading beneath the veil.

"*I cannot,*" she exhaled, the words escaping like a breath she'd held too long.

"But you will," Elias said. His hand found hers once more. Grounding. Unyielding. "You will lead with wisdom and grace...and I will be beside you every step."

The crowd murmured in anticipation as Adalja lifted her veil, revealing a face streaked with tears. Taking a steadying breath, she stepped forward to the raised platform.

She looked out across a sea of unknown faces, her chest tight, her gloved hands clasped at her stomach. She didn't know how to begin. They never prepared her for *this*.

No book, no script could offer her the confidence—or the comfort—to speak at her parents' funeral.

She swallowed, drawing a much-needed breath, unmoved by the shifting feet and awkward silence. Then, with a wave of courage and desperation to finish the task, she spoke:

"Pembrians...Worthyns," she began, her voice frayed but growing stronger with each word, "I wish I could ease your sorrow. I can only offer an oath: I will lead with my father's candour and my mother's dedication. I will—"

"What of the war?" A voice interrupted from the crowd, cutting through her resolve.

The question rippled through the gathering like a stone cast into still water, fuelling worried murmurs.

"Aye! Will we be pulled into Worthyn's struggle?" another voice barked—harsher, more accusing.

Adalja hesitated, her heart racing. The faces before her blurred, their worried, expectant gazes blending into a single, suffocating mass.

"N-No...I—I do not wish for violence," she stammered, her voice faltering. "I will take every measure to ensure peace."

But her words did little to calm the unrest. The murmurs swelled, voices rising in a cacophony of doubt and fear.

Amidst the chaos, her gaze swept over the crowd, desperate for an anchor. Then she saw it—a familiar face, standing out among the sea of strangers. Her breath caught, the world narrowing to that single point, her racing heart slowing as recognition dawned.

Olivja.

Thread XXV

ᚦᛖ ᛒᚢᚱᛞᛖᚾᛋ ᛟᚠ ᚺᛖᛁᚱᛋ ᚦᛖ ᛒᚢᚱᛞᛖᚾᛋ ᛟᚠ ᚺᛖᛁᚱᛋ ᚦᛖ ᛒᚢᚱᛞᛖᚾᛋ

ᚨᛞᚨᛚᛃᚨ

The familiar woman was, of course, the only person Adalja requested *not* to see.

In the dim light, the woman stood, draped in blood-red silk that clung to her like a warning. Adalja's fingers twitched at her sides, lost for words at the vision before her. Red in a sea of black—an insult in this place of mourning. Yet the woman stood unashamed in her culture.

Gold jewellery gleamed against her honey-toned throat and wrists, stark against her dress. Her body was rigid, carved from stone, an the scowl on her face seemed etched into her features, brows drawn tight over eyes that burned with anger.

But it was the way Olivja's gaze lingered—faint tremors at the corners of her eyes—that betrayed the depth of her hurt. A cold sickness twisted in her stomach. Olivja's shocked expression pressed down harder than the grief of her parents' death ever could.

"F-Forgive me..." were the only words able to escape the princess' surprised, trembling lips.

The outraged crowd assumed it was for her faltering speech. But truly, the words were meant for the silent Heiress in the back of the room, face lit beautifully warm from the candles she stood near.

"As your *Queen* was saying..." Elias began as he approached the stand, picking up the speech that was already crashing and burning.

Her suitor slid his hand into hers, weaving their fingers together tightly. Brazenly. A fierce glint in his eye, ready to unite their people.

"I know many of you worry for what is to come of our union," he said through his mask. Though he spoke loud enough for the entire room to hear, Adalja couldn't make out a word. His voice was muffled by the intensity of the gaze she was locked within—a screaming conversation louder than it all.

The thick incense clawed at her lungs, each breath heavier than the last, as though the very air in the room had turned to stone. Her fingers trembled, seeking solace in Elias's steady grip.

His hand was warm against the cold dread settling in her bones, grounding her in a moment she didn't want to face. He squeezed her hand gently, thumb trailing across the knuckle of her thumb in slow repetition.

"Together, Adalja and I will prove ourselves worthy. She shall be the pride of our people—I swear it."

Adalja inhaled sharply looking up at him, wincing as she knew that each adoring word that left his mouth was a sharp stab to the Ragnarvik heiress' heart.

Why couldn't she have listened? she nervously thought, her eyes darting between her old friend and new lover.

"Pray, all of you, make your way to the feast hall. We shall join you shortly. For now, let your Queen be granted a moment of solitude with her family, to mourn and to seek the guidance of God in this trying hour." Elias spoke in a direct tone, his free hand gesturing towards the three exits of the circular room.

Everyone slowly shuffled out, mumbles and whispers echoing throughout the room.

Adalja kept her gaze on the crowd, watching the exact spot where she'd seen Olivja. As the crowd trickled out, Adalja spotted the Norsewoman marching towards the three of them in the centre of the emptying room.

"*Heavens*," Brahms grumbled in frustration as he finally noticed the upset heiress.

Stepping forward, Brahms resumed his usual guarding position as if he were in armour...he would have needed it to defend against Olivja.

As the last of the crowd filed out, the knot in her stomach tightened—leaving an emptiness that echoed in the silence now settling over the room.

"Heiress Olivja," Elias greeted, his free hand extending towards the upset woman. "We were not expecting you."

Olivja snapped her gaze up at the tall prince with a scoff. "We? I'd wait for the wedding before you speak like that." Her voice lost its bite, but her glare remained—a silent fury that cut deeper than words.

Adalja couldn't hide her guilt, heartbreak, or the thunder booming inside her. Silent tears rolled down her cheeks, and it was clear the heiress noticed—her jaw clenched as though cursing her own mouth.

Elias' brows were raised, and Adalja knew that under that dark mask lay a surprised yet darkened countenance. Brahms stood by, jaw clenched tight, holding back to avoid overstepping.

The princess spoke up before either tense man could, her heart racing wildly. "Olivja, *I beg*—for my parents, I—"

"Do not speak for the dead," she began, the words silencing Adalja like a slap. "I *demand* to know why you denied me my farewell from them, Adalja," Olivja snapped angrily, clenching her jaw tightly with fists at her sides.

"*Demand?*" Adalja asked, newfound anger flashing across her tear-streaked face. Her lips parted in disbelief, her gaze flickering across Olivja's contorted face.

Adalja glanced up at Elias, who waited for her to continue, releasing her hand as if granting space for her anger.

"You demand this of me? And on this day, no less?" Adalja scoffed, sweeping her curls from her flushed face. "I asked for but one thing—only *one* thing!"

"This is not about you! This is about *them*, Princess...About *me*! *My culture*!" Olivja spoke with raw anger, disregarding Adalja's words entirely. "Why shun *me* from their wake? Why cast me out from their send-off? What grave sin have I committed that you'd *shame* me like this!?"

"Even Hel would grant me this farewell," Olivja seethed. "But you—you turn me away as though my grief is a crime!"

Adalja's heart plummeted, her breath catching at the way the heiress spoke—especially so close to where her mother and father lay.

"You bar me as if I am filth! As if I do not have the right to stand beside them!" Olivja shouted, eyes burning with tears as she pointed towards the dead Pembrooks. "Is that what you see?"

Adalja's eyes narrowed at the Ragnarvik woman's challenge.

Rage rose—a new kind of fury—boiling back to the surface like a stew left too long on the flame.

"You do not have the right to speak to me like this, Olivja! Not today, when I am mourning and giving my farewells!" Adalja's words were sharp, laced with guilt-tinged anger.

She knew Olivja was hurt, but the burning fury inside her could not be contained. The pain of failing her parents once again—even in death—was more than she could bear.

Adalja inhaled shakily, eyes watering as rage overtook her. "You will show them respect—"

"How is my being here *disrespectful*? I only wished to *mourn*! *Why?* Because they *hate* me? Is there anger towards me so eternal that it extends beyond Hel!?" Olivja shouted, cursing her parents, scoffing as though it was amusing.

She breathed heavily as she continued, "Perhaps, I am doing you all a favor—if they *despised* me so much, maybe my presence will raise them both from the dead—"

"*Enough*," Elias said sharply, sliding one foot in front of Adalja as Olivja stepped closer, subtly separating them. His hand brushed back towards Adalja's hip, an attempt to ground her as she trembled.

From behind Elias, Adalja saw Olivja mirroring her expression—disbelief, though in two very different ways.

"You speak like *faith-born* fools!" Olivja yelled. "You ban me from here and call it *honour*?!"

"I believe it is best you leave, *Ragnarvik*," Brahms sneered in a vile tone, eyes blazing angrily as he stepped forward, finally having a word in the argument.

The princess wanted to stop the tumbling boulder, but she was locked in place, paralysed by emotion. She knew deep inside Olivja was in the right, but so was she.

Adalja had to make a choice. And she chose to stand by her parents—as the princess always did.

"*What*?" Olivja asked, her anger faltering into a crackling gasp as she searched Brahms' eyes for any hesitation or withdrawal.

"Leave—*now.* I am Sir Brahms of the Pembrooks, sworn knight—you will *not* speak of Queen Natja or the King in such regard," Brahms spoke with pride that bartered no interruptions.

The sweet, silly boy Adalja and Olivja had grown up with was gone—replaced by a man of royal honour and duty...but being prideful and demanding in the face of an angry Olivja was not the right choice.

"So, *I'm a* blot on your name, *Sir Bramble*...But you let *him* be here with you?" Her words were harsh, broken as she motioned towards Elias with both of her open hands. "He's worthy of grief, and I am not?!"

Adalja heard the shattered tone of the frantic, furious woman.

Brahms scoffed a few times, a sound of disbelief with embarrassment and frustration at the use of such a nickname. Before he could fire back, Adalja spoke up.

"Elias being here is not of your concern *or* the point, Olivja, and you *know it*," Adalja said with furrowed brows, though her quivering lip gave way to her guilt and sadness. She didn't want to send her away, but with Olivja's lack of respect for her choices, Adalja knew this was all she could do—the only *right* thing left to her.

"Truly, that is my *only* point," Olivja retorted.

Then Elias stepped forward, gently reaching for the heiress' wrist, ready to end their quarrels.

"If you do not wish to listen to Sir Brahms' order, you will have to answer to me," the prince spoke in a low voice, irritation heavy on his words.

Shock flashed across Olivja's face. She snatched her hand away and raised it, taut with power. Adalja gasped at the quick and hostile action, throttled by her ability to resort to it so quickly.

In one swift motion, she slapped Elias across the face, striking his masked cheek with a sharp crack.

Elias barely reacted, his head turning only an inch, eyes shut. Even with most of his face hidden, Adalja could see the tight clench of his jaw beneath the fabric.

The impact of flesh-to-mask echoed in the quiet room, bouncing off the curved walls and back at them.

"Answer to that, *Eli*," Olivja growled, her hand still raised from the slap, ready to deliver a second if challenged again.

Brahms responded instantly, gripping Olivja by her shoulders with an unforgiving force.

The Norsewoman yelled in protest, but it was useless to fight against his anger. Swiftly, Brahms shoved Olivja towards one of the exits, her gasp punctuating the motion as she stumbled and fell onto the cobblestones.

She winced, and Adalja flinched forward, hesitating to assist the heiress.

Everything that could have gone wrong had gone worse.

Adalja couldn't have defended her even if she wanted to. Her chest clenched to think Olivja's stubbornness had turned a day of grief into one of anger.

Elias was the one to move, his step calm and calculated as he tried to help Olivja to her feet.

"Liv..." he sighed, his voice heavy with disappointment, shaking his head. He extended a hand to her, but she only glared at the offer.

"I can help *myself*. You've done enough," Olivja growled out through gritted teeth, shoving his hand away, pushing herself upright.

Elias stepped back and returned to Adalja, grasping her gently. Still shocked and numb from the moment, she allowed his hand to entangle with hers once more.

"Let me take you home, Princess," he spoke with a gentle tone, glancing at Brahms who was busy glaring at Olivja.

Adalja merely nodded, unable to tear her eyes from the distressed heiress as she struggled to stand. Elias guided her out of the Worthyn crypt against the deep ache in her chest.

As the three of them exited the room, Adalja stole a final look at Olivja, who was huffing—hands raking back through her hair, growling like an animal, fighting tears as blood trailed down a scraped arm.

Her fingers twitched at her side, aching to turn back, but she forced herself forward. The sound of Olivja's growl clung to her ears like a curse.

"Well..." Brahms spoke first through the uncomfortable silence with a huff. "That's *one* way to earn a spirit's fury," he mused, trying to lighten the air around them, though his voice held no amusement.

Adalja shot him a warning look. Elias fought a stifled chuckle as they made their way back to the carriage. The snow had thickened; their breaths, though soft, billowed in small puffs in the dense air.

No words were shared on the ride back to the castle. A thick silence hung over them as Adalja kept her reddened eyes downcast to her lap. Elias sat beside her, a comforting anchor in her ocean, while Brahms watched them from across.

"I wish to be alone," Adalja spoke in a hoarse tone as the three of them finally returned to the Worthyn castle. She pushed her snow-sprinkled hood down once they were in the foyer—nose and cheeks flushed from the cold and tears.

"*Alone*? Will you risk such folly, Princess?" Brahms asked, his hand rising to her shoulder to halt her. "What of the killer? You wish to walk undefended?"

She looked at his hand, her stomach twisting painfully. She hated the reminder that her parents were slain in cold blood, and the person responsible was still out there.

"I...I know your heart seeks to keep me from harm," Adalja whispered as if sharing a secret. "But my mind is tangled, and I am lost in it. I need time..."

Though she wasn't sure what would untangle her, *truly.*

Adalja reached her hands out to grasp theirs with a gentle and reassuring touch. Then she slipped away, walking off into the night, her steps echoing against the stone floors.

She wandered her way through the halls, unsure of where to go. She didn't want to be in her room, the silence too loud and far too close to Olivja's resting quarters. Adalja wanted to avoid her for as long as she could.

For a moment, a dark thought was born of guilt and trespassed into her mind. Perhaps things would be easier if the killer found her and finished off her lineage for good.

The vagrancy of her walk and swirling mind had her moving like a spirit without purpose. Her feet moved in tandem with the winding paths of her thoughts—left when she was reasoning, right when angry. She froze in place whenever the grief weighed her down.

And eventually, something led her to the gardens. Her heart. Her brain. Or perhaps fate.

She approached the doors, tugged them open, and released herself to the winter air.

She didn't care if the first snowfall was heavy, powdering every surface in the garden she could see. The silence and chill welcomed her frigid thoughts. With one deep breath, she pulled the black hood of her cloak over her head and stepped out into the cold garden.

Snow blanketed the hedges and trees, softening their edges into ghostly forms. Fountains stood frozen, their icicles glittering like teeth in the light. The statues—forgotten remnants of a time before—gazed solemnly into the quiet evening, their stone eyes blind to the world that had moved on without them.

Adalja's boots crunched softly against the stone path as she approached the one at the end. Less worn than the others and half-swallowed by snow, the figure held a torch in one hand and what looked like a fruit—split open, seeds exposed—in the other. Frost clung to the folds of her stone robe, as though even she had surrendered to winter's silence.

Adalja had come to escape. And yet even now, her thoughts trailed back to Olivja.

She paused, breath misting in the air, fingers lifting towards the statue. Her hand hovered in the space between them, drawn to the duality she couldn't quite explain.

The torch. The fruit. One seemed to burn, the other beckon. As if both held answers she wasn't meant to understand.

Olivja had called this one *Persephone*—but Adalja knew nothing else of her. Still...something about her was familiar. Perhaps the beauty, or maybe it was the choice that lay in her hands.

Adalja reached out, curious to touch, to get a glimpse of this woman's story.

Before she could, the voice of a man she was beginning to adore stirred the frost behind her.

"Careful, My Princess. Touch that pomegranate, and you'll be tempting more than the winter frost."

Adalja jumped, hand retracting back under her cloak as she turned to Prince Elias, who had seemingly followed her in. His black cowl was back over his head, being painted by the snow as he took careful steps closer to her.

It was unexpected, the way his mask was down around his neck, his sharp features in full view.

A shiver ran up her spine—caused by more than the icy air. She was surprised to see him, yet more at ease that he'd found her instead of anyone else.

"Oh, Prince Elias, I was only—"

"Freezing?" he asked her with a teasing cocked brow as his eyes slowly analysed every inch of her trembling, frost-touched frame before returning to her gaze.

In the snow, his eyes reflected brightly, an enchanting green. Once he was close enough for her to feel his warmth, she turned away from the statue, forgetting her curiosity in the stone hands.

His scent—mint and pine—carried on the crisp air, and she all but melted into the becoming comfort of Elias: his warmth, his steadiness, the quiet hush of him.

"No," the princess laughed softly, her eyes crinkling at his playfulness that she welcomed warmly. "Are *you* cold, My Grace? I must confess, I was under the impression that princes were meant to be impervious to such things."

Her tone was light, almost flippant. Though if she were being completely honest with herself, she hadn't truly felt the coldness of the storm raging on, having almost forgotten it entirely.

He chuckled softly, shaking his head slowly. His breath was warm and steady as it puffed against her face, a teasing smirk pulling at the corners of his lips.

Adalja fought to keep her smile in check, pressing her lips together as she waited for his response. A small sense of pride swelled within her for managing to bring out a laugh from him, even in the darkest of times.

"Even I have shivered once or twice, I will confess..." Elias trailed off as his hand reached up to brush a snowflake from one of Adalja's curls that had fallen free.

"Could I tempt you to come inside for some tea, My Lady?" he asked, his eyes trailing her small frame, touch warm as it lingered against her cheek.

The princess shook her head, stubbornness outweighing the temptation of his offer.

A few moments of silence passed before Adalja's voice cracked through it.

"Do you believe they'll find the person?" she asked, breaking the moment's fragile peace, though her eyes still held his cautious gaze as he towered over her.

Elias faltered, his hand slipping from her cheek.

"...Princess?" he asked, his eyes narrowing slightly as he studied her face, searching for meaning, feigning confusion.

"Whoever harmed them..." she said faintly, her voice full of uncertainty.

"Do you?" She pressed again, more fragile this time, her words cracking as the lump in her throat rose, threatening to steal her breath. Tears welled up in her eyes, and she looked away, ashamed of their sudden return.

Her heart raced when he stepped closer, his hands settling gently on her arms over the fabric of her cloak. He offered a small smile and rubbed his palms up and down her biceps in long, soothing passes—trying, with more tenderness than she expected, to warm her.

Silence filled the space between them once more, his expression full of contemplation.

Finally, Elias sighed, his breath forming a small cloud in the cold air. His hands stilled before gently squeezing her arms. He leaned in, closing nearly all the space between them—her back now pressed to the statue behind her.

"I cannot swear much to you, My Lady..." he exhaled, his voice barely louder than the snow, as if it might swallow the words whole. "But I will do everything in my power to avenge them."

Adalja closed her eyes and let out a slow breath. It wasn't enough to silence the winds inside her—but in that heartbeat, Elias reached up, cupping her cheeks in his unexpectedly warm hands.

Her eyes flew open in surprise.

His thumbs brushed tenderly along her cheeks, as if trying to ease the ache written there—to promise, in silence, what words could not undo.

"Prince—"

"No."

His voice cut through gently but firmly, rejecting the formality. His brows furrowed, eyes locked on hers like he was searching for something deeper. "Enough of this...What you require now is warmth and care."

He stepped closer. Their bodies hovered, nearly touching, and the radiating warmth of him left her frozen in place. Her chest rose and fell in quick, shallow breaths, soft clouds spilling from her parted lips.

All around them, the snow fell in a hush, soundless and steady—encasing them like a snow globe. And in that quiet, shaken world, Elias Worthyn was at its centre.

"Elias..." Adalja breathed, her voice barely more than a whisper, trembling with nerves as his gaze dropped to her lips.

"Yes, Adalja?" he murmured, his voice like velvet, warm breath ghosting against her skin as he leaned in closer.

A shiver coursed through her—from something much deeper than temperature. And with that same shiver came a pulse of heat, one that melted not only the flakes as they touched her skin, but the ice that had fallen around her heart.

The air between them trembled with something new. Something electric.

"What if we don't find them...?" Adalja asked softly, her words catching in her throat. "What if I'm..." She couldn't finish. The thought of becoming queen—of bearing that weight alone—terrified her. Tears stung at her eyes, unshed but aching.

Elias' hands tightened just enough on her face, still tender, still careful. *Reminding* her of his presence.

"Do not let fear take root in your heart," he said, voice steady and low. "I swear it—on my vow, on my heart, and on the strength of my kingdom—that no gods will let such cruelty go unanswered."

He paused, his tone softening as he leaned closer. "Let me be your peace, just for this moment. I will protect you...for as long as I draw breath."

His promise left Adalja frozen in time. And yet, her emotions burned against the cold.

She melted beneath his touch—stilled, breathless, and overcome by the quiet strength in his hold. It steadied her. Anchored her. Like he could be the constant she so desperately needed in the tempest closing in around her.

Lost for words, her thoughts tangled in feeling. Her eyes searched his face, finally landing on the intensity in his gaze.

"Elias..." she whispered, her breath a fragile wisp against his lips. "You need not be that for me. I ask not for such a vow."

"Never have I needed anything more, and for that, I seek nothing but your love."

The princess watched Elias intently, her pulse quickening as she saw it—the unspoken truth in his eyes. Her heart skipped. For a fleeting moment, time seemed to stretch, her breath catching in her throat.

He was going to kiss her. That much was clear, and her fingers trembled at her sides, betrayed by the nervous anticipation that clawed at her.

As those final, breathless words escaped his lips, she realised, too late, there was no turning back. His face drew closer, his presence overwhelming, and her mind screamed in soundless panic.

Oh gods, oh gods...!

Then, in the space between heartbeats, he closed the distance—his lips capturing hers in a kiss that was tender, yet fierce, a promise made flesh.

Adalja froze, overwhelmed by the suddenness, as his arms wrapped around her.

She felt like a snowflake—adrift in a world not her own, yet falling exactly where she was meant to. A tender, fleeting thing, melting beneath the warmth of a single touch.

Slowly, cautiously, she leaned in. Her eyelashes fluttered closed as her body responded to his warmth, her hesitation melting like the snow beneath their feet.

Her mind, once a swirling torrent, became the calmest waters of a crystal blue ocean. His lips were soft, supple, and moved with practice, as if he'd been thinking about this moment for eons.

She sighed into his touch, his taste reminiscent of herbal tea, allowing herself to be led by him and his lips. Adalja slid her hands blindly under his cloak, her numbed fingers grasping his shirt for warmth and balance.

The move spurred the prince on, urging him forward until her back pressed firmly against the stone platform of the long-forgotten statue.

Elias' hand slid up, tangling into the princess' curls. He tilted her head back to deepen the kiss, eliciting a breathy gasp as her lips parted. His other hand slid down to her hip, squeezing gently.

The kiss burned like a hearth, sparking heat between them in a way that made her feel both welcomed and protected. She wanted to stay in that fiery connection, even if part of her was unsure about the kiss itself.

She hadn't expected their first kiss to come on the day of her parents' funeral. But it carried a special weight—a pull of need and unity that deepened their blossoming connection.

It was sugar to ice—melting, sweet.

He drew back, but their lips lingered, brushing softly with every ragged breath.

Her eyes opened slowly, pale blues searching his deep green. They shared a look of quiet curiosity, wondering if it had been the right move—if the feelings were truly reciprocated.

And Adalja? She was unaware of how to feel.

In an instant, her mind was overrun with *Elias.* She was certain that was his plan—to kiss her and make her feel light and airy again. But she hadn't expected it to work so well.

His eyes trailed slowly to her lips, lingering for a moment as he bit his bottom lip.

Elias released her hair, his finger tracing from the corner of her jaw to her chin, holding it there. Adalja shivered at the feeling, and he grinned in return.

"You're quite short, Lady Adalja." His soft voice was dampened by the snow around them.

Her suitor's smile grew in tandem with her growing blush, and before she could apologise for it, his hand joined the other on her hip. With one swift motion, he lifted her easily onto the stone platform, perching her in front of the woman's carved gown.

Now at a perfect height—*his* height—their eyes met naturally.

He stepped closer, pausing before her knees, his hands gripping the cold stone on either side as he leaned in. His nose brushed gently against hers, a teasing smirk tugging at his lips as he studied her closer.

"Much better," he said, grinning. Adalja stifled a nervous giggle, her bashfulness getting the better of her.

"I agree, My Lord..." Her eyes dropped to his lips, expecting another taste of his warmth.

Slowly—almost painfully—he leaned in again, pausing a breath from her lips as his warm breath teased her skin. Then their lips met in a kiss deeper than the last. Her cold fingers slid into his hair, accidentally pushing his hood down. The soft brush of her touch sent a shiver through him.

Elias' lips moved with determination this time, parting hers as he claimed them fully. The kiss was wet and gentle.

A smile tugged on his lips, and she smiled back; both were eager for the tantalizing kiss to continue. Her hands pulled him in, her heart aching for more of Elias.

Their closeness—the kiss, the warmth—felt necessary.

The need to feel loved—especially after losing such a big part of herself—was finally being met. She wanted Elias, and he was showing her he felt the same—for once, it was with someone she knew her parents approved of.

In the cold air, their heavy breaths mingled in soft clouds between them.

His hand slipped, inching towards temptation as it slid up her knee, squeezing gently over the fabric of her dress. As it slid higher, she arched into him, giving way to his fingers as they curved around her hip and rested at the small of her back.

A soft sigh left her lips as her eyes fluttered open. He pulled back, his low-lidded gaze heavy with desire and unspoken intention.

"*Adalja...*" he exhaled, his voice low and reverent, like a prayer carried on the snow. She looked to his lips watching how they wrapped around her name.

At first, she thought she might kiss him again, but as she met his eyes, a pang of guilt struck her chest—guilt she couldn't place.

Snowflakes clung to Adalja's lashes, their delicate frost making her blue eyes gleam with a crystalline brightness. Her gaze flitted between his green eyes, which shimmered like fresh spring grass against pale strands of his icy hair—a striking contrast to the wintery stillness around them.

Adalja's lips parted as she struggled to find the words, a whirlwind of emotions rushing through her.

Elias watched her intently, his mask still gathered loosely around his neck. His teeth grazed his bottom lip in a moment of silent contemplation, his gaze searching hers as though trying to decipher the flood within her.

"Thank you..." Adalja breathed out, keeping a steady gaze with him.

His fingers slowly slid up her cheeks and cupped her face once more. "You thank me? For making you endure this cold longer?" Elias teased her, his thumbs brushing against her cheeks tenderly. "You're very welcome."

She smiled, her eyes fluttering shut as she leaned against his warm hand. At the mention of the temperature, the warmth subsided. The cold from the stone finally seeped through her gown.

"Is the Fair One ready for her tea now?" he asked, a playful smile curling his lips as he glanced at the bashful princess.

He didn't wait for her reply.

In one smooth motion, he slid an arm beneath her knees, his other hand pressing firmly to her back. Careful yet confident, he swept her effortlessly into a bridal hold. The suddenness drew a surprised gasp, her hands instinctively clutching his shoulders as his warmth wrapped around her—a striking contrast to the chill.

"I'm quite warm already," Adalja teased with a bashful grin, leaning against his shoulder.

He carried her out of the snowy garden with a quiet chuckle. She enjoyed hearing him laugh—she needed it. She needed *him.*

"As am I." Elias pressed his lips to her temple with a gentle kiss.

Adalja glanced back at the statues, giving Persephone one final look before the castle's warmth welcomed them inside. She was pleasantly surprised—grateful—for the way her garden visit ended.

For Elias had done more than warm the chill of winter's first snow.
He had chased the ice from her skin—and kindled something far deeper beneath it.

Thread XXVI

With a swift push, Olivja flung open the Worthyn doors, her shoulders rigid with fury. She dropped her arms to her sides, fists clenched tight as she stormed up the grand foyer steps.

"Madame Olivja!" a knight shouted from behind, his earlier calls in the courtyard still unanswered. "Lord Vincent demands your presence!"

She spun on her heels at the top of the stairs, her tear-streaked glare sharp enough to stop the knight in his tracks. He seized her left forearm, and the rough grip ignited the fury already simmering beneath her skin.

"*Release me!* You think I'll bow after the day I've suffered? You're mad!" Olivja cried, yanking at his grip, her eyes blazing with rage and tears. "Let me be, or I'll MAKE YOU!"

She struggled harder, prompting the knight to snatch her other arm in a clumsy attempt to restrain her. "I am not some tame girl to be pulled like a dog!" Olivja shouted, fury crackling in her voice. She was done being dragged and pushed around.

The knight was adamant about following his orders, but the Norsewoman met him with unrelenting fire. She drove her foot into his thigh, unleashing the grief and resentment she'd buried since the funeral.

He stumbled back, stunned by the heiress' wild defiance—unheard of in holy halls. He stepped forward again, hand darting towards her arm with renewed urgency.

"Olivja?!" boomed a voice to her right—someone familiar.

She turned, her tear-blurred gaze locking on him, breath coming in fast, shallow bursts.

Vincent strode towards her in sleek black, a stack of books balanced in one arm, his masked face unreadable. His green eyes flicked from the knight to Olivja, narrowing when they caught the tears on her cheeks.

He went to her in a flash, dropping his books to the floor as both hands cupped her tearful face, scanning her for evidence of any wounds that the knight may have caused.

"Vincent!" Olivja growled, jerking from his touch. "I am well! Enough!"

He caught her arm and tilted it, revealing a bleeding scrape that deepened the frown on his face. He let go before she could shove him off and turned fully to face the knight.

"You *harmed* her?" Vincent asked, voice low and sharp, fists curling at his sides.

The knight swiftly stepped backwards and hands raised in defence.

"N-No, Your Grace, never!" he stammered, ripping off his helmet to reveal sweat-matted dark hair and wide, fearful eyes. He dropped to one knee beside Olivja, head bowed. "Please forgive me, My Lord!"

"Your orders were to bring her to me unharmed," Vincent said, stepping closer, towering over the cowering knight. "If you failed in that, then only your blood will make it right."

"Vincent, *be still*!" she shouted, stepping forward to grab his wrist with both hands, stunned by his sudden fury. "It was my own doing! That is enough!" She looked between Vincent and the knight, willing them both to listen.

Both men turned their heads towards the erratic woman, bewildered by the red heat flashing across her face.

Vincent's posture softened, and when he noticed her grasp on his wrist, she let go. He straightened, gaze dropping again to the scrape on her arm. He left the knight kneeling and turned to her, voice gentler.
"Very well then, Olivja—explain."

"I want to be alone, Vincent! This rage is mine to hold—not yours to fix!" she shouted, unbothered by how it might wound him.

She was so consumed by anger and despair—she *welcomed* a good smack from Vincent. *No,* that would only make her angrier. So she turned to leave, but as always, he caught her forearm and tugged her sharply back around.

"Princess, *do not* walk away from me. You are *hurt,*" he said, voice soft as his eyes searched her grief-stricken, puffy face. Still holding her firmly, he demanded, "If not my knight, then who? Who is to pay for this act, Olivja, just give me a name—"

"Let. Me. Go. While you still have fingers!" Olivja shouted, furious not just at the grip, but at being forced to explain herself at all. Her fury was a dragon's fire, and she didn't want Vincent caught in the blast.

He had always been protective—she knew that—but right now, it was unwelcome. She could take care of herself...but even as a child, Vincent never believed in her strength. She shook her head, jaw tight, refusing to stop tugging at her trapped wrist.

Her mind flashed to Elias and Adalja, parading as lovers at the funeral—touching, caressing, clinging. Then came the memory of Brahms, of being dragged down again, *in front of* Adalja. It sickened her, but those betrayals weren't ones she could share with Vincent. That made it worse.

She was a ship lost at sea—sails shredded by winds she couldn't command, caught in a storm she'd summoned. It wasn't just their betrayal. It was her own. Each time her thoughts wandered to what could never be—what shouldn't be—she crashed against the jagged rocks of her own doing.

"I've no words for you, Vincent. Be gone! I swear, if you don't unhand me—" she yelled, voice cracking. "It was all my own foolishness...so *please*! *Let me be*!" She was desperate for solitude, for *peace.*

Gods, his grip is forged by dwarves!

Vincent stood silent, weighing her words. After a moment, he sighed and glanced briefly at the knight, yet his grip on her never loosened. Somehow, his hand stayed clasped around her, no matter how much she pulled—like trying to break free from dried clay.

"Have this mess brought to my study and the afternoon tea prepared," Vincent said to the knight. Then he stepped closer to Olivja, just as an animalistic growl tore from her clenched jaw.

His heavy hands slid up to her biceps. She shoved at his chest as he stepped closer. He lifted her elbow, brushing gently over the inflamed skin of the wound Brahms had given her.

"Did this happen at the funeral, Olivja? You were not meant to be there..." he mumbled, ignoring her struggling as though it didn't exist. His brows furrowed with concern. "Where was Elias when this happened?"

Her jaw clenched at the name.

"Oh, *Elias*? He watched! Watched me fall, watched me bleed! Took the sting of my hand for it too—just the same as you!" Olivja snapped, a bitter laugh slipping through her tears.

She blamed Elias for every ounce of her pain—Vincent still saw him as some faithful protector of her.

Vince's emerald eyes seemed darker than before. Still, he remained calm and silent, even after the knight left—despite her coldness.

She knew his kindness was meant to draw her out—but she was surprised by how easily it worked. She didn't want to tell him what happened—but she *craved* validation. Even if it was from Vincent.

"He let someone hurt you?" His voice dropped an octave, low as a dark chord—sending chills down her spine.

She swallowed hard, her anger pausing just long enough to wonder how her words might harm Elias. Before she could defend him, he spoke again.

"...I'll be having a word with him about that. But I must say—it is good to know your defiance spares none," Vincent said, his tone dull at first. Then a faint chuckle escaped. "...What on earth were you hoping to accomplish by going there?"

"*I beg you*—forget it..." Olivja muttered, turning away, though he tilted his head to follow her gaze.

He sighed and released her hands, stepping back. With both palms raised in quiet surrender, he waited.

She didn't quite understand why she felt the urge to speak. Maybe it was Adalja's betrayal—choosing Elias—that drove her back towards Vincent. *No.*

She trusted him—because, as foolish as he was, she knew him. He had earned that much.

A shaky sigh escaped her lips, bringing the backs of her hands to wipe at her eyes, shocked by her own vulnerability.

"*Ugh*...Pabbi would not set foot there—said they deserved a funeral fit for Jarls, not this farce. So he made me carry his blessing in his place..." Olivja said.

She crossed her arms now that he had let her go and continued, her voice sharp. "But the *Pembrooks?* They cursed me with their last breath, wanted me gone. No one welcomed me—only snarls and cold stares met my arrival."

She paused, scoffing as her anger flared again.

"Even so, the Pembrooks were my blood once—before even *you* walked beside me, Vincent—and yet I was sent away from their dying breath. *Me*!" Olivja shouted—not at him, but at the world, at Adalja, Elias, Brahms. But Vincent happened to be the only one listening...

He was always the only one who ever listened.

She shook her head as hot, angry tears slid down her cheeks. "Either they are *fools* who know nothing of death's weight in my people's ways...or they hate me so deeply, they'd honour the dead before giving me peace!" Her lip quivered, but she pressed on—knowing she wouldn't get the chance to say it to anyone else.

"I should have been there, standing strong as they passed beyond—but they kept me away. And yet Elias is welcome? How can that be just?" Olivja asked with a sharp motion of her hands.

She knew Vincent would always protect his brother above all else, but once she began, it was impossible to stop.

"I—I would not spill his name lightly," she added quickly. Her tears returned, hot as betrayal throbbed in her chest and knotted in her throat. "But—I was meant to stand beside them. Their loss burns in me...*deeply.*"

Ashamed and spent, she let her head fall. She was done speaking. It no longer mattered.

But just as her gaze dropped to the floor, Vincent lifted it, pressing a finger beneath her chin. His eyes were gentle as they read the heartbreak in her face. And yet, as always, he spoke with that same ruthless edge.

"Foolish girl. You're meant for *far more* than standing beside dead nobles," Vincent said flatly, letting his hand fall once their eyes met. But her gaze didn't waver—her chin didn't drop.

"Forgive me for saying so, Liv, but the Pembrooks are not worth these tears..." He shrugged, though his expression darkened. "It pains me, watching you fight for scraps of recognition."

"*Pains you!? It pains* me, Vincent! I am in pain, all the while your *brother* gets everything I—" She caught herself just in time and turned her eyes away again.

"Elias *had* to be there, Liv—he's *marrying* the Pembrook woman," Vincent said, his eyes narrowing. "In the grand scheme of things you mean *nothing* to them," he mumbled darkly—not to insult her, rather he spoke matter-of-factly. Oddly, that hurt worse than anything.

"You're wrong, I—" she paused, a lump catching in her throat.

She had been foolish for ever thinking she could be considered—*acknowledged*—by people other than her own. Suddenly, she had a lot more to think about. And all she wanted to do was run from it.

"Forgive me..." she cleared her throat. "Your tea grows cold. Go, before I bring more ruin to Midhelm," Olivja finished coldly, unable to look him in the eyes.

"Heiress Ragnarvik...*apologising*? That's not like you," he said quietly and Olivja could hear the smile hidden behind his mask. His brows knit in real disappointment as he shook his head.

"You can handle my ferocity, but a simple betrayal leaves you whimpering like a child? Are you not stronger than this, Olivja?"

He was reprimanding her.
Lovingly—mockingly—and she scoffed as she recognised it.

It was a simple comment, but enough to halt her tears entirely. Just the thought of appearing weak in front of the man she'd competed with for years froze her in place. Adalja's betrayal cut deeper than Vincent could ever know, but still—she was ashamed of her weakness, especially after putting on such an unwavering front. Being vulnerable with him was the last thing she ever wanted.

"Aye...I am."

"Then you should know, darling, that noble souls keep their tears hidden from the eyes of the world," he said softly, stepping closer. His gloved fingers unfolded with care, brushing away the wet tracks on her cheeks, a touch both gentle and commanding.

Her jaw tightened, confusion flickering like a shadow in her eyes. His gesture was tender, yet it carried a flare of ownership—mocking or protecting, she could not tell which. The ache between them was raw and sharp.

"But I am no noble soul...and you are not—" Her voice cracked.
She drew a shaky breath, voice low, *gentler*.

"You are naught but Vincent."

And they both paused, looking at each other in understanding or...perhaps misunderstanding. Who really knew?

He smirked, shrugging like it was no surprise. "Right you are, Liv. Sharp as ever, I see..."

When her tears soaked into his gloves, his hands dropped without hesitation to grip her biceps. He gave her a reassuring squeeze—hard enough to steady her but not enough to hurt. His touch was a chain dragging her back from the edge.

"I say..." He cocked his head, eyes narrowed, sizing her up. "We owe them thanks for casting you out."

"Thanks?" she spat, cheeks burning as his breath fanned her face.

"But of course," he said with cruel amusement. "In their foolishness, they've handed me the perfect excuse to tend your pathetic, broken heart, princess."

Her cheeks flared hotter, fury and shame warring inside her. Of course he'd choose this moment to twist the knife.

She slammed her hand into his chest, stepping back sharply to break his hold. Folding her arms she shook off the fog, meeting his arrogant gaze with fire.

"You're a bastard, Vince," Olivja snapped, a bitter smile flickering before she shoved it down with a glare. "Now leave me alone. I want no part in your *tending—*"

He laughed, low and knowing. "Oh, my dear. If that were true, you wouldn't have bared your soul to me. Heavens, you're truly distraught over this—"

"I am *not* distraught!"

"No?" He turned sideways, offering his elbow like some gallant gentlemen to a distressed damsel. "Well then. If you crave solitude, I'll see you to your chambers before the vultures swarm. You can stew in your pride, 'not distraught' and all," he said, brow arched.

Olivja hesitated, rage and relief and something softer twisting tight in her chest like a knot. She wanted away, she knew that. But she couldn't deny that the anger felt lighter. No. It was still just as strong, only now she had Vincent to unleash it on.

But...she wasn't—was she?

Swallowing, she stepped forward and placed a hand around his arm while her expression slightly relaxed.

If not for their history, she might have enjoyed his presence. She understood why noblewomen envied her place as his bride.

For a fleeting moment, she wished it were that simple—that she could enjoy it, embrace it, live it. But she would never submit to the role of a nobleman's wife. And yet, it angered her that it was Vincent she had to refuse.

On their way, an awkward silence befell them. She begrudgingly appreciated Vincent's uncharacteristic restraint. His quiet escort surprised her, and she didn't fail to notice it. As they reached her room, a wave of relief crashed over her.

"Here we are, my Jewel..." Vincent's voice was quiet, almost soft, as he let go of her arm and opened the door.

Inside, a young maid was setting a tray of tea and pastries on the wooden desk. Once the royal's presence was noticed, the girl hurriedly finished and fearfully scrambled out of the room.

She scoffed. The tea was for *her?*

Once Vincent let her go, she stepped into her room, fists clenched at her sides. Her deep red gown trailed across the cold floor, mirroring the weight dragging through her thoughts.

Knowing it couldn't last, she counted her steps to see how many she could take before he spoke again. It was only after the second step that he cracked.

"If it pleases you, Olivja, I'll escort you to the crypt whenever you wish—should you desire to go again," he said and cleared his throat. "You—you were right...You deserve to mourn."

Those weren't the words she expected. She half turned, brows furrowed in confusion.

"Despite what they all think of you, you deserve closure from that wretched family," he mumbled before stepping into the room after her, heading towards the tea.

What they think of me?
She swallowed dryly. The phrase tumbled in her mind like stones in a rushing current. Her lonely gaze shifted to her freshly made bed.

"Let it be known...the Great Vincent has at last bowed to my right..." Olivja exhaled and stepped towards her bed frame, longing for rest, wishing to sleep away the remaining heartbreak and confusion.

"I'll send a raven. None shall doubt my lady's truth," Vincent said dryly, rolling his eyes at her as he reached the desk.

The sound of ceramic clinking filled the quiet space as the prince poured a cup of steaming tea.

She closed her eyes, hugging the bedpost—the only affection she could offer the world.

After a short moment, she heard his steps growing closer, approaching from behind. His hand fell to her hip. When her eyes opened, a plate holding a full teacup hovered in front of her. Taking it proved more challenging than expected.

"Your pity *stings*, Vincent," Olivja whispered, staring deeply into the crimson tea.

The cup stayed in front of her, held tightly in his strong grasp...tight enough for him to shatter it, and yet it remained steady.

"I have no pity, Liv. This is *patience*," Vincent murmured, his voice low and calm, "but *God knows I'm running out of it.*" His words whispered warmly against the side of her head.

She responded with a scoff, voice strained as she said:
"Then leave. You think tea can fix me?"

In the tea's surface, she saw Vincent's eyes. They weren't angry, they weren't rolling in annoyance. Just soft. They were *kind*. For *her*.

"*Heavens no*. I'm not a fool. But it's a start..." he said with a soft chuckle. The cup trembled briefly in his hands before he sighed. "You need *something*, Liv...and apart from this damned tea, I am all you have left."

Olivja bit her bottom lip, nursing it as her brows lifted in wounded confusion, unsure how to feel—unsure how to respond.

Eventually, she whispered:
"What an awful thing to say."

And yet, Vincent was right. Adalja had cast her out. Brahms wounded her. Elias took her place. Dagrun sabotaged her. Her mother abandoned her.

Tragically, Vincent was the last thing holding her together.
Him—and a steaming cup of horse-dung.

"Indeed...for you and me both," he whispered, his breath against her ear now. "Stop fighting me, Ragnarvik...*Drink*." His order was calm but swift, and her hands balled into fists.

As much as she hated it—with everything else put aside—she saw a peaceful future by his side. Images of Adalja and Elias flashed before her and she swallowed the tightness in her throat. If Adalja could do it...why not her?

Vincent was teaching her to choose her battles wisely—showing her that not everything was black and white. And against her better judgement, he was gaining her trust again.

She reached out with both hands and took the cup from the plate. Without a word, she lifted the warm liquid to her lips and drank. Then she closed her eyes once more. She wasn't accepting him, not yet. But she needed peace—and he was giving that to her.

"I say this with all due respect: you deserve more than this, Liv, *spiteful as you are*," Vincent murmured with a soft chuckle, pressing his other hand to her hip as she drank.

Olivja sighed, warmth flooding her face as she exhaled, sending fragrant steam swirling from the cup. The tea was flavorful and calmed her nerves instantly.

"Take your time," his words lowered to a whisper as they neared her ear.

He had removed the bottom half of his mask at some point. She knew because his lips brushed her bare shoulder. Not quite a kiss...just a presence.

Her fingers tightened around the cup. Pulling the porcelain from her lips, she swallowed, ready to curse him for his touch. But he spoke again.

"I'll let you enjoy your *aloneness*, princess," his warm yet chilling words sent goosebumps where his lips touched. He gave her hip a parting squeeze, then withdrew.

As he reached the door, she turned at last to watch him go. Confused and heightened, Olivja clutched the cup to her chest, her heartbeat strong enough to ripple the remaining liquid.

"I am not alone!" she called out, voice unsteady, unsure why she felt the need to correct him at all.

For the first time, the Ragnarvik heiress faltered.

"Right again, Liv...you never will be," pausing at the door, he turned slightly, glancing at her over his shoulder. "I'll walk this path with you, till the end." With a soft rustle of fabric, he flipped his hood back into place and slipped through the door.

And Liv was left in silence with all her confusion and uncertainty.

She looked down. Tea leaves swirled at the bottom of the cup.

If he's all I have left...
The thought clung to her like frost.
...then I truly am alone.

THREAD XXVII

ᚦᛖ ᛒᚢᚱᛞᛖᚾᛊ ᛟᚠ ᚺᛖᛁᚱᛊ ᚦᛖ ᛒᚢᚱᛞᛖᚾᛊ ᛟᚠ ᚺᛖᛁᚱᛊ ᚦᛖ ᛒᚢᚱᛞᛖᚾᛊ

ᛒᚱᚨᚺᛗᛊ

ANGRY AT HIMSELF, AND THE SITUATION, Brahms excused himself once they arrived back at the castle. Adalja had refused his care, and frankly, he needed a break from everyone.

In times like this, it became hard to keep his frustrations under control—or quiet. He had always been a dutiful servant—nothing more. No one listened to him, no one took his advice, no one followed his direction. Not once in his entire life.

He had no say in anything. Ever. And he was tired of it. He was tired of being invisible while irresponsible royals were handed everything—even when they didn't want it.

Olivja was one of the few royals who knew how to get a decent rise out of him, especially because she didn't listen to *anyone.* She was able to do whatever she wanted, and no one would lay a hand on her.

Well—until Vincent, he thought, letting out a dry laugh.

It was a terrible thought, but truly, he envied her freedom—and resented her disregard for anyone but herself.

The display at the funeral confirmed any and all negative opinions he had of her. He couldn't believe she'd show up just to make a scene.

His fists clenched as he recalled the events. He stormed down the halls towards his quarters.

"Brahms!"

Annoyed to be interrupted, he froze and cracked his neck, hoping to shake off the tension as he half-turned.

From the corner of his eye, he saw a large figure approaching fast. Finishing his turn, he lifted his hands defensively—just as Vincent charged.

Knowing he couldn't defend against a royal, he braced himself as the angry prince grabbed hold of his shirt and flung him back into a painting, holding him there like a nail to a board.

Wide-eyed, the knight grabbed his assailant's wrists, breath ragged with shock.

"Explain to me why Olivja returned from the funeral with injuries!" Vincent shouted, veins bulging across his neck, arms, and head.

Brahms was unsure of how to respond.

He had stepped between Olivja and Elias to prevent a fight, and slightly injured her in the process. But that was nothing compared to the wounds he'd left on her before...or the ones she could have given the prince.

However, that wasn't something he could casually admit. Admitting that he was at fault for causing injury to a princess was enough to warrant a severe punishment, but lying would bring much worse.

His anger deepened immediately at the thought that Olivja had told Vincent. She must have known that this would be his response...

His eyes darkened and he inhaled sharply, unsure how to respond—but his anger towards Olivja clouded his judgment.

"My Lord, had your *viking bride* followed orders, I wouldn't have had to stop her from fighting with your brother," Brahms sneered, unable to mask his passive aggression.

Vincent chuckled—undoubtedly at the image of Olivja fighting Elias—but the amusement vanished as he spoke again.

"I care not if she holds an axe to your *throat*. You will bear it as the loyal hound you are," he began, lowering his voice to a brutal growl. "Should I catch you laying a hand on Olivja again, *I will feed your corpse to the wolves.*"

Brahms wasn't in the right mindset to be threatened, especially by someone he already didn't like. Gripping Vincent's forearms tightly, he pressed forward, forcing the prince to stumble backwards into the hall.

"Aye, that's rich comin' from you," Brahms scoffed, flicking his wrists like he was gearing up to punch. "You harmed 'er long before I did."

If Vincent knew Brahms like the princesses did, he'd recognise the thickening of his accent as a warning.

The prince's jaw clenched, his eyes widening before narrowing into a seething glare. His breath caught, a muscle in his neck tensed, and his fists curled at his sides—Brahms had struck a nerve.

It felt good to draw that out of him. He'd never admit it, but in that moment, he understood why Olivja was so defiant.
He could get used to it.

"You...compare yourself to *me*?" Vincent scoffed, disbelieving, as he stepped back towards the poor knight and shoved him into the wall.

Brahms felt his breath against his face as the prince snarled: "You wouldn't last a breath against me. You are nothing without an order. You don't move unless I say so—so let's try *this*. *Sit*."

The prince slammed his knee into Brahms' groin, sending him crumpling to his knees.

Brahms groaned, clutching beneath his ribs in a futile grasp for comfort against the pain. The breath fled his lungs, silencing him. Held up by his shirt, Brahms dangled as Vincent smirked.

"That's a good boy," Vincent said flatly, glaring as Brahms struggled to breathe. "Now, you will be wise to keep that foul name out of your mouth when speaking of Olivja."

Again, with the dog references.
He hated it—almost as much as he hated Vincent. And that hatred only deepened, his teeth clenched so hard they ached, holding back the words he wanted to spit.

The prince loomed over him, head dipped like a vulture circling its prize. With deliberate precision, he slid his fingers into Brahms' hair and yanked his head back—just gentle enough to mock, firm enough to dominate.

"Your loyalty to the Pembrooks means *nothing* to me. I will see you gutted and replaced before you draw another breath—"

"Vince." The calm voice echoed from the hallway to their right.

Dropped in an instant, Brahms collapsed to all fours, dragging in the breath he'd lost.

"Elias."

When he looked up from the floor, he found Elias and Adalja—both soaked, their cloaks dripping. Adalja slowed, confusion tightening her brow.

"What is the meaning of this?" Elias hissed, striding forward, fists clenched at his sides.

"Perhaps you could tell me, Elias. *You* were the one who saw it happen," Vincent snapped, his fury intensifying now that it had shifted to his brother.

Brahms glanced down the hall, making brief eye contact with Adalja who lingered just behind Elias.

There was a pause between all of them. Elias looked from Vincent to Brahms. His stare lingered on Brahms' for a beat too long before shifting—sharpening as they met his mirror.

"Now is not the time, brother, and you are in no place to punish Brahms."

"Well, if no one else will..." The growl came with a brutal kick to Brahms' gut, toppling him onto his side.

The impact stole his breath. He curled inward, arms clutching his stomach as pain flared through his ribs.

"Vincent, *enough*!" Elias barked, stepping forward.

The long-haired prince scoffed, palms facing the rafters with a bitter smile. "What is this!?" He laughed, though it dropped into a sneer. "You'd defend a pathetic knight, but not *Olivja*?!"

Elias fell silent, and Brahms caught the flicker of regret that crossed his face. He clenched his jaw, eyes dropping to the carpet between them.

"Olivja threatened the peace of the *entire* wake. She deserved no defence," Elias shot back, a dark challenge flashing in his gaze as they raised to glare at his brother once more.

Vincent's eyes burned. "So, that's how you regard her now? Merely a problem to be managed? I wonder, brother," he broke off with a sharp scoff, "how Olivja would take such *loyalty* from your lips."

He stepped back, his arms wide.

"Go on, play the noble prince—it becomes you *well*. But do not lay blame at her feet when she strips you of absolution and leaves you in memory. Count yourselves fortunate I was not there to defend her."

Elias scoffed, the sound tight with frustration as he stepped back. The words seemed to land in old wounds Vincent knew how to hit. Worse still—Brahms and Adalja had seen it all.

Elias clenched his jaw, rage and denial warring across his face before he turned sharply on his heel to leave—refusing to give Vincent another word.

Vincent let out a humorless chuckle, contempt simmering in his glare.

Adalja reached for him, catching his arm before Elias could storm off.

"*Eli...*" she murmured, voice faint and uncertain.

Elias stopped, shooting her a sharp and silent look of warning. Without a word, he pulled his arm free from her grasp and kept walking. Adalja stood frozen, her hand suspended in the air before slowly curling into a fist and falling to her side.

Vincent's gaze lingered on Princess Adalja, razor-sharp and unreadable. "Be wary of him. He has a *habit* to flee when courage is called for."

Adalja didn't respond. Her shoulders sagged, lips parted—but no sound came. Vincent shook his head, exhaled through his nose, and stormed off in the opposite direction of his brother.

Brahms slowly stood, straightening the formal clothes he'd been loaned—now wrinkled and dirtied from Vincent's tirade.

Adalja's parted lips quivered, then pressed shut, her frown deepening beneath a flush of guilt. Brahms caught the tremor in her fingers as she reached towards him, hesitation plain in every movement.

Disappointment flickered in his dark eyes—not sharp or cruel, but resigned, as if he'd expected nothing more.

"Do you understand why this happened?" Brahms muttered through clenched teeth, brushing dirt from his sleeves with trembling hands. He winced, the motion sending pain through his ribs, a bitter scoff catching in his throat.

Adalja flinched. "No...I don't understand," she whispered, eyes searching his face. She touched his bicep, a quiet offer of comfort.

Brahms didn't soften. He tilted his head back and closed his eyes, summoning patience. "*Olivja happened,*" he muttered, voice low and rough with anger. "Told Vincent I harmed 'er. So he came for *me*."

Adalja blinked, lips parting in disbelief, but no words came. She shook her head. "I...I can't imagine she would—"

"Are you really going to excuse her after today?" Brahms snapped, his voice sharp like a blade. The raw disbelief in his voice made Adalja wince.
"I'm tired of her, Adalja. *I'm tired of all of this*."

The words surprised even him, but once said, they flooded out.

"You all get to run around, say what you want, *do* what you want...Olivja ruins my one chance at-at *feeling* like I was more than some," his voice broke—words sticking in his throat as he swallowed hard, clenching a fist at his side.
"Some *dog*."

Adalja's brows drew together. "You are no dog—"

"No?!" Brahms barked, making her flinch. He ran his hands through his hair, tugging in frustration. "That's all I've ever been to you—obedient as a *beast*! I follow commands, eat when told, shit where you say, and keep still 'til summoned. And what do I get from it?"

He flung a hand towards his clothes—once fine, now wrinkled and torn from Vincent's assault.

"Look at me! A moment to feel like I belonged, like I was worth something—and she couldn't even let me have that. I *always* get the short end of the stick, Adalja."

Adalja's lips trembled. Her chest heaved as guilt laid heavy, but she couldn't form words before Brahms went on.

"Every time I try—*every time*—I'm reminded that I'm nothing to any of you. Not to Olivja, not to the public. Not even to *you*."

Adalja's breath hitched at the accusation. Before he could say more, she reached for him, grasping his arm and tugging him into a hug.

Brahms stiffened, rigid against her. His anger simmered beneath the surface, his arms limp as her grip tightened.

"Forgive me, Brahms," she said against his shoulder, voice cracking with unexpected emotion. "You're my truest friend...you *do* matter. Hear me when I say this, you are more than some *knight* or-or some *pet.*"

He stayed frozen, breath hitching. Then, reluctantly, he raised his arms and wrapped them loosely around her. The anger didn't leave him, but the tension dwindled.

Even now, he felt unheard—as if pity was all she could offer. She knew what it meant to be powerless, but it wasn't the same. He mattered to her...but to no one else. He was kingdom fodder. If it came down to it, his life would be taken without hesitation—as long as a royal got to live a moment longer.

Maybe it was the taste of normalcy. Maybe it was the loss of his only purpose. But for the first time, he realised he wanted to live for himself—not for royals.

"I know about a thousand men who would disagree...and *one woman*," he said hoarsely.

That was when the betrayal hit him—heavy and unmistakable, pressing down over everything else. Olivja had always seemed above conformity, untouched by rules or ranks. But in the end, she'd turned him in.

The only reason he'd dared to lay hands on her was *because* he trusted her. He wouldn't make that mistake again.

She pulled back, meeting his eyes.
They both knew what this looked like—like Olivja was done with them. Brahms blamed himself, at least in part. But he hadn't imagined it would end like this.

"I'll speak with her—"

"I don't want you to." His voice cracked, emotion breaking through. "If I matter—like you say—then she'll come to me on her own. And if not...I'll know where I stand."

Adalja and Olivja were closer than he'd ever been. He knew if Adalja said a word, Olivja would crumble—for *her*. He wanted her to approach him on her own.

The princess bit her bottom, worry flickering in her eyes. Olivja wasn't the apologising type. Which meant this friendship was hanging by a thread.

She nodded faintly and stepped back into the hug. It was the only thing she could do—respect his wish.

Hugs from Adalja always meant something to him. He hadn't had many since they arrived at the Worthyn's. So he held on—despite how unlovable he felt.

His body relaxed. He wrapped an arm around her, pulling her close. Chin resting atop her head, he shut his eyes tight—fighting the tears rising fast behind them. The wounded knight's other hand rose, hesitant at first, and tangled into his princess' curls to anchor himself.

"I love you, Brahms." Her voice trembled as her arms curled around his ribs, holding tighter. She pressed her face into his chest, like she could shield them both from everything outside. "I'm glad beyond measure that you were there today."

Brahms stilled, taken aback by the sincerity in her voice. He chose instead to focus on the warmth of her embrace and the faint, familiar scent of cinnamon and snow that clung to her.

He exhaled slowly, "Aye, aye...I love you as well." His words were rough, but his hold tightened, his large hand settling protectively between her shoulder blades.

For a moment, there was nothing else. No Vincent. No Olivja. No kings, no orders. No expectations. Just the rise and fall of Adalja's breathing. Just the weight of her love, warm and real.

THREAD XXVIII

ᚦᛖ ᛒᚢᚱᛞᛖᚾᛋ ᛟᚠ ᚺᛖᛁᚱᛋ ᚦᛖ ᛒᚢᚱᛞᛖᚾᛋ ᛟᚠ ᚺᛖᛁᚱᛋ ᚦᛖ ᛒᚢᚱᛞᛖᚾᛋ

ᛟᛚᛁᚠᛃᚨ

EDITH GENTLY TWISTED the Dottir of Ragnarvik's hair into a fishtail braid, her wrinkled fingers working the thick hair masterfully. A dark brown gown with red trimmings loosely flowed to the floor, covering her bare feet. Olivja admired herself in the mirror, enjoying the darkness.

The heiress stood in front of the grand oval mirror, staring at herself as she thought about the recent traumas.

"Amma..." Olivja began quietly as a cold breeze from an open window caught a few strands of her hair. "Did you know them well?"

"No...but your mother and father did," Edith said beneath her breath, struggling to tie the end of her braid with a red ribbon.

Olivja's hair was long enough for the heiress to tie it off herself. She turned around, gently taking her braid from Edith. The older woman continued gently, a serene smile on her face as she marveled at her heiress.

"In a way I knew them as well, but only from what they told."

"And what did they tell?" Her interest was piqued. Olivja knew very little of her parents' individual relationships with the Pembrooks.

All she knew was that her father and Phillip were close; she had read their letters they had exchanged for the past ten years...That's how she got her letters to Adalja, by sneaking her own onto her father's messenger raven.

Edith sighed, reaching around Olivja to grab the small jewels that she had been instructed to hold. As the heiress handed them to her, she continued...

"The history between your parents and the Pembrooks is deep, all four of them were knots in the same net...I would not be surprised if your mother makes an appearance when she hears of their death."

"She would come 'ere?" Olivja scoffed, handing a final red jewel to her maid. "Hard to believe...she's no friend to any soul, least of all the Worthyns."

Edith stayed quiet and finished her accessories, stepping away to grab her fox-hide cloak, the auburn fur lining her hood and trim.

"Why ask me of the Pembrooks, child? Your heart knows them better than I ever have." Moving back to the Jarl's Dottir, she wrapped the cloak around her shoulders, fastening it with a bear claw button at her collarbone.

"I wish to avenge them...yet each time the thought crosses my heart, guilt strikes like a blade," She admitted bashfully. "I loved them...and then I hated them 'til their deaths. I know not how to feel—"

"Why must you feel any way at all?"

Olivja paused and stared blankly at her Amma as she considered it.

"We are complex, Olivja—never solely defined by our actions." Edith's voice was firm now, her gaze unwavering as she looked up at the Jarl's Dottir. Her hands gently gripped Olivja's biceps, offering both support and strength. "You seek praise of them, so your vengeance feels righteous. But tell me—does justice choose sides? Do the gods?"

Olivja remained silent, her eyes narrowed, as if weighing Edith's words.

"The Pembrooks were good people," Edith continued, her voice softening. "Simply victims of this wretched world, just as you."

Olivja's gaze lingered on the floor, troubled, before she lifted her eyes. "...So, you think I should help them as well?"

Edith's grip tightened slightly, her eyes narrowing with purpose. "Our people listen to the pull of their spirit. They trust the fire within them and walk paths forged by their own will—not weighed down by doubts or the chains of the unknown." She paused, as if considering her next words carefully.

"The Norns know you'll find your way. Now, all there is for you to do is...move forward."

The words settled heavily in Olivja's chest, the sacredness grounding her. Her Amma released her arm and stepped back, allowing Olivja space to process.

Olivja turned towards the mirror, her reflection staring back at her with new purpose. She felt the stirrings of a new destiny in her heart, one that would lead her to avenge the Pembrooks and win Adalja's heart.

She would fulfil this—*one way or another*. But the road ahead was unclear.

Avenge dead royals?
The idea seemed impossible—an act of defiance against whatever forces that had claimed their lives.

Edith's advice was meaningful, but dangerously reckless for someone whose heart was already so steadfast. Olivja didn't know where to begin, but the fire in her chest told her one thing for certain: she wouldn't stop until she found her way.

With her Amma by her side, Olivja was escorted through the narrow, stone-lined halls towards the grand dining room.

The morning still hung over her, a dark cloud that grew heavier with each step. As they reached the threshold of the dining hall, the familiar sounds of clinking cutlery and murmured conversations met her ears.

At the long, polished table, Elias and Adalja sat together, speaking in hushed tones, though their conversation seemed more a formality than anything truly intimate. Brahms stood a little farther away, his presence almost as imposing as the towering columns that lined the room.

Olivja's chest tightened, an unfamiliar sense of displacement sinking in. This was the same hall where she had once sat comfortably among them, but now, it felt like a world apart.

And Vincent—the only person who may have been interested in her presence—was nowhere to be found.

As she stepped into the room, all three of them turned their gaze towards her. It was like being examined by a tribunal, and each of them had a different verdict.

Adalja's eyes were filled with disappointment. Brahms' gaze was colder, edged with resentment, as though she had wronged him. Elias, though, couldn't even look at her. His eyes flickered towards the table, then to the far wall, avoiding her like she was some sort of dangerous animal...and she felt that way.

She was exposed, vulnerable in a way she had never experienced.
A wave of anger rose in her chest.

Edith, the steady presence at her side, took charge without asking. She pulled out a chair at the table—directly across from Adalja—and motioned for Olivja to sit. The action was too deliberate, as if Edith had made the decision for her that she couldn't quite make for herself.

Olivja sat stiffly, her body rigid with tension, immediately locking eyes with the princess. Adalja's gaze was sharp, her lips pressed together in a tight line—but her disappointment was evident.

It wasn't just in her eyes; it was in the way she held herself, the way she subtly turned her shoulder away—towards Elias. The room seemed to shrink as Brahms and Elias, like two quiet sentinels, continued to watch them, their stares heavy and full of unspoken words.

She hates me.
Olivja shook her head, tearing her eyes away.
They all hate me.

For a moment, she considered standing up and walking out. She hadn't realised how furious she was with them until this moment, seated beside them.

Her hands clenched into fists beneath the table, nails digging into her palms as anger pulsed through her veins.

She wanted to speak—say something, anything—but she wasn't sure where to start. The words were trapped somewhere between her heart and her throat, unwilling to break free. She wasn't sure if she was angry with them, with herself, or with the whole wretched situation they found themselves in.

Before she could speak, a maid approached her with a soft clink of porcelain, setting a small plate of a morning meal in front of her. The scent of warm bread and fruit wafted up, but Olivja barely noticed.

Without thinking, Olivja stood, her chair scraping loudly against the stone floor. She slammed her hands down on the table, and in that instant, the entire dining room seemed to hold its breath.

The air was thick, frozen. Her voice was louder than she intended, a raw, jagged thing that cut through the silence.

"I should not have done what I did. So be it. I cannot take back the blow—but I'll not pretend it meant nothing." The words left her lips with an almost painful finality, her cheeks flushed with the sting of embarrassment.

Her teeth clenched as she spoke, the sound of it grating against the stillness. She wasn't entirely sure who she was apologising to—perhaps all of them—but it felt like something she had to say. And yet, she couldn't ignore the hope that they would apologise to her in turn.

"I loved them as well," she added, her voice thickening. She swallowed hard, fighting the wave of emotion that threatened to rise in her chest.

No, she told herself. *Not here, not now.*

She fought back tears of rage, the bitter kind of grief that made her want to scream. "And so did my father. When you turned me away, you also turned him away...I was angry."

Adalja's eyes softened, glossing over, but she didn't speak. She kept her gaze fixed on Olivja, waiting for something more, some hint of remorse, some spark of understanding.

Olivja wanted to hear *something—anything*—that would make the weight in her chest feel a little lighter. But before she could look for the words that would change this moment, Elias spoke up, his voice gentle but firm.

"Your apology is not needed," he said with a sigh, his tone carrying an almost comforting weight. His eyes met hers briefly, the kindness in them palpable, though it wasn't quite enough to pierce through her anger. "We understand."

We.

Something inside Olivja snapped at the sound of his voice, the softness of it clashing with the bitterness that clung to her heart. She shot him a look that could've melted stone, a searing gaze full of contempt.

"I wasn't speaking to *you*, Eli," she snapped, her grip tightening so hard on her utensil that she thought it might snap in her hands. She practically growled the words through clenched teeth, her frustration bubbling to the surface. "Only to Adalja." She finished the sentence quickly, as though she had to spit it out before saying something she'd regret.

Her eyes remained fixed on the princess, whose expression had shifted into something sad—too sad for Olivja to bear.

The look in Adalja's eyes pierced through her, and Olivja couldn't stand it anymore. She turned her head away sharply, focussing on her plate, trying to keep the wrath from uncoiling.

But as the tension seemed ready to break completely—

BAM.

The sound of the dining doors crashing open cut through the stillness like thunder, and Olivja's head jerked up in surprise.

Vincent stood in the doorway, a wild look in his eyes and a stack of papers in his hands, hair loosely tied back. He strolled into the room, his presence almost too big for the space, like a stormfront rolling in.

"Ah, excellent. I'll not have to repeat myself," Vincent's voice boomed with unrestrained annoyance, and Olivja's posture relaxed.

Thank the gods.

Vincent strode to the table, making a beeline for the seat next to her, right across from Elias. Olivja sank back into her chair with a heavy sigh, a mixture of annoyance and, surprisingly, relief.

Was this moment ruined, or had it somehow been *saved* by Vincent's sudden entrance?

Without missing a beat, Vincent slammed the papers down onto the centre of the table with a loud thud, a slight grin spreading across his chiseled face.

"I have uncovered the hands behind the deaths of the Pembrooks."

The room fell silent.

As if on cue, Adalja stood from the table, her face drained of colour. Elias followed suit, his movements slow and deliberate as the shock registered. His hand silently moved to the princess' lower back, as if bracing her. The air seemed to crackle with tension as they processed what Vincent had said.

"Three witches from Perdyr," Vincent continued calmly despite the gravity of the situation. "They were slain as a warning to stop these unions. If we hadn't found them when we did, our darling Adalja would have met the same fate."

Olivja's breath caught in her throat. She hadn't expected this, not at all. Her heart skipped a beat, her mind racing as she tried to process the revelation. She never imagined it would unfold like this...and so soon.

Vincent slid the papers across the table to Elias, who hesitated before picking them up, his eyes scanning the documents with suspicion.

"How were they found?" Elias asked, narrowing his eyes, his gaze flickering over the parchment.

"The poison used led us to their village on the outskirts of Perdyr...I had the Wise Man check to be sure," Vincent replied, his words precise, almost too calm given the circumstances.

The Wise Man was their local herbalist, able to trace and dissect such a thing.

Olivja's stomach twisted. She felt a sinking sensation, as though her entire world had just been turned upside down.

This was supposed to be *her* fate. Her path was already set, and now it was crumbling like the bread on her plate.

"And if you still doubt me, brother—those wretched women confessed the moment they were found. Told my scout it was their brew. Their wicked work," Vincent finished, a note of satisfaction creeping into his voice.

The room remained frozen in stunned silence, but Olivja couldn't focus on anything except the sharp, biting realisation that this discovery—this truth—would change everything...would *ruin* everything.

Olivja barely glanced at her meal as the discovery settled over her like a thick fog. The food, once inviting and warm, had lost all appeal. She pushed the plate aside, her mind consumed by a rush of conflicting emotions.

Her eyes watered, but not for the same reason as Adalja's. She wasn't mourning the Pembrooks the way Adalja had, but rather the death of her own dreams—her own purpose.

"They admitted to it?" Brahms spoke up, his voice full of fragile hope as he stepped closer to the table, his eyes shining with desperate optimism.

"They deny it now that they're in shackles," Vincent scoffed, leaning back with pride as he lifted a chalice of wine. "After all, fear has a way of reshaping the truth."

She couldn't stay silent. The need to speak was unbearable, and she didn't even know why she said it:

"Wouldn't the rival jarldom take pride in killing the Pembrooks?"

Her voice was heavy with suspicion, a challenge thrown into the mix, hoping—no, *needing*—there to be a hole in his story. The words hung in the air, unsettling the room.

Everyone turned to her with a mix of confusion and disbelief, as if she had broken some unwritten rule.

"I only mean..." Olivja nervously continued, pushing through the silence. "If they know they're to be executed, why not proudly announce their involvement?" Her words were sharp, cold.

Vincent's face darkened, and he scoffed.

"Had they escaped, they might've celebrated their betrayal. But now that they're in chains, their oaths to Perdyr mean little." He shot her a look of disbelief, his gaze bitter. "Pride such as yours is rare, Liv," he continued, and the barb stung, but Olivja didn't flinch.

Olivja knew that Norse loyalty ran deep...so his accusations—that Perdyr people were cowardly, bothered her deeply—even if they were their enemies.

Elias handed the papers to Adalja, whose gaze was still fixed on the pages, though she seemed unable to process them.

"The execution is set for the morrow," Vincent continued, his voice steady despite the chaos surrounding them. "The knights post word of it as we speak."

Olivja's heart twisted.

The morrow? So soon?
This was supposed to be her moment—*her* redemption. And now it was slipping through her fingers like sand. Right into Vincent's hands.

Ever the hero. Even when she wished for him not to be.

"And where are they?" Olivja couldn't keep the bitterness out of her voice, the helplessness rising in her chest. She refused to believe it. She had to find something...but she was grasping at straws.

Vincent crossed his arms over his chest, still grasping his chalice. He looked almost smug, as if his work was done.

"Locked away...they're witches, after all." He shrugged, as though the matter was settled. "But worry not, every soul will have a chance to see them before they die...even their foolish gods."

Olivja's mind spun.

Witches? The word meant something far deeper to her than anyone else in the room, and it gutted her.

Her mother was a witch...she was raised as one in her early years. She shook her head, hands clenching tighter.

Adalja's voice was a whisper, but it hit Olivja with the force of a wave.
"...I did not believe the day would come..." The princess' tear-streaked face was a mirror to the devastation in the heiress' chest.

But Olivja couldn't allow herself to feel sympathy. Not yet. Not when everything she had fought for had been snatched from her.

"Believe it, Princess," Vincent said with a new, almost fanatical intensity, leaning forward across the table.

His eyes gleamed with something darker now, a fervor that sent a shiver down Olivja's spine.

"Avenging your parents will bring me the greatest pride," he flattered Adalja, and for a brief moment, they shared a meaningful glance—one that made Olivja's stomach twist painfully.

It was too much. Olivja couldn't stand it anymore. Her heart was slowly crushed with each word spoken. The taste of bitterness in her mouth was overwhelming. She didn't belong here. She couldn't even look at them anymore.

Her lungs forgot to breathe again.

The rest of the meal continued around her, but Olivja was no longer present. She absentmindedly poked at her plate, pushing the berries around with a numb gaze, unable to hear their voices. She wanted to scream, but instead, she sat in silence, feeling lost.

Once everyone had excused themselves, she stood, her chair scraping across the stone floor.

She left the dining room without another word, pulling the hood of her cloak over her head to shield her from the cold gaze of the others. Her footsteps echoed in the empty halls, steady and purposeful, though her mind was a whirlwind.

Trust the fire.

Her amber eyes burned with a quiet flame beneath the hood as she walked towards her next destination.

The Dungeons.

She didn't know what she was doing, but Amma told her to believe in herself...That's what she was going to do.

She casually strode down the halls. She wanted to see these *so-called* witches for herself.

Her family respected witches—Völvas they called them—but knowing more about them was limited to those who practised. Her mother was one, which meant in some way, Olivja was one as well...perhaps that was part of the reason she was pulled to their cells.

But as she reached the dungeons, she caught sight of a knight in blackened leathers and chainmail, standing post at the rounded door. She slipped behind a pillar, catching her breath. Of course the killers would be heavily guarded.

So she waited, for hours, peeking around the stone. Passing knights knew better than to interrupt her or question her—they knew her well as the defiant Norsewoman.

She ended up sitting on the ground, slumped in exhaustion as she waited. *Gods, she could never be a knight.*

But then—

"*So this is where you've been hiding from me?*"

Liv gasped, crawling on her hands and knees to peek around the stone. She knew that voice. *Kai*—one of Vincent's knights.

There, at the dungeon door, the blonde-haired man had come up, in polished silver armour, his helmet tucked beneath his arm. His other arm, however, was extended, gripping the top of the dungeon door. His stance hovered over the black-leathered guard, head tilted.

"*If I were hiding...you wouldn't have found me.*" The short one glanced up, his head tilting ever so slightly. His dark hood fell away, and a sharp smirk glinted—one that seemed sharper than any blade the man might have carried.

"*Then perhaps I should drag you off somewhere darker—give you a proper place to hide,*" Kai murmured, voice low and seductive in a way she had never quite heard from him before.

Olivja covered her mouth with her hand, an open-mouthed smile on her lips. *Of course men stir your blood, Kai.*

The man in the leathers shifted, paused, and then reached out, taking a firm hold of the front of Kai's armour, dragging him back from the dungeon door and off to their *dark corner*.

If not for the pressing matters, she would have followed them. But she took the opportunity and crawled the rest of the way to the dungeon door, her gown trailing behind her, picking up sediment like a mop. When she reached it, she stood, cracked it open and slithered inside.

She descended the dungeon steps, her fingertips trailing across the cold stone. She reminisced about all the times spent there as a child...and how silly and dangerous it had been.

No wonder she was so rowdy. The memory pulled a scoff from her throat as she stepped into the open dungeon floor.

She stepped carefully, taking note of the empty cells, nosily peeking into the ones with other prisoners.

And then she found the cell with three women.
They were dressed all the same. Black gowns, fur cloaks, long dark hair. They all turned in unison, their dreadful expressions widening at the sight of her.

She paused. Stared. And then spoke.

"They call you witches..." Olivja said bravely, speaking to them in Norse—if they were truly Völur, they would understand it.

Taking a deep breath, she pushed forward, stepping closer to the bars. *"Is it true?"*

"Highborn Olivja...Dottir of Solvig, child of fate..." the middle völva straightened, taking a careful step towards the bars. *"You have come to save us."*

A sting of relief and upset hit her. It was clear they were Völur, they were Norse. Vincent was telling the truth.

"I have asked you a question," Olivja uttered, her breath quickening as anticipation rose in her veins.

A second völva rose from her crouch, pushing back her hood as she approached the bars. *"Yes, honourable one,"* she said, her brown eyes steady with confidence. *"We are what they claim...but we would never forsake the ancients, as they suggest."*

The immediate denial of the murder shook Olivja to the core. She believed them in an instant. It was in her blood to trust, fear, and respect Völur.

While other cultures shunned them, casting them as demonic or unnatural, the Norsemen understood the truth of the Völur—their deep reverence for nature, order, and fate. But their sacredness could not prove intention alone.

She stood there, her hands clenched into fists beneath her cloak, trying to suppress the uneasy emotions swirling inside her.

"Then the poison was not concocted by your hands?" she asked, her voice steady but edged with a quiet force.

The third völva slowly lifted her head, her gaze drifting towards the iron door. Her hood obscured her eyes, but Olivja could see the tear-streaked cheeks and the flushed nose—her face was faintly glowing in the dim lantern light, like stardust caught in shadows.

"I did. Alone, Highborne..." the witch's voice was weak, almost a whisper, as she addressed her with such respect. She seemed to collapse into herself, her words heavy with guilt as she quietly cried. *"My sisters carry no guilt—"*

Before she could finish, footsteps echoed down the stone corridor. Olivja turned to see Elias entering the dungeon floor, his hood falling back to his shoulders, leaving only a mask to cover his expression. His gaze met hers immediately, a silent curiosity passing between them.

He approached, cloak flourishing behind him, and took a quick look at the imprisoned women before looking back at Olivja with a tilt of his head. "You've come to question them?" he asked quietly, lowering his brow. "...Or *befriend*?"

She took a deep breath, truly wanting nothing to do with Elias at a time like this.

"You came here as well, Elias—I could ask the same of you." Her tone was full of resentment; all she felt around him now was jealousy, anger, and abandonment.

"Perhaps I followed you. We've yet to speak of the slap you gave me." Elias cocked an eyebrow.

"*Ha*! Do you intend to punish me for it?" she taunted, tossing back her hood to match his. "...I have nothing more to say to you, Elias. I know where I stand."

Elias sighed at her, his sad eyes the only thing she could dissect. He stepped closer, glancing over at the celled women. "I seek only to know the truth of what they've done, and—while we're here—what *I've* done to earn your anger."

"Don't trust your own blood? I'll be sure to let Vincent know that..." she scoffed while occasionally glancing at the women. Apparently, she didn't trust him as much as she thought either.

"I have little trust in how *swiftly* they were found," Elias said matter-of-factly. "Like you, I thought it best to hear it from their own lips."

"Well, your brother seems certain," Olivja whispered, voice wavering in the uncertainty the thought brought, tossing her glare to the stone floor.

"You fear he is wrong?" Elias asked, shifting slightly.

"I fear what may happen if he is wrong, Your Grace," Olivja mumbled weakly, slowly raising her angry eyes to his. "Blame kills more than any poison or blade...it's the darkest curse a mouth can speak."

She had no more to say to him, nor to the Völur. She couldn't speak with them in private any longer now that the Worthyn man was present. Perhaps, if she found a moment, she would try again...but she knew she didn't have much time if the execution was planned for the next day.

Olivja's heart ached as she turned away, leaving the white-haired prince with the dark-haired witches, her heart swirling with hope.

Perhaps, the true killer was still out there.

Thread XXIX

ᚦᛖ ᛒᚢᚱᛞᛖᚾᛋ ᛟᚠ ᚺᛖᛁᚱᛋ ᚦᛖ ᛒᚢᚱᛞᛖᚾᛋ ᛟᚠ ᚺᛖᛁᚱᛋ ᚦᛖ ᛒᚢᚱᛞᛖᚾᛋ

ᚨᛞᚨᛚᛃᚨ

Adalja glanced up at the cloud-choked sky, her eyes tracing the leaden curtain over the winter-blanketed forest beyond the castle grounds. The light was dim, heavy, as if the heavens themselves were weighed down by sorrow.

Her breath rose in soft puffs as she sat curled in the window nook, watching the way snow clung to the branches like abandoned spirits.

A low sigh escaped her lips, and for a fleeting moment, she entertained the thought that her mother and father had spoken to their God—perhaps begged him to paint the world in mourning shades.

The storm felt personal. A message. A veil. And in that cold tapestry of snow and silence, she allowed herself a smile, imagining her parents watching from beyond, knowing their killers had finally been found.

Three women. Three *witches*.

Her mind, like her curls, was untamed—two loose braids hung down her back, but wild strands sprang from them, dusted with static and frustration, framing cheeks pinkened by the chill and her restless thoughts.

She still didn't understand. Why take her parents? What was there to gain from such cruelty? It wouldn't stop her marriage...if anything it only made it all the more important. Even now, with the culprits caught, unease clung to her skin like damp wool. There was relief, yes—but also grief, sharp and splintered.

She exhaled and shut her eyes for a moment, her fingers twisting the fabric of her skirt in her lap. But peace was short-lived. The door creaked open with no warning, shattering the quiet.

Prince Elias stood at the threshold.

He was a vision of winter himself—his black cloak powdered with snow, hair tousled from the wind. Concern creased his brow as he took in her tear-stained face, small in the window where he had left her hours before. His hands curled at his sides, leather gloves pulled taut at his knuckles.

Her teeth sank into her cheek. There were moments lately where she recognised herself in him. In subtle gestures, in silences, in the ways they both bore their grief like a crown too heavy for their heads. And that brought her a comfort she hadn't known she needed.

He said nothing at first, simply stepping further into the room. She nodded slowly, her knees pulled up to her chest again, a quiet resignation settling over her.

"What is the reason for your surprise visit this evening?" she asked finally, her voice light but hollow, floating like frost on glass.

Elias' ever-green eyes met hers—so often clouded by pain now.
"To see how you fared, My Lady...and..."

He moved to sit beside her on the wide nook's ledge, a quiet habit they'd created together, careful not to disturb the stillness too much. She shifted slightly, resting her chin on her knees again as her braids fell forward, framing her like twin ropes.

"And?" she asked, barely above a whisper.

His gaze lingered on her, thoughtful and far away. For a moment he looked as though he might not answer.

"...I thought perhaps...if I spoke softly enough, you might smile for me again," he said at last, voice gentle and sincere, a curve tugging at the corners of his mouth. "Even if it be but for a short while."

She studied him, eyes narrowing with curiosity. In a time like this—how could he tease? She tilted her head, a touch of disbelief ghosting across her features.

"Such bold words," she replied dryly, though her voice held no venom. "I don't believe the finest jester even could—I mean no disrespect to your humor, Your Grace."

She spared him a soft laugh, one that didn't quite reach her chest, but it was something. His responding smile was quiet, knowing. He seemed content just to see her try.

"No? You doubt my abilities?" he teased, brow raised. "I can be *quite* persuasive...unless of course, you'd rather I get the *real* Jester in here..." He leaned back slightly, feigning offence with a shrug.

"No!" Adalja gasped, eyes wide, hand darting to his forearm. "Not that thing—please—" She swallowed, panic rising. "Elias, why should I smile, hm? Three women are soon to be tried by—"

"*Has she said yes yet?*"

The interruption startled her. Her head whipped towards the door, where Brahms stood with a crooked smile, his casual stance framed by the doorway. His silver armour was gone, replaced by snow-damp, simpler clothes—soft, warm. A man returned to his truer self.

Adalja scoffed, a breath of reluctant amusement leaving her lips.
"The two of you are plotting against me?"

Brahms strolled in, ruffling snow off his cloak as Elias chuckled beside her. The men exchanged a glance—one of easy camaraderie—and something in Adalja's chest loosened. The idea that her prince and her knight might actually become friends, allies...It meant more to her than she could name.

"I *believe* she was about to say yes," Elias grinned.

Adalja eyed them both, her lips curling slowly into something near a smirk. They looked far too pleased with themselves. "Yes to...what, exactly?" she uttered.

"To going to Fairtide with us...?" the prince hummed, lips rolling inwards.

She gasped.
The offer hung in the air like bait she wasn't sure she should bite.
Gods, she wanted nothing more than to escape with them...

"Well?" Brahms prompted, eyes bright. "What do you say, Princess? You owe me a puzzle-jug." He waggled his brows and Adalja laughed, a real one this time.

"Puzzle-jug?" Elias asked, curiosity sparked.

"Adalja was in this white—"

"*Brahms*," she hissed, cheeks blooming with colour as she cut him off.

Brahms threw up his hands in mock surrender. "What? 'Tis a celebration!"

Adalja's smile faded.

"Celebration?" she echoed, voice sharp.

"Yes, Princess. Your parents will be resting easier now. Justice is close." His words were meant as comfort, but her expression darkened.

Celebration? How could anyone celebrate more death? Relief was not the same as joy. And she could not pretend that the trial of three more lives was something to toast.

Elias, sensing the shift in her mood, stepped in quietly. "On the contrary. It's to ease your mind, My Lady. Something to help you forget—for just a while. Be free."

Free.

The word lingered.

Without her mother's hand pressing down on her every move, without the weight of her father's expectations, she was freer now than she'd ever been. And yet, it tasted bitter-sweet.

"I suppose..." she drawled, voice teasing, her mouth curving into a slow, reluctant smile. "I find myself yielding to your wishes." She raised her hands in surrender and swung her legs off the nook. Elias was already rising, hand extended to help her up.

"I'll lead," he said with a wink, and she took his hand. "Perhaps I shall surprise you and conquer the puzzle yet?" he added, tugging his cowl and mask back into place.

She looked up at him, the smile still clinging to her lips. "You cannot conquer that which you do not comprehend."

The three of them—princess, knight, and prince—walked from the room together, Adalja at the centre of their protective orbit. Her fingers fidgeted at her side, mind still drifting. She found herself thinking of Olivja, of her sharp tongue and even sharper heart, and the chasm that still remained between them.

Guilt pressed against her chest like a blade.

Still, for now...she walked forward. Eager to forget it all.
Even if that meant her too.

THEY ARRIVED BY CARRIAGE at ghostly Fairtide, let out before Odin's Horn. The town, emptier than *Skuggadagr*, had returned to its usual vacancy.

A soft veil of snow blanketed the roof of the tavern and, despite the emptiness around them, the amber glow seeped from beneath the window shutters, telling of life and warmth.

Adalja sighed with a smile, hair quickly sprinkled with snowflakes, starkly showing against her dark curls. Elias stepped in front of her and pulled up the hood of her cloak, tugging at it to secure it.

"Come now, lovebirds, it's freezing out here," Brahms teased, a touch of sourness in his tone. He stepped towards the tavern, pushing the door open with his backside, eyeing the two royals.

Adalja stepped away with swiftness, eager to enter, and walked into the warmth of the tavern. Elias soon followed with a deep breath, stepping into the candle-lit space. The air was thick with the smell of roasted meat and spilled ale, and the hum of lively chatter mingled with the sharp clink of mugs.

"Well, this is...*charming*," the prince said as the door shut. A few townspeople glanced their way, silencing some of the tavern folk.

Adalja felt shy, almost humiliated, knowing the whispers were all about her. She looked down—until Brahms pulled her towards the farthest corner where the barrels of ale waited.

"Three tankards of ale and a puzzle-jug, my friend." His voice was deeper, as if trying to impress the burly man behind the counter, sliding across a small pile of copper coins. Brahms added, "Hold a moment...you've fought in the war, haven't you?" he asked with a smirk.

The large man grunted with a nod, chuckling while slamming down three larger-than-Adalja's head tankards.

"*Brahms*," Adalja hissed, slapping his arm with a warning in her eyes as she turned to face him.

"What?" he asked, feigning innocence as he leaned on the counter with one arm. "I wasn't wrong."

"Your mouth runs faster than your mind sometimes," Adalja laughed, surprised at his calm demeanor, noticing how at ease he seemed tonight. She wished she could feel the same.

She glanced around the tavern, growing uncomfortable with the stolen glances from the patrons. What was once a place of comfort now felt foreign...like she no longer belonged. Adalja was farther from the person she dreamed of being than ever before.

"*Oi*," Brahms called, his voice lowering as his fingers suddenly cupped her chin, forcing her gaze to meet his. "You are to relax tonight, dove. That's an order. No one here is in their right minds, so...Simply be as you are, as you *always are* when we are here."

Adalja smiled softly, heart swelling at his words. But as she opened her mouth to protest, he shook his head—still holding her chin, flustering her further.

"You're 'Adalja the Free Woman' tonight. Not Princess, nor *Queen*," he cooed with a wink.

"No, *please* don't," Adalja groaned, grimacing at '*queen*', a title she wasn't sure she'd ever fully accept.

Brahms chuckled, nodding before continuing. "This is a good thing—*trust me*. I'll make sure you're both safe tonight." He glanced towards Elias, who was trying hard to fit in among the unruly patrons while also desperately saving their table.

The sight made Adalja snicker.

Brahms took a deep breath, settling back into his serious tone. "Aye, you can cry later. Tonight, we get properly muddled and maybe even dance about it—let's mourn like vikings do!"

Adalja let out a shaky breath, shooting a glare at him. "*You cannot use that term here, Brahms—*"

Brahms rolled his eyes with laughter as his grip shifted to her cheeks.
"Let us try this once more..." he said, squeezing her cheeks together in tandem with his words like she was some broken puppet. "*Yes, sir, you're always right—*"

Adalja smacked his hand away with a playful glare before he could finish. He leaned up against the railing, crossing his hand beneath his chest with a stupid grin on his lips.

"*Ah*, there she is...like a true Norse-warrior!" he cheered sarcastically. Adalja rolled her eyes—but the smirk on her lips stayed, unshaken.

Brahms nodded towards the ale. "Come...before our prince gives our table to a brute."

Adalja giggled as she picked up a tankard and the puzzle-jug, and Brahms held the other two.

"Certain you've got that? With that unpolished step of yours?" he teased, raising a brow.

"Oh, hush," Adalja shot back with a snicker, "unless you'd like me to push you down myself." She placed her mug on the table where Elias sat. The prince curiously looked around with wide eyed excitement—or perhaps paranoia.

"Don't tell me you've never been to a tavern, Your Grace?" Adalja cooed, her tone a mix of shock and amusement as she sat beside him at the round wooden table.

Elias flushed at the question, clearing his throat while Brahms set down their drinks.

"I—" Elias hesitated, then cleared his throat again. "Perhaps...once. But that was a long time ago, Princess. Places like this are hidden gems in Worthyn." He smiled sheepishly, cheeks pink.

Adalja found herself warming at the reaction, enjoying the rare shift in the usually composed prince. He only grew more bashful at Adalja's affectionate gaze.

"*Hm,*" Adalja hummed, a mischievous smirk tugging at her lips, "How lucky we are to grant you this time then." The two locked eyes, though swiftly broken by Brahms' voice.

"Who's the first victim of the night?" Brahms asked, his tone playful, eyes gleaming with anticipation as he looked between the two while holding the puzzle-jug vase.

"I think it must be our princess." Elias motioned with his head, surprising her with his choice. "Word is you're quite the champion," he added with a knowing look at Brahms, who sported a sheepish smile.

Adalja glared at Brahms, but only for a moment before she relinquished her pride, standing with a deep breath.

Brahms handed her the vase—its neck carved with intricate holes. The goal was to drink as much wine as possible without spilling...though of course, the game was impossible and always ended in disaster.

"My dress..." Adalja trailed off, glancing down. The light blue fabric would be ruined by the mess of the game. She'd never cared with Brahms—but Elias? She didn't want to ruin whatever image he had of her.

"Your gown matters little, sweetling," Elias said softly, raising an eyebrow. "'Tis your heart we mend tonight."

He was right.
Tonight was about forgetting, about relaxing, and what better way to do that than to lose her senses to wine.

"DRINK! DRINK! DRINK!" Brahms chanted, banging his hands against the table, attracting too much attention for her liking. Elias watched with a gleam in his eye, tilting his head to watch her methods.

With an eye roll and a daring smile, she cupped her hands around the neck, sealing the holes with her palms, and carefully tipped back the vase. She drank slowly—not a sip, but the entire carafe emptied in one go. As intended, the wine spilled down her palms, arms, and neck—staining her maroon.

With a loud gasp—and maybe even a small burp—she finished. The surrounding patrons erupted into laughter and cheers as the princess, or rather the queen, set down the empty vase. Adalja fell into a fit of coughing and giggling. Elias watched with admiration, the blush still settling on his cheekbones.

Brahms raised his tankard, grinning as he turned to Elias. "Now it is our turn, Elias. Share a drink with me."

Elias smirked, and nodded quietly. They raised their tankards and Brahms scooted closer, looping their arms at the elbows. They both brought the mugs to their lips and tilted with shared grins, drinking the entirety in one fell swoop.

Brahms had to pause, coughing alongside Adalja who was still recovering, while Elias was the last to release air. When he finished, the prince let out a loud burp, sending them all into fits of laughter.

They drank again, taking turns with the holey contraption. Adalja's heart raced with anticipation—eager to feel alive again.

As the night wore on, their laughter drowned out every other conversation in the tavern. Adalja's light blue dress was now streaked with purple stains from their wild drinking games, and for the first time in a long while, she felt a reckless sense of freedom.

Her gaze drifted to the empty seat, and a quiet grief crept in—wordless, but heavy. No matter how much she tried to enjoy the moment, her mind remained stuck. She wished Olivja could see her like this—living freely, something the heiress always seemed to do so effortlessly.

She tried to appreciate the warmth of the tavern, even as her mind wandered. Lost in the haze of her thoughts, Adalja's gaze drifted to the men.

At the centre of Odin's horn, Brahms twirled Elias with a drunken flourish, their fingers locked tight as they spun between tables and swaying bodies. Elias' laugh was breathless, his boots slipping slightly on the tavern floor, but Brahms caught him with a hand to the waist—close, steady, smug.

The two moved in rhythm now, chest to chest, as if the ale had melted away the world and left only them, flushed and grinning in the hearthlight.

Elias, usually so reserved, seemed lighter, his expression open and unguarded. His eyes held a warmth and intensity that made Adalja's chest tighten, though she couldn't quite place why.

Brahms, ever mischievous, leaned in to whisper something private to Elias, a secret shared only between them. The two of them grinned widely, unable to tear their gaze from one another. Brahms' eyes sparkled with a look that Adalja had seen a thousand times before, but this time it was...different.

The moment Elias noticed her watching, however, he recoiled slightly from Brahms, his playful demeanor shifting. Brahms, his brow knitting in confusion, followed Elias' line of sight and spotted Adalja sitting alone at the table.

Without hesitation, the prince straightened himself, his charm effortlessly slipping into place as he made his way towards her.

"Adalja," Elias called in his slurred speech as he waltzed up with a slightly swayed step, hands reaching out for her.

"*My Lady...*" He beckoned her, curling his pointer finger back towards himself a couple of times with a drunken smirk on his lips, his cat-eyes set on her.

Adalja's gaze slowly drifted from his outstretched hand to his eyes—half-lidded, coal-lined, alluring, with a drunken gloss. She giggled, shaking her head, unwilling to slide off her chair—afraid of how the wine would hit her when she stood.

"I fear I've become too merry to move, My Lord," she mused, taking a final sip. Warmth spread through her limbs. "I'll stay right here."

And, as though anticipating her rejection, he took another slow step towards her, his presence pulling her deeper into the moment.

"You break my heart, Princess." Elias pressed a hand dramatically to his chest, wounded. "And yet, still, I would crawl to you," he teased, closing the distance until her eyes were level with his chest.

Adalja's world blurred around the edges, her nerves bundling with the warmth of the spirits coursing through her, leaving her feeling both carefree and oddly comfortable. His finger found her chin, tilting her head upwards to meet his gaze more directly.

"What manner of mischief is this?" she asked, her voice airy, as she leaned slightly towards him.

She knew this was far too much affection for unmarried suitors to share in public. But the Norse never cared...

And she didn't want to push him away. Not when his warmth was something she secretly appreciated.

Elias chuckled softly, tilting his head as his eyes roamed her face, taking her in fully. "I'm simply admiring the woman I'll be marrying," he said, feigning nonchalance as he wet his lips.

At the same time, he slowly squatted in front of her. "Tell me what you make of it, my love," he hummed, punctuating his flirt with a hand trailing up her skirt—far too forward, far too drunk.

Adalja blushed and let his hand linger, silently challenging him to see how far he'd really go. But as they stared into each other's eyes, her stomach twisted with nerves and she conceded. She playfully swatted away his wandering hand.

"You've a silver tongue, sweet prince—one that surely sees much practice," she teased, reaching for the pitcher again. As she moved, Elias caught her outstretched hand with his free one, tugging her towards him with the kind of strength he typically hid.

She stumbled out of of her chair, landing against his chest, laughter escaping her lips as the world tilted briefly around them. His quiet chuckle vibrated beneath her cheek, grounding her. Without letting go, he shifted his grip—his fingertips traced a line up her palm, slow and deliberate, sending a trail of chills along her skin before his fingers gently laced through hers.

"Elias!" Adalja gasped, her voice tinged with shock.

Her cheeks burned with a heat she could scarcely contain as she pressed her free hand firmly against his chest. She pulled back enough to meet his gaze, her eyes wild and unsure, until his arm slid around her waist, drawing her back to him.

Flustered, Adalja yielded to his touch, allowing him to lead her further from the table and into a playful sway, the music from the tavern wrapping around them like a gentle spell.

"What? Not *interested* in a dance with me—*hic*—my girl?" Elias teased, leaning close enough that his lips brushed her ear. She could barely hear him over the music—but she felt him clearly.

"How dare you question me?" Adalja laughed, but it was short lived as he gripped both of her hands, pushing her outward before pulling her back in with a smooth, practised step.

She sighed deeply and shrugged, realising she couldn't escape the dance—and didn't entirely want to.

"Curse your persuasion..." she trailed off with a giggle, her eyes twinkling as Elias spun them in a wide circle, swaying them both to the rhythm.

She smiled up at him, and he smiled back, picking up the pace. He danced them in a flower-like pattern, spinning her out only to yank her back into him. As she fell into his chest once more, her stiffness melted. But, just as it did, his face lowered to hers—mere inches from her parted lips, her breath heavy.

"May I?" Brahms' voice interrupted, deeper from his own spirits, but more tense than she'd expected.

He pulled at Adalja, but she held fast to Elias' hand, tugging Brahms in towards them instead, eager to dance in a carefree circle.

Laughing, they pulled him along, spinning in circles as if they were children in a sunlit meadow. Adalja revelled in the freeing sensation, dancing with the two men she adored.

As they swirled to the lively tavern music, others joined in—young and old alike, eager to share the joy. But soon the spinning and the warmth of bodies unsettled the princess' stomach, and the room began to tilt around her.

With a stumble, she broke away from the dance, her steps unsteady, and sought a quiet space to sit and collect herself, her head swimming from both the drink and the whirlwind of movement.

Then, a mention of Olivja caught her ear—a thread of conversation from nearby women. Her heart hammered instantly. Adalja's brow furrowed as she caught the cruel words.

"*She's* to wed him? I cannot fathom what he sees in her," one woman scoffed. "He could find better by candlelight and coin, *right over there...*" She pointed to a hay-covered bench in the far corner. The women erupted into laughter.

Adalja's sights locked onto them across the jumbled crowd, a table away. The dim-lighting casted shadows across her pale frame, bathing her in a darkness that mirrored the anger she hardly felt.

"If he's not cautious, he'll find himself *cursed*—and worse, our entire kingdom with him."

"How many times can one lie with a *witch* before she casts her spell upon you in the night?" The women drunkenly burst into shrill laughter again, but Adalja had heard enough.

They spoke of Olivja as if she were nothing more than a foreign woman tainted by witchcraft, and the anger boiled over inside her. She stormed towards the noble women's table without a second thought.

The tavern quieted as Adalja's voice rang out, slurred but sharp.
"You dare disrespect the heiressh of Ragn'rvik?!"

The woman stuttered, her confidence crumbling before Adalja's glare. "Y-your Majesty Pembrook, no...you must have mis—"

"Misheard?" Adalja's voice cut through the air. "I could have your *head* for yer lies—and more for dis'on'ring royalty."

"Please, Princess Adalja, we did not mean—"

"*Queen*," Adalja corrected, her tone icy, the power of her heritage—and wine—surging through her. The women shrank back, but she didn't let up.
"Queen Pembrook."

Elias and Brahms appeared at her side in a flash, concern on their faces, but they didn't intervene. Adalja's gaze flicked to them for a moment before she returned to the women with renewed fury.

"Ha—the *Queen* has a soft spot for *vikings*!" she mocked for the last time.

Without thinking, Adalja snatched one of their mugs and splashed its contents in the woman's face, splattering ale across their fronts and even a few pagans seated behind them. The tavern gasped in unison.

Elias and Brahms looked equally stunned, though Brahms smirked in quiet approval—even if he fought it. Adalja, stood tall, eyes flashing with pride and surprise.

The woman, dripping in ale, stood with a contorted face and squinted eyes.

"How *dare you*?!" she yelled out in outrage as she gasped and wiped her face with her dress sleeve.

But Adalja knew she was in no kind of danger; her status as royalty made her untouchable.

Elias gripped the princess by her bicep, yanking her smaller, swaying frame into his chest. "Apologies, ladies...carry on!" he called with a smile, holding her close as he slowly backed away from the table.

Once far enough from the mess, Elias stepped back, holding her shoulders.

"*Adalja*...!" he hissed, his lips curling up into a silent smirk, unable to deny the enjoyment of watching his usually kept princess act so ruthlessly.

"*What*?!" Adalja snapped, brows raised, eyes swimming in her drunken haze. "Didn't you hear th—"

"We should go," Brahms' voice cut through the tension, his hands nudging them both towards the door.

The stares of curious and judgmental patrons made her stomach churn, but before she could think about it, dizziness hit her like a wave. She stumbled past them, slammed through the door, and collapsed at the side of the tavern, retching into the cold night. Her dress caught a good portion of the mess.

"*Oh...gods...*" she muttered weakly, feeling humiliated but not sorry, not at all.

Brahms' laughter rang out behind her as they burst through the door, cutting through the discomfort. "I do not believe my EYES! AHA!"

Adalja glared, lips pouting, her face flushed with cold and embarrassment. "Look'away..." she slurred, but Brahms only laughed harder

Elias moved to her side, his arm slipping around her waist to steady her. "Easy, sweet one," he murmured, voice thick with drunken concern—yet still smiling. "I've got you."

The dizziness still spun, but she leaned into him, feeling his warmth and support.

Brahms dramatically called out, *"GOD!! HEAR US!* Call out this *beast* inhabiting our dear Princess!" His voice echoed in the empty town and across the seas.

Adalja and Elias both grumbled, "*Silence*," in unison.
She could feel Elias' chuckle rumbling in his chest.

Brahms chuckled, wiping tears from his eyes. "*Ah,* I yield, I yield...he wouldn't listen to us sinners anyhow," he said as he got into the carriage with them, sighing in satisfaction.

Adalja, still dizzy, collapsed onto the seat, her head resting in Elias' lap.

"Heavens, Adalja, I've seen kingdoms fall with more grace than you," Brahms teased, but she only groaned in response.

"M'a force of *nature*," she muttered, a slurred giggle muffled against his stomach, making Elias laugh. As the carriage lurched, Adalja winced, clutching Elias' thigh. "Make the spinning stop, *pleasssse.*"

He held her tighter, fingers combing back wild curls from her face. "Perhaps lying down isn't the wisest choice, My Lady...though I think we've found the court's true danger," he teased, flashing Brahms a grin.

"Not witches or warriors—it is *this* woman after spirits."

A small giggle slipped out despite herself.

The rest of the ride blurred—her head swimming somewhere between sleep and nausea.

When they finally reached the castle, Brahms offered to help her, but Elias shook his head.

"She's my responsibility," Elias said steadily, scooping her into his arms without effort. Her arms instinctively curled around his neck, seeking balance and warmth. "I'll see to her tonight," he added, his tone softening as he glanced at her flushed face.

"How kind and brave of you," Brahms laughed softly. "...though I'd suggest a healer—and a bucket," he said with a teasing grin, eyeing her pale, queasy face.

Elias smiled. "Come—before our God smites us for our sins tonight."

Thread XXX

ᚦᛖ ᛒᚢᚱᛞᛖᚾᛊ ᛟᚠ ᚺᛖᛁᚱᛊ ᚦᛖ ᛒᚢᚱᛞᛖᚾᛊ ᛟᚠ ᚺᛖᛁᚱᛊ ᚦᛖ ᛒᚢᚱᛞᛖᚾᛊ

ᛟᛚᛁᚠᛃᚨ

A soft knock jolted the heiress where she sat, loosely covered by her fur-covered bedding. Edith, who had been nalbinding in the corner, stood from her chair and approached the door. The maid's long white nightgown flowed with a soft draft that flowed into the room as she opened the bedroom door.

"Lord Vince...Good evening," Edith slightly bowed her head.

Lying in bed, Olivja's stomach plunged as her eyes flew open.

"May I come in, Madam?"

At the request, Edith briefly turned to look back at Olivja. They exchanged a short look and the older woman cleared her throat.

"The heiress is nearly ready for bed, sir—"

"Not to worry. I am only looking for the others...I figured Olivja may know where they were," he said, a bit louder.

Unfortunately, hearing that he was looking for Adalja piqued her interest.

Moving the covers aside, Olivja stepped out of bed and approached the door. Clad only in one of Jarl Dagrun's oversized, long-sleeved tunics, she stayed close behind Amma and the door, the safest place for her. She peeked around the corner, eyes lifting.

Vincent stood in the flickering light of the corridor, his imposing figure framed by the shadows.

He wasn't wearing his cowl, only his mouth covering, so his hair hung loose in white, milky waves that tumbled past his shoulders—damp from bathing, with a few strands still dripping slowly down his back.

A long-sleeved nightshirt, loose and slightly wrinkled, clung faintly to his skin where it was still wet, the fabric darkened in patches and shifting with each movement. It draped over his broad shoulders and was tucked haphazardly into his pants.

He was barefoot, the stone floor chilled beneath him, grounding the quiet tension that clung to his every breath.

His hands, bare and calloused, rested at his sides, though they twitched faintly—betraying the storm simmering beneath his composed exterior.

Even dressed for the bed, there was an undeniable weight to his presence, a dominance that filled the space and made the air feel heavier.

Vincent's eyes swiftly moved from Edith to Olivja, his eyes crinkled into a smirk. At the sight of her, he tugged his mask beneath his chin with a single finger. "Apologies princess, I'll let you rest—"

"Have you checked her room?" Olivja asked gently, crossing her arms beneath her breasts.

Vincent laughed and gently pressed his other hand against the heiress' door. "You thought I'd check your chambers before *hers*?"

Olivja blushed, not having realised how risky, how stupid, her comment was and swiftly shook her head with a nervous laugh. "I—am tired, forgive me."

"Too tired to join me? I'm sure Adalja would much rather see your face than mine," he cooed, pushing the door open and out of Edith's hands, causing the older woman to scowl.

Unfortunately, Olivja did not think that was true, but she also couldn't sleep knowing Adalja was missing.

The Norsewoman grabbed a small red shawl that hung on the brass coat hanger beside her bed and quietly shrugged it onto her shoulders. As her actions silently showed her agreeance, Vincent's smile grew and he returned his mask back over his mouth.

"Very well," she said reluctantly, stepping out of her room. Her figure was shaped nicely by her loose brown locks as they cascaded down her back, strands occasionally drifting across her bare thighs.

As they walked together, they stayed in silence. Occasionally the two of them would split off to open separate doors, but Adalja was nowhere to be found.

On the far east wing, where the princes stayed, a library and several studies awaited their search. She was thankful of her familiarity with the castle as it made her feel comfortable looking for the princess on her own.

Oddly, the longer their search went on, the less she wanted to find Adalja. Her thoughts swirled with questions...

What is she doing alone with them? Why is she hiding?

Olivja became unsure of whether or not she wanted to know the answers.

She reached for the door that led to Vincent's study, a room she had spent too much time in. As her hand wrapped around the brass knob and the door clicked open, Vincent's voice boomed.

"Olivja!" he swiftly called, jogging to meet her.

"What—"

Two knights came forward, shuffling loudly in their metallic gear. They called, panting once they arrived, "We've found them!"

SWIFTLY, THE KNIGHTS LED THEM to the main room, Olivja gazed down at the scene from the top of the stairs with Vincent. Her stomach dropped and she deeply regretted joining Vincent on the hunt.

Elias stood tall, looking down at a sleepy Princess Adalja as she lay in his arms, Brahms standing close by.

The three looked up at them as they entered, and Elias mumbled quietly. His posture shifted as he turned towards Brahms, lowering Adalja to her feet.

Quickly, he handed the noblewoman to the knight, and she leaned her full body weight against a flushed Brahms.

It only took a few seconds for Olivja to understand that all three of them were drunk.

"What in God's name?" Vincent laughed gently, opening his arms with a welcoming presence as he approached. "We've been looking everywhere for you!"

Olivja followed Vincent down the steps, her movements languid and quiet. She trailed a few paces behind as he descended with sharp purpose. At the bottom, Elias turned slowly to face his brother, his flushed cheeks betraying his nerves.

"Forgive us, Vince," Elias began, his voice measured but tense. "Adalja wished to see the town, and Brahms offered to escort us. Things...got out of hand. I've handled it."

Vincent stopped a few feet away, crossing his arms as his gaze bore into Elias. "Oh? Have you?"

Olivja lingered beside Vincent, her eyes finally settling on Adalja. The princess looked remarkably content, despite the circumstances—her flushed cheeks and easy smile was evidence of her drunken state.

Olivja's expression hardened, resentment flickering across her face.

Adalja seemed oblivious to it all, her carefree demeanor twisting something in Olivja's chest. She had never seen Adalja drink before, and the sight unsettled her in a way she couldn't quite name.

Vincent's voice cut through her thoughts, cold and exacting. "Explain yourself, Elias. What do you mean by 'handled'? For if it had truly been dealt with, Sir Brahms would already be facing punishment for taking her from the castle." His tone dropped, icy and accusatory. "And yet, I find no astonishment in it—this is not the first time you've let him slip."

Elias' face darkened at his suggestion and his hands coiled into fists.

However, before he could say much else, the drunk princess grumbled: "*Perhaps you should have joined us—*" Unfortunately, loud enough for everyone to hear.

"Pardon me, Princess?" Vincent's tone was laced with amusement and disbelief as he scoffed, tilting his head at her.

Olivja could see the fear that painted Brahms' face as he held onto the weak, sloppy princess. But Adalja was put together enough to continue.

"*Prince Perfect—*" Adalja growled while trying to take a step forward, but Brahms desperately held onto her.

"My family's dead—*hic*—I think I'm quite deserv'ng of-a drink!" Adalja called with a small hiccup, glaring at Vincent to the best of her ability.

"Adalja—*stop—*" Brahms could be heard desperately, fearfully, mumbling to the princess, who was far too deep to stop.

"Pr'haps if *you* had-a drink—*hic*—you wouldn't be so *tight-laced*!" she continued with a giggle before Brahms swiftly covered her mouth, his eyes wide and apologetic. As Adalja continued rambling behind his hand, Vincent's demeanor darkened.

He took a step towards them, and at the same time, Elias swiftly took one as well, blocking his way.

Vincent's hands immediately shot up, grabbing the fabric that covered Elias' wine-stained chest.

Olivja, with wide eyes, looked between the four of them.

"Leave her be," Elias said confidently, his voice low. "She had one too many pints, that's all."

"I'm more than capable of handling a wild woman—*but I've had my fill of that knight of hers*," Vincent growled, making it clear he had no interest in punishing Adalja—only Brahms. He tightened his grip on Eli's shirt, raising his voice. "If he's to guard our women, he's to be held to the same standard as any other knight of ours."

"He's mine to correct, just as he's mine to pardon," Elias snapped—every bit as aggressive as Vincent. From behind them, Olivja couldn't see the glare that was exchanged between brothers, but her own eyes widened in admiration.

Adalja's muffled mumbling still carried beneath Brahms' hand. Vincent's hardened stance finally eased. He sighed, stepped back towards Olivja, and crossed his arms in quiet defence.

"*You and your knights*...Why didn't you think to invite us to your celebration, *Eli*?" Vincent drawled, mocking the nickname with theatrical disappointment.

Olivja found herself wondering the same, bristling quietly at the exclusion.

"Your presence wasn't requested, brother," Elias retorted, tossing his hood back onto his shoulder. "Do you not have your own *wild woman* to tend to?"

At the response, even Olivja grew upset. She wanted to chastise him, all three of them in fact, but right as she took a step forward, Vincent's arm jutted out, stopping her from moving towards the group.

Her breath quickened. She wasn't about to let herself be used as a weapon—but Vincent spoke before she could.

"I can handle mine. It's clear you cannot say the same," Vincent defended Olivja, but at the expense of the blue-eyed maiden.

"Perhaps you should get Adalja to bed before you spoil her further...I'd hate to see a woman wasted in front of you."

Elias hesitated. He glanced at Adalja, who was barely paying attention anymore.

"Then you'll have to excuse us..." Elias muttered. He nodded to Brahms, and together they escorted the drunk woman down the hall.

Olivja lingered, watching her three old friends leave without a second look to her. Her throat knotted.

She watched until Adalja was no longer in her sight, expecting *one* of them to look back...but they didn't. Her hands tightened into fists.

Vincent lowered his arm once they were out of sight, but it didn't matter, Olivja had already turned on her heel, heading back towards her room swiftly.

She was furious, tired, and betrayed. Here she was, trying to fight the notion that her friends were casting her out, and they continuously were. She stomped back up the stairs, her hair puffing out as she hurried along.

"Liv!"

Perhaps it was always a habit of Vincent's to chase after an infuriated Ragnarvik. A soft tone of amusement could be heard in his voice again as he called for her repetitively, chuckling at how angry she was, following her closely.

"Olivja—Stop! Look at me!"

Like before, his hand caught her wrist before she could reach her chambers, and he held her from retreating further. Her head snapped back towards him, a couple tears exposing themselves on the apples of her cheeks.

When his eyes noticed her tearful face, all amusement left him. Yanking away his mask in one swift motion, he closed the space between them, his eyes darting across her face as both hands found hers.

"What on earth—"

"Tell me, Vincent...is your heart full now?!" Olivja, remembering everything they had spoken about, snapped at him. She wasn't necessarily angry with him, but he was the easiest, more readily available target.

"What? What are you insinuating?" he asked with a scoff, shocked that she was projecting onto him. His grip was firm on her wrists and yet, for the first time, she wasn't attempting to pull away from it.

"You spoke and so it is—you're all I have!" Olivja's shout diminished to a mere whisper as she spoke. "And tonight, the gods have answered as you swore they would. They are no friends of mine...I should have listened to you..."

She let him hold her wrists because she was afraid of pulling away and losing him too, of losing absolutely everyone in one night. She relinquished control of her tears, no point in holding them back as Vincent had already seen them. She couldn't look him in the eyes, so she looked down at his chest, her body trembling with rage.

"*Naturally*," Vincent sighed with a grin. "...Let it be known, Liv has finally submitted to my right..."

When he saw how broken she was, he sighed again, only this time it was shaky and more genuine.

"Come now, what did I say about tears?" His tone was light, almost mocking, as though he were trying to diffuse the tension with humor.

But Olivja was too overwhelmed for it to work. He slid his hands down from her wrists, gently curling his fingers around hers as though he meant to kiss the back of her hands. Instead, he simply held her hands in that delicate, intimate way, his gaze softening as he met her eyes.

"*Forget them*, Olivja—they've already forgotten you, as plain as day...Do not bow to them by offering your tears." Vincent shrugged his shoulders, making light of the deep betrayal she felt.

She wished he understood the true depth of her feelings.

She looked up at his face, shaking her head while contemplating his words. She despised how right he was, how effortlessly she found herself agreeing with him, and how alike they truly were.

Even as children, they had been so similar—perhaps that was the real reason they clashed so fiercely then...perhaps that was the reason they saw eye-to-eye now.

She wanted to tell him that Adalja had completely broken her heart too many times to count, that Olivja was tired of being a victim to her own heart.

She tried to wrap her mind around why Adalja wouldn't invite her...why her presence was so detrimental to their pleasure—that she was better off alone in her room. She looked down at her hands, her lip quivering as intensely as her fingers.

The sight of her tearful, pained face elicited more emotion from him. "Princess, if it's spirits and a night on the town that you desire, you and I can go *whenever* you like—"

"No, Vincent! Let the others drink themselves blind. I'll not join them! *Ugh*!" Olivja groaned frustratedly, her heart aching as she imagined Adalja holding her hands instead of him.

But unfortunately, her jealous rage quickly overwrote those images with ones of Elias holding Adalja's instead. Her jaw clenched and she snatched her hands away from him, pushing them up to cover her tearful eyes.

"I wish only to be loved...to be seen—for someone to care if I vanish with the morning mist." She whimpered into the dark of her hands. "...I am so weary of being forgotten...I have gathered the scraps of others' love for too long...gods know I *ache* to be chosen..."

"Olivja," Vincent's voice came closer but she continued angrily.

"Answer me!" she shouted tearfully, dropping her hands so she could hug herself tightly as she desperately looked to him for an answer.

"What is so wrong about me? What is it that renders me of no worth? Gods, even *you* want *nothing* to do with me—Let the wind carry me, then. If none will hold me close, I'll vanish like smoke!"

She gasped as his hands snatched her face once more, holding it up to his gaze. His shadow loomed over her, jaw tight, eyes blazing, breath hot and sharp between his teeth.

"Do you truly not see that I care for you, Olivja!?" he shouted at her, cupping her cheeks.

"Do not *drag* me into the *failures* of your other companions because you are *hurt*!" His fingers dug harder into her damp cheeks, trembling with restraint, his breath ragged and shallow—as if her words had cut something raw inside him.

"They know not the depth to which you have been carved into me...I could *never* forget you, even were I to wish it."

Her breath caught, a mixture of shock and something colder flickering in her eyes. The confession in combination with the physical aggression rendered her dumbfounded. She jerked her face slightly from his grip, her voice trembling with both outrage and hurt.

"Could never forget me!? You abandoned me just the same as them! For countless winters!" Olivja whimpered, pushing her hands against his firm chest, failing to yank herself free of his strong grasp.

"You lie...you lie to me—I am nothing!"
Her strength faltered as her sobs continued, her entire world crumbling at the thought that Vincent cared for her as deeply as he claimed—at the thought that he cared more than everyone else.

"Lie?" he growled, a bitter laugh escaping him as his eyes flashed with frustration. "Do you think I *enjoy* the *hold* you have on me?!" His hand squeezed her cheeks tighter, forcing her to look at him, only him.

"Stop—You are hurting me, Vincent!" she shouted, her words edged with both fear and pain, but hardly heard amongst his declaiming.

"I've never spoken truer words in my life—you are a thorn in my side—"

"Let me go!" she shouted and his other hand caught her wrist as she tried to throw it against him, holding her still, backing her into the stone wall beside them.

"*Never*, Olivja! *God*—you are *torment* made woman...but we are *bound*. You and I. We always have been. And I've nothing else. No one else." His voice hissed, the hurt clear beneath his anger.

"Vincent, no! This path will *only* bring *ruin*—we can't—I *can't*—" she whimpered, her tears dampening his fingertips as he gripped her jaw tighter, keeping her head still against the wall.

The air between them was thick with both anger and self-assurance, and something else—something unspoken, old and raw.

His gaze flickered between her tear-filled eyes and her quivering lips, his own chest heaving similarly to Olivja's. He was furious, like her, but there was something deeper—something darker in him that she didn't quite understand.

"I am *far beyond ruined, Olivja.*"

The torchlight was few and far between along the corridor, each flame guttering in its sconce, too weak to chase the shadows from his face or the stone walls around them. Darkness clung to his features—made him seem carved from it.

He pulled her closer by the hip, his fingers bunching the fabric of her tunic. The fire's dim glow caught the edge of her cheekbone—the rest of her swallowed by shadow.

"These paths have been carved into our bones since our birth—we have no say! They'll force us to walk them no matter—We *have no choice* in this life. And yet, with every *loathing* breath, I choose to be yours." His voice broke on every word.

Their lips brushed with each word, a sensation that had Olivja pushing at his chest.

"Vince—stop—" she grunted, his breath warming her lips. She couldn't take it. *"Enough!"*

Her heart raced in her chest, her hands trembling as they pressed harder, failing to create space between them.

Because she couldn't push him away.
Gods, she knew she could, but she wasn't.

She hated how he made her feel, but it was undeniable—the heat, the pressure, the desire to know how Adalja felt with Elias, the need to prove that she could do it too.

If he was all she had, she *wouldn't* push him away.

"*Look at me*!" he growled, tilting his head, desperate for her gaze. She couldn't see him—not really. The shadows swallowed his face even up close, leaving only fragments: the gleam of his eyes, the tension in his jaw.

"You do not belong to this world, nor to the courts, Olivja." His words came in ragged grunts, as though he despised every letter that left his mouth.

The prince's hand trembled against her wet cheeks. As if trying to reclaim control, his other hand gripped her hip and yanked her tighter against him.
"*...But you belong to me.*"

He angled her face towards his, just as she parted her lips to shout—
His mouth crashed onto hers.

Olivja gasped, her hands frozen against the firmness of his chest. Her amber eyes shot open.

No—no—this isn't happening—

She was kissing him.
Tasting him.
Feeling him.

She jerked back, but he followed, chasing her lips like he'd been starved. Their bodies collided—no space left between them but the thick air they barely breathed.

Then why...why did her hands grip his shirt instead of push him away?

His breath—wine and rosemary. The way he held her face. The press of his hips against hers. She was being pulled in. *Into him.*

Lofn...forgive me.

Her eyes squeezed shut, her lips parting with a breath of surrender. She accepted his kiss—and with it, perhaps, the fate she had fought for so long.

For a moment, she couldn't tell if she did it because she had no choice...because the world expected it of her...or because it was the only way to cling to the last piece of herself before it shattered completely.

Vincent exhaled into her as the kiss turned sharp, almost violent. It wasn't passion—it was defiance. A clash of will and pride. A desperate need to prove something—to each other. To themselves.

They were both trapped. And this kiss...

It was their quiet rebellion. Their only language in a world that had stripped them of choice.

His hand slid into her hair, gripping the strands with ruthless tenderness as his mouth parted and claimed hers again.

Pain stirred before pleasure. Confusion before longing. And still—she didn't pull away.
And he knew she wouldn't.

Her fingers slid up his chest, curling around the collar of his white nightshirt. She tugged—softly, almost questioningly—as if needing him to steady her, to anchor her in the ocean of everything they were. Or maybe...to drive the moment deeper.

Deeper into him.
Into what they were becoming.

His tongue pressed between her parted lips, tantalizingly exploring her mouth, her own tongue a warring force. Their teeth and tongues collided as the kiss surged hotter, more desperate, a dance of dominance from both sides.

A strangled, almost desperate, groan escaped his lips from the back of his throat, echoing into her mouth, causing a wave of warmth to spread upwards from her fingertips.

His grip tightened in her hair, tilting her head to reach deeper while he firmly grappled with her waist. Vincent's lips only parted from hers to reconnect with her jaw, trailing open-mouthed promises towards her ear.

Her breath was shallow, eyes shut as she let herself succumb to the enigmatic pleasures, focussing only on the feeling of his body against her—nothing else, *no one* else.

Gods, she knew she didn't want this. She knew she never wanted him this way—*no man this way*. She knew her heart belonged to Adalja, so why, *why* did this feel right too?

Her hands slid up into his wet hair, gripping at the nape of his neck, sending chills down both their spines.

As his lips reached her collarbone, her shawl fell away, tumbling with the remainder of their restraint. He worked his way back up her neck, his breaths hot and heavy until they were back on her own, crashing down with a deeper need than before.

He was desperate, eager, *starved*...like he had been waiting for this moment for his entire life. Olivja could feel it in the way his hands trembled against her, in the way his breath was quick and sharp, and in the way he savored every second.

"Vince," she exhaled his name, the word stopped by his tongue as it pressed into her mouth again. Olivja groaned, taken aback by his forwardness, by the way he grabbed her, and the way his hand slid beneath her shirt and grabbed overtop her linen drawers.

His teeth found her bottom lip, tugging as his mouth moved away, only instead of trailing kisses, he nibbled his way down the other side of her neck. Her bare thigh was grabbed, hoisted up around his waist as his hips achingly pressed further.

She inhaled sharply, be it from the sweetness of his mouth or the sudden realisation of what they were doing and *what would happen if she didn't stop it.*

Her hands tightened in his hair as his hips rolled again, a desperate grunt spilling from his lips into the crook of her neck.

She couldn't. She couldn't do this.

"*Vincent.*" His name came out a breathy whimper, a fragile boundary she hoped—prayed—he would not cross, no matter how desperate he was.

He froze. His breath lingered, heavy and hot against her skin. Hers shuddered through his hair.

And then, slowly, he pulled back.

They were left with nothing but stunned, wild stares. Her neck prickled cold as the heat of his spit began to cool, and still his hands clung to her like he didn't quite believe he had to let go.

Neither of them could have imagined this was how the night would end.
Not like this.
Not standing inches apart, staring like strangers into each other's eyes—shocked, breathless, undone.

Olivja's cheeks flushed.

Vincent let out a trembling sigh, as if bewildered by their kiss—as if he hadn't been the one to start it.

He looked at her again, more carefully this time, like memorizing something he feared he'd never touch again.

Then slowly, his hand slipped from her hair and returned to her cheek. His thumb brushed the corner of her mouth, wiping away the glistening trace of his kiss, the remnants of everything they didn't say.

His piercing green gaze locked onto hers, his brows drawn in, curved upwards at the centre.

"I...I apologise..." he murmured, the words thick with unspoken shame as his hand slid out from beneath her shirt.

She stared up at him, her breath caught in her open mouth; her composure and words, stolen by the intensity of his gaze, his touch, and the lingering echo of his lips. With a frustrated scoff, he shook his head, his thumb gently lifting her chin to close her mouth for her.

"*... What have they done to us, Olivja.*"
Vincent's words were dark, yet gentle, like he was silently cursing everyone who had any involvement in the forcing of their marriage...or perhaps something else?

She didn't know how to respond, she was unsure herself what this meant, or what this would do to them. She hesitated, her eyes darting back and forth as they searched his face.

"It's," she gulped, "it's not like you to apologise, Vincent." Olivja exhaled, her words shaking at the same rate as the rest of her limbs, shivering with anxiety and adrenaline as she tried to dilute the intensity of their moment.

"...Don't get used to it, Ragnarvik, your lips have only ever tempted me this once." A sad, yet dashing, smirk cut through the dark tension between them, pulling the both of them back to a more familiar version of their relationship. "I shall not make it a habit."

His finger and thumb pinched her chin lightly, his eyes were sad, almost angry, a sharp contrast to the kindness in his tone. Something was hidden beneath, and Olivja was fully intrigued.

"*Good...*" Olivja returned quietly, her body still shaking with nerves at the thought that they had kissed.

Bittersweet was the truth that Vincent—of all men—held the honour of her first kiss from a man. She was grateful it was him; it could never have been anyone else.

"Are you still *angry* about the Pembrooks?" Vincent asked, still holding her chin.

Unshockingly, the kiss had momentarily overpowered all feelings of betrayal and anger she held. She didn't want to admit that he succeeded.

"No...I suppose not...Now my wrath burns for you alone," Olivja continued with a playful sigh, unable to truly process anything that had occurred while he was still in front of her.

But Vincent enjoyed her snide remark. Another chuckle escaped him as his hand slid back up to her cheek, offering a slight tap from his palm in exchange for her rudeness.

"*Good*...then all is quiet once more," he finished charmingly, taking another look into her eyes before stepping back a hair.

Suddenly, he squatted in front of her and her cheeks flushed. While keeping his eyes trained on hers, his hand found her fallen shawl. He held it up for her, his freehand finding purchase against her thigh, thumb brushing absentmindedly.

Olivja stilled, her throat tightened, so she cleared it.

His eyes flickered in the breath of torchlight, shimmering with something beneath—a quiet mirth dancing in their glow.

"Your clothes have fallen, my girl," Vincent teased, and she snatched the shawl from him before he could finish it.

"Don't look at me like some whore," she hissed.

Though he wasn't finished.

Before standing, he pulled her thigh close and pressed a kiss to it, closing his eyes like he savored her taste.

Her cheeks burned with a fire unknown to her and she looked away, fingers curling into the red fabric of her shawl. The taste of her old friend still lingered on her tongue and it sent chills down her spine.

Without more words, his hands dropped from her thigh and he stood slowly, taking a shaky step back from her. He pulled his mask above his nose and his cowl over his head without keeping eye contact, his eyes lingering elsewhere, the same as hers.

For the first time since she arrived, his strong confidence faltered as he looked anywhere but her eyes. It felt strange...because no matter how hard either of them tried, their love was like a blade balanced on its edge—sharp, precarious, and impossible to wield without drawing blood.

"Has it, Vincent..." she asked him before he could leave. "...all gone quiet?"

With his expression hidden, only his eyes told the truth of his dark thoughts. "Was it ever, Olivja?"

And she had nothing more to say to that.

After exchanging mutual glances, he nodded at her.
"May sleep find you gently, princess." His voice was low and quiet, an edge to it that made her want to reach out and stop him.

Slowly, he turned down the hall to his own wing of the castle. Despite the way he took his time with her, he stormed off quickly, as though the weight of their intimacy had finally landed.

And again, she was left alone.

Olivja lingered there for a moment longer, her bare feet brushing the cold stone floor as she stared at the empty hall. The flicker of distant torchlight played shadows along the walls, a poor distraction from the churn of her thoughts.

Eventually, she turned back towards her chambers, her steps slow, as though each one might convince her to go after him.

When she reached her room, the fire had burned low, leaving the space dim and cool. She shut the door behind her with a quiet click, pausing to take in the stillness. The faint scented smoke from the fading embers and incense filled the air as she crossed to her bed, her fingers brushing over the edge of the fur-lined covers.

Sliding beneath them, she pulled them up to her chin, the coarse warmth a stark contrast to the chill clinging to her skin. She lay there, wide-eyed, staring up at the wooden beams above her. They seemed heavier tonight, pressing down like the weight in her chest. The silence of her room was deafening, amplifying every errant thought, every flicker of what had transpired.

After all...she just kissed her best friend, and worst enemy.

Her cheeks remained flushed, her mind spinning as it lingered on their kiss...on Vincent. Her lips rolled inward, pressed into a thin line as her thoughts circled back to the way it felt—how overwhelming, how consuming.

She had never kissed anyone with such intensity, with such emotion. All her life, she had been so sure she would never give herself to a man—had taken pride in that certainty—and yet...

Her arms tightened around her covers, her knuckles white in the moonlight.

She knew who she was. She was confident in her heart, in her love for women. That had never wavered.

And yet, as her fingertips brushed over her bottom lip, she couldn't deny the pull—the aching confusion that told her she would do it again.

Not because he was a man, but because he was her best friend.
Because he had her, and she had him...*always.* Because he was *Vincent.*

He had always been Vincent.

If he was to be her bonded soon, maybe it was easier to surrender than to fight.

Odin, what has maddened me?

Since when has Olivja ever willingly bowed to anything? And how is it that Vincent is the one who makes her willing?

Her fingers traced absent patterns against the fur, her breaths steady but shallow. She felt hollow yet full, like she was carrying the enormity of something she couldn't name.

For once, she wished her mother was there. She knew Highwife and Jarl Ragnarvik had a complicated relationship; her mother loved women too, and yet she was still with her father.

She sighed heavily, feeling more alone than ever before, because now she didn't even have herself to hold onto. Staring at those beams, she didn't dare close her eyes—not yet. If she did, she feared she might see his face, hear his voice, and lose herself all over again.

Her door slowly creaked open and she sat up on her elbows, gazing at the door as though she had summoned him by thought alone.

Slipping like a shadow against the amber light from the hall, Vincent stepped through the small cracked door and shut it with his back.

His mask was gone. So was his shirt.

Her chest tightened, and she struggled to find her voice. "Vincent—"

"Olivja..." he interrupted her, only to go silent. His eyes lingered on the ground, unable to meet hers from across the room.

Her chest heaved beneath the blankets and she sat up a little higher, eyelashes batting in confusion and a bit of relief.

"I...simply needed to check on you." His voice was weak and quiet, but it was a weakness that she had heard from him before, one that filled her with a deep sense of nostalgia, of yearning.

"Hel's Gates—you came with no clothes and only concern?" Olivja asked, loud enough for him to hear across the room.

"I had to." His expression was illuminated by the dimmest of candle lights, and yet the shadows betrayed his gentleness as his gaze begged for her.

"You're all I have, Olivja, all I've ever had...I'd do far more, for far less." As he spoke, his posture softened as though he was waiting for something, someone, to make him feel human again.

Her lungs clenched, heart rattled and her hands gripped the bedsheets. She was ready to turn him away, needing her rest before such a big day, her mouth opened with a weak refusal. "Vince—"

"I can't be alone tonight, Liv." His interruption was honest, fragile; it was almost as if she was speaking directly to his heart and not to the man carrying it. He finally lifted his eyes which caught the moonlight perfectly, a shimmer lighting up the glossy sheen.

Her breath caught, his words striking a chord deep within her. She wanted to argue, to push him away, to steel herself against this vulnerability—but the look in his eyes made her pause.

They were raw and unguarded, full of something she couldn't name. Vince looked lost, like a man unravelling, held together only by the thread of her presence. Olivja had seen that look...she knew what he was asking for, because he had asked for it before.

Without a word, she shifted to her right, making space beside her. Her heart thudded painfully in her chest as she lay on her side, his movements quiet and deliberate, like a shadow slipping through the dark.

He slid beneath the covers with a slow, careful grace, the warmth of his body immediately chasing away the chill of her solitude.

Her breath hitched as his hands found her thighs, tracing a path upwards with a touch that was both hesitant and certain. Liv shivered as his calloused palms pressed lightly against her back, pulling her closer as his arm slid beneath her.

In one fluid motion, he nestled against her, his face burying itself in the curve of her chest. His damp hair was cold against her skin; his breath was warm, ragged and uneven, as though he had been holding it in for far too long.

Her arms moved instinctively, wrapping around him, her hands brushing the bare, solid expanse of his back. The moment her fingers skimmed the raised, jagged lines cutting across his skin, she froze.

Scars.

So many more than she remembered. Some faint with time, others still angry and rough beneath her touch. Olivja's breath caught in her throat, the warmth of him fading as something colder took its place.

What have they done to you?

She wanted to pull back, to see them properly, to trace each one and demand to know the story—but not now. Not while he was vulnerable and warm in her arms, letting her hold him like they were still children hiding from a storm.

So she stayed silent, blinking hard against the sting behind her eyes.

Later, she promised herself.
Later, when they weren't wrapped in the fragile hush of night, she'd ask. She'd force him to tell her every truth he'd hidden beneath his skin.

For now, she just held him a little tighter, fingers splaying gently over every wound like a quiet apology—for not knowing, for not being there, for not being able to stop whatever had carved into him so cruelly.

She could feel the tension in him, the way his muscles coiled beneath her touch, and her breath stuttered at the intimacy of it. With her head resting gently above his, her shallow breath fanned his scalp.

With every inhale, she breathed in more of his freshly bathed scent—rosemary, chamomile, and, as always, that lingering trace of amber. Her eyes fluttered shut—just a moment—while she relished in his warmth.

The quiet vulnerability between them spoke volumes as Vincent sought solace in her presence, needing her more than anyone had ever needed her.

"Vince..." Olivja breathed, her voice cracking as her fingertips tangled in his hair, their long locks weaving together like threads in a vivid tapestry.

But he stayed silent. His arms tightened around her waist, pulling her flush against him, holding her as though he was afraid she'd slip away, as though he'd lose himself in the process.

"*Don't*," he murmured against her, his voice muffled but urgent.

It was then that Olivja heard the quivering in his voice. It was then that she noticed the trembling in his arms and shoulders. And then, wetness, staining her tunic, dampening her chest.

He was crying?

Tears came to her own eyes at the feeling, and she pulled him tighter against herself.

Oh, Vincent.

She willed it all back. She would be strong for him.

"Please, Liv...*let me stay...*" he exhaled against her breasts, his voice hoarse with emotion.

Their breaths mingled in the quiet space between them, the air charged with unspoken words and emotions too heavy to name.

"*I will*," she returned with a whisper of her own.

Her heart ached at the vulnerability in his tone. Yet the strength of his need pressed against her chest as heavily as his body did. She exhaled shakily, resting her chin against the top of his head with a quiet nod.

For a moment, she let herself get lost in the sensation—the way his bare skin felt against hers, the strength in his hold that belied the fragility she could feel in him. She didn't know what to say, so she said nothing, her hands moving in gentle, soothing patterns along his back.

This wasn't the first time they had slept together, and apart from their kiss, it felt the same as it did when they were young; only two souls, relying on each other for warmth, for support. And no matter how much they fought that day, or how annoyed they were with each other, things always ended up better.

She stayed awake longer than him, ensuring that her fragile prince fell asleep. He needed it more than her, that much she could tell. And it felt right—almost healing—to be held in his arms again. To see the young, fractured boy beneath the surface, even if that sight cut deeper than she expected.

When his hold slackened and his head grew heavy against her chest, she allowed her own eyes to close. His warmth, his scent, his presence—it wrapped around her like a cocoon, pulling her into a restless but peaceful slumber.

And as her mind slipped away, her last thought was that, in this fragile, fleeting moment, maybe, they had somehow found each other again.

THREAD XXXI

ᛟᛚᛁᚡᛃᚨ

THE FAINTEST LIGHT OF DAWN filtered through the cracks in the wooden shutters, casting pale streaks across the room. The cold air hung heavy with the lingering scent of smoke and the shared warmth of the night.

Olivja stirred, her eyes blinking open to find Vincent still nestled against her. His serene face caught in early light, white lashes and strands of hair resting on his cheeks as his breath came slow and steady.

Her gaze lingered on him, caught in the gentle beauty of his features. In sleep, he looked younger, almost like the boy she used to know—the one who shared her secrets and weathered her sharp tongue with that cocky resolve. It was strange, seeing him like this after everything.

Her chest tightened. She hadn't expected to see this side of him again. Vulnerable, unguarded. *He'd hate her for thinking that.*

For all his sharp edges and storms, something in Vincent still tugged at her, a quiet ache she dared not name. In moments like this, when the walls between them seemed to vanish, it was easy to remember why she'd once loved him in her own way.

But morning had come, and the moment, fragile as it was, couldn't last. Carefully, Olivja shifted, easing his arm away from where it draped over her waist. His fingers twitched against her back, his body stirring faintly, and she froze, holding her breath. After a moment, his breathing evened out, and she slipped free of his grasp.

Her feet touched the cool stone floor, and she winced at the chill. Glancing back to ensure he hadn't stirred, she grabbed her robe from the chair near her bed and wrapped it tightly around herself.

The silence in the room was deafening as she tiptoed to the door, her heart pounding despite her careful movements.

Olivja moved quickly, the hem of her robe brushing against the cold stone as she made her way to the bathing chamber.

The thought of warm water offered reprieve—cleansing not just her skin, but the chaos tangled in her mind.

When she reached the chamber, she closed the heavy wooden door behind her with a soft click. The air was damp, the faint smell of chamomile and oats clinging to the steam that hung in the space.

As she slipped out of her robe and nightwear and stepped into the bath, the heat enveloped her, coaxing a soft sigh from her lips. For a moment, she sank beneath the surface, the world muted and weightless. It was only here, in the quiet solitude of the water, that she could allow herself to unravel.

Water, the sea, had always been her refuge, a place that welcomed all and silenced all. Beneath its surface, the world went quiet, as if the chaos of life couldn't follow her there.

It was peaceful yet deafening, a paradox that somehow made sense. The water asked nothing of her, gave her no commands, no expectations—it simply existed, vast and unyielding. It cradled her sorrows and swallowed her whole.

She remained under the surface, eyes open as she gazed at the rippling waves above her. As her lungs burned, she released her breath and watched as the bubbles escaped her, imagining them as her worries and fears, vanishing back into the world as they popped at the surface.

The sea, the water, comforted her.
It held her better than anyone ever could.

She sat up suddenly, gasping for air, water clinging to her lashes, her eyes dry and stinging. Her chest rose and fell in frantic rhythm, her fingers gripping the edge of the tub as though anchoring herself back to reality.

Adalja.

And she gasped again at the thought.

Why was she her first thought after finally breathing again?

The name struck her like a bell toll, reverberating through her mind, relentless and unyielding. Of all the memories and faces to surface in her moment of solitude, why hers?

The thought clung to her like the water dripping from her skin, impossible to shake, and yet she did not try.

Because Adalja had a way of finding her, even in the spaces she thought were hers alone, in the spaces only Olivja controlled. And her heart ached sharper than her stinging eyes as she told herself she was alone in that feeling; convinced Adalja no longer cared.

"She looked so happy...without me," she sighed in her language, her voice echoing softly through the bathing room. She scoffed, anger flaring.

Every time she thought she was over her, her mind flickered to the three of them, her old friends—effortlessly enjoying themselves without a second thought for her. She cringed at how Adalja lived so blissfully without her—the way she undoubtedly had for the past decade.

Everything seemed stacked against her: the Pembrook deaths, the lost letters, imposed marriages, and the crushing weight of isolation.

She stared at her knees, folded in the water like jagged cliffs rising from the Ragnarvik shores, void of emotion, unsure how she could continue to pursue that love—or why she even wanted to.

And then her mind shifted to Vincent—someone desiring and deserving of her love, yet she couldn't give it to him, not as she wanted...not fully. Not with her heart split.

It was the day he was supposed to execute the three women in charge of the Pembrook poisoning. For a moment, she wondered if that was the reason for his vulnerability the night before.

Then she recalled their kiss—the way his hands moved across her body like a warrior wielding his weapon—and her chest clenched, her fingers tightening around the sides of the tub.

It was all so unfair, so unjust.

Her eyes glanced at her knees again, and for a moment, she imagined herself a boat trapped between them. One way brought her pain but granted her direction and stability—the other way brought Vincent pain and left her boat without a sail, without an anchor.

Yet, for reasons beyond her strength to unravel, she was willing to abandon ship and swim if it meant reaching Adalja's heart.

"Have the gods cursed me?" Olivja chuckled, her eyes fixed on her reflection in the water. The ripples fractured her face, distorting it until it looked as unrecognizable as she felt.

Clenching her jaw, she stood, letting warm droplets return to the pool of fragrant water beneath her. She expected the bath to revitalise her, but her entire body ached, mirroring the pain she carried.

As she stepped out, she sighed, reaching for her linen towel on the brass stand. She tucked the corners around her breasts.
The door clicked open.

Pausing where she stood, she became thankful that she had covered up when she did.

"If this is your attempt at seeing me naked, Vincent...I've already finished," Olivja sighed, her back to the door, fully prepared to turn him down with all her might.

"Is that who you were expecting?"

Olivja turned at the sound of the pristine voice.

Standing with one hand on the doorknob and the other holding her robe shut was the beautiful Pembrook.

She looked as though she had wrestled with the gods themselves through the night—her beauty undiminished, but with the weariness of battle evident on her face. She was half-dead yet still a goddess, untamed and unbroken, like the first light of dawn breaking over a battle-scarred field.

Hel. She was Hel.

And her disheveled form stirred a bitter jealousy that clung to her heart, mixed with an unyielding pull of desire.

It truly was as if the gods had cursed her, making Adalja both a temptation and a reminder of what Olivja could never quite reach, no matter how hard she tried.

"Perhaps," Olivja smirked coldly, riled by the hint of jealousy in Adalja's tone—almost angered by it. "Or...maybe I was waiting for you."

"That seems to be our story, doesn't it?" Adalja grumbled, frozen at the door, her tired blue eyes waiting for permission to enter.

Liv couldn't believe her eyes.

Had she subconsciously manifested this moment?

All the pain that had once gripped her body now surged to her fingertips, making them ache with need. She swallowed her shock before speaking, irritation tinging her voice despite the excitement beneath.

"On the contrary, *madame*, *we have no story*." Olivja's tone was hardly kind, frustrated that once again their relationship was misinterpreted.

Turning away, she strode casually towards the vanity on the right wall, turmoil churning within her. Looking down at the beautifully woven fabric of her robe, Olivja cleared her throat.

"Did you have *fun* last night, princess?" she hissed, toying with random bodily care items on the counter.

"I did...it was a good night for me, though my mind tortures me with pain," Adalja admitted quietly.

Her anger backfired. That was the one thing she *didn't* want to hear.

But somehow, she cherished the faintest victory in knowing the princess hadn't emerged unscathed from her haphazard night. She stifled a dry chuckle at the thought of the spirits tormenting her in the early light.

But her frustrations crept back in. The thought of Adalja having a great time—drinking, dancing, and gods knew what else—with Elias made her want to vomit. Her breath became shallow.

"Oh...good. Good, that's welcome news," Olivja said through a clenched jaw, biting hard enough to crack a molar. "*Then be off,* before I make your day worse than it's already destined to be...since you *clearly* lack the desire for my presence."

"Olivja—"

"No, Adalja. Save your words. You said it yourself, *you had a good night*. Why let some meaningless *'heathen'* ruin anything more for you?"

Olivja's hands clenched into fists, her body tense with the urge to shout, to demand something from Adalja—something that wasn't merely a part of her attention but all of it. But today was the wrong day for this fight.

She could feel the grief settling in her bones, the looming shadow of the execution hanging over them, and she knew the anger in her chest wasn't going to make things any better.

Still, as she looked at Adalja, the woman who should have been hers, Olivja's stubborn and unbridled anger outweighed all else.

Adalja had nothing to say—and it filled her with a sliver of cathartic relief. She wanted the woman to hurt as she had hurt her, but she knew the princess would never truly understand her pain.

Her hands gripped the counter's edge, her breath shaky as she fought back rageful tears. She wanted to brag about her evening with Vincent, to make her jealous...but Olivja couldn't bring herself to taint the memory by using it as a weapon.

She wanted to keep that moment to herself—unsure if she'd ever get another like it with him. A unique treasure of sorts that she wanted to protect.

"I'll get out of your way," Olivja uttered, the anger drained from her voice, leaving only quiet pain. "Before the water runs cold..." Her eyes stayed fixed on her trembling fingertips, silently hoping Adalja would grasp the weight behind her words.

She held her breath, waiting. Her gaze stayed fixed on the porcelain bowl before her, too nervous to meet Adalja's reflection.

"Very well..." the princess murmured.

The door clicked shut, and Liv's eyes shot up to the mirror.

Adalja had closed the door behind her and stepped carefully towards the bath, avoiding Olivja's gaze—a gesture both infuriating and gratifying.

The heiress watched her every move in the mirror, palms slick as she clenched her robe tighter.

But, while *her* fingers were clenched, Adalja's grasp unfurled. The Pembrook's silk robe cascaded like water down her bare skin, revealing every perfect curve.

Olivja's breath caught, her face flushing as her dreams unfurled before her—every expectation somehow met. The shock rooted her in place, fear creeping in that this was all just a dream.

Had she fallen asleep in the bath? Was she drowning—was this the gates to Valhalla?

Eager for it to be real, Olivja turned her head slightly, still holding her breath. But seeing the princess—seeing her—was worse.

"*Gods...do not put me through this, Adalja.*" Olivja exhaled as she leaned back against the wooden counter, the strength of her emotions threatening to collapse her.

She dared not let her knees buckle, not here, not now, not at the sight of her.

The anger simmering beneath her skin became unbearable—Adalja knew how deeply Olivja felt, yet she would disrobe in front of her?

"I am here only to *bathe*...you may *leave*," the princess declared. Adalja's head turned slightly, casting her a fleeting glance before facing forward again, her indifference slicing through Olivja like a blade.

But the heiress could feel the tension. It was as thick as the steam.
And she craved it, sought more of it.

For a few agonizing seconds, Olivja allowed herself to drink in the sight of her—the elegant curve of her spine, the soft glow of her damp skin in the candlelight. Her stomach twisted painfully, butterflies morphing into sharp, cutting edges.

Adalja had given her butterflies before, but never like this—never so violently.

As Adalja lifted her leg and stepped into the tub, the water rippling around her, Olivja finally exhaled. Watching her sink into the bath was a momentary reprieve, a fragile truce.

But as the steam curled upwards and blurred the edges of her silhouette, Olivja's thoughts darkened.

This bold unveiling—what was it if not a silent invitation?
Or was it a taunt? A cruel, calculated reminder of what Olivja could never truly have?

Her jaw clenched. She wouldn't let herself be toyed with, not by Adalja.

If she was being teased, she'd return the favour.
If Adalja meant to provoke her, Olivja would show her how dangerous that could be.

With a steady breath, she stepped away from the vanity, letting her linen towel slip to the floor like a discarded pretence. She approached the tub, naked and vulnerable but burning with determination.

"You mock me?" Olivja questioned, crouching down behind Adalja, her voice low and sharp. She leaned in, her breath ghosting against Adalja's ear, sending shivers down her spine. "You're without heart, Addy."

The words were cold, almost cruel, but Olivja couldn't stop them. She was drowning in the flood Adalja had created, desperate to pull her down with her.

Her trembling fingertips ghosted over Adalja's shoulder, brushing her gently.

Adalja tensed instantly, the water rippling as her body reacted to the touch, yet she stayed frozen, silent.

"You know that to be far from the truth," Adalja finally whispered, her voice steady, the words slicing through the heavy air like a blade.

"Do I?" Olivja scoffed, her fingers tracing the side of the tub, a mixture of anger and reverence. "You've not shown it to me. Not once."

There was a pause, and Liv hoped her words had hurt. "You'd bare your body to me...but not your heart...?"

"You'd bare your body to *him*..." Adalja grumbled, her blue eyes fixed on her knees beneath the water. "But you'd curse *me* for being sworn to Elias?"

Olivja froze.
There it was again, *Adalja's jealousy,* hot and targeted.

Though she never intended to make her upset this way, she had to admit it felt good. Jealousy was but a fraction of the rage the princess had inflicted upon *her.*

Let her feel it. Let it remind her of her desires.

The Norsewoman smirked, leaning her head against the tub.
"Curse you? Never. But him—I'd damn with a smile..." Olivja said, her tone biting as her fingertips danced over her back, teasing the edges of her own fury.

The princess' shoulders rose and fell faster, her breath heavy with anger.

"And what better way to curse Elias than to bathe with his woman." The words dripped with venom, but the way Adalja shivered under her touch only fuelled her fire. Liv's lips curved into a bitter smile.

"You will not—"

"Aye, but you've already done half the work for me, Adalja, *all on your own,*" Olivja hummed as she leaned in closer, pressing her lips to the princess' shoulder.

Her skin tasted of honeyed oat and something that was uniquely and entirely her own.

Adalja remained silent, her breath hitching slightly as Olivja leaned in closer. The steam thickened, wrapping around them like a cocoon—there was no escaping the heat that simmered between them.

"Are you upset I was expecting Vincent?" she prodded as her hands moved with purpose, brushing Adalja's dark hair aside to expose more of her neck.

The princess didn't respond right away, but that was fine.
Olivja knew the answer.

The Norsewoman leaned in and brushed her mouth against the crook of Adalja's neck, *coaxing* her admission, or *submission.* It mattered little which it was. She'd take either.

She placed three kisses there before Adalja finally shuddered.

When she broke her silence, her voice was a faint echo, barely audible over the crackling candles. "Yes," was all she could manage, before a fourth kiss stole her breath again.

Triumph rushed through her body, as though she'd won the first battle of her *own* ten-year war. The Norsewoman bit the inside of her cheek, resisting the urge to celebrate too early.

"Don't be upset. You should be pleased that you are not him," Olivja said, her lips grazing the princess' skin with each word.

"Why?" Adalja exhaled, like she'd been holding her breath too long.

"I wouldn't whisper for him." Olivja sighed, her breath brushing the shell of her ear. "I wouldn't reach for him this way." She shuddered, bringing a hand around to grasp the front of Adalja's neck gently—*possessively.*

"Nor would I *kiss him this way...*" Liv added, pressing her lips to the line of the princess' jaw.

"Liv—"

"I can hold back no longer, Adalja," Olivja breathed. "I am filled with need for you."

Heat pooled in her stomach, becoming unbearable behind her princess, her hand tightening just enough to claim.

The noblewoman's breath hitched audibly, goosebumps rising along her neck as Olivja kissed her skin again, slower this time, trailing her lips towards her bicep.

"Olivja—we *mustn't,*" Adalja whimpered, but her protest crumbled beneath desire. Water streamed down her raised arm as she reached back. Her hand, soaked and trembling, found Olivja's cheek, pulling her closer.

The princess couldn't deny the pull—the hunger. And once Olivja knew it to be true...

It was over.

The heiress leaned forward, licking the length of her neck with slow, indulgent cruelty, her breath branding each patch of skin.

"Then, shall I find Vincent to finish what you've started, *Fair One*?" Olivja grinned against her skin, savouring the use of that horrid nickname, and pulled back to let her think it was over.

But it wasn't.
Gods, not even close.

She straightened, hand sliding deliberately up Adalja's neck, gliding over water-slicked skin until it reached her jaw. With firm yet gentle pressure, she tilted Adalja's face back, forcing her to meet her gaze.

The sight stole her breath.

Adalja's flushed cheeks, half-lidded eyes, and parted lips spoke louder than any protest could. Her words said restraint, but her expression was greedy.

The steam rising from the bath enveloped them, its humid embrace clinging to their skin, amplifying every sensation. Gently, Liv's thumb stroked her lower lip, memorising its softness, practically able to taste Adalja from look alone.

Still, she pressed for a response.

"Answer me," Olivja demanded, her voice firmer now, the desperation in Adalja's gaze fuelling her resolve.

The princess' cheeks flushed, whether from jealous frustration or the pull of desire, both of which stirred something deep in Olivja. She held her head back, waiting, her breath steady but eager.

"Don't go to him," Adalja whimpered, her breath soft but desperate, her hands seeking purchase against Olivja's wrist.

She was trembling—*nervous.*

"*Why shouldn't I?*" Olivja asked as her eyes devoured the soft noblewoman.

She knew it was a cruel thing to manipulate her at a time like this, but she wasn't perfect. She wanted to hear how badly Adalja needed her, even if—in this moment—it was purely lustful.

She'd take whatever she could get from her.
Olivja was shackled to the love she bore this woman.

"I don't *want* you to," Adalja whimpered truthfully, barely audible.

And in that moment, the reins had been handed to the princess. Because Olivja would do *anything* for her.
Anything to satisfy the woman's wants and needs.

THE WORDS SHATTERED EVERY RESTRAINT Olivja had clung to.

Relief and desire surged through her, crashing over her like a tidal wave. Her chest heaved, eyes glistening—on the verge of tears from the sheer magnitude of it.

Without hesitation, she closed the distance between them, savouring the electric tension as their noses brushed, their breaths mingling over parted lips.

She closed her eyes and let herself feel it—every dream, every letter she'd written in desperation, every night spent clutching her pillow and pretending it was her. It was *real* now.

And with a shaky sigh, her mouth captured Adalja's in a kiss so tender it bordered on reverent.

It was slow. A delicate, testing dance, as though exploring the fragile thread between them. The princess' lips were soft, inviting, but still—unmoving. She did not yet kiss back, only moulded to the shape of Olivja's longing.

But Olivja pressed on. She cupped both sides of her face with desperate strength and tilted her head to deepen the kiss. Adalja tasted like morning tea and honey, and her cheeks, damp from steam, fit into Olivja's palms like a promise.

And as if undone by touch, Adalja's mouth parted. Their breaths mingled. Olivja shuddered. Dainty fingers threaded through Liv's damp brown waves, pulling, searching, for more.

And Olivja, grateful and groaning, gave it to her.

Everything inside her burned. Every limb, every nerve. Because the woman she loved was finally in her grasp, begging for her through touch alone.

Perhaps the gods had not cursed her after all. *Perhaps she was blessed.*

Then Adalja moved. Their lips parted with heavy, gasping breaths as the princess turned to fully face her.

For one aching second, Olivja feared it was over—that she had gone too far.

But no.

With a great wave of water, Adalja lurched forward, seizing Olivja's face and bringing their lips together once more—this time with a desperation that stole the air from the room.

They kissed again and again, their mouths crashing in growing intensity. The steamy air curled around them, thick and close. Adalja's hands slid to Olivja's waist, fingers trailing paths up her slick sides, mapping her like sacred land.

Olivja groaned softly into her mouth, the sound reverberating straight to the pit of Adalja's stomach.

Driven by need, the heiress stepped into the bath. Water sloshed over the edge as her bare body sank into the steaming depths.

She didn't stop.

Bracing herself on Adalja's shoulders, Olivja pushed forward, pressing their bodies together until the princess' back met the curved warmth of the tub. The contrast of water and heat and flesh made them both gasp, their lips parting before crashing together once more.

"...'Livja," Adalja murmured between kisses, her voice soaked in longing. Her hands tangled in Olivja's soaked hair, nails grazing the nape of her neck, drawing a shiver that slid down the Norsewoman's spine.

"You...set me ablaze," Olivja breathed, her lips trailing down the edge of Adalja's jaw to the sensitive curve of her neck. Her teeth grazed the delicate skin beneath her ear—and the sharp gasp she earned in return drove her wild.

"No faith-blooded boy could make you burn the way I do," Olivja breathed against her collarbone, her voice thick and rough with hunger.

And as if in answer, Adalja's thighs parted beneath the water—welcoming her closer.

The princess was a siren in Olivja's waters. And even knowing the danger, the Norsewoman dove willingly.

Olivja's hands roamed beneath the surface, reverent in their exploration—tracing Adalja's hips, waist, ribs—memorizing each sacred curve and freckle.

Their legs tangled. Olivja pressed against her—skin to skin, slick with water and heat, everything too much, too perfect.

"He may worship your name," Olivja breathed into her ear, "but I'll make you *forget it*...and take you the way a queen *should* be taken."

One hand gripped the edge of the tub, the other sank into the curve of Adalja's hips, dragging her closer. Olivja's lips dropped to her chest.

"Slow...deep," Olivja groaned, grinding into her. "*Claimed.*"

Adalja whimpered, arching into her, nails dragging jagged lines down Olivja's back. Marking her with her love.

"I want you to—" she gasped, "*Gods*...take me like one of your own."

Olivja smiled, dark, hungry. A lover's smile. A *conqueror's*.

She's crying out for me—and I've only just begun my raid.

The bath's warmth was nothing to the fire between them—a blaze that devoured thought, doubt, everything but this moment.

Their kisses turned frantic, leaving them breathless. Olivja's hand slid beneath the surface, fingers grazing the soft skin of Adalja's inner thigh.

"You want to be one of us, Princess?" Olivja grinned as Adalja's body flinched. She stilled her hand, let it linger—made her wait.

"But can your soft little body handle my viking hand?" she whispered, eyes locked on hers.

Without any hesitation, her lover nodded. "*Ruin me with them*," Adalja begged, her voice barely above a whisper, hands trembling with want.

Her head fell back against the tub's edge—surrender written in every curve.

Olivja didn't wait. She claimed her completely. *Properly.*

Their passion spilled over like the water around them, drowning them in unrelenting need. Drowning *her* in Adalja.

Every sensation—her skin, her breath, her lips—devoured her whole. And the way she whispered her name, moaned it, *cried it*...It made Olivja's heart race. And Liv was greedy for it.

She wanted to hear Adalja cry out in pleasure. She wanted to take every ounce of closeness and make it *matter*. For desire rose only where love had long endured—and hers had endured for years.

"*Freyja*," Olivja panted into her mouth, "has marked you as mine."

Each touch was a promise. Each moan a vow.
Years of longing—hunger, ache—finally answered.

Soon, even the bath couldn't hold them. The need for solid ground overtook all else.

They parted, breathless. Eyes dark—pupils blown wide with desire. Olivja's hands slid to the backs of Adalja's thighs. With a low grunt, she stood—lifting her from the water with practised strength.

Cool air hit their skin, but it quenched nothing. Olivja lowered her gently to the cold stone. Adalja gasped, back arching to escape the chill, reaching for her fire.

"I have you," Olivja cooed, coaxed. She pressed against her, molding their bodies together like pieces of an ancient puzzle. "Let me warm you."

She planted her palm beside Adalja's head and pulled back to drink her in—Adalja beneath her, just as she'd imagined. Her body thrummed with desire.

The world outside vanished. Even time paused.

Amber eyes burned hotter than anything Olivja had ever felt. Adalja was *finally* beneath her—waiting, watching. Lips parted. Cheeks flushed. Chest marked in bruises.

Perfect.

Olivja could have wept.
Instead, she smiled—at Adalja. At her gift.

"This fire began with you. It ends with you, " she said between shallow breaths, parting Adalja's legs like the golden gates to Valhalla.
"...I'll make this worth the gods' gaze."

With a shuddered breath, Olivja's lips traced a path of devotion up the princess' body.

Everything Olivja craved lay beneath her lips—beneath her teeth. A feast of woman and goddess, meeting her hunger with breathless whines for more.

Their bodies locked—inevitable as fate. Every movement, every gasp brought them closer to a place they'd only dreamt of.

"You're so beautiful beneath me..." Olivja moaned, voice breaking. "*It's cruel.*"

But this was the opposite of cruelty.

It was reverence. It was surrender.
It was *bliss.*

By the time they were undone, Adalja was gasping, her body quivering beneath the force of Olivja's love.

Ruined and proud.
She'd taken it like a warrior.
And Olivja—breathless, spent—was overcome with pride. With *devotion.*

She was no noblewoman any longer.

Liv hovered above her, chest heaving. The steam rising from their skin felt like proof of something divine.

"My Adalja," she purred, reaching for her face, brushing her glistening cheeks.

"I'll carry the memory of this on my hands until I die." The Norse vow spilled like a spell from her lips—one she didn't bother to translate.

And though the princess did not understand the words, she nodded. She leaned further into Olivja's warm palm, smiling, eyes closing.

She wore her pleasure like a crown.

Olivja's heart fluttered as Adalja's icy eyes opened. She parted her swollen lips to speak—

Knock. Knock. Knock.

"Princess Adalja?"

Olivja stayed perfectly still, smirk curling at the thought of someone catching them like this.

Adalja responded the opposite way—pleasure vanishing from her face in an instant. Fear filled her. As her head darted towards the jiggling handle, Olivja caught her cheeks in both hands—gently forcing her gaze back.

"*Shh*—look at me, *princess. Get to the door.* I'll stay hidden," Olivja whispered, knowing that, no matter how much she longed to be seen, Adalja's need for secrecy mattered more.

They held each other's gaze—for as long as they could—silent gratitude passing between them.

Another knock sent Adalja scrambling, snatching her robe from the wet floor.

Olivja crawled behind the tub, her own robe in hand, hugging her knees to stay out of sight.

The door creaked open. Olivja stayed silent, smirking faintly as she listened to the final notes of their stolen moment.

"Oh—Thank *goodness* you're well, Princess...I was waiting in your room for dressings."

"Lady Sapphire...Forgive me, I—I fell asleep in the bath."

"You're freezing, My Lady!"

"Yes...will you help me to my ch-chambers, please."

Their voices faded as the wooden door clicked shut, leaving Olivja radiant. A beaming light in the dim bath.

She took her time, replaying every second—blushing, fingers trembling with the memory of Adalja's skin. She remained lost in thought until the stone grew too cold beneath her bare skin.

With a grin that wouldn't fade, she tiptoed to the door, successfully sneaking back to her chambers. The only evidence of their meeting was the separate pairs of wet footprints trailing on the carpeted floors.

Her cheeks flushed pink, she gripped the front of her robe tightly and cautiously opened the door, expecting the room to be empty.

Instead, her breath caught when her eyes landed on Vincent, standing silently beside her bed, head bowed as his fingers drifted over his linen shirt, smoothing it with absent care.

His head lifted at the creak of the wood, and she stood there like a stranger to her own room.

"*Ah*, there you are, princess," Vincent said, his eyes flicking over her appearance with a faint smirk. "Decided against having me tend to your bath this time?"

His tone carried a teasing lilt, but his usual stoic demeanour seemed lighter, as though good sleep had restored some of his composure.

Yet to Olivja, the illusion was long fractured.

What once might have seemed noble or self-assured, now struck her as something different—a carefully constructed facade, more martyr than hero, built to shield the vulnerable truths he worked so hard to hide.

She scoffed, soft and low, masking the vulnerability that crept into her tone.

"You fought so hard for sleep, I figured I'd grant you the peace of it—just for a while." Her voice was steady, but her shallow breaths betrayed her unease.

Olivja's grip tightened on the front of her robe, the damp strands of her hair clinging to her back as she stepped further into the room.

The soft click of the door sealed them in—two figures suspended between the memory of last night and the question of what it meant.

Though her mind wandered to Adalja and her breathless voice. She clenched her jaw, a rush of guilt and excitement clashing inside her like an unforgiving sea.

"Such a considerate princess," Vincent chuckled and slowly moved around the bed towards Olivja, his eyes low-lidded as he looked down at her.

He stopped an arm's length away, gaze trailing over her as if he could read her perfectly. In turn, she tightened her grip on her robe, as though to conceal what had transpired moments ago.

His smirk softened a fraction. "I shall leave you to get ready, my jewel."

The change of conversation threw her off centre for a moment, a familiar tension rising within her as she realised what he was referring to.

"Vincent." Her voice halted him as he stepped past her towards the door.

They both turned, locking gazes.

"Tell me...y-you've no questions left unanswered?" Her voice quivered, as though her body rebelled against the question.

She longed to hear him give her the certainty she craved—the assurance that the three Völur women were truly responsible for the death of the Pembrooks. Most of all, she needed to know he was certain within himself.

Killing a Völva carried grave consequences in her culture...and Vincent? He was about to execute three.

If he just spoke to her, if even a fraction of him was unsure, it would be enough. She'd help him deal with it—fix it—make everything right again. She could save not only the women, but *him.*

She needed to know what he was thinking. *Desperately*.

As he looked at her, head tilting with an expression of twisting confusion, she asked again.

"You've looked into their souls, and found no mercy there? This is the end you choose for them?" Olivja's voice was steadier this time, urging, as she held her breath for what would come.

For a moment, he only looked back at her with his piercing green eyes.

In the quiet seconds of their unwavering gaze, she saw something she hadn't noticed before.

His eyes were brighter—had they dulled over time without her realizing? And yet, just as quickly, the brightness faded, replaced by the same shadowed anger she'd grown to recognise.

"What are you asking me, Olivja?" Vincent's brows furrowed deeply, his expression sharpening as confusion gave way to frustration—and perhaps even betrayal.

"You must see the storm within me," Olivja said softly, her eyes searching his for understanding. "If there's even a shadow of innocence—would you still let them hang?"

Vincent clenched his jaw, his eyes flashing with anger in the span of a single breath. Yet he stayed calm as he closed the space between them.

"There is no innocence within them, my love," he said, his hand sliding up her arm before gripping it gently but firmly. "I am sure of it." His tone left no room for argument.

And Olivja couldn't stop herself.

"But...the one who made the poison could hardly speak—her guilt nearly undid her..." Her voice softened as she searched his face for the answers he withheld. "She bore the blame without protest, to shield her kin. Tell me—what kind of murderer carries herself with such honour?"

His eyes darkened; his brows furrowed with anger.

"One who is about to die, Olivja!" Vincent's voice rose. His fingers flexed as his grip on her arm tightened, pulling her closer until his chest was against hers.

His tone sharpened, tinged with disgust, as he went on. "You spoke with them? Sought them out?"

Olivja swallowed hard, standing her ground. "I had to be sure—"

"And you hid this from me?!" he cut in, disbelief thick in his voice.

"Vincent, they are my people!" she shouted, fear and defiance tangled in her tone.

"No. *I am*, Olivja. They know *nothing* of you—care naught. *I do*!" His voice dropped into a growl, venomous and raw.
"*Or have you forgotten me*?"

His gaze flicked down to where his hand gripped her arm, and a flash of guilt and sadness passed through his expression.

In an instant, he released her, stepping back as if realising he had nearly broken his promise. A moment of silence lingered between them, thick with unspoken words.

"If that's how you feel, princess, so be it. Allow me to save you the pain of watching them die. *You will stay here.*" He stormed to the door.

"Vincent, no! Do not twist my words—I never asked to be hidden!" Olivja shouted, following him to the door, her robe clutched desperately around her. "I asked for truth, not a prison!"

Throwing it open, he barked at a knight stationed outside, completely ignoring her calls.

"See to it that she does not leave this room," he ordered, his voice clipped and commanding.

Without waiting for a response, without so much as a glance back at her, he marched away—and the door slammed in her face before she could reach him.

Thread XXXII

Outside Adalja's door, the steady bustle of maids and knights went on as they readied the castle against the creeping chill of winter.

Vincent's commanding voice echoed in the halls, though muffled by her door. The princess could hardly register the morning's noise—her mind was swirling. Even her gaze had gone distant, fixed lifelessly on the open window as the memory of the bath replayed in her mind.

Olivja's body. The press of their lips. The way their bare skin had fit together. She stared up at the wooden beams overhead, heat rising again as she relived every detail.

It was everything she had ever longed for. The thought of being ravished by a pagan had tormented her for years...and how wondrous, how merciful, that it was with one who loved her. With Olivja. She had taken her purity—and with it, her breath, her heart, her very soul.

All the unspoken desires surged to the forefront of her mind. A soft, blissful sigh escaped her, mind fluttering to impure places—until a voice pulled her back.

"Lady Adalja?"

She jolted, blinking rapidly and turning towards Sapphire, who stood holding up two gowns.

That's right. She cleared her throat. She was supposed to be getting ready.

"I...thought dark blue, Your Highness," Sapphire said with a sweet smile. "It belonged to your mother..."

Adalja, eager to forget what lay ahead, waved her hand towards it and nodded.

She remembered her mother wearing it once...though now, it felt like a sin to wear it, after what she had done with Olivja. It was long, blue, trimmed with white lace that trailed from the tight sleeves, around her breasts and down the centre line.

A pleased smile crossed Sapphire's face as she approached, ready to help dress her mistress. Adalja, without thinking, dropped her robe.

A soft gasp escaped her maid, and Adalja glanced down at herself.

Sparing love bites and bruises dotted her skin from her collarbone to her hips, down to her knees—a trail of Olivja's unspoken claim. Her stomach flipped, and a bright blush crept up her cheeks. A quiet laugh escaped her, her heart full, unexpectedly warm.

Sapphire's eyes widened, but she turned away just as quickly, modestly focussing on the gown in her hands. Her movements remained gentle, free of judgment—assuming, incorrectly, that the bruises belonged to Elias, Adalja's intended.

So, for now, the truth remained safe.

Adalja's thoughts drifted again as Sapphire slid the heavy gown over her shoulders.

She thought of the execution—of the witches, and their fate. Elias and Brahms deemed it necessary, but even now, she wasn't sure. The Pembrook killers were about to be punished for their crimes, and yet Adalja's heart remained dark and numb. Her red haired fastened the last ties and draped a dark blue cloak around her.

"You look beautiful...and strong, Princess Adalja," Sapphire said softly, stepping aside to reveal her reflection—tall and solitary.

She didn't feel strong. Or beautiful. But in her reflection, she saw her mother—and beside her, the enduring love of her father. Clenching her jaw, she raised her chin a little higher.

She was prepared to witness her parents' deaths finally avenged. In the very least, it was something to be thankful for—closure.

As the carriage arrived at Worthyn Town Square, she heard the low murmur of the gathered crowd.

Brahms stepped out first, his armour gleaming under the afternoon sun. The carriage door swung shut on its own, leaving her alone with Elias. Her eyes stayed trained on her lap, her hands twisting together.

"Are you ready, my love?" Elias' voice was soft, gentle, breaking through the deluge of Adalja's thoughts. He had pulled down his mask, revealing a look of genuine worry as he extended a hand towards her.

"No," she answered immediately, the word slipping out before she could think. "Yes? I—I don't know..."

Her eyes glistened with fear, her brow knitting as she struggled to respond. A wave of emotion hit her and she turned sharply to the right, covering her mouth with her hand as she fought back a cry.

Her sleeve dampened as tears spilled over, her shoulders shaking from the strain of holding it in.

"I...I have yet to see a life taken," she cried, wracked by the truth and fear of it.

The weight of the crown, the looming gallows, the deaths meant to be celebrated, pressed down on her, shrinking her until she felt invisible.

But she wasn't. Not to *him*.

The seat beside her shifted. Elias moved closer.

He reached for her, gently pulling her hands from her face. One hand cupped her cheek, his thumb brushing away tears as he lifted her face to his. His eyes held nothing but warmth and understanding, a quiet patience that almost undid her.

Without a word, he leaned in, his lips finding hers with a tenderness that made her breath catch. The softness of his kiss drew a quiet sob from her. Her fingers gripped his coat, grounding herself as her heart tumbled forward.

"*Elias,*" she exhaled against his lips.

Her quiet plea seemed to urge him on and he pressed closer, his arms caging her as though he could shield her from the world outside. Their bodies molded tightly together in the corner of the carriage, each seeking comfort in the closeness. Her tears slid into their mouths like shared pain.

Her mind swirled with confusion—Olivja, her parents' loss, the deaths of three women...and now, the feelings she held for Elias.

He pulled away from the kiss, his breath coming sharply as he opened his eyes. Their gazes met—blue and green locked in a silence too heavy to name. He kept his nose against hers, sighing shakily against her lips.

"I am your strength, Adalja...*let me* be your strength." His voice was soft but firm, the words brushing her as gently as his thumb on her cheek.

"If the burden breaks you, let it break me too. I'll carry it all and you with it." He spoke with quiet urgency, searching her eyes for a sign—any sign—that she could do this. That with him beside her, she wouldn't fall.

"When the time comes, hide in me. You need not watch," he whispered, his thumb brushing the curve of her cheek as he held her face gently in his hands. His lips met hers—slow, deliberate. Then again, softer still.

"I will guard you, Adalja," he murmured into her mouth, each word a promise sealed with another kiss, warm and lingering. "...from all that frightens you. *Evermore.*"

And then he kissed her again—deeper this time. A kiss that stole the breath from her lungs and pulled a whimper from the depths of her soul.

When he finally pulled away, her lips still parted, her lashes fluttered like they were waking from a spell. Her gaze clung to his, dazed and wide, the world around them nothing but silence and heat.

She didn't know what to say—or how to feel.

These kisses felt different—her emotions clouded, uncertain. Yet his affection pulled her back from the edge, echoing loudly through her.

Carefully, she nodded in his palms.

After a moment, he pulled back, his hand sliding from her cheek to her own, squeezing gently before guiding her from the carriage. Together, they stepped out into the cold, their breaths visible in the frosty air as the low hum of the gathered crowd grew louder.

The bustling town square spread before them like a sea of restless bodies, villagers bundled in patched cloaks and furs, their faces painted with a mixture of anticipation and dread.

Snow clung stubbornly to the cobblestones, crushed underfoot by the shifting crowd, while banners bearing the Worthyn crest, the wolf and the dagger, fluttered in the brisk winter wind.

Knights in polished steel stood at the perimeter, their helms glinting dully beneath the pale grey sky. Their hands rested on sword hilts or spear shafts, a silent wall of authority that kept the people from pressing too close.

Smoke curled lazily from nearby chimneys, carrying the scent of burning wood and faint traces of roasted chestnuts, as street vendors hawked their wares despite the morbid occasion.

The raised wooden gallows loomed ahead, its dark, weathered beams stark against the wintry backdrop. The ropes of three nooses swayed gently, creaking with each gust of wind—a grim promise of justice yet to be fulfilled.

As they were escorted forward, the steps groaned under their boots, the sound oddly amplified in the heavy stillness of the square.

Adalja stood beside Elias, who positioned himself close to Brahms. The knight was silent beneath his helm, his stance rigid, his hands clasped tightly behind his back as though holding himself in check.

Adalja's heavy gaze lifted to the centre of the platform. There, beyond the ropes, stood Prince Vincent—tall and cloaked, his hood casting his face in shadow beneath the noonday sun. In one hand, he held a roll of parchment—no doubt the final decree.

The faint murmur of the crowd swelled as more villagers filled the square, their voices like the low roar of an encroaching tide. Somewhere in the distance, a baby cried, silenced quickly by its mother. Yet above it all, the ominous creak of the ropes and the biting winter air dominated, a reminder of what was to come.

Klaaang. Klaaang. Klaaang.

The chapel bell rang three times—a symbol of the deaths they were about to witness—as Vincent stepped to the edge of the platform.

Adalja's breath caught in her throat. She stood as tall as she could, though the quick rise and fall of her chest felt painfully obvious. Elias grasped her hand beneath their cloaks, his hold firm. He gave her a glance and a subtle nod—one only she would notice.

It was happening.

The crowd fell into hushed silence, the final moments resting squarely on Vincent's shoulders. She was grateful it was him giving the speech—the stares alone would have shattered her.

He stood tall, his regal posture unwavering. The wind tugged at the hem of his cloak as his voice rose above the square—clear and strong, even behind his mask.

"Today, justice shall be met."

His gaze swept over the gathered crowd before settling on the three figures before him—three women whose fate was sealed by the very actions that had stolen her parents' lives. From where Adalja stood, she couldn't see them. She was grateful for that.

"Their crime is unforgivable. These women—these witches—sought to poison the Pembrook family, to rip the heart from Midhelm itself. Their treachery cost us more than two monarchs...it nearly cost us the war, the crown's security, the very *foundation* of Worthyn's past and future!"

A murmur rippled through the crowd, but Vincent's voice cut through it like a blade.

"They have been found guilty, and today, they will answer for their sins. The poison they brewed—the one that tore through darling Adalja's father and stole her mother's life—was no accident. It was a plot born of pride, wrath, and *Dark Magic*."

He paused, his expression hardening. The words stung, bringing fresh tears to her eyes. The crowd murmured at the mention of 'Dark Magic.'

"To those who still believe their loyalties are safe with Perdyr—let this be a warning... *Worthyn does not forget. Worthyn does not forgive.*"

The crowd erupted in cheers as Vincent's words echoed through the town square.

"FOR WORTHYN!"
"WITCHES!"
"BURN THEM!"
"FOR QUEEN ADALJA!"

The shouting made her choke back a sob. She squeezed Elias's hand tightly, trembling with conflicting emotions.

The kingdom's unspoken loyalty wrapped around her like a cloak, their fury burning bright in memory of her parents—an undeniable, fierce validation. Yet beneath it all, the shadow of the coming deaths settled heavy in her chest, weaving sorrow and guilt into every breath.

Vincent opened his hands to the eager crowd. They fell silent once more as he stepped back, his gaze fixed on the witches as he addressed them one final time.

"May your souls find peace."

As Vincent finished, the guards stepped forward, ushering the witches ahead. Their hands were bound, their faces pale, each carrying the weight of fate in a different way. The crowd's murmurs swelled as the women climbed the wooden steps, the boards creaking underfoot in the cold air.

It was the first time Adalja saw them. Her heart sank. They looked heartbreakingly beautiful—and so very sad.

Disappointment coiled in her gut. She had expected anger, venom, the sharp glare of villains—but when their eyes met, all she saw was a heavy, solemn quiet.

They couldn't be the ones responsible for such a heinous crime.
These were the killers?

The first witch was silent.
Her eyes were red from weeping, tears streaming down her face as she stared at the ground, unwilling—or perhaps unable—to meet the eyes of the crowd. Her shoulders trembled as she walked, a quiet sob escaping with each step.

The second was visibly frantic. She twisted in her bindings, her face a mask of fear and desperation. Her eyes darted to the crowd, to the princess, then back to the executioner.

"*Bik ek thik!*" she cried, her voice cracking as she struggled against the knights. "We beg! The aesir see us—*thoo* must see us!"

"*Thoo*—We are *kvenger* of the gods... not liars, no *morthingr*! Spill our blood wrong—this land remembers...! Blood stay forever!" Her words were wild and desperate, a mix of norse, pleading for any chance to escape the fate she knew was inevitable.

But her cries fell on deaf ears. She tilted her head to the sky and cried out, "*Odin*! Hear our cries! Release us!"

The third witch stood rigid with fury.
Her fists clenched in the bindings, jaw set, eyes burning with rage as she glared at Vincent from beneath her dark hood. Her breath came in shallow, controlled bursts, and though she remained silent, the fire in her gaze spoke volumes.

As they reached the top of the platform, the knights roughly positioned them beneath their nooses. The women stood still—each reacting in their own way—but all bound by the fate they would share in death.

The executioner approached, his hands working efficiently to adjust the ropes around their necks.

The first witch, her sobs quiet but persistent, bowed her head, almost as if accepting the inevitable. Softly, she mumbled something to herself...

The second witch, still pleading, was held tight by the guards, her body writhing in fear as the noose was placed around her neck.

The third witch, silent and furious, stood tall beneath the rope, eyes blazing with hatred towards Vincent.

And Vincent stared right back at her, unmoving.

The air was thick with tension. Their kingdom's fate, Adalja's vengeance, all rested here.

"STOP!"

A SHRILL SCREAM CUT THROUGH THE AIR, reverberating across the tense silence. Adalja knew the scream well. Her heart froze.

Heiress Olivja came charging towards the wooden gallows, her boots slapping the cold stone as she hurried up the steps.

Her hair was a wild tangle of braids and waves, and her linen dress was hastily gathered in her hands. She was breathing heavily, as if she had run for miles...

In a frenzied panic, Olivja bolted to the knight who stood by the latch that would release the planks beneath the witches. With a desperate cry, she shoved him with all the strength she could muster.

He staggered back, caught off guard, and fell right off the platform into the crowd of Worthyn people.

Her outburst was cut short. Two knights seized her from behind, yanking her away from the lever by her arms.

She fought like a wild animal, thrashing and wriggling in their grasp, her feet kicking against the wooden boards in a futile attempt to break free.

"They're innocent—they are sacred! Vincent—Listen to me! Do not kill them!" she shouted, her voice cracking as her words echoed through the square, pleading for mercy.

Her chest heaved with desperation as her eyes locked onto Vincent's, raw with fear and anguish.

"Please!" she cried again, her throat raw. "They are not the villains you seek! I know it!"

The knights pulled her back towards the edge of the stand, but her gaze never left the witches—nor her suitor.

Adalja's tears hadn't stopped since their arrival, and they came faster now at the sight of Olivja, forced to her knees.

The Norsewoman cried out as her arms were wrenched behind her back, her struggles slowing under the strain. The Ragnarvik heir searched the crowd, her eyes pleading for an ally—for proof she wasn't standing alone. But Adalja looked away.

She couldn't bear it. She didn't understand it.

Why now? Adalja clenched her fists, cursing Olivja's timing—this was supposed to be closure, the moment to finally lay her parents to rest.

First the funeral...now this?
She was furious—resentful, grieving, lost.
Why is she doing this?!

"HERESY!"
"SHE'S A WITCH!"
"HANG HER!"
"HEATHEN!"

The crowd erupted at the sight of a Norsewoman defending witches. Guilty or not, they were still witches—still Norse. That was enough.

Olivja thrashed, her face streaked with tears, as Vincent raised his hand to silence the crowd, his fury fixed on the heiress.

"*ENOUGH!*" Vincent shouted, his voice so loud and full of rage that it silenced the entire square.

He turned towards the witches, pointing with a finger heavy enough to kill on its own.

"Look at how shamelessly these witches stand there! Look at what they've DONE, corrupting my bride's mind, turning her against me! Their deaths will purge them of their sins; they will serve as a lesson to all who defy ME!"

"NO!" Olivja screamed, her voice fierce and unwavering.

She struggled against the knight's iron grip, her fury unyielding despite the pain. "You are blinded by vengeance, Vincent! If you kill them now, you risk damning your own soul—cursed to walk in darkness just like our enemies! LISTEN TO ME!"

And he did listen—but not to her reasoning. He heard only her defiance.

Vincent stormed across the platform in a blur, his cloak flying behind him as he moved towards Olivja.

Adalja stepped forward on instinct, her pulse thudding in her ears, and Brahms moved with her. But neither of them could take another step forward. Elias gripped them both, holding them in place, stopping them from reaching Olivja.

Adalja looked up at him with wide, pleading eyes, silently begging him to let her intervene. But Elias didn't return her gaze. His focus stayed on Olivja, and as Vincent reached her, Adalja buried her face against Elias' side, unable to look.

CLAP...CLAP...CLAP

Vincent's blows rang out, sharp and brutal. Olivja's pained cries echoed in the hush that followed. The entire square stood in shocked silence, as though the blows had landed on them all.

When Adalja finally pulled her face from Elias's chest, she saw Olivja—head bowed, breath ragged, still trembling with rage from the force of the slaps.

The knights dragged her to the front of the stand. Again, Adalja flinched forward, desperate to help—and once more, Elias held her back.

"He'll kill her," she whimpered to Elias, hoping he would act with her. But he didn't budge.

"He won't."

Adalja's breath quickened as she looked up at Elias's stone-cold expression. How could he be sure? Was she about to watch Olivja die?

The cowering princess looked back to the front, her tears dried up by shock and adrenaline.

She was no longer angry at Olivja for interrupting, but furious that she would risk her life like this.

Her hands shook as Vincent stepped towards the Norsewoman in anger. What would she do if Olivja was forced onto the stand like the witches?

Vincent's sharp tone cut through her thoughts like a knife.

"You will watch these women die, Olivja." Vincent's voice was cold. "And with them, their cursed hold on you."

One knight lifted her head by her hair, forcing her fiery eyes to lock onto the condemned. With Olivja restrained, Vincent turned away from her, his anger now set on the witches.

"Do it," Vincent commanded, wasting no more time, his voice carrying through the square.

Not even a final word. *Just death.*

"NO!" Olivja screamed one final time, yanking with the last of her strength. "ODIN, FREYJA! TAKE THEM—!"

The same knight clamped his hand over her mouth. Her cries stopped—no more screams to interrupt the execution.

With one harsh movement, the executioner pulled the lever. The floor beneath the women opened. The women jerked, their feet kicking, their bodies suspended in the air. The crowd held a hushed, collective breath, watching as the witches met their end.

The first witch's body hung limp, her tears now silent in death. The second still struggled for air—but her pleas had stopped. The third remained defiant, her body still—her anger unrelenting even in the face of death.

Olivja fell to the floor, weeping loudly, breathing like a rabid beast, wriggling against the knight's hold.

Vincent stood motionless, watching the finality of his decree unfold.

Adalja looked away, a hand desperately covering her mouth as her stomach heaved at the sight of the struggling women.

Justice for Adalja's parents had been delivered—but now, more deaths sat on Worthyn's shoulders...*and on hers.*

The town stayed quiet and still until the witches hung like cursed marionettes—broken puppets used only to justify death and war and division.

Eventually, a few people drifted away as the execution came to an end. Somehow, they could go about their day as if it never happened. While they returned to their routines, Adalja stood shattered—longing only to sob and sleep.

Was this what passed for normal in Worthyn? How could she ever rule such a place? Doubts swirled—about herself, about this kingdom she never chose.

The knights pulled Olivja to her feet, her body limp in the face of her failure.

"Put her in the dungeons..." Vincent's calm voice sliced through the tension. "I'll decide what to do with her."

She lifted her gaze, momentarily freed from dread.

Olivja's eyes burned as she was shoved from the platform, defiance still blazing in her gaze. She was marched towards the iron carriage—the same one that had held the witches before.

Adalja could not tear her eyes away, terrified that something even worse might happen to Olivja—haunted by the thought that this might be the last time she would ever see her.

Once the defiant Ragnarvik was secured in the carriage, Elias let go of Adalja and Brahms. He stepped forward to join Vincent, who had his temples in his hands, his face drawn with strain.

The two brothers spoke in hushed tones, but Adalja barely noticed. Her mind was racing, her heart pounding in her ears.

Freed from restraint, Adalja's feet moved on their own—her body acting without permission. She cast a final, lingering glance at Olivja's carriage, the cold iron bars separating them.

Her heart clenched. With one last shaky breath, she turned and slipped from the platform, breath quick with adrenaline.

Her steps were soft at first, tentative, but as she neared the edge of the crowd, she found her stride. She slipped into the shadows, her movements quiet, swift—every instinct urging her to remain unseen. The chaos of the moment shielded her; the murmuring crowd and distraction of Vincent and Elias kept all eyes elsewhere.

Adalja pressed herself against the rough stone of a nearby building, her breath shallow. She crept through the darkened alleyways, her mind a blur of worry and fear. But as she stepped forward, the reality of the moment crashed over her.

Her legs buckled beneath her, and before she knew it, she was on her knees, her hands clutching at the stone beside her. The tears came suddenly, hot and uncontrollable, spilling down her cheeks. She couldn't stop them.

The sight of Olivja—her strength, her desperate sense of justice—taken away. The witches—their lives snuffed out in an instant. The relief of having justice for her parents' deaths—stripped from her.

Adalja knelt frozen, hands flying to cover her eyes, breath shallow as voices blurred into a distant hum.

She didn't know how long she stayed there, kneeling in the alleyway. The fear, the guilt, the grief held her in place, and the tears wouldn't stop.

After a long moment, Adalja wiped her face with the back of her sleeve, chest tight, breaths ragged.

Just when she thought she had nothing left, the faintest scent reached her—a delicate, familiar fragrance that stopped her in her tracks.

The smell of nutmeg and cloves, soft and comforting, swirled around her as she wiped her nose. Her mother's perfume...the one she always wore.

Adalja froze, her hand still pressed to her face. For a heartbeat, everything around her seemed to fade, and all that remained was the memory of her mother's presence—her warmth, her voice, her kindness before it was all stripped away by the trials of life.

Then, the sharp sting of reality returned.

She glanced down at the dress she wore. The fabric, though now worn from time, still carried that same scent, faint but unmistakable.

Adalja had chosen to wear it today in some vain hope that her mother's strength might pass into her, that perhaps she could find courage in the fabric of that dress.

But as she sat there, crumpled and broken in the dirty alleyway, it felt like a cruel reminder of the woman she had lost, a woman who might have been able to help in this moment—the only one who might have had the power to change everything...

Tears pricked at the corners of Adalja's eyes once more, but she held them back. She couldn't afford to fall apart again, not when so much was at stake.

She couldn't stay here. Not like this.

Her heart pounded as the final choice settled in:
Go back to Elias—or find Olivja.

It felt wrong to even consider Olivja while wearing her mother's dress...and yet, not for a moment did she truly consider going back to Elias.
She had to leave—had to go to her.

She took a steadying breath, pushing herself up, letting her fingers brush the fabric one last time as if to borrow her mother's strength.

"I long to be more like you," she breathed as if the wind might carry her words to wherever her spirit lay. "But, forgive me...I am not."

And with that, she rose and left the alleyway behind, leaving shadows and doubts in her wake as she followed the only path she could bear to walk.

Thread XXXIII

"Apologies, Princess," one of the few knights grumbled as they guided her down the narrow steps to the dungeons. Their heavy steps echoed across the stone floors, exhibiting the emptiness within the cells. No whining, groaning or growling—all things that were common for castle prisons.

Olivja, rage fuelled, kept her eyes forward and her jaw clenched.

Cautiously, they walked her to the farthest cell at the back of the dungeon, pausing in front of it so the jailor could unlock the gate. A shrill metal scraping filled the room as the door was pulled open, prompting the guards to release the shivering woman.

Aggressively, she stomped inside, crossing her arms as the gate slammed behind her. She didn't bother fighting with the knights.

Her anger was only to be directed towards Vincent.

Their footsteps echoed and receded, shutting her in the dim dungeon, completely alone with her anger.

You'd best know what you're doing, Vince.
Her thoughts screamed as her adrenaline trembled throughout her.

The stone walls seemed to magnify the cold temperature as it penetrated her fur boots. She had left her cloak in the castle, leaving her in a linen dress that was not made to handle the brutal dungeon environment.

Nay. Don't question yourself...you did what had to be done.

The heiress chewed on her bottom lip as it quivered, trying to refrain from crying.

A Norsewoman in a nobleman's dungeons never ended well. She knew the sort of consequences she had earned for speaking out in public against a royal figure. Suddenly, she wasn't so sure her defiance was worth the cost...

Vincent was finally treating her decently, the women she tried to save were dead, and now, she was locked away with an array of punishments waiting for her.

Left in contemplation, she wondered what she was willing to pay for justice—when justice gave nothing in return.

She shook away the thoughts. Olivja's values were what drove her to ensure that those women felt defended and seen in their last moments. The grief in their eyes, the unwavering confidence in Vincent's...

She was right about their innocence, she was sure of it.
But what did it matter now that they were dead?

A lot of good your feelings do, Olivja. They can't save you now.
She criticised herself, clenching her fists at her sides, the tears she had attempted to withhold spilling onto her cheeks.

She paced the cell to steady her breath, the image of the hanging Völur seared behind her eyes. Visions of revenge clawed their way to the front of her mind—

No.

She didn't want to hurt Vincent. Even after all he'd done—after the way he treated her—she still couldn't bring herself to want his pain.

Pacing like a trapped beast, Olivja wore a path into the dirty stone floor, fury simmering beneath her skin. Her rage alone was *almost* enough to keep her warm.

But, like every caged animal, someone always came to prod it.

Footsteps descended the dungeon steps once again and Olivja stubbornly turned away—facing the back of her cell. She was unaware of who was approaching, but the hairs on her arms and neck stood with each increasingly loud step.

Eventually, the footsteps stopped. The imprisoned Norsewoman swallowed dryly.

But it was no executioner who called to her. A soft, warm voice filled her ears like an angel's breath.

"Olivja?"

And the dark-eyed heiress swiftly turned, her hair standing more than it would have for anyone else.

Adalja stood just a few feet from the cell door, arms crossed beneath her chest, her expression laced with disappointment. She wasted no time.

"What were you thinking?" she exhaled, voice sharp with accusation.

Olivja had been naive to believe her lover had come to help. She should've expected anger.

Of course. She comes to scold, not to stay.

A bitter scoff slipped from Olivja's lips as she flung her hands up.

"*Gods, Adalja*. What use are my thoughts? No one's ever cared for them, save to have me chained...or struck for speaking them aloud."

"Speak not in that manner. I care—"

"Do not find your courage now that I am *caged*."

The interruption landed like a blade, silencing Adalja and cementing the tension between them.

"Why did you come here? Tell me—was this visit meant to soothe me, or salt the wound?" Olivja's words, resentful and exasperated, filled her cell as she moved closer to the front wall of iron bars.

Adalja, confused by her tone, scoffed as well. "What have *I* done that you look at me so? I am not the hand that placed you here, Olivja."

She slipped her strong arms through the bars and leaned in, resting her forehead against the rusted beams. A subtle, taunting smirk touched her lips.

"Aye, that is the truth—not *you*, your husband," Liv said. "Let's ask Eli how he feels about your being here—with it, we shall tell him what you begged me at sunrise."

It became clear the subject struck a nerve. Adalja stepped forward, too quick, too defensive, her hands curling into fists at her sides.
"He's not my husband."

"Ah, then I'm not just a friend," Olivja said, cutting in with quiet sharpness. "Only lovers mind words like that."

She didn't look away. Her amber eyes stayed locked on Adalja's face, watching the way it flushed and faltered.

Olivja softened, voice low now, almost reluctant. "You know its true..."

A thought bloomed—this might be the last time she ever saw Adalja alone. And if so, then the truth deserved breath.

"Olivja, you mustn't say such things!" the princess hissed, glancing over her shoulder as if the shadows might be listening. Fear shivered through her posture, and she didn't speak again—only stared, eyes wide and searching.

The heiress took a deep, quivering breath, trying to keep calm amidst an awful situation.

"Apologies, *My Lady*...but shall I act as though I feel nothing?! I am no *court-trained creature*—I won't live behind false smiles."

Their eyes locked, resentment clashing with frustration. There was nothing more Adalja could say to that.

Olivja had already sworn to bury her feelings for Adalja, but that was *before* the princess dragged her into the bath.

It was *she* who stirred this storm, who woke the beast that now refused to sleep.
The heiress had tried to hold it back—fought to keep her hands clean.
She would not bear the blame alone.

But, staring down at Adalja through the cold bars of a cell brought her more grief than ever. And the sadness on the princess' face—quiet, unreadable—only deepened the shameful ache.

Olivja shook her head and drew back from the iron, another sigh slipping past her lips.

"And here I was, foolish enough to believe you meant me no harm," she murmured, voice like flint. "Go on, then—return to your precious Elias. He's trained you well enough."

Instantly reddened, Adalja stepped forward, her octave increasing in anger.

"Trained!? Heavens, Olivja, what would you have me *do*?! Defy the Worthyns alongside you and get us *both* killed?! At least this way I can still help!"

"*Lucky,* was I?" Liv laughed in her face. "And if they'd hanged me like a traitor, what grand gesture would you have made? A prayer? A *sigh*?" Olivja knew better than to get much angrier with her, but the question still stood.

Her eyes filled with tears, because she already knew the answer;
Adalja would have done nothing.

"Late for kindness, don't you think?" Olivja asked, her voice cracking in pain. "So go—do as the rest do. Leave me, before you bring more ruin."

Adalja, chest heaving, growled as she glared at the jailed woman. "*OH!* You have caused ruin upon yourself on your own...I've done nothing wrong!"

Stunned by Adalja's blindness, Olivja gripped the cell bars until her knuckles turned white.

"Nothing? Adalja, you've *completely—*" She cut herself off, drawing a slow breath. She only ever held back for Adalja.

A dark calm settled over her, masking the storm beneath. She pressed on quieter, jaw clenched tight, restraining the fury rising within. "You've left me to rot, *just like before.*"

Adalja raised a hand to the bridge of her nose, her words faltering through a frown. "Olivja, your life hangs by a thread and you fixate only on our *affair*? This is not about us!"

Calm shattered; she scoffed, her voice rising with fury.

"Ha! Since we crossed into this kingdom, Adalja, they care *only* for *us*. We're pieces in their foolish royal game and you ask me to bow quietly!" As she spoke, her Norse accent thickened every fierce word. "You ask me to abide by their rules—to let you marry him! I'd sooner meet death!"

Adalja, tearful and heavy-breathing, shot back, "And after your display on the stand, you might just succeed!"

Olivja growled, frustration boiling over. Even now, at a time like this, Adalja made it seem she truly cared for Olivja—as if the heiress' life hadn't already been a long chain of misfortunes and betrayals. Maybe she did care...but not enough to act. Not enough to tell the truth.

She had enough.

Adalja drew a slow, shaky breath, averting her gaze. "I am trying to help you, Olivja. Don't cast my feelings aside. If harm comes to you, I...I beg you to see the greater design—"

"I'll burn every damn design that dares to bind you to another," Olivja declared, voice ringing from her chest. "And if the flames take me too, then I'll welcome death. This is not what your heart seeks—I feel it, deep within."

"It's not what my heart seeks, Olivja—but even if it were, how could I risk all for one so reckless with consequence? One who would rather be right than live?"

"Aye, I know—the thought of me at your side must seem madness." Olivja ran her hands through her loosely braided hair, knotting it further.

Her hair mirrored the chaos in her mind as she murmured, "If I were a man, perhaps my reckless blood would charm you..." Then, raising her voice to be heard, she fixed her cold glare on her lost lover.

"Maybe then you'd lay your choice at my feet, not his!"

"...how dare you..."

"You've seen what I am," Olivja cut her off. "Born to dare the wrath of gods and queens alike." Her stubborn smirk crept back—one she'd never fully tame.

They stood silent, eyes locked—opposites that held the same fire. Anger melted into desire, and Adalja quickly dropped her gaze, shaking her head to clear the confusion.

Both knew this talk was a dangerous path. At last, Adalja found the strength to end it, turning away—but Olivja was not done.

Before the princess vanished from sight, Olivja's voice rang clear through the empty cells:

"Would you let them kill me?!"

All Olivja saw was the back of Adalja's gown and how it froze at the sound of her voice.

The brown-eyed lass leaned entirely against the bars again, arms stretched overhead, fingertips buzzing with adrenaline.

Olivja knew—this might be their last moment together.

Slowly, Adalja turned and stepped to the cell once more. The very image of poised, sorrowful beauty fuelled the jailed Norsewoman.

"There's my good noble-girl," Olivja breathed, pressing her face against the bars, heart glad Adalja had returned to grace her final moments. "You follow orders so sweetly—his, mine...makes no difference, does it?"

Her tone was soft, yet beneath it lay sharp edges of possession and relief—a hunger to claim Adalja wholly, no matter how she masked it. Their shared bath whispered truths Olivja would never forget.

Adalja's cheeks flamed, even in the cold dungeon's gloom.

The princess' brows drew down, and she shook her head slowly, eyes lifting to Olivja. "How could you ask such a thing?"

"You said it yourself—I'm a daring heathen." Olivja's smirk lingered, even as the winds of dark fury churned beneath. She fought to spare Adalja's pride—even now.

She shrugged, a bitter chuckle escaping. "Tis a fair question...if your husband wills it, this might be my final moment."

Adalja's anger flared at the word. She stepped forward, chest nearly brushing the bars. "Olivja, he's not my husband—but just for that, yes, I *would* let them kill you."

Though blunt and swift, her answer was no veil to Olivja.

Scoffing softly, she studied Adalja now close, eyes tracing every curve and line, drinking it in while she could. She cared not how brazen her gaze lingered—if this was the last time, *she'd claim it all.*

"You wound me, princess," Olivja said, pouting mockingly—before her grin returned. "Gods, after everything—you still lie. *Poorly*, might I add. And for whom? No crowd. No court. There's only us here, dove."

Her voice dropped lower, no longer angry—soft now, and warm. "And only I see your heart as it truly is."

But even in the warmth of her tone, Adalja stepped back. Her cheeks burned brighter. She shook her head, and when she spoke, her trembling voice betrayed the boldness of her words: "You have no grasp of what burns within me, Olivja."

"Then *tell me.* You showed it so freely this morning." The words trembled with desperation, but still carried their weight. "You need not hide it from me, Adalja."

"There's nothing to hide."

"They could hang me for this..." Liv said. "Would you truly let me walk to the rope still doubting what I meant to you?"

Her words thickened the air. Silence swallowed them again.

Adalja's sorrowful gaze said everything—but not enough. She dropped her eyes to her fidgeting hands.

Olivja stayed still, eyes locked on her—desperate.

"This is not where our story ends," Adalja whispered, lifting her gaze with quiet certainty. Tears shimmered in her eyes. "But yes...I would."

At last, Olivja's strength—and restraint—broke.

She reached through the bars, seized Adalja's waist, and dragged her close until their bodies met iron. Adalja gasped, flushed and breathless.

One of Olivja's hands held her firm against the bars. The other gathered her skirts, dragging them upwards until her bare palm met the skin of Adalja's thigh—cold, bold, unforgiving.

She squeezed *hard,* claiming one of the many places her mouth had worshipped that morning.

"Need I remind you..." Olivja exhaled, her breath fogging in the cold air. "Your body belongs to me now."

A desperate whimper escaped Adalja's lips. "I know—"
But Olivja didn't let her finish.

Olivja seized her face, yanking her forward into a kiss that stole their breaths. It wasn't tender—it was raw, all fury and desperate passion.

Adalja met her with equal heat, threading her fingers through Olivja's auburn hair as if anchoring herself there.

It could've been their last kiss. They both knew it.

Olivja growled against her lips, her free hand gripping the back of Adalja's neck. She held her there like she could will time to stop.

She broke the kiss and squeezed her neck, a silent plea trembling in her fingers.

"Now tell me the truth," Olivja breathed, their lips still brushing. Her voice broke. "*Say that you love me, Adalja.*"

But she didn't wait for an answer. She kissed her again—harder. Her tears turning the kiss salty—no longer sweet.

"Liv..." Adalja gasped into her mouth, yanking her hair. The heiress welcomed the pain—it felt like proof.

The princess lifted her lips, parting them like she was about to speak.

Olivja looked into her eyes—those soft, ocean eyes that always gave her away. She knew that there was love behind them...why else would she kiss her this way? Why else risk everything—now, of all times?

A gentle sob left Olivja's mouth, silently begging for the truth...but it never came.

"*Adalja!*"

A voice, loud and furious, boomed from the far end of the dungeon.

The women jolted apart, scrambling in opposite directions. Vincent stormed to the cell—he had seen the kiss. He seized Adalja without hesitation, gripping both wrists hard.

"What do you think you're doing?" the prince hissed, voice like venom.

Adalja crumbled beneath the fire of his glare, and Liv hated herself for it.

"Vincent, enough! Release her! Whatever rage you carry, it belongs to me!" Olivja shouted, her voice breaking with fury, fear, and helpless tears as she stood caged behind the bars.

They had made a mistake—she knew it. The sight of his hands on Adalja made her palms burn, as if her rage could melt iron.

"I tried to help you, Olivja—I kept you from being hanged out there—*this* is how you repay me!?" Vincent snapped, tightening his grip until Adalja let out a fragile cry, dropping her head in shame.

"Let her go!" Olivja cried, white-knuckled as she clutched the bars. She never thought she'd feel relief at the sight of Elias—but there he was, jogging towards them, with Brahms lingering behind.

"I'll handle her, brother. That's enough!" Elias called sharply, moving to Adalja. Vincent dropped her the moment he heard Elias' voice.

"Be sure you do," Vincent hissed, his voice like venom, low but sharp enough to slice through the room. "*She kissed her.*"

Elias and Brahms froze, the accusation hitting like a crack of thunder between them.

Brahms straightened, shoulders tense, but it was Elias who truly faltered.

The taller twin's breath hitched, pain flickering fast across his face—then something darker.

Vincent's jaw clenched. His eyes dropped to the floor, not in shame, but as if his thoughts dragged them down. A slow, quiet envy pooled beneath the silence, unspoken yet palpable.

He was already seething from the execution, but now he had seen Olivja's heart. And that chilled her to the bone.

She had made her choice—and now, she was reaping it. The hurt in his eyes only stoked the fire she had ignited at the gallows.

He stepped towards the cell door, blocking Olivja from the world beyond. Her eyes pleaded, wide and desperate.

"*No—Elias, please,*" Adalja whimpered, hidden from Olivja's view. "Don't leave her here!"

"Come, Princess. Now." Brahms' low voice guided her out with Elias. Their footsteps faded down the corridor.

Olivja looked down at the ground as the sense of abandonment returned. Of course it would end like this. It was all her fault. She had risked everything—but for what?

A lot of good your feelings do.

She hated herself for being swayed so easily—hated herself even more for not choosing submission when she still could. Her feelings numbed with fear—the kind that settled deep when left alone with an angry Vincent.

The soft rattle of keys signaled the beginning of the end.

She stepped back quickly, retreating to the farthest wall. Her tear-filled eyes rose to meet his.

The shrill creak of iron on stone echoed through the dungeon as her cell swung open. She considered making a run for it—but with the hooded knight beside the prince, she knew she wouldn't get far.

Vincent stepped inside.

"I believed we understood each other, Olivja," he said, voice laced with pain, the disappointment unmistakable.

"What a damned mistake I've made." The words weren't for her—they were muttered to himself.

With a sharp motion, he tore off his mask and hood, revealing fury behind his eyes. The fabric fell to the floor like the weight of his trust.

The hooded knight followed, shutting the gate with a resounding clang. He carried a coil of rope and a flogger. Olivja shuddered at the sight.

She had never been whipped, but the unknown—the threat alone—only tightened her resolve. Clammy hands clutched at her dress, an anchor in the raging tempest.

"You spoke out against me—*publicly*!" Vincent's voice cracked like thunder as he gestured towards the gate. "In front of the entire kingdom, Olivja! *Do you not see what you've done*!?"

"You tried to keep me from the execution, Vincent! You weren't *listening* to me!" she fired back, her voice loud and laced with desperation. "You killed them at the first hint of guilt—no trial, no truth, no chance to speak! *Why?*"

Without warning, Vincent closed the space between them and slammed his palm against the wall beside her head. The crack echoed through the dungeon, shaking her to her core.

Olivja screamed and flinched, silenced by the sheer nearness of his fury. His hand had stopped a breath from her cheek—the near miss sent shivers down her spine.

"Because I will be KING, Olivja!" he roared, his voice filling every corner of the cell. "I don't need to prove myself to you, to anyone! You know *NOTHING*!"

His voice burned like flame, and her tears spilled like wax from a candle too close to the heat. He struck the wall again—louder this time, sharper, closer to snapping.

She cried out, shrinking beneath the crushing strength of his fury. Never had she felt fear like this. Each strike chipped away at her resolve, leaving her trembling.

"You know nothing of what it takes to *hold* truth—to *survive*! You're naive to the weight of death, blind to the sacrifices that come with rule!" he shouted at her and his hand clamped to her face, rough and bruising.

She sobbed, her head jerked with every furious syllable.

"But you will never know, Olivja, because I have shielded you from *EVERYTHING*!" His voice cracked—a ragged, broken cry, spilling the weight he carried: fear, betrayal, hurt.

"F-forgive me, Vincent, please...I swear it, I only chased what I thought was right!" Her voice broke through her sobs, every word soaked in regret.

She regretted everything that had led to this moment—and yet, it was only the beginning of his anger. She knew he couldn't hear her over the storm in his mind. She was but a leaf in thc whirlwinds of his rage. Winds she alone had summoned.

For the briefest moment, his fingers softened against her cheek. She whimpered.

His gaze darkened, shaped by something that looked like hatred...but she knew better. The tears in his eyes told a different story—one he'd never name.

She met his stare with a quiet apology, her eyes pleading for forgiveness without a single word.

His gaze dropped to her lips, and his thumb traced them—painfully gentle, as if touching something already lost. When he spoke, his voice was barely a breath.

"Is that what you call right? *Kissing her*?"

Her breath caught. Her heartbeat faltered.
There was no undoing what she had done.

His lip curled in a disgusted snarl, and once more, he tightened his grasp.
"Tell me why," he hissed, raspy and low. His fingers dug bruises into her cheeks as he waited for an excuse they both knew wouldn't cut it.

"Vince..." she whimpered, using his name in a desperate attempt to soften his anger. But she had no words—no explanation that could repair the damage.

In her search for Adalja's heart, she had dug herself into a hole and now it was too deep to escape. There was no saving her, and she knew it. The kiss. Her public display of defiance. It was enough to have her killed.

All she could do was hope the Vincent she knew—she trusted—was still somewhere inside. That he wouldn't hurt her for such treason...or rather, for breaking his heart.

"I never meant to—"

"TELL ME, Olivja!" His shout rattled her soul.

He slammed her head against the cold stone wall. She sobbed sharply, both hands flying to his forearm, clawing at the painful hold.

"DON'T, VINCENT!" she screamed, her voice cracking from the blow. "Please-please—forgive me, I-I—"

The true horror of her emotions, of her decision, had manifested as him. His anger, his betrayal, his heartbreak now hung over her like a volcanic cloud.

Beneath him, consumed by hopelessness, Olivja finally realised—
She had lost *everything.*

"TELL ME why you've done this—why you've forsaken yourself! Why you've forsaken *ME!*" His voice cracked, desperation bleeding through his rage.

His hand moved to her neck, tightening, as his voice dropped to a venomous whisper—for the final time.

"Speak it true, Olivja...*before I lose myself completely.*"

Her breath hitched as she processed every word. Her resistance faltered as she looked up at him.

"I *love* her."

The admission came as a whisper, slicing her throat and lips like glass. Maybe that's why she said it so softly—to spare herself the pain. To soften the blow.

She barely said it loud enough for him to hear, as though the truth might lose its weight if spoken softly—as though it could save her from death.

Telling him the truth ruined everything—*everyone.*
Adalja. Their marriages. Vincent. What remained of their bond.
And yet, the one risk she cared least about was the only one truly in danger: *herself.*

But she couldn't lie to him any longer, to anyone. She couldn't—even if she wanted to.

Where she thought his eyes would soften, they hardened. His grip on her neck and wrists tightened, and she choked out a sob.

Vincent let out a strained breath. His composure unraveled. His hands trembled, losing all sense of strength as he gazed down.

"After all this time—*after everything*—you say *that*?" He paused, shaking his head as though fighting an internal battle she couldn't understand. *"No..."*

"No. *You won't love her.* You'll hate her. I will...*make you...hate* her."

With a sharp yank, he dragged her towards the wooden post in the corner of the cell.

She gasped, her lungs burning as she fought to breathe.

He pinned her wrists above her head, binding them tightly with rope. She thrashed against his hold, panic overtaking her.

"We were meant to do this together," he growled, his voice cracking with emotion.

"*Together*, Olivja. And now you—no. I won't—I won't let you..." His words were as disheveled as he was, fuelled by an undeniable rage.
"I will not lose you to this."

His hands trembled as he worked, his anger spilling over like a dam about to burst.

"Vincent, allow me to speak!" Olivja begged breathlessly, her voice breaking. But her desperation fell on deaf ears. With a final sharp pull of the rope, she was stretched to the post.

He stepped back, growling as he raked his hands through his hair. "God, Olivja—you've said enough! You've said FAR too much. And now I—I have to fix it...fix *you*."

His pained exhale echoed in her ears, as though this were some twisted, ironic fate.

"I never meant to betray you," she sobbed. "Vince—please, please, show me mercy!" Dread set in, knowing nothing could stop what was coming. It hollowed her—left her numb. She had never begged for anything in her life.

"I am, princess. *This is.*" His voice dropped, cold and unyielding. He cupped her cheeks, his touch disturbingly gentle as he wiped her tears away.

"No one will know about this, Olivja—I promise. I'll keep you safe," he added, his hands tightening around her cheeks for a moment. "So I must—I *must* do this..."

"Vince—"

"If you can't control yourself, Liv...I'll do it for you." His eyes shut tight, trapping them in eerie silence.

Then, just as quickly, his eyes opened. He stepped back, breathing heavily—as though the darkness of his decision had finally settled on his chest. His gaze drifted to the flogger. Silent. Decided.

"*Go ahead.*"

Without warning, the flogger stepped up and his hands tore through her linen tunic-dress. She screamed, thrashing as the ropes carved into her arms, her whole body jolting in panic.

She begged, sobbed—but it was useless. Her back was bared. Stripped of cover. Stripped of mercy.

Pain. Sharp. *Searing.* It tore through her like fire.

A scream burst from Olivja's lips, filling the narrow cell. It broke into a strangled gasp as the brutal reality of the first lash sank into her flesh.

She curled her hands into fists, nails digging into her skin, trying to hold herself together as tears burned her eyes. Her body trembled, locked in place by shock. The pain pulsed outward, dizzying, stealing her breath.

Only one lash and she was shaking. It cracked something deep inside her. A pain beyond imagining.

Anything. She'd give anything not to feel that again.

"Vincent! Wait—please—Y-you gave your word—stop—!" Her voice broke, gasping. But the words didn't reach him.

He dropped his voice, jaw trembling, eyes full of something raw and broken. He stood tall, fists at his sides, fury rippling off him in waves. It sent a shiver through her—skin prickling with goosebumps.

"If pain is the price for your safety, Olivja, so be it...*I'll bleed for this as much as you will.*"

THREAD XXXIV

ᚦᛖ ᛒᚢᚱᛞᛖᚾᛋ ᛟᚠ ᚺᛖᛁᚱᛋ ᚦᛖ ᛒᚢᚱᛞᛖᚾᛋ ᛟᚠ ᚺᛖᛁᚱᛋ ᚦᛖ ᛒᚢᚱᛞᛖᚾᛋ

ᚨᛞᚨᛚᛃᚨ

THE SILENCE IN THE HALLS sent Adalja spiralling further into the dark pit of her fears. Each step echoed a sharp reminder of what had happened.

Brahms walked silently behind them, following closely as the prince dragged the princess forward in a surge of indignation.

His once-inviting green eyes had turned to piercing darkness beneath a hood pulled tight, a mask resting low on his nose. His brows furrowed, never once meeting her tearful, pleading gaze.

Her heart shattered and pounded at once, sending cold numbness to her hands.

The only real sensation was the slow, almost absent-minded curl of his fingers digging into her flesh.

"E-Eli—"

"*Silence.*"
Elias growled, dragging her around the corner. His voice sent chills through her, and she obeyed at once, dread blooming behind her eyes.

A lump stung her throat each time she swallowed between panting breaths, her short legs struggling to match his furious pace.

Her head snapped back towards Brahms, desperate for someone—anyone—to help. The princess' unruly hair mirrored the chaos in her mind. When their eyes met, his face was grim, deliberately turned from hers. He was angry with her too.

Her heart twisted, like a vice tightening cruelly around it.

Adalja didn't know what to do, what to think—only that nightmarish fear coursed through her for both herself and Olivja.

"*Elias, please—*" Her voice cracked as she yanked her arm free, shattering the frost that had gripped her bones since the moment they were caught.

Elias spun, forcing her back with a furious step until her heels struck the stone wall. His masked face was mere inches from hers as he held her against the wall. He refused to let her speak, slamming his free hand against the stone beside her head—a rage only his brother could match.

Her breath hitched, trembling, as she looked up into his narrowed gaze of pure anguish and betrayal.

After a long, silent beat, Brahms finally spoke. His voice strained with concern as he looked between them, Adalja's eyes flicking towards him.

"Prince Elias, this..." Brahms trailed off as he moved closer, his boots heavy against the stone floor.

"Did you know?" Elias' voice was a whip—sharp, relentless—his glare fixed on Brahms. His grip tightened, pressing Adalja harder into the cold wall.

"What? No—"

"Don't you lie to me," Elias growled, fury vibrating through her bones. The force of him was so overwhelming, she could barely breathe. He tilted his head towards Brahms, his fury thickening with every word. "Did—you—know?"

The sight of the only men who had ever stood by her colliding in a storm of fury and betrayal tore her apart. She wasn't just losing them. She was unravelling *all* of their bonds. The shame of it suffocated her.

Brahms stepped forward again, his voice quiet but firm. "Olivja's *always* been this way, Elias—she's an untamed *Pagan. That's all.*"

The words stung, and a sick knot twisted in Adalja's stomach. Olivja was already locked away for her own crimes—yet now paying the price for a kiss that had shattered everything between them. A kiss Adalja had wanted too.

The guilt pressed heavily against her chest. Blaming Olivja felt cruel when, deep down, Adalja knew—the blame was on her shoulders. She had sealed Olivja's fate with her own hands.

Adalja shook her head, her voice trembling with urgency.
"Elias, if anything happens to her...I-I won't survive it." A cry fell from her lips, desperate. Fragile.

His head snapped to her, eyes like twin daggers—green and merciless—cutting the breath from her lungs. His anger was a living thing, choking the space between them. Adalja recoiled, her heart splintering further beneath his gaze.

"You will not speak of this in these halls," Elias growled, his voice low and dangerous. He stepped closer, tearing off his mask, his breath hot against her skin as the tip of his nose brushed her cheek. "Do you understand me?" he whispered fiercely—his voice both a command and warning.

Her whole body flinched as Elias' fingers dug harder into her arm, silencing her with a force that could break bone. Adalja nodded weakly. Brahms fell silent, his gaze heavy but unreadable. She was left to drown in the stillness between them.

He pulled her from the wall, guiding her down the corridor, her feet barely managing to keep up.

Every step was fire. Each one burning away Olivja's love. Brahms' loyalty.
Elias' trust.

She was slipping from everything she knew. With each passing second, her life crumbled beneath her feet.

Elias ordered Brahms to remain in the hall, then shoved her into her chambers. She stumbled in panic, her heels betraying her under the sudden roughness—never expecting such contempt from him.

Her room was as dark as Elias' presence behind her. The weight of two worlds pressed on her chest. Her red, swollen eyes met his, flinching as he slammed the door shut.

"What were you thinking?" he hissed, his hand flying upwards as his face twitched with fury.

She'd never seen that look on his face before—jaw clenched, eyes sharp with fury. Her breath caught. She stepped back, slow and cautious, as if one wrong move might set him off further.

The world tilted slightly, her head light, like the dizzy warmth of wine—but this was colder, sharper. It churned in her gut instead of blooming in her chest. Her eyes searched frantically for the man she knew, but a stranger stepped towards her instead.

Elias' voice barked, sharp and cutting through the tense air: "How could you do this—to me, to Olivja—to *us*?"

Vulnerability flashed across his expression, but it vanished as quickly as it appeared, replaced by the sharp angles of his glare. In two long strides, the prince closed the distance between them.

Adalja's breath hitched as she tilted her head back to meet his burning gaze, her knees threatening to buckle in submission. Before she could collapse, his hands seized her biceps, holding her upright.

His blazing eyes locked onto hers, searching for something, anything—a shred of honesty, perhaps.

Adalja's panicked breaths came quick and shallow as he pulled her in. His grip shifted, one hand snapping to her jaw with firm authority. She froze under his intense stare, her wide eyes pleading as his breath fanned over her face.

"Speak, Adalja...*please.*" His voice dropped to a strained growl, a mixture of desperation and command.

"I—I..." Her lips quivered as her voice faltered, the words caught in her throat. Wild thoughts swirled in her mind, but no lie came to her. She was lost, fumbling for words she didn't have.

"*I don't know.*"
The words finally rose—choked—ripping through her vocal cords and spilling from her lips. Tears welled in her eyes, tracing paths down her cheeks, dampening his thumb and fingers where they gripped her face.

The truth burned between them, a painful realisation that neither could escape. She wasn't lying—and that truth tormented them both as their gazes locked.

Elias' jaw clenched, his nostrils flaring with each laboured breath.
"Why were you down there?" he growled, his voice low and threatening, his gaze fixed on her lips like a predator in wait.

He stepped closer, and she retreated instinctively. His grip tightened, drawing a wince as her lips compressed beneath his hand.

Adalja's nervous hands rose to his wrist, trying to ease his grip. Her fingers tugged feebly, and after a tense moment, he released her. She stumbled back, holding her sore cheeks, her small frame quivering with each uneven breath.

"I knew not what would befall her, Eli," she whispered, her voice breaking.

"She is Vincent's *devotee*, Adalja," he hissed, each word sharp as a blade. "He would never hurt her."

"Olivja—"

"Do not speak her name to me!" His voice cracked like thunder, cutting her off.

His pacing footsteps echoed through the room, his hands raking through his hair in frustration. It was as if he were trying to physically tear the anger from himself, but it clung stubbornly.

"Elias, please," Adalja said, lips trembling as she stepped towards him, eyes wide with desperation. "You must understand."

He stopped abruptly, his gaze snapping to hers, pinning her in place. "*Make* me understand!" he shouted, his voice cutting through the air like a whip.

"What manner of thought possessed you? Was I a fool to believe our bond ran deeper than this...?" His hands sliced through the air in wild gestures, punctuating his words. "How many times have I asked you to trust me? To confide in me?"

"I do trust you, Elias!" she cried, the words bursting from her with raw urgency. But her desperation only seemed to deepen the rift between them. Her chest ached, a deeper kind of hurt blooming inside her.

She was losing him, losing *them both* to this forbidden love, to the web of guilt and longing woven through their hearts, their loyalties. She had thought they shared a bond, but now she feared it was slipping through her fingers like sand, much like her relationship with Olivja.

Adalja reached for him, fingers twitching, but his next words stilled her.

"Then why do you feel a stranger to me, now?" His voice broke, quiet and raw.

The anger in his eyes dimmed for a moment, replaced by a haunted pain. Both of them stood on the precipice of something they could not undo, the consequences of love and their choices hanging heavy in the air, impossible to escape.

"This—is strange to me as well," she said, her voice barely audible. "I...I have barely begun to understand it myself, Eli. Please..." Her voice cracked, each word a fracture in her resolve.

"Understand *what*!? *What* is strange?! You have said *nothing, Adalja!*" Elias roared, his patience unravelling. He stormed towards her, backing her against the wall.

"Tell me," he begged, "what has borne this...?"
His hand found her jaw again, though gentler this time, as he leaned in close. Their bodies met, the space between them vanishing as he pressed forward, his hand sliding to rest at her neck—not forceful, but firm.

It wasn't a suffocating touch, but one that held an unrelenting grip—a need to keep her from slipping further away.

The door creaked open, drawing both their attention.

Brahms stood in the doorway, his expression taut with concern. He hesitated, unwilling to intervene but ready to act if the prince's anger escalated.

"Elias." Brahms' voice was sharp, *warning*.

Even so, the prince didn't release her immediately. He drew her forward, fingers sliding back and pressing just beneath her jaw.

Adalja's breath hitched, her heart racing as she stared into his eyes, which blazed with hurt and frustration.

And then, it came. The truth that none of them were ready to confront.

"My love for *her*, Elias."

The words slipped out, unbidden and unstoppable. They hung in the air, heavy and irreversible.

Adalja's chest heaved as her confession settled over them all.

The silence that followed was suffocating, her words lingering in the air like held breath.

The force of her own truth left her unmoored. Her legs trembled, as though the earth beneath her had shifted without warning, and she had nothing solid to cling to. The raw honesty terrified her; the words echoed in her mind like a mantra she couldn't swallow.

She couldn't believe what she had said—no, what she had admitted out loud for the first time.

But the truth was undeniable: she loved Olivja.
Somehow, saying it aloud felt like both a liberation and a curse.

Her chest rose and fell rapidly as her thoughts raced. Memories of Olivja flooded her mind; the way her laughter lit up even the darkest moments, the softness in her gaze when no one else was looking, the whispering strength she carried like armour.

And now, standing here with Elias' piercing gaze on her, all of it burned brighter, sharper, as if daring her to deny it.

For a moment, there was only silence, save for the soft rustle of the winter wind outside. Brahms' eyes darted between the two, his expression a mix of shock and disbelief...maybe even anger, but he said nothing, his lips pressed into a thin line.

Elias froze, her confession slicing through them like the crack of lightning.

"You have woven lies around me from the beginning..." he scoffed at her, looking down with a disgusted expression as though he no longer saw the woman beneath the facade.

"No—'twas not so!" Adalja tried to plead, desperate fingers curling around themselves. She clung to his chest and pushed at him all at once. Her eyes were locked with his as his fingers flexed momentarily.

"How long have you let me believe I was enough for you?" he shuddered.

"That is enough, Elias!" Brahms said through gritted teeth as he stepped in to aid the princess.

Adalja's eyes flickered to Brahms, then back to Elias, unable to look away for long. She wanted to hug Elias, to apologise, to try to explain...but she remained unmoved, frozen in time.

His lips curled into a bitter smile, though there was no warmth in it. "Of all the things you could have said, Adalja..."

Adalja could see tears brimming in his eyes, and for a moment, she couldn't tell what he felt.

His expression held a dark, unbridled anger—yet his very presence breathed fear, like that of a lost lamb. She was unsure of which emotion to fear more.

She opened her mouth, but no sound came out. The way Elias looked at her—like she was a stranger, like she had betrayed him in the worst way—made her want to vanish into the shadows.

Elias shook his head, a dry, humourless laugh escaping his throat as a single tear fell from his eye.

"Do you even recognise the weight of those words?" His voice cracked, his emotions warring within him, clashing together—pride clawing for outrage, heart aching for understanding, mind spiralling into a labyrinth of outcomes.

"Do you not realise what could have happened to you if it was my *father* who caught you instead of I!? He'd...he'd make you fear darker depths than death itself, Adalja—make *me* fear those depths. I—" He staggered a gasp, his words spilling from him, frantic, as if searching for answers only he knew.

Her heart ached with the thought that her truth was his undoing.

"My father...he—" His voice broke on the word, but he stopped himself, clamping his mouth shut as though even speaking it aloud might summon his shadow.

Brahms shifted uneasily, taking a hesitant step towards Adalja, his gaze sharp and wary.

"My Lord..." A quiet call to ground the prince.

But Elias shot him a sharp look, his hand snapping up to silence him.

Adalja's lips quivered, her breath hitching as tears pooled in her eyes—on the brink of falling.

"I never meant to hurt you, Elias," her voice faltered, the sorrow needling into her, relentless. She hugged herself, trying to hold together the pieces.

"*Never meant to.*" His laugh was sharp, cutting through the air like a blade. "You *have* hurt me, Adalja, but in ways you could *never* comprehend," he hissed, his green eyes wild with indiscernible emotion.

"You—you could *die* for this," he choked out, his hands cupping either side of her face as though he was shielding her from the world, from his anger. "If my father finds out—he *will* kill you."

"Enough." Brahms finally stepped up to them. "You're frightening her, Elias. Look at her," he said firmly, his voice a low rumble.

Her chest tightened at the sound of his voice—steady, unwavering, just like always. Tears welled again, unbidden, blurring the shape of him as he stood there—still defending her. He owed her nothing, not now, not with her lies and betrayals.

"I have no wish to frighten her, Brahms," Elias muttered, his voice dropping to a near whisper—as though to himself.

He looked down. His hands slipped to her wrists, thumbs brushing softly along the insides where her pulse trembled. She could feel the tremor in his touch.

"The price for loving a witch...*is carved deep in stone.*"

The words chilled her spine. She pressed back into the wall, her heart hammering.

Elias' gaze flicked to Brahms, then back. For a heartbeat, his face softened—just a flicker of the man she'd trusted. But it was fleeting. The shadow of betrayal loomed too large.

"Elias, I beg you," Adalja whimpered, reaching out—desperate for him to see her pain. "If what you say is true—then help her. I cannot bear this night without knowing if she is safe!"

Elias stepped back slowly, his shoulders rising and falling with measured breaths.

"Then I'll see to it that Olivja is well," the wounded prince mumbled, eyes falling to the stone floor.

Without a glance at Brahms or Adalja, Elias swept from the room.

The door swung shut behind him.

"You've truly done it now, Addy, and not for the better..." Brahms sighed, eyes burning with loud disappointment. "How could you let her warp your mind? What were you *thinking*?"

She couldn't face another battle of questions she had no strength to answer.

"Olivja has done nothing, Brahms. I have cared for her always...and you, of all people, know this!" she cried, heart at war with the world.

"What I know is *this*—if you didn't have *him*," Brahms said, gesturing to the door where Elias had stood, "you'd be facing the same death as those who stole your parents. And what would that gain you? Satisfaction? A moment of pleasure?"

"I would have gained *LOVE*!" Adalja cried back at him, breathless—she wasted every drop of strength on those words—on the idea of true love.

"*I* love you...*Elias* loves you—" he gritted out. "Your *parents* loved you..." Each word drove him closer, heavier than the last. "And you would throw it all away for the love of *some Viking*? She *cannot* be worth that much!"

Her breath caught. A sharp tightness bloomed in her chest as his words sank in—slow, deliberate, like a blade pressing down rather than striking.

"She is worth *everything*!" she cried, stepping from the wall, gesturing wildly as her devotion spilled out. "She embodies all I have longed for, and all I have sought to become!"

"With her I feel I've never *breathed*—like I've spent my entire life *choked*, *gasping* beneath waves." Her hands trembled at her chest, clawing as though to rip the feeling out. "And she does not merely *save me*, Brahms. With her—I am *truly* myself."

Brahms froze, shoulders dropping.

"I've spent my life walking blind in faith. I will do it no longer! I do not want this life—I want *her*!" She took in a shaky breath, looking down at her open palms, trembling as she imagined Olivja's hands in them.

"She makes me believe in a love that isn't caged...nor crafted as a treaty...but in a love that is so free, so *profound,* the Gods themselves would fall from the sky to congratulate me!"

"And I know she feels the same," she finished with a fragile whisper, her voice breaking alongside her heart.

Adalja stood in silence, tears slipping down as she gasped for the breath her words had stolen.

She hadn't been ready for how it would feel—to bare her heart like this. And now, with the cost of love burning in her hands, she knew it was too late.

No amount of love could mask the risk of it.

She lifted her gaze to Brahms, finding his face dulled, eyes numb to her pain.

"All of this, Adalja...yet, *you kept it from me*. From *her*." Brahms spoke into the silence, thick as smoke. "And now you've made us into *fools*..." His voice faltered, the quiet sound of his heart breaking in front of her.

"What if he kills her...?" Adalja choked out, her tears blinding, her guilt all-consuming.

His eyes narrowed, glare sharp enough to freeze her where she stood.

"What if...? *GOD, Adalja*!" Brahms growled, making her flinch. A bitter laugh escaped him, thick with disbelief. "What if he kills *YOU*? Has *that* thought crossed your mind? Has it?" He threw his hands up in surrender.

"I am not the one in a cell with Vincent!"

"Who says you won't be? *Elias*? What power does he have?" Brahms snapped, brows raised in disbelief. "What am *I* supposed to do if he fails!? How am I to protect us from this?" His dark eyes locked with hers, searching for reason in her madness.

"You would risk *my* life for *her*?" His voice broke with the final question, fear bleeding into his anger as he stepped in close.

Adalja stood in shock, breath caught, the image of him dying for her desire turning her stomach.

"No..." she whispered, the lump in her throat tightening as though her own heart begged to be torn out. "I would *never* let anything happen to you, Brahms. I-I only worry for her." Her voice shrank with the last words, her eyes falling shut in shame.

"Perhaps, Adalja...you ought to start minding your own being," Brahms said through clenched teeth, "*and spare a thought for those who truly care for it.*"

Adalja said nothing. He was wrong. *She was far from selfless.*

Brahms stepped back, sighing before he spoke again. "You have not cared for that woman in over a *decade*. And now—*now* you choose to confess it all?" He scoffed, stunned.

"Do you truly believe throwing yourself at a *pagan's* feet will mend what has been broken?" He paused, but didn't let her answer. "It will not. And if you are not cautious, Princess, you will lose all that *truly* matters...*if you have not already.*"

The words sank heavy in the room. She dropped to the floor beneath them, small again—unsure, unsteady. The war in her mind dragged her heart down, sinking in the cavity of her chest like a stone.

Brahms stood in silence at the edge of her room, arms crossed, letting her grieve—but refusing to leave.

The isolation slowly sunk its claws into her as she curled in on herself, her sobs the only sound left.

Thread XXXV

ᚦᛖ ᛒᚢᚱᛞᛖᚾᛊ ᛟᚠ ᚺᛖᛁᚱᛊ ᚦᛖ ᛒᚢᚱᛞᛖᚾᛊ ᛟᚠ ᚺᛖᛁᚱᛊ ᚦᛖ ᛒᚢᚱᛞᛖᚾᛊ

ᛖᛚᛁᚨᛊ

Elias shut the door behind him and leaned heavily against it, dragging in a shaky breath. Adalja's confession pressed against his chest, sharp and unrelenting.

Olivja. Of all people, it had to be her.

He clenched his fists, his mind a battlefield of confusion and anger. For so long, he had kept his emotions measured, controlled—Adalja had shattered that with a single truth.

The prince pushed himself off the door and began walking the winding corridors of the castle, each step echoing his unrest.

He wasn't rushing—at least, that's what he told himself. Olivja would be well. She always was—more or less. Still, his feet carried him towards the dungeons with purpose.

This wasn't for Olivja, not entirely. It was for Adalja—for the anguish in her voice when she begged him to check on her.

The chill of the stone stairwell bit into his skin as he began to descend. He faltered at the top, his thoughts a whirlwind.

He saw Adalja again—trembling with shame, yet defiant in her love.
Brahms—with his maddening, unwavering loyalty.
Vincent—snared in the same chaos, perhaps deeper than any of them.
And Olivja—*damned Olivja*—standing at the centre of it all, so effortlessly destructive without ever trying.

His heart twisted as her name echoed in his mind.

He had always accepted love in all its forms—love that defied the faith-borns' rigid tenets. But it wasn't the sight of two women kissing that gnawed at him.

It was *her*. It was this tangle of lives that never should have crossed like this—never should have collided with such force.

The thought of Olivja being in love with Adalja—it was too much. It made sense in a way that infuriated him.

Of course, it had to be *Adalja*. The one person he could not share, the one bond he could not sever. And yet, that wasn't what left him breathless, wasn't what made him sick with himself.

It was the anger—the selfish, ugly anger—that he had no right to feel.

Of all the women to steal Adalja's heart, it was Olivja.
And of all the women Vincent was tied to, it had to be someone like her.
Openly defiant, boldly sinful.

But she was also his friend, someone he cared for more than he ever admitted, and someone who carried her own unseen burdens.

His teeth clenched as he descended further, faster now, the stone walls narrowing around him. He welcomed the cold, let it seep into his skin, hoping it would quiet the storm within.

Halfway down the steps, a sharp echo rose from the depths below, bouncing off the walls.

He froze, his hand gripping the wall as his ears strained for another sound.

There was a moment of heavy silence, then another reverberating noise—low, guttural, and too far away to make sense of.

A shiver crawled up his arms. He swallowed hard and continued downwards, his pace quickening, his heartbeat a steady drum in his ears.

Whatever waited below was too late to stop now.

SNAP!

Another sharp echo resonated in his ears, a painful memory surfacing at the sound of a whip. He flew down the remaining steps, landing hard as Olivja's shrill cry echoed off the stone walls.

"*Enough.*"

His brother's cold voice echoed, followed by a louder THWACK—and a sharper, more desperate scream.

He sprinted towards the cell where they'd first found Adalja.

As he reached it, his stomach dropped—his heart too.
Now at the bars of the cell, he heard and saw *everything*.

Olivja hung from a wooden post, arms stretched above her head, bound by coarse brown rope. Her dress had been torn open—her back raw from the lashes of a hooded figure, flogger in hand.

Vincent paced, breathing heavily, muttering to Olivja—or to himself.

Elias's trembling hand pushed open the iron door, the screech announcing his presence. At the sound, Olivja's eyes snapped towards him. Shock and desperation flooded her bloodied expression.

Her eyes lit with desperate hope, while Elias's dimmed with horror.

"*—Elias—*" she coughed, sobbing, tugging weakly at the rope that held her upright. She was a sweaty, tear-streaked mess—eyes wide, like a doe cornered by hunters, pleading for mercy she knew would never come.

"Call not for him, *Olivja*...you know he won't help you." Vincent growled, flashing a murderous look at Elias.

Elias stepped closer, breath quickening, heart sinking.
"What have you done, brother..." he whispered, hands faltering at the sight of Vincent unravelling in his rage.

His eyes flicked over it all—the splattered blood, the hooded whipper, the trembling muscles of the Ragnarvik heir...he was stunned into silence. But that silence burned into anger.

"What HAVE YOU DONE!?" Elias shouted at him.

Never had he imagined Vincent would hurt Olivja so viciously—no matter the crime.

Vincent stopped pacing and turned to Elias, palms open to the ceiling. "What does it look like, Eli?" he exhaled, breath ragged, eyes gleaming with madness.

Torture. Jealousy. Hatred. That's what it looked like. Not love. Not Preservation. *Control.*

Elias' fists clenched as he shook his head in disbelief. "If Dagrun knew of this..."

"HE WOULD THANK ME!!" Vincent roared, stepping closer—his vest soaked in the stench of blood and sweat. He pointed towards Olivja. "I am *saving her*, Elias!"

"How is this saving her, Vincent? *Look at her*!" he demanded, heart breaking at the sight of two people he loved—reduced to bloody ruin. His eyes flicked from Olivja's torn back to Vincent's sweat-slicked brow. "You *must* stop this—she's had enough."

"And if I stop and Father comes home?!" Vincent shouted, his voice cold enough to chill their spines. "When he hears what Olivja's done—the way a *Pagan* spoke against his court...the way she kissed a *woman*—what do you say he'd do to her if not *ALREADY DONE* by *me*!?"

The question left Elias stunned and silent.

Their father was capable of far worse than a lashing—they'd experienced it firsthand. Elias knew Ezekiel would descend upon her in seconds if he came home and she wasn't *dealt with*.

His hands trembled at the realisation that, in some twisted way, Vincent was right. As much as he wished he could—he was helpless before their father.

He looked down at the cobblestones, stepping back as he debated how to go on.

"And what of the wedding...? She can't be covered in wounds when you marry—her people will see." Elias grasped for any excuse to outweigh the dread of Ezekiel's vindictive return. "If you continue, brother, she'll be beyond curing."

"She will survive this..." Vincent's voice was low and dark as he turned back to Olivja, who had been granted a moment's peace during their argument. *"She's strong...like me."*

The words sent a chill down his spine; his fingernails carved crescents into his palms.

"...And what of her maid? What do I say when she asks for her?" Elias pushed one last time, desperation clawing at his voice. "This won't go over well for the Ragnarviks, brother—you're hurting one of their own—"

"Then keep them away...at least until I'm finished with her." Vincent stepped towards Olivja, whose head hung limp in the silence that followed.

Elias's eyes burned. His body froze.
He was afraid. And that fear overshadowed all else.
That fear was what backed him out of the cell, face blank with shame.

Olivja lifted her head in silence, her gaze meeting Elias' as he closed the heavy iron doors.

He looked away, unable to bear the guilt of denying her relief.

He told himself he'd apologise later.
Later, he would explain that Ezekiel's punishment would've been far worse than Vincent's.

Vincent took her chin and lifted it, both of them wearing the same pained expression as their eyes met.

Elias' heart raced, his nerves frayed by that old, familiar ache—watching abuse unfold and doing nothing.

He left the dungeon before more of it could be seen, the sounds of her pain were more than enough to shake him.

As he reached the top step and pushed open the dungeons' door, he was met with wide blue eyes. Not Adalja's.

Nimble's.
His father's jester.

The others called them 'it.' A thing. A trick. But Elias knew their name.

They were strange, yes. Haunting, absolutely. But they belonged to the castle. They'd been there for him when no one else had.

Their head was tilted, arms slack by their sides. And in one hand, a small piece of chalk.

Elias looked down.

They had drawn a picture. A broken heart—jagged, cracked down the centre in two strokes, like it was done with a trembling hand.

When Elias looked back up, they were gone.

A shuddering breath escaped him.

This wasn't like most of their visits...they didn't draw this to make him feel good, or to make him laugh...no.
This was something else.

Disappointment, acknowledgement, *heartbreak.*

He stared at the empty space where the jester had stood—until Olivja's echoing cries forced him to move.

As he climbed the stairs to Adalja's room, Elias's mind swirled—vacant and uneasy. He wondered what this would do to his bond with Olivja.

What made him feel worse was knowing that not a hair on his body felt any anger towards his brother. Even after all of that.

Their bond ran deeper than any marriage, any conflict, any trial.

There was no question—he would abide by Vincent's wishes, and keep them away from Olivja until he was done.

No one truly grasped the malice of King Worthyn. And if it came down to it, Elias would protect himself, and his brother, above all else.

But in that dungeon, he saw a version of Vincent he hadn't seen in months—broken, angry, afraid. And it terrified him.

It appeared that the more the marriage plans unfolded, so did his brother.

THREAD XXXVI

ᚦᛖ ᛒᚢᚱᛞᛖᚾᛋ ᛟᚠ ᚺᛖᛁᚱᛋ ᚦᛖ ᛒᚢᚱᛞᛖᚾᛋ ᛟᚠ ᚺᛖᛁᚱᛋ ᚦᛖ ᛒᚢᚱᛞᛖᚾᛋ

ᛒᚱᚨᚺᛗᛋ

BRAHMS HAD STAYED WITH ADALJA THROUGH HER TEARS, giving in to the desire to console her, unable to keep his anger from showing—especially when she was crying like a child.

Adalja's panic finally dwindled, though her face remained flushed and tear-stained, her anxious feelings conquering all else as she worried over Olivja.

"She's well, Adalja," Brahms assured. "Elias will handle it, I do not doubt it."

"Do you believe Vincent would harm her?" Adalja ignored his reassurance and paced around her room, hugging herself tightly around her corset.

"By law or rage, he could end her life!" Her voice rose with worry, her eyes still shedding tears.

"No...he wouldn't. I am certain of it." Brahms, sitting on her bed, held his helmet in both hands, looking at the floor as though the cracked stones could offer reassurance.

"Elias will keep her safe...and all will be as it was, Princess."

The jealousy and resentment that stirred when it came to Olivja was deeply ingrained in his persona. Even so, Brahms was anxious for the well-being of the Ragnarvik woman.

Somehow trouble always found her.

However, as awful as it sounded, Brahms was glad it wasn't them who stood in Vincent's path.

A sudden knock at the door jolted Brahms to his feet, clearing his throat.

"You may enter," Adalja called shakily, wiping her tearful eyes with the backs of her hands.

Thankfully, an exasperated Elias entered the room. Brahms took a small step forward and drew a deep breath.

"Well?" he asked swiftly, and the room filled with a heavy silence.

Elias, shutting the door behind him, nodded.

"She is well...she simply needs to rest and to stay hidden for a few days until the town quiets down and forgets about her outburst. She set them off quite easily."

A weight fell from Brahms' shoulders as he heard that Olivja was fine. Adalja, releasing an audible sigh of relief, clutched at the necklace around her neck.

"Thank goodness," she whimpered and turned towards her bedroom window.

An awkward silence sat in the air.

By now, everyone was aware of Adalja and Olivja's complicated relationship.

Brahms kept his eyes on Elias...for a handful of reasons.

He was surprised by how calm Elias seemed. Olivja had spoken up against his brother publicly, and immediately following, his bride-to-be was seen embracing her.

It was more than enough to reduce a man to shambles. And yet, Elias was unwavering and stood tall...almost too tall. Despite his relatively positive attitude, his demeanor remained dark and melancholic.

The prince's eyes darted around the room, revealing how his thoughts wandered. But never once did those emerald jewels land on Brahms...which was unusual. Typically, he couldn't escape Elias' gaze.

"I shall go," Elias said, clearing his throat as he turned to leave, taking a final glance over his shoulder at the distressed princess.

It was obvious that he wanted more from that conversation, but Adalja, still peering out her window, said nothing more. Her thoughts were tunneled on one thing—or rather, one Norsewoman.

Brahms tried to give Elias a look of reassurance—perhaps thanks—but the prince ducked out of the room without another glance.

He watched the door, feeling disappointed that Elias left so quickly and he wasn't going with him. Looking back to the window, he sighed seeing the princess still sulking at the sill.

"I…will go too," Brahms said, slowly stepping towards the exit. "Uuunless you need me, for anything?…Adalja?"

A moment of silence passed before she realised he was even speaking, pulling a heavy sigh from Brahms. It became clear to him that Adalja was not interested in any company or conversation. Her worry bled off her like dye in water.

"Princess…Elias confirmed Olivja is well…What more do you need to feel at ease?" he asked, a bit louder to ensure she heard. Frustration flared in his chest, and he tried his best to hold it down—let it sink into his teeth instead of letting it out on her.

Adalja finally turned her head. Her eyes were red from the tears that seemed never-ending since her arrival at the Worthyn castle. She hugged herself and looked down at her feet.

"There is no ease in me," she admitted weakly. "Not where it concerns Olivja."

There was a pause, and then a chuckle escaped Brahms.

"She has *never* been an easy one," he said with a scoff, lifting his helmet. "Yet still, you cannot stay away." Brahms snickered, sucking at his teeth trying not to further tease her in such a fragile state.

As Brahms slid his helm back over his head, he walked towards the door, his armour softly clinking as he reached it.

Whether his comment upset her or she was too lost in thought to hear, he wasn't sure. He glanced back a final time, shaking his curly head in exasperation at the disinterested princess.

"May sleep find you well, Addy," Brahms sighed, closing her bedroom door gently as he stepped into the hallway.

A shiver ran along his spine and limbs. For whatever reason, something in the walls in the hall chilled him to the bone.

Typically, Adalja was his only concern, but he spent too much time around Olivja to be confident that she wasn't getting into trouble.

For Adalja's sake, he set his mind on ensuring Olivja was safe in bed.

After checking her room and finding it empty, Brahms made his way down towards the dungeons, hoping to not find Olivja still there.

His heavy footsteps echoed and bounced along the dungeon walls as he descended the steep steps. Soft mumbling and distant whimpers bounced back. Cries and whimpers were common sounds for dungeons, but he had patrolled the Worthyn dungeons before...these sounds were new.

As he descended, incoming footsteps urged him to pause.

A hooded knight approached, head low, black armour splattered with dark browns and purples—dried blood—a flogger in his hand.

Black armour...
He suddenly remembered the short knight who had teased him before.

A chill ran along his spine as he realised he had been flippant with a *punisher.*

Slipping back against the cold walls, he allowed the other to pass while his mind succumbed to worry.

Clenching his jaw, he reached the bottom floor and at the end of the wide room sat Olivja's cell. Quickening his pace, Brahms sped towards the back of the dungeon, glancing into each cell as the whimpering grew louder.

Did he lie to us? To me?

He immediately replayed Elias' words in his mind. The prince had been careful not to say what happened to Olivja, but he'd made it sound as if she were well—*unharmed*.

As he came to the front of Olivja's cell, it was clear that wasn't the case. With a deep breath, he gazed into the dimly lit cell.

Vincent stood inches from a seemingly unconscious Olivja, cupping her cheeks, whispering to her softly.

The heiress—tied to a post—bled profusely, her back painted with lashes from an apparent flogging. Her once beautiful tunic, now recklessly torn, exposed her trembling body.

A wave of horror, anger, and shock washed over the knight as he stared at what looked to be a lifeless, tortured version of his childhood friend. He caught sight of Vincent, wiping his thumb across her blood-splattered cheek, a heavy exhale huffing from his nose as he nudged it against Olivja's.

Thankfully, Brahms' face was hidden behind his armour; as Vincent turned to look at him, his true emotions remained hidden.

"...Sir Brahms..." Vincent's tone was raw and low as he took a step back from Olivja. "If you don't mind... she'll need assistance to her chambers."

Pulling a small handkerchief from his pocket, Vincent wiped away red smudges he had cleaned from Olivja's cheek as he approached the iron gate.

"Y...yes. Of course, Your Highness," Brahms stuttered in fear at first, but very quickly readjusted his tone, standing straighter as he remained as nonchalant as possible. "Have a good evening, My Lord."

In Vincent's eyes, the encounter at the funeral made it clear—Brahms had no concern for Olivja and her pain meant nothing to him. He couldn't be more wrong.

Vincent passed without a second thought, and Brahms stood frozen for a moment, waiting to hear his retreating footsteps before engaging with Olivja.

Once the sounds of his echoing stomps reached the stairs, Brahms yanked his helmet off of his head, tossing it carelessly to the ground. He ran to the heiress, his eyes wide and glassy.

Quickly, his trembling hands lifted her drooping head. He had seen lashings before, but they were nothing like this. This had gone too far...even a brutalised knight could attest to that.

Her head fell limp, her eyes completely shut, sparking deeper panic in him.

"Liv," he called to her, his breathing turned to gasps as she remained unresponsive. He tapped her face several times, and when she showed no reaction, he began assuming the worst.

"Olivja!" Brahms cried louder. He held her face in one hand while the other undid the tight ropes that had carved gouges into her flesh.

"*By God's wounds...*" He grunted and cursed, using all his strength to undo the knots that had tightened over hours of pulling.

Eventually, the rope fell to the floor, and her arms dropped to her sides—waking her from unconsciousness. She cried out in pain, gasping for breath. Olivja's eyes fluttered open as shallow sobs spilled from her lips.

Brahms very quickly held her up by her hips, repositioning her face to his.

"*Shh*—I have you—it's *Bramble. Look.*"

When their eyes met and she realised Vincent was gone, a trembling cry escaped her lips. His heart tightened and throbbed all at once.

"What were you thinking, Liv?" Brahms whispered shakily, wiping sweat and tears from her drowsy eyes.

Tormented and manipulated, her expression carried a weakness that Brahms had never seen from her. Her once amber eyes were now a darker shade, as though the fire behind them had been completely extinguished, leaving an empty, forgotten gaze.

"Forgive me," she whimpered, her voice hoarse and raspy, and he knew what caused it. *Screaming.*

"Do not—do not ask forgiveness for *this*," he said, shaking his head, voice low and rough. "Save your apologies for other things...later, perhaps." A faint chuckle followed, meant to lift the heaviness from the air.

Typically, he considered himself bad with words, but Olivja used to be someone he could make laugh or, in the least, snicker, especially in inappropriate moments. And yet, as he attempted to make a jest, she stayed silent and unamused.

Her head fell limply against his palm, her eyes fluttering shut as she failed to keep herself awake amidst the pain, exhaustion, and blood loss.

Brahms swallowed dryly, unsure of how to proceed. "Olivja, I need to get you upstairs."

"Leave me," she begged, turning her head away from him, tears and sweat spilling off her cheeks. "Please—I—I can't move..."

And unfortunately, she was right. Any sort of walking or manoeuvring would jolt her back, and after being whipped for God knows how long, Brahms knew it would be excruciating no matter how he did it.

Gulping, Brahms took a closer look at the open wounds carved into Olivja's back. Some of the older lashes were already darkening as they coagulated. However, her back was more wound than skin.

He realised that she likely wouldn't be able to walk, let alone move her upper body. He sighed heavily. Now it made sense why Vincent had seemed happy to give him such a task; he knew it would be impossible for Brahms to move her peacefully.

"Liv...listen to me, truly, I'll be as gentle as I can," Brahms tried his best to sound confident, but his voice was as nervous as he was. "Just let me get you out of 'ere."

Knowing she was going to resist no matter what he did or said, he reached out and began moving her on his own.

Despite her cries and gasps of pain, he pressed on. He did it quickly, wanting to get her into position without stopping to readjust.

He came in close and lowered her arms onto his shoulders, a shrill groan vibrating in her throat. While keeping her arms as elevated as possible, he grabbed her thighs and lifted her, holding her chest to chest like he would a child.

Brahms knew this would apply the least amount of pressure to her back, and so, despite how awkward it was for her to be against him, he did it.

The two were never affectionate towards each other. They hardly even hugged...and that wasn't necessarily because Brahms didn't want to.

Olivja made it known that she would rather die than be touched by Brahms. And yet, as he carried her out of the dungeon, her head fell limply into the crook of his neck without any resistance.

She melted into him, shaking like a frightened animal. As he carried her through the halls, each step elicited a cry, whimper, or groan from the injured Norsewoman.

He could tell she was trying to be quiet, but she failed each time. Ironically, while his steps weakened her, they only strengthened his rage.

Seeing her reduced to a helpless victim angered him more than he wanted to admit.

It wasn't like her to act this way, and it exposed the true depth that Vincent's punishment had dug.

Brahms wanted to help her, avenge her…but the reality of the situation made it nearly impossible. Vincent was likely going to get away with this, and a knight like him could do nothing but watch.

"Hold on, Liv." His words were a hastened whisper as he increased his speed, trying his best to maintain a smooth ride for her.

She groaned, her hands trembling, trying to find a piece of armour to cling to.

"We're nearly there," he mumbled quietly to her as he climbed the castle steps, reaching the halls of their rooms. His breaths were heavy against her hair, and he clenched his jaw to keep her steady.

When they arrived, he carefully pushed open her door and shut it behind himself.

Inside, a worried Edith was sitting at Olivja's desk, wearing nothing but her nightgown, her hair done in a loose braid.

Brahms hadn't had the chance to speak privately with Edith, but he knew her well…or he had, prior to leaving with the Pembrooks. A sharp pain passed in his heart seeing her ageing face.

She turned towards the door, her eyes wide as she saw Olivja's mangled back.

"Brahms?" The older woman immediately stood from her chair, gasping. "*Gods above…*what happened?!" she exclaimed, rushing to his side as he entered the room.

"Vincent," he grunted, moving to her bed. He knelt onto her mattress as Edith flung the fur blankets to the ground. He was thankful that the maid was here...he didn't want to handle Liv alone any longer.

"Lay her down, quickly," Edith's words were precise and quiet as she reached out to help.

Edith carefully helped lay the heiress on her belly, placing her palms down flat beside her head. Getting Olivja down was easier than picking her up, but as her body was able to relax, the adrenaline subsided and the true pain of her wounds started to show.

"I need to get her aid." Shakily, Edith moved to her desk chair and swung a dark robe over herself, preparing to leave. "I will be back, my Olivja," she added and swiftly left the room, shutting the door behind her.

Olivja grunted loudly into her pillow, and her once flat hands curled into fists as they gripped her sheets.

Brahms looked down at her with worried eyes, swallowing hard. He wasn't sure what to do now. He wanted to be more helpful...but being around Olivja like this was a difficult task.

Immediately following the first grunt, the Ragnarvik woman cried out in pain, her breathing becoming shallow and swift as her sobs began.

Even Brahms could tell that this was dangerous.

"Olivja." He tried to be gentle and knelt beside her bed, placing an awkward hand on top of her shaking fist. "She'll not be long now...y-you're strong."

After a few short moments of stifling her suffering, Edith returned with a basket of supplies.

Brahms knew he didn't want to be around for this part. Brahms pulled his hand from Olivja's. But, before he could step back from the bed, she gasped.

"*Don't leav*e," the wounded woman begged into the white fabric of her pillow, her shoulders twitching.

Brahms would give her hell for this later. The last thing he desired was to be there while Edith picked and cleaned her wounds.

His hand started to shake as he realised he couldn't say no to her...not while she was like this.

Sighing shakily, he laced his fingers with hers and took a seat beside the bed.

Edith conjured the ointments needed to properly clean such wounds, but thankfully, she also knew to give her something for the pain. She reached over Olivja and handed Brahms a small wooden bowl.

"Make her drink," Edith said tiredly, still breathing heavily as she returned to grinding the herbs.

"What is this?" he asked while bringing the red liquid to Olivja's lips. Brahms knew better than to refuse her.

"Poppy," Edith sighed. "It will ease the pain."

And after hearing that, Olivja took it well, willing to consume anything to drown her agony.

Unfortunately, though, Edith couldn't wait for the flower to kick in before beginning; her wounds were already starting to form scabs and close at the ends.

"Are you staying?" the old woman asked while ripping away the remaining fabric that covered Olivja.

He hadn't considered that carrying her up the stairs was *not* the hardest part.

As Edith questioned him...Brahms deeply wished to say no and walk out of that room obliviously. In fear of his true wishes spilling out of his frightened lips, he silently nodded.

Edith was pleased that he agreed to stay, and the moment she began picking and cleaning Olivja's wounds, it became obvious as to why. Brahms' service quickly went from moral supporter to physical restrainer.

For the first thirty minutes, while waiting for the poppy to cloud her senses, the pain of the cleaning process was excruciating.

Olivja, bearing the full force, wailed into her pillow while her hands dug into the sheets. Reacting on their own to the pain, her hips and legs jolted involuntarily—the stinging ointments inflicting additional torment.

Swiftly, he held both of her wrists and pressed them down, preventing her from pulling away from Edith's quick and desperate hands.

He didn't like doing this. He wanted it to end as much as Olivja did...maybe more.

Brahms was thankful that he had grown so much over the years. When they were younger, Olivja gave him a run for his coin. Even now, as she writhed in agony, she was strong.

In fact, as he looked down at his childhood friend, bearing the unbearable, he painfully acknowledged how strong she was—and always had been. A knot caught in his throat.

A sharp, shrill cry left her lips, and Brahms shakily exhaled, looking back to glare at Edith. He knew it wasn't her fault, but he was tired of seeing her this way.

He never wanted to see this again.

"I know, child," Edith whimpered, panting. Her eyes were teary. It was very clear that it pained her to hurt her heiress.

"My—fault—" Olivja sobbed, her shoulders and arms shivering in shock. "Forgive me..." Her quickened breaths turned into hyperventilation as she repeated, *forgive me*, again and again.

Brahms hated imagining how many times Vincent's flogging must have forced those words out of her. But as angry as he was, he knew that her anxious breathing would only bring her more pain.

"That's enough now, Olivja. You're with us..." Brahms growled, interrupting, trying to knock some sense into her. He moved one of his hands up to hers, squeezing it with reassurance. "*Breathe.*"

In response, Olivja tried her best to take a deep breath. As if on cue, the poppy finally flooded her system, and as she exhaled, her sobs quieted to whimpers.

Her contracting muscles melted into the mattress, and her skin softened...as though every fiber in her had instantly relaxed. As her body eased, the preparation of her wounds did as well. Edith was able to work quicker, and while Olivja was still in pain, she could handle it without needing to be restrained now.

Still, Brahms—whether consciously or not—continued holding one of her hands.

Edith sighed as she dropped the bloody iron forceps into a bucket of water. A thick white cloth was brought out, and Brahms' final task was to help wrap the heiress in the bandages.

With Olivja sedated, the two of them were able to clean up and tuck her in for sleep with ease. Edith, her hands full with supplies and bloodied rags, moved to the door first. She gave Brahms a nod before exiting, likely to go get cleaned up herself.

The knight, still sitting beside the close-eyed Olivja, sighed shakily, exhausted and ready to leave. He slowly stood, but as he did, his hand was squeezed a final time.

"Bramble," he heard her whisper and looked down.

Olivja's eyes—puffy, tearful, and darker than they ever had been—gazed up at him.

"...speak no word of this to her."

He locked eyes with her and took a sharp breath. Even now, after being brutally flogged and painfully fixed, Olivja was still worrying about Adalja above anything else.

Adalja was part of the reason she was beaten in the first place, and yet, amidst her struggle, her first coherent comment was about Adalja. It shook him to the core, forcing his preconceived notions and opinions of Olivja's childlike infatuation to shift. It was more than that, and he finally believed it.

He sat back down and gave a shaky nod, swallowing hard.

"She will not learn of this," he strained, unsure of whether he would keep his word. He watched as her eyes closed once more and lingered there beside her for a moment longer.

Once she finally fell asleep, Brahms considered his duty complete.

Carefully, he let go of her hand and stood, double checking to make sure she would stay asleep before moving to her door.

He opened it and glanced back towards Olivja.

His heart throbbed with darkness more than ever before. It was no coincidence that it came from knowing Olivja more deeply than he ever had.
And yet...he was just as lost as before. Perhaps even more.

He found himself lost in thought, standing in front of the Prince's room. He was angry Elias had lied—angrier still that he had let Olivja suffer, and even more so that he now had to keep this a secret from Adalja.

The knight's hands were clammy from simmering anger, jaw clenching with frustration as he reached for the wooden door. Brahms struggled with whether he should intrude on the man's personal space, but his righteousness outweighed all other options.

His fist came down hard three times on the wood before he stood tall in wait. His heart hammered in his chest, trying to focus on the right things to say. To not speak on emotion alone.

"...Sir Brahms?"

Brahms blinked, eyes snapping up to meet the masked prince now that the door was opened.

"*Elias,*" he breathed the name quietly, trying to contain his composure and not burst out in justified anger.

"Yes?" Elias glanced around the halls, on edge, before his green eyes returned to Brahms.

As their gazes met, the frost on the edges of Elias' face softened. He nodded towards his bedroom, inviting Brahms in.

For a moment—only that one moment—Brahms' heart fluttered, his fingers buzzing with electricity at being invited into his sleeping chambers. But the reminder of why he was here struck hard the moment he stepped past the doorway.

Elias shut the door behind them.
"What brings you *here*, Brahms?" he asked, tilting his head slightly down at the shorter man.

Brahms' eyes flickered over every surface of Elias' room, making mental notes to bring up later...if things went the way he was silently begging for them to go.

"Do you know where your brother is?" Brahms asked, eyes squinting at the prince, wondering if he'd lie to him again.

There wasn't much that Brahms drew the line at, not much he stuck his claws in, but loyalty, honesty, *duty*...those were nonnegotiable.

No matter what his heart whispered when he looked at the stoic prince, this was something he could not turn his back on. And in the silence, he'd already gotten his answer.

Elias cleared his throat, stepping closer to Brahms.

"I'm not certain...What makes you ask?" His tone was tight. Brahms' anger flared at the way he spoke—so dismantled from his usual demeanor that sent a chill through the knight's body.

"Do you not know?" Brahms asked, raising his brows in speculation.

"Brahms? Are you well?" Elias asked, avoiding the question as he stepped closer, quickly towering over him.

The deflection of answering only pushed his frustrations further down a path of no return.

"Is Olivja *well*?" Brahms retorted, challenging the prince to answer honestly. Brahms never broke eye contact, his gaze fixed and searching for any hint of deceit.

"I gave word to you and the princess, as I recall." Elias shook his head. His hands lifted for a moment as if wanting to reach out to the knight—then dropped to his sides once again.

Elias sighed, running a hand through his already-disheveled hair, his face still half covered by the dark fabric.
"What...is the reason for your questions?"

Brahms scoffed, his restraint snapping at the deflection of his question once again. Lying without lying...it was almost worse.

"You must have forgotten the smallest of details Elias..." Brahms trailed off, eyeing the prince with a narrowed gaze.

Elias' eyes widened slightly at the nasty tone. "No...I-I," he stammered.

There it was again.

Brahms inhaled deeply before speaking again.

"'Tis comical, truly," Brahms sneered. "You spoke not a *word* of how Vincent lashed her—left Olivja to *bleed in chains.* Is that *well* to you?"

Elias looked like he could be sick, even if his face was partially hidden.

"Brahms..." Elias breathed out nervously, raising his hands defensively. "I...I had no desire to scare Adalja. Lying was never what I sought..." His words trailed off, clearly unable to give a good reason for what he'd done.

"You lied to *me,*" Brahms said, stepping back from Elias to create distance. But Elias was quick to close it, following his retreat.

Brahms raised his hand at the prince to halt his advances, knowing he was trying to make up for the dishonesty.

"You do not understand," Elias exhaled, his eyes worried as he realised Brahms didn't want him near. He paused mid-step and straightened. "I cannot defy him...I am...afraid of what he will do."

The words were mumbled, almost incoherent, but Brahms was desperate to find a good enough reason for breaking his trust and leaving Olivja as tattered and beaten as she was.

"You *fear* Vincent? He is *your* brother, Elias." Brahms shook his head, unable to listen to the excuses. "How do you think Olivja felt?"

"No..." Elias closed his eyes, inhaling deeply. "Not *Vincent*...my father." He sighed, almost choking on the words as if admitting the fear was a punishment in itself.

Brahms faltered in his anger for a moment, seeing the look that crossed Elias' eyes—but the rage to avenge Olivja won.

"Your father did not raise the lash. *Vincent* put Olivja to torment. You let him strike her until she was raw!"

"It is a lesser sentence than Ezekiel would happily give that woman...I do not *ever* wish to see harm to Olivja..." Elias trailed off, sitting at the edge of his bed slumping over as if defeated. "She is my truest companion," he admitted, eyes flickering sideways to give Brahms one long glance before returning his sorrowful gaze to the stoned floors.

"Is that how one treats a friend? Is that how you make sense of her suffering? And what of your lies? Am I to forgive them?" Brahms asked, stepping towards the prince wearily, afraid of falling under his charming spell.

He hadn't expected to see such vulnerability in the face of accusation.

"Still, you do not understand," Elias snapped, anger slipping into his voice. "Let it be said—Liv was lucky to escape with so little. And if protecting Adalja means deceit, then I shall wield it...*as shall you*." Elias spoke more sternly now, lifting his head with a commanding glint in his eye.

"You cannot ask that of me, I am no liar."

"*You will be*, should your love for her be more than mere words," Elias returned, matching Brahms' harshness.

Brahms flinched, his jaw tightening as he looked away, anger warring with reluctant agreement in his expression.

Silence hung between them, Elias' words sinking in like heavy stones. The prince's gaze was unrelenting, daring him to challenge the truth he'd laid bare.

Brahms exhaled sharply through his nose, his fists clenching before he crossed his arms over his chest—as if to stop himself from lashing out.

He stepped back, pacing a few strides to release the tension gripping his chest. But the heat of Elias' stare burned into his back, his words still lingering, cutting through Brahms' resolve.

He hated it. Hated that Elias was right. Adalja could not know.

When Brahms finally turned back, his anger had dulled into something quieter, more cautious. Elias had slumped slightly, his elbows resting on his knees and his head bowed, the flicker of his earlier anger giving way to exhaustion.

"Why are you afraid of him? King Ezekiel?" Brahms asked, his voice softer now, though the frustration hadn't entirely faded.

He moved slowly, cautiously, as if approaching a wounded animal. Sitting beside Elias with a deliberate space between them, his hands clasped between his spread knees, he sighed heavily and waited, his mind bracing for something awful.

"Vince and I have never known love from that man," Elias said with an emotionally distant tone, his eyes hollow as he stared at the ground.

Elias' hands rubbed against his thighs, clearing his throat as if to brace himself. "My father *is* malevolence...he is a walking punishment, and he does not forgive," Elias answered quietly.

And the prince continued: "Olivja, *a Norsewoman*, spoke out in front of the entire town against Vincent. She was *lucky* he was not near. But even a whipping may not be enough to save her if he hears of it."

They sat in silence together for a few minutes as Brahms digested the heavy-hitting words.

"And you believe that justifies your brother's actions?" he asked bluntly, not finding it in himself to beat around the bush right now.

The silence that followed was more than enough of an answer. But then Elias broke it with a hushed voice.

"Vince is only doing what's necessary. To keep her from being killed, to prevent an *uproar*, Brahms." Elias shook his head. "Our people do not take kindly to Norse-folk...least of all, my *father*."

Brahms clenched his jaw, the anger seeping back in quickly, and he pushed himself up from the prince's bed.

"I cannot stand by someone who allows torture in the ways I saw tonight," he responded, clenching his fists at his sides. "Pagan or not. She is my ally."

It pained him to have to be like this with Elias, but he saw no other choice. He would have done anything in his power to stop such an act.
And he didn't even like Olivja.

If Elias truly cared, he should have done the same.

"It is clear where your loyalties lie," he said, more to himself than Elias.

The whispered admission made Elias shoot up, shaking his head with pained eyes. "Brahms, no, it isn't. It doesn't change who I—"

"I do not wish to hear more of your *lies*, Elias," Brahms said quickly, not wanting to hear the broken tone of the prince as he turned his back to him. "Save your words for Heiress Ragnarvik."

THREAD XXXVII

ᚦᛖ ᛒᚢᚱᛞᛖᚾᛋ ᛟᚠ ᚺᛖᛁᚱᛋ ᚦᛖ ᛒᚢᚱᛞᛖᚾᛋ ᛟᚠ ᚺᛖᛁᚱᛋ ᚦᛖ ᛒᚢᚱᛞᛖᚾᛋ

ᛟᛚᛁᚡᛃᚨ

ONCE THE LASHING STARTED, TIME BECAME ELUSIVE.

Olivja lost track of how many lashes she received or how long she was tied to the post. She couldn't even remember how many times she begged Vincent for it to end.

Each strike bled into the next, a relentless rhythm of agony that warped the edges of her reality. The world around her seemed to slip away, her body a distant thing, nothing but a vessel for punishment.

At some point, the pain grew so vast her mind retreated, curling in on itself in a final act of preservation. It shut down entirely, retreating into a haze just to escape the burn.

She had long since broken—but the whipper showed no mercy.

When she next opened her eyes, Brahms hovered nearby—but her mind, still thick with pain and fear, couldn't fully grasp him. Pain still haunted every inch of her skin, but its edges had dulled, softened by something creeping into her bloodstream.

She remembered Edith's touch, but even that became distant, as if her hands were hovering just beyond reach. The relief and care she offered only broke her thoughts further, like a desperate spark that fizzled out too soon.

By the end of her cleansing, she lay face down in her bed, bare from the waist up, her body heavy with the effects of strange vials whose liquid shimmered with unnatural sheen.

As the first drop touched her lips, the warmth spread through her, the pain slowly being replaced by something else—a derivative version of peace.

It settled in her veins, and the pain of the lashing faded, replaced by a warm, languid calm.

Her body, once tense and raw, relaxed as if the weight of the world had melted away. Her mind drifted, thoughts floating like wisps of smoke, distant and unimportant. The room around her blurred, its edges softening, as if seen through a veil.

She drifted above herself; light, detached, as though her body was no longer her own—untethered, weightless. Her awareness of pain had been replaced by a sweet numbness, like a dream too soft to hold.

In that moment, nothing mattered but the fleeting, gentle peace brought by the vials.

Her eyes closed...

They opened to a soft touch on her cheek.

Through her fogged gaze, she saw...
Baldr...?

No.
It was a man.

Vincent—or perhaps Elias?
His face warped and shifted like a mirage that flickered in and out of focus.

His features blurred, softening into a glowing, dreamlike haze. His face lost definition, melting into gentle curves, and his green eyes glowed, too luminous, like those sung of in old myths.

He sat beside her bed, and she could only blink as his hand swept across her cheek, unreal and distant. The sound of his voice drifted towards her, stretched and disjointed, like a far-off echo she couldn't quite grasp.

Every movement he made was exaggerated, slow, as if suspended in a thick haze.

"*Vinnn...?*" She tried to speak, her words spilling from her lips like molasses—thick and sluggish.

"*Shh...*" His voice, soft and oddly soothing, made her eyes flutter, her mind fighting to stay awake. " ...It's me... "

Hearing his voice and his presence inches from her, her breath quickened, spiralling into shallow, panicked gasps.

Her hands shook as a wave of panic clawed up her spine, an instinctive fear coiling in her chest, tightening her ribs like a vice. She could still feel the sting of betrayal and the ache of wounds not yet healed. And now he was here—when she was most vulnerable.

"N—n..." Her lips barely shaped the word. "*G—et away...*"

She tried to sit up, to drag her body from the bed—but the poppy anchored her, the mattress pressing like iron chains.

Move, she willed herself, terror pounding in her mind.

Her heart raced, each beat a frantic alarm. All she could do was watch as he leaned closer, his gaze intense, shadowed with a look she couldn't read—dangerous, unknowable.

She shook her head, desperation flaring in her eyes. "*...please...*"

But Vincent only shook his head gently, almost sorrowfully, as if her fear wounded him more than anything.

He raised a hand to comb through her hair, his touch firm, pressing her down—not in comfort, but control. He stroked her hair with a heavy hand, his voice low and unyielding.

"No...*shh...shh*," he murmured, his voice soothing but coldly final. "Stop—stop, Olivja... No more pain. Only my protection. *I promise*."

But his words felt like chains tightening around her.

Promise? The word struck her like a curse, not a comfort.

His voice wrapped around her like a trap, dragging her deeper into the mattress, into her own fear.

She lay still, despite how desperately her heart was hammering in her chest, staring up into his green eyes with a trembling gaze she didn't recognise in herself. His words echoed in her head, like whispers down a long, winding tunnel, fragile with something that went beyond kindness.

"I never wished for this, Liv... these *burdens*—your *pain*... and yet I am bound to them, all the same." His voice broke, sounding almost childlike, as though he, too, was lost.

She didn't know if it was the tincture flooding her veins or the sound of his voice—but a flicker of old warmth stirred inside her.

"Vince..." she exhaled, her lips barely shaping his name. Her eyes welled with tears, her hand trembling as she tried to reach for him.

*Forgive me...*she thought, but her body was leaden, numb.

He took her hand and squeezed it gently, leaning close enough that their breaths mingled.

"Look at me..." Vincent's voice trembled.
She fought to hold his gaze—to see the man in his pleading eyes, not the monster who had broken her.

When her gaze faltered, he took hold of her face, his hand firm yet somehow gentle. "*Look at me... listen to me*," he exhaled, almost desperate.

Her weary amber eyes found his. He exhaled, clutching her tightly—though she felt almost none of it. Her other hand gripped the bed sheets tightly, the tension in her knuckles betraying the stress she tried to silence.

"I hate who I've become... " His voice drifted, the words blurring together as her senses dulled again.

He leaned closer, their foreheads almost touching. "Everything's changed... since I left... make it right. I swear I will."

A gentle pressure brushed her lips—a faint, remorseful embrace.
She blinked, recognizing it as a kiss...but before she could react, he pulled away to whisper:

"*I'm in love with you Olivja...* "

Her eyes widened. Her breath stilled.
His did too.

"Since the day we met... I have been ...all my life," he murmured against her lips, clearer this time, his voice thick.

She wished she'd truly heard it. Wished she could understand the weight it carried. Still...she could feel her heart pounding.

"And I can't lose you ... but *God*—it's like you *wish* to be lost," he squeezed her cheeks, a sob catching in his throat. "*... I need you ...* "

"Vincent..." Her voice was a broken whisper.

She wanted to tell him she loved him too—or that she *had* once.
Their love was strange—nothing like what others imagined—but real enough to shatter when betrayed. Real enough that part of her wanted to trust him again, wanted to kiss him back.

Why didn't she?

His eyes softened, almost as if he could sense her thoughts.
"... you love her... " he whispered with quivering lips, his hand slipping back into her hair.

"But you *can't have her*, Olivja. Do you hear me?" His voice hardened, his grip tightening, making her heart beat faster. "You *can't*. I won't let you—And if I have to take you away from here, I will. *I will.*"

Her tears broke free, silent and unending.

The words sank into her fogged mind, heavy and hard, twisting into something darker with each repetition. *I will.* His words clung like shackles, binding her thoughts and muddling her fear with the ache of the unknown.

Her right hand weakly rose to press against his chest—to push him away, or maybe to hold him there. She couldn't tell.

"I don't...*mm-understand...*" she whimpered, voice faint and thick with exhaustion. "You...hurt me...say y'*love me*?" Her eyelids drooped, her hand sliding from his chest as the poppy fought with her.

He caught her hand, pressed it to his chest, brushing his thumb gently over her knuckles as if trying to comfort her. "*Yes*, Olivja... I won't let you risk your life for unreturned feelings."

A spark of clarity pierced the haze.
"Love...'s worth every risk, Vince," she murmured—weak, but certain.

"*A curse by any other name is still love,*" he rasped.
His hand gripped her cheek again, harder this time.
"And even were it not. What you feel is not *love*... Love *stays* when you reach for it—not vanishes when you're close enough to touch it—she does not love you!" Vincent's jaw tensed, bitterness flickering in his eyes.

A breath passed between them. His thumb brushed tenderly along her cheek, as though tracing the edge of his ruin. Olivja smiled sweetly against his hand, amusement blooming from the hopelessness.

"Then...what of your love...*Vinny*...?" she hummed. "You're...*cursed*...just as much as I?"

"So be it...Let us curse the whole damn world—because your love is *mine*," he growled, eyes locked on hers. "You're mine, Olivja. *Finally mine.* So I don't care if you think you love her. It changes *nothing*, do you hear me?"

Now, both hands gripped her face, his voice trembling as he fought to anchor her through the haze.

"*You're mine, Olivja.*"

"*Yes...*" she whimpered, finally yielding—though she no longer remembered what he'd asked.

Then, slowly, he closed the space between them again.
His lips found hers once more. This time, she met him halfway.

The kiss was slower, heavier, like molten metal pouring from his anguish, grief, and unspoken remorse into her parted lips. Each press of his mouth burned with desperation—a silent plea for forgiveness she could feel in her bones.

The poppy dulled her pain but sharpened her awareness: the heat of his skin, the tremble of his hands, the ache between them.

His fingers slid through her hair, tangling at the base of her skull as if to anchor her, as if letting go meant losing her forever. A soft, whine escaped her, lips parting for him as his tongue sought hers with a fervent need that sent sparks along her spine. Her skin flushed under his touch, her breaths coming shallow and quick as his kiss grew bolder.

The world outside of them ceased to exist.

She craved this—*him*. A love that, at least in this dreamlike state, didn't wound or unravel her. A love that felt real, tangible, safe.

The rational part of her knew it was fleeting.
Knew she could never speak it aloud.

His lips broke from hers, only to return with renewed hunger, claiming her again and again—like he couldn't bear even a breath's worth of distance.

His body pressed closer to the bed, his chest heaving as though he couldn't breathe without her. She gasped as his teeth grazed her lower lip—a spark in the fog, pooling heat low in her belly.

A soft moan slipped from her, involuntary, as her fingers lifted to cup the side of his neck—loose, but wanting. His name formed on her lips, but he swallowed it in another kiss—this one rougher, raw with desperation.

He groaned, deep and broken, the sound vibrating through her. It wasn't until dampness brushed her cheek that she realised he was crying.

His lips moved to her jawline, then her cheek, then her neck and shoulders, before returning to her mouth. His breath came in gasps, his hands still cupping her face. His trembling fingers brushed at the tears, unsure whether they were hers or his.

"*Forgive me*," he whispered against her lips, voice cracked and raw. But he didn't pull away—not yet.

He kept kissing her, gripping her face like it was the only thing anchoring him to this world.

And maybe *she was.*

She opened her eyes as he finally drew back—a thin string of saliva connecting their lips like the last thread between them. Then it broke, like a strand of spider silk caught in the wind.

A strained silence followed, thick with all they hadn't said.

Her lashes drooped; her vision blurred. His fingers brushed her cheek, sweeping away tears she hadn't noticed.

He exhaled, barely audible, "... *rest, my girl*... You're safe now."

As the drug took hold, her mind slipped into a dreamlike haze—fragments of their laughter as children, the warmth of Adalja's touch, the sting of the whip—all blurring into a fog of fear, regret, and something like love, twisted and tangled beyond recognition.

Just before sleep claimed her, she thought she heard him whisper, almost to himself...

"*Were we born to a gentler world...* "

He leaned in as her breathing slowed, brushing his lips to her hair—an apology, a farewell, and a desperate hope she would never remember he carried.

Thread XXXVIII

ᚦᛖ ᛒᚢᚱᛞᛖᚾᛋ ᛟᚠ ᚺᛖᛁᚱᛋ ᚦᛖ ᛒᚢᚱᛞᛖᚾᛋ ᛟᚠ ᚺᛖᛁᚱᛋ ᚦᛖ ᛒᚢᚱᛞᛖᚾᛋ

ᚨᛞᚨᛚᛃᚨ

That night, Adalja couldn't sleep.

She lay awake in bed, eyes fixed on the ceiling, silent tears slipping down her cheeks as her thoughts spiraled through the pain of the day.

Every thought led back to Olivja—her face, her voice, the memories they'd shared. Despite the pain she'd caused, despite the distance she had kept, Adalja longed for her still.

Why was it that no matter the trouble, her thoughts always returned to Olivja?

Even when she was the root of her troubles, all she wanted was to see her again.

Her thoughts tangled into a restless web, and soon, they drove her from the bed. She couldn't lie there any longer. Her mind raced.

Adalja threw off her covers, skin chilled by the night air, and reached for her cloak at the foot of the bed. She stepped into the shadows of her chamber, her bare feet whispering towards the door—towards Olivja.

She eased the door open, her heart pounding, and let it creak shut behind her. Clutching her stomach, she made her way down the corridor to Olivja's door.

When she reached the door, it inched open—slowly, quietly—as if welcoming her.

A tall figure emerged, unmasked and unhooded.

Vincent.

His gaze was dark—displeasure shadowed with something Adalja couldn't name. He closed Olivja's door with slow deliberation, his jaw tight as he turned towards her.

The air between them chilled like morning fog, heavy with unspoken tension.

Adalja parted her lips to speak, but the weight of his presence—his fury, his coldness—pressed down like a wall she could not breach.

"Oh...g-good evening, Prince Vinc—"

"Return to your room, Princess." His voice cut through the silence, sharp and immediate—like he saw straight through her fragile composure. "She does not wish to see you."

Adalja froze, her breath catching in her throat. His words hit like a slap—cold, sharp, and final.

"D-did...she say that?" she asked, voice faltering as she stepped back, clutching her cloak tighter.

Why is he speaking this way to me?

"I—I only wish to speak with her, if I may—"

"You believe I'd fabricate her words?" His tone hardened, fury simmering beneath every syllable.

He stepped closer, the space between them shrinking with each breath. "You've led her on this wild chase...and still, you lack the courage to fight for her. Even now, you wait until she sleeps. *You're too late, Adalja.*"

Her heart twisted as his words sank in with terrifying clarity.

What had Olivja told him in the dungeons? Did he know everything?

Adalja's thoughts spiraled. Her voice failed her.

"You're blind to how deeply you wound her," Vincent scoffed, fists clenched at his sides as bitterness thickened in his voice.

He stepped forward again, resentment pulsing off him like heat. "I won't let it continue."

"I never meant to hurt her, Vincent!" Her voice trembled as she fought back tears. The knot in her chest tightened, guilt seeping into her skin like poison.

She'd tried to protect Olivja, tried to stay away—but all she'd done was make it worse.

"I've always cared for her—"
Vincent didn't give her a chance to finish.

With another step, he loomed over her, driving her back against the wall, the heat of his fury pressing her into the stone. His chest hovered close, the tension between them sharp enough to crack. He slammed his hands against the wall, caging her in place.

"If you mean that, you'll *stay away* from her, Adalja," he said low, quick, and venomous. His eyes darkened, shadowed with threat. "Otherwise, the punishment won't be so kind...and you'll both share the witches' fate."

Her breath caught. The fear she'd buried clawed its way up.

The witches—their fate had been cruel. Final. Merciless...
She understood what he meant.

Then, without a word, Vincent stepped back—breaking the moment with bitter finality. His boots echoed down the hall as he turned sharply, leaving her alone with the weight of his words.

Adalja stood frozen, her chest rising and falling with a sudden rush of emotion. She glanced towards Olivja's door, her thoughts tangled in Vincent's accusations. His words echoed sharply in her mind, the sting of guilt tightening in her chest.

Be it his threat—or something deeper gnawing at her heart—she returned to her room. She shut the door behind her, pressing her forehead to the cool wood as her eyes slid shut.

Am I the one hurting her?

The question gnawed at her, cutting deeper than anything Vincent had said. She couldn't shake the truth in his tone—nor the creeping reality that Liv's pain might be her fault.

Adalja moved farther into her room, her mind racing. Her gaze dropped to her hands.

She'd come so close to seeing Olivja tonight—but now, she couldn't. She wasn't sure she had the right to anymore.
And even if she did...she was *afraid.*

And perhaps that was the difference between her and Olivja:
Adalja wasn't willing to risk her life for love.

Only a day had passed without seeing Olivja at meals before suspicion quickly took root.

With each day, the silence around Olivja's absence sharpened, the uneasy murmur of excuses hollow and unconvincing.

"Need I remind you of her feelings towards you?" Vincent said bluntly whenever she asked, never softening the harsh truth.

The others had their own ways of keeping Adalja at arm's length.

"Your time's claimed from dawn to dusk, Princess...as is Olivja's," Elias assured her with practised politeness, deflecting whenever concern flickered in her eyes.

When caught, Brahms would mutter, *"I brought her meals earlier; she is well,"* but always avoided her gaze.

After *a week* of strained reassurances and averted looks, Adalja knew—something was wrong. It was no longer enough to let them pacify her. She needed to see Olivja for herself.

Late one evening after dinner, she waited for the dining hall to empty. Once sure no one would follow, she slipped through dim corridors, quietly determined to visit her Norsewoman.

No knights stood at Olivja's door—a sight that brought Adalja both relief and a twinge of anxiety.

Would Olivja be angry for her absence? Or hurt by this sudden intrusion? Each question weighed heavily as she approached, her breath shallow.

She stopped, took a steadying breath, and lifted a trembling hand to knock. A soft rap echoed against the oak as she paused, waiting.

Surely, if Olivja were well, she would answer...
The silence sank like a stone in Adalja's chest.

She knocked again, pressing her ear against the wood, straining to catch any faint rustle—bedsheets shifting, a soft sigh, a footstep. But the quiet stretched on, heavy and suffocating.

Without another thought, her hand found the silver handle. It clicked softly as she turned it, and she slowly pushed the door open, peeking through the widening crack.

She froze, hands flying to her mouth.

Olivja lay face down on the bed, an arm dangling limply over the side, her back wrapped in blood-soaked cloths that had faded from white to mottled, translucent red. Dark stains dripped down to the cold stone floor.

Despite the horror, Olivja looked peaceful, her face softened by sleep, breaths slow and rhythmic.

Adalja closed the door behind her, eyes never leaving Olivja's sleeping form, chest twisting with pain and disbelief.

The room was dim, shadows dancing along the stone walls. Her gaze drifted left, where a fire crackled, sending faint warmth through the cold air. A small cauldron hung above the flames, steam curling from its surface. Inside, white cloths boiled in an herbal brew, the sweet scent of chamomile and honey drifting through the air.

Someone had cared for Olivja all this time—tending wounds in silence, sparing no detail. But no one told her. No one even hinted at Olivja's condition...

Did Elias know? Did Brahms?
Her fingers clawed at her cheek, chest tightening with fury at the thought.

How long had they kept this from her? Guarding Olivja's suffering behind layers of polite words and veiled looks?

Stepping closer, Adalja's footsteps echoed softly against stone. Her eyes stung as she fought back tears.

Beside the bed, a small table held dozens of empty glass vials and jars. The cloths on Olivja's back were dripping—thin and translucent over the wounds beneath, revealing deep, jagged lashes.

Her skin was swollen, a raw landscape of purple and red welts spreading like fire up her back. Adalja's stomach churned. Tears slipped down her cheek—one, then another, then another. Her hand trembled over her mouth as Olivja's suffering washed over her.

Did Vincent do this?
The thought took hold, icy and undeniable, as she stared at the brutal marks. The realisation set her blood ablaze with a helpless rage.

Her mind spiraled, imagining the punishment—the cruel lash of the whip, Olivja's cries filling the air. The image was unbearable, filling her with fierce, protective pain.

Slowly, she lowered herself beside the bed, hand hovering above Olivja's shoulder. She wanted to hold her, brush a stray lock of hair from the heiress' face, offer comfort—but the wounds looked too painful. She wouldn't risk waking her.

Instead, she stayed close, silent tears falling, heart breaking for Olivja's pain—and for the blame resting partly on her own shoulders.

Her hand gently grasped Olivja's limp one as it hung over the bed. Her thumb trembled as it caressed the back of the hand. A subtle gesture conveying only a fraction of the affection she longed to give.

"Mmm...sneakin' in...on a woman's sleep, hm?"

Olivja's slurred, sleepy voice lifted Adalja's tearful eyes. A single amber eye met hers; the other squished against the bed's side.

"Liv!" Adalja gasped, a soft sob escaping as her second hand rose, gently touching the side of Olivja's face—the kind of touch only lovers shared.

"I'm here now. What did he do? How long have you suffered?" she asked with another gentle sob, brushing strands of hair from her sweaty face.

"*Gods...so...beautiful,*" Olivja whispered, unaware—or uncaring—of the moment's severity and intensity.

Adalja was caught off guard—her eyes widened, tears pausing briefly in the face of Olivja's drugged affections. Her heart twisted, sorrow and tenderness flooding her chest. She didn't know whether to laugh or cry, whether to smile at the sweetness or weep at how out of place it felt in this dark moment.

Her fingers trembled as they brushed another lock of hair from Olivja's flushed face, her thumb grazing the soft skin of her cheek.

"Y-you would flatter...at a time like this?" Adalja whispered with a shattered chuckle, her voice breaking.

She swallowed thickly, trying to regain composure, but the sight of Olivja so vulnerable made it impossible to hold back tears. "I beg your forgiveness, Olivja...I should have come sooner."

"*Thoo laeknar sairth...*" Olivja spoke tiredly in her native Nordic tongue.

The heiress had often spoken Nordic when they were young. Adalja tried to learn, but the words never stuck. Now, more than ever, she wished they had.

"I—I can't understand you, Olivja..." Adalja said softly, scoffing gently.

The wounded woman sighed, turning her head just enough to nuzzle into Adalja's hand—seeking comfort without knowing why.

The soft brush of fevered breath against her palm sent a shiver up Adalja's arm, her stomach tightening with a fluttering heat she fought to ignore.

She swallowed hard, then let her thumb trace slowly over Olivja's cheekbone—slower than intended, afraid to break the moment.

"*Aye...*" Liv responded with a weak smile, eyes closing as her lips found the inside of Adalja's palm, placing faint kisses that sent zaps of electricity up her arm. "*Mm...*I said...you heal *all* my wounds..."

Heavier tears streamed down her rosy cheeks at the painfully tender admission. Olivja lazily looked up, shaking her head in tiny movements, confused by what was happening.

"Do not...*weep,*" Olivja spoke faintly, her voice heavy and unsteady. "*I am well...sleepy...*" She smiled slowly, hazily, as if trying to comfort Adalja even when compromised.

Adalja's heart shattered with every word.

She wanted to shake her, make her understand the gravity of what had been done, see how badly she was hurt, how deeply everyone had failed her. She wanted to scream, curse the world—but instead, she whispered:
"You're not well, Liv...*far from it.*"

Her fingers pressed harder into the side of Olivja's face, as if she could make her whole again with genuine touch alone. The rawness, helplessness, and desire to protect crashed through Adalja—a flood of emotion she barely contained.

"I hate this," Adalja choked, leaning down to press her forehead gently against Olivja's, the heat of feverish skin searing into hers.

"I cannot bear seeing you in pain...*I have so much shame...Forgive me*—I can't—I can't lose you, Olivja."

Olivja let out a soft, sleepy laugh, though it sounded more like a sigh than anything. "You won't...'m not...losin' you..." Her words slurred, fading as she fought against the medicinal haze. "Not 'fter all of *this*—" she laughed again, but it was fragile, a fading echo.

Adalja smelled the faint sweetness of her breath—a sharp, piney scent that clung to the air. Poppy, she realised, and she shuddered.

How much have they given you?

Her heart ached—not just for Olivja, but for the helplessness within herself, for how little she could do to stop the pain that lingered inside.

"Did you come 'ere...only to cry? Hm?" Olivja asked, her voice barely above a whisper, but still teasing. She raised a trembling hand and rested it against Adalja's cheek, her fingers feverish and unsteady.

The touch, soft as it was, carried too much. It broke something in Adalja—a fragile dam she'd held back for far too long.

She leaned into it, barely, just enough to feel the strength of her. Just enough to pretend, if only for a breath, that things might still be right again.

"No...I—" she began, but her voice caught.

Gods, how many times had she rehearsed it in silence, in shame, in fear. Now here she was, kneeling before her—breathless, heart thudding so loud she feared Olivja might hear it.

"I came here to tell you that I..." She swallowed hard, eyes flicking down for the briefest moment. Her courage trembled. Her fingers curled gently around Olivja's hand, grounding her. "*I love you.*"

The words didn't come out like in the daydreams. They came out quiet. Uncertain. *Human.*

But they were true.

Her chest felt cracked open, raw with the vulnerability of it—of saying it too late.

"I love you, Olivja..." she said again, breath shaking. "And I will forever regret that it took so much—so long—to see it."

Olivja's eyes fluttered, struggling to focus, and despite the poppy clouding her mind, a soft, dreamy smile crept across her face.

"I know."

It was barely murmured—slurred and weak. Not the words she longed to hear, nor as soft or loving as she'd dreamt—but still, Adalja's heart fluttered all the same.

Liv reached out weakly, brushing Adalja's cheek with the backs of her fingers. "...Always knew."

Adalja paused for a breath.
Stupid. Naive. Slow.
That's what she was when it came to loving Olivja.

Yet the Norsewoman never held it against her. She never looked at her with blame or bitterness. Liv waited. She loved her all the same—no matter how long it took.

The princess didn't know what to say, so she closed the distance between them, pressing their foreheads together in an intimate, feather-light touch.

They remained that way, smiles tugging at their lips, noses nuzzling gently—yearning for a deeper embrace that couldn't come...not yet. Not until she was better.

"You did...*you were right...*" Adalja whispered, breath catching, her eyes burning with tears as she let go of her pride.

The Norsewoman's eyes fluttered as she swallowed the lump in her throat.

"*Close your eyes*...I'm not leaving your side, Liv."

Olivja's presence eased away as the poppy took hold. Adalja's fingers brushed her cheeks tenderly, lingering until the pained Norsewoman slipped into deep slumber.

She settled beside the bed, legs folding beneath her as she lowered her head to rest on the mattress's edge, beside Olivja. Even feverish, the warmth of her skin was comforting.

For the first time in what felt like eternity, peace settled over her—here, with Olivja, if only for this fleeting moment.

Adalja's eyelids grew heavy, the intensity of the day pulling her down, and she drifted to sleep right there, on the floor beside Olivja's bed.

Her cheek rested against Olivja's arm, the steady rhythm of her breath a quiet lullaby.

At last, the fear of being caught faded—surpassed by the far greater fear of losing her.

Thread XXXIX

"*Adalja…?*"

A weak, raw voice stirred her from sleep. Blinking the haze away, Adalja's blue eyes met Olivja's. They were feverish, bloodshot, and filled with something unfamiliar—fear, or perhaps anger.

"Olivja…" Adalja murmured gently, reaching out to touch her face. Her fingers paused as she noticed the sweat beading heavily on Olivja's forehead, her expression tight and stricken with pain.

"G-get…*ow*…" Olivja's voice came in broken demands, each word a struggle through clenched teeth. Soft, choked grunts escaped her, and Adalja could see the agony pulsing through her.

"Liv, *you're safe,*" Adalja raised her head slowly, groggy from waking, voice low and soothing. "It's me…*I'm here.*"

But Olivja's eyes flashed, and her brows drew together.

"Get…*OUT!*" she screamed. The rawness of her voice tore through the room as she turned her face away, burying it into the pillows, her muffled cries choked and twisted in pain.

Adalja stumbled back, her heart seizing as she hit the floor. The fierce rejection cut deeply.

Her mind raced watching the way her body arched with every pulse of pain. The cloths covering her wounds had dried, the raw skin beneath inflamed and angry, the herbs and poppy having long since faded.

Fighting through her own fear, Adalja reached out again, grasping Olivja's fist as it clenched the sheets, desperate to comfort her.

"Please, Liv—let me help you!"

"No!" Olivja's hand jerked away her touch as if burned. She struggled, pushing onto her elbows, a look of agony and fury twisting her face.

"I don't *want* you here..." Her voice was strained, torn between desperation and accusation. "You're the cause of this...*of—of all that I suffer*!" Her breaths came in shallow gasps, her eyes darkening with something closer to hate than Adalja had ever seen.

Their eyes met, and she froze as she saw the pained, tear streaked face of her lover.

Adalja's throat closed, words dying before they even reached her lips.

Her heart cracked with each breath Olivja took, every ounce of pain on her face like a dagger twisting in her chest. She wanted to fight back, to apologise, to explain herself—but the look in Olivja's eyes stopped her, holding her in place.

"F-forgive me," Adalja's voice trembled, barely a whisper. She took a shaky step back, eyes glistening with unshed tears. "I'll—I'll seek Edith, Liv, I—"

"Be gone!" Olivja sobbed, her voice breaking as her body tensed, arms trembling so violently that Adalja could see it from where she stood by the door. "*Please...please...don't look at me—not like this!*"

Adalja's heart shattered as she watched the strongest person she knew reduced to sobs and strained cries. The image of Olivja—so fierce, now vulnerable and broken—was too much to bear.

All the strength Olivja had, all the pain she'd borne alone...and Adalja was powerless to take any of it away.

The door flew open, and Edith, her maid, rushed to Olivja's side, her hands steady and practised as she reached into the basket of tinctures she'd brought with her, seemingly unbothered by Adalja's presence.

"Olivja, *my child*!" Edith gasped, already preparing a dose of poppy.

"*Amma—h—hyalpa mehr*!" Olivja's voice, fragile and raw, cut through the air, her Nordic plea for help wrenching something deep within Adalja.

"*Ek bith* ..." Her voice trailed off as she buried her face in the mattress, a haunting sound that went on even as Edith helped her.

"*Hush*...hush now," Edith murmured, though her voice betrayed the worry she fought to conceal. She worked quickly, trying to soothe Olivja's trembling with each drop of the tincture, layering blankets around her to ward off the cold before the true work began.

Anything to help...anything to ease the torment that had gone unseen for far too long.

Adalja stumbled back, her hand catching on the doorframe as she slipped out of the room.

Her vision blurred.
Olivja's suffering rained down on her while guilt clawed up her throat. She couldn't stay—couldn't stand to watch her like this knowing she was part of the reason for her agony.

As the door shut softly behind her, the echo of Olivja's muffled cries clung to her, driving her back a few paces down the hall as if retreating from the sound itself. Her mind spun with guilt and anger.

Did Olivja even remember their words together? Had it all faded into the haze of her pain?

Her sorrow turned to fury as her thoughts landed on Vincent—the man who'd done this to her.

Her pace quickened, her bare feet echoing down the hall, her dress wrinkled and tear-stained, worn too long. She couldn't help Olivja now, but she could face him and demand justice for the wounds he'd left behind.

She no longer cared for what it meant for her. She only cared about Olivja.

Turning sharply around a corner, Adalja collided with a solid, imposing figure, the force stopping her dead in her tracks. Her tear-filled eyes trailed upwards to meet the gaze of Jarl Dagrun, a towering, broad-shouldered man.

She gasped.
Maybe he, Olivja's father, had the authority to make things right.

"Jarl of Ragnarvik—" she began, but she faltered as the sharp scent of ale hit her.

His gaze narrowed, fixing on her face. His linen shirt was rolled to his elbows, exposing some of the many sprawling tattoos that inked his body. His eyes—heavy, dark with the weight of too many nights spent like this—searched her expression.

"Tears...do you weep at every hour, child?" His voice was thick with drink, but there was a strange comfort in the rumble, a steadiness that reminded her of the all he used to be.

Nostalgia washed over her like a crashing tide, drowning and reviving her all at once. She longed to run to him, the way she used to when the world felt simple...so she did. She was tired of not doing what she desired.

She closed the space between them, slamming into his burly chest with a soft cry, taking in his smoky, ale-soaked scent. It was just as she remembered.

The princess' tears streamed onto his tunic as his arms slowly, but firmly, wrapped her in a deep embrace.

His chest was suffocating and he squeezed as though he had been desperate for affection and warmth the same way. His breath stuttered, and his heart thudded faster against her cheek.

"There there, *Björnling*," he sighed above her, the nickname churning something deep in her heart.

Safe. It was the only word she could place to the warmth of being in his grasp as he towered so high above her she could barely reach his chin.

"R-Runey..." she whimpered, the name spilling from the oldest parts of her memory. She tried to steady her breath, her chest heaving.

"It's...it's Liv!" Her head lifted, looking up to him with wide, begging eyes. "Vincent, he...he harmed her—whipped her! Til she bled!" Her voice cracked, and the words caught in her throat. "I-I saw it myself, she—she..."

She couldn't finish. The images, the horrors, were too much.

Dagrun looked down at her with confusion, his ability to comprehend hindered by his drink. For a moment, his arms slackened.

"Harmed her..." he said, though more so to repeat what he had heard.

"Ah...*daughters*..." he sighed, his pierced lip curling at the corner of his mouth as a sad smirk appeared. "The curse that forever bleeds the father dry..."

The words froze her in place. Why did they sound so familiar? As if he'd spoken them before, maybe even to her own father in the past.

The realisation hung in the air, and for a brief moment, she thought those words might be the beginning of his tirade—the spark that would ignite his fury.

But instead, he simply stepped back, his hands gently removing the princess from his chest. He gripped her biceps gently, a final moment of reassurance before nodding his head.

"Thank you, Adalja," he mumbled.

Without another word or glance, he stepped past her. A heavy darkness seemed to settle over him, glooming the halls with each massive footfall.

Adalja stood there for a moment, caught between disbelief and confusion.

Was that it? Was that the extent of a Norseman's rage? Of his feelings for his own flesh and blood?

"Dagrun! Wait!" she called out, her voice rising, more from shock than anger, as she watched him turn his back on her—*on Olivja*.

"You must help her!" she shouted down the hall, her echo magnifying the emptiness she felt.

If not her own father, then who? Who would avenge Olivja, if not him?

Adalja knew herself well enough—she wasn't capable of vengeance. She could hardly stand the sight of Olivja's pain, let alone strike back at the one who caused it.

But she needed someone...*anyone*.

For a moment, the Jarl froze mid-step, a slight twitch of his head signaling he had heard her. He turned his eyes slightly back towards her, a flicker of something passing across his face—something deeper, older. Regret, or maybe shame.

She clung to that brief hope, but it had faded as quickly as it came. His gaze turned cold once more, and he continued forward, leaving her standing there, the echoes of his footsteps growing louder in the silence.

Adalja stood motionless, her breath catching in her throat, the pain of Olivja's suffering growing like a parasite in her chest.

Was she the only one who still cared? The only one who understood what had been done to her?

The world around her felt distant, as though she were fading into the shadows with each passing moment.

"Please, Dagrun," she whispered, her voice now barely a plea.

But the Jarl was already gone, his form swallowed by the hall's gloom, and Adalja was left alone with nothing but the echo of her own broken resolve.

THE REST OF THE DAY WAS LONG.

Adalja avoided her room.
She cared little for her appearance, her mind consumed by other matters—Olivja, vengeance, the witches, Vincent, Elias, Brahms.

All that mattered were the feelings she had long repressed, ones that overwhelmed her now, rushing to the surface like a tide.

And yet, despite all the emotions churning inside her, she felt utterly alone.

She wandered the halls, the dungeons, the gardens, circling the castle like a restless spirit.

Knights eyed her oddly, faint maids whispered about her, yet she was too lost in herself—too consumed on what to do—to pay attention. Her thoughts were tangled, her words uncertain and unspoken.

By the time the evening sun had set, she found herself inside the dining hall, the warmth of the fire failing to reach her icy skin. The cold winter air had seeped into her bones, turning her flesh as pale as death itself.

The scent of roasted pork and freshly baked bread teased her senses, and she followed it, hoping to find a moment of peace before anyone else arrived.

But she was wrong.

She had barely taken a sip of wine when the silence was broken by the unmistakable sound of footsteps. Vincent took his place at the far end of the table, and soon after, Elias sat directly across from her, followed by Brahms who stood tall near the entrance.

The tension in the room seemed to increase with every passing moment, growing thicker at the thought that Olivja wouldn't be joining them—again.

None of them knew that Adalja had discovered the truth, and as they carried on with their dinner, her anger grew heavier.

Brahms was the first to approach her, his usual easy demeanor replaced with concern. He leaned down slightly, studying her with a tilted head.

"Adalja...where have you been?" he asked quietly, his voice laced with genuine worry. His hand landed gently on her shoulder, and she flinched, startled by the contact.

He pulled his hand back instantly, a furrow creasing his brow. "You're near frozen. What has become of you, My Princess?"

"*I saw her.*"

She mumbled the words, faint, but they were enough to make Elias' head snap up from his plate. His expression tightened, searching her face—as if hoping he'd misheard.

Vincent dropped his utensils at her revelation, and Brahms straightened instantly.

"*WHERE IS HE?!*"

Suddenly, a booming, angry voice echoed from somewhere inside the castle. A warning to what was about to come.

Adalja's eyes widened, her fingers instinctively gripping the edge of the table in fear.

But just before anyone could truly react, the doors to the dining hall burst open with a crash.

Dagrun stormed in, his heavy boots thudding against the floor with each step, his cloak floating behind him like the cape of a Norse god.

His face was flushed, his breath ragged from whatever fury had brought him here. His eyes scanned the room, landing on Adalja first, before sweeping across to Vincent.

Adalja stood in a flash, fingers prickling as her blood surged.

Vincent stood as well, but with less urgency, bringing a cup of wine to his lips as though an angered Norseman wasn't the scariest foe to face.

After locking eyes with the long-haired prince, Dagrun stormed forward, rushing him.

Elias stood from the table, kicking his chair back in shock as the Jarl of Ragnarvik grabbed hold of Vincent's vest, knocking his cup to the floor in an instant.

"You sit here in comfort, *drinking*, while she suffers? Did you think me blind to it?!" Dagrun's voice, thick with his accent and boiling rage, filled the hall. "Stand and answer for what you've done to Olivja, or I'll see you dragged by your hair to the gods!"

The dining hall fell into a heavy silence. The maids froze like statues, and not even the Worthyn knights dared intervene.

The rage of the Ragnarvik Jarl was a rare sight, and they were all witnessing it firsthand.

"Do you truly believe I meant to harm her?!" Vincent shot back, his voice cold and unwavering. "Mercy's no softness, Dag. At times, it's the cruelest kindness of all!"

The words hung in the air, sharp and biting. Vincent's defiance, though bold, only seemed to fuel the fire in Dagrun's eyes.

Even if Vincent's claim were false, it mattered little; the Jarl's fury was already ignited.

Without another word, he yanked Vincent towards him by his collar, lifting him off his feet with surprising ease.

Dagrun growled, his voice a low rumble as he leaned in close, his breath hot with fury. "You speak of mercy?"

"Dag—*DON'T*!" Adalja screamed, and with that, he threw Vincent to the ground with a savage force.

The sound of Vincent's body hitting the stone floor echoed through the hall, the impact making the very walls seem to shudder.

The Jarl stood over him, a towering shadow of rage.

"*Words like mercy won't save you now, boy...*" Dagrun hissed, falling to his knees above him, one hand gripping Vincent's chest, pinning him to the cold stone while raising his fist.

Vincent gasped for air, his pride faltering for the first time as he found himself at the mercy of the southern Norseman.

Dagrun's eyes burned with fury, and Vincent could see the full force of the Jarl's rage pressing down on him, unstoppable as the tide.

His fist came down—once, twice, three times—before a maroon splatter decorated the floor.

He wasn't planning on stopping, desperate to put forth the same amount of pain that Vincent did on Olivja.

Adalja wanted to stop him, and yet her feet were frozen to the floor, her body shocked—in fear of the power that was the Ragnarviks.

Even Brahms stood still.

Vincent grunted loudly, putting up his hands in fear of another strike, desperate to get away from the imposing fatherly figure.

But he wasn't finished.

Dagrun hit him until his mask fell weakly to the ground, until his grunts went quiet and even after that.

"No!" Adalja shrieked finally, not willing to see another death at her hands.

She lunged forward and Brahms took a strong hold of her from around her waist, pulling her back from the monster she had summoned.

"ELIAS!" she called for her suitor—Vincent's only chance at surviving this.

But Elias only stood there, eyes wide and watering, breathing as heavily as Adalja—yet his expression was numb, like he'd seen a ghost.

"E—li—" Vincent's desperate, strained cry slipped from his lips, faint but piercing.

Elias didn't hesitate; he rushed to Vincent's side, his sudden movement snapping the Worthyn knights into action.

Two, three, then four knights struggled to tear the furious Jarl from his target, each one grappling with Dagrun's brute force. Then they finally managed to hold him back.

"You have FORSAKEN ME, SON!!" Dagrun's bellow shook the walls, his voice cracking as the betrayal seared through him, his last hope crumbling.

His growls and curses echoed down the corridors, descending into guttural rage as the knights pushed him further back, eventually dragging him towards the dungeons.

Elias knelt beside Vincent's unconscious form, his jaw clenched with worry.

"Gothel!" he yelled, calling for the advisor who was nowhere in sight. "Get him to her—*now*!" He barked, urgently motioning to a few knights as they carefully lifted Vincent's limp body.

As Elias moved with them, his focus entirely on getting Vincent to safety, Adalja was left alone in the aftermath.

It took a moment for the truth to sink in...then it hit her all at once.

This was entirely her doing.

A vengeful act—a rageful one—all in the name of love. She couldn't help the regret that coursed through her at the sight of Vincent so beaten, so hurt.

She stumbled back, breath hitching in shallow gasps.

Her mind raced.
Dagrun's fury, the broken form of Vincent, Elias' desperate call for help—it all swirled together, a surge of emotions she couldn't contain.

She covered her mouth to stifle a sob, her chest heaving as the gravity of it all hit her. The streaks of Vincent's blood smeared across the floor made her stomach churn, her fingers trembling as she pressed them to her lips, desperately fighting the urge to scream.

Her eyes darted wildly around the room, searching for something to hold on to, someone to make sense of the chaos.

And then she saw Brahms.

Pacing near her, his helmet clutched in one hand, his chest rising and falling unsure of whether to help the other knights or return to Adalja. His eyes—solemn, shadowed with disbelief—found hers and held.

It was enough to crack her.

She shook her head frantically, biting her lip to keep the sob from tearing out of her throat as he stormed towards her. In seconds, his arms were around her.

He pulled her close, holding her tightly, almost crushingly, as though she might shatter if he let go.

"*Shhh*...I have you," he murmured, his voice rough, strained. "It is done, Addy. You are safe."

But it wasn't done. It would never feel done.

She buried her face in his shoulder, her fingers clutching at him as if she could claw herself out of the moment. Her body trembled, silent sobs wracking her chest as her tears streaked his metal armour.

"I can't do this," she whimpered, believing she was not worth easing. "Release me, Brahms...please. *This is—all—my fault...*" Adalja's breaths were little but short gasps and shuddered.

So his arms did not yield. He held her tighter.

"Steady now, Addy," he murmured softly, almost beseeching. "Breathe...before you come undone."

Outside, the wind howled through the castle walls like a warning.
The bloodstains on the stones glistened in the firelight, stubborn, unyielding.

And Adalja felt it—deep in her chest—that this night would haunt them all.

Thread XL

ᚦᛖ ᛒᚢᚱᛞᛖᚾᛋ ᛟᚠ ᚺᛖᛁᚱᛋ ᚦᛖ ᛒᚢᚱᛞᛖᚾᛋ ᛟᚠ ᚺᛖᛁᚱᛋ ᚦᛖ ᛒᚢᚱᛞᛖᚾᛋ

ᛟᛚᛁᚠᛃᚨ

Olivja's lashes fluttered as dawn pried her from the poppy's false calm. Light brushed her face—warm yet intrusive—but the softness of her bed deepened the dream's lingering strangeness.

It was the same dream, repeating endlessly through her healing.

In it, she waded through icy waters, clutching a torch that flickered weakly against the darkness. Around her, voices rose: Vincent's cry, Adalja's scream, Brahms's wrath, Elias's desperate pleas—loud and unforgiving. Then a cold wave crashed down, snuffing the flame.

The darkness swallowed her whole.

She lay still, head heavy, the room drifting in and out of focus, as if the last threads of a sweet, haunting fog were finally loosening their grip.

Her body felt worn, strangely distant, as if the pain had dulled into an ache drifting along the edges of her awareness.

When she blinked fully awake, her gaze trailed around the room, noting the gentle flicker of the fireplace across the room. There was a dim familiarity in the glow, but something—something felt missing. Or was it someone?

A shiver touched her skin, and she drew her fingers to her temple, attempting to press away the faint, maddening ache that pulsed there. Shadows of memories teased her—laughter, cries, a voice softened with affection, the ghostly pressure of a hand clasping hers, perhaps even a kiss?

But the more she strained to grasp them, the further they slipped, scattering into fragments she could hardly name.

She tried to sit up, and the fog shifted again, bringing flashes of Vincent—his emerald eyes, the cold press of his voice...the words that felt like only a whisper. Her breath hitched, though she could not place why.

And then, another. A name brushed her lips, light as a murmur: *Adalja*. The syllables felt like warmth she knew she had once held close, but now, like embers, they left only a faint glow and no heat.

The fog of whatever Edith had been giving her left her unaware of anything beyond the pain before the first dose and after it faded—

Everything in between was gone.

As she lifted herself, a soft groan escaped her lips. Her back throbbed with a dull ache, but she recognised that the hardest part of her healing was behind her—her physical healing, at least.

The scars Vincent had carved into her *spirit*, however, ran far deeper than flesh, wounds that no amount of rest or time could ever mend.

Carefully, she reached behind herself, her fingertips trembling as they searched for the remnants of her wounded back. As her fingers traced the rough, raw edges, she winced, instinctively curling them back at the sharp sting lingering beneath her skin.

The scars were jagged and unkind, but healed enough to suggest a return to normalcy. A jolt of panic struck when the door to her room opened, her body tensing, fearful of seeing Vincent...or perhaps Adalja—anyone who might have played a part in her suffering.

But it was Edith, her eyes wide with relief at the sight of Olivja, now unclouded by the haze of the poppy.

She entered quietly, shutting the door gently behind her, carrying a small basket of tinctures and ointments. She approached the bed without hesitation, seemingly unbothered by Olivja's state of undress.

Keeping her clothed must have been impossible during her healing.
She had been bare from the hips up for...

"How long...have I been like this...?" Olivja rasped, her voice hoarse, spent in endless screams.

"Two weeks it has been, My Lady," Edith spoke regretfully, setting her basket down beside the bed with a grunt of old age.

The revelation hit Olivja like a blow, sinking her stomach and tensing her muscles. A wince escaped her clenched jaw.

"Weeks?" she echoed, struggling to steady her voice, knowing that any surge of emotion would worsen her state. Liv took a shaky breath through her nose, her voice tight. "W—what have I missed? Has the wedding taken place—*agh*—"

She tried to turn towards her Amma, but the scabs on her back throbbed, pulling painfully at her taut skin. Frustrated, she remained still, breathing shallowly, each breath sending an ache rippling across her ribs and back.

"Oh Olivja, you wake from your haze and still only worry about the marriages..." The older woman mumbled to herself in Norse while looking through her basket of medicinals.

When she stood again, she held a small vial of deep brownish-red liquid. Liv raised a hand, stopping Edith before she could offer it.

"No," the heiress spoke quietly, her voice steadier than she felt. "Not anymore...I need my mind clear...whatever's left of it."

Her Amma hesitated, worry etched into her face, but Olivja managed a faint, defiant smile, despite the pain. "*Please.* I wish to face the rest of this as myself," she quietly begged.

The older woman studied her for a moment longer, searching for the smallest hint of doubt or hesitation that might prompt her to argue. But Olivja's resolve remained unshaken.

With a subtle nod, Edith returned the vial to its place in the basket. She lowered herself onto a wooden stool beside the bed, her movements slow, as if carrying the weight of her own thoughts.

For a brief moment, Olivja could almost feel the presence of others who had sat beside her during her long rest.

Edith's heavy sigh broke the silence, her mood darkening as she settled in.

"Then..." her Amma began softly, her voice heavy with unspoken weight, "I hope you are well enough to face the news I've brought, child..."

By Edith's standards, Olivja was far from ready to hear what had occurred during her rest.

DRESSED ONLY IN A LONG-SLEEVED, beige tunic that skimmed the floor and her fox fur cloak, Olivja stormed down the halls, ignoring the sharp pains jolting through her core with each step.

She didn't care who she passed or who might be watching—nothing mattered but finding her father.

The news that Elias had imprisoned him sent waves of rage through her. Her father had acted on her behalf, recklessly, and it stoked both fury and sorrow. The thought that he had avenged her in his own reckless way made her eyes sting. How she wished she'd seen it—the look on Vincent's face, the force behind her father's blows.

But now, once again, someone she loved was held by Elias.

At the dungeon hall, two large Worthyn knights stood with spears crossed over the door, blocking her path without a word.

But nothing would stop the Jarl's Dottir.
She stomped towards them, driven by the same fury that had carried her this far.

"You would bar a Norsewoman from visiting her Jarl—her *father* in his cell?!" she shouted, her patience fraying with every throb of pain.

"Princess Olivja, we have strict orders not to allow *anyone* in—"

"*HEIRESS* Olivja—and I WILL BE your *queen* in the coming weeks!" she snapped, her voice rising.

"Are you defying me? Are you prepared to be punished for this insolence? Are you prepared to fight a Ragnarvik?!" She shouted louder this time, fury driving every word past hesitation. "Have you *forgotten* my blood?!"

At her height, Olivja stood eye-to-eye with their quivering chins, their nervous breaths misting the air—visible proof of the tension she'd sparked. She held her ground, meeting their wary stares with a gaze that refused to waver.

After an uncomfortable pause, they shared a brief glance and finally stepped aside, each moving only enough to let her through.

She resisted a smirk, sighing instead—part relief, part frustration. Playing the villain, the unrelenting force, had become second nature.

Since Vincent's brutal punishment, every soft part of her had been carved away, leaving only a hardened shell—defiant, resigned to being the outcast. And she accepted it now.

Without another moment's hesitation, she flew down the winding stone steps of the dungeon. Her bare footsteps echoed sharply through the narrow passage as she forced her battered body onward.

She ignored the ache in her side and the tremor in her legs, moving faster with each step until she reached the bottom.

The air was damp and stale, thick with the scent of stone and moss. Fear surged as memories of her lashing clawed back into her mind. She breathed through it, passing a row of empty cells—each one a silent shadow in the murk.

Then she saw him.

Jarl Ragnarvik was slumped on the cold floor, his wrists shackled to a heavy iron ring embedded in the stone beneath him.

His clothes, though smeared with dust, were otherwise pristine—his face unmarked despite the struggle she'd heard about. She had pictured him bloodied, bruised—battle carved into his skin.

But he was just as she remembered, a warrior brought low but never broken.

When he raised his gaze and saw her, his tired brown eyes lit with recognition—and a flicker of hope.

Tears pricked at Olivja's eyes before she could stop them. Her resolve shattered in an instant, the pain of her back lost to fear as she stumbled forward.

He rose and moved quickly to the front iron bars, towering well past the top of the cell door.

"Pabbi." The word tore from her in a whisper, broken and thick with grief, as she lurched towards the cell and gripped the bars to stay upright.

Her legs quivered beneath her, drained of strength, yet she clung to the bars with fierce desperation.

Her father's tattooed hand reached out, fingers slipping between the bars to grasp hers. His voice, weary but gentle, carried a quiet promise of comfort amid the dungeon's gloom.

"*Valk...my strong girl...*" he murmured in their native tongue, and warmth settled over her like the weight of an old cloak.

She squeezed his hand with all the strength she had. The cold iron pressed into her skin as she tried to pull him closer, but the chains held him back. She glanced up at him, brows knit in fierce protectiveness as tears streamed down her cheeks. The sight of him in chains made her stomach turn.

Olivja spoke only in their tongue, untrusting of those who might be listening.

"They have no right to do this to you. This—this is a crime against our people. I—I'll tell Mama!"

His gaze softened, a small, sad smile crossing his lips. *"No, Valk. I am here by my own hand...I chose to wield my anger, to strike as I did. None bear that burden but me."*

"I bear that burden! I do!" Olivja sobbed, knees buckling as she collapsed to the floor, her body shaking.

She gasped for breath, her voice thick with guilt.
"I've forsaken you, pabbi—I've failed you... The fault is all mine." She clutched the cold stone beneath her, desperate to anchor herself in a reality she couldn't escape.

Dagrun's face twisted with sorrow and love. Dropping to one knee before her, he held her hands firm, refusing to let go. He spoke gently, his voice a comforting rumble in the stillness of the night:

"Aye...My Rose...why do your thorns always turn in upon yourself?"

"Do they, pabbi!? Do they!?" Olivja's voice cracked, raw and desperate, her eyes wide with fury and anguish as she looked up at him.

She shook her head, the helplessness too much to bear.
"I only cause pain and anger—if they turn upon me, it is because I deserve it...I deserve the pain—not you, not Adalja, not Vincent—"

She paused, chest heaving as the truth of her self-condemnation took over.

"I cause all these horrors! And yet, I do not wish to change," she whispered, her voice quivering with shame.

"I am broken, pabbi...My mind is consumed by jealousy, hatred, vengeance, pride, and yet I..." She faltered, her words dissolving under the crush of her own self-loathing.

"I can't change. I can't stop being this—this heathen," her voice cracked, and she looked away, unable to meet his eyes. *"But everyone desires it of me. And I bring so much suffering because of it..."*

Dagrun's gaze softened, his fierce expression melting into something gentler, but resolute. A flicker of fire remained—unyielding, and only what a father could possess. He reached out, calloused hands cupping her face as he lifted it to meet his gaze, chains rattling softly.

"Listen to me, Valk," he said, his voice steady but filled with conviction. *"You need not change for a soul. You are the woman you've chosen to be. The woman our gods guide. And you are no heathen."*

He brushed away more tears, his eyes glossing over with some of his own.
"I may not have always been there...but I have always seen you. You are everything I have ever prayed for—everything I could wish for in a child."

He paused, his voice dropping to a soft growl as his thumb traced her cheek, brushing away a tear. *"I am proud of you, Olivja. Proud of who you've become. No fate, no alliance, no amount of suffering could ever change that."*

A heavy sob broke in tandem with her heart, her eyes shutting tightly as his warmth overwhelmed her.

Her father's words were both a balm and a blade.
It was hard to believe him—hard to trust *anyone* after so many years of defiance and solitude. His praise and encouragement was familiar, but too sweet to accept. How was she to trust the words of a sober man, when she had long relied on drunken promises?

They were words she thought she may never here from him. Words she didn't feel she deserved. But she hadn't known how deeply she needed to hear them until they landed. Her eyes fluttered open, staring back into an identical gaze.

"Pabbi...what if they kill you for this?" Olivja whimpered. *"For protecting my foolish choices? I-I could not live with myself if—"*

Dagrun cut her off with a soft chuckle, a dry rasp in his voice.
"King Ezekiel is our ally. Killing me would only seal Perdyr's victory," he said with calm that reassured her—though his tired eyes betrayed the depth of thought he'd given to the matter.

"There's no honour in taking my life. They know it. Our people know it. You need not fear for me."

Still, Olivja's heart ached with unease. Every decision felt like it pushed her father closer to a precipice. *"But I spoke against them—the Worthyns. They could—"*

"They will not," he said, tone firm, slicing through her doubt like a blade. His sharpness steadied her—but didn't wholly convince her. *"And that is not for you to worry about, my Wild Sun."*

The nickname, always so soft in his mouth, carried the strength of a command now.

"*You do not carry the burden of these alliances on your shoulders alone. You must know that.*"

His words settled over her like a warm embrace, one he could not give her. Olivja searched his eyes, needing more. Years of drunkenness made this moment feel distant—like seeing him through a veil she desperately wished she could cross.

"*Pabbi...*" Her voice cracked, fragile and uncertain as she searched for the courage to tell the duty that has haunted her for so long.

Dagrun's brow furrowed, and he leaned in slightly, urging her to speak. "*Child?*"

Olivja took a deep breath, her chest trembling as guilt twisted inside her like a wound that wouldn't heal.

"I have to move against our alliance—again," she whispered, her voice trembling, as though asking permission from her father. *"They murdered the Völur...witches, they called them."*

She shook her head, hot tears cutting paths down her cheeks once more. *"They were innocent—I know it."* She choked on the words, throat tight in fear of his disapproval.

"I have to find the truth. I cannot live in lies," she whispered like a vow. *"This path—I did not choose it. Odin marked it upon me, this much I know, pabbi..."*

Dagrun's expression softened further, his gaze holding both understanding and a quiet pride.

"Then...find the truth, Valk," he said quietly. *"You are the voice of our people. You carry our power, our strength, and no one shall ever silence you. Worthyns may wear crowns, but it does not make them true."*

He gave her a firm squeeze, his hands rough and grounding. *"You come here to ask for my approval, eh? When have you ever needed that before?"*

Olivja stilled at his playful reminder of the defiant child who always walked her own path no matter what was laid before her.

Why *was* she seeking permission?
The question made her scoff at herself, embarrassed by the lapse into vulnerability. But as her gaze met his, she sighed shakily.

"No, I...I am not seeking approval, fodir. I am warning you," she said with a dangerous smirk, a mischievous glint in her eyes, one he knew well. *"This truth I find may crumble the very kingdoms we hold dear."*

Her father, despite her reckless words, smiled and his lip ring glinted in the dim light. His greying facial hair curled as shallow wrinkles creased with a low, amused chuckle.

"My rose...how much you are your mother now..." he said softly, his eyes darkening as memories stirred. *"The sea may crash against the shore...but..."*

"—the land remains," they finished the Ragnarvik saying together, the words flowing between them like a river that had never stopped running.

Dagrun's expression softened, but there was an undeniable strength in his gaze. *"When your waves calm, I will be here to ground you, Valk."*

The words carried more weight than she expected—a vow not just as a father but as someone who had seen the tempest within her and would face it, no matter how fierce. As always, they saw each other.

Not as burdens or thorns, but as family. As blood.

She leaned closer between the bars and their foreheads met, her father's hands cupping her cheeks with a firmness that said, '*I will never let you go*'.

They remained there, father and daughter bound in defiance, each drawing strength from the other in the dungeon's silence. His cold hands warmed against her burning skin, and for a moment, it felt like they were the only two in the world.

"I love you, Pabbi." — "I love you, Olivja."

The faint murmur of knights at the top of the stairs signaled that their time together was nearing its end.

With a heavy sigh, Olivja pulled back, taking his hands from her cheeks and holding them in her own. She stood a little taller, her resolve hardening like steel.

"*I will find who killed your companions, pabbi. I will avenge you, as you have done for me. I will prove to the gods that I am worthy of Adalja's love. I will make things right.*" She said louder, clear and purposeful, as though she wanted everyone—especially the gods—to hear her vow.

"If Odin has put you on a path, let us ask him not for mercy, but for sight," Dagrun murmured. *"May he show you the truth, no matter how grim. Let him guide you where I cannot follow."*

Olivja let out a shaking breath, feeling the words trickle over her like the waterfalls in her jarldom. She smiled weakly, as if the gods had already heard and sealed the path ahead.

Together, they whispered an old prayer to the Allfather under their breath: *"Odin, let no lie blind us. Let no crown silence us. May your ravens watch over us."*

She squeezed his hands, their eyes meeting with a depth of understanding only those bound by blood and fate could share.

Her promise lingered in the air, thick with the unspoken truth that this mission might cost them everyone they held dear.

"May fate be with you, Olivja—as am I...*always.*" His voice, a low murmur, carried the weight of years of wisdom, love, and pain shared between them.

His words were a solid foundation beneath her feet, the strength she would carry into the storm ahead.

A final silence passed between them—a single shared breath before she turned.

Olivja moved quickly, glancing towards the narrow passage out of the dungeon. The knights were drawing closer, their footsteps echoing ominously at the entrance.

Her heart pounded, her breath ragged—but purpose steadied her, sharpening her focus like never before.

She crept through the dark passage, her body pressing against the cold, damp stone walls as she made her way towards the exit. The heiress reached the wooden door, her hand hovered over the cold metal handle. Slowly, ever so quietly, she cracked it open, its hinges groaning with age.

She slipped through, her movements swift and silent, the evening torchlight wrapping around her like a cloak. Olivja slipped into the shadows of Worthyn, her promise to her father and the gods now a fire burning in her chest.

She knew it true—
WHAT LAY AHEAD WAS CARVED BY THE NORNS LONG BEFORE TONIGHT.

Passage III: Hjarta í Myrkri

[A Heart in Darkness]

Thread XLI

ᚦᛖ ᛒᚢᚱᛞᛖᚾᛊ ᛟᚠ ᚺᛖᛁᚱᛊ ᚦᛖ ᛒᚢᚱᛞᛖᚾᛊ ᛟᚠ ᚺᛖᛁᚱᛊ ᚦᛖ ᛒᚢᚱᛞᛖᚾᛊ

ᛖᛚᛁᚨᛊ

Elias had to give his brother time—time to simmer, time to cool before attempting a visit. And perhaps, he needed some time himself.

In his room, he sat quietly, staring at a letter Gothel had handed him moments prior.

A silver coin spun between his fingers—a nervous trick he'd learned long ago. Olivja had scolded him for it often as a child, but now, no one was around to correct him.

His mind drifted to memories of their childhood, when fear of their father's anger bound them together, back when the only person each had in the world was the other.

Now look at us...

For some reason, his mind flashed to Brahms, and he scoffed, an unexpected ache catching him off guard.

That meddler, he thought, scoffing in disbelief at how quickly his little white lie about Olivja's condition had reached Brahms. Somehow, the knight had seen right through him.

Lying, like sleep, was a necessary evil. Elias didn't like to do it, but it had become natural for him to run from the truth.

A shameful feeling lingered; the memory of Brahms' disappointed look striking him harder than he'd like to admit. He shook his head as though trying to clear away the tangled mess of emotions weighing on him—shame, confusion, and loyalty all colliding.

What mattered most was his brother; it had always been that way. But Brahms and Adalja were slowly gaining his favor, and it frightened him.

The care he once gave so freely to Vincent was being pulled in pieces, and he didn't know how to stop it. He didn't know if he *wanted* to. All he knew was that he couldn't lose his brother—not now, not ever.

The coin slipped from Elias' fingers, clattering to the stone floor before rolling all the way to the door. He sighed. The sound bothered him—not because it was loud, but because of how it echoed.
Sharp. Hollow. Alone.

Like that coin, his brother had fallen—slipped from grace—and the thought unsettled Elias more than he cared to admit. Vincent's rage and distance towards Olivja had shown a side Elias had never seen before. A side that left him wary.

But who was he to judge? The same could be said of him.

He dragged his hands over his face, groaning softly.

And then—a soft scrape of metal against stone made him freeze. Elias slowly peeled his hands away and glanced down.

The coin had returned.

It lay motionless at the foot of his chair, gleaming faintly in the torchlight. His eyes lifted—slowly, carefully.

There, crouched by the door, was the jester.

Nimble.

They squatted low, knees spread wide, their impossibly long braids coiled like snakes on the floor in front of them. Elias hadn't heard them enter. Hadn't felt a shift in the air. And yet—they were here.

Their head tilted. Blue eyes calm. Curious. Hands resting delicately on the stone.

Elias stared, then scoffed softly, a reluctant sound leaving his lips. He leaned forward and plucked the coin from the stone floor.

"...Thank you," he murmured, flicking the coin across his knuckles with a practised grace.

Nimble had taught him that trick. God, it felt like a lifetime ago.

They'd given him his first coin as a boy—small, copper, worn from the hands of a hundred court jesters before them. But to Elias, it had meant everything.

He looked up again.

Nimble hadn't moved—a crouched gargoyle, perfectly still, watching.

Elias raised his brows, then flicked the coin back towards them. It rolled gently across the floor.

Nimble snatched it up with startling speed and tucked it into their palm. With a flick of their wrist, a second coin appeared—seemingly from nowhere. Then both danced over their knuckles in perfect sync, flipping, twirling, vanishing, reappearing. One shot into the air, then vanished before falling.

When Elias blinked again, the coin was delicately caught between Nimble's teeth.

He laughed—just once, quick and quiet—but real.

A true smile crept across his face, uninvited. Warmth stirred in his chest like something half-remembered. He'd nearly forgotten what it felt like to grin without guilt. To forget, even for a breath, the ache of war and expectation.

Nimble always had that effect on him. Strange, eerie, wordless—and yet somehow always knowing exactly what he needed. Though, he remembered the days when they had a voice.

A sharp, clever thing. All bite and laughter, like wind through broken glass.
He missed it more than he'd ever admit.

Now, her silence said even more.

He looked away, trying to bite down the smile, shaking his head. He didn't want to feel better.
Not yet.

And then—The sound again. Metal. Spinning.

He looked back. Nimble was gone.

In their place, before the cracked door, two coins spun on their axis—one his, the other unknown. One had already slowed, but the second seemed to spin forever, humming like a thread pulled tight.

Elias stood sharply, drawn to it. He dove for the faster one, catching it before it stilled. Once the coin rested in his grasp, he let out a breath he hadn't realised he was holding.

But when he opened his palm, that breath stilled once more. What he held was no coin at all.

It was his brother's wax seal disc. Heavy and silver, etched with a precise *V*.

After a moment of staring, his throat working with uncertainty, he closed his fingers around it. He brought it to his chest, holding it there like a gesture of fealty.

Vincent needed him.
Even if he didn't know it. Even if he'd never say it.

Elias rose, more certain now. He snatched the letter from his desk with a flick of distaste, pulled his hood over his head, and fit his mask into place. He left the wax disc and the coin behind on the table and slipped out into the corridor—just as silently as Nimble had.

Vincent's room was close to his own, and perhaps that was why it felt so difficult to stay away.

Despite his anger, Elias knew his brother was suffering. The bruises were more than physical; they marked a deeper pain. They hurt his soul...shattered the safe, fatherly image Dagrun once carried. He knew this because that pain ran just as deep in him, even if he hated the actions that had brought them here.

Reaching Vincent's door, the knights posted outside allowed him entry without a word. The door closed softly behind him as he pulled back his hood, leaving his mask in place—though he couldn't say why.

His gaze fell upon Vincent lying on the bed, bare-chested, his face a mess of bruises: a swollen eye, split lip, darkened cheekbones. Vincent's eyes met his, cold and resentful, though Elias knew the anger wasn't truly meant for him.

Elias approached cautiously, taking a seat beside the bed, fingers idly playing with the letter, unsure of how to begin.

After a long silence, Vincent finally grumbled, "What do you want?" His voice was low, bitter, as though any more disappointment would shatter him completely.

Elias sighed, leaning back in his chair. "Can't I check on my brother in his time of need?"

Vincent's gaze sharpened, suspicion flaring in his expression. He saw through Elias easily, knowing there was more to this visit.

"*Very well*," Elias admitted, a hint of a smirk tugging at his lips. "I'm here to strike you while you're down. Did I not say this would happen if he found out you harmed Olivja?"

Vincent scoffed, eyes narrowing. "You rub salt in my wounds and call me a fool in one breath? You truly think I've no notion of what I do, Eli?"

"Do you?" Elias asked, matching his brother's scoff with one of his own.

"Every step I take is measured...and I've ever been the wiser of us, even still," Vincent cockily retorted, lazily turning his head the other direction, uninterested in sharing what truly lied in his mind.

Elias' patience snapped and he stood, unable to contain his frustration. "If there is some grand design at work, then speak it, Vincent! You hanged three witches, had me cast Dagrun in chains—If your heart seeks vengeance for Mora—"

Before Elias could finish, Vincent surged from the bed like a beast unchained, seizing him by the throat. In a blink, he drove Eli backwards with such force the wall groaned under the impact, a picture frame crashing to the floor as the entire room seemed to jolt from the violence. Elias' boots scraped against the stone, his breath caught beneath Vincent's tightening grip, eyes locked with the war that raged in his brother's.

"Do not speak of her!"
Vincent's face twisted in fury, his voice a raw roar reverberating through the room.

Elias held his brother's gaze, his own filled with sorrow, not fear. The mention of Mora had struck a nerve, awakening a darkness in Vincent that Elias hadn't anticipated. He looked back at him, apologetic yet unyielding, realising he had made a mistake bringing her up.

Vincent's rage faded as suddenly as it had appeared, and with a pained grunt, he released Elias, collapsing. Instinctively, Elias caught him, helping him back to the bed.

Once Vincent was lying down again, Elias returned to his chair, steadying himself with a deep breath. He knew better now than to bring up Mora again.

Softly, carefully, Elias spoke again: "If *she* is not the heart of this, then speak what is. I have *never* kept my secrets from *you*, brother...you owe me as much." His voice was low, a mix of urgency and vulnerability, bracing himself for whatever truth Vincent had been hiding.

Vincent kept his gaze to the right, fixed on the open window, the cool breeze stirring loose strands of his hair as he sighed. Slowly, he turned back to his brother, his expression grim yet honest.

"I've no mind to remain chained by Ezekiel. I cast them off long ago," he began, his voice low and edged with defiance.

He didn't look Elias in the eyes as he spoke, each word carrying a weight that was years in the making. The use of their father's full name made him sit up, knowing that whatever was about to be said was buried deep.

"For decades he has shamed our blood—beaten us, turned us upon one another, poisoned us with falsehoods and cast us off the moment his reach proved too great." Vincent's voice was tight with years of bitterness, each word a small release of all he'd held back.

"He shaped us as weapons to swell his pride, hid us from the world so his name alone would gleam. To him, we've been naught but tools. But no longer, brother. I'll not be the pawn in his game, nor the *mud on his boot*." His jaw clenched as he spoke, the pain in his gaze cutting through even the dim light of the room.

Elias said nothing, though his fingers tightened around the letter until the edges crumpled, nearly tearing. He'd heard these sentiments before, felt them even, but the force of Vincent's anger was something else entirely.

"His crowning move," Vincent continued, his voice low and fierce, "was to sell us off. To him, these marriages are his victory, his path to securing the power he craves, solidifying his lies one last time. But I say—" Vincent's eyes flicked to Elias, a dark glint in them. "I say, let these marriages be his undoing. Let them turn and ruin him; let them be the reason he loses *everything*." The words held a calculated edge, a bitter finality, proving he had been honing this plan in secret.

He paused, his voice dropping to a dangerous murmur. "I would do anything to bring justice to our family, Elias. *Anything* to undo the wrongs he's set upon us. No matter the cost on my soul...no matter the cost of *any soul* that stands in my way."

Silence befell the room at the same time that the sun set, enveloping the room in an unexpected darkness. A chill began at his fingertips and ran all the way to his shoulders, causing Elias to slowly remove his mask. He looked up from the letter, locking his eyes with Vincent.

"Brother..." Elias began, his voice weak, brought forth by the memories of their evil father. "You speak of the horrors of our father while boldly announcing the retire of your morals...you are drowning in your resentment—"

"And I will die in it," Vincent immediately snapped, but quickly his voice tapered into something more gentle, more hopeful, "...*unless*...unless I bring that man to his knees."

Again, there was a silence as Elias contemplated his words.

He, too, wished nothing more than for their father to suffer for the crimes he committed...but Vincent's resolve frightened him.

Vincent was a stubborn man—a man of justice, shaped by Olivja—and just as he feared her audacity, he dreaded what this new determination meant for his brother...and for himself.

"All I ask...is that you consider the aftermath of your path, Vincent..." Elias treaded carefully. "Will you cut down all those who stand in your way? Are you willing to become a monster to slay one?"

Unfortunately, the tone in Vincent's voice hardly changed. He took no time responding as he brought his eyes to his fists in his lap, "I already have."

Elias froze.

Already have...killed?

The thought pounded in his skull, his heart beating quicker at the thought of Vincent, throwing away lives in the name of revenge.

He didn't know what to say. He looked down at his clenched hands, because he didn't want to believe it. And in his brother's eyes he saw no lie. Just confidence and hard truths.

"Will you abandon me now?...Is my *vengeful* spirit undeserving of your love, brother?" The tone of the wounded prince was not accusatory, but laden with sorrow, as if he truly believed that his quest was enough to sever the bond they had shared for so long.

Their identical eyes met, and Elias clenched his jaw, fighting back tears as his loyalties were once again put to the test.

How could he abandon Vincent? How could he throw away everything they had—everything they had been through—over his hatred for their father?

Every inch of Vincent's pain, every ounce of his brother's fury, pressed into Elias like a blade to his chest. Just because Vincent was choosing a darker path, did it mean he was no longer his brother? No longer his closest friend?

His heart wavered from the question, but Elias drew in a deep, shaky breath, steadying himself before he spoke.

"You will never lose my love, Vincent," Elias said, his voice unwavering, though the words felt heavy with their weight. His jaw set firmly, and he spoke as though offended by the mere suggestion.

"I may not join you on your quest for justice...but I am your eternal ally. *Evermore*, brother."

For a long moment, neither of them moved. Then, slowly, Vincent reached out, his hand trembling as he grasped Elias' forearm in a firm, desperate hold. Elias, caught off guard, mirrored the gesture, his grip tight with unspoken emotion.

Without another word, Vincent pulled his brother into a tight embrace.

The years of tension, anger, loyalty, and sorrow flooded in that moment. Their hearts beat in time, an unspoken understanding passing between them in the silence. Elias hugged him fiercely, the weight of the world momentarily lifting from his shoulders as he clung to the only person who had ever truly known him.

In that moment, they were not the sons of a tyrant, nor the men caught in the throes of war. They were simply brothers, bound by blood, by memory, and by love—no matter the paths they would walk.

They remained locked in each other's arms, the quiet comfort of their bond wrapping around them like a shield. It was a rare, fleeting moment of peace amidst the chaos that had consumed their lives.

The steady rhythm of their breaths was the only sound, an echo of everything they had been through, and everything they had yet to face. But it didn't last long.

As time passed, Elias' weight pressed too heavily on Vincent's injured frame. He pulled away first, clearing his throat as he tried to rid himself of the sudden surge of emotion.

The truth had to be spoken, and there was no room for weakness now.

Without a word, Elias reached for the letter, the true reason for his visit. It was heavier than it should have been.

As his fingers brushed against the paper, the gravity of what was to come hit him. He couldn't avoid it any longer.

"Now, will you share with me what is in writing?" Vincent's voice cut through the silence, sharp as ever.

He'd noticed the letter long before Elias even reached for it. His eyes glinted with a knowing suspicion, and Elias could feel the hollowness of his brother's gaze.

Elias swallowed hard, the words sitting like stones in his throat. He wasn't sure how to deliver them, how to tell Vincent the truth without breaking the fragile peace they'd just found.

His hands trembled as he unfurled the letter, his heart racing.

"...Word of the execution, and Dagrun's imprisonment...it reached the battlefield, brother..." Elias began, his voice barely a whisper, as though the very mention of it might shatter the stillness.

He tried to soften the blow, to prepare Vincent for what was coming, but he knew it wouldn't be enough.

Vincent's brow furrowed, a flicker of understanding passing through his eyes. He was already reading the letter in his mind, piecing it together before Elias even finished.

Finally, he met his brother's gaze and, with a heavy heart, delivered the words that would change everything.

"He rides for us."

Thread XLII

ᚦᛖ ᛒᚢᚱᛞᛖᚾᛊ ᛟᚠ ᚺᛖᛁᚱᛊ ᚦᛖ ᛒᚢᚱᛞᛖᚾᛊ ᛟᚠ ᚺᛖᛁᚱᛊ ᚦᛖ ᛒᚢᚱᛞᛖᚾᛊ

ᚨᛞᚨᛚᛃᚨ

Adalja wandered the halls, moving along shadowed walls like a cat in the night, a single candle burning upon her iron plate.

She hadn't left her bedroom since the night of Dagrun's arrest. The guilt kept her from showing her face, blaming herself for yet another horrible thing to befall Olivja.

Brahms had been glued to Adalja's side as much as he could help. He provided her comfort and comedy, as he always had. Elias occasionally stopped at her room. Even after the truth had come between them, he was still the one to bring her meals.

Adalja's eyes flickered over the paintings that scattered the walls as she made her way to the library, hoping to find solace through a book. Or perhaps she was simply missing Olivja.

She had not heard from or seen her since she had screamed at her to leave. The moment twisted and grew hazardously in the back of the princess' blistering mind.

And then—like a dream, or a nightmare—the faint jingle of bells echoed down the hall ahead of her.

A shiver slid down her spine.
It was down there—the thing she'd seen haunting the walls of Worthyn since her arrival.

She knew those bells. That quiet, mocking trickle of sound. The jester. It was beckoning her, or perhaps warning her.

Adalja's fingers curled tighter around the candle plate, stomach clenching.

She crept down the hallway to the library, her light blue fabric flowing like waves down her back. Her hair was relaxed, gentle curls bouncing with each step as she neared the large door.

And then she saw it: white chalk scrawled on the stone beside the door like a warning...or an invitation.

Adalja quickly looked around, blue eyes scanning the dark halls for the lanky beast. But the corridor was empty. Only the faint jingle of bells remained, as if the jester truly lived in the walls.

Slowly, her eyes trailed up towards the wooden rafters, bracing to catch it swinging above her. She raised the candle, the dim aura casting the wood in flickering shadows. But, thankfully, no Jester was among them.

Only Adalja haunted the halls now. And the art. And the bells.

She looked back at the chalk, stepping closer. Adalja's heart pounded, loud and frantic in her chest as she moved the flame to illuminate the artwork.

Drawn across the stone wall near the library door was a woman's figure—smudged but deliberate—with long, wild hair, arms outstretched, holding a messily drawn crown engulfed in flames. Above her, the shape of an eye—open, disturbingly focussed.

And then the quiet swallowed her. The bells stopped in an instant. As if it was *pleased* she'd seen its masterpiece.

She gulped. Goosebumps prickled her skin and her eyes darted to the library door.

Then...right beside her ear...
Jingle.

With a loud scream, Adalja dropped her candle and burst through the library door, quickly turning and closing it behind her, breathless. Eyes closed to tight, she rested her head back against the door, hand firmly holding the latch shut so the jester could not enter.

You are well, you are safe. Tis but a trickster. That's all.

She inhaled slowly through her nose, exhaling through pursed lips. She had never known fear like the kind the jester stirred in her. It made her smirk, disbelieving of how much it shook her...but the smile faded the moment she opened her eyes.

Every candle in the library was lit, casting a warm glow over the shelves and books. The table in the center was covered with pages and quills, a mess that poured onto the floor and nearly stretched to the door.

Her heart shot up to her throat, constricting painfully.

Someone else was lurking through the library.

Her hand tightened, ready to yank the cold metal doorknob before she could be spotted. But then the beautiful image of Olivja peeked slowly from behind a large shelf. Her wide, fearful eyes mirrored Adalja's.

The Norsewoman sighed as she stepped fully out from behind the bookshelf, dressed in her dark cloak and a long beige tunic that lay flat against her body.

"What are you doing here?" they whispered at the same time, voices sceptical yet edged with relief.

"I thought you were the jester," they said again in unison.

For a moment, they only stared at one another, eyes unblinking. Olivja clutched a book, her gaze drifting in thought. She tapped the leather cover thrice before letting her eyes fall back on the princess.

"L-liv..." Adalja stumbled over her words as she inched towards her. "You're walking...that's...that's wonderful," she choked out, throat tight with nerves.

As she grew closer, Olivja stiffened and stepped back. Adalja caught it. So she froze, chest clenching.

"You should be resting," Olivja whispered, an air of concern laced in her hushed tone. Her jaw clenched as she placed the dark brown book on the table beside her.

She stepped towards Adalja this time, and the noblewoman felt a weight lift from her chest as she drew in a silent breath, her eyes flickering over the heiress. But it became clear that Olivja was not interested in the same way. The heiress turned to a shelf and began flicking across books, barely paying any attention to Adalja.

The princess clenched her jaw. Her hands were so sweaty suddenly.

"As...as should you," Adalja said, raising her hand slightly to gesture at the wounds Olivja had barely recovered from. When her hands returned to her sides, she wiped them on her gown, swallowing the nerves.

"I do not need lectures, princess..." Olivja sneered, turning to face her, arms crossing. "You may leave."

"I will not," Adalja quickly replied. "Do not push me away..."

"You're right. *How dare I,*" she said dryly, tilting her head. "I am doing what must be done. What you've *wanted* me to do since coming here. And there is no more *time* for me to suffer in your games, Adalja—my people need me."

"I never wanted *this*," she whispered. After a brief pause she pressed on, "And you should be healing, that is what is important."

"My fodir sits in *chains*, Adalja," Olivja snapped with a shaking angered breath. "You do not get to counsel me. Now, go."

But the princess shook her head. "I cannot..."
The admission was pathetic, but it came out—a trembling whimper—before she could stop herself. She was afraid of leaving and facing the jester, and desperate to remain beside Olivja.

The heiress growled quietly, frustration rolling off her in waves as her breaths staggered. "What are you doing, Adalja? Why trouble my ears with your words *now,* of all times?"

"I...I wish to help you," Adalja mumbled, eyes flickering away nervously, "t-to be with you."

Olivja laughed low, her eyes closing for a moment as if in disbelief. The sound made the princess glare in frustration; the heiress minimized every single thing she said. And then she turned away, snatching the book from the table before disappearing into the dark rows of the library.

It was obvious that she wanted little to do with Adalja, and that was justified. But the princess was as stubborn as any other Norse person. She wouldn't let her slip away again—not now that the truth was out. Not now that everything was falling apart.

"*Olivja*," Adalja whispered through gritted teeth as she walked after the fading silhouette of her, but the woman did not budge, did not look back, and she did not answer.

As the princess drew nearer, her hand shot out, daringly stopping the heiress in her tracks with a firm grip on her bicep. With a harsh yank, they were facing each other once more.

Olivja glared down at her. And while her amber eyes made the princess go still, it was not in submission—not yet, anyway. Still, she could not deny the tightening in her chest at the warmth of golden skin beneath her palm.

She was bewitched by her closeness, entranced in the shadow of night, hidden between the pages of Worthyn's castle. The princess bit her lip, brows twitching upwards.

"*Unhand me, Adalja...*" Olivja drawled angrily, driving the noblewoman back until she stumbled into a bookshelf.

Soft fingers grazed the wood behind her as she was pressed into a wall of words, her cheeks flushed. Her blue eyes flicked to Olivja's lips for the briefest moment before meeting her intense brown gaze once more.

"Liv..." Adalja breathed, her hands unsteady, lifting to grasp the folds of Olivja's cloak. "...let me share your burdens, I beg you." She didn't even try to hide the way she pulled the heiress closer. But Olivja's hands stayed in fists at her sides.

"No. I'll not see you torn apart for the sake of my fire. I'll face the gods themselves if I must—for justice." She uttered, letting out a heavy breath against her face. "And you could not do the same... *You have shown me that.*" Olivja quietly added, tilting her head at the short princess. "So stay away, Adalja."

"I *can* do the same! I-I want to help," Adalja whimpered the words, though she did not believe them herself. Yet she wanted Olivja to believe—wanted her to see the strong woman she ached to be.

"YOU—" Olivja cut herself off from yelling, not wanting to alert anyone of their presence in the library, jaw clenching as her eyes burned with fury and betrayal. She never broke her gaze from Adalja, her breath heavy but quiet.

"No. You do not wish to *help.* You wish for relief from your guilt. You are *only* here because you are *ashamed*. And because you *pity* me," Olivja scoffed. "Do not demean me with this sorrowful *act*. Go."

Before Adalja could even blink, Olivja stormed off around the corner to the other side of the bookshelf, leaving her in her shamed thoughts.

Adalja wanted to cry—*again*—frustrated over being dismissed. Her fists clenched at her sides, determination burning in her chest.

"Olivja!" she called as she rounded a shelf.

An audible groan echoed from the shield-woman. She stopped, turning to meet Adalja again, hands tightly coiled.

Olivja's stare glimmered like polished citrine, illuminated by the candlelight seeping between the gaps of the shelves. Her skin glinted like gold and it took her breath away—even when warred by her angriest expression.

The princess took a small step closer, her hands nervously fidgeting at her chest.

"Is it demeaning? My affections? My care? Is that truly how you f—"

"Gods, I've had enough, Adalja!" Olivja shouted, tossing her book onto the shelf. She ran her hands up her face, combing back her wild hair and gripping it as though the Adalja's presence unraveled the very threads of her consciousness.

"I have not!" Adalja cried out, her fingers now clutching at her skirt. She was ready to sprint towards Olivja if she were to be refused again. Taking another step forward, Adalja declared, "I am ready now—*truly!* Olivja, I will not stop—I care *not* about the risks any longer!"

The Norsewoman growled, "You speak of risk as if you've tasted it." She pointed at her with a heavy finger. "Yet you'd never stake a thing for me—not then, not ever! Don't you start this now once everything else has burnt!"

"Is that what this makes us? *Burnt?*" Adalja asked in a broken whisper, gaze narrowing at the Ragnarvik heir. "Is this how it ends? Our tale turned to ashes—unfinished?" she whispered, her voice choked, unable to let go of this even if Olivja had enough. "*What about me?*"

She gasped, unable to finish as Olivja stepped forward, closing the distance between them until she was caged between strong forearms. Her back slammed against the bookshelf, knocking bound literature to the floor with quiet thumps. She looked up, like a doe caught in the mouth of a bear.

"*Now* you ask for my consideration? Begging for my gaze like a starving thing...Is that hard for you, princess? *Hm*?" Olivja exhaled, looking down at her with a scrunched face, her anger on full display.

"Maybe I ought to make you *wait...kiss* you, take you to my *bed*, and leave you in the cold—*just as you did to me,*" Olivja hissed, her voice cutting through the silence like a blade, her hands clutching the wooden bookshelf until her knuckles blanched.

"Perhaps then you will taste but a shard of the ache I have borne for you—perhaps then you'll know how I've felt for the past *ten years*..."

Olivja lowered her head.
Her lips hovered Adalja's so close they shared the same breath.
The tip of Olivja's nose dragged deliberately up the bridge of Adalja's, her touch as searing as fire on bare skin.

"*Gods,*" she exhaled with a shudder, "but I can't do that to you."

"For no noble heart like yours should ever bear the burdens I suffer for you."

Adalja's eyes shimmered with want, with love, at those words. Even in her worsts, Olivja's words laid her upon an altar. Her chest rose and fell in rapid, shallow breaths—thrumming with a longing that refused to be denied.

And then, in a wave of barely restrained chaos, Olivja's lips crashed against hers. Fierce. Hungry. *Possessive.*

The kiss wasn't a simple claim—it was a battle. It was grief and fury and longing, a tempest that demanded surrender.

Adalja gasped against her, wide-eyed for a heartbeat before yielding completely, her mouth opening under Olivja's assault as if craving destruction and salvation all at once. She melted, desperate for every touch, every scrap of her.

Liv moved like she was losing herself to the need to claim her, to leave their love branded into their spines and the spines of the books around them.

Without thinking, Adalja's hands slid to Olivja's back, clutching at the fabric of her linen, forgetful of the wounds she carried. She pulled the heiress closer, as if they could fuse into one.

A low, pained groan slipped from the back of Olivja's throat, raw and unguarded, though she used the kiss to smother the sting of her back. Her hand slipped into Adalja's curls, tangling with purpose before tugging her head back with an almost bruising force. They broke apart, gasping for air, their gazes locking in a moment that burned hotter than fire.

Time seemed to pause, the space between them heavy with unspoken words and undeniable want.

Her hand slipped from Adalja's hair, fingers trailing with deliberate care down to her jaw, where she grasped it firmly. Her thumb grazed across Adalja's wet, parted lips, the mocking touch igniting a flame low in the princess' belly.

"Desperation wears you well," Olivja whispered, her voice dark, laced with something dangerous and consuming.

Her blue eyes dilated, the heat burning from her fingertips to her spine—every nerve alight. She was unravelling under Olivja's gaze, the cruel warmth of her whisper, and the sharp edge of her touch. Her body thrummed with need, her resolve breaking like the tide.

Driven to prove her devotion, Adalja surged forward, showing Olivja just how desperate she truly was.

Standing on her toes, she tilted her head and pressed her lips against Olivja's with the force of a crashing wave, as though she intended to drown them both in their shared love and torment.

Olivja sighed into her mouth—a sound laced with relief and longing—but it was cut short as Adalja's tongue sought hers, their lips parting to explore the depths of their souls. They moved in perfect chaos, heads tilting in opposite directions, each kiss more fervent than the last, as if they were trying to consume the very essence of the other.

Strong hands moved with purpose, slipping down to the hem of their dresses. Liv hiked the fabric higher, her fingers grazing the warm skin of Adalja's thighs. The soft brush of their bare legs meeting sent a jolt through them both, a shared gasp breaking the feverish rhythm of their kiss.

With a sudden, deliberate motion, Olivja gripped Adalja's hips, pulling her sharply downwards, her knee pressing firmly between Adalja's legs. The impact knocked another book to the ground, but neither cared.

Adalja couldn't hold back the sounds that erupted from deep in her chest, raw and untamed. Her hands flew from Olivja's back to her hair, tangling in the silken strands with an intensity that matched her desire. She tugged hard enough to draw a low, restrained sound from Olivja—a mix of pain and pleasure that sent a fresh wave of heat through Adalja's body.

"Look at you, princess...*breaking* beneath me," Olivja exhaled into her mouth, her voice a dangerous purr, each word weighted with triumph and want.

She tugged Adalja's hips closer, her nails trailing up her sides in a slow, deliberate motion. The gentle scratch of her touch left a wake of goosebumps across Adalja's curves, as if Olivja sought to mark her in ways that would linger long after this moment was over.

"Liv," Adalja whimpered, unashamed of her desires, of her devotion to this woman. She gasped into her open mouth, taking in her warmth, her scent, and touch—dissolving like the sugar in her tea.

And for a moment, Olivja indulged, biting down onto Adalja's lip before trailing open-mouthed kisses along her neck, heavy breaths betraying her restraint.

But then her lips stopped.
Her hands slipped from her dress.
And Adalja was left breathing heavier than ever before.

Olivja pulled back just enough for their noses to still touch, and Adalja's eyes opened.

She saw Liv's smile, and yet, in her eyes, all she saw was pain. A darkness brought on by the deepest of heartbreaks, the finality of her choice.

"*Oh, my sweet little dove...*how could you risk everything," her words poured like poisoned honey, luring her in, "..for a heathen as reckless as I?" She gently grabbed Adalja's hand and closed her eyes as she pressed a wet kiss to her palm. "For someone who'd rather be right than...*yours*?"

The words invaded Adalja's ears like smoke. Olivja's eyes slowly opened, glaring at Adalja with a coldness that froze both of their hearts.

"Wh—what...?"

Then she remembered, stomach twisting in despair, that those were the dreadful words she had spoken to Olivja before the whipping. Words she regretted. Words she had hoped Olivja did not hold onto. *She did.*

She tried to pull her hands away, but Olivja held them firmly, shaking her head with a soft scoff. She pushed Adalja's hands back to the wall of books, pinning her there like punctuation to her final point.

"Never will you be mine, Princess. Forgive how long it's taken me to agree."

Adalja's heart shattered, hearing the damning words from Olivja's mouth, eyes widening up at the angered woman.

Olivja stepped back, releasing her hands, breaking the final connection between them. She eyed Adalja with cold indifference before turning away, departing to the sea of shelves without another word, touch, or glance—leaving the princess stunned and desperate.

The princess stared breathlessly into the shadows. Anger, confusion, arousal and heartbreak all mixed dangerously within as she stood helpless, trapped by words on all sides.

With a final whimper, Adalja shamefully stormed out of the library, tears brimming, hot and heavy. Her steps were loud against the stone floors, carrying the weight of her anger and heartbreak.

This was it—the end of her and Olivja.
The final straw had broken them.
And she could only blame herself.

Without thinking, Adalja left the castle, driven by nothing but the desperate need to escape. She couldn't face the truth of the life she was in now—not yet.

Her sobs caught in her throat as she passed two Worthyn guards, who said nothing, only watched in silence as she disappeared beyond the doors.

As she descended the stone steps into the garden, snow fell heavily around her. The cold bit at her bare skin, but she didn't care.

The nightgown plastered to her as the wind tugged at the thin fabric, yet the fiery howl of heartbreak burned too brightly for the chill to penetrate. Her breaths came sharp and shallow, her vision blurred by new, heavier tears.

Now outside, in the biting solitude of the night, Adalja sobbed aloud, her boots crunching loudly over the snow-dusted cobblestones.

She passed the stables. Beyond them, the forest loomed, its shadowed treetops silhouetted against the falling snow.

As she crossed its threshold, the quiet engulfed her. The snow-muted silence of the trees was suffocating, and yet it was the only solace she could find. Her steps slowed, and finally, her knees buckled beneath her.

Adalja collapsed onto the frozen ground, her sobs spilling like icy rivers down her cheeks.

This feeling...it was new to her: *rejection.*

Why would she throw me away?

She cried harder, hands fisting into the icy snow beneath her. She threw a clump of snow towards a tree.

I thought she loved me!

She cradled herself, her shoulders shaking violently as her cries echoed through the woods. She cursed the gods in her mind, fury and sorrow twisting in her chest like a cruel knot.

She hated the life she and Olivja were forced to endure. Her heart ached for a normalcy she knew they would never have. If she could, she would carve out the pieces of herself that felt too much, that failed too easily, that feared too greatly.

But then—*snap*.

The sharp crack of a branch broke through her anguish, yanking her back to the present. Her cries stopped abruptly, and she sniffled.

"...*Olivja*?" she called weakly, eyes softening with hope.

She does love me!

The silence that followed was deafening.

Adalja's tear-blurred eyes darted through the shadowy trees, the snowfall casting a ghostly haze over the forest. Her chest heaved as her breaths fogged in the frigid air.

"Come out! You're frightening me!" she shouted, her voice cracking from the strain of her sobs. She scrubbed her hands across her cheeks, wiping at the tears, replacing them with snow.

No response came.

The silence stretched, thick and ominous. Her pulse thundered in her ears as she braced herself, forcing her cold, trembling frame to move.

She straightened.
Large hands came from behind.
She was snatched with sudden, brutal force.

One hand clamped over her mouth, muffling her scream, while the other coiled tightly around her waist, lifting her off the ground.

Her stomach lurched as her muffled cries spilled against the attacker's rough palm.

Adalja flailed, her legs kicking wildly as she fought to free herself. Panic surged through her veins like fire, her screams rising as she tried to twist in the iron grip.

The hand covering her mouth shifted upwards, pressing over her nose now, forcing her silence.

Her mind spiraled as the lack of oxygen sent her body into overdrive. She clawed at the hand over her face, her muffled screams growing weaker as her chest burned.

She couldn't see her attacker, couldn't turn her head to look. Her thoughts raced, flashing to Olivja—how ruinous things were left. Then to Elias. Then Brahms.

A sob wracked her chest as she realised, with chilling clarity, that this could be the end. She was going to die!

Tears streamed freely from her eyes as her body fought instinctively, kicking and twisting, but her strength was fading fast.

The harder she struggled, the more her lungs burned for air.

Her vision blurred, then dimmed. Her limbs grew heavy, her muscles slackening as her body surrendered to the encroaching darkness.

But, right before the cold took her, a strong accented voice brushed her ear. *"You are safe now, tiny one."*

And then the forest faded into black.

Thread XLIII

ᚦᛖ ᛒᚢᚱᛞᛖᚾᛊ ᛟᚠ ᚺᛖᛁᚱᛊ ᚦᛖ ᛒᚢᚱᛞᛖᚾᛊ ᛟᚠ ᚺᛖᛁᚱᛊ ᚦᛖ ᛒᚢᚱᛞᛖᚾᛊ

ᛟᛚᛁᚠᛊᚨ

The night was endless after Adalja had left her.

The Norsewoman spent the rest of her evening combing through every page of any book that had *anything* to do with Perdyr; their culture, the Völur, poisons, mapped apothecaries.

Her mind was firmly set on discovering the truth—for once, not even Adalja was a distraction.

Their time together had left much to be desired, but destroying the princess' interest in her was the only way to be sure that she wouldn't be hurt by whatever trail she left behind.

The flickering candlelight danced on the worn pages of the ancient texts as the hours slipped away. She barely noticed the slow creep of dawn breaking through the narrow windows of the library, or the aching in her back from sitting too long in one position.

Vengeance consumed her entirely—eclipsed all else.

But as the first rays of sunlight stretched across the floor, the silence was shattered by hurried footsteps echoing down the hallway.

The sound of armour clinking, the rustling of tunics, and the shouts of men in command reached her ears. It was a sudden burst of chaos that pulled her from the pages and back into the present moment.

Her heart skipped a beat. She stood, and only then did the exhaustion set in.

Her legs protested, a sharp ache shooting up her spine. As the blood rushed to her head, her vision blurred and she brought her hand up to her forehead.

After steadying herself, she carefully made her way to the door, cracking it first before she stepped out into the hall.

Worthyn guards passed her without even a glance, jogging in full armour across the castle. With no choice but to follow, she let the current of armored men pull her forward through the twisting halls.

The heiress' pulse spiked, mind already racing with the possibilities of what could be happening. As she neared the main foyer, the noise grew louder, the urgency more palpable.

When she entered the grand hall, she was met with a flurry of knights rushing to and fro, their heavy boots thudding against the stone floors. Their faces were grim, their movements swift and purposeful.

Her eyes scanned the room, landing first on Elias, who was barking orders at several of the older knights, and then on Brahms, who stood near the prince, his face drawn in concentration. His posture was rigid, his usual relaxed composure replaced with a tension that told her something serious was unfolding.

What in the Gods names...

She strode across the room, weaving through the men as they scrambled about, her presence going unnoticed in the chaos. She approached Brahms, her voice cutting through the air with an edge of urgency.

"What madness is this?" she asked, her gaze flicking to Elias, who was now turning to join them.

Brahms' eyebrows shot up at the sight of her. This was the first time she had been seen by anyone apart from the Pembrook woman. But as quickly as the shock came, it morphed into something darker, something cold and hopeless.

"I...It's Adalja," Brahms began, his eyes telling her a story she didn't want to hear. "She's been taken, Olivja...by Perdyr."

Olivja grasped at her chest, breathing as quickly as a war drum. The words struck her like a cold-plunge. At first, they didn't register—only echoed in her mind. Then the shock hit.

Her vision blurred, tears welling in her eyes before she could even comprehend what had been said. But soon after, they bloomed into reality, and a wave of terror and sorrow overwhelmed her.

A hollowing tore through her heart, as if it had been ripped out entirely. Immediately, memories of their final, bitter exchange filled her mind—Adalja's last words, her pleading, her desperate hoping.

Instead, Olivja had turned her away...she had been cruel to her.
Had the pursuit of vengeance already truly cost her so much?

A helpless sound escaped her lips, unable to contain her dismay.

Elias stepped closer. Regret clung to his expression like soot—thick, smothering, impossible to wipe away. It was the look of a man who had failed as much as anyone.

"We must go—now! Why stand here with your tails tucked!?" Olivja shouted, her body already shifting towards the grand entrance, desperation in every step.

She needed to move, to act. She needed to find her—before it was too late, before she was lost forever. But as she turned, a hand gripped her forearm, pulling her back sharply.

"Olivja, all our men are scouring the land as we speak. The command was given the moment word reached us." Elias' voice was firm, but there was a tremor hidden beneath his words.

"You cannot go and hazard your own life. If they aim to break these unions, you are certain to follow."

Her chest seized.

"You called them murderers! Have you forgotten?! For all we know, she lies cold in the earth already!" Olivja shouted, her voice cracking with the weight of her panic.

She yanked her arm free as the sound of boots thudded like drumbeats in her skull. She couldn't be still—not when Adalja's life hung in the balance.

The ache in her heart only deepened as she turned away. Both men stood there, still as statues, as though their very presence in her pain made it worse.

For a fleeting moment, there was silence. And then, almost too quietly, Olivja's voice broke through the heavy air.

"*You*...you let her slip through your fingers—how?" The words were bitter. She glared at Brahms, blaming him in her heart, for she couldn't bear to face the deeper guilt that gnawed at her.

"No, Heiress, do not lay blame at Brahms' feet." Elias' voice cut through the tension like a knife.

His hand shot out, pressing against Brahms' chest as though to shield him from the blade of her daggering accusations. His eyes were full of urgency, but also something else—something desperate, and a little afraid.

"This duty is ours—to bring her home. And we shall not fail."

For a moment, Olivja's gaze met Elias'. There was something different in his eyes. Something that made her skin crawl, that made her blood turn cold.

How could she trust him, when he had been the one to imprison her father, the one who had stood by while Vincent harmed her? His words rang false, like promises she had endured too many times. The resentment burned through her, searing her thoughts.

But she swallowed the harsh words that threatened to spill out. Elias' confidence was *barely* enough to quiet her anger.

"We shall see her safe again...I swear it, Liv." Elias' brows furrowed, and his voice, though calm and sure, carried a quiet desperation.

Again, they exchanged a glance, one far more respectful than the last—a silent understanding passing between them. It was as if Elias could see the depths of the pain in Olivja's heart, a pain that no one else in the castle could truly comprehend.

The venom she had been ready to pour out died in her throat.

She wanted to shout, to rage at him, to make him feel her pain. But in that moment, there was nothing left but the sound of her heart breaking all over again, and the realisation that, no matter how much she resented him, he was the only one who could return Adalja to safety.

As Elias, Brahms, and the entire fleet of Worthyn Knights rushed from the castle, a deep sense of helplessness settled over Olivja, heavy and suffocating.

She closed her eyes tightly, trembling as she covered her face with shaking hands.

"*Odin, Freyja—bring Adalja safely back to my arms. Guide these foolish men. And I will bring justice to your sacred daughters,"* she whispered, her voice barely steady.

And after a breath of allowing her voice to be heard, she moved. Olivja stormed deeper into the castle.

She knew all she could do was continue her search for the truth in their absence.

Elias and Brahms' broad assumptions about Perdyr's involvement left her with little faith that they'd find Adalja—she feared they would end up chasing shadows.

But if she could uncover the true killers behind the Pembrook massacre, she would know exactly who had taken her princess.

A single knight was ordered to follow Olivja, and he lingered far behind, keeping a respected distance from the irritable, erratic woman.

Her mind was set on a destination she dreaded but knew she had to reach—Vincent's study.

The guilt of turning to him after all that had transpired clawed at her, but it was the only place she could think of that might hold something valuable.

She pushed the door open with haste, the quiet creak of the hinges mocking her sense of urgency. Closing it behind her, Olivja's breath caught in her chest as her eyes scanned the room.

Every step into his study felt like trespassing on a ghost. His presence lingered here—not in scent or sound, but in the quiet way the room seemed to watch her.

It was the same as she remembered, filled with old books and scattered papers—a sanctuary of heart and secrets. Her heart wrenched...just a bit.

Her fingers brushed over the surface of his desk, searching for anything out of place, anything that could lead her to the truth.

A sharp thrum raced through her ribs as she sifted through the papers, unsure of what she would find...unsure of what to expect. She wanted to find his evidence, she wanted to follow the trail he had started.

While rummaging through Vincent's things, she lingered over his books with a scoff. And despite herself, she found she had to read a little:

"My mind is plagued with nightly screams,
Yet shadowed 'mares 'tis not what it seems.
For 'tis sweet dreams I've come to dread,
When peace doth come, I'll know I'm dead."

For a moment, her eyebrows joined. A flicker of concern painted her expression.
But then she scoffed again.

Ever the brooding fool, spilling his heart in ink. You'd think his writing would have improved with age, she thought, a faint, amused fondness flickering in her despite all he'd done.

Her thoughts shifted—how was he now? How well could he move? Would he be upset if he found her here?

The worries sent a shiver through her, and she quickly dropped the poetry. The stack of papers tumbled down with a heavy *thump,* jarring the table.

Klink-klink-klink.

The sound of glass rolling on the stone floor drew her gaze beneath the wooden desk. She leaned down, scanning the shadows until her eyes caught sight of a small vial, rocking gently back and forth, as though nudged by an invisible hand.

Her brows knit together as she bent down fully, her fingers carefully grasping the empty glass.

The cork was still firmly in place, and a slim black string wrapped around the vial in a delicate macramé weave. She turned it over, studying it, until her eyes fell upon tiny etchings on the bottom: *YEW*

She gasped, her lips forming the name silently.
Yew, a Völva's plant, one she had worked with before...

A prickling sense of dread rose in her as she recalled the haunting warnings her mother had given her of the Yew Tree's strength. It carried death, rebirth, connections to Hel...

She raised the vial, holding it up to the torchlight. A bit of darkened liquid still remained at the base. A chill ran along her forearm...an omen, an instinct.

Immediately, she knew it was the poison used to kill the Pembrooks. It had to have been what Vincent found...*why else would he have this? He was no practicing pagan.*

Clutching the vial tightly, unwilling to lose her first clue, she set to work, rifling through scattered papers with her free hand, searching frantically for its original resting place.

WARN—

The bold word caught her eye on a paper sticking out of a different leather journal. With uncertain fingers, she reached for it. Slowly, she raised the page to her face, her breath catching as her eyes scanned what was written:

WARNING: THE YEW'S KISS

Beware the brew thou holdest; *it is the drink of endings. Take heed and follow these instructions precisely, lest the potion claim an unintended soul.*

Dosage: *One sip, no more, no less. Too much, and the death may come too quickly, raising suspicion; too little, and the heart will falter but live.*

Timing: *the heart will slow within the hour. Death to follow within two.*

Concealment: *The taste of Yew is subtle but bitter. Mask it within a spiced wine to ensure it is swallowed in full, leaving no trace of its dark work.*

Warning: *Under no circumstance should this potion touch thy skin or eyes. It is poison even upon the flesh.*

Remember, with the Yew's Kiss, there is no remedy, no second chance.

It is a path only travelled once.

She dropped the vial in an instant, and from her height, it shattered against the rough stone floor with a sharp, violent *crack*.

The small glass pieces skittered across the surface, scattering like broken promises.

She took a step back from the desk, her breath shallow, still clutching the small paper to her chest as though it were the only thing keeping her grounded.

It was written in a trembling hand, like the creator struggled to write in common tongue. Like it was written *for* someone who could not understand Norse.

If the Völur had created this poison for themselves—why write a warning?

Her gaze dropped to the shattered vial on the floor. Her mouth went dry at the sight of the dark, translucent liquid pooling among the shards.

A wave of nausea washed over her.

She didn't want to believe it—not him, not Vincent.
But the evidence was undeniable.

Could he really be the poisoner? The thought was like a punch to the gut. All this time, she had been fooled.

A subtle, creeping sensation tugged at her thoughts, and then—she felt it. A soft, unsettling tingling in the palm of the hand that had been holding the vial. Her heart skipped a beat, a cold sweat breaking out across her skin.

Her breath caught in her throat, panic clawing at her chest. Slowly, she lifted her palm, eyes fixed on it as though expecting something terrible to unfold before her.

The tingling grew stronger, and for a long moment, all she could hear was the frantic pounding of her heart in her ears.

Footsteps echoed from the hallway, growing louder, each step a drumbeat of dread in her chest.

She gasped, her heart racing, and in a frantic blur, she darted towards the nearest bookshelf, scrambling to hide herself in the shadows of a room too open to conceal her. She pressed her back to the thickest part of the shelf, forcing herself to remain as still as possible, her breath shallow, a low roar filling her head.

The heiress covered her mouth with the hand that hadn't touched the vial, fighting to silence the panicked sob that threatened to escape her.

The door to Vincent's study creaked open, and her stomach dropped.

Her eyes stung with tears, the fear threatening to crush her.

No guards. They were all sent to find Adalja. Which meant, with cold certainty, that the only person who could walk through that door now was the man who owned it. The one who had set this trap.

Vincent.

She froze as the air in the room thickened with the threat of his presence.

She *wanted* to trust him. She *wanted* to believe that this was all the evidence the witches had given him, but something gnawed at her, a deep sense of unease that wouldn't shake.

Being seen with this—whatever *this* was—could never be overlooked. No matter what, it would raise questions, suspicions. Even if he was innocent.

Her breath came in shallow gasps, desperate to calm her frantic pulse, but her heart pounded too loudly as if it could hear the danger closing in.

Footsteps—slow, deliberate—came from behind her, too close to the desk. Then, they stopped.

Olivja's blood ran cold.

She forced her eyes towards the door, the one left ajar at the entrance of his study. *I need to run...* Her mind screamed with the urge to flee.

Maybe if she ran fast enough, she could find Edith or her father, and make herself safe.

But there was no time to think.

With a burst of adrenaline, she pushed herself up and bolted from behind the bookshelf. Her footsteps were loud, each one like a hammer striking against the silence of the room, as her body moved with frantic desperation.

Just a few more steps. She could see the door, feel the cool air beyond it.

But then—*a yank*—her dress was wrenched backwards, pulling her violently back into the room.

"No!!" The word tore from her throat as her back hit the ground. "Vincent, *stop*!" she shouted, while scrambling to her hands and knees.

She pushed up to sprint, barely able to lift herself before a heavy weight slammed down on her back, crushing her into the cold stone floor.

Pain vibrated through her back, her scabs breaking open as her ribs strained under the pressure with each frantic breath she took.

A strong, merciless hand wrapped around her neck, choking off her cries while a second covered her mouth and nose.

The pressure mounted; her chest locked as she fought for air. The hand at her throat was relentless, unyielding.

No!

She thrashed with all the strength she had been taught to use, but he was heavy—too heavy for her to lift without breath.

Desperation surged within her, and somehow, she managed to bite down on the delicate skin of the palm covering her mouth. A fleeting hope—one final, frantic attempt to plead, to make him hear her.

"Vincent!! Please—PLEASE, you swore!!" Her voice cracked, broken with sobs, her chest heaving with the strain. But before she could finish, his hand slammed down over her mouth again, cutting off her cries, careful this time to avoid her teeth.

The air in her lungs grew thinner as the sharp pain in her chest grew unbearable. Her lungs screamed for relief, but it wouldn't come.

The world around her blurred—her limbs went heavy. The cold grip of unconsciousness reached for her, curling around her like a noose, pulling tighter with each passing second.

"Don't make this harder, Olivja. It'll all be over soon..." he growled, fighting to hold her still, using all of his body weight to subdue her.

She couldn't see his face, not from this position. She thought maybe looking into his eyes would stop him from hurting her, but not with her chin anchored to the stone floor, not with everything around her spinning in dizzying circles.

This can't be it. Not like this.
Not when she was so close—so close to the truth. Not when she had finally uncovered the lies. Not while Adalja was gone.

Tears spilled from her bloodshot eyes, streaming down her face as she stared at the open door—the doorway to freedom, to escape.

The bright light poured through it, stark against the dark room, shining like a beacon. It was bright. *Too bright.*

She shook her head violently, a desperate, instinctual attempt to break free.

I can't die like this. I have to live. I have to—The page.

Her mind grasped at the last thing she could hold onto—the one thing that still had meaning.

Her only chance.
It was just within reach, barely an arm's length away. Her fingers, slick with sweat and desperation, grazed it only to have it yanked from her grasp.

Her one goal, to avenge the Pembrooks, her father, Adalja—taken from her.

Her soul ached. The grief, the helplessness, the pain of everything she had lost—it consumed her, thrumming through her chest.

And through it all, she felt him. Vincent.
He was doing this. He was taking her life from her.

With every last shred of her strength, she clawed at the back of his hand, her nails digging into his flesh in a final, desperate attempt to make him feel something. Anything. But there was no mercy in him. No hesitation.

"Forgive me," his voice hovered above her, strained as the backs of his hands became raw from her scratching. "*Shh*...be still."

Her chest was on fire. It was like her heart was being torn apart from the inside.

But the fight was fading. Her hands dropped, weak and lifeless, falling limply to the cold stone beneath her.

Her body went heavy, her limbs losing their fight. There was nothing left—no strength, no breath, no ability to keep going, despite the endless reserve to keep going.

Her fingers scraped the stone as though reaching for something she couldn't have. A final, hopeless attempt to free herself, to find her way out of this nightmare.

But there was nothing.

As the darkness pulled her under, memories rose to the surface, bright and unbidden.

She saw a familiar nature trail—the old path they used to run when they were children, where the sunlight crackled through the trees and shimmered against the rushing river.

A boy jogged ahead of her, face streaked with dirt, eyes shining with a fierce, determined light.

"Come on, Olivja!" His voice echoed, young and hopeful, filled with a warmth that now seemed impossibly distant.

It was Vincent, her childhood friend—before he was anything else. Before the world turned dark.

"I'm coming!!" She giggled, glancing behind her to catch the gaze of Elias, jogging to catch up.

In her mind, she was small again, running to catch up to him as he grinned over his shoulder, daring her to keep up. Her mind was desperate to find a light in the darkness of Vincent's choking hold.

As they reached the riverbank, Vincent leapt from rock to rock with effortless skill, landing on the far side with a quiet grunt. He was always so fast, so sure-footed—always just beyond her reach.

Desperate to catch up, desperate to prove herself, she took a leap too large for her balance. Her boot slipped on the slick, glistening stones, and in an instant, the force of the rushing water swept her into the river.

She was a strong swimmer, but not with her cloak's heavy fabric dragging her down, clinging to her skin like a shroud. The clasp choked at her neck, its weight dragging her under as moss and freshwater soaked every inch.

Her body tumbled with the current, striking rocks and hidden crevices, each blow jarring her, scrambling her sense of direction.

The wet fabric wrapped over her mouth, blocking even the smallest gasp of air. She tried to scream, but water filled her throat instead, choking her with its cold, relentless pull.

Her limbs thrashed, her fingers clawing at the fabric, desperate to peel it away. She was sinking, deeper and deeper, her vision blurring.

This is it, she thought. *I'm going to die*.

Her life began flashing before her—a scattered, panicked jumble of faces and places.

She thought of her father, stern yet proud; her mother, whose warmth felt so distant now. She thought of Adalja, of her jarldom, of all she hadn't yet done.

Even in the murky depths of the river, she knew she was crying, the salt of her tears mixing with the cold rush around her. Her limbs grew numb, her chest burning for air.

Then, suddenly, a strong hand seized the back of her, pulling her sharply out of the water. She was still choking as water drained around her, but there was air—precious air.

"Y-you almost *died*, Olivja!" Vincent yelled, his voice trembling as he leaned over her, too consumed by his emotions to mask his terror. "What—what would I have done if you had—are you even *listening* to me?!"

She nodded weakly, still catching her breath. Slowly, her small hand reached up and gripped his, holding his fingers with what strength she had left.

In that moment, nothing else mattered—not her pride, not the sting of failure, only the fierce relief of being alive and feeling Vincent's steady presence beside her.

Vincent froze, his eyes widening in surprise and what looked like reluctant relief.

"M-my fault..." she croaked, her voice hoarse, a tiny cough escaping as she admitted her mistake. She rolled onto her side, shivering, but with a faint, weak smile creeping onto her face.

"*Tch. Aye,* everything's always your fault...*ninny*," he muttered, his voice thick with leftover worry but laced with the usual teasing.

Her cheeks burned at the insult as she glared up at him.

"If you *hate* me so much, then why did you even *save* me?" she snapped back, though her voice was barely a growl.

A bit of river water still lingered in her throat, making her cough and splutter as she spat into the dirt.

Vincent's face twisted, equal parts annoyance and something softer she couldn't quite name. "Because...because you're *you*, Olivja!" His voice was gruff, but his gaze softened enough to betray his worry. "Do you think I'd just...let you die?!"

She tried to suppress the warmth rising in her cheeks, turning her face away to hide the small, exhausted smile forming on her lips. "I...guess not," she mumbled.

Elias stood beside them, hands tightly clenching his small cloak as though ready to give it to her. "You really shouldn't shout at her, Vincent...she almost drowned," he said gently.

Vincent let out a scoff, his voice slipping into a mocking imitation.
"*You really shouldn't shout at her, Vincent...*" he parroted in a high-pitched tone before rolling his eyes.

Rising from the ground, he extended his hand to Olivja with a smirk. "She can handle it. She's strong...*like me*."

Their eyes met, his green gaze steady and full of something she couldn't quite grasp—but maybe, she thought, it was respect. Something about that moment, that trust, made her feel invincible, like she could take on anything as long as he was there.

AND THEN—SHE FELT HERSELF WRENCHED BACK, the warmth ripped away as the cold stone pressed into her cheek.

Reality came rushing back.

The weight on her back was heavy and relentless, his hand wrapped tight around her throat. Her vision swam, the last traces of light from the doorway bleeding into a haze.

"*Vincent*," she tried to whisper, her voice barely a breath.

The fierce will to survive surged within her, but her body betrayed her, limbs growing weaker as darkness claimed her.

She thought of the river, the laughter, the reckless strength she'd once felt beside him. She thought of his poetry and his hair. Their friendship. His lips. His hands. Their banter.

And now...now there was only the silence, her spirit slipping further and further away, until the darkness finally pulled her under.

And then the hall's bright light touched her...as though the violent hand was removed from her neck and replaced with a gentler one, one that caressed her cheek and fell over her eyes with a welcoming warmth...

And to her, he whispered with a softness that didn't belong in that room. That didn't belong in this moment.

"*Don't be afraid, Olivja...You belong to me.*"

Her eyes fluttered closed, a final tear slipping down her cheek, and then—*nothing*.

THREAD XLIV

ᚦᛖ ᛒᚢᚱᛞᛖᚾᛋ ᛟᚠ ᚺᛖᛁᚱᛋ ᚦᛖ ᛒᚢᚱᛞᛖᚾᛋ ᛟᚠ ᚺᛖᛁᚱᛋ ᚦᛖ ᛒᚢᚱᛞᛖᚾᛋ

ᛒᚱᚨᚺᛗᛋ

BRAHMS' HALF-GLOVED HANDS GRIPPED THE REINS tightly, his knuckles aching beneath the worn leather, but he didn't let up. Their journey began midday, leaving only a few hours before the sun would slip behind the mountains.

He kept his gaze fixed on the snow-dusted horizon, unwilling to meet Elias's eyes as they reached a clearing beside Brookhaven, the northern river that split Midhelm in two.

Elias dismounted first, his fur-lined cloak swirling in the sharp wind as he cast Brahms an uneasy glance. He said nothing, though the silence between them felt like a taut wire, ready to snap.

Adalja's disappearance weighed down on him like a wet cloak he couldn't remove. His chest was tight, his hands trembling with agency. He feared for his princess—feared what he would do if he failed to save her. In a matter of weeks, every royal he sought to protect, had been taken from him.

But he forced himself not to think of it. The image of his princess—cold, afraid, harmed—was too much for him.

Though it would be dark soon, Brahms was willing to ride all the way to Perdyr and back if it meant ensuring Adalja's safe return. But now, Elias' safety was in his hands as well. He couldn't let anything happen to the prince.
Even if he was still upset with him.

Brahms swung stiffly from his horse, the cold biting through his boots and creeping up his legs as he went to untie the pack.

The clearing they chose was surrounded by dense pines, stretching tall against the evening sky. Snow-covered plains gleamed brightly through gaps beyond the river, endlessly rushing despite the winter chill.

Far to the east and west, dark silhouettes of distant mountains stood stark against the setting sun. The air was sharp, cold enough to sting their throats with every breath, and carried the faint scent of pine and freshwater.

Brahms moved through the motions of setting up camp with an unyielding determination, brushing off any offers of help from Elias with curt nods and muttered refusals.

He drove the stakes for the tents into the frozen ground with quick, forceful strikes, his breath fogging the air with each exhale. His heavy wool cloak flared around him as he worked, the fur-lined collar brushing against his flushed cheeks.

His thick, padded tunic and leggings provided some warmth, but the cold bit at every exposed patch of skin, numbing his fingers and toes despite the gloves and boots he wore.

When Elias reached out to assist with the bedrolls, Brahms shot him a steely look before snatching the roll from his hands, handling it himself. Each task became an outlet, and he welcomed the strain on his muscles, anything to keep him from snapping outright.

By the time he had the fire pit arranged and the flames flickering brightly, a heavy silence had fallen around them, thick and sharp as a blade.

The fire cast flickering orange light across the snow, its warmth a small but welcome reprieve against the bitter cold. Brahms glanced towards the dark forest, his breath curling in frosty puffs as he worked, hardly registering the wintry landscape's harsh beauty.

Somewhere in the back of his mind, he knew this was the last stretch of peace before they reached the chaos awaiting them in the north.

The crackling of the fire and the rustle of Elias' movements seemed louder in the strained quiet.

Brahms stood beside his horse at the edge of camp, ensuring the beast was warm and secured.

Behind him, Elias was fussing with something near the fire, but Brahms didn't turn to look.

He didn't wish to speak with him. He was here only for Adalja—if he could have gone alone to save her, he would have.

He'd barely spoken to the prince since that night. The lie—the cover-up—had buried itself deep. But he was only a knight, and had no place speaking to Elias. That truth made the silence easier to bear.

He busied himself with his horse, checking the saddle and adjusting the reins, but eventually, he ran out of things to occupy himself. Now and then, a snow hare skittered past or a fish flopped in the river.

It was serene...or it would have been if not for the ache in his mind.

With a reluctant sigh, he turned back towards camp. Elias sat hunched, hood pulled low, his face half-obscured by a woollen scarf. He was hunched over the fire, steam rising from a small pot in his gloved hands.

The scent of roasted vegetables drifted towards Brahms, mingling with burning wood, and drew a low, insistent growl from his stomach. It was as though his body moved without his mind's permission, drawn to the fire's warmth and the promise of food.

Elias straightened at his approach, holding out two wooden bowls filled with steaming carrots, mushrooms, and parsnips.

Brahms hesitated, his pride warring with his hunger. Accepting the bowl would feel like surrender, as though he were forgiving Elias for the lies about Olivja. But the wind's bitter bite and his aching stomach won out.

"It need not carry meaning, Brahms," Elias called—his voice firm, but gentler than it had been earlier. "*Take your food.*"

Brahms took the bowl from him without a word and retreated to the opposite side of the fire. He sat on a log, cloak barely chasing the chill, careful not to meet Elias' gaze, his eyes fixed on the meal.

The warmth rose from the brown broth, and his stomach growled louder in response. His hand, encased in a fingerless glove, scooped up a spoonful, and he brought it to his mouth. The rich, hearty flavor hit his tongue, and a sigh of satisfaction slipped from him as the warmth spread through his chest.

For a moment, all Brahms could do was focus on the meal—on the soothing silence that allowed him to ignore the unease stirring beneath his skin.

He ate several more bites before he realised Elias was still watching him. Brahms slowly glanced up, meeting Elias' unmasked gaze—he must have taken it down to eat.

His eyes were sharp, unreadable, as though he was trying to decipher something unspoken. The tension between them thickened, hanging heavy in the air like the scent of the fire that crackled softly between them.

He took another bite, chewing slowly, as if trying to swallow down the knot in his throat. This time he remained staring at his prince. A silent challenge that said: 'go on, ask me what's wrong.'

And it worked.

"You're...still brooding over me, Brahms?" Elias asked, voice cautious, testing the waters. His empty bowl sat between his hands, his posture tense, waiting.

"Not *brooding*," Brahms muttered, his words sharp, but the undercurrent of something else—something darker—was impossible to ignore.

He met Elias' eyes for a brief moment before looking away, his gaze dropping back to the vegetables, still swirling the spoon in his bowl.

"...*Untrusting*," he finished, his voice rougher than he intended. Each word seemed to cut through the air with a bitterness that clung to his tongue.

Elias didn't respond immediately. The silence stretched between them, thick and uncomfortable—like Brahms' words had left a mark in the cold air.

He could feel Elias' gaze on him, but he refused to look up this time, unwilling to face whatever expression his prince might be wearing.

There was no softening of the tension, only the harsh reality of betrayal and unspoken accusations hanging in the space between them.

"You don't trust me?" Elias finally asked, his voice quieter now, almost tentative. "Brahms...I told you why I kept her fate from both of you—Not all truths are meant for the light." He paused to clench and unclench his jaw.

"You know Adalja better than I do—was I wrong to assume she would have acted rashly if I told her the truth?"

"You were right about her, I'll not deny it," Brahms said quickly, his gaze hardening as it shot up from his bowl, a look sharp enough to pierce steel.

"But you erred in thinking *I* could not withstand the truth." He pushed himself to his feet, unable to stay still any longer, his anger too alive to be contained in stillness.

"It makes me wonder, Your Highness, what other truths you'd keep from me," he continued, his voice biting, raw. "Is it that you think so little of me, My Lord, that I stood beneath your confidence?"

Elias didn't flinch, his response soft and patient, though his eyes betrayed the hurt beneath his words. "I believed our bond to be greater than this, Brahms," he said gently. "I regard you higher than any knight in my service—'tis for that reason I kept it from you. I wished not to bring you pain."

"Well, because of your lie," Brahms scoffed, chest tight, "instead of one friend pained, there were three."

His words hung in the air, heavy with the truth that Elias' decision had shattered more than trust.

"You lie to protect *me*?" Brahms continued, throwing his hands up towards the evening sky, as if seeking an answer from the very heavens.
"That is *my duty. Not yours.*"

He crossed his arms, though his twitching brows betrayed the hardness in his voice.

Elias' gaze softened, the sharpness in his posture faltering.

"I apologise, Brahms," the prince said, his voice quieter now, sincere and laced with regret. "The last thing I desire is to bring you pain. If you swear the falsehoods wound you more than any truth ever could...then let this be the last of my lies."

Brahms stood there, his heart torn.

True regret shadowed Elias' face now—the sharpness in his eyes dulling, widening, his brows lifting in a pained curve. The sorrow clung to the air between them, heavy and inescapable.

It made his chest tighten, and for a moment, Brahms wanted to reach out, to forgive him, to ease the tension between them. But the words caught in his throat, out of reach.

There was too much to let go of so easily, and it wasn't his place to forgive on behalf of Olivja. His fingers tightened around the bowl, as if clinging to restraint.

"...I thought you said this meal meant *nothing*," Brahms grumbled, the words coming out a little softer than intended.

Deep down, he couldn't stay angry at the first person to ever cook him dinner.

Elias smirked, a glimmer of amusement breaking through the solemnity of the moment. "Had I not lied, you'd have let yourself starve," he said—his voice light, though sincerity still lingered beneath it. "As I said...*not all truths are meant for the light*."

Elias stepped closer, stopping just a foot away, the fire's warmth crackling between them. His gaze softened as he tilted his head slightly, palm open for the empty bowl.

"Say you've forgiven me," he said quietly, his voice calm, though a glimmer of desperation sat behind his words. "And I'll serve you...another helping."

Brahms hesitated, the remnants of his frustration still hanging in the air. His chest tightened at the memory of their argument, the sharp words and the tension that had built up between them.

But something in Elias' eyes, something almost tender, made the anger slip away—just a little. He couldn't quite put his finger on it, but it was there, an unspoken understanding that made him tired of holding onto his grudge.

Perhaps it would be smarter to ease the tension and work together on our dangerous quest...
You're a weak man, Brahms.
He thought, for a breath, before he smirked.

"...You'll have to work for it," the knight muttered, his voice quieter now, the sharp edge of his irritation beginning to fade.

"*Ah*," Elias sighed, a soft chuckle escaping him as he nodded, the corner of his mouth lifting into a smile. "I look forward to proving myself to you, then."

Brahms felt the blush creeping up his neck—though with his darker complexion, it would be hard for anyone to notice. Even if they did, he'd blame it on the winter air.

He glanced away quickly, more from the sudden warmth in his chest than anything else. The prince had this way of making everything feel so...personal. The way his words lingered, like they were speaking to more than just the moment.

A prince, he thought. *Proving himself to me? What have I gotten myself into...* He scoffed softly, trying to mask the strange fluttering in his chest, but his eyes betrayed him as they flicked upwards.

Elias seemed to catch the flicker of his inner thoughts. His grin widened, smug and knowing, and a dangerous spark gleamed in his emerald eyes.

"Are you planning to give me the bowl, Brahms—or hoping I'll come and take it?"

Brahms lifted an eyebrow, his voice taking on a teasing edge, the familiar banter returning. "I'd like to see you try, Your Highness—"

Before he could finish, Elias moved with a quickness that left Brahms momentarily stunned. In a blink, Elias snatched the bowl from his hands—effortless, as if he'd done it a hundred times before. Brahms staggered back, eyes wide, his face heating despite the cool night air.

Elias, however, only chuckled, a rich sound that filled the space between them, his grin easy and confident as he returned to the fire.

His fingers worked quickly, refilling the bowl with the vegetables, his posture casual, as if they had been exchanging nothing more than pleasantries.

Brahms, still caught off guard, watched him with almost involuntary admiration.

For a moment, Brahms couldn't help himself. His eyes lingered on Elias as he bent down to tend to the fire, watching the way the flames reflected off his light hair, the line of his back, the fluid grace in his movements.

Elias was everything Brahms both wanted and wanted to be—tall, poised, noble in ways he couldn't quite describe. Handsome, in a way that made Brahms almost uncomfortable. He was more than a prince, more than an ideal—someone Brahms couldn't quite figure out, no matter how much he tried.

The glance turned into a stare, and before he realised it, Brahms was lost in thought, caught somewhere between admiration and a deep, unspoken longing.

It wasn't something he had allowed himself to feel in years. Certainly not for someone like Elias—yet the prince had a way of getting under his skin, making him forget the distance that kept others at bay.

It was Elias who broke the silence. His voice, rich with amusement, slid through the air like a teasing melody.

"Are you staring at the meal that hungrily?" he asked, tone light but pointed. "...Or at me?"

The question struck Brahms like a lightning bolt. His heart skipped a beat and his stomach flipped, the words barely registering as his mind scrambled to make sense of them.

Is he...flirting with me? At a time like this?

The thought spun rapidly, drowning out everything else. His head swivelled instinctively, checking that no one else heard...
But they were alone. Only the squirrels bore witness to their exchange.

He hated how easily his anger, his frustration, melted with every word Elias spoke, like some kind of magic undoing his resolve. His composure, so carefully constructed, crumbled with a glance, a teasing sentence.

Brahms' gaze darted down to his hands, searching for answers. Anything to avoid Elias' gaze, which seemed to peel back every defence, every layer. He was a knight, a man of discipline and control—yet here he was, a mess of confusion and vulnerability.

When Elias approached with the bowl, Brahms' hands were suddenly clammy. He took it without thinking, the movement mechanical, his eyes still elsewhere.

"Th—the meal, m'Lord," he stammered, his voice betraying him. It came out softer than he intended, unsure, the words barely more than a whisper as he tried desperately to maintain some semblance of control.

Elias' voice dropped, smooth and teasing, the shift in his tone sending a shiver down Brahms' spine.

"And here I was, thinking we'd sworn off lies—you and I."
His grin grew, wicked and knowing, as his emerald eyes lingered a moment too long. "Thankfully...you're quite easy to read."

Brahms swallowed hard, a lump forming in his throat as the prince's stare bore into him. But Elias turned without a word, his retreating steps light, almost lazy—like none of it mattered at all.

Brahms stood for a moment, hand clutching the bowl, knuckles white from cold and pressure, pulse pounding in his ears. He couldn't recall the last time he'd felt this...off-balance.

His mouth was parted, dry—unable to believe what had just happened. He glanced at his horse as though the animal could offer him some sort of clarity. The horse, however, seemed completely uninterested in the emotional turmoil of its rider, lazily chewing some dry grass.

Brahms sat, quickly finishing his vegetables, the warmth in his chest mirroring the comfort in his stomach. Yet his mind soon drifted back to the prince's words and that playful, knowing smile. He wasn't sure how he was meant to feel—annoyed, amused, or something else entirely.

As the the last streaks of daylight disappeared, Brahms rose from his log, still stuck in his mind.

He walked towards his gear, retrieving his sword—the rigid chill of metal cooling his hands. Stars peeked above, moonlight reflecting across the snowy landscape, casting a steady glow despite the dark night.

Brahms took a seat by the fire, the blade gleaming in his grip as he methodically sharpened it with his honing stone, the rhythmic sound of steel against stone echoing through the air.

The night settled around him—calm, still, save for the occasional hiss of the fire. It was a quiet kind of peace, one that allowed his thoughts to swirl as his blade slowly took on a finer edge. He silently wished his mind was as easily sharpened.

Evening stretched on, the night air growing colder as the sun sank farther. The crackle of fire and steady scrape of steel were Brahms' only companions beneath the vast, starry sky.

He glanced up for a moment, his eyes catching the beautiful wonders above. Brahms rarely had the opportunity to leave the Pembrook kingdom, let alone embark on a long voyage. Despite the growing unease in his stomach, he tried to enjoy the beauty before him.

A soft shuffle of footsteps pulled his attention from the stars to the prince, approaching the campsite with reins of his tan steed in hand.

"Stargazing, Brahms?" Elias asked, his voice light as he guided his horse towards the white one Brahms had borrowed.

Brahms looked away quickly, embarrassed to be caught staring at the heavens. He shrugged and mumbled, "I don't get to see them often..."

Even in the reflection of his pristine sword, the shining constellations glimmered above him.

"I wasn't mocking," Elias replied quickly, sensing Brahms' discomfort. He tied the horses together at a brance, then sat besides Brahms' on the log. "I enjoy it as well."

Brahms could feel the prince's presence, his warmth seeping into his right side. His hand movements grew shakier the closer Elias got.

Get it together.
Brahms cleared his throat, forcing himself to speak as casually as possible.

"D-do, uh...do you know much about them?" His voice faltered, betraying nerves as he tried to make conversation, as if their closeness wasn't enough to shake his composure.

"Vincent does...I only liked to stare, but he *insisted* on teaching me," he spoke dryly despite the hint of nostalgia in his tone.

He lifted a strong hand towards their left, pointing with his first and second finger. "*Fratres*...brothers. Our favourite."

Brahms tried to follow his gaze to the constellation, but his eyes couldn't quite make it out. His body was too tense, too aware of the proximity between them. His heart raced, and the air around them felt heavier, more charged.

Elias noticed his struggle and paused, glancing at Brahms out of the corner of his eye. Without a word, he shifted slightly closer, leaning towards him. His fingers moved gently through the air, guiding Brahms' attention closer to the hidden constellation.

"Look up there, towards the east—just above the tallest tree. There are two bright stars, close together...and just beneath, a few more stars, like arms stretching out to one another...Do you see them?"

Brahms squinted, trying to make sense of the pattern, but no matter how he adjusted his gaze, he couldn't see it. His frustration was clear, his breath quickening, and his heart thudded harder in his chest.

Elias watched him for a moment. Then, slowly, he moved closer, hand rising to Brahms' chin. With a gentle yet insistent touch, he tilted Brahms' head back, his cold fingers warm beneath the jaw.

Brahms tensed in seconds.

"Don't fight it, *stargazer*," Elias murmured, his smirk evident in his tone, his voice low, nearly a whisper. "Let me show you."

Brahms felt like a stone as the prince's fingers held him steady, urging him to keep his gaze fixed on the sky. The touch was soft but commanding, his breath brushing against Brahms' ear as he guided his head upwards.

"Look," Elias said again, his voice softer now, his hand still firm beneath Brahms' chin, guiding his head upwards. His other hand came around the other side of Brahms' head, pointing towards the sky. "You see it now, don't you?"

The stars came into focus—two bright points, identical in their brilliance, standing proud in the dark sky. Their light felt almost tangible, flickering in the quiet night.

But Brahms couldn't focus on them.
The warmth of Elias' fingers beneath his chin, the closeness between them—it was too much. The touch alone was more intense, more *heavenly,* than any constellation he could have ever spotted.

Brahms only muttered, "*I do,*" his voice thick.

He couldn't bring himself to swallow, nor could he take a breath without it catching on something invisible and new. Even as Elias lowered his hand, the prince's touch lingered, making Brahms' heart race.

He turned to face Elias, but the moment was already slipping away. Elias was looking at him now, his gaze unreadable, a silent curiosity flickering in his eyes.

But then the prince rose from the log with a swift movement, as if he could erase the moment.

"When we get back to the castle, I can teach you more, if you'd like..." Elias' voice was soft, gentle, though his body remained distant. He tossed leaves into the fire, staring into the flames, back turned to Brahms.

"Do you teach *all* your knights about the stars?" Brahms scoffed, his words sharper than he meant, an attempt to mask the vulnerability that threatened to break through. It was easier to push this away than to face whatever had passed between them.

"I'll say it again..." Elias' voice dropped quieter now, sincerity clear beneath the words, "You are unlike any knight I've known." He offered one last glance over his shoulder before nodding, a quiet dismissal that sent a pang through Brahms' chest.

Elias turned towards his tent, stepping inside without another word.

Brahms' gaze lingered on the empty space where Elias had stood, the air thick with the unspoken. He stayed still for a long moment, sharpening his sword as the night pressed down on him.

Eventually, Brahms stood, his heart still pounding in his chest, and made his way to his own tent. He undressed quickly, but even as he lay on his bedroll, the image of Elias' eyes, the softness of his touch, replayed in his mind.

He closed his eyes, trying to block it out, but the sensation lingered—
How close Elias had been, how everything had shifted in that fleeting moment...

As he drifted off to sleep, his thoughts were consumed by Elias, the taste of his breath, the warmth of his touch.

The air between them had been thick with something neither of them had named yet—but Brahms could feel it, deep in his chest, stirring something he wasn't ready, nor ever expecting, to face.

THREAD XLV

ᚦᛖ ᛒᚢᚱᛞᛖᚾᛋ ᛟᚠ ᚺᛖᛁᚱᛋ ᚦᛖ ᛒᚢᚱᛞᛖᚾᛋ ᛟᚠ ᚺᛖᛁᚱᛋ ᚦᛖ ᛒᚢᚱᛞᛖᚾᛋ

ᚨᛞᚨᛚᛃᚨ

ADALJA GROANED.

Her eyes fluttered open slowly, vision blurred by sleep.
A pounding headache throbbed between her temples, her throat was raw—parched, either from screams or the cruel absence of water.

Cold seeped into her bones, but different than the cold of the snow she had been kneeling in.

As her eyes adjusted, she drew quick, shallow breaths, the memory of her last moments flooding back—strong arms, a giant hand, and a deep Norse voice.

With a sharp gasp and a groan, she pushed herself upright from the cold, rocky floor. A torch flickered on the wall, casting weak, wavering light—barely enough to reveal the room around her.

Rough stone walls closed in on all sides. The floor beneath her was hard and uneven. Across from where she sat stood a single wooden door, heavy and iron-banded. The space was small, clearly not built to hold people—at least not often. Crates and barrels were shoved carelessly to the far edges, as if someone had cleared the room in haste just to make space for her.

From the rafters above, bundles of dried herbs and branches hung suspended on rope, swaying faintly in the draft. A few stretched animal pelts were pinned to the beams, and from rusted chains dangled gutted fish, drying and stinking up the air with a sharp, sour rot. In one shadowed corner, a tangled mass of rope and netting coiled like a massive spider's web, forgotten and thick with dust.

She shuddered. She was no longer in Worthyn.

Brushing tangled curls from her face, her lungs burning in the chill, panic clawed at her chest as she scanned her bleak surroundings.

"Oi! You...yer finally awake!"

Adalja jumped at the booming voice. Her head snapped towards the door, eyes narrowing at the figure she could barely see through the small, barred window. A man's voice carried through.

"Did ye have a sweet rest, princess? At this rate, I thought ye'd sleep through the whole damn war," he chuckled, clearly pleased with himself and his joke.

With a loud creaking metal sound and a jolt, the wooden door was pushed open and she was met with a mountainous man, standing taller than the door itself.

Her gaze *immediately* flickered to the massive weapon he held—an enormous, double-edged axe, smaller than him but *towering* over her. A shiver ran through her as she noted the sharp glint of its edges.

Instinctively, she rubbed her neck, dread pooling in her stomach of what it could be used for. Despite her fear, she glared at him, more confused than scared.

The warrior bent his head to fit beneath the door, stepping in with booming footfalls. Adalja pushed herself back, eyes wide, whimpers spilling from her like a frightened animal.

"If ye fancied escape, forget it..." his mock-serious expression exaggerated by his furrowed brows. "I'm no fool to let ye slip away."

The words hung in silence as he stood tall, glaring down at her, planting his axe down to the ground beside him...and then—

He let out a belly laugh, the sound rumbling deep from his chest.

Adalja watched with wide-eyes, panting the same as before.
This warrior laughs before he kills, she thought, whimpering. She stayed silent, unwilling to engage, to anger, despite his apparent friendliness.

The man loomed over her, a beast of a figure. His body was covered in dark, rune-like tattoos, including one over his right eye. Though his head was a beautiful array of curly ginger hair, falling around him like a lions' mane. At the end of his face was a large beard, neatly tapered into a small braid.

"I should tell you..." he mused, tilting his head as he looked her over, "Ye snore like a stuffed pig but look like a queen...but I suppose ye are one now, aye?"

His dark brown eyes narrowed as if assessing whether she was truly queen-worthy. The Norseman's gaze seemed distant, in a far off land of the past. For a moment, something flickered—nostalgia, regret, or maybe scepticism—but it was gone as quickly as it came.

"I—I am," Adalja rasped, her voice hoarse from dehydration. The words rang hollow, a painful reminder of her situation. "S-so I would advise you to let me go...k-kind sir," she cleared her throat, struggling to keep her tone steady.

The man inhaled sharply, then burst into laughter, as though she'd told the funniest joke he'd ever heard. His booming guffaws only deepened her sense of frustration and helplessness.

"By the gods, yer a funny little thing!" he said with a broad grin.

Adalja's head throbbed as a low, rhythmic drumming echoed in the distance. The muffled roar of a Norse town stirred to life outside the building. Her eyes darted back to the man, wondering if the call of the drums would herd him as well.

"Ah! Hear that, princess?" he asked excitedly, dropping onto a wooden stool near the door in her cell. The poor wood creaked under his massive weight as he set his axe against the doorframe casually—*knowing* she would not dare go for it.

"The village wakes...and soon they'll be whisperin' yer name," he snorted with laughter. "Aye, don't fret, pet, they're not expecting ya—you're a bit...tied up right now." And then he winked, as if the joke wasn't at her expense, as if she had any ounce of interest in humor at a time like this.

And yet, despite the anger bristling in her frame, the glare she carried, he continued sweetly.

"I am Björn, son of Björn, tiny one...and you, Princess, I know by name and by face." The man spoke, leaning towards her, tilting his head slightly.

His accent was strong, that of a Norseman, but something was lilted in it. It was not like Olivja's or Dagrun's...perhaps a Northman? Chills ran along her skin as she realised where she was.

Perdyr.

Her thoughts spiraled, fear gripping her chest. Would they kill her? Would she meet the same fate as her parents? Her breath hitched, uneven and shallow, as she watched the man closely.

"Do I not speak yer common tongue well enough? Or have the mice taken yer tongue?" Björn chuckled, smiling at his own jests, and her brows furrowed, a pout forming on her lips as she stayed silent.

"Hah! Yer a bold thing to look at me so," he mused. "You glare like a wolf pup, why so?" He asked, curiously eyeing her.

Even if Adalja were to stand on the bench she was certain he'd be at eye level, and it intimidated her. The muscles in her face unfurled instantly, a nervousness settling within that she may have upset him by accident.

"You stole me from my lands," she blurted out.

She wanted to know if she were to be killed soon or if a fate worse than that awaited, but she was too afraid to speak the question.

The princess trembled with the thought that she may never see Olivja, Elias, or Brahms again. Her heart ached wondering what torture Brahms was putting himself through with her absence knowing he would take this personally.

"*Aye,* I carried ye from yer lands...Took you as easy as plucking a lamb from the field," Björn said with a snort.

"This is no laughing matter," Adalja cut in sharply, her voice cracking despite her effort to sound calm. "Tell me, is this vengeance for your witches? Or are you here to see my bloodline ended for good?"

She surprised even herself with the force of her words. It was the bravest she had sounded since her capture—bravery born not from courage, but from sheer exhaustion.

Björn's grin faded. A chill ran through her.
His eyes darkened as they swept over her face, heavy with thought.

The silence that followed grew thicker than the air in the cell.

When at last his lips curved into a small, knowing smile, it wasn't cruel—it was almost wistful, like he'd glimpsed a ghost.

He drew a deep breath, his voice low and even.
"We are not the ones for you to fear, Princess...*I bring you no harm.*"

"You took me from my kingdom," Adalja shot back, her fiery gaze locking onto him. The words burst out sharper than intended, her fear now frayed into anger.

How dare he speak such lies with such a calm tongue?
These were thc people who had stolen everything—her home, her family, her future.

Björn shook his head, his expression taking a more serious note that silenced Adalja.

"*Worthyn* Kingdom is *not* yer kingdom, Princess..." He trailed off with a scoff of disbelief and something else she couldn't figure out.

The man glanced around the empty building before looking back down at her. "It was not to harm ye—we pulled ye from the jaws of death." He spoke as if the words would be easy for her to swallow.

"I do not trust your word...You take me unwillingly, lock me in a cell, kill my parents—"

"Aye, and *that* is where you err," he corrected quickly with a sharp tongue that made her flinch. "Do not lay their deaths at the feet of my people."

"You lie. I will not hear this from *you,*" Adalja growled, trying to contain her anger. "You stole me to stop my marriage—to win this war—'twas not for me!"

"These marriages are only to fuel a war ignited by lies spun from a troll in king's clothing," he hissed with a disgusted tone.

He scoffed angrily at her. "Björn cares not if ye hear him. He did what he must to see you safe—he has no remorse."

Her fingers curled inward, nails digging into her palms almost tight enough to bring forth the blood that burned inside her.

"Then what do you say happened to them, Sir Björn?" Adalja called to him, her voice angry, untrusting.

Björn looked off into the distance, a deep and silent yawn escaping him. "If we were not the ones to kill them, tiny woman...Who else is there?" he asked quietly, leaving her to sit in the silence of his question. "Who gains from Natja's death?"

The thoughts that pierced her mind sent a shiver down her spine. The world began to crash around Adalja.

Her thoughts turned to Elias in an instant, the pieces slowly connecting in her tired and weary mind.

"I do not wish to believe the things you are telling me, Sir Björn," she admitted in a hushed tone. "You turn the blame upon my allies...?"

"I do," Björn scoffed. "I am your ally now, tiny one." He wore a growing grin, playful in nature, yet his words were frightening.

"*Ally*?" Adalja asked with a fragile tone. She was nervous—more than nervous—asking a question like that to a man who owed her nothing.

"I thought so..." Björn nodded. "Strange way to treat a friend, eh?" His voice turned stiff, hard. Björn sat silently for a moment, adjusting his seat on the wooden stool. The creak of the old wood filled the quiet as he gazed up at the ceiling. Finally, he braved himself to meet her eyes.

"I may've erred—but I'd stake my blade it was you that night, wearin' the look of a *pagan*, slipping through the dark of Fairtide..." His grin grew wider, like he had *caught* her in the act of some lie.

Her eyes went wide, her heart sunk.

"M-me?" Adalja stuttered, breaths uneven. "I know n-not what you speak of, sir Björn—" She swallowed tightly, playing the fool.

"Aye, I remember—you were there with yer suitor. Ye tossed an axe into a beam for a piece of silver, splashed a whore with mead, left the tavern in shambles," Björn chuckled, leaning back against the stone wall. "But ye were sloshed like a longship—I don't blame ye forgot the whole damn thing."

The princess froze, the memory coming back, though incredibly fogged. She barely remembered that night...she had wished it stayed that way.

She cleared her throat, "Must have been...a *different* princess—"

"*BAHAHA!!*" Björn held his stomach as he laughed, wiping a tear from his eye. "Nay, do not call me a fool, *Pagan Princess,* the gods know the truth," he spoke through his laughs, taking a settling breath at the end.

Adalja bit her cheek, embarrassed by it all. For a moment, she wished he had killed her instead of making a fool of her. She glanced down at her tattered dress and sighed.

"Aye, *Adalja,*" he called to her, voice calm as still water and she looked up at him.

"That strength, that *wonder,* in you—you've the heart of the North," he said with a serious tone. "That alone makes you worth saving. 'Tis just one more reason I took you from the faith-borns."

His dark eyes stared deeply into hers and, for the first time, she felt *seen*. Seen in a way she could have never imagined. Seen as one of *them*.

She blinked, her eyes glossing over and she quickly looked away, her breath stuck somewhere between gratitude and confusion.

Adalja didn't know how to respond. He told her something she had longed to hear her entire life. And why did it hurt that it was from someone who was supposed to be her *enemy.*

But the moment was shattered as the sound of a horn echoed through the area.

Björn turned towards the door at the sound before looking back at the dirtied princess. "It is the eating hour. Björn will return with bread," he announced, his tone leaving no room for argument. "Or mayhap, a sweet little cake for the pagan princess."

"Sir Björn! Wait—" Adalja begged as he stood. She scrambled to her feet, brushing off her dirtied gown.

He grunted, snatching up his executioner's axe and lifting it as if it weighed nothing. Then he paused, turning his head towards her. "Call me Björn-Björn, all of my friends do, tiny one."

Adalja shook her head quickly, ignoring his request. "Please, I don't wish to stay here, sir," she softly begged, afraid to take a step closer now that he had the axe in his hand.

"Where else would you go, dove?" Björn shook his head with a chuckle.

"Sit tight—I'll be back soon to stir your spirit some more. But until then, best make yourself look dead. The *rats* like to pick at pretty things like you." The jest rolled off his tongue, but it made Adalja's stomach twist.

She glanced around herself with a weak whimper, hugging her dress tightly to herself, paranoid with a new fear, far worse than death—*pests.*

Her gaze flickered to the dark corners of the room, searching for movement, and when she looked back up, Björn was already gone.

The door shut with a cold finality, leaving her in the dim, quiet cell to wonder what fate would come next.

THREAD XLVI

ᚦᛖ ᛒᚢᚱᛞᛖᚾᛊ ᛟᚠ ᚺᛖᛁᚱᛊ ᚦᛖ ᛒᚢᚱᛞᛖᚾᛊ ᛟᚠ ᚺᛖᛁᚱᛊ ᚦᛖ ᛒᚢᚱᛞᛖᚾᛊ

ᛖᛚᛇᚨᛊ

The sounds of the morning birds pulled Elias from his dreams. The soft trill of the distant songbirds stirred him awake, their melodies reaching him through the thin beige walls of the tent.

The morning air was sharp, seeping through every gap in the canvas and chilling the tip of his nose. But it wasn't only the cold that lingered—*it was the thought of last night.*

The feeling of Brahms beneath his touch, the quiet intensity between them, and his breath catching in the stillness. Elias traced those memories in the quiet of the morning, a small smile tugging at his lips.

His thoughts had been lingering on the knight more than he ever expected. It was a feeling he hadn't expected, but somehow it felt like it belonged—or had been there all along—nestled beneath the surface of his thoughts.

A strange, pleasant warmth remained in his chest as he sat up, though it was quickly tempered by the biting air.

Rubbing a hand over his face, he stood, his limbs heavy from sleep, and reached for his linen tunic, draped at the foot of his bedroll.

The world outside was painted in white, a blanket of snow covering the trees in a soft, muffled stillness. The air was icy, sharp with the tang of pine and cold earth, each breath forming a plume of mist that hung momentarily before dissolving.

His boots crunched in the snow as he stepped forward, surveying the campsite. His eyes flicked to Brahms' tent—unmoving. The knight was heavy in sleep after such a long ride.

Elias' grin tugged at the thought of Brahms tucked under his blankets, his usual tough exterior softened in sleep.

There was something charming about how even the hardest men betrayed their gentler side when at rest.

He turned towards the nearby river. They needed fresh water for their flasks and to wash the bowls from supper the night before. It would be unbearable to soak his hands in the stream, but the chore couldn't wait.

As he approached, the chill in the air deepened. The river was full of icy rocks, the surface dusted with snow and edged in jagged ice that broke off in chunks in the rushing current.

Elias knelt by the bank, breath forming visible puffs as he bent down at the edge. The cold stung his fingers immediately, making him wince. His breath hissed between his teeth as he worked quickly, filling their flasks and scrubbing the bowls as best as the freezing conditions allowed.

Despite the pain of the moment, he couldn't push away the thoughts of Brahms. How strange this pull was—this magnetic tension that only grew stronger now that they were alone.

It felt impossible to hold back the flirtations—the gentle praises slipping from his lips as effortlessly as smoke curling into the air, too fleeting to be taken back.

It was dangerous, yet he didn't want to stop. The desire to pursue him had been simmering ever since their first, innocent conversation outside Adalja's room...

Adalja.

Thinking of his betrothed made his heart ache, and suddenly all of his playful thoughts of her knight were blanketed in worry. He wondered for her safety, and longed for things to be right between them—whatever that meant for him, for Olivja.

He pushed those thoughts aside, focussing desperately on the cool rush of the water. Splashing it over himself, he took in a sharp breath, needing the chill to clear his mind.

For a brief moment, he felt free from everything—even his growing feelings for the clumsy knight.

But as he leaned forward to rinse the last bowl, water dripping from his hair and jawline, the crunch of snow nearby made him freeze.

He wasn't alone...
Elias turned, his heart pounding.

Two massive figures stood between him and the camp, their shapes dark against the morning light. Their eyes were cold, focussed on him with an intensity that sent a shiver down his spine.

They were Norse-born, unmistakable by their broad shoulders, wild hair, and bright green and gold tunics that gleamed faintly in the early sunlight.

The weight of their gaze told him they hadn't come to greet him with pleasantries...

Elias' hand instinctively slid to his waist, searching for the hilt of his sword—but it wasn't there. His stomach sank as the realisation hit—he'd left it back in his tent. Foolish.

His body tensed, every muscle on edge.
This wasn't the peaceful solitude he'd hoped for.

"Prince Elias of Worthyn..." A chuckle sliced through the tension like a blade.

The Norse woman stepped forward, her dark skin gleaming beneath an iron circlet. Long, blonde braids swung as she moved, the broad axe in her hands shone with a deadly promise.

"You stray at the edge of your lands...*alone*? Do you long to meet your god so soon?" Her voice was deliberate, each word like a dagger.

This wasn't random; she'd been waiting for this. He could feel it.

Elias fought to steady his icy breathing, meeting her icy gaze. He could almost hear his father's voice drilling into him during training, but the weight of her presence pressed down like a mountain.

Behind her, the other figure stepped into view. The second warrior slung the shaft of a massive spear across his shoulders, gripping each end loosely like he was stretching after a long day's work. His brown hair fell in wild, rope-like strands, almost matching the dark tattoos curling over his skin.

He looked Elias over and let out a groan.

"*Hel's breath,*" the man exasperatedly sighed. "Quit toying with your food, Kara." He glanced around lazily, as though expecting reinforcements.

Elias' eyes darted back towards Brahms' tent—*still unmoving.* What once felt endearing—his sleepiness—had become the bane of Elias' existence.

"Killing me won't end the war, Iron-born!" Elias raised his voice, praying it was loud enough to wake Brahms. "Perhaps we can come to an agreement! There's no need for bloodshed!"

Kara's lips curled into a sneer as she stepped closer, her shadow falling over him like a storm cloud. The leather wrappings of her axe creaked as she tightened her grip, and a cold bead of sweat traced its way down the back of Elias' neck.

"Kill you?" she scoffed, turning briefly to her companion before fixing him with a glare as hard as iron. "Worthyns earn no mercy—"

She lunged without warning.

Elias reacted instinctively, sidestepping her broad stroke with a speed born of years of training. His boots stomped into the snow, the icy crust breaking beneath his weight as he propelled himself forward with everything he had. The campsite wasn't far. If he could just reach Brahms—

The breath was ripped from his lungs as the broadside of Kara's axe crashed into his back, sending him sprawling into the snow. He struck hard, the frozen ground beneath the powder unforgiving.

The world spun, his ears ringing as cold snow pressed against his face, its sharp chill mingling with the fiery pain in his ribs.

Gasping for air, he clawed at the ground, the frost burning his fingertips. Before he could react, the haft of her axe came from behind, sliding cold and sharp across his neck. She yanked him upright, like a wolf caught in a snare.

"Admirable, little wolf," Kara growled, her accented voice as cold and cutting as the wind. "But it's me who bears the true beast's heart." She drew her weapon tighter against her chest, the motion wrenching his throat harder, choking him with ruthless precision.

Elias' vision blurred, the brilliant white of the snow and the sharp blue of the sky fading into grey at the edges. His hands clawed uselessly at the haft pressing against his windpipe, every desperate inhale scraping against his throat.

The other warrior approached, his boots crunching heavily through the snow. A lazy grin spread across his face, his breath curling in thick clouds around him. The spear rested casually across his shoulders as he paused just a step away, head tilted, studying Elias like some strange curiosity.

"*This*? This is the great heir that pitiful old fool calls his pride?" he mused with a laugh, the sound echoing in the still, frozen air.

He let the spear fall to the snow, which groaned beneath its weight, then stepped forward—slow, deliberate. With one massive finger, he brushed a strand of Elias' hair from his face, his grin spreading wider.

"Let him boast while he still draws breath. He won't when we're through."

Elias twisted weakly, the frost-laden air tearing at his throat as he tried to draw a breath. His strength was no match for Kara's iron grip.

The Norseman's fist slammed into his abdomen without warning, the impact tearing through him like a thunderclap. Snow flew from the force of the blow as Elias doubled over, a strangled grunt escaping his lips. His knees buckled, but Kara yanked him upright again, the haft of her axe tightening mercilessly against his neck.

"Brahms!" Elias gasped, his voice hoarse and desperate as he called for his knight. His gaze darted towards the distant tent, its canvas rimmed with frost, but still frustratingly silent.

How are you still asleep!?

A chuckle vibrated against the shell of his ear.

"See how quick he howls for his pack?" Kara hissed in his ear, her breath steaming in the frigid air. The wooden haft pressed harder against his throat, cutting off his voice before he could cry out again. She laughed low, a mocking sound that scraped against his pride. "The pup fears the claws..."

Her comrade stepped closer, the glint of steel catching Elias' eye as the barbarian drew a dagger from the hide-wrapped hilt at his belt. The blade shimmered like ice, reflecting the pale winter sun struggling to break through the clouded sky.

The man examined it for a moment, his grin broadening with grim satisfaction.

"A cut for every life?" the Norseman mused, his voice dripping with malice. "Worse punishments there be, young prince—our dead Völur know it well."

The mention of the Perdyr witches sent an icy dread curling in Elias' chest. This was no battle of war—this was vengeance, plain and burning.

He strained harder against the hold, panic beginning to creep at the edges of his composure. He wanted to shout that they had the wrong brother, to beg forgiveness for the reckless actions of the other Worthyn prince. But the haft held him silent.

The dagger moved, catching the faint glare of the sunlight as the warrior brought it down with precision.

Shink.

Elias flinched, teeth clenched as the blade carved down his sternum, slicing through his shirt like paper—straight into his skin. The pain flared hot, radiating outward, but he swallowed the groan, forcing himself to stand rigid. He could handle a cut or two...it wouldn't be long before Brahms found him...*It couldn't be.*

The Norseman tilted his head, watching him like a curious animal. "Silent? That's not like your kind...Let's see if we can change that..."

He slashed again, this time across Elias' ribs, blood blooming against his shirt. The sharp sting stole the breath from his lungs, and his fists clenched against the pain.

Kara tightened her grip around Elias' neck, forcing him to remain upright and still, a cruel smile tugging at her lips as she leaned in close, her voice a low whisper in his ear. "What's the matter, little wolf? Too prideful to whine?" She kept her hold firm, her eyes gleaming as she savored his struggle.

Her attention never wavered from Elias, even as the Norseman took a step back, processing where he would lay his blade down for the third time.

The sound of steel slicing through the icy wind rang loud and clear, cutting through the stillness like a blade through frost.

Only it wasn't the Norseman's blade that sang.

With a raw battle-cry—more a wail than a roar—both warriors turned with bored expressions, watching as Brahms came charging from the camp, sword raised high, cloak curling behind him. There was no gleaming armour or polished helmet to mark his charge—only a linen sleep shirt, loose pants, and bare feet sinking into the snow. His hair was tousled, the cold wind threading through it, and his eyes were still heavy with sleep.

The warrior had plenty of time to bend down and snatch up his spear. The battle cry was a poor choice.

Heavens above. I'm finished.

Elias fought to keep his eyes open.

The barbarian turned swiftly, parrying Brahms' first blow with the shaft of his spear. The Norseman drove a boot straight into Brahms' gut, knocking the breath from him with a sharp grunt as he was hurled backward, rolling through the snow.

Before he could rise, the spear came sweeping low towards his ribs. Brahms twisted just in time, the tip slicing through the space where his torso had been a heartbeat before. But the Norseman didn't let up. A second swing came sharper, faster—Brahms rolled beneath it, scrambling for footing as the snow slipped under his bare heels.

He regained his stance, and at once the two began to circle—one massive and merciless, the other smaller, honed, his blade poised. The cold wind howled past them in a hush of anticipation.

Elias' breath caught. God, Brahms was fast. Not just quick-footed—but precise, sharp as frost, moving with skilled grace. Even bruised and breathless, there was a fire behind his eyes that made Elias' stomach tighten. A blush crept across his face, shamefully warm against the cold.

Then, the Norseman lunged. The spear shot forward, quick and vicious, nearly driving into Brahms' gut again. He dodged, barely, the edge slicing a thread from his cloak as he ducked the follow-up blow. Steel rang against steel.

The spear came again, thrust hard towards his chest—Brahms blocked it with a twist of his sword, but the sheer force knocked him back, feet sliding across the powder-white ground. Brahms adjusted his stance, chest heaving, eyes fixed, locked like a predator.

Elias swallowed hard. That look—fierce, determined—he'd never seen Brahms like this before. And now he couldn't look away.

The Norseman grinned and charged again—but this time, Brahms stepped into the blow, spinning in close, too close for the spear's reach. His blade flashed upwards.

The warrior barely had time to react before the steel met flesh—Brahms' sword slashed clean across his abdomen with a thick, ripping sound, a brutal arc that sprayed crimson across the snow.

The man staggered back, gasping, his boots slipping in the powdery ground. Brahms gave him no quarter.

The Norseman's dagger came up in a desperate attempt to parry, but it was no match for Brahms' skilled and furious onslaught

"*Brothir*!!" Kara's voice rang out in the bitter air, sharp and filled with an uncharacteristic fear. She struggled against the moment, a force of nature suddenly faltering as she watched her comrade's impending fall.

But Brahms was unrelenting.

With a final, savage blow, his sword cleaved across the Norseman's neck. The kill echoed across the frozen landscape, a sharp contrast to the eerie quiet. The sickening squelch of steel through flesh was matched only by the shocked gasp that escaped the man's lips. His wide eyes locked onto Brahms for one fleeting, frozen moment before he collapsed into the snow.

Blood pooled rapidly around the fallen man, staining the once-pristine white in a stark, dark red. Steam rose from the warmth of it, swirling faintly in the freezing air as silence descended once more.

Elias exhaled sharply, a tight knot in his chest loosening. He had been right. Brahms had saved him...even if for a moment he doubted it.
But there was no time to relish in it. Kara's iron grip on him remained unyielding.

She looked down at the body of her fallen comrade, her chest rising and falling with every breath, her eyes wide with disbelief. A low, guttural growl escaped her lips as she stared down at him.

"Again...Worthyn sheds my people's blood without cause or care..." Kara growled, her voice low and dangerous. She tightened her hold, her haft still pressed to Elias' neck, the wood digging into his skin. Elias choked, his heart pounding with a mix of relief and fear.

Brahms raised his bloodied sword, his eyes locked on Kara with a cold, unwavering determination.

"Release him," Brahms ordered, his voice a dark promise. "Fail to yield, and I'll see a life repaid for every mark upon my Prince."

Kara smirked at the challenge, but as she met Brahms' eyes, something in her faltered. The grip of her axe loosened for a moment, her breath freezing in her chest as she seemed to hesitate.

"*Lokhjart...*" she mumbled in Norse, her voice loud enough for them both to hear. Her gaze flicked to her dead comrade at their feet, then back to Brahms. Her body language shifted, the hardness in her stance softening.

After a few deep, steadying breaths, she spoke again, louder, with a trace of respect in her words. "You fight well...like one of us."

"Clearly, I've the better blood," Brahms scoffed, his sword held high, eyes never leaving hers. "Unhand My Lord, or meet the same fate."

The silence between them was thick, charged with tension, as the two warriors faced off. Brahms stood firm, his posture ready for whatever Kara might throw at him next.

The blood on his cheek and the scrapes on his bare feet only added to the fierceness of his presence, his gaze unyielding. Elias watched him through low-lidded eyes as his head was held back, unaware of the deep blush on his cheeks.

Kara's eyes narrowed, lips curling into a tight snarl. "You fight...for dis *weakling...*?"

"You've heard me once. There'll not be another warning," Brahms said, his voice low, but filled with a deadly promise.

He rolled his neck to each side, as though preparing for the fight of his life—ready to do whatever it took to protect Elias.

The prince smirked.

Kara growled in frustration, her grip tightening around Elias' neck one last time before she released him with a vicious shove, knocking him to his hands and knees in the snow.

The force of her push left Elias breathless, but he didn't have time to recover. Kara stepped back, her voice heavy with anger and something like resignation.

"I've done what you ask. Now let me take him," she demanded, her voice steady despite the cold edge of grief, as her axe was dropped to the snow. "Dead or living, he's mine to burn."

Elias glanced back at her, then towards Brahms, his expression betraying a flicker of curiosity about what decision would follow. Worthyn knights had been ordered strictly against allowing the barbarians to recover their dead—something Elias didn't fully agree with but wasn't bold enough to challenge.

Brahms' jaw tightened, his sword still raised defensively. His breathing quickened as he mulled over her request.

After a moment, he relented, though his voice carried a nervous tension he couldn't disguise.

"...Very well," the knight said, his tone sharp with unease. He shot Elias a quick, pointed look. "Make it quick."

Kara stepped forward without hesitation, her focus fixed solely on her fallen comrade. She ignored Elias entirely, moving with purpose. When she reached the body, she crouched beside it, her movements steady and deliberate.

With a grunt of effort, she hoisted the lifeless form onto her back, the display of strength a grim reminder of the fight she had spared them from.

She paused only briefly to retrieve her axe from the snow, its handle glinting faintly in the pale light. Without a word or glance back, she began her retreat, trudging slowly through the thick drifts, her burden a silent testament to her resolve.

The swirling flurries muffled the sound of her steps, erasing her presence bit by bit until she disappeared entirely into the forest, swallowed by the snow and the silence it carried.

Brahms stood like a sentinel, his sword still raised, the tension in his frame easing only when she was completely out of sight. Slowly, he lowered his weapon, though his knuckles stayed pale around the hilt.

His eyes dropped to Elias, his expression softening for a breath—but only just.

Elias, still reeling from the fight, slowly pushed himself upright. His fingers dug into the snow beneath him, the cold biting into his palms. His breaths came shallow and quick, the adrenaline in his veins still racing—but when his eyes met Brahms', a strange calm washed over him, silencing the fear.

"You're late," Elias said, his voice strained but laced with gratitude.

Brahms' lips twitched, a faint smile ghosting over his face. "Perhaps next time you will let a servant do the work born to them," he said, his tone steady, though his teasing edge was unmistakable. "These tasks are *clearly* too heavy for a prince."

Elias let out a shaky laugh, more from relief than anything else. The weight of the situation was starting to lift, but his pulse was still racing.

He could feel his heart slowly returning to its normal rhythm as Brahms stepped closer, sheathing his sword. There was something calming about having him near—something grounding in the midst of the chaos.

"I'll...keep that in mind," Elias weakly replied, the words feeling almost too small for everything that had happened, too trivial for the way Brahms had pulled him from the edge of torture.

He knelt beside Elias and his sharp, brown eyes scanned over him, taking in the torn shirt clinging to his body, the blood streaking his skin, and the dampness in his white hair from where the snow had melted.

"Mark me, you're a sorry sight..." Brahms sighed, the barest flicker of concern in his voice. Then, with a low mutter about stubborn princes, he shrugged off his own cloak and draped it over Elias' shoulders.

The warmth of the thick fabric, still carrying Brahms' body heat and his charming scent—cedar and leather—enveloped him like a shield against the biting cold.

"...thank you, Brahms." The prince's teeth chattered, his freezing fingers tightly holding the cloak shut at his chest.

Elias glanced up, catching sight of the knight's broad shoulders and furred, strong arms now exposed to the winter air. The sight did little to steady his racing heart, and for a moment, the tension of the battle faded into something softer.

But, it was the way Brahms looked at him—almost too long—that made his heart beat a little faster.

"Don't thank me for this," Brahms grunted, his tone gruff but soft enough to convey something Elias couldn't quite put into words.

He slid his arm under Elias', lifting him with ease, as though he didn't weigh a thing. Elias marvelled at the strength in the knight's arms—how easily Brahms held him and his body.

Despite the cold temperature, he was burning hot, Brahms' touch sending waves of warmth across his frame. It was a small moment of tenderness—a knight lifting his prince—but to Elias, it meant everything.

How does he do that? he wondered. *How does he make everything feel so...natural?*

The blush on Elias' cheeks betrayed him, a warmth that had nothing to do with the injuries or the freezing remnants of snow.

As Brahms carried him back to their campsite, his thoughts flickered briefly to the way Brahms had stepped in—without hesitation, without question—throwing himself into the fight, not for honour, not for glory, but for Elias.

He could have been more patient. He could have waited for an opening, but no, Brahms had come for him. *Immediately—once he woke.*

Brahms carefully laid Elias onto his bedroll inside the tent, the cold air biting at their exposed skin.

As the prince's body sank into the soft blankets, the comfort was short-lived.

The pain from his injuries came crashing down on him—sharp, fiery pulses that coursed through his chest.

The punch to his abdomen left a constant pressure, and the cuts on his chest throbbed with a biting sting. Everything the adrenaline had dulled was now demanding attention, and Elias couldn't suppress the gasp of pain that escaped him.

But even as the agony crested, Brahms' presence softened it, even if it did little for the tightness in his chest.

Brahms didn't hesitate. He knelt beside Elias, his fingers moving with practised precision to brush Elias' wet hair away from his face. The touch, though gentle, was firm.

Like everything about Brahms—there was care, but also undeniable strength.

Elias shuddered slightly, unsure if it was from the cold or the sudden wave of self-consciousness that washed over him.

"Well, I hope your chores were worth it," Brahms muttered, his voice low and focussed as he glanced over Elias' injuries.

His gaze shifted down to Elias' torn shirt, his eyes narrowing slightly. "I need that off," Brahms said quietly, his tone leaving little room for argument.

"E-eager to undress me?" Elias scoffed, trying to be overly forward as though to retain some sort of control over the situation.

Brahms responded only with a glare, his worry and eagerness to fix his wounds overshadowing the intimacy.

Elias' breath caught, a nervous flutter in his chest. He hadn't expected the knight to be so...direct, especially not when it came to his shirt.

The winter chill outside no longer bit—or maybe it was the heat that surged to his cheeks.

This is ridiculous, he thought, his thoughts scrambling as he awkwardly shifted, half-laying down and half-sitting up.
It's just Brahms...it's just a shirt.

But as Brahms moved to help him, his hands steady and careful, Elias felt exposed in more ways than one. He was used to being in pain, but being seen like this—vulnerable, his chest and abdomen exposed to Brahms' critical eye—felt different.

His stomach twisted, both from the lingering sting of his wounds and the strange, sudden awareness of the knight's proximity.

Brahms' fingers worked with efficiency, tugging at the torn fabric of Elias' tunic until it was fully removed over his head, exposing the prince's chest to the cool air.

The cold hit Elias' skin like a shock, and he couldn't stop himself from flinching, every bruise and cut suddenly feeling more raw than it had before as his abs clenched. The self-consciousness deepened for some reason, wishing the warmth of the blanket were enough to hide him from Brahms' gaze, but it was futile. The knight was here to tend to him, after all.

Brahms took a long look at his chest—or perhaps his wounds—and a small blush came to his cheeks. Regardless of whatever was swirling in his mind, his hands moved expertly as he took a cloth and began dabbing at the cuts along Elias' chest.

The action was methodical, though there was an undeniable softness in the way his fingers grazed against Elias' skin. Each touch sent a jolt through the injured prince, one that had nothing to do with the pain of the wounds.

These cuts were nothing compared to the wounds he had sported before and yet, he let him tend to him, the knight who had fought for him and now cared for him without a second thought.

It felt like a privilege to be the one Brahms would go to such lengths for, and Elias' heart swelled with a strange mixture of gratitude and complete admiration.

Not for a second did Elias' green gaze leave Brahms' handsomeness...
He liked this look on Brahms—the focussed, worried, careful expression that tensed his entire face. His eyes dropped to his lips—

"I know you're trying to prove yourself to me, My Grace." Brahms' sudden voice pulled his eyes away.

He glanced up at Elias through thick lashes, with the faintest hint of a smile. "But to give your life for me would wound me all the more." His voice was rough but laced with amusement.

Elias met his gaze, his own smile tugging at his lips despite the exhaustion and flustered feelings settling over him.

"Well...forgive me, *sir*," the prince cooed, unable to tear his eyes away for even a second.

Brahms' lips twitched as he inspected the wound on Elias' side with a critical eye, his expression focussed as he leaned in again to carefully wipe blood from the surrounding areas on his chest and cheek.

This time, he didn't shy away from any touches or closeness; instead, he welcomed it, feeling the unspoken bond between them grow stronger with each brush of Brahms' hand.

"...Best we move, this place offers no cover," Brahms suddenly grumbled, his worried thoughts weighing heavily on his facial expressions, though there was an underlying softness in his voice as he finished tending to the wounds.

The thought of their danger pulled his head from the clouds in the worst way. Elias let out a tired sigh, knowing Brahms was right.

"Might be worth looking at the map—perhaps we've strayed too far into *Viking* territory," he suggested, his voice barely audible.

Just then, his knight applied a cleansing tonic to Elias' open cut, the sharp sting burning like salt in the wound.

Elias gasped, cursing under his breath. "*Heavens, Brahms!*...Easy..." His body tensed as the burn of the remedy cut through him.

Brahms looked up at him, eyes gleaming with a mix of amusement and concern.

Elias bit his lip, trying to hide the discomfort, though the flush of his skin betrayed him. His gaze dropped, his eyes following Brahms' every move, especially as he pressed a cloth to his cut. The knight's breath brushed against his skin, warm against the chill of the air, and Elias' pulse quickened.

The closeness was overwhelming.
The heat between them left Elias unfocused, Brahms' arms circling him to wrap the bandage around his chest. Their faces hovered a breath apart, and the prince was afraid to breathe at all.

Each touch, each movement was an intricate balance between a fierce knight and a princess' right hand. There was no hesitation in his actions, no discomfort in the way he handled Elias' body, but the man could sense a quiet intensity in his knight.

It was as if Brahms was afraid to break something too fragile, despite both of their strength. The contrast left Elias both comforted and...awfully aware of how much Brahms cared.

His chest ached as he considered the likelihood that this was the exact way Brahms took care of Adalja. A subtle smirk grew on his lips.

Of course he'd be this gentle...

"I'll not let you bleed your life away, My Prince," he scoffed. Brahms grinned and added, "All finished...returned to *perfection,*" as he tied the bandage at his sternum.

Brahms sighed deeply as he straightened up, rubbing his hands over his thighs to dry them.

Perfection? Elias thought, a wry smirk tugging at the corner of his lips.
Was that truly a compliment?

Brahms glanced at Elias' belongings, neatly arranged as if by some unseen hand—clothes folded, weapons placed properly. Atop a small, folded table rested the map, carefully spread out.

Without another word, Brahms moved towards it, his gaze scanning the parchment with practised ease. For reasons Elias couldn't quite understand, the pain rushed back.

Brahms ran a strong finger over the map, plotting their next move with quiet precision, trailing up Brookhaven.

Elias watched him for a moment, silently wishing he would return to his side. So instead, he pushed himself up. His gaze fell to the neatly bandaged wounds, and something in him unraveled. He silently hoped they'd scar...

He walked across the tent, while continuing to be warmed by the knight's furry cloak, and peeked over Brahms' right shoulder at the map. It was as though a spark ran between them, the proximity causing a subtle tension.

Elias noticed the way Brahms stiffened, though his attention remained on the map. He smirked, amused by the knight's subtle nervousness, but chose not to tease him. He stepped aside, not wanting to distract Brahms after all he'd done.

Brahms pointed to a small axe on the map.

"There," he said, his voice low. "The Axe, near the Worthyn settlement. We ride there today, and in a day's time, we'll be at Adalja's side..." His finger tapped the axe as he glanced over his shoulder. The two locked eyes, and Brahms finished with a mumble: "And everything will return to the way it was meant to be."

The words hung heavy, and Elias caught a note of something deeper in Brahms' voice—something that spoke of dread. His brow furrowed.

Elias reached out, wanting to touch his shoulder, wanting to offer reassurance...

"Brahms—"

"I'll see to the camp and ready the horses," Brahms interrupted him, tone firm but not unkind. Without another glance, he turned and left the tent, leaving Elias...in *his* cloak.

The prince wondered if he hadn't noticed he still wore it, or if perhaps he *wanted* him to...

A deep ache settled in Elias' chest, something far deeper than any physical wound.

And, in that cold aloneness, wrapped in his knight's scent, the cloak lost its warmth.

THREAD XLVII

ᚦᛖ ᛒᚢᚱᛞᛖᚾᛋ ᛟᚠ ᚺᛖᛁᚱᛋ ᚦᛖ ᛒᚢᚱᛞᛖᚾᛋ ᛟᚠ ᚺᛖᛁᚱᛋ ᚦᛖ ᛒᚢᚱᛞᛖᚾᛋ

ᚨᛞᚨᛚᛃᚨ

The northern night was unforgiving in a way she'd never known.

Winter crept through the cracks of the stone cell like death itself—its fingers cold and searching, brushing against her skin with cruel intent. The chill sank through her thin nightgown as if she wore nothing at all. Each breath was a shard of ice stabbing her chest.

Desperate, Adalja crawled across the frozen floor and curled beneath the wooden door. A single torch burned faintly above, warmth seeping through like smoke. She had already tried—and failed—to reach one of the pelts from above. This was her only hope.

She pressed herself against it, starving for even the smallest scrap of warmth. Her teeth chattered violently, and though she couldn't see herself, she knew her lips were the same shade of blue as her dress.

She cupped her hands to her chest, exhaling into them, desperate to summon the barest hint of heat.

If I freeze to death here, she thought bitterly, *I'll haunt Björn and all his kin until the end of my days.*

A sound—footsteps, then a door opening down the corridor.

She shot upright, limbs trembling from cold and stiffness. With a groan, she fumbled for the small wooden stool, dragging it to the door with numb fingers. She climbed atop it, clutching the iron bars with hands that barely obeyed—just tall enough to peer out.

Then came Björn.

He strolled in with a grin, axe across his back, looking far too warm for a man surrounded by snow and stone.

When he spotted her clinging to the bars, a smile tugged at his lips. "Morning, tiny—" he began, but stopped short. His grin faltered as his eyes narrowed. "You shake with glee to see Björn Björnson?" he asked, tone light but edged with concern.

She shook her head quickly, lip trembling. The cold made words brittle in her throat. "I-I'm f-f-f-freezing..." she stammered, her voice barely cutting through her chattering teeth.

"Didn't try the door, did you?" He chuckled. "Gods, I left it unbarred."

Adalja stared at him, blinking.

Perhaps she hadn't tried it...because the thought hadn't once crossed her mind. Not once today had she truly considered running. She recalled now—there had been no screech of iron when he'd left, no shifting of the bar. He'd told the truth.

Am I a fool? she wondered.

Before she could answer, Björn moved. Slowly, he pried the door open.

Adalja stood, still perched on the stool—nearly eye-level with him, bathed in amber light from the hall.

With a smile, he held up a small cloak in his hands. His eyes gave it a quick once-over before meeting hers.

"The gods know you're no giant, so I fetched furs for a dove," he teased.

He stepped towards her with the cloak, movements deliberate but gentle. She quickly reached for the cloak, grasping the furs with desperation.

She slipped into the cloak quickly, sighing quietly at its perfect fit. It hugged her figure in a way the other hadn't. Its clasp was curious—a curved claw from some beast long dead. She let her fingers linger there, her lips twitching at the faintest smile.

She looked like one of the shieldmaidens she used to pretend to be as a child.

"*Ah, there she is*—a true Pagan Princess—draped in furs at last," Björn teased with approval.

The cloak tickled her ankles, soft furs warming her arms and chest. Her fingers brushed the edge, and it felt heavier than it truly was. Not from weight—but from meaning. From the simple fact that it was a Norse cloak.

And it felt...*right.*

Björn said nothing. He only looked at her, eyes soft with an emotion she couldn't name. Their gazes locked—just for a moment—and the cold seemed to loosen its grip between them. It wasn't quite affection, but it was something close.

But reality returned quickly, like a wave crashing on stone. Still, the warmth of the cloak remained—his unspoken gift.

"Tiny one..." Björn choked out before clearing his throat and stroking his beard. "It wears well on you."

His voice was tight, a little lower than before. Then he stepped back, picked up his own cloak, and slung it over his shoulders with practised ease.

"I am grateful," Adalja murmured. Curiosity and confusion tangled in her chest as she tried to make sense of him...this strange new kindness.

"Keep it close. North winds are no friend to noble blood," he smirked, nodding once before stepping out of the cell again—this time leaving the door wide open.

Adalja remained where she stood, clutching the cloak tightly around her. She watched him go, her fingers adjusting the collar as her eyes followed him with quiet wonder.

She went to sit back down but Björn interrupted her with a sharp clear of his throat. *"Ahem—"*

The princess glanced up and there he was, still standing at the door, one hand on his hip, the other to his axe.

"Is it fear that keeps you here...or comfort in your cage, little dove?" he said, voice echoing slightly in the hall. He jerked his head, wordlessly saying, '*Come on*'.

Her blue eyes widened.
Was this a trick? Some sort of Norse practice to gain her trust and then sling her up by her wrists when the moment was right?

She swallowed hard, heart pounding—because despite her brain screaming warnings, *she wished to trust him.*

She didn't know if any of the other Perdyrians would have shown her such care. She still didn't know what it meant—but she was grateful.

The princess stepped forward, boots tapping lightly on the uneven stone as she moved into the corridor beyond. The faint scent of mead and smoke clung to the air, mixing with the sharp tang of dried herbs and leather.

She paused at the threshold, peeking both ways down the narrow back hall. It was nothing like she expected.

Instead of stone walls and endless rows of barred cells, there were thick timber beams, low doorways, and storerooms stacked with barrels, crates, and sacks of grain. Bundles of nets hung from the rafters, swaying gently in the draft.

It was too...alive. Too coarse. Too far from Pembrook's polished corridors and Worthyn's cold, pristine dungeons—yet far more put-together than any Ragnarvik corner she'd explored as a child.

"Never sat in a cell before, have you, little royal?" Björn's voice broke her thoughts, deep and warm with a chuckle as he strode ahead. He reached out to shove open a crooked door that creaked on its hinges.

Adalja stiffened, clutching the fur tighter around her shoulders. She decided not to answer—surely he knew the truth.

"I have not either," he called over his shoulder, his tone half amusement, half weight. "We've no need for cages 'ere—not when law and gods rule the land. Only they can hold a soul." Björn grunted with approval at his own words.

Then, with a spark of mischief glinting in his eye, he pushed the door wider for her.

Adalja's jaw clenched as she stepped through, curling further into the safety of the cloak. Though she soon found it no longer needed—
Beyond the door, warmth hit her like an embrace.

As she stepped into the heart of the building she realised: This wasn't a dungeon at all. She was being kept in the back of a tavern.

She could hear the muffled hum of voices down the hall, the clatter of mugs on tables, and the faint rise of laughter that came in waves. The air smelled of smoke, stale mead, and roasted meat, making her stomach grumble—barely heard over the sound of soft music.

As he led her into the tavern, heads turned. Silence fell over the warmly lit room, and her cheeks burned. They were all staring at her.

She swallowed hard, eyes flicking to Björn. He nodded at the tavern-goers before ushering her to the main door and leading her outside.

THE FIRST THING SHE SAW beyond the tavern was stone—towering, strong, and ancient.

The keep of Perdyr loomed over the square like an ancient beast. Its towering levels were hewn from dark, weather-bitten stone, the kind that seemed to drink the cold. Massive timber roofs jutted out at steep angles, built to bear the weight of endless winters, their edges rimmed with long-frozen icicles that broke off like teeth.

At its core, two colossal wooden doors—bound in rust-streaked iron—stood shut. Great braziers flanked the entryway, spitting fire against the wind, while black smoke slithered from the narrow chimney stacks above, merging with the breath of the people huddled in the square below.

Adalja's breath caught in her throat. The wind struck sharp and unkind, making her gasp and clutch her cloak tighter.

This was no ramshackle camp of war-torn raiders. It was a fortress, a true jarldom—built to last, carved into the bones of the north like it had grown from the very earth itself. The magnitude rivaled the Pembrook castle, which had been standing for nearly a century.

The town square was a patchwork of cobbled streets, their stones dusted with a thin sheen of frost. Carved wooden beams jutted from the corners of the structures, each etched with runes and bears—sleeping, roaring, even dancing.

A clang of metal echoed, surely a blacksmith at work in the market square. A woman with baskets of hides was shouting in Norse, likely enticing buyers.

At the tops of stone towers flapped the banner of Perdyr—a crest she had not yet seen—green with a golden bear, curled around a bundle of wheat.

She drank it all in—the sight, the scent, the sound.

This was Perdyr.
A jarldom hidden from the eyes of Midhelm for a decade, standing strong.

How?
That was all she could think.

How, after ten long years of war, did this jarldom still thrive—how did they fight and live in the same breath—how did a jarldom so vast, so full of life, become the enemy?

She felt dropped in a place of legends, and her eyes glazed over with admiration as she stood at the tavern door.

Her new cloak felt heavier now, bearing the weight of *Perdyr*.

Children's laughter rang out in the crisp air as they chased one another across the stones, hurling clumps of snow with bright, flushed cheeks.

The sound pulled her back, bittersweet and sharp, to Ragnarvik—when she had played this same way with Olivja and Brahms.

A little girl darted past her in simple woollen skirts and boots like young Olivja had worn in those days. Adalja's chest tightened, tears threatening as she thought of her.

Gods, let her be safe.

"Aye! Tiny one!"

Björn's voice boomed across the square, jolting her from her thoughts.

Before she could turn, something struck the back of her head—a snowball bursting against her hair in a spray of ice and powder. She gasped, spinning on her heel as snow trickled down her neck.

There he stood, grinning like a great fool, another snowball hefted in his massive hand.

"Too busy watching the little ones to learn your history?" he called, his voice full of teasing warmth.

Before she could reply, he hurled a second snowball. She flinched, sidestepping just in time with a gasp. The snow landed just shy of a patron in the tavern behind her. She gave a reluctant laugh.

The moment felt strange, wrong even, to smile in such a place—but her cheeks ached with the effort to hold it back.

"*My* history?" Adalja asked, clutching the cloak tighter as Björn strode over.

"Well...*all* of our history," he said with a shrug, though his voice now carried a weight that stilled her protest. "By day's end, you'll understand but *a part* of the truth behind every blade drawn in this war."

Unease twisted in her gut. She pressed her lips together and inhaled sharply; the icy air stung her lungs like shards. She nodded, unsure of what the day would hold, her nose turning pinker by the second.

He jerked his head and began guiding her down the winding streets lined with thatched homes and barter houses, the road wide enough for carts and horses. Adalja, wide-eyed and jittery, drank in every detail.

Björn's eyes lingered on her over his shoulder before he turned forward.
"Your loyalties are with us, little dove," he called back, his voice low now, edged with something dangerous. "With *Perdyr*—in ways you cannot yet understand."

As they rounded a wooden building, Adalja couldn't tear her eyes from it. Something about the little house caught her eye—darker than the others, quieter.

Charms hung from the beams, bones and feathers swaying in the wind. Strange symbols were painted over the wood, different from the other buildings, and the air smelled of smoke and herbs.

It wasn't a place for silver.
Something in her bones whispered: this was where the witches traded. And it called to her—

Oof.
She bumped into the broad back of Björn Björnson, who had stopped without warning.

She peeked around and before him stood a tall, broad-shouldered woman with mismatched eyes and a glare that could sour milk.

"*Valdie—*" Björn began, but the woman cut him off, speaking in rapid, aggressive Norse.

They argued in sharp bursts, too quick for Adalja to interpret.

After a tense beat, Björn shifted, giving the angry woman space. Together, they turned to stare at Adalja—and she swallowed hard.

"H-hello, Madame," Adalja offered, her voice barely above a whisper.

"*Tch.*" The shieldwoman rolled her eyes from her to Björn.

They exchanged a few more words before she turned and stormed off, braided hair tossing in the wind.

Björn cleared his throat and moved on without a word, as if the encounter hadn't happened at all.

But Adalja, full of intrigue, pressed him. "Who was that?" The princess asked softly.

When he didn't answer, she tried again.
"Where are we going?" She tilted her head to look up at him, breath puffing in the cold air.

"No more questions," Björn said, his brows furrowed in thought. "Only follow." As he spoke, Adalja sighed, remembering that she was, in fact, *still just his prisoner.*

Eventually, they stopped at a horsehall—an open, timber-framed structure longer than any stable she'd seen.

Dozens of horses stood tethered in neat rows beneath the sloped roof, steam rising from their flanks in the cold. The air was thick with the scent of damp hay, leather, and sweat.

Riders moved in and out with purpose, some speaking in low Norse, others laughing as they unsaddled beasts twice the size of those in Pembrook.

They walked between the rows. Adalja smiled at every beast—and horse—that looked her way, the hay crunching softly beneath her boots.

"Skarde!" Björn's voice rang through the hall, deep and commanding.

A sharp neigh echoed in answer, rich and powerful.

Björn laughed and jogged towards the rear, where the largest horse stood waiting.

Adalja hurried to follow—then stopped dead at the sight of the animal. Her breath caught.

Taller than even Björn, the dark brown stallion stood like a shadow forged of earth and fire, scars carved across its flanks pictures of old battles. Its mane was braided in small, tight pleats, and its heavy hooves stamped the ground in excitement at its master's return.

Björn wasted no time. He saddled Skarde with practised hands, murmuring words Adalja didn't understand—his voice low and soothing, as if speaking to kin. Then, with a final tug at the leather straps, he led the stallion out into the pale morning light.

"Have you ridden before, tiny one?" he asked with a grin, patting Skarde's flank with a force that might've bruised a man.

"N-nothing like this—"

"Hold fast. I'll see you mounted."

"*What*!?"

Before she could protest, his hands were at her waist, lifting her as though she weighed no more than a sack of grain.

She gasped sharply as she was hoisted onto the saddle, settling at the front with wide eyes and a death grip on Skarde's thick, braided mane. Her breath came in short, fast bursts. Even in stillness, she could feel the power beneath her. Slowly, her eyes lifted.

She had never sat so high in her life.

The Norse town sprawled out before her—it was even more beautiful from above. Her heart thudded in her chest, not from fear, but *awe.*

Then Skarde shifted.

Björn climbed up behind her, settling easily into the saddle. She caught his scent, ash and honey, surprised by the gentleness of it. His warmth pressed against her from behind, his arms reaching around her as he took hold of the reins.

"There we are," he rumbled, the sound of it almost a purr.

With a soft whistle, Skarde moved—deliberate and unhurried through the frosted streets. Adalja held tight, her heart thundering as the Norse world passed by below her.

She had never felt smaller. And yet...somehow, never stronger.

Hours later, the sun dipped low, bathing the sky in a wash of pink and orange.

At last, the towering stone buildings gave way—and in their place came the faint, distant cries of seabirds.

The path turned to dirt as it wound up a steep hill, the sounds of civilization fading behind them. Only Skarde's hooves echoed now, striking the hardened earth beneath them.

The cold sharpened here, biting through the heavy cloak Björn had given her. The furs did little to shield against the relentless wind.

As Skarde crested the hill, Björn brought him to a stop. Below them stretched a vast valley, cleaved in two by the Northern Fjord.

Mountains and rocky cliffs unfurled towards the northern sea, its waters icy blue as they spilled into Midhelm. The river, wide and deep, carved a striking boundary through the valley.

Its vastness made the silence feel eerie, unnatural.

'Wide' didn't do it justice—it was a force of nature, a fjord that cut through the valley like a deep scar.

On the far side of the fjord stretched the lands of Pembrook.

Farmlands dotted the landscape, neat rows of soil basking beneath a sky that somehow seemed brighter. Small homes and chapels, smoke curling from their chimneys, nestled into the hillsides. A distant figure moved with purpose, tending to livestock that grazed freely on the frost-bitten grass.

But that was not the side they stood on.

Perdyr's side...
Adalja could only describe it as a *graveyard.*

Here—the land lay blackened and barren, a desolate expanse of scorched earth.

What once may have been homes, fields, and livelihoods were now nothing but ash and rock. The fire had consumed everything, leaving behind a jagged, lifeless terrain, as though the earth had been flayed down to its bones.

Tall trees stood like charred fingers, extending out from the underworld, a forest of black and white. The barren forest separated the dirt path from the scorched fjordside.

It was unnerving—a stark line of separation between life and ruin. The river was too perfect a barrier, its waters a mirror of the fjord's duality.

One side scarred and silent, an eternal testament to suffering; the other side alive and thriving, almost mockingly so.

The divide was so absolute that it felt intentional, as though some divine hand had drawn the line and spared one side while condemning the other.

But why? Why would anyone allow this...?

She sat there, caught between the worlds, struggling to comprehend the enormity of what lay before her.

Björn cleared his throat.

"This is what war leaves behind," he said quietly. His playful demeanor had vanished since they reached the destruction. "Blood...ash...*scars.*"

And with that, he snapped the reins, urging Skarde down the dirt path, into the burned forest—into Perdyr's burned reality.

Adalja kept her eyes forward as they proceeded through the bone-thin trees and ashy deadfall.

When they broke through the treeline, she sat face to face with what remained.

Charred timbers and blackened stones littered the ground, the acrid scent of ash lingered on the winds, like even the air had been scarred in ruin.

The buildings grew sparse, their silhouettes crumbling into the snow. Some leaned precariously; others had collapsed under the weight of years.

Adalja's eyes watered. One hand rose to clutch her chest while the other tightened around the horse's mane.

Björn's presence behind her felt distant now, a shadow amidst the wreckage. She barely heard the crunch of hooves in the snow, her focus fixed on the deathscape around her.

Something caught her eye—a small, tattered doll half-buried in the snow. Its faded features stared blankly back at her, its stitched smile grotesque against the backdrop of ruin.

A child's toy.

Her throat tightened as she imagined small hands holding it, the child long gone, stolen by the horrors that had ravaged this place.

Her hand trembled as it moved up to her mouth, eyes desperate to look away, yet when she did they fell on a sight far worse—

Bones.

They jutted from the snow in ghastly defiance, pale and jagged against the frozen earth. Some were shattered, others crushed, as though discarded in haste. Her stomach churned, bile rising in her throat.

The silence around her was suffocating, broken only by the distant creak of weathered beams and the rustle of wind through lifeless branches.

"This was the birthplace of Perdyr," Björn said, his voice low and thick with loss. "Born of the sea, same as all of us. Homes clung to the hillside, livestock grazed, fishermen thrived. The paths were never still—not for a single day. But now..."

He fell silent for a moment, his eyes hard, jaw clenched.

"*Now, it is but a stain...*" he trailed off, not needing to say more.

The charred remains of the village spoke for themselves.

She wanted to close her eyes, to shut out the sight of it. But some stubborn part of her refused.

There was no escaping this. *No turning from it.*
Just as there had been no escape for Perdyr's people—no mercy from the brutality of war, of *Worthyn.*

Amid the silence, he turned Skarde and rode deeper, leading her further into the devastation.

Adalja swore she could hear faint whispers and screams of the past carried on the ashy wind.

Björn tugged the reins, and they came to a halt between what remained of a once-living aisle of homes.

Only the stone frames of two doorways stood now—weathered yet defiant.

Björn's weight shifted behind her, and when she turned, she found him already on the ground, walking towards the ruins on the left. His broad frame towered over them, his cloak picking up flurries in the wind.

Björn's eyes were hard, yet glassy, burning into the rubble with the fury of a pagan god.

"Was this...your home?" Adalja's voice was soft, almost afraid—drawn out by the grief written so plainly across his face.

He didn't answer at first. Instead, he took in a sharp breath and stared at the ruin, as though willing some remnant of life to stir from within.

At last, he spoke.

"Aye...our hearth." His voice was thin and breathless, the last word catching on a wound carved long ago.

"Astrid blessed me with two beautiful girls. Freydis and Frigg. My *youngs. My blood,*" he whimpered the last part.

A single tear slipped silently down his cheek, vanishing into the thicket of his beard. He raised a broad hand and ran his palm slowly along the top of the stone frame.

"This roof held their *laughter*. These fields held our *sheep...*" His voice cracked, and he swallowed hard.

"Now..." he exhaled slowly, trembling. "Now the ash holds their bones. And Freyja—*their souls.*"

The words hit Adalja like a blow to the chest. She looked at the charred remains of the home and opened her mouth, but no comfort came.

What could she offer a man who had lost everything? Especially knowing it was her own people who took it from him?

Björn kept going, as though each word bled from a wound he couldn't staunch.

"They called us *heathens. Vikings,*" he scoffed bitterly, speaking to the wind. "But I did not cross seas to be here—this is the soil I was born to...The soil *my kin* were born to."

"When Lilli died, they rained helfire upon us in the dead of night. No honour. No warning. And the land..." he paused, shaking his head, "she never forgot. Never forgave."

"Sir Björn..." Her voice faltered. The lump in her throat rose and swelled. "I...I did not know," she whispered, though she knew her words were salt on a gaping wound.

His voice dropped, restrained rage seeping out.

"Why would they tell you the truth, *eh*? They want a victory. They want glory. Not honour," he growled. "The faith-borns stole my peace. They carved me into a warrior—*for their greed alone*." His grip on the stone tightened until his knuckles went white.

"And I strike with such fury, they curse the night they stirred it in me."

At last, he turned his head towards her, something ancient and aching behind his eyes.

They stared at each other—Adalja taller atop Skarde, her breath shuddering.

"*Why*..." Her voice trembled with guilt. "Why did you bring me here?" Adalja asked.

Björn sighed as he stepped towards Skarde. He pressed a large, firm hand over her knee, his sad eyes softening for the first time since they arrived here.

"To show the truth. To help ye see with clear eyes why we took you from their kind."

"But I am faith-born, Björn—of their blood, of the crown. I am your enemy!" Adalja called to him from above the horse.

Björn shook his head and turned back to his home. "Spoken without sense."

Her breath caught and she shook her head. With a desperate scramble, she fell off the side of Skarde, barely managing to catch herself against the uneven stone.

She glanced towards Björn, who barely turned to look at her over his shoulder.

"I am unworthy of your mercy, of your truths...I should not be here!" Adalja couldn't hold back the tears any longer, her hands clutching at her chest.

"You ought to strike me down—as you would *any* who have wronged your people!" she cried, chest heaving as their eyes connected.

Björn slowly turned to face her, head tilting as if he was inspecting a mere insect that bothered him. Adalja's body trembled for a moment, but she held firm in her demands.

"You beg for my blade?" Björn asked, his voice quiet, unmoving.

Adalja exhaled sharply through her nose, sharp and insistent as the tears streamed. "If it is justice you seek, then spill my blood! Be done with it! End the marriage—the *war!*" Her hands clenched at her sides, shaking from the weight of guilt.

The Norseman took a step closer, but he did not speak.

She stared up at him, desperate to bring reprieve to a generation wronged.

"Please!" the princess cried, her voice cracking as it echoed against the stone.

Before another word could leave her lips, Björn moved.

In one swift motion, he reached behind him, his massive hand curling around the haft of his axe and yanking it free. The blade caught the last light of day as it rose, a cold gleam flashing across her face like lightning before the storm.

Adalja gasped. Her body tensed, stance faltering for a breath as the heavy weapon hovered—alive with threat. Her eyes flicked towards the gleaming edge, catching the cruel reflection of her own fear in its shine.

Björn exhaled—a guttural, bone-deep sigh, like the belly of a mountain stirring. His boots thudded against the ground as he advanced, steady and unrelenting, each step pounding like war drums in her chest.

The weight of him—his height, his fury, his grief—cast her in shadow. His body a silhouette against the setting sun behind him. It swallowed her.

She braced herself.

Her chin lifted on sheer will alone, though her stomach coiled with dread. She clenched her jaw and forced her eyes shut, refusing to scream. To flinch. If death was to come, she would not meet it whimpering.

"I spill no kin's blood."

The last words she'd ever hear...

She turned her face away as the axe's cold edge touched her throat.

A single tear slid down her cheek.

A final breath escaped her.

Then—A low chuckle. And then another.

The metal pulled back.

She cracked one eye open, confusion overtaking terror. Björn stood before her now, leaning heavily on the axe, its blade buried harmlessly in the earth.

"You are brave, Adalja," he said, voice touched with amusement, yet steady as stone. His head tilted as he added, "You are no dove..."

Her heart thudded again—but not from fear. From disbelief.

Then, softly, he said: "Your mother was my friend once. I owe her this—keeping you safe."

Adalja's breath caught. Her lips parted, but no words came.

My mother?

Her thoughts stormed, threatening to collapse her. The frost on her skin was nothing compared to the heat blooming in her chest—guilt, confusion, disbelief.

Slowly, almost unwillingly, her clenched fists unfurled. Her palms were damp with sweat. She hadn't realised she'd clenched them so tight. Her shoulders, once locked with fear, slumped—hollow from the strange relief of surviving what she'd just begged for.

"You knew my mother?" She managed, the words small, brittle.

Björn nodded. In one smooth, practised motion, he swung his axe back over his shoulder and secured it in place.

"Aye. Many in Perdyr did." His tone was low, distant—like words carried from another time.

The words struck her like a blow. She turned, following him as he walked back to Skarde. Her breath came fast and shallow.

—that cannot be true..." she said, voice quaking. "Perdyr...they *killed*

hand on his horse's reins. He didn't face her right away.

"With all I've shown you..." he muttered, voice rumbling like thunder. "You still cling to that lie?"

Then he laughed—soft, tired. Not cruel, not mocking. Just...disappointed.

"*Perhaps you are a faith-born—so easily fooled*," he said, almost to himself.

Adalja could hardly hear him through the roar in her head.

She stood rooted to the spot as the northern wind howled past, lifting the ash and soot of a ruined world into the air. She stared at the blackened earth—the charred bones of something greater than herself—when the question rose, unbidden and trembling, from her lips.

"If not Perdyr...then who...?" Her voice was hollow, torn. When she looked up, her eyes found Björn's again.

He held her gaze, dark eyes filled with old grief and the fire of a truth long buried.

"The guilty blame the loudest."

The words struck harder than any axe. And in the silence that followed, Adalja realised that the enemy was not in the North—

It waited in Worthyn.

Thread XLVIII

ᚦᛖ ᛒᚢᚱᛞᛖᚾᛊ ᛟᚠ ᚺᛖᛁᚱᛊ ᚦᛖ ᛒᚢᚱᛞᛖᚾᛊ ᛟᚠ ᚺᛖᛁᚱᛊ ᚦᛖ ᛒᚢᚱᛞᛖᚾᛊ

ᛒᚱᚨᚺᛗᛊ

Brahms tugged at the reins of his horse, Elias following, as they neared the small inn that bordered both Worthyn and Perdyr. They had spent hours travelling since the attack, growing closer to Perdyr—to Adalja.

The inn, a sturdy wooden structure with walls of thick, dark timber and a sloping thatched roof, stood just outside the treeline in a small clearing. Beside it, Brookhaven flowed endlessly, a large water mill churning on the opposite side. The sound of rushing water, creaking wood, and the occasional flap of gathered fish filled the night air.

The building was nestled against a cobblestone street that was overgrown and long forgotten, with a small, low sign swinging in the wind, bearing the faded name of the establishment: ***'The Broken Axe'.***

Brahms smirked to himself as he unhooked a small pack of clothing from the back of his horse. The thought of having yet another night alone with Elias—even if it felt selfish—was exciting.

"I reckon we could both do with a proper night's rest, no?" he asked the prince while stealing a glance, taking note of the revelry seeping from the warmly lit building.

"A drink is what I'd prefer," Elias called as he grabbed his own pack with a grimace, his free hand clutching the wound on his chest.

Elias walked ahead of him, and Brahms purposefully lingered behind, eyes following his every move as the prince swayed with a confident step...though it faltered at the brightly painted sign above the inn's door.

NO WEAPONS, written in common tongue as though it were meant for *them*.

The two men looked at one another silently before their eyes drifted back to the sign. After a few moments of thought, they slowly discarded their weapons in a large pile of unattended belongings near the door.

Brahms clenched his jaw, not liking the idea of being completely helpless after what they had experienced earlier, but if Elias trusted it...then so did he.

Inside, the flickering hearth cast long, dancing shadows across the low-beamed hall. The fire's heat did its best to push back the creeping chill that bled in through the timber walls, but the warmth was patchwork at best.

The scent of smoke clung to the air, thickened by stale ale, damp wool, and sweat. Laughter echoed off the wooden walls—deep, guttural, Norse-born joy that mingled with the clinking of mugs, the quiet strum of a lone lute, and the low murmur of stories being traded over half-finished plates.

Along one wall ran a heavy beam, worn smooth by years of drinkers leaning elbows and mugs against it. Barrels of ale and mead sat near the hearth, firelight catching the curve of their staves. Stout tables and benches filled the space, their surfaces scarred by blades, burns, and brawls.

Every inch of the room held life: travellers curled beneath furs under tables, an old man snoring in the rafters, two children bundled by the hearth like pups, and a woman resting her head atop her husband's lap while he drank around her sleeping form.

Brahms was surprised to see such a barbaric peace, thriving only hours away from the Worthyn camps.

But then he caught sight of a few nobly dressed folk, standing out among the thick crowd—those of Worthyn or Pembrook. Yet they bore the same fire in their eyes, drinking and laughing like the rest.

Brahms and Elias lingered near the entry, the light of the hearth catching in their cloaks as they waited in the haze of heat and noise for the innkeeper to show himself.

When he did, the tall, broad-shouldered Norseman—with a mane of wild, blonde hair and an extravagant, brightly coloured tunic—came around the corner.

He flashed a grin, his eyes twinkling with mischief as he swept his arms wide in a welcoming gesture, looking over Brahms and Elias.

"Ah, two strong souls seekin' shelter in my humble hall," he boomed, his voice carrying across the room. "Welcome, strangers, to the Broken Axe. We break bread first, barrels second...and if the gods smile, we'll *share* the furs after."

He chuckled to himself, then leaned in slightly, lowering his voice to a mock-serious tone as he continued, "Before the ale flows and the feast begins, hear me well—this is my hall, my sanctuary in Midhelm."

"No quarrels, nor blood spilled under this roof. No talk of battles or war songs. Keep your hands to yerselves—unless you mean to share more than mead and laughter." He threw a wink their way, eyes lingering on Brahms, which made his cheeks flush.

Elias seemed to have caught it as well. Even with his mask covering most of his expression, Brahms picked up on the subtle shift.

"Aye, for in the Broken Axe, we drink as kin! No blades—only bellies full o' ale and good folk at your flank," the innkeeper finished, striking a large grin and an exaggerated bow.

"I've space for tired bones anywhere you can find, and warmer company for those who fancy it. So—what'll it be? Mead? A full belly?" The innkeeper tilted his head towards Brahms, making him feel more flustered, eyes roaming his figure. "Or mayhap...something more *tender*?"

Brahms crossed his arms, tilting his head up at the innkeeper with a small laugh. "*Oh*? *Tenderness*?" he repeated, ready to fill his final night as a free man with more than wine.

"Sleep and a drink—that is all," Elias said with a curt tone, stepping forward and slightly in front of Brahms.

His green, low-lidded eyes shot him a sideways glance, sending a chill through the knight that urged him to be silent.

Brahms felt the weight of Elias' dominating presence, the tension radiating off of him like a wave about to break. It wasn't the kind of tension that came from the threat of enemies or the strain of battle—it was something different...like jealousy.

When the prince turned back to the innkeeper, the Norseman's eyes went a bit wider.

"A pleasure to have you, Prince Worthyn," the innkeeper suddenly chuckled, bowing again ever-so-slightly.

Both men were slightly taken aback by the Norseman's politeness despite him *clearly* knowing who the prince was. There wasn't even a hint of resentment or distaste in his tone.

"Up the stairs—try not to break the bed or spoil the sheets, aye? The room is mine."

"Only one room?" Before Brahms could stop it, heat bloomed across his cheeks.

"Aye. Not many get walls and a door at the Broken Axe," he muttered. "But he's of royal blood, and I've got sense enough not to have it spilled on my floors..." The innkeeper's words hung in the air.

"Though, if *you* prefer not to share..." He pointed a seductive gaze towards the curly-haired knight. "You can sleep with me in the storeroom, *mirthling.*"

Brahms' jaw dropped—just a tad—but he snapped it shut before the prince could see.

Elias' eyes slowly narrowed, the green depths shrinking under a shroud of darkness from his hood and presence.

"He sleeps with me." The prince's eyes remained cold, his posture still as he nodded silently, holding out a small pouch.

He sleeps with me, replayed in his mind like a battle cry. Though Brahms stood stiffly, pretending not to feel the sudden pressure building in his chest or the way his breath came a little too quickly. He cleared his throat, rolling his lips inward.

The innkeeper smirked, allowing the pouch to fall into his palm. He brought it to his eyes and peered inside, his grin growing.

He met Elias' gaze, forcing himself to swallow the lump in his throat as he offered a smile and a nod.

"I will join you shortly, My Lord."

Elias, ever perceptive, tilted his head slightly, raising an eyebrow. "You wish for me to walk into the warrior's tavern *alone*?" he questioned, a smirk tugging at his lips. "And to think I believed you *concerned* for our safety."

"Forgive me, I simply..." Brahms muttered, forcing a small smile that didn't quite reach his eyes. "I need a moment." His voice was thick, the words and worries stuck on the back of his tongue.

Elias simply nodded, the playful glint in his eyes softening ever so slightly before he turned towards the door.

"See to it you don't keep me waiting." With that, the prince lifted the mask back over his nose, hiding away his chiseled features.

The door closed behind him, and Brahms was left alone with his thoughts.

THREAD XLIX

ᚦᛖ ᛒᚢᚱᛞᛖᚾᛋ ᛟᚠ ᚺᛖᛁᚱᛋ ᚦᛖ ᛒᚢᚱᛞᛖᚾᛋ ᛟᚠ ᚺᛖᛁᚱᛋ ᚦᛖ ᛒᚢᚱᛞᛖᚾᛋ

ᛒᚱᚨᚺᛗᛋ

A SIGH ESCAPED HIM, his shoulders sinking. Brahms lowered himself onto the edge of the bed, his body taut with the tension of the evening that had only just started.

The thought of Elias inches away, sharing the same narrow space, sent a shiver through him—an ache of anticipation, fear, and something he refused to name.

And then, Adalja—her absence lingering on his mind like a bruise. They were so close... Was is wrong to indulge as a free man on his final night? He dragged both hands over his face, exhaling sharply as if he could press the chaos from his skull.

He needed to pull himself together.
Wanted to get through the night without falling apart.

After several minutes, he rose, inhaling deeply as he tugged his linen tunic off. The warmth of the room met his golden skin as he tossed his head back with a sigh.

Finally, with a fresh, beige shirt on—stitched with brown yarn—he was ready to face his prince once more. Catching his reflection in the round plate above the bed, the knight quickly ran a hand through his curls.

Brahms descended the narrow staircase, carefully avoiding the sleeping bodies. The sounds of the hall grew louder as he neared the bottom.

The low hum of conversation, laughter, and the clinking of mugs mixed with the crackle of the hearth. The wooden steps creaked underfoot, and the heavy scent of roasting meat and ale filled the air once more.

“He returns.”

A flash of movement caused Brahms to still on the final step.
The innkeeper smirked as he swung in front of him, leaning against the bannister. His eyes wandered Brahms’ frame in a way that made him feel...noticed. Far too noticed.

Brahms shifted, but the innkeeper’s tone—low and teasing—intrigued him.

“*Aye*, I sensed tenderness was of your liking,” the innkeeper cooed, his voice carrying a subtle flirtation. His gaze lingered far too long, dark eyes glinting with amusement.

As Brahms stood on the final step, the Norseman—taller and broader than he—had to look up slightly to lock eyes.

Heat crept up Brahms’ neck, though he quickly masked it with a grin of his own.

The attention stirred something unexpected in him. For a fleeting moment, he pondered how long it had been since sharing a bed with anyone. He wondered if everything he had been feeling towards the prince was simply borne of desperation...

There was only one way to find out.

“If you’re offering tenderness, I’d be rude not to take it,” Brahms said softly, leaning against the nearest post with lazy confidence—though inside, his heart was beating faster than he’d admit.

The Norseman raised an eyebrow, stepping closer still.
“Then tell me what you’re looking for, *mirthling*.”
His heavy Nordic accent was low, full of suggestion.

A shiver of uncertainty ran through him, but it wasn’t entirely unwelcome. He gave the innkeeper a small smirk, trying to appear unaffected. His thoughts, however, kept returning to his prince.

He knew better than to pine after Elias—a prince devoted to Adalja. It was never going to end the way he desired.

Perhaps a distraction was what he needed to steer his heart away...

With slow deliberation, Brahms shrugged, his lips curving into a faint, tight smile.

"Perhaps a drink first?" he asked, his voice steady despite it all. "To *loosen* myself."

He gave the innkeeper a small, pointed look, allowing himself to indulge. Not like it would matter in the long run. He'd never see this man again.

The innkeeper's smile widened as he stepped closer, still far enough to maintain the teasing distance.

"There's plenty for you to drink here…" the innkeeper trailed off, eyes flickering to Brahms' lips. "Though not all from barrels."

Brahms gave a half-hearted chuckle, though his throat tightened at the implication.

God help me, he thought, tilting his head slightly, a little grin playing at the edge of his lips.

"I'd sooner know your name, sweet giant, before I run you dry…*of drink*," Brahms said, his little grin curling slowly into a daring smirk.

"Viggo…" he answered, voice low and growling, closing the space between them until their chests brushed.

"But call me what you will—so long as I'm claiming you," he murmured, licking his bottom lip before gripping Brahms' waist.

He had no time to enjoy the closeness.

"So *this* is how my coin is spent, Brahms?" Elias' voice cut through the air.

Brahms practically died, the smooth but biting tone like a knife to the neck.

Viggo sighed, letting go so he could take a slow step back.

Behind him, tall and glaring, stood the prince, masked head angled at both of them. His sharp eyes flicked to the innkeeper before returning to Brahms with raised brows.

"*Ah*, the man's keeper," Viggo said, straightening up and stepping back from Brahms as if sizing up Elias. Sensing the shift, Viggo's grin widened as he raised a brow at Brahms.

"Best not leave your knight alone," the innkeeper hummed to Elias.
"He'd ride like a shieldmaiden of the sheets."

Brahms' heart stuttered, his stomach lurching at the comment—half insult, half praise.

Elias' hand reached for Brahms' before he could respond, a shiver jolting down his spine. He tugged him past Viggo, who sighed and watched them vanish into the warm, bustling room.

"*Elias*," Brahms hissed, the soft grip on his hand feeling like a quiet claim.

But the prince said nothing, guiding him to a small table, weaving between resting bodies and drunken patrons—none of whom glanced their way.

Their hands stayed linked until they sat—finally parting only once they'd settled across from each other. Neither wanted to let go.

The prince leaned forward onto the table, hands clasped. His cat-like eyes drifted, but the glint in them was sharp, filled with mischief as he sucked at his teeth.

"So, Brahms," Elias said, voice low but with an unmistakable edge. His tone was playful, but there was something possessive underneath, a thread of authority Brahms hadn't expected.

The knight blinked, his brow furrowing, gaze darting around the tavern before settling on the prince—tense and uncertain in a place like this.

"Yes...?"

Elias crossed his arms with a small, teasing smirk, his voice dropping into a low, purring tone. "Have you brought me to a place where you're already *well known*?" Elias asked.

"Wh-what? No—I...I don't follow." Brahms gave a nervous chuckle, uncertain whether to laugh or bristle. "Explain your meaning..."

The edge in Elias' voice caught him off guard. His gaze fell to the two full mugs—untouched. He'd kept the man waiting too long.

The prince's eyes narrowed faintly, his tone sharp but deceptively soft. "You seemed rather at ease with the innkeeper. It's a fair question, is it not?" His voice was intoxicating. Casual but threaded with just enough challenge to make Brahms shudder and go quiet.

Elias tilted his head, eyes expectant—though he left little room to answer.

"Go on," the prince pressed, his eyes crinkling as he smiled behind his mask. "Your *keeper* deserves to know." The label bit softly—but there was warmth beneath it.

Brahms hesitated, toeing the line between irritation and flustered amusement.

"*Prince Elias*, I cannot be blamed if others are *drawn* to me," Brahms muttered, gaze lowered, voice rougher than intended. "Were I less noble, I'd wager you burn with envy..."

He glanced up through his lashes, mouth twitching.

Elias unravelled his hands so he could lean over the table, green eyes burning with jealousy as they trailed across his face.

"*Perhaps you're right...*" he murmured, too close for Brahms' comfort.

But that's not to say it bothered him.

The thought that his prince had gotten jealous over him filled him with a sense of pride and relief. Proof that the tension, the looks, the *feelings* were not figments of his imagination.

They had to be real. *Why else* would he pull him away from another? Why else would he look at him like *that*?

God, it rattled him.

He swallowed hard and leaned in. "Don't let me keep you waiting any longer, My Lord..." Brahms teased, clearing his throat as he pushed one of the tankards closer to Elias.

The room was filled with warmth, both from the fire blazing in the stone hearth and from the energy of its patrons. The flickering torchlight cast deep shadows across their faces, giving them a sensual glow that magnified the tension in the air.

After finishing their first round, Elias began rolling a coin across his fingers. The restless trick caught Brahms' attention and held it.

Brahms watched those long, deft fingers coax the coin over each knuckle; smooth, deliberate, like even idle motion obeyed him. Heat stirred low in the knight's stomach, his jaw tightening as he forced his gaze away.

God, he shouldn't let his thoughts linger there...shouldn't let them linger on how skilled those hands were.

A couple of amused, or perhaps pleased, glances passed between them as they both continued to drink.

For the first time since their journey began, Elias didn't seem untouchable. He was just...a man. *A very handsome man.*

And like this—drinking, surrounded by heathens—he almost felt attainable.

Brahms was no stranger to tavern flings. For whatever reason, others found him desirable...and the knight took every inch of that attention.

He was but a poor orphan boy, with no one to love.
Why wouldn't he?

Brahms' vision softened, the edges of the room blurring as the mead worked its quiet magic. And his gaze kept straying, drawn to Elias, to the curve of his lips, to those saint-like eyes that seemed to whisper sin in the glow of the firelight.

As the evening wore on and the ale took root, their conversation ebbed and flowed like the music—each word slurring, each laugh spilling easier, and every glance lingering longer than it should.

Brahms found himself leaning in, his guard slipping. They played a few tavern games, and Elias tried teaching the knight to roll a coin across his knuckles. But Brahms' hands were too thick, too strong for such grace, and each time the coin clattered loudly against the table, it earned him a displeased glance from a nearby patron.

The inn soon quieted. Bodies slumped in sleep, breaths deep and snoring. Even the hearth's pops had shushed.

But the prince and the knight remained awake, eyes on each other, the remnants of their drink in hand. And in that lonely quiet, they felt more comfortable than ever before.

They faced one another, Brahms with one elbow propped on the table, the other hand resting on his thigh. His knee bounced beneath the wood his eyes trailing across sleeping patrons.

Across from him, the prince mirrored his posture, though he held his tankard low, cradled in the hand resting on his lap.

Elias shifted, nudging his stool until his leg brushed Brahms' under the table.

The space between them smouldered, heat curling in the narrow gap, the faint scent of him—warm skin and resin—mingling with the spice of mead sitting heavy in the hall's air.

"I must admit," Elias cooed with a half-grin, his voice lower now, a hush born of respect for the sleepers around them. "It pleases me...to see you unguarded at last."

"Is that so, Your Highness?" Brahms murmured, smiling as he licked a trace of mead from his bottom lip, his gaze finally returning to the prince.

"It is." Elias let out a soft chuckle, leaning in slightly, his breath warm with the sweetness of drink. "Your eyes—your stare...it has purpose now. I feel it."

His voice was softer still, no longer teasing, but edged with something deeper—something that settled between them like a secret.

"You're ever watchful, like the shadows themselves might rise against you...but not tonight." He paused, eyes never leaving Brahms. "Tonight, your gaze is set."

The words settled low in Brahms' stomach, tight and heavy. Elias' gaze held him in place—steady, knowing.

"You've been burning holes through me all evening," Elias whispered. "*Admit it.*"

A sharp breath escaped Brahms—half laugh, half nervous exhale. His face flushed, warmth rising that owed more to Elias than to the drink.

He tilted his head at the prince, eyes narrowing slightly with a challenge, lips twitching between a smirk and a confession.

Oh, to be bold, or to be bashful—that was the question.

His gaze flicked around the room, quick and quiet. No eyes lingered on them. No one watched. Just the low murmur of embers and the scent of fire-warmed wood.

And so, with a courage born of longing and a touch too much mead, Brahms let his hand slide from his thigh to the prince's, fingers curling gently around his knee.

He leaned in slightly, close enough to feel Elias' breath stutter, to see his lips part. And then he stilled—testing, watching for cracks in the prince's restraint, for surrender in his stillness.

The world narrowed. Every doubt dissolved. There was only Elias now, and Brahms' heart pounding in his chest.

"*I admit it,*" Brahms whispered, his voice hoarse with want, his gaze dropping to Elias' lips, already bracing to close the distance—to taste what had haunted him for nights upon nights.

And Elias began to lean in to, his mouth curling into an open smile.

But just as their lips were about to meet...

The floor creaked.
A sharp, unmistakable groan of wood underfoot.

They both startled, pulling apart like boys caught beneath the moon. Their flushed faces turned towards the sound—just a drunken noble stumbling down the steps, casting a groggy, unimpressed glance before staggering out the door, likely to relieve himself.

Silence followed, thick and suffocating.

Their eyes met once more, but where Brahms hoped for laughter, or even a shy return to what nearly was, Elias faltered. His gaze dropped. The flush on his

At the door to their shared room, his eyes fell to the handle. His skin was clammy. His jaw clenched. He waited in the hallway, playing the whole night back in his mind. Nervousness gripped him like a disease.

He shivered with desire and pent-up frustration, rubbing his hands over his face—then across the front of his pants—trying to calm himself.

"*If yer not goin' in there—I will.*"
A barely intelligible grumble escaped from a haggard woman slumped at his feet.

Brahms' eyes widened and slowly shifted downwards, but she was already snoring again, her face matted with dirt, a small beast's bone dangling from her parted lips.

He swallowed dryly, taking it as a sign, and stepped into the room, eyes shamefully pinned to the ground.

A steadying breath filled his chest—
But as soon as his gaze lifted, it vanished.

His prince was already tucked beneath the furs, lying on his side, facing away from the door. The bandages across his back pulled taut over tense muscles, outlined in the soft golden light spilling through the open doorway.

The muscle in Brahms' jaw twitched, nerves warring with the ache to be close to him.

He stepped inside—movements slow, deliberate, careful not to shatter whatever fragile peace Elias had carved out in the knight's absence. He shut the door with a soft click and tiptoed deeper into the room, drawing a sharp breath as he moved.

When he reached the edge of the bed, his throat caught.

He preferred to sleep shirtless.
But Elias was already without his.

Why did it suddenly feel wrong to take his off too?

His hands hovered at the hem of his tunic, curling and unfurling with hesitation. After a pause, he decided: if he wouldn't be touching him, it was harmless. And probably better to sleep *comfortably*, given what tomorrow held.

With a quiet sigh, the tunic came off. Then the boots. He left his trousers on, though loose at the hips.

Then came the final challenge: getting into bed with his prince.

He was trembling like a leaf in a windstorm. But he was exhausted—and drunk—and Elias looked like everything a man might pray for.

So, as silently as he could, Brahms climbed onto the bed, the mattress dipping beneath his weight.

With a shuddered breath, he lay on his back, his hands folded stiffly across his sternum like a sickly priest.
But he *had to* sleep like a priest.

Because even now—even here—he would not dare defile the space between them that Elias had made.

Brahms closed his eyes, begging for sleep to reach him. But against his wishes, the room spun—half mead, half burning desire to have Elias. The warmth of the bed dulled the ache in his spine—but not in his head, nor in his heart.

Right as he pressed his palms over his face to try to dull the ache...There was a soft rustle of furs.

And the prince shifted beside him.

Brahms' eyes cracked open, instinct pulling him from the cusp of sleep. He held his breath as Elias rolled gently onto his back—then, with the slow, half-conscious weight of someone long asleep, he turned towards him.

His face had softened in sleep, his expression gentle...*handsome,* perfect.

And suddenly religion lost all meaning.

Because before him lay a god—and there was no book, no priest, that could tell him otherwise.

Then Elias moved again, brow furrowing like a man searching for warmth in the middle of some dream.

And before Brahms could fully comprehend it, the prince's head settled softly against his chest. He fit right beneath his collarbone, head nuzzling slightly, as if Brahms were an item of comfort to him.

And the knight froze—not daring to shift. He would barely dare to breathe. His cheeks flushed, nerves buzzing from the space beneath Elias' head, radiating out in slow, electric waves.

Elias' breath was warm and steady, each exhale brushing the hairs on his chest in slow, deliberate rhythm. One of his hands rested between their bodies, his knuckles grazing Brahms' ribs, like the movement was natural.

The knight's heart was thundering—gods, it was pounding loud enough to wake the heavens themselves. But Elias didn't stir.

He only exhaled again, soft and steady, a faint hum slipping from his lips—like a man who'd finally found what he'd been unconsciously reaching for. As if he had been waiting for Brahms all along...and now, here he was.

And Brahms welcomed it.

The prince was warm. *So achingly warm.*
He knew—let the cruelest winter howl beyond the walls, let the storm claw and scream around the inn—he would need no fire, so long as Elias lay beside him.

He could feel every breath, every shift, every quiet vulnerability in the way Elias curled against him. Not out of lust, not from drunken heat, but something gentler...like trust, like wish.

He hadn't planned to touch him. *Gods knew he hadn't.* He hadn't imagined Elias would fold into him like this, like they were lovers hiding from the world beneath borrowed furs. But he relished it.

Because tomorrow, they would fight. Tomorrow, they would find Adalja. Tomorrow, this fragile moment would become a whisper in the dark, nothing but a dream blurred by ale and duty.

So, with the last of the liquid courage still burning in his veins, Brahms let his hand drift—tentative at first, cautious.

His fingertips found the back of Elias' neck, slid across to his shoulder, and rested there. His skin was soft, warm from sleep.

Brahms' thumb moved in slow, deliberate circles, not for seduction, not for want—just reverence. Quiet, sleepy reverence.

He hadn't gotten what he thought he desired that night.
But perhaps this was better.

So he stayed there, wide awake, memorizing the rhythm of Elias' breath against his bare chest, imagining a world where they had no titles. No restrictions. Only hope. Only the shape of each other beneath the furs.

Before sleep could take him, Brahms turned—slowly, gently—shifting his weight, careful not to disturb the moment. He slid his arm around Elias' waist, palm pressing lightly against the small of his back.

Elias made no sound, no protest. Instead, he leaned in, his lips brushing the crown of Elias' head, where the faint scent of him lingered—the pine enticing, the mint maddening.

Elias molded to him so seamlessly. Like they had always been meant to fit this way.

A sharp twist knotted in Brahms' chest at the unspoken trust in how Elias offered himself—unguarded, unconscious.

The rhythm of Elias' breathing, the warmth of him pressed close, the way his hand rested without fear between them—he was everything Brahms had ever wanted.

And in that certainty, in the stillness that wrapped around them like a second blanket, with his prince quietly curled against his chest...Sleep finally took him.

THREAD L

ᚦᛖ ᛒᚢᚱᛞᛖᚾᛋ ᛟᚠ ᚺᛖᛁᚱᛋ ᚦᛖ ᛒᚢᚱᛞᛖᚾᛋ ᛟᚠ ᚺᛖᛁᚱᛋ ᚦᛖ ᛒᚢᚱᛞᛖᚾᛋ

ᛒᚱᚨᚺᛗᛋ

THE MORNING AIR WAS CRISP, carrying the sharp bite of snow as Brahms tightened the last strap on his horse's saddle. Thick snowflakes drifted from the grey sky, settling on the yard of The Broken Axe and softening the sounds of the waking world.

Despite the cold seeping through his half-gloves, a lingering warmth burned beneath his skin—whether from the sting of the frost or the memory of the night before, he couldn't say.

The memory of Elias' breath, the way their skin had met, and the quiet weight of the prince curled against him—it all played over and over in his mind, just as vivid as the fresh snow underfoot.

"Your stirrups are too high," Elias' voice broke through the stillness.

Brahms glanced up, finding the prince jogging down the wooden steps of the inn, two bowls of steaming porridge in his hands.

Snowflakes dusted his tousled hair, while his cloak hung loosely over his shoulders, the white flakes catching on the fur trim. His hood was pulled tight over his head, the mask resting around his collarbone, giving him an air of nonchalance as he approached.

"I tended the royal livestock for five years, Your Grace. I daresay I know my way around a horse," Brahms muttered, adjusting his saddle with a grunt.

Elias smirked faintly, his eyes squinting, but there was a tenderness in his gaze that softened the sharpness of his usual wit.
"And yet, it is still wrong."

Brahms rolled his eyes, more to end the conversation than because he believed Elias.

He adjusted the stirrup with a bit more force than necessary, his flustered mind controlling his actions under the prince's scrutinizing gaze. It made the knight's skin prickle with a self-consciousness he hadn't expected, and he tried to push it aside.

After a moment, Brahms turned towards Elias, catching his eyes as they moved from the bowls of porridge to the prince's face. He crossed his arms defensively, his suspicion rising.

Elias always seemed to have an agenda, especially when he was bringing him food. Brahms narrowed his eyes.

"*What*!?" Elias quickly caught on, scoffing as he extended a bowl to him. "Do you have any notion how long I waited in line for this? I was pressed between two ravenous barbarians the *entire* time!"

Brahms' lips twitched.

"Well, forgive me if I've grown suspicious of your meals, Prince Elias," he retorted. "After all, the last one was a *trap*."

Elias' expression softened. Caught between fond amusement and a touch of disbelief, he sighed dramatically. "Brahms, it is a hot day-meal. Are you truly going to refuse it?"

Brahms parted his lips, prepared to press the point about Elias' hot morning meat, but the words stalled in his throat.

Elias' smile, his teasing tone...it made him want to drop the act, to stop being so defensive. And yet, his suspicion was what finally got the prince to smile.

"So...is this some sort of peace offering, then?" Brahms asked, his voice less certain than he'd intended.

Elias raised an eyebrow, his smirk deepening.
"Are you at war with me, *stargazer*?"

Brahms hesitated, the usual guard he kept up slipping for a moment as he looked at Elias with a mixture of frustration and something else he couldn't quite name. He was tired, flustered, and confused.

After a long, drawn-out pause, he sighed in defeat, the corners of his mouth twitching upwards despite himself.

"Verily, yes," Brahms muttered, reaching for the bowl, his fingers brushing against Elias' in the process.

The touch sent a strange warmth through him, but he quickly pushed the feeling aside, trying to remain unaffected.

Elias chuckled softly, his eyes flicking to Brahms, a glimmer of affection hidden behind his usual sharp gaze. "How many bowls of porridge does it take to get a knight to smile?"

Brahms didn't respond, focussing instead on the meal as if it could offer him some sort of escape.

But in that moment, there was no denying how easily Elias had disarmed him—how effortlessly his presence seemed to soften the edges of Brahms' stoic demeanor. It left him feeling more exposed than he cared to admit, and for a moment, he almost regretted how close they'd become.

Elias took a deep breath, his tone shifting. "Our evening weighs on your mind?"

Brahms was caught off guard, halfway through swallowing a spoonful. His throat tightened as he choked, coughing heavily as the hot porridge burned its way down.

His eyes watered from the effort, and when he finally managed to clear his throat, his voice came out rough, raw from the struggle.

"Y—yes..." Brahms rasped, clearing his throat again as he glanced at Elias, trying to mask his discomfort. "But...the blame is not yours, Elias." The words spilled out before he could stop them, a small, unintended admission.

"I merely hope the night granted you good rest, *My Lord*," Brahms added, his tone awkward and uncertain.

He assumed his prince had no recollection of curling beside him, and therefore, no idea what it stirred within Brahms. For that, he couldn't hold it against him. Only hold it close to his heart, a secret of his own.

Elias' expression softened, his gaze touched with something between regret and confusion. "I...did sleep well," he said quietly. "Did you, Brahms?"

The knight looked up sharply, his gaze catching Elias' before he could stop himself. The sincerity in the prince's voice made his stomach churn, leaving him exposed.

For a fleeting moment, Brahms hesitated, unsure if he could bear the unspoken truths hanging between them.

"I did." It came out rough and unpolished, startling even himself.

Brahms' eyes darted to his bowl, pretending to busy himself with it.

"Good," Elias sighed, as though something had been weighing on his mind. "Eat quick, the daylight bleeds now."

"Aye, My Lord," Brahms agreed, his voice soft but heavy with all the words he couldn't bring himself to say.

Elias hesitated, his gaze lingering on Brahms for just a moment longer. Then he stepped away, pulling his eyes down to his porridge as though diminishing the intensity between them.

"We need to devise a plan," Elias mumbled, bringing the wooden spoon to his mouth, taking a small bite of the steaming food.

"There is no need...I have seen to it already," Brahms responded quickly, motioning towards the back of Elias' horse.

There, piled high in a chaotic mound, was a collection of fur-lined gear and weapons, ropes tied haphazardly to keep it all in place.

When Elias noticed it, he froze. His breath caught for a moment, and he slowly turned back to Brahms, his eyes wide with disbelief.

Brahms was smirking, proud of himself.
"I thought a disguise might serve us well—"

"You stole from them!?" Elias hissed. His whisper-yell was sharp and low, a blend of horror and disbelief.

He darted towards his horse with urgency, his eyes flicking back to the loot, as if it might vanish the moment he looked away.
"*Heavens*, Brahms, how did you even—"

"They were distracted by...*evening-meat*," Brahms muttered between bites. He shrugged nonchalantly, moving to the side of his horse while shoveling the rest of his breakfast into his mouth.

He was ready to mount when the sudden slam of wooden doors shattered the quiet.

The knight's attention snapped to Viggo and a smaller warrior storming out of the inn, clad only in sleep shirts and breeches. Their sleepy faces twisted with rage.

The hairs on the back of Brahms' neck stood on end.

The two Norsemen glanced at the spot near the inn entrance where their surrendered weapons and armour *should* have been. Brahms had taken all of it.

Despite the risk, a smirk played across his face.

The two men charged down the steps, their fury evident as they caught sight of the thieves, fists clenched and ready to strike.

"Go—GO!" Elias shouted hoarsely.

In one fluid motion, the prince vaulted onto his horse and tossed the porridge at the charging Norsemen in a dramatic splatter. He snapped the reins and his cloak billowed like a dark wave. The horse's hooves thundered against the snow, and with another crack of the reins, they shot down the winding path into the forest.

Brahms scrambled onto his own horse.

Just as he swung his leg over, Viggo lunged forward, shouting in fury, his heavy boots crunching through the snow.

"CURSE YOU, Worthyn SCUM!" The innkeeper bellowed, narrowly missing the hem of Brahms' cloak as the knight urged his horse forward.

Adrenaline surged through Brahms as he pressed his heels into the horse's sides, racing to catch up with Elias. The air was sharp with winter's bite, and Viggo's angry yells faded into the distance.

Brahms laughed, the thrill of the chase lighting a fire in his chest.

THEY RODE NORTH, through the forest, the cold biting at their faces, until they were sure no vengeful Norsemen could follow their tracks. Snow-covered ground stretched behind them, disturbed only by fresh hoofprints. They slowed their horses as they reached a clearing.

Brahms dismounted with a practised motion, boots landing with a soft thud, echoing in the stillness of the forest.

He moved towards the pile of gear on Elias' horse, fingers eager for the warmth of fur-lined cloaks and tunics. The cold air of the north seeped into his bones, urging him to hurry.

Elias dismounted, his cloak fluttering like the shadow of a wraith. Silently, they unpacked the pile of clothes and gear.

Brahms stripped off his gloves, pulling a thick tunic from the pile. It was rough-spun but warm, thick enough to shield him from the cold.

"Here we are," Brahms muttered, shaking snow off a fur-lined cloak.

The plan to impersonate Perdyrians was more daunting now.

His stomach churned as he glanced at Elias, who began unlacing his tunic. Brahms turned away, the tension between them palpable. He undressed quickly, the icy air zapping his skin of warmth.

Pulling on the tunic, Brahms took a surprising notice of how the fur felt against his skin—rough but comforting. He secured the hide pants with leather straps and adjusted the cloak over his shoulders.

When he turned, Elias was already dressed, his tall frame wrapped in a brightly coloured tunic and fur. He looked more like a warrior than a prince.

Brahms adjusted his own armour straps and slid on fur-lined boots. The final touch was the iron helmet: Brahms' long and studded, and Elias' was smooth and short, covering only the top half of his face while the bottom was obscured by his black mask.

The clearing was silent except for the rustling wind and the occasional shift of the horses. Brahms glanced at Elias and grinned.

"I daresay we look the part," he commented, adjusting the strap across his chest.

Elias' gaze was unreadable through the narrow holes of his helm.

"I pray this ruse holds," Elias said dryly, his voice muffled by the cloak's hood. "The longer we linger, the sooner they'll be upon us."

Brahms nodded, pulling his cloak tighter. Though the thick furs offered warmth, the fear of failing clung to him like frost. They mounted their horses once more, their Norse disguises adding a layer of danger to the already tense journey.

The centre of Perdyr was several hours away, and as they travelled, the enemy presence intensified.

Each time a Norseman passed, the two impostors went unnoticed, their disguises effective.

As the morning sunbathed the sky in hues of grey and blue, they slowed their approach. Brahms' stomach churned with unease.

They didn't speak Nordic; they were noticeably smaller than the average towering Norseman and the massive weapons were unwieldy in their hands. Failure seemed a heartbeat away, yet they pressed on, driven by the urgency of rescuing Adalja. He knew how they were going to get inside Perdyr, the fear came from finding Adalja and somehow getting her out.

Thankfully, the pile of weapons on their back would serve as an easy way in.

The closer they got, the more desperate he became to perfect every part of their plan. Brahms was already rehearsing what he would say, practicing his Nordic accent, lowering his voice abnormally, clearing his throat anytime he didn't get it quite right.

"W—we 'ave found deese weapons *—aHEM— we've come t' return 'em—Odin's will*—no...ah—We COME WITH ARMS for the war, b—brothir—"

"Sounding good, *highborn*."

He hadn't realised Elias was trotting quietly beside him the entire time, the helm casting his peripheral in darkness.

He jumped, turning to look at him, his helmet unbalancing on the top of his head to the point where he had to hold it still so it wouldn't fall off.

Elias was watching him.

That damned smirk tugged at the corners of his lips as he chewed, slow and deliberate. The crunch echoed softly between them. Brahms felt his cheeks burn. He couldn't hold his gaze—his eyes darted between the glint of the fruit and the curl of Elias' mouth.

"Apple?" Elias asked, his voice low and careless as he tilted his head, extending the half-eaten fruit towards him. His other hand held steady on Juniper's reins, relaxed as if this were nothing.

But Brahms felt everything.
"*Hm*?" he managed, his fingers tightening on his own reins as his heart clawed against his chest.

Elias didn't press. Just inched the apple closer, his smile quiet now, curious. The offer lingered in the space between them, tender and stupidly intimate.

Brahms took it without thinking. His fingers brushed Elias' knuckles for a split second—warm skin, soft calluses. The heat in his chest swelled to his ears. He nodded once, but his appetite had already curled and fled like mist.

Still, he held it. Looked at it.

A crescent hollow of bites, shining with saliva and soft toothmarks. His mouth went dry, then wet all over again. He glanced up. Elias hadn't looked away—his green eyes were locked on him, unreadable, a little amused.

A little something else.

Brahms hesitated, then sank his teeth into the apple—right into the place Elias' mouth had been. The flesh gave easily—crisp, wet, and deliciously sweet. His lips curved against the fruit.

It was the closest thing to a kiss he'd ever get from him.

He chewed slowly, swallowing thickly as he dared one last glance. Elias hadn't blinked. He was watching him still—sharp, soft, and unflinching. And only when Brahms swallowed did Elias finally turn back to the road ahead, as if nothing had passed between them.

But something had. *He knew it.*

The warmth settled low in Brahms' gut. He could still taste the sweetness. Still feel the ghost of Elias' mouth pressed into the bite he'd stolen.

And gods help him—it was the best damn apple he'd ever had.

But the warmth of the moment quickly vanished as they reached the final stretch of land. To their left, a dull, steady thrum seemed to rise from the valley. The faint echo of war drums, heavy as a heartbeat, drifted across the snow-laden land. Every now and again, a horn's low wail carried on the air, haunting and distant.

Brahms froze at the hill's crest, his breath catching as the sight unfolded before him.

The jarldom of Perdyr—a place he'd never imagined he would see—lay in ruins, a shadow of what used to thrive in this land.

What once was a pine forest all around them, seemed to have been ripped from the roots by a god, tossed to grow in death.

The winter sun hung high, bleaching the snowy cliffs and jagged fjord in a blinding glare. The wind whipped around them, biting deep as it carried a far darker scent—burned wood, smoke, and a faint, metallic tang he couldn't quite place.

Directly ahead, nothing but blackened earth stretched to the horizon on this side of the fjord.

The trees—once proud and unbroken—were now twisted, skeletal husks clawing at the sky. Ashes danced on the cold gusts like lost spirits, as though the land itself longed to forget the violence that had torn it apart.

Only barrenness remained. The wind whispered of cruelty. The land was alive with death.

Brahms shifted uneasily, his hands flexing around the reins.

He had never been this close to war before. Never stood so near a jarldom bled dry.

Elias remained silent beside him, his jaw tight, green eyes scanning the horizon with grim familiarity. The war was no longer distant—it was hours away, perhaps less—and Brahms could feel the urgency coiled in his chest.

Brahms was startled to find the same heaviness in the prince's eyes.

He would have expected pride, or disdain, from the leader of Worthyn's forces. Instead, there was...shame.

It struck him then: perhaps Perdyr's theft of Adalja had been a desperate act, a final attempt to save themselves from a kingdom willing to burn the world to ash.

"Let's move," Elias urged, his voice steady and deliberate.

The certainty in his tone filled Brahms with confidence—they would find her, and she would be safe.

Elias said nothing more, guiding his horse forward along the barren trees, following along the burned land silently.

The charred trees and snow-muted landscape shielded them well, their passage unchallenged as they moved deeper into enemy territory. The tension was thick, but Brahms trusted his plan.

To their enemies, they were nothing but two of their own. Not a Worthyn prince or Pembrook knight under furs, but kin of the same waters.

The trees and ash embraced them in its silence, broken only by the crunch of snow under their horses' hooves and the occasional rustle of wind through brittle branches.

Brahms gripped his reins tightly, his tension mounting with each step deeper into the woods. His eyes darted from tree to tree, half-expecting an ambush from the shadows.

"What then, when we are past their gates?" Brahms asked quietly, his voice low but edged with unease.

"We hold ourselves as any Northman would," Elias replied, his breath visible in the cold air. "I'd advise you to keep at that accent—lest it betray you."

Brahms scoffed under his breath, his attempt at humor a weak mask for his growing anxiety. "You said it was convincing—"

"I lied."
Elias' smirk was audible, though his gaze never left the path ahead.

Before Brahms could respond, a sudden noise snapped through the quiet—a rapid crunch of footsteps in the snow to their left.

Both men turned their heads in unison, their movements sharp and instinctive.

Brahms' hand flew to the hilt of his sword as his pulse quickened. Though they were both warriors, they felt like deer, grazing in a land of bears.

A figure stumbled out from the snowy trees, disheveled and desperate, and Brahms flinched.

It was a woman, clutching herself against the cold, her hair tangled with twigs, her clothes drenched from snowmelt. She trembled violently, her wide, searching eyes filled with raw desperation.

"H—Help!" She coughed, her voice hoarse and weak.

Brahms' heart sank to the snow. He knew that voice. Without thinking, he spurred his horse forward.

"Brahms! Wait!"
Elias' sharp command rang out behind him, but Brahms didn't stop.
He couldn't stop.

As he neared, the woman collapsed to her knees in the snow, her arms wrapped tightly around herself to stave off the biting cold. She shook uncontrollably, her words stuttered and frantic.

"F-f-forgive me...I should n-not have run...Please, ret-turn me to B-Björn—please—I shall not run again! I s-swear it. I'm-m-m...s-o c-c-cold..." Her voice cracked, the words tumbling out in a jumbled mess of fear and exhaustion.

Brahms slid off his horse in one swift motion, wrenching and tossing his helmet to the ground with a dull thud. His heart pounded as he took a step closer, his breath visible in the frosty air.

"Adalja..." he gasped, his voice soft but urgent.

At the sound of his voice, she blinked up at him, her expression one of confusion. Her pale lips trembled as though she were struggling to piece together the moment.

"B-Brahms?" Her voice wavered, barely above a whisper.

Relief flickered across her face, followed by a flood of tears as recognition finally took hold.

With a strangled sob, she staggered towards him, collapsing into his chest. Brahms caught her easily, his arms wrapping around her vibrating frame as though to shield her from the cold and everything that had haunted her.

"Heavens, Adalja, you're *freezing...*" Brahms muttered, his voice tight with worry. He enveloped her in his cloak, wrapping it around her frail body. She clung to him, her reddened fingers icy against his neck, her sobs muffled against his chest.

The sound of Elias approaching broke through the haze of the moment. Brahms glanced up to see him scanning the treeline, his gaze sharp as he tossed a heavy fur cloak towards Brahms, his movements brisk and practised.

"Bring her to her feet. The longer we wait, the closer they draw," Elias ordered, his voice low but urgent.

Brahms caught the cloth deftly and wrapped it around Adalja, shielding her further from the cold. With quick, practised movements, he helped her up, lifting her onto Elias' horse.

She nestled tightly against his back, her head hidden beneath the hood of the fur-cloak, her hands tightly gripping the sides of his torso. Elias turned his horse, and took off back the way they came, securing Adalja's safety out of the clutches of Perdyr.

Brahms watched them leave for a moment, his chest heaving with the reality of their success—how easy it was.

His eyes scanned the trees, waiting for the trick, the scheme of it all. But nothing leapt from the shadows.

With a sharp exhale, he mounted his horse.

Relief cracked through his chest like sunlight splitting winter clouds.

Adalja was alive. She was with them once more.

For the first time in days, he allowed himself a deep breath. He followed after Elias' fleeing horse, leaving behind the quiet, skeletal woods of Perdyr for Worthyn.

In the windblown snow, only their hoofprints remained—marks soon to be swallowed and forgotten.

Thread LI

ᚦᛖ ᛒᚢᚱᛞᛖᚾᛋ ᛟᚠ ᚺᛖᛁᚱᛋ ᚦᛖ ᛒᚢᚱᛞᛖᚾᛋ ᛟᚠ ᚺᛖᛁᚱᛋ ᚦᛖ ᛒᚢᚱᛞᛖᚾᛋ

ᛒᚱᚨᚺᛗᛋ

They found a small clearing, nestled deep within the forest. It wasn't much, but the towering, frost-covered trees shielded them from the biting wind.

The ground was packed with snow, fractured by patches of frozen grass stubbornly poking through. A heavy pine branch sagged nearby, bowed under the weight of snow—a natural shelter for their fire.

"This will do," Elias muttered, dismounting and gesturing for Brahms to follow.

Together, they worked in practised silence, setting up camp.

Brahms had anticipated the cold, gathering dry wood earlier. Within minutes, the fire caught, its warmth spilling into the frozen air and bathing their camp in a soft, golden glow.

Adalja moved stiffly as she dismounted Elias' horse, exhaustion and cold weighing down each step. She led the horse closer to the fire, hands trembling as she draped blankets over the animals.

Brahms watched her, relief mixing uneasily with concern. She had escaped—but how? And at what cost?

As the firelight brightened, Adalja's figure emerged clearly against the dark forest backdrop.

Elias approached, his barbarian helmet tucked under his arm. He murmured softly, voice low and deliberate, plucking a twig from her hair with careful confidence.

Brahms caught fragments of their words, carried on the biting wind.

"Are you certain you're well?" Elias' brow furrowed, his hand brushing lightly against her shoulder as she leaned wearily against the horse.

Adalja's hands stilled briefly as she secured the blanket over the animal's back. "I'm well, Elias," she said softly, though the slight tremor in her voice betrayed her. "*Truly*."

"You're still freezing," Elias exhaled, gaze sweeping over her as if assessing injuries she wouldn't admit. "And...you're trembling."

"I'm not," she replied quickly, though her fingers shivered as they struggled with the knot.

Elias' hand gently covered hers, halting her fumbling.

"Let me," he said quietly, finishing the task with deft movements. She said nothing, too drained to resist.

They lingered by the horse a moment longer, Elias' voice low enough that even Brahms, seated near the fire, couldn't catch the words.

Adalja nodded occasionally, distant and unfocussed, her gaze lost beyond the snowy clearing.

The two of them moved towards one of the tents, their shadows dancing across the canvas wall. Brahms watched briefly before turning back to the fire.

Elias carefully guided her inside, slowly closing the flap behind himself. He stepped away from her, squatting beside a small sack near the tent wall. He rummaged through it, his back to her.

The tent was warm—too warm, almost suffocating after the biting cold outside. A faint tallow scent clung to the canvas, the lantern's flicker soft but unsteady, painting his sharp features in shifting gold.

Adalja's hands fumbled with the cold fabric of her gown. The princess' body trembled even within the tent, winter's bite lingering cruelly.

He stood, turning with a fur-lined gown, folded in his hands. "Here, my love...take it. I will not look."

Elias placed it in her hands and turned back to his chest without any hesitation or second looks.

She watched, still, her hands curling into the warm fabric. But her body—stricken with cold—would not obey her.

Her gaze flicked once, then again—catching Elias tugging off the Norse armour they'd worn to slip unseen into Perdyr.

A pang of guilt struck her as she thought of the way she had abandoned that jarldom. She hadn't thought she'd survive the night—running through the snow, lungs burning, Björn's words lodged in her mind like a curse.

Foolish to leave, perhaps...but how could she stay, knowing Olivja might be in danger?

Adalja didn't realise she'd been staring until Elias stripped off the tunic clinging to his frame. The motion was slow and deliberate, careful of bandages she chose not to acknowledge. Pale light kissed the hard planes of his shoulders and back—skin warm and shimmering against the cold world beyond the tent.

Their eyes met. His greens—sharp, searching, heavy with questions. Her blues—uncertain, guarded, but drawn to him all the same.

A ripple of heat swept through her, melting frost into a blush. Flustered, she turned away sharply, breath catching.

"You *ought* to get dressed, Adalja, *please*," Elias murmured, voice low as he stepped towards her. His palms brushed her from behind. "You're like ice."

Adalja froze, muscles taut as his hand lingered—warm, careful.

"You needn't worry, Elias," she whispered, too quiet even for herself. But her chattering teeth betrayed the lie.

His thumb brushed her chilled skin—a ghosting touch that sent another shiver rolling through her. Her limbs ached with coldness, muscles locked tight as she forced a steady breath.

"I *always* worry for you, Adalja," he said softly, breath warm behind her. "Do you need my assistance...?" he whispered.

She nodded, her hands clenching around the folded gown. She kept her eyes on the canvas in front of her as Elias' warmth came closer.

Slowly, her suitor's hands moved to the thin ties of her nightgown. His fingertips—warm as fire—brushed her neck, and she stiffened.

His hands were gentle, steady but unhurried. The fabric was damp and clinging to her skin, and she felt the tremor in his breath as he loosened the ties. Slowly, carefully, he drew it down her shoulders, letting it fall and pool around her snow-soaked boots.

The air between them seemed to thrum, heavy and warm, unlike the winter air outside.

She tried to steady her breathing as cool air licked her bare skin, her body exposed to him. She couldn't see his face, but she felt the weight of his eyes.

The backs of his fingers slid down her spine, featherlight. Elias' touch was cautious and warm, brushing down the expanse of her back.

Adalja shuddered under his touch as it paused at the small of her back.

His hands sent a sharp shiver racing through her, though she couldn't tell if it was from cold, shyness, or something else entirely.

"I know not what I would have done had I not found you," he whispered, his breath warm against her neck. He placed a gentle kiss against her shoulder, his hands curling into her hips.

"Had they touched you, Adalja..." he said, voice hoarse. "All of Perdyr would have felt my wrath..." His threat trailed off—laced with quiet protection and possession.

Adalja bit the inside of her cheek before finally answering him."...I am unharmed, I swear it, Elias."

Silence, gentle and comfortable, passed between them. And then, his arms extended around her, encasing her in a tight, warm hug. He pulled her bare body to his, his front warming her back, sending a chill through her veins.

"And it will stay that way," he whispered, his lips brushing the top of her head. "For as long as I live."

He took the gown from her and his arms retreated, leaving her feeling breathless. Though the dress was not yet around her—the cold no longer gripped her.

He bundled the dress and guided her arms into the sleeves, his touch gentle but firm. He slid it over her head, smoothing it down along her sides. The silence was loud, but it fuzzed on the edges with warmth and familiarity.

When he finished tying the back, he stayed close, his breath warm against her ear, his hands warm and firm on her hips.

"There," he murmured, his voice low and raw. "Better?"

Adalja nodded faintly, still staring at the floor of the tent. But before she could retreat, one hand reached past her shoulder, fingers curling lightly under her chin. Her breath caught as he turned her head back towards him, his thumb brushing the edge of her jaw.

"Look at me," Elias said quietly.

She didn't resist. Her heart pounded, but not from fear.

Her eyes met his—greens deep and unguarded, flickering in the glow. There was no malice there, no hidden sharpness...only worry. Only him.

"I came far too close to losing you," he said, voice unsteady. "And I know not how I should endure a world without you."

Adalja's lips parted to speak, but her words died as his thumb brushed her cheek, slow and reverent.

And then—his mouth found hers.

The first brush of his lips was light, almost hesitant. A question.

Adalja let out a shaky breath, her body tipping instinctively towards him, leaning back into the warmth of his muscular frame.

His lips met hers a second time, and she accepted it.

This time, when he kissed her again, she turned fully in his arms, fingers bashfully brushing the landscape of his chest. The kiss deepened, his hand sliding from her jaw to cup the back of her head, cradling her gently as though she might break.

And perhaps she still would.
But she knew she would be safe in Elias' arms.

BRAHMS

Eventually, the two of them emerged, dressed once more in their royal attire—Adalja in a warm winter dress and cloak.

As they joined Brahms, the princess broke the heavy silence with a faint, teasing smile.

"You look good as a Northman," she said, her voice soft but threaded with humor. Her gaze flicked to Elias. "But *you*—I much prefer as a prince."

Brahms chuckled, the sound easing the tension—if only briefly.

"It's too cold to change," he replied, glancing down at his *borrowed* gear. "So I suppose I'll stay a barbarian a little longer."

His smile faded as his thoughts turned practical—the memory of Adalja stumbling through the snow still fresh. He leaned forward, his brow furrowed.

"How *did* you get out?" His tone was careful. "I was ready to cut through an army of giants for you."

Adalja's expression, once soft, flickered. Her gaze dropped to the fire, eyes hardening.

"They...let me," she said at last, her voice fragile. "They granted me a walk...and I took it to flee."

Elias frowned, disbelief plain across his face.
"...They let you wander?" Suspicion crept into his voice. "Why?"

She didn't answer immediately.

Her shoulders tightened, shrinking under their scrutiny.
"I do not know," she finally said, her voice weak. "Perhaps...perhaps they are not who we thought they were, Elias."

Brahms glanced at him, confusion mirrored in both their eyes.

Elias pressed gently, placing a gentle hand over her knee. "What is it you mean, Princess?"

Adalja hesitated, pulling her cloak tighter around herself—as if warding off the North itself.

"They revealed much to me...s-spoke truths I scarce believed," she stammered, her voice catching. "Truths of the war. Of Perdyr. They said..." she trailed off, her lips pressed inward, as if sealing the words away.

Brahms leaned in, shadows gathering in his expression. "Go on."

"That they bore no guilt for my family's deaths," she whispered, the words splintering in her throat. "They said..." Her eyes flicked to Elias, wide with fear. "*It was Vincent who killed them.*"

The words struck like a thunderclap.

Brahms' jaw clenched. His body stiffened as his mind raced. They had left Olivja behind—alone, unprotected—with Vincent. A man capable of unspeakable violence.

Adalja's voice cut through the tension—quiet, but no less urgent. "I had no choice but to flee—to bring warning to you, and to her. If their words hold truth...then Olivja is in grave peril."

Brahms rose abruptly, fists tightening.

Elias shook his head. "Vincent wouldn't hurt—"

"He already has!" Brahms snapped, his voice sharp with frustration. He turned towards Elias, eyes blazing. "You saw with your own eyes what he did to her, Elias. How can you stand in his defence?"

Elias flinched, but held his ground. "These could be lies. They seek to turn us upon ourselves. They know what these unions will bring. Do not let them twist your mind."

Adalja shook her head, tears brimming. "If they knew what was at stake, why not end me?" she asked, her voice faltering.

She looked so small, so fragile in the firelight—and Brahms realised she'd been carrying that question since her escape.

"They kept me warm. Treated me kindly. They sought not to harm me." Her voice carried a steadiness that unsettled even the quiet snow—conviction. "If they meant to end these unions, why free me? Why warn me of *him*?"

The fire crackled softly, filling the silence that followed.

Brahms shifted his gaze to Elias, whose eyes were fixed on the flames. Something in the prince's expression—tight, wary—gnawed at Brahms. It wasn't doubt. It was *knowing*.

"I..." Elias began, but his words faltered, gloves tightening over taut knuckles. He was unsure how to continue, and Brahms had enough.

"Don't be blinded by blood, Elias," Brahms said sharply, voice low and seething. "If they wanted her dead, why spare her? *Think*. Adalja's right—Perdyr was trying to keep her safe...from *him*."

Elias didn't respond immediately, his jaw tightening as if he were clenching back words he didn't want to speak. His gaze remained fixed on the fire, the weight of Brahms' accusation hanging heavy in the air.

Finally, the knight muttered, almost to himself:
"Olivja was right..."

The words settled like stones in Brahms' chest, a bitter truth none of them could ignore.

They all thought of Olivja's outburst at the execution—the rage, the defiance in her voice when she'd dared to speak against Vincent. Maybe she hadn't known the full truth, but she had trusted her instinct. She had *seen* something none of them had been willing to see. And now, the three of them sat here, a days ride from the kingdom, knowing they hadn't believed her when it mattered.

Brahms' harsh words to her weighed heavily on his shoulders; he'd blamed Olivja for *everything*...and now danger loomed.

Adalja's voice broke the standoff, raw and pleading. "...We must return to her."

His heart twisted at the desperation in her voice. The firelight illuminated her face, pale and tear-streaked, and for the first time since he'd found her, he saw just how much the ordeal had drained her.

She looked ready to collapse. But as much as her words tore at him, he knew the truth—they were in no shape to ride through the night, not in this cold, not in this storm.

"Even if what Perdyr claims is true," Elias finally said, looking at both of them with deep sadness in his green eyes.

"*He loves Olivja...*" he whispered. "I know that as deeply as I know my own name."

Silence fell again, each of them wrestling with what to believe.

Could Vincent kill the Pembrooks and love Olivja? Could they both be true?

Brahms couldn't believe it. It challenged everything—killing his king and queen was unforgivable.

His hands clenched into fists as he considered the paths he would take when they returned. His gaze shifted to Adalja, whose face was frozen in dread, her mind swirling with the unknown.

Elias stood, slowly brushing snow from his cloak.
"We need to rest, no matter..." he said, voice firm but measured. "We shall find no truth if we perish in a storm before we return."

Brahms wanted to speak up, but Elias didn't give him the chance as he gestured towards the tents.

The prince's voice fell quiet, almost saddened in its restraint.
"I'll take first watch. You two—rest."

Adalja hesitated, her eyes flicking between the two of them, but her exhaustion won out. She nodded faintly, her shoulders slumping as she turned towards the tents.

The knight stared at his prince in disbelief and anger, unsure what to believe—but his princess needed him. He needed to be by her side.

Brahms followed, catching up to her before she could enter.

"Wait," he said softly, his hand brushing her arm to stop her. She glanced at him, her expression wary but curious. "Let me make sure you're comfortable."

She opened her mouth to protest, but Brahms cut her off with a smile. "Do not tell me the Northmen have turned you stubborn. Come—let me help, will you?"

Adalja sighed, giving him a small nod of consent. He ducked into Elias' tent first, checking the blankets and tucking the bedroll tightly to keep out the cold.

The tent was simple, a small shelter against the elements, but it would do. He turned back to her, offering his hand to help her inside.

"Here," he said softly, guiding her to sit on the bedroll.

She curled her knees to her chest, shivering beneath her cloak. He crouched beside her, unfolding the thickest blanket and draping it over her shoulders.

"Thank you," she murmured, her voice so faint it barely reached him.

"I've done nothing worth thanking, truly," he replied, his tone gentle but firm. "I would see the whole world burn before I let harm befall you, Princess. You know this."

Adalja's glassy eyes met his, full of exhaustion and something he couldn't quite name. "What about...for Olivja?" she asked after a long pause, her voice barely above a whisper. "Would you do anything to keep *her* from harm?"

Brahms froze, her question catching him off guard. For so long, his only concern had been Adalja's safety. It was why he had stayed by her side, why he had sworn to protect her above all else.

But he couldn't deny that the thought of Olivja needing his help stirred something deep within him—a fire that burned just as fiercely. He let out a quiet sigh, shifting to sit on the ground beside her.

"No," he admitted, his voice low.
"But," he paused, choosing his words carefully, "she'd never ask that of me. *Nor accept it."*

Adalja nodded, studying him with tired, questioning eyes. "Do you truly believe she's in harm's way?"

His throat tightened. He didn't want to lie to her, but the truth weighed heavily on his chest.

"I believe..." he hesitated, running a hand through his hair. "We've all misjudged Vincent...and Olivja...she knows it more keenly than we do."

Adalja's lips trembled, her gaze dropping to her hands as she clutched the blanket tightly around her shoulders.

"I should have done more for her," she whispered, her voice breaking. "At the execution...I ought to have found my tongue."

Brahms reached out, placing a steady hand on her shoulder. "I ought not have raised my voice at her," he said quietly, the regret heavy in his tone. "But hear me...Olivja would not have you take this burden upon yourself. None of us foresaw what was to come."

He paused, his hand curling over the blanket, trying his best to reassure her. He drew a shaky breath and forced a small smile. "But now we will set it right—all of us, together. And when that time comes...we may speak our regrets, and beg for forgiveness on our knees."

Adalja let out a weak laugh at his jest. Her eyes shimmered with unshed tears, and she nodded faintly, leaning into his touch for the briefest moment before pulling back.

"Rest now," he said, his voice quiet yet resolute. "We ride at first light. We *will* see her safe again."

Adalja didn't respond, but the tension in her shoulders eased as she lay down. Her movements were slow, weighed down by exhaustion. Brahms tucked the blanket around her, making sure it would keep out the night's chill.

When she finally closed her eyes, he lingered for a moment longer, watching the rise and fall of her breathing. Only when he was sure she was settled did he step out of the tent, the cold night air hitting him like a slap.

He glanced towards the fire, its flickering light casting long shadows across the snow. Elias was seated where Brahms had left him, his face partially obscured by the glow. But Brahms didn't have the energy to confront him again about Vincent—not tonight.

Crossing the camp, he ducked into his own tent, unwilling to face the prince again tonight. He shed his cloak and boots before sinking heavily onto the bedroll. His body ached from the ride, and his mind buzzed with restless thoughts.

The fire outside crackled softly, its faint warmth a small comfort in the biting cold.

Somewhere out there, Olivja was waiting.

He thought of her—her defiance, her anger, and the way she'd looked at him during her outburst at the execution.

She hadn't been wrong.
She had seen what the rest of them were too blind or too afraid to see...

Brahms closed his eyes, leaning back against his pack.

He had failed her once.
He wouldn't fail her again.

As exhaustion pulled him under, the last thing in his mind was Olivja's face—unyielding despite betrayal, proud and mocking when he would inevitably apologise for *everything*.

Tomorrow, they would ride.
Tomorrow, they would begin to set things right.

THREAD LII

ᚨᛞᚨᛚᛃᚨ

THE HORSE'S RHYTHMIC TROT over the uneven path offered a small comfort as they rode through the dense trees at the edge of the Kingdom of Worthyn.

Heavy clouds sagged low above them, casting a grey pallor over the land, as if the sky itself mirrored her anxiety. Tension thickened the air, and Adalja couldn't shake the knot of unease that had taken root in her stomach since leaving camp.

Wrapped tightly in Elias' cloak, Adalja shivered, her hands instinctively tightening around his waist as she pressed her chest to his back. She tried to ignore the cold creeping in around them.

The ride had been mostly silent, broken only by the occasional quip from Brahms, who—despite their situation—still managed to bring levity.

"And what strange Northman skills did they teach you, hm?" Brahms asked with a smirk, guiding his horse to ride alongside Elias's mount.

They'd discarded all the stolen wares, leaving Brahms in just his tunic and cloak. His eyes flicked to Adalja with quiet intent, as if trying to lift the heaviness of their journey.

Adalja smiled in spite of herself, the knot of worry in her chest beginning to unwind. "I certainly learned how to lay you flat in combat," she replied, her tone light despite the dread gnawing at her over returning to the castle.

Her thoughts drifted to Björn. She hoped he wasn't too angry about her escape—even knowing they might never cross paths again.

Brahms' gaze lingered on her hands, wrapped tightly around Elias' waist, before flicking up to meet hers with a curious glint in his dark eyes.

"With those dainty limbs? You wound me deeply," he said, placing a hand over his chest in mock indignation. "I travelled far and wide to find you, Addy—battled great warriors!"

Adalja giggled quietly, unable to suppress it. "Is that truly meant to dazzle me?" she shot back, grinning.

Elias shot Brahms a sidelong glance, one brow arched in mild amusement. "*We,*" he corrected, a playful glint softening his usually solemn gaze. He gave Brahms a knowing look as he gently tugged his reins, guiding the horse around a fallen tree blanketed in snow.

Adalja glanced between the two, then pressed her face to Elias' back, seeking shelter from the biting wind. Even the horses shuddered, huffing as they quickened their pace against the chill.

"Ah, yes...*we*," Brahms echoed with an exaggerated sigh. "I suppose I should be more grateful for your company on this journey, Prince Elias."

Though his voice held a teasing edge, Adalja sensed the genuine fondness beneath it. Brahms might jest, but he valued Elias.

The prince, unusually quiet, softened at the sound of her laughter. His posture eased as he glanced down at her hands, still wrapped securely around his waist. His fingers brushed hers, then gently pulled them tighter. He didn't say more, but the gesture spoke volumes—protective, even in silence. His usual stoic edge gave way beneath her touch.

Brahms rolled his eyes as he rode closer to them. "You should've seen it, Adalja," he called dramatically, grinning as he pushed ahead, eyes flicking to Elias now and then. "I saved Prince Elias' handsome rear from two barbarians. It was—"

"One barbarian," Elias cut in, his face flushing beneath the mask. "The other retreated," he added with a scoff, recalling their time spent together to save the princess.

Warmth crept into her chest now that Brahms and Elias were with her again, letting her forget—if only for a moment—everything else that swarmed around them.

"Aye," Brahms drawled with a laugh, casting Elias a knowing smirk as he trotted ahead.

She stole a glance at the distant silhouette of Worthyn Castle, just beginning to rise through the trees. A familiar tightness returned to her chest as they neared—unsure what waited for them, or what danger they might be walking into. With every step closer, the worry burrowed deeper.

"Prince Elias!" a guard called, slamming the butt of his spear against the stone. The horses stomped and startled in response.

Elias and Brahms tugged their reins together, and Adalja clutched tighter as the horse reared, then settled.

They waited a moment as the gates creaked open.

Adalja lifted her gaze to the towering castle before them, her eyes scanning the high windows—searching, hoping for a glimpse of Olivja. But her heart lurched.

A memory struck like a blade...the last time she'd stood in this place. Olivja had pushed her away. She had made it clear she was done with her.

Yet perhaps...time apart had softened what lingered between them. Maybe absence had made the heiress miss her. A subtle hope. A flicker of light in the dark.

Adalja clenched her jaw and held Elias tighter, grounding herself in his warmth. She repeated quiet reassurances in her mind: that everything would be well, that Olivja would hear her out.

What came after—she had no way of knowing.

Elias gently rubbed her frozen hands, his steady touch pulling her from spiralling thoughts. He lifted one of her hands, pressing a firm but delicate kiss to her reddened knuckles through the fabric of his mask.

After a brief hesitation, she sat up straight to ease off his back, and he slid from the saddle with practised ease. Adalja stayed on the saddle as Elias guided the horse to the stables, leading it into a stall beside Brahms, who had just dismounted.

"What shall we do now?" Adalja asked. The question dangled like a noose—ominous, inescapable.

Brahms glanced up, his focus shifting from the gear, to Elias, and then to her. His gaze held a silent question.

"Well..." Elias said first, his tone firm but kind. "We'll get you to the fire and into a warm bath. Your lips are pale as winter's breath."

Adalja exhaled—a sigh that released more than just air. She reached for Elias' hands, her own fingers stiff and trembling, and slid down from the saddle with as much grace as the cold allowed.

"And all else can wait until later," Brahms added, his voice low as he continued tending to the gear. He led his horse into the stall beside Elias', locking it in place with familiar ease.

Adalja nodded, her breath beginning to steady.

They weren't wrong—rushing in wouldn't solve anything. Her gaze drifted again to the looming stone walls, silently praying Olivja would be waiting...forgiving. *Understanding.*

The three of them approached the castle, Elias taking the lead. He guided them up the icy, snow-laced steps. At the doors, a guard stepped forward and opened them without a word, offering the Worthyn prince a respectful nod.

Elias returned the gesture, his hand finding the small of Adalja's back as he gently guided her inside. Brahms followed close behind, his eyes downcast, shoulders heavy with what was to greet them.

Then, breaking the heavy silence, a voice rang through the hall—sharp, commanding, and unmistakably unfamiliar.

"My prodigy returns—and with his prize in tow. Princess Adalja, no less. I knew it would be you, Elias—the one to bring her back to safety."

The voice echoed through the foyer. And for the first time, Adalja saw him. *Ezekiel Worthyn.*

The King descended the stairs with a grace that belied his power, chin held high and palms turned upwards in a theatrical display of superiority.

Tall and commanding, his long black hair flowed like a dark river down his shoulders, framing pale skin that seemed to glow against the stark contrast of his obsidian eyes. Clad in regal black and silver, he wore a silver crown that gleamed coldly atop his brow, with twin robes fastened at his shoulders sweeping behind him like moving shadows.

A hooded knight trailed at his right in tight black leathers and chain mail. The lanky jester followed on his left, descending the stairs on her hands, bandaged feet pointed skyward.

The King's grin stretched wide, but his eyes remained untouched by it. The man she'd only heard terrifying tales about stood before her now—a looming figure within the castle.

Her breath caught. He embodied every imposing detail her imagination had conjured. A shiver slid down her spine as Ezekiel strode forward and pulled Elias into a tight, unwelcoming embrace. His smile remained fixed—colder than any greeting she'd ever known.

Elias seemed to shrink beneath his father's touch. He hesitated before returning the embrace, his gaze flicking to Brahms and Adalja before he muttered, "Lord Father."

"I was not expecting you so soon," Elias added, his voice tight with discomfort.

Ezekiel let out a low chuckle as he pulled back, grasping Elias' shoulders. The bells in the jester's hair jingled as she flipped to her feet, crouching into a corner of the foyer.

"Are you not pleased to see me, son?" Ezekiel asked with a smirk that said he already knew the answer.

Adalja studied King Worthyn with a mix of curiosity and unease.

His dark eyes swept over Elias, assessing him more like a product than a son. Adalja noted how his gaze lingered—sharp, calculating, and cold.

It struck her then—no matter how unlike him they seemed, the twins still carried him. In their skin. In the cat-like shape of their eyes.

Adalja scanned the foyer, hoping to find Olivja—but instead, her gaze landed on Vincent, standing several steps behind Ezekiel. Her eyes swept over him once—something about him was different. Off. At first, she mistook him for a second Elias—until she realised it was a bruised, fractured Vincent.

The proud locks that once framed his face—symbols of strength and confidence—were gone, replaced by a rough, uneven cut.

The sight hit her like a blow—sharp and unexpected.
But it wasn't his hair alone that unsettled her.

His split lip and the dark bruise under one eye stood out—a harsh contrast to the bright, vivid green of his gaze. The prince's jaw clenched tight with tension, and his eyes—those familiar eyes—now held a hollow sadness she'd never seen before. The gaze he fixed on her was no longer warm or bold. It was cold now—tainted with contempt, and something deeper still: dread.

He didn't look like the Vincent she knew. This man was hollowed, changed. And the shadow of whatever had broken him was impossible to ignore. He took a slow, stiff step down from the platform—then another.

The truth sank over her like a winter fog, cold and suffocating: something had broken him while they were apart—and that something wore a crown.

"And sweet *Adalja*," Ezekiel drawled, savoring her name. "I've waited quite some time for this greeting."

A chill ran through her, as if every sick thought he'd ever harbored had colored his tone.

He dipped his head in a faint bow, long hair spilling over his shoulders, one hand to his abdomen—yet his eyes never left hers.

"It's a pleasure to meet your acquaintance, Your Royal Highness," Adalja said weakly. The words tumbled out without thought—her mind too preoccupied with finding Olivja.

But now, it was Elias who had the king's full attention—the golden child, the unchallenged heir, praised for every success.

Ezekiel's voice boomed with pride, "Your return to my castle, Princess Pembrook, is most welcome..." He stepped forward, opening his hand out for her, a faint gentleness in his tone.

Elias swallowed hard and glanced down at her.

Adalja was too afraid not to oblige. She took a small step forward, and the King seized her hand, yanking her the rest of the way towards him.

"A much finer version of your mother...What a shame, what happened..." He mumbled, lowering his head. "I offer my deepest condolences." His lips lingered too long on her knuckles—but she remained still.

From behind, she caught a flicker of movement—Vincent stepping forward, his brows drawn low in anger. But before he could reach them, Ezekiel released her.

Adalja stepped back to Elias, who drew her in protectively as his father straightened.

"My boy—a true man, with her by your side..." He chuckled, as if she were a treasure to be claimed. "Come now, show me the joy that fills your heart to have her back," Ezekiel smirked, arms crossing over his chest as he gestured towards Adalja.

Elias gave a faint, nervous laugh, as he tugged his mask beneath his chin. His eyes flicked to her lips as if weighing a decision.

Before she could react, before she could protest, he surged forward, his kiss crashing onto her lips with a desperate, searing intensity she hadn't expected. The sudden force stunned her—eyes wide, lips frozen in place. But Elias' desperation pushed against her resistance, pulling her into it with a roughness she wasn't used to—and never expected of him.

Her body gave in, melting against his as her eyes fluttered shut—shielding herself from the watching eyes of Vincent, Ezekiel, and Brahms.

"*Elias*!" she breathed against his lips, the word barely escaping as his kiss deepened, his grip tightening on her hips.

Her heart hammered painfully in her chest, and though she didn't understand the sudden flood of passion, she found herself giving into it—more out of fear than anything else. Fear of what Ezekiel would do if she refused to play along—if she disrupted the show.

Ezekiel stood taller, chest puffed, clearly savoring the sight of his son's boldness.
Vincent, off to the side, glared—appalled, though she didn't quite understand why.

"Ah, that's the spirit!" Ezekiel roared, clapping his hands together.

The jester mimicked its king, shaking its head side to side to jingle the bells in tandem with Ezekiel's claps. The sound echoed through the hall, a mix of mockery and triumph.

"Such is the way of a man who claims what is his—no faltering, no doubt. Bold and resolute. A true heir of Worthyn." His laughter rumbled through the room, eyes glinting with approval.

The kiss broke at last, leaving them breathless. Adalja stood, wide-eyed and parted-lipped, staring up at Elias. His quick breaths matched hers, his gaze darting across her face in search of forgiveness. For a moment, silence stretched between them, both stunned by the violence of the kiss, their faces frozen in mirrored disbelief.

Brahms cleared his throat first, the sound slicing through the silence like a razor. The sound was strained, and then Vincent scoffed—angry and sharp—snapping her attention to him.

"Enough of this. Olivja—where is she?" He tried to speak with authority, but his voice cracked halfway through. As he descended a few more steps, Ezekiel paused and turned to meet his other son's eyes.

Vincent glared at Adalja, but beneath it, confusion and worry twisted his features—unsettling her.

"What? Oli—" Adalja stammered, mind racing with fear. "Sh—she's not here?" The words tumbled out, and her chest clenched.

Had Vincent done something to her? Were her nightmares now unfolding before her? Was she too late?

"Why isn't she with you?" Vincent snapped. His shoulders trembled, breath quickening, fists clenched at his sides.

"That thought crossed my mind as well..." Ezekiel's voice cut through the air—harsh, cold—and sent a chill up Adalja's spine. Her stomach twisted, a hollow dread spreading through her. She glanced at Brahms, but his gaze flicked between her and Elias, unreadable.

Then Elias' hand slid under her arm, wrapping around her waist with unexpected force, pulling her in before she could react.

Her thoughts spiraled, the weight of the moment crashing down like icy water. *What did Vincent mean? Where is she?*

She tried to pull away, but Elias held her firm, his fingers pressing into her hip, his narrowed eyes silencing her.

"Lord Father?" Elias' voice broke through, laced with controlled concern. He tilted his head, trying to draw the king's focus back. "What are you speaking of? Where is Olivja?" His voice stayed calm, but the stiffness in his jaw betrayed what he held back.

Adalja's hand clenched his shirt. Her vision blurred at the edges as panic churned in her chest.

"She is gone." Ezekiel said, flat and final. The three of them froze where they stood.

Gone...?

Her lips parted, anger rising beneath the panic—but Elias squeezed her waist sharply, cutting the words off with a wince.

She closed her eyes, silently submitting to the pressure of his grip, her body tensing in response. When she looked up, her eyes searched his face—wide with fear, pleading for answers. But Elias refused to meet her gaze for more than a second.

He felt like a stranger now—colder, distant, unreachable. A shield had dropped over him—maybe to protect himself, or her, in some twisted way.

Brahms looked pale and hollow, more frightened than she'd ever seen him. His eyes flicked between her and Elias.

"Now...Ah, Sir Brahms..."

Ezekiel's voice was light, almost pleasant—though kindness wasn't what followed.

"The rat responsible for their deaths...You've lost not only your precious queen, but your princess as well." He stepped towards Brahms.

The princess' heart sank. She stepped forward to defend him, but Elias was faster, yanking her back with a bruising grip.

"I return to find another princess gone—and you, a rogue, standing with my son?" He loomed over Brahms, who stammered, trying to explain himself. "Since you were kind enough to save her, I'll show you mercy—a chance to be broken and trained by my men, rather than executed."

A deafening silence fell between them. Terror seized Adalja by the throat.

"Yes, My Lord...my apologies. I take all the blame," Brahms spoke softly but stood rigid, his eyes locked on King Worthyn.

"You will no longer be watching over our darling Adalja," Ezekiel said with a sly smile. The possessive tone made her flinch. "Now go," the King commanded, his voice velvety with command—its cruel undertone unmistakable. He waved a hand with lazy finality. "You have much to learn."

At once, the hooded black knight emerged from Ezekiel's shadow, like a summoned spectre. His blue eyes gleamed beneath the hood, his grin spreading as he rolled his neck—bones cracking like winter branches.

Adalja's breath caught sharp in her throat. Her gaze whipped from Elias to Brahms to Vincent—frantic, searching. But no one moved. No one stopped it.

Brahms didn't flinch. He stood tall, jaw set, eyes fixed forward like stone.

The knight approached.

Then—without a word—he cocked his arm back and slammed his fist into Brahms' face. The impact thundered through the hall.

Even the king recoiled, brows lifting with fleeting surprise.

Brahms dropped like a felled tree. A sickening crack followed, then the wet splash of blood on stone. He let out a low, guttural groan, pain ripping through him as his hands clutched his face.

"Brahms!" Adalja shrieked, her voice cracking. She lurched forward, but froze as two silver-clad knights seized him—dragging his bloodied body like a sack of meat.

The black knight followed in silence, his cloak and shadow swallowing the light as he vanished down the dark corridor.

Adalja fought Elias' grip, clawing at his arms, but he drew her back, shielding her.

"No—no!" she sobbed, her voice cracking as he cradled her against his chest. She buried her face in his tunic, her cries muffled against the fabric.

Brahms was gone.

And the king watched with idle satisfaction, as if the violence were nothing more than theater.

Elias rubbed his thumb gently along her hand, a soothing gesture that failed to reach her heart as Ezekiel stepped closer.

"P-please see me to my chambers, My Lord," she cried against him, her voice trembling and raw.

Elias nodded, jaw tight. "Yes, My Lady," he exhaled, his gaze fixed on Vincent—who turned and left—jaw clenched, eyes shadowed with concern. "Please excuse us, Lord Father..."

As Elias led her down the corridor, Adalja's thoughts churned in the silence between them.

She glanced up at him, eyes wide, brimming with tears. "Elias—Olivja, she...she would not vanish so, I—"

"I am aware, Adalja."

"And Vince..." she whispered, eyes distant. "He looked...His hair—"

"*I am aware*, Adalja," he sighed through clenched teeth as they rounded a corner.

"Elias—"

"*Adalja*." His voice was low but firm as he stopped at her chamber door, halting her with a steady hand. He pushed the door open with one hand, gently guiding her inside before letting go.

"We cannot speak of this now. I...*I must go.*"

He lifted a hand to cup her cheek, and she shook her head, lips parting in silent protest. "Adalja...*sweetling,*" he murmured, his thumb tracing her cheekbone, fingers trembling.

"I will find Olivja. I will mend this—*let me.*" His other hand rose to cradle her face fully. They stood there, still and suspended, as his green eyes searched hers with silent desperation.

These were not times for defiance—not with so much unknown.

"Tell me she lives," Adalja croaked out, body trembling, voice ragged. "*Please...*" An ache bloomed in her chest as she reached up, curling her fingers tightly around his wrists.

"I need to speak with Vincent," Elias murmured tearfully, voice tight, as he leaned in and pressed his forehead to hers.

"...Promise me you will not leave your room," he whispered, his eyes squeezing shut as if the words cost him dearly.

"Elias..."

"Swear to me you'll stay in your chambers, Adalja. Please—it is not a request." His voice was low, edged with urgency as he leaned closer.

His masked nose brushed gently against hers—a silent vow, full of warmth and warning. The warmth of it tightened in her chest, curling around her heart like a fist.

"I promise," she whispered, swallowing hard. His hands tightened on her cheeks for a fleeting moment, as though he couldn't bear to let go.

Then, with a deep, reluctant breath, they fell away.

"I will return to you," Elias promised, the words faint but certain, his green eyes never leaving hers as he stepped back towards the door.

Adalja nodded, too choked to speak, watching him slip from the room like a man stepping into the jaws of fate.

The door shut behind him, and silence swelled around her, heavy and suffocating. The stillness felt alive somehow, aching through the castle walls like a wound. A cold draft curled along the floor, biting at her skin as she stood frozen, her eyes fixed on the door.

For one helpless, foolish moment, she hoped—hoped the unruly Norsewoman she loved would burst in and sweep her into her arms.

But that moment never came.

Adalja's chest caved inward. Her knees gave way beneath her, and she sank to the floor beside her bed. Tears carved hot trails down her cheeks as sorrow's heavy flood broke over her.

Olivja was gone.

And she was certain it was by the same hand that had slaughtered her parents—the same man with the broken, boyish face who stood vacant in Olivja's absence. His shortened hair, his battered frame...was it all a mask?

The thought clawed at her chest, pressing so hard her ribs felt ready to split.

Her fears turned darker, her thoughts spiralling around Ezekiel—the shadowed ruler. Had he orchestrated this too? Had all of it been part of some greater web of cruelty?

Adalja doubled over, her body curling into itself as sobs wrenched free.

"Where are you, Olivja...?" she choked, pressing her face into the edge of her bed, clutching the sheets so tightly she thought she might tear them apart and weave a new fate from the threads.

But no fate came. No answer. No hope.

If Olivja still lived, Adalja knew—it wasn't Perdyr who had taken her.

Now, bound by her promise to Elias, all Adalja could do was wail into the hollow night, clutching her heart as if she could hold it together by force. She cried for all that had been lost, for all that was to be lost, and for every grief her heart had yet to name.

Thread LIII

ᚦᛖ ᛒᚢᚱᛞᛖᚾᛊ ᛟᚠ ᚺᛖᛁᚱᛊ ᚦᛖ ᛒᚢᚱᛞᛖᚾᛊ ᛟᚠ ᚺᛖᛁᚱᛊ ᚦᛖ ᛒᚢᚱᛞᛖᚾᛊ

ᛖᛚᛁᚨᛊ

The castle walls stood darker now, as if his father's shadow clung to every stone. The corridor torches burned low, their light flickering weakly against the suffocating stillness.

Elias moved swiftly, his boots echoing in the empty hall as he headed for Vincent's room.

Every knight he passed stood straighter, their hands firm on their swords, their eyes averted. Ezekiel's presence had settled over Worthyn like ashfall, stifling and unrelenting.

His mind raced, looping through the chaos of their return. Olivja was gone. Brahms, taken—dragged off to some unknown fate by his father's right hand.

And Vincent—the way he looked.
Elias' heart ached at the memory of him: standing tall despite the bruises, the bloodied face...and the hair, cut short.

What had father done to him?

The thought twisted in his gut, driving him faster.

Vincent needed to answer for Olivja's disappearance. But more than that, Elias needed to see him—to know he was still breathing, still himself after Ezekiel's wrath.

His brother's chamber loomed ahead, the torch beside it casting jagged shadows over the wood.

Elias hesitated, his hand hovering above the latch.
He needed answers.
He needed his twin.
Jaw tight, he cautiously pushed the door open.

The room was dark, lit only by pale daylight seeping through the arched window and the dying embers of what had once been a raging fire.

Vincent sat on the far side of the bed, head in his hands, his bare, bruised back arched and turned towards the door.

Elias stepped inside and closed the door softly behind him.

Despite the fear looming over him, Vincent didn't move—not even a flinch—as Elias entered. Either he was so used to *someone* barging in, or he no longer cared what happened when they did.

Elias lingered by the door, still as a shadow despite the desperation in his chest.

The weight of the past hours—Olivja's absence, Ezekiel's return, Vincent's bruises—pressed down on him. His gaze drifted to the empty space on the right side of Vincent's bed.

A shaky sigh escaped him. The silence between them stretched thin, too heavy to hold for long.

Eventually, Vincent shifted, casting a dark, sidelong glance over his shoulder. His left eye was swollen, the skin an ugly blend of purple and red, glossed over as though he'd been crying.

Elias stepped closer, heart sinking as Vincent slowly rose to his full height. He towered as always, though only a hair above Elias. His breathing was ragged, each breath shallow and uneven.

The closer Elias got, the worse Vincent looked. His hair was uneven and jagged, as if hacked off in a fit of rage. Thin red streaks marked the edges of his scalp where the blade had cut too close.

The sight turned Elias' stomach.

"What happened, brother?" Elias' voice trembled, betraying the nerves coiling in his chest. He stepped cautiously around the foot of the bed, desperate to meet his eyes.

Vincent met his gaze, his voice low and simmering with rage.
"Tell me true—what *you* think happened, *brother?"* he spat, venom sharp enough to cut. "Father returned."

Elias didn't flinch, though his hands trembled at his sides. He forced himself to remain steady.

"What became of Olivja? I must know." He asked, voice firm.
He hadn't meant it as an accusation, but the demand bled through all the same.

"Excuse me?" his brother hissed, green eyes burning with betrayal.

"What *madness* is this, Elias?! Did *father* ask you to question me!?" Vincent roared, his voice cracking with the force of his emotion. "I know not! How many times must I say it?! I KNOW NOT WHERE SHE IS!"

His brother staggered back, clutching his head with both hands as if to keep his thoughts from tearing loose. He dropped heavily onto the bed, each breath breaking into a frustrated groan.

Fingers tangled in his hair, tugging for a relief his hands could not give. Everything familiar had been stripped from him—torn away by Ezekiel.

"I—" Vincent's voice broke into a sob. "I was certain she was with *you*..." The words tumbled out, raw and aching. His hands dropped to his face, shoulders heaving with sobs Elias hadn't seen in months.

The strongest, most unbreakable man he knew, reduced to this—shattered and helpless. It gutted him.

Elias longed to reach out, to close the distance, but his feet stayed rooted, useless beneath him.

"Father warned me..." Vincent's voice was muffled behind his hands, quivering with grief. "He warned me what would befall me if she did not return with you..." His hands clenched into fists, knuckles white.

"If not with you...then where is she, Elias?" he shouted. "WHERE!?"
In a sudden burst of fury, Vincent sprang up, seized the bedside lantern, and hurled it at the stone wall.

The glass shattered with a deafening crash. Shards scattered across the floor as the flame flared—then caught on the debris. A small fire licked at the floor, casting wild shadows across the room.

Elias didn't hesitate. He snatched a loose sheet from the floor and smothered the flames, stamping them out in seconds. His heart thundered, but he barely heard it over Vincent's ragged breathing.

As the room stilled, Elias looked back to Vincent, now slumped on the bed, face buried in his hands again.

The room was wrecked, but Vincent was the most broken thing in it.

Elias swallowed hard, his own voice shaky as he spoke. "Then what of the Pembrooks, brother? What of *their* fate? Your hand had a play in *that*, did it not?" His words were gentle, careful—because Vincent looked like he was teetering on the edge of his sanity.

For a long moment, Vincent didn't respond. His head hung low, his shoulders trembling. When he finally spoke, it was barely above a whisper.
"Yes...It was I. Their deaths were all my doing, Elias."

Slowly, he lifted his head, his face unnervingly calm despite the bloodshot eyes and tear-streaked cheeks.

"But I swear it, brother," he whimpered, locking his gaze with Elias'—their identical eyes a reflection of two very different souls. "I did not kill my Olivja."

The silence between them stretched, their gazes locked in an unspoken battle. But Elias couldn't endure the sight of his brother—so broken, so far removed from the man he had once known.

He turned away, dragging a hand across his face, his chest tight as he struggled to steady his breath. He stopped at the window, his fingers gripping the cool stone of the frame, staring out across the vast land for a shred of clarity.

"Why?" Elias asked at last, his voice wavering with anger and disbelief. "Why kill them, Vincent—why the Pembrooks?"

"Father was going to take everything from them. Every coin. Every man," Vincent said sharply, his words coming fast as though he had practised this justification a thousand times over in his mind.

"With Adalja as the remaining heir, he can take nothing. Pembrook laws allow the husband to inherit the throne...it all belongs to you, Elias—to you and Adalja—no one else."

There was no hint of remorse in his tone, only cold conviction. The certainty in his voice sent a chill through Elias, muscles bulging as he gripped the windowsill harder. He stared out at the trees beyond the castle walls, the weight of Vincent's actions pressing down on him like a plague.

Anger flared in his chest—not only at what his brother had done, but at the sheer audacity of keeping it from him.

"And you hid this from me?" Elias asked firmly, his voice low but trembling with emotion. "We might have faced it together, Vincent. *Together*. Yet you chose to hide it. And now—three women slain to bury your sin. How could you?"

"I did this for *you*! For *us*! Can you not see it? Imagine the power he would have wielded with the Pembrooks in his grasp. He would have controlled everything! *Even Adalja*!" Vincent barked, stepping forward, his voice rising with desperation. "Do not turn your back on me, Elias!"

Elias spun around, his movements sharp and full of fury as he closed the space between them.

"I would *NEVER* turn my back on you, brother! How many times must I declare that!?" he shouted, his voice breaking as his eyes filled with tears. "*Never*! You're pained by my doubt, and yet this entire time, you've doubted *me*! *Shielded* me from your plans, *why!?*"

The room fell silent, the air between them thick with unspoken anguish. Vincent's chest heaved as he stared at his brother, his jaw clenched with fists at his sides.

"I did doubt you, Elias," Vincent said after a long pause, his voice quieter now but no less sharp. "Because you don't have the gall to do what must be done."

He paused, allowing the words to settle—to *cut*.

"Father would have twisted this family into nothing but his pawns if I let him. I saw how he looked upon Adalja...upon Olivja—as though she were naught but a *tool* to be used. I could not suffer it then—I shall not suffer it now!"

Elias shook his head, his voice full of disbelief. "So you've twisted *us*? Made us pawns in *your* game instead, Vincent?"

Vincent took a step back, his expression hardening. "We were made into pawns long ago—by *him*. This is *his* game, Eli, always has been. But I swear to you, he shall not have this victory. I care not what it does to me!"

"Listen to what you just said, brother!" Elias's voice cracked, and he gestured towards Vincent's bloodshot eyes, his bruised face, the shattered remains of the lantern on the floor. "Look at *yourself*. Look at what this has done—to us, to *Olivja*! This is no game! This is *destruction*, Vincent!"

For a moment, Vincent faltered, his gaze dropping to the floor.
Then his resolve hardened again as he lifted his head to murmur:
"But a small price to pay for vengeance."

Elias stared at his brother, his chest tight with emotion. He could see how deeply the hate for their father had settled in Vincent's bones, in his gaze, in every word he spoke.

This was no longer about family—it was about revenge.

"Then what happens next, brother?" Elias asked quietly, his voice heavy with sorrow. "What will you do *now*? What move comes next in this *game* of yours, Vincent? For I fear the depths of your wrath...the fury that knows no end. And Father—he has no more use for you, now that Olivja is..." He couldn't finish the sentence.

"Ezekiel always has a use for me." Vincent's voice broke as he sank back onto the bed, his face hidden in his hands. "Until he's sure, he'll keep me alive...and likely *beat* me every day until she returns...mould me into the perfect son...into *you*." He motioned weakly to his new short hair, scoffing in disbelief.

"He'll force the marriage between you and Adalja and then..." Vincent trailed off, his voice quiet and defeated. "*I do not know*, Elias. Without her...I'm nothing—nothing but a tool to break Ezekiel."

Eli bit his cheek at those words. They hurt. But what hurt more was knowing how right he was. His eyes stared at the broken shards of glass for a moment before a chill gripped him.

"I need you to swear to me," Elias said nervously, swallowing before he continued, "that you will not hurt Adalja or Brahms. They are not pawns—they are people...*my* people. I care not what else you do, but swear to me you'll leave them unharmed."

Vincent's gaze lingered on Elias, his bloodshot eyes unblinking.

For a moment, he didn't respond, as though weighing his brother's words. The air in the room was thicker now, the silence pressing down like a weight neither of them could lift.

"*Promise me*, Vincent," Elias whispered, stepping closer, his voice a mixture of desperation and pleading. "I can't stand by if you hurt them...they've done nothing to deserve such."

Vincent clenched his jaw, his expression tightening as the chasm between them grew. He dragged a hand through his ruined hair, fingers catching in the strands, sharp with frustration.

The gesture caught the light, a flash of pain in its wake—a reminder of how their father had carved the boy he once was into something unrecognizable.

"I cannot promise such a thing," Vincent said, his voice tight and bitter. "Not where Ezekiel is concerned. I know not what I'll be made to do to survive what's coming." He paused, his jaw easing, just enough to speak again.

"But I'll try," he added, quieter now—as if the words cost him. "For your sake...I'll do all I can to spare them."

Elias shook his head, jaw clenched as frustration flared anew.

"Try?" he repeated bitterly. "This is not a matter of trying, Vincent. I need your word. Something firm—something I can hold to. Because I cannot trust you as you are now! You've kept too much in the shadows." His hands trembled now, control slipping with every word.

Vincent's eyes dropped to the floor, unable—or unwilling—to meet Elias' gaze. He rubbed his forehead, the gesture sharp with frustration at being forced to agree.

"Very well...I swear it, Elias," Vincent muttered, the words strained. "I will not harm them. For *you*..."

Silence settled thick between them, Vincent's words lingering like smoke.

Elias exhaled slowly, his shoulders dropping in relief. He knew Vincent meant it, in his own broken way, and that was enough for now.

"Good," Elias said, his voice firm as he nodded. "I'll not suffer you to cast me aside again, Vincent. No more secrets. No more seeking vengeance alone. We stand in this together—whether it pleases you or not."

Vincent's lips curled into a bitter shadow of a smile, but he didn't argue. For the first time in a long while, the chasm between them felt narrower.

"I hear you, brother..." Vincent murmured, a flicker of vulnerability breaking through. "But *this*...this is not a burden I can draw you into."

Elias' resolve hardened, his voice steady as steel.
"I cannot accept that. You are the only one who has been fighting—"

"Because I am the name he curses most, Eli!" Vincent shouted, lifting his gaze at last—eyes shadowed with grief. "I am ruin...but you—you still have a future. Whatever chance, whatever life I had was torn away with *Olivja*."

The words hung like the ash in the air—too heavy to breathe.
Neither spoke, but at that moment, Elias understood—finally, fully.

He couldn't help Vincent on his journey, not when he had so much to lose: Adalja, Brahms, *Vincent*.

His brother—as dark as it was—only had himself left to lose.
And maybe not even that.

There wasn't a soul left in this world keeping Vincent tethered to humanity—not even Elias. Vengeance had devoured him, and Elias couldn't find it in himself to blame him. Vincent sat there—bloodied, battered, and hollowed by what Ezekiel had done to him.

This was his brother's mission alone...and though Elias feared what that meant, he knew nothing could stop him now.

Because there was no wrath like that of a man with nothing left to grieve.

Their eyes met, and in that silence, a fragile agreement passed between them.

Elias turned away, stepping to the window. His knuckles blanched against the sill once more, struggling to steady his breath.

Vincent remained still, his gaze softened—not with peace, but with a dangerous numbness.

The silence stretched between them, thick with the residue of their shared past—and the distance of their diverging futures.

"Why not run, Vincent?" Elias shuddered, a last, desperate attempt to pull his brother back from the brink. But even as the words left him, he knew they would fall on deaf ears.

This wasn't the first time they had spoken of leaving their cursed lives behind.

"I could've walked away with all I had. But I stayed..." Vincent said with a hollow scoff. "That debt will shadow me forever, Elias."

"What happened to Mora was not your fault—"

"It was," Vincent cut in, sharp and unyielding, before the argument could take root. His voice was sharp, trembling. "And same as her, Olivja is gone. And Father will have my head for it..."

Elias swallowed hard, staring at the gaping, empty hole in Vincent's bed, stained with absence.

He dared not say it outright—but the thought had gnawed at him since the moment he came back. His father's hatred hadn't changed. Not for Olivja. Not for her mother, Highwife Solvig. And least of all, not for Vincent himself.

"He won't kill you for this..." Elias whispered, voice low and wary. "But...I fear Father's wrath. And his hatred—"

He froze, eyes wide, the truth settling in with a cold finality. Vincent looked up slowly, locking eyes with Elias.

He didn't want to believe it. But how could he deny what he already knew? His father was an evil man with an eternal vendetta against Vincent, against Solvig, against *love.*

And therefore, against *Olivja.*

"...when...when did Father return?" Elias asked quietly, his voice weak with dread.

"Moments after I found her missing—" Vincent's breath froze. He shook his head, answer warring with implication. His chest heaved as he rose from the bed. He staggered to the nearby wall, bracing himself with clenched fists.

Neither needed to speak. The truth loomed between them—dark, undeniable.

"If not at Perdyr with Adalja, then..." Elias hesitated, voice faltering.

"No. *Enough*." Vincent growled, his knuckles whitening against the cold stone. His breaths turned ragged, so erratic Elias feared he might collapse. "*Do not speak another word*, Elias—"

"It had to be father who harmed her, Vincent. If you swear you had no part in this, then—"

"NO!" Vincent's roar shattered the room. His fist slammed into the wall, the force reverberating through stone.

The crack that followed wasn't in the wall. It was in him.

"NO! *NO—NO—*!" He shouted it like a mantra, his voice growing more fractured with each one. His legs buckled, and he dropped to his knees, clutching his head as a guttural growl tore from his throat.

"It can't be TRUE! It is *NOT*!" Vincent cried, his voice ricocheting off the stone walls.

But it was true. It had to be.
There was no other explanation.

With the knights gone, and Vincent bedridden—
Their father had killed Olivja.

Elias' blood ran cold. He could only stand there, helpless, as his brother shattered—grief and fury spilling from every crack.

Ezekiel had taken from him *again*, and now Vincent was nothing but a shattered, bleeding shell.

Tears welled in Elias' eyes. He longed to comfort him—but what words could ever reach that kind of pain? How do you ease the loss of someone you loved? A lover. *A friend.*

The thought tore at him, and yet he stayed where he was, silent and still, knowing Vincent had no one else.

"*My Olivja...! My sweet girl...*" He sobbed against the floor.
Vincent folded over his knees, body heaving with sobs, hands clawing at the cold stone beneath him. "*I'll kill him...I'll burn him to the ground...*"

Elias let his own tears fall in silence, guilt gnawing at his chest. He wasn't worthy of this grief. Yet it spilled from him anyway.

The thought of Olivja's last moments, alone with Ezekiel...it made him sick. They both knew of their father's anger, his hatred, his ruthlessness.

And there had been no one here to help her.

Minutes passed, broken only by the sound of Vincent's muffled cries.

Somehow, Elias found the courage to speak again.
"We will avenge her, brother."

"No." Vincent lifted his head, his tear-streaked face pale, his eyes so bloodshot they'd lost nearly all their white.

What remained in his gaze wasn't grief, it wasn't even *human*. It was pure unrelenting rage. It was the collapse of a soul.

"I will," he growled, voice low and venomous. His fingers curled into the stone beneath him, grounding himself for what came next. "I will make him suffer...I will deal with him the way he's dealt with *everything else.*"

Elias took a hesitant step forward. "Vincent—"

"*In blood.*"

Vincent's words were final—his tone hollow, yet brimming with violent resolve. His breath slowed. The fury simmered.

Elias wanted to stop him, to make him wait, to think—but he knew better. Vincent's mind was set—unmovable as stone—and nothing Elias said would break through.

He nodded, the lump in his throat making it impossible to respond. He couldn't stop his brother, and a part of him didn't even want to try.

Elias lingered, his hand twitching at his side as if he might reach out. But he didn't.

Vincent's grief was a whirlpool, violent and consuming. Elias knew better than to swim with him.

His brother stayed on the ground, hunched over his knees, fists pressed into cold stone. Vincent's breath came in harsh, uneven bursts as the grief surged back.

"Leave me, Elias," he muttered, his voice cracking.

Elias flinched. "Vincent, I—"

"*Go!*" His voice was more pain than man, "I can't stand you here any longer..."

Elias swallowed, chest tight. He stepped back, his boots scraping softly against the stone. He hesitated near the doorway, his hand brushing the cold stone frame as he looked back.

Vincent remained crumpled, head bowed, fists pressed to the floor—as if his grief alone could crush him.

Elias' voice was soft, barely audible as he whispered, "I am sorry, Vincent. " He paused, letting the words settle in the still air. "I hope you know that."

He didn't wait for a response—there wouldn't be one.

With one final glance, Elias turned and slipped into the corridor, drawing the door closed with a gentleness that belied the weight inside him. The soft click lingered in the silence, a note of finality that would not be undone.

He stood there, unmoving, staring at the dark stone across the hall as though it might swallow him whole. Then, before sense could stop him, he drifted forward until his brow struck hard against the wall. He pressed his knuckles into the unyielding surface, teeth clenched, while the vision of Olivja—gasping, breaking, beneath Ezekiel's grip—burned through him.

He did not know what to do now.

While his brother writhed in torment, he was meant to return to the bed of the woman chosen for him. To hold her, kiss her, comfort her. To play at love, while knowing his brother would never again taste the embrace of the woman he truly cherished.

And Olivja...Eli's truest companion, his oldest bond.

His heart fractured beneath the thought of her.

He drove his knuckles against the wall. Tears came hard and bright, falling like stones polished by the sun, catching light before breaking upon the floor.

"Forgive me..."
For not being there.
For not listening.
For loving Adalja.

The words barely left him, a ghost of breath cast into the emptiness, hoping some echo of her still haunted these halls.

No.

She deserved more than these halls. She deserved more than apologies.

Yet the bitterest truth was this: *Vincent deserved nothing more than her.*

And now...
She was gone.
And soon...
So will Vincent.

Thread LIV

ᚦᛖ ᛒᚢᚱᛞᛖᚾᛊ ᛟᚠ ᚺᛖᛁᚱᛊ ᚦᛖ ᛒᚢᚱᛞᛖᚾᛊ ᛟᚠ ᚺᛖᛁᚱᛊ ᚦᛖ ᛒᚢᚱᛞᛖᚾᛊ

ᚨᛞᚨᛚᛃᚨ

Weak morning light filtered through the heavy curtains of Adalja's chambers, the golden hue doing little to chase away the chill that clung to her.

She gasped awake, her chest heaving as her eyes flew open as she sat up from her bed. Her hand flew to her throat, as if she could tear free the last remnants of her nightmare.

In her mind, she could see it—the image of Olivja's lifeless body, cold and pale, as if death had stolen her warmth and left only a shadow behind. The vision was so vivid, so sharp, that for a breathless moment, she believed it was real. Adalja pressed her hands to her face, her heart slamming against her ribs.

"Olivja..." she whispered, her voice cracking with grief. The hollow ache in her chest threatened to drag her under again. She curled her knees to her chest, fighting the urge to crumble completely.

As she shifted in the large bed, her brows furrowed. She'd remembered falling asleep crying on the floor, so how did she end up in bed? Adalja sniffled, rubbing her nose with her sleeve, and that's when she smelt it.

The faintness of Elias—mint and pine—clung to her clothing, and she blushed realising he must have put her to bed. But he was no were to be found now.

Her thoughts shifted, dragging her out of the momentary haze.

Dagrun. He remained in the dungeons.

The memory crashed over her, grief replaced—if only for a moment—by duty.

Olivja was gone, but her father still lived—imprisoned and abandoned in the cold stone depths. She wondered if he even knew what had happened...

Adalja rubbed her puffy eyes, hair falling in loose strands around her damp, tear-streaked face. She breathed deeply to steady her shaking hands.

She couldn't afford to be weak now.
Olivja wouldn't have wanted her to be...

Her bare feet hit the cold stone floor, and she stood, pulling a thick robe over her shoulders.

Without hesitation, and ignoring the promise she'd made to Elias, she left her chambers. Her steps were quick and purposeful, despite the exhaustion weighing her down.

The hallways were quiet at this early hour, the castle steeped in the stillness of dawn. A few servants glanced at her as she passed, but none dared to approach. Something in her expression—unyielding resolve—kept them silent...or perhaps it was the wild disarray of her appearance.

When she reached the entrance to the dungeons, two knights stood guard, their hands resting on the hilts of their swords. They straightened at her approach, exchanging uncertain glances.

"Princess Adalja," one said cautiously. "It's a blessing to see you within these walls again, my lady. We're heartened by your return. How may we serve you?"

"My business is with Dagrun," she said firmly, her voice steady. "Let me through."

The knights hesitated, shifting uncomfortably. "Your Highness...the Viking?" one asked, trailing off.

"He is no *Viking*! And I know he's down there." Her finger jabbed towards him, patience worn thin. "Now open the door."

They exchanged another glance, but neither dared to argue further. With a nod, one of them unlatched the heavy iron door, the hinges groaning as it swung open.

"Be wary, Princess," he said softly. "He's become quite...barbaric in that cell..."

Adalja didn't reply. She stepped through, descending the narrow stone staircase that led into the dungeons.

The air grew colder with each step, the oppressive chill settling into her bones. The dim light from the torches barely reached the damp stone walls, casting long shadows that seemed to stretch endlessly.

"*EZEKIEL!!*" The voice echoed louder in her ears than off the stone walls—Dagrun's desperate cry. She gasped, surging forward at a quicker pace, desperate to reach him.

At the bottom of the stairs, the dungeon opened into a long corridor lined with cells. The air was thick with the stench of mildew and damp earth. The sound of water dripping echoed faintly. The silence pressed in—until his voice rang out again.

"ANSWER ME!" This time, a loud clang followed—metal against metal.

Her eyes scanned the cells as she ran forward, her breath catching when she saw him.

Dagrun stood against the bars, eyes wild and red-rimmed from sleepless nights and long-lost tears. His once-proud figure looked diminished, his broad shoulders hunched as though the grief and captivity had crushed him. He'd been left to rot in that cell all this time...

A soft sob escaped her as fresh tears welled in her eyes. Adalja approached his cell, gripping the cold iron bars, unafraid of him—even now, worn and wild.

"Dagrun!" she cried, her voice breaking as tears sprang to her eyes.

"Adalja—" His breath of relief misted in the cold dungeon air.

The dungeon was freezing, and she gasped as one of his shackled hands pushed through the bars, cupping her face. His hand was like ice, calloused, caked with dirt from days in his cell, and yet the touch was soft, gentle.

"Sweet Adalja..." Dagrun whimpered, his tears falling like anchors while hers clung like rain. His voice cracked around her name, as if saying it gave him a reason to hold on.

He looked broken—his eyes downcast, his pierced face streaked with dirt and grief, the once-tight braids in his hair fraying into disarray. He looked exactly how she felt inside: like a soul pulled from the wreckage.

"Olivja—is she with you?" he asked, lifting his gaze, searching her face like a man reaching for shore. "I've not heard from her—the knights give no word..."

Adalja's breath caught.

His eyes.
They were nearly the same as Olivja's, a bit darker...and sadder, lacking the same defiance and resolve. She stared into them, and for a moment, neither of them breathed.

Then a tear slid down her cheek. His shackled thumb brushed it away with a gentleness that shattered her. And her silence gave him the answer.

His hands trembled against her skin.

He nodded once. Then again...slower. As if his mind was still trying to deny what his heart already knew.

"I see..." he breathed, softer than a man ought to speak. As if louder words might break the world.

Adalja bowed her head, her voice barely escaping.

"We know not where she is, Jarl..." She hesitated, the truth tightening in her throat. "I fear—I fear she—"

"Oh, Adalja..." Dagrun's voice cracked again, higher this time, a fragile breath before a fall. "If she walks with the gods...do not fear for her."

But he was the one trembling. His hand, rough and cold, shook against her cheek. And she sobbed.

She closed her eyes tightly, letting the chill of his touch seep into her skin. It was the only thing anchoring her—the only thing that didn't vanish when she reached for it. He was the last piece of Olivja she had left. And even he was behind iron.

Why was everything she loved always just out of reach?

"I ought to have listened to her more..." she whispered through her sobs, her small hand wrapping tightly around one of his fingers—rough, calloused, worn. She clung to it like a relic. Like a memory she didn't want to fade. "*Gods forgive me.*"

She squeezed harder. As if she could hold onto the pieces of Olivja slipping away through her hands. But no warmth came from it. No comfort.

Just the hollow ache of what could've been.

"She deserved more of my heart than I gave..." The words shattered something between them.

Dagrun's jaw tensed. His expression flickered—just briefly—with pain too deep for tears. And yet, when he spoke, his voice was soft and true.

"She may be gone," he whispered, "but love still reaches her. She will feel it, wherever she walks now." His second hand reached through the bars, cupping both sides of her face, steadying her with the quiet, bone-deep strength of a Ragnarvik.

The touch felt like a lifeline—warm, grounding—but it made her ache all the more.

Because Olivja could never hold her again. She would never feel her skin, never hear her laugh rise into the wind.
Death had carved distance between them that no horse, no ship, no god could cross.

"How...?" she whimpered, her voice cracking from the strain of grief. "Please—tell me how to love her still."

Another tear slid free. Dagrun's gaze never left hers. His grip on her face tightened just enough to hold her in the moment.

"The thought that love ends with death..." he began, voice firmer now—anchored in something older than both of them, older than grief. "That is a coward's lie. Spoken by those who've long forgotten what love truly is."

He leaned forward, like he was passing her a sacred truth.

"Love is not flesh and bone. It is the soul's fire—it stays. It lingers in what we do, in the sagas we carry forward. It's there in every act of honor, in every tale spoken to keep her name alive."

Adalja's breath caught. Her tears paused, just for a heartbeat, as she stared up at him.

"The sea may crash against the shore, Adalja...but the land—*the love*—remains." He spoke it like a phrase passed down. A saying etched into memory. A promise. Maybe he had spoken it to Olivja once.

The sting of her absence burned sharper, but his words settled deep—like soil laid over a grave. Heavy, yes. But necessary.

"Do not abandon her now," he whispered. "Carry her closer."

The silence that followed was full. Adalja could hear her own heartbeat, steady and aching.

Carry her closer.

She closed her eyes again, clinging to the thought. Perhaps love didn't end. Perhaps it was only the beginning of something deeper, something that could still burn brightly in her heart even after Olivja was gone.

"I will," she said with a shaky breath, her voice barely audible. "I will carry her with me...always."

"Good." Dagrun nodded firmly. His rough hand slipped away from her face, the moment dissolving into the cold, unforgiving presence of the bars between them. "Because...I have something for you. Something of *hers*."

Her eyes widened, her hands going still against the bars as she searched his face for meaning.

"In my room," he continued, his voice quieter now, "under the bed—there's a chest. Full of letters. Your father's hand. *Olivja's*. Mine." He sighed shakily, his words weighed down by grief.

"Your father kept them all this time. Said it was right they return to me. But...with how things have gone—" He faltered, his hand briefly resting on the bars as he gathered his composure. "They carry words meant for your eyes, not mine."

The letters.

Adalja gasped, her chest tightening as a flood of emotions threatened to overwhelm her—excitement, relief, and an unrelenting desperation to read the words from Olivja that she never had the chance to hear.

"Go," Dagrun urged softly, a faint, quivering smile tugging at his lips as he saw the surge of hope in her eyes. "Find them. Find her love."

Adalja stepped back, her eyes lingering on his familiar, yet broken face for just a moment more. Then, driven by an urgency she couldn't contain, she ran up the stairs, her feet barely touching the ground as she rushed towards Dagrun's room, towards any piece of Olivja she could cling to.

As she pushed open the heavy doors, the bright foyer greeted her, its sunlight momentarily blinding. She squinted, her vision slowly readjusting. When her eyes opened again, they landed on a towering figure.

"Darling Adalja." Ezekiel's voice slithered towards her, sending a chill straight through her chest.

He was standing too close, his hands reaching out to capture her arms. She jumped at his touch, a jolt of panic thudding through her. She looked up at him, standing there in her nightgown, cheeks flushed with a mix of surprise and fear.

"Well met, as if by design," Ezekiel continued, his voice smooth but dripping with condescension. "You've much to prepare for the evening's hour...and yet look at you—wandering as one in a dream, princess."

His words dripped with mock kindness, but the underlying patronizing tone made her blood run cold. He didn't wait for any response, his eyes passing over her with disinterest as if she were of no consequence.

Without sparing her a second glance, he turned away, his sharp command echoing through the hall.

"Have her escorted to her room, and then to my son's...we wouldn't want to lose her a *second* time." He snapped his fingers, and at once, the knights moved, their steps synchronised as they approached her.

One of them placed a firm, yet gentle hand on the small of her back, urging her forward.

Adalja hesitated, her heart pounding as her thoughts returned to Olivja's letters—waiting beneath Dagrun's bed. She glanced back at Ezekiel as he descended into the dungeon, but there was no time to waste, no space for her to make her own choice.

She looked up at the knights—silent, emotionless figures who did nothing but obey, their presence cold and unyielding. Ezekiel's command loomed over her, pushing her towards the unknown.

THREAD LV

ᚦᛖ ᛒᚢᚱᛞᛖᚾᛋ ᛟᚠ ᚺᛖᛁᚱᛋ ᚦᛖ ᛒᚢᚱᛞᛖᚾᛋ ᛟᚠ ᚺᛖᛁᚱᛋ ᚦᛖ ᛒᚢᚱᛞᛖᚾᛋ

ᚨᛞᚨᛚᛃᚨ

ADALJA SAT IN THE MIDDLE OF ELIAS' LARGE, ORNATE BED, the soft silk of her silk gown clinging to her damp skin as she twisted her wrists in the ropes that bound her to the headboard.

The room around her was eerily quiet, save for the occasional clank of knights' footsteps in the hall, or the faint rustling of wind against the window. The air thickened as if the very walls were closing in around her with each passing minute.

It was Ezekiel's idea to leave her tied...and the echo of his words made her anger flare.

"So you'll give my son no cause for struggle."

The bed was too soft—mocking, even. The pale grey and black colours of the room only deepened her sense of disconnection.

Her hair, once flowing freely, now lay in delicate curls, combed through after a bathing. Her makeup—meticulously applied to cover the dark circles under her eyes—had begun to smudge with the dampness of her silent cries.

She tugged at her wrists again, the ropes biting into her skin—a cruel reminder: she wasn't free. A prisoner, even in love. Yet the coarse rope felt gentler than the reality that awaited her.

Even as tears pooled in her eyes, she pressed her lips together, willing herself to stay composed, to not ruin the illusion of the woman she was meant to be.

The door creaked open, and a faint chill washed over her.

Her white-haired prince stepped into the room. As he saw her tear-streaked face, his own eyes welled, his expression twisting in shock.

"*Elias!*" Her voice broke as she yanked at her wrists.

Elias rushed to her, a shadow darkening his face. He cupped her face, thumbs brushing beneath her eyes.

"*Forgive me, Adalja...*I have you now. I'm here..." he whispered, and her body slumped with relief.

Once her tears stopped, he turned to the ropes, tugging frantically.

He stopped short.

The door creaked open—
King Ezekiel stepped in, and the room darkened.
Adalja's stomach turned.

He wore dark, draping robes, a pointed silver crown resting atop his ink hair. He smirked at the two sitting in bed. Adalja drew her knees closer, nausea blooming in her gut as he stalked forward.

"Lord Father." Elias shot to his feet.
"What is the meaning of this?" he asked, blocking Adalja's trembling frame.

"I am here to witness the consummation, my son. To be certain you honour your duty—as a man and as her lord." He crossed his arms, a smug glint in his eyes.

Her face drained of colour. Elias looked just as pale, his eyes flicking sideways to Adalja.

"No..." Adalja whimpered, shaking her head at Elias, who stood frozen in place.

Ezekiel tilted his head slowly, a smirk forming before he chuckled. A dark sound that raised the hairs on her arms and legs.

"Lord Father, th-this is meant for *after* the vows, we cannot, in good faith—"

"You are to be sent to the battlefields come morrow, my son. There will be no time for *bedding*. You will do it now—"

"No," Elias said sharply, voice firm with command.

For a moment, reassurance bloomed—fragile, fleeting. Safe, even.
But not for long.

"No?" Ezekiel laughed at his son's defiance. "I will not ruin *all* of your fun, my boy. I'm only here to *confirm* it. You should be grateful I am allowing you to defile her early."

"Lord Father, I will not allow this—"

Ezekiel came closer with a boldness that silenced all—even the wind at the shutters seemed to still. His eyes bored darkly into Elias, now standing less rigid, his confidence faltering.

"You have no choice." His father chuckled darkly. "And you do not order me, *boy*. You will *allow* what I say and nothing more."

It was a simple sentence, but the warning sat heavy.

Ezekiel waited, as if half-expecting further defiance from Elias, before he nodded with a smirk.

"*Good*. Now...let us resume," he said, repositioning himself across the room, settling into the oak chair beside Elias' desk.

"Lord Father—"

Ezekiel only stared, his face void of the smugness it once held. They had no choice.

"You will have her submit, as is her place, and I shall bear witness to it, as your King and your father." His voice was matter-of-factly—only adding to the sinister weight of his words. "I will not speak it twice."

It shook them both to the core. Even their eyes failed to weep in front of the King.

Adalja clenched her jaw, dragging her gaze from Ezekiel to meet Elias' as he slowly turned.

"Elias..." Adalja whispered, a sound more whimper than word.

Her prince came closer, his face shadowed with duty. With a trembling hand, he slowly pulled back the blankets, revealing her bare legs as he kneeled beside her. His movements were slow and controlled, as though afraid he might hurt her.

Adalja looked up at him as he shifted closer, his hand gliding over her towards the knots at her wrists. He hovered above her.

"Let me help you out of these first..." he murmured gently, his fingers returning to the knot as her hands twisted for freedom.

"*At-at-at*...my son. The ties are tradition—they shall not be undone," Ezekiel said firmly, his tone leaving no room for argument. "Your mother and I weren't much keen on them, but you'll learn to love them all the same."

The vile comment left Ezekiel's mouth with ease—like a tale he'd told dozens of times. Adalja's stomach churned, sick with dread. She was about to become one of his wedding stories he would tell to his courts.

Elias' gaze, dull and dazed, lingered on the rope before his fingers moved—hesitating, then slowly curling around her wrists.

"I'd much prefer silence," he growled through gritted teeth, not at her, but at the man behind them.

His eyes dropped to Adalja's.
She saw it—*regret*.
A quiet sorrow for what he was being forced to do.

Her breath hitched. She closed her eyes for a moment, bracing herself, then nodded. A small, solemn gesture of consent.

It was nothing like she had imagined her first time would be, nothing like what she had once dreamed. Yet it was him, and for that alone she tried to be thankful. If it was inevitable, she could only surrender to it.

Elias shifted, his movements deliberate as he repositioned himself between her legs. Adalja inhaled sharply.

His touch was careful—detached. His hands, firm yet distant, rested atop her outer thigh, just below the edge of her gown. Lace and silk brushed her skin as he lifted the fabric—just enough to reveal the barest glimpse beneath.

Her fists clenched where they hung, suspended above her head, wrists bound to the wooden headboard. Her breath trembled, but her eyes never left him—tracking every cautious, calculated motion.

Then, with a sharp tug, Elias drew the blanket over them both, pulling it high to shield her as best he could. A barrier of cloth between her body and the perverse gaze that watched from across the room.

"Ah...Look at the pair of you—soft as wine, are you?" Ezekiel chimed in, a showman's smirk curling his lips, as though he knew their secrets better than they ever could.

She swallowed hard, her heart pattering faster at the realisation; his father truly meant to stay and watch. There would be no escape.

Elias leaned in close. "I have you...*breathe...*" he whispered, sharing a gentleness no one else could hear—not even his father.

She let a slow breath roll from her parted lips as he leaned in even closer, his lips brushing the shell of her ear.

"*You're safe with me*," he promised. His voice was firm, even in its softness, as his lips feathered against her ear, sending a chill through her.

She *did* feel safe with him. If it had to be anyone, she welcomed it being Elias. Adalja swallowed the dryness in her throat, accepting the role forced upon her—accepting this was who she had to be now.

Elias' wife.

His touch moved slowly between them, his lips tender as they brushed beneath her ear and trailed along her jaw towards her lips.

He hesitated as he came face to face with her, his breath fanning her face as she looked up at him. Their eyes locked in silence as he tugged down his trousers—only revealing what he must.

"I trust you," she whispered against his lips, breathless. Still, her eyes stayed fixed on his face, too afraid to look anywhere else.

He captured her lips in a gentle, languid kiss, a stark contrast to any they'd shared before.

This one felt like a reassuring touch, one of love and genuine regret. His mouth moved slowly against hers, their lips melding together perfectly as she let her eyes flutter closed, needing to forget where they were and who was watching.

"Enough of this hesitation, Elias—*get on with it*," King Ezekiel snapped, urgency sharpening his voice.

Adalja wanted to curl into herself as Elias positioned himself. His glare burned down at her body. Not meant for her, but for his father.

His eyes returned to Adalja's before he kissed her again.
A distraction from the pressure they were both about to endure.

She winced into his kiss, her eyes clenching shut as he bedded her—slow, steady, and full of unspoken apology.

His chest heaved as he rolled his hips into her, slowly, several times. A tear slipped from her eye, caught gently by his thumb.

A chill traced both their spines as Elias leaned closer, hiding his face against hers while his other hand reached for the headboard. Instead, his palm wrapped around her wrists—his gentleness speaking the sorrow he couldn't voice.

His grip on her hip tightened with each deepening thrust, soft grunts pressing against her ear. For a moment, only the rocking of the bed and heavy breaths filled the room.

"There's the man I raised!" Ezekiel bellowed—startling them both, shattering the fragile concentration shielding them from their pain.

Adalja flinched slightly, her hands tugging at the ropes enough to make her skin burn. As he continued, Elias' fingers curled around hers in quiet reassurance.

Though soon, his breaths turned to grunts, and Adalja answered with whimpers, letting the prince claim her lips with loving kisses.

He released her wrists, shakily cupping her cheek instead. His eyes brimmed as he looked into hers—both red and wet with tears; a mirrored ache, a shared pain.

"*I've got you, darling,*" he exhaled, voice trembling.
His movements slowed, breath still heavy. She winced, leaning into his damp, firm touch.

"A true Worthyn." His father grunted—sated, proud, as though Elias had proven himself at last.

Her heart ached as she tugged at the ropes again, as if she might somehow break free.

Elias shook his head, closing his eyes tightly as though he could escape from this moment. He groaned, the sound catching, choked pain rising in his throat.

She wanted to disappear entirely, but Elias' weight above her anchored her to some twisted semblance of love, carried with each push of his hips.

"I love you, Elias," she moaned, lips parted in a breath, desperate to cradle him with words—the only way she still could.

It was the first time she had spoken it aloud, but she had to. She longed to. *He was the last she could ever love*, and she would love him with all that remained of her.

His tear-filled green eyes met hers, relief flashing across his face as he lowered his brow to hers, foreheads gently touching.

"I love you," she whispered again, breath trembling against his skin.

He kissed her with protective comfort—a slow, tender contrast to the urgency below, where his movements grew strained, trembling with the weight of ending. His hand eased from her cheek and found purchase against her bound ones once more, as if he was bracing himself even now.

He grunted softly into her mouth, then louder, breath hitching against her lips as though the pleasure, the pain, the rawness of it all was being pulled from him with every thrust. Each push came heavier, more desperate, as if he could pour every apology into her before the moment finished.

And perhaps that was enough—for at last, Ezekiel left.

The door shut behind him, leaving them alone once more.

"Elias," she breathed into his mouth, her eyes fluttering open only to find his still clenched shut.

"Eli—" she whimpered, but his tongue swallowed the sound, lost in the fever of the act. She kissed him again, a trembling exhale spilling into him: "It is done." She tore her mouth aside to release the words, desperate to be heard.

He lifted his head, locking eyes with her—his tear-reddened gaze finding hers. His body trembled as his movements slowed to a stop.

"Rest now," she cried. "It's finished." Her words were breathless, her heart breaking at the sight of Elias so undone.

Sweat beaded across his brow, his hair in disarray, lips parted in ragged panting. He released her fingers only to cradle her cheek, his thumb brushing her skin with a trembling breath.

His head dipped in a faint nod, though his eyes darted once to the place where his father had sat, still wide with fear. When they returned to her, they faltered—falling to where their bodies were joined.

With a strangled grunt, he withdrew—swift, careful, yet broken. Their bodies parted, and with it the fragile illusion of unity.

Clothing was pulled on in silence until they were no longer one but returned to themselves. His hands flew to the ropes, a sob breaking loose in his throat.

They had survived, perhaps—but the pain, the grief, lingered in every part of them.

"Adalja, forgive me, *please,*" he begged, shaking his head as tears streamed faster than before.

As soon as the ropes were undone, he cupped her face, gently forcing her to meet his gaze.

She wrapped her arms around his neck, drawing him into her chest as they both wept, softly yet unrestrained.

His sobs muffled into the crook of her neck as her hand tangled in his hair, hushing him through her own dread.

They lay together, granting one another the space to feel—to mourn the devastation forced upon them.

In that shared silence, they found a fragile comfort neither dared to break.

Elias spoke first, his voice breaking against her skin, tears soaking into the fabric of her gown. "I would give all to undo this...*Forgive me, my love.*"

Adalja gently nudged him back, urging his gaze to meet hers. Her fingers trembled as they brushed the tears from his cheeks.

"*Please*, I do not blame you," she whispered, soft sorrow threading through her voice.

Even in the face of her mercy, Elias could not stop crying. His eyes darted away, unable to meet her gaze. He shook his head, his throat working to hold back the sobs rising within.

"Elias...?" she breathed, heart aching at the sight of him unravelling. "This marriage is not ruined because of this. My love for you will not diminish—"

"I have no place beside you, Adalja...I am not deserving of this," he cut in, a whimper escaping him as he turned his face, pressing a hand over his mouth, as though holding back something deeper—something buried in shame.

Adalja choked on a soft cry; his anguish pierced her soul.
"My sweet prince...*hush now*...why do you say such things?"

Elias' voice came low, almost broken:
"Because Adalja—I have no place beside a woman."

He faltered, his chest shuddering as though the words themselves wounded him.

"It is men who hold my heart."

A heavy silence followed.

He said it like it seared him.
It shattered her.

She needed a moment to cradle the sorrow of his revelation. Her heart ached—not from heartbreak, but from the torment he had endured—by his father, and by her.

"*Oh...Eli*," Adalja breathed, a quiet, aching whimper.

She reached for him, her hand moving with care to cradle the back of his head, and gently guided him back into the crook of her neck. He cried there, and she let him—no longer hiding his sorrow, no longer alone in his truth.

She understood.
The fear. The weight. The cost of carrying a secret like that for so long.

And more than anything, she felt honoured that he had chosen her—trusted her—with it. Even if it came at a painful time for him.

"*Forgive me, Addy,*" he choked out, his back no longer steady—racked with fear, stripped by shame.

But she shook her head.
"You do not deserve to feel shame for such feelings," she whispered against the crown of his head.

"My heart shall ever be a place for you—*no matter the rest.*" Her voice cracked on the words, heavy with emotion, but she knew he needed to hear them.

Elias' sobs softened, his head nodding faintly against her. He didn't speak, didn't move much—but he didn't pull away either.

They shifted, slowly, and Elias drew her onto his chest. His face was pink with tears, his eyes puffy, lips parted as he lay back against the pillows. Though he stared numbly at the ceiling, his burdens had not *completely* extinguished the life in his gaze—dimmed, yes, but not gone.

He held her tightly, as if afraid to let go of his truest companion. And Adalja sank into him, wrapping herself around his quiet, impossible strength.

His fingers curled protectively at her side. His other hand moved in slow, calming paths up and down her arm.

She lay her hand across his chest and listened to the steady rhythm of his heartbeat. Proof they were still alive...even after everything.

Her eyes were closed, her hand gently clenched in his tunic for comfort. Then she felt it—that subtle skip in his heartbeat—just before he spoke.

"I love you, Adalja," he whispered, his breath trembling. "*I swear it.*"

And she believed him.

A tear slipped free, trailing down her cheek as she smiled into the warmth of his chest.

They would forever be tied together; a bond no betrayal, lie, or death could break. A tether that would defy the odds of fate, bound in ways only they would ever know.

And with that silent vow, they lay in stillness, holding fast to the only comfort left to them: *each other.*

Thread LVI

ᚦᛖ ᛒᚢᚱᛞᛖᚾᛊ ᛟᚠ ᚺᛖᛁᚱᛊ ᚦᛖ ᛒᚢᚱᛞᛖᚾᛊ ᛟᚠ ᚺᛖᛁᚱᛊ ᚦᛖ ᛒᚢᚱᛞᛖᚾᛊ

ᛖᛚᛁᚨᛊ

Knock. Knock. Knock.

"Come now, son!" Ezekiel's loud voice rang out, followed by a deep, rumbling laugh from outside the door. "Spare the poor lady her burdens and make merry!"

Elias sat up slowly, rubbing the exhaustion from his face with the back of his hand. His chest was heavy, and his mind swam in the aftermath of the night.

"Stay..." Adalja breathlessly begged, her fingers trembling as they curled around his bicep, her face twisted with fear at what he might face on the other side.

"I must go, my love, but I shall return," he promised, his voice quiet and strained. He exhaled a shaky breath, trying to steady himself. "I have never failed a promise to you, nor shall I begin tonight."

Leaning in, he placed a soft kiss on her cheek, the briefest touch that lingered. He hoped it conveyed all the gratitude, pain, and regret.

That kiss, like so many other things between them, was a fleeting moment of tenderness amidst the chaos.

The two shared a final, wavering glance before Elias pulled away. He fixed the clasps on his vest, lifted his mask, and set it in place to hide the storm brewing in his expression.

The last thing he wanted was to face his father after what he had done to them, but there was no choice. He couldn't keep Adalja close when his father was already closing in. He didn't trust Ezekiel enough to let him near her, not after all that has happened.

Elias gave her one last look before stepping out of the room.

In the hall, Ezekiel stood tall, a wicked grin playing on his lips. Vincent followed, stone-faced, his eyes lowered in quiet understanding. His brother had always known—better than anyone—who Elias truly was.

"And now, we celebrate as men," Ezekiel boomed, slapping Elias heavily on the back, directing him down the hall towards the king's study. His grip was firm, almost suffocating, like he was trying to pull Elias further into his world.

Elias shot a dark, sideways glance towards Vincent, whose glare was sharp but silent. Nothing good would come from this night—it never did when they were summoned by their father.

Vincent trailed loosely behind them, his posture stiff, his silence louder than any words. The way their father clung to Elias like this—pushing Vincent aside, always setting him in the shadow—cut deeply into Elias. He hated the favouritism, hated the reminder of how much Vincent was always left in the dark.

When they reached the study, Ezekiel entered without hesitation, striding towards the massive wooden table where most of his royal dealings took place. On top sat several carafes of mead, their amber contents catching the low torchlight, the thick aroma already blooming through the air—warm, indulgent.

Elias inhaled without meaning to.
It smelled like what always came next: excess. Escape. Numbness.

Above them, hanging upside-down from a thick beam, was Nimble. They plucked slow, delicate chords from the lute strung across their chest—faint, distant notes that hovered like smoke.

Ezekiel slapped a heavy hand down on the table.

"We drink, my son! To victory! To blood! To the future!" He poured himself a full goblet, gold spilling over the silver rim, then shoved the carafe towards Elias with a grin that held too many teeth.

"Down you come, pretty Thing," he called up to the ceiling while reaching his chair.

Nimble's fingers froze on the strings.

"Give me a show...let me look at what's mine," their father added. His voice, oddly gentler now—almost a plea. Not quite a command. Not quite affection. Something warped and in-between.

Ezekiel leaned back in his chair, eyes leaving his sons entirely. He watched the jester instead—his broken centrepiece.

Nimble twisted. Their lute slid across their back as pale hands gripped the beam.
Then, without ceremony, they dropped.
This time, they didn't land with grace.

They hit the ground with a hard thud, their thin frame collapsing to the floor in a heap of limbs and bells. The lute clanged against stone, and the room seemed to flinch with the noise.

Ezekiel chuckled softly to himself, amused by them in all ways.

"Do not stop until I say," he murmured.

From the floor, the jester's legs curled up and over—folding above their head in a slow, inhuman arc, like something boneless. Their body twisted and writhed as they pushed up into a bridge, then flung into a backbend that snapped their heels over their head.

Elias remembered this. These *performances*. These grotesque displays that his father so loved. The way Nimble became a thing to be bent, and thrown, and shaped into whatever Ezekiel desired.

His father's little creature.
His *delicate abomination*.

Elias' hands curled into fists as the jester kicked their legs towards the ceiling and spun in a tight circle. Their braids jingled faintly with each flick of their limbs. One leg pointed to the stone, the other skyward, their hands bearing their entire weight as they moved with eerie grace.

Even Vincent was still, silent. His face unreadable—but his eyes, like Elias', were full of something closer to sorrow than awe.

Only Ezekiel smiled.

"Perfect..." he cooed into his drink. "*My broken doll.*"

Nimble lowered their feet to the floor again, arched into a deep, unnatural bend, and slowly pulled themself upright. They kept moving—flipping, twisting, contorting.

Not like a dancer. Not like a court jester.
Like an eel, knotting to evade a blade.

And Ezekiel? He drank. He watched. He hummed. He let the pretty illusion keep him warm.

Eventually, his eyes returned to Elias, the jester momentarily forgotten.

"Now," he said, voice rough with mead and amusement, "you've earned your share, haven't you?"

A long pause.

"Tell me...what was she like? A fire in her like her mother's?"

Elias met his father's gaze for a moment, the bitterness swirling inside him. He grabbed a silver goblet, filled it with the amber liquid, and raised it to his lips. The mead burned slightly on the way down, hot and sweet.

He didn't want to drink it. Didn't want to play this game. But he had to, didn't he?

He glanced over at Vincent, who had already taken a seat across the table, eyes staring down at his untouched cup. Vincent's jaw was clenched, his posture rigid with restraint. Years of being overlooked wore on him just as much as the weight of their father's expectations.

"Drink up, Vincent!" Ezekiel bellowed, pouring a cup for his brooding son and pushing it towards him.

Vincent's eyes flickered to Elias once before he relented, taking his drink up in a delicate, bruised hand without a word.

The two brothers clinked their cups, the sound hollow in the tension-heavy air. Neither truly wanted this celebration, but it was expected.

"None like the fire in Olivja, though...The pleasure it would have given me to see a Worthyn tame a beast like that." Ezekiel's voice dropped to a growl—timed perfectly as Vincent brought the cup to his lips. He drank without thinking, forced to swallow as if to toast the very words.

Ezekiel smirked. "But...*alas*."

Elias' eyes shot to Vincent, who slowly lowered his drink and set it on the table with a thud—his face numb, blank.

For the briefest moment, Elias told himself Olivja was better off dead than tied to Vincent's bed, the way Adalja was to his. He could only imagine the horrors that would have transpired behind those doors.

"To my kingdom," Ezekiel declared, breaking him from his dark thoughts, raising his cup high. "To *my* bloodline."

Elias took another sip, tasting the bitterness of both the mead and the moment. This was the life they were trapped in—honour without love, legacy without meaning.

And so, they drank—the twins less than the king.

At some point, his empty goblet slammed down onto the table, and Ezekiel spoke again, his voice taking on a more menacing tone.

"Concerning the Pembrooks...a sorrowful end. A shame indeed, wouldn't you say, Vincent?" His tone was harsh, accusatory—the anger was clear. They caught it in seconds, exchanging a glance before responding.

"Yes, Lord Father," Vincent said dully, his voice flat. He hadn't touched his mead since the first sip, though he reached for the cup again.

"*Hm...*" Ezekiel chuckled darkly. "Which of you thought it wise to kill them?" His voice grew sharp, anger rising with every word.

Both boys went still. *Silent.*
And so he continued.

"You thought I'd be taken in by your fake hanging? Even Olivja, simple as she may be, saw through your trick—now SPEAK!"

When he yelled, Nimble's bells rattled and clanged. They had fallen to the floor again. Perhaps to make Ezekiel laugh, to lighten the tension...or maybe even in fear. But as swiftly as they fell, they resumed their dance, only now their eyes stayed on the king.

Elias' stomach churned. He already knew where this was going, and his body tensed, his hand tightening around the goblet.

"Lord Father—if I may, the Pembrooks were—"

"*For once*, my son, I care not what you have to say," Ezekiel interjected, grinning, his eyes narrowing with venom.

And from the corner of his eye, Elias saw Vincent—always so controlled—tilt back his cup and down the remaining mead. He set the empty goblet down slowly, wiping the corner of his mouth with a smirk that didn't quite reach his eyes. His voice came calm—*too* calm.

"You demanded results. The marriages are secured. I assumed you'd be pleased." He shrugged, nonchalant, as if daring Ezekiel to strike him. "If that's not what you meant, I beg your pardon. You mustn't leave such matters to a simpleton like me...lest I bring ruin to all."

Elias froze. His eyes widened as he stared at his brother, silently pleading with him to stop.

But Vincent stood firm. His expression, vacant. His resolve, unshaken. It was as if he had already accepted this confrontation as inevitable—*welcomed* it. Like he needed to push as far as possible, just to convince himself that whatever followed...was deserved.

"PLEASED!?" Ezekiel roared. His face turned red as he rose in a flash, arm sweeping across the table in a violent burst. Goblets, papers, and mead crashed to the floor in a thunderous clatter.

Shock rippled through the room.

But Vincent didn't flinch.

The bells had gone silent.

Nimble knelt in the centre of the room, their chalk-covered hands trembling against their bare stomach, eyes wide and locked on Ezekiel.

"Leave," the king growled, as though aware of how deeply he was frightening them. Nimble hesitated for only a moment before crawling out, braids and bells dragging softly behind. Ezekiel's breathing was ragged, his chest rising and falling with fury.

"Were this truth to reach the ears of our allies, they would forsake us in an instant," he hissed. "And if the Ragnarviks learned the Pembrooks died by *our* hand—there would be no future left to grasp. All would be lost!"

Elias' heart pounded, as if it was trying to break through his chest and run away. He stepped back from the table, breath quickening, eyes darting between his father and Vincent.

And still—Vincent was calm. He swirled the final drops of mead in his goblet, as though the king's fury were nothing more than background noise.

"Well..." he cooed, his voice smooth, yet laced with something far more dangerous, "...blessed thing we still have Dagrun, isn't it? All you need do is release him—and the Ragnarviks will come flocking to your aid, *Ezekiel*."

A chill ran through Elias. But a fire sparked in the king.

"*Put. That. Down.*"
Ezekiel's voice turned to ice—quiet, deadly, pulsing with fury as his fists clenched at his sides.

Vincent obeyed. He placed the cup down with slow deliberation, a sardonic grin tugging faintly at his lips.

But Elias knew it wasn't over. Not by a wide measure. The tension in the room was suffocating. Elias's blood ran cold; the threat in the air was palpable.

Without warning, Ezekiel lunged, his hands crashing into Vincent's chest with a guttural snarl. Before anyone could react, the king seized him, hurling him to the ground with a sickening thud.

The sound reverberated through the room, leaving a stunned silence in its wake.

Vincent didn't flinch. He lay there for a moment, still and quiet, his chest rising and falling with slow, deliberate breaths. Then, with a movement as casual as before, he pushed himself up from the floor, his expression unchanged.

But Elias knew the damage was done.

His heart roared in his ears, and the violence pressed down on him. He couldn't bear it anymore—the crushing weight of his father's rage, the sickening sound of Vincent's grunts of pain.

Without a word, Elias backed away, each step feeling heavier than the last. It was the final blow to his night—enough to break him.

He watched as Ezekiel leaned in close to Vincent, his hands reaching for him again, and it was too much.

Elias turned, forcing himself not to look back.
He couldn't.

As the door clicked shut behind him, Elias' breath caught in his throat.

"*GET UP, BOY,*" his father's voice echoed through the thick walls, a brutal command that made Elias' heart and stomach sink to the floor.

The sickening sounds that followed—flesh colliding, Vincent's muffled grunts—made it worse, as though his heartbeat had synced with the violence in that room. It dragged him back, pulling him into the darkness of his memories, to when they were children, cowering beneath their father's wrath.

Elias' eyes watered, but he didn't allow the tears to fall.
Not here. Not now.

Not while Vincent had a truer reason to cry.

He turned, his feet moving almost of their own accord as he stepped away from the room, the cries behind him growing louder with every step. His chest tightened, each beat of his heart thudding hard against his ribs.

Where could he go?

He couldn't seek Brahms. And Adalja...he couldn't bear to look her in the eyes, not like this. Not after everything.

So he left the castle.
His steps were heavy. His mind, numb.

The cool night air met him like a slap to the face as he climbed up to the terrace on the roof. The stars above blinked quietly, offering little comfort for the flood of sorrow inside him.

Tears spilled freely down his cheeks. His hands trembled as he braced himself against the stone ledge. He stared out over the shadowed kingdom, desperate to think of *anything* other than the violent echo of their father's rage.

For a moment, all he could hear was the rush of his own breath. The relentless beat of his heart.

And as the wind stung his face, Elias thought of better days—days when the halls were filled with warmth, Vincent would race him to the roof, when laughter lived in the walls, and when he didn't feel like he was drowning.

But those days were gone. Now, it was only him up here.
Alone.

Tonight, the past had finally caught up to him.

The burden of being a brother...had proven too steep.

THREAD LVII

THOUGH THEIR NIGHT BEGAN IN MISERY, it ended in something softer—almost sweet.

Elias returned after an hour or two, sliding silently into bed beside Adalja.

Heavier than when he left. Quieter than before.

She felt the silent apology in the way he pulled her close, his face buried in her hair.

For the first time, Adalja slept in the arms of someone she knew would keep her safe—someone who loved her, even if not in the way she wished deep down. They simply held one another until exhaustion claimed them both.

But now, the other side of the bed lay empty, and Elias was nowhere in sight.

The morning of her wedding dawned quietly, but Adalja awoke with a heavy heart.

She lay in Elias' bed, still warm where her prince had been just hours before. The memory of his arms wrapped securely around her sent a strange pang of longing through her chest.

Soon—in the eyes of the court, of God—they would be one.

Adalja sighed, rubbing the sleep from her eyes as flashes of the night before replayed in her mind—the sound of his barely contained sobs, whispered confessions, and vows.

She understood who he was now, what he wanted—and what he did not. Yet the ache of his absence radiated through her.

Yawning, she pushed the memories aside and swung her legs over the mattress's edge. A soft groan slipped from her lips as her body tensed beneath the day's weight.

She needed to bathe—to shed the emotions clinging to her like a second skin.

Slipping out of her silk gown, she reached for a robe and wrapped it tightly around herself. The soft fabric brushed her skin, and her heart clenched with quiet pain, recalling the last time she had worn it...

"Lady Adalja?" A soft knock.

Sapphire's gentle voice slipped through the cracked door as it creaked open. "It is time to get ready, my dear," she whispered low, her smile small and tight.

Adalja gave a stiff nod, her stomach twisting with unease. Her voice came cold and flat—mirroring the tension caged within her chest. "*Indeed.*"

After her bath, she was led back to her chambers. And in a short hour, before the grand mirror, Adalja scarcely recognised the woman gazing back.

A queen. A bride. A soul aching for a freedom she had only begun to glimpse—before it was cruelly wrenched away.

The gown was breathtaking. White lace clung to her form, silver accents tracing every delicate curve. The corset cinched her waist mercilessly, while the puffed shoulders made her feel less a woman and more a doll—dressed, arranged, and set on display.

Her long curls were delicately twisted by Sapphire's hands, pinned apart from a few loose strands framing her face. Silver beads were sewn throughout—like fallen tears of an angel.

Her crown—delicate yet commanding—rested atop her head, the final reminder of her Pembrook royalty.

She had not worn it since her arrival at Worthyn Castle, and oddly—it seemed to fit tighter. Somehow, it no longer felt hers in ways she couldn't describe.

Forged from pale silver, it was set with soft pearls and flecked with small cabochons of deep lapis and shimmering moonstone—their cool hues reflecting her new queenship of Pembrook. Its slender, tapering points rose like the spires of her homeland's castle—elegant yet unyielding.

Today, it felt heavier. A final reminder of who she once was, and what she was about to become.

Despite the radiance, despite the beauty of it all, tears blurred her vision.

"*This is not what your heart seeks...I feel it.*"
Olivja's voice echoed in her mind as she stared at her reflection, hands clutching the gown at her thighs.

Olivja was right.
She had always been right.
And it felt cruel that Adalja could only now recognise it.

Sapphire approached slowly, her expression tinged with admiration.

"You look ever the queen, Adalja," she said softly. She swallowed hard, then lowered her voice to a gentle murmur. "For the final touch...your mother wished for you to wear this."

She held up a stunning, white-laced cloak, hooded and bordered in deep grey fur—likely from some wild animal. Its stitching was careful, loved, worn—something she hadn't even known her mother possessed.

Adalja's eyes watered as she reached out, her fingers brushing the soft fur as a lump formed in her throat.

"My *mother*?" Adalja whispered, her voice cracking as she clutched the softness like it might bring her parents back.

It was a painful reminder of their absence, and it twisted her heart.

Her eyes fell on a rune—stitched with careful practice on the inside near the hood.

The Ragnarvik Rune.

Her fingers grazed it, and her eyes widened.

It *couldn't be.*

Her mother—the one who had scorned Norse culture like a disease, who loathed the Ragnarviks—had chosen this for her wedding day?

There was something buried beneath the seams, a memory, a trace of something older. A whisper of the Pembrooks' time among the Ragnarviks...
Perhaps her mother's hatred hadn't been entirely honest.

But she smiled. Because not only would her mother be with her through this, but *Olivja.* It felt like a final sign from the gods—a sign of where her heart truly belonged.

She pulled it over her shoulders, wrapping herself in the last remnant of motherly love. Her mother's scent still clung to it—but not only hers. Traces of her father lingered, too: his warm, nutmeg musk.

Her eyes shut tight, anchoring herself in the scent.
In them—In their final wish for her.

THE HEAVY SILENCE OF THE CASTLE SURROUNDED HER, broken only by the faint echo of her footsteps on stone.

Adalja clenched the sword-shaped clasp of her cloak, her trembling fingers betraying her nerves. She blinked rapidly, willing away the tears that pooled in her sea-like eyes.

The air was thick with melted wax and incense, wafting from towering iron candelabras that lined the hall, their flames flickering in the torchlight. Shafts of pale winter light filtered through narrow windows, casting a muted glow across the grey stone.

This was a place built for endurance, for command, for war—not for warmth, not for comfort, and certainly not for weddings.

Her maid's voice, soft and sweet, cut through her thoughts.

"You will lead with grace, My Queen," Sapphire murmured, her tone laced with unspoken sadness. Adalja's chest tightened at the words—the title's burden settling deep beneath her ribs.

"I...I truly wish to," she whispered, barely audible.

She pulled her hood over her head, the fabric pressing into the points of her crown, and followed Sapphire though the ballroom. Ahead, the great doors remained shut—the garden path, her aisle, waiting just beyond.

The soft hush of her silk shoes upon the stone marked her passage, quiet as a fluttering dove.

A faint rustle in the shadows made Adalja falter.

At first, she thought it only a trick of the flickering torchlight.
But then, she saw him.

Vincent.

He stood half-shrouded in darkness, leaning against one of the towering pillars. A man—or the shell of one—was half-lit by flickering torchlight, his expression caught between contemplation and agony.

His green eyes locked onto hers, and the despair in them struck her like a physical blow.

His black eye was worse than before—swollen further—and his split lip had reopened, a faint streak of blood trailing from where it had been hastily wiped. Dark bruises marred his cheekbones, and his jaw was tender—its skin darkly tinged with purple.

Adalja's heart cinched, tightening until it ached.

She had seen him less than a day ago, and though he'd already looked shattered, now he seemed reduced to little more than dust.

Some part of her longed to go to him; another knew the remnants of Olivja hadn't just left her hollow, but had emptied him too—perhaps even more.

For today was supposed to be his wedding day as well.
And now, it was not.

A chill ran over her skin, sharp and icy, as though the air itself carried the weight of her unspoken fears.

She didn't need to ask who had hurt him—she already knew.

His knuckles were raw and abraded, as if he'd fought back, though the tremor in his hands betrayed the toll it had taken. Like a little boy. Like a man who'd lost everything.

He limped as he pushed himself off the stone, wincing with each movement, though he tried to mask it with the tightness of his jaw.

Adalja froze, her breath hitching in her throat. She wanted to speak, to ask what had happened, but the words lodged in her chest like a stone.

Vincent didn't move closer. He didn't speak. He stood still, watching her with an intensity that felt almost unbearable.

His frame sagged beneath a silence heavy as winter's chill. And in his eyes—those haunted, green depths that watered—was something she couldn't name.

A yearning. A sorrow. A farewell.

The moment stretched between them, silent and heavy, until Vincent finally straightened with visible effort.

He gave her a single, lingering glance—his expression pained, like a man at the edge of a precipice.

Then, without a word, he turned and limped into the shadows—his footsteps fading until they were consumed entirely.

Adalja stared after him, her chest tight and aching. She didn't notice the tears burning in her wide-open eyes until Sapphire's gentle tug brought her back to the present.

"My Queen," Sapphire said softly, her hand resting on Adalja's arm. "We must go."

Adalja nodded, her movements stiff, and turned back towards the towering oak doors leading to the gardens. But before she could take another step, a familiar voice, deep and resonant, called her name.

"*Adalja.*"
The sound froze her in place.

She turned slowly, pushing her hood back to reveal her tear-streaked face.

Jarl Dagrun stood at the entrance to the grand ballroom, his broad frame imposing yet comforting.

He was transformed from the last time she'd seen him in the dungeons. His kingly garb was immaculate: a dark red jerkin over a long-sleeved brown tunic and tailored pants, a single white flower pinned to his chest.

Golden beads were woven into the intricate braids of his hair and beard, each catching the light like tiny suns. Despite the sharpness of his appearance, there was a softness in the way he stood, like the day's long shadow clung to him, and he shouldered it without complaint, for her.

Like a father would.
Like her father might have.

"Runey...?" Her voice cracked as his name left her lips, heavy with disbelief.

Her feet moved of their own accord, quickening as if pulled by some unseen force.

When she reached him, his massive arms enveloped her, drawing her against the warmth of his chest. The embrace unraveled her carefully guarded composure, and she sighed deeply into him.

He smelled of firewood and sage, a scent so grounding and familiar it almost cleansed her of the torment clinging to her heart.

Here, against him, her fears seemed to lift, if only for a moment.

"...Young Vincent asked me to walk you, and I'd not let another lead you to the altar," Dagrun said gruffly, his voice as warm and comforting as his embrace.

Adalja tilted her head to look up at him, and her breath caught at the sight of his brown eyes, glassy with unshed tears.

She knew this moment, this kindness, wasn't meant for her. It was meant for Olivja—*his daughter*. Something he'd never get the chance to do.

Her lips parted, but no words came, only a trembling exhale.

Dagrun's shaky breath betrayed the way he shattered. One of his large hands rose to cup her cheek, his thumb gently brushing away her tears.

"She would have been...*so proud* to call you her wife," he said, his deep voice faltering with grief.

A soft sob escaped her lips as she leaned into his touch, her soul unravelling at his words.

Together, they stood in the silence, bound by the shared pain of what could have been.

Dagrun pulled her close once more, his arms tightening around her as though he could shield her from the world.

After a long moment, he stepped back, his hands sliding down her arms to clasp her delicate fingers. His gaze lingered on the sword-shaped clasp of her cloak, and a faint, bittersweet smile curved his lips.

"*Aye*...they'd see you in this, wouldn't they..." he murmured, his voice thick with emotion.

A humorless chuckle escaped him, his broad shoulders bouncing ever so slightly. "It is good to know Natja still held it close, even after all these winters. My soul will rest easier knowing it."

"Y...your soul?" Adalja asked hesitantly.

"Solvig," he said simply, his voice softening as he reached out to touch the clasp.

"She spent months crafting this for your mother, as though the Norns themselves blessed her hands. It was completed just in time for the wedding..." His voice broke as his fingers fell away, and he took her hands again, enveloping them completely.

"...Your father may not stand among us, little Adalja," he continued, his beard quivering as he fought back tears at the mention of King Pembrook. "But I feel him still...I've no doubt he stands beside you now."

He brought her hands to his lips, placing a reverent kiss on the backs of her fingers. His head bowed low, his towering frame leaning towards her in a gesture of devotion.

"We *always* will," he exhaled, his words an offering, his tone as steadfast as a vow.

After another moment passed, Dagrun straightened himself, clearing his throat as he guided her hand to the crook of his elbow. His touch was steady, grounding.

"...Now, it is time for us to build something better," he said under his breath.

Their eyes met in a final, quiet understanding before the grand doors to the garden creaked open.

A gust of cold wind swept inside, carrying with it the scent of winter and stone. Beyond the doors lay the ceremony grounds: a cobbled aisle flanked by towering, stone-carved gods, their solemn faces watching over the proceedings. A place she remembered well.

Each step forward dragged the shackles of destiny as Adalja moved with Dagrun by her side.

Servants and knights stood in reverent rows along the aisle, their gazes fixed respectfully downwards. A few dared to glance at her, their expressions betraying fleeting glimpses of sympathy, curiosity, and admiration.

A small band of troubadours plucked at harps and lutes, their wedding tune scattering across the stone like falling crystals.

At the end of the stone path stood Elias, waiting at the Persephone statue. She loomed tall, her outstretched hands beckoning Adalja forward.

Elias' figure stood stiff but poised, his formal black-and-silver attire immaculate. But once his eyes fell on her, his posture relaxed, and a peaceful, contented expression settled over him.

She was pleased to see him no longer trapped by his mask, his hair neatly done apart from a few strands that fell across his forehead. Beside him stood the priest, robed in white and gold, his hands clasped before him as he awaited their approach.

Adalja's chest tightened with each step. Her heart pounded against her ribs, not from fear or doubt, but from the sheer enormity of the moment. Dagrun's arm remained steady beneath her hand, his presence a quiet, unwavering support.

As they neared the goddess, the echoes of their footsteps on the stone filled the air, mingling with the soft rustle of cloaks and whispered prayers from the gathered crowd.

By the time they reached the priest, the world's burden had settled heavy across her shoulders. And yet, Dagrun's final squeeze of her hand reminded her—she was not carrying it alone.

Elias' ungloved hands reached forward, receiving her from the Jarl. He guided her the final few steps—a silent reminder of his devotion and protection.

She stepped in front of him, a bittersweet feeling clinging to her heart.

She wished she could cry. She wished she could look at him and feel all the things she once felt for Olivja.

But she couldn't. And yet, she was grateful—truly—that it was him she had been made to marry.

The priest began the ceremony, reading from a page that declared their union—the power of their love, and all that came with it.

Adalja kept her eyes on Elias, and he did the same.Neither cared to hear what others had to say about their love, their connection.

When it came time for their vows, the priest pushed his book forward—two silver rings rested upon its surface. Elias reached for hers first.

"With this band, I declare my eternal love for you, Adalja," Elias said softly, pinching the ring carefully between his fingers.

He drew her left hand gently towards him, his gaze locking onto hers with quiet admiration. The weight of their shared burdens, their secrets, and their unwavering loyalty lingered in the cold air between them.

"I swear," Elias continued, his voice steady but laced with quiet emotion, "to stand at thy side—not as husband, but as thy partner in all things. Through storms that shall rage, through fires that shall try us...I shall be thy shield and thy sword, thy truest friend, and thy sworn truth. *Evermore.*"

Adalja's breath caught, tears welling in her eyes as she stared into the sincerity of his expression. Elias slid the cold band onto her finger with gentle care, his touch as warm as his words.

Her lips parted, trembling slightly as she began her vows. "And...with this band, I do pledge my love to thee, *Elias,*" she said, her voice low, certain.

"I vow to honour thee—not only as my husband, but as my truest friend. To see thee as thou art, and to hold dear the man who has borne me through my darkest nights. I shall share thy burdens, guard thy secrets, and walk beside thee...*evermore.*"

She paused, her voice breaking as she continued. "Let this sacred union bear witness that love endures all things, and by its grace, peace shall reign."

With deliberate care, Adalja slid the matching band onto his finger.

Elias' smile grew—soft, bittersweet—as he closed his fingers over hers, their hands clasped in a bond stronger than words.

The priest nodded, his voice breaking the spell of their private world.

"By the exchange of these vows, these bands, and the grace of God, may your union be blessed in eternity."

Elias cupped her face then, his thumbs brushing away the tears that had spilled onto her cheeks.

"We will do this hand in hand," he spoke for only her to hear, his tone carrying both reassurance and quiet determination. "*Always.*"

Adalja's lips curved in a watery smile. "Together," she breathed. "Always."

He leaned in. His movements were slow and deliberate, as if giving her the space to retreat should she wish.

But she didn't.

When their lips met, it was soft and tender, a kiss that spoke of trust, of mutual devotion, and of the promise that neither would have to face their battles alone.

The crowd erupted in applause, though the moment belonged only to them.

As they pulled apart, Elias pressed his forehead gently to hers, his breath warm against her skin despite the cold.

"I love you, Adalja."

"And I, *you*, My King."

Hand in hand, they turned to face the gathered witnesses, their faces composed, their bond unbreakable. With the echo of their vows resonating in their hearts, Elias and Adalja began their final walk down the aisle.

The crowd's cheers softened, becoming a distant hum as she focussed on the stone ahead. She held her chin high, no longer afraid of what the future might bring—together, they would face it.

The sound of their steps echoed across the stone, and as they neared the grand doors to the gardens, Adalja took a deep breath, knowing that this was not the end, but a new beginning.

"Cheers...and good tidings to the newly bound!"

A voice shattered the fragile peace of the moment, booming from the shadows of the garden.

Slowly, Adalja and Elias turned, their hands entwined. The handful of knights and maids stationed along the aisle stirred uneasily, shifting their weight as the air thickened with tension.

At the far end, beneath the looming figure of Persephone, Vincent towered.

His hair was disheveled, damp with sweat, clinging to his face. His eyes, dark and hollow, burned with sleepless fury.

Dagrun knelt at his feet. His face was twisted in pain, Vincent's fist tangled in his braids, yanking his head back.

Steel glinted in the sunlight—Vincent's sword pressed hard against the jarl's neck, rising and falling with each labored breath from Dagrun's chest.

"A parting gift," Vincent called. His voice was almost serene, too calm, but the smile that curled his lips trembled with barely caged rage.

Tears rimmed his bruised eyes, but they shone like glass—unshed, unbreaking.

His gaze lingered on Elias for a breath. Then it snapped—like a whip—to the man among the knights.

His father.

"*For the man who taught me all I ever knew of love,*" Vincent finished, his voice like a death knell.

Elias' voice cracked as he stepped forward, his hand slipping from Adalja's grasp.
"Brother—"

"*STAY* where you are!" Vincent barked, his words cutting the stillness like the sword in his hand.

His grip on Dagrun tightened, his knuckles as pale as the stone gods surrounding them.

"All of you. Stay."

Adalja's heart thundered in her chest. Her gaze flickered to Ezekiel, who rose slowly from his place at the front. His hands curled into fists at his sides, but his face remained eerily still, save for his eyes—burning with silent fury as they locked onto his son.

But no one moved.
No one dared.

Vincent tilted his head, his smile twisting further as he leaned closer to Dagrun, his voice softening, laced with venom.

"Do you think he'll mourn you, Dag?" He let the words hang in the air, his focus momentarily drifting back to his father. "Or will he thank me for sparing him the trouble of a *heathen?*"

Adalja's stomach turned violently.

Her mind raced—fragments of Olivja flooding her thoughts. Her knees threatened to buckle, and for a moment, she swayed.

This couldn't happen.
Not to Dagrun. Not to Olivja's remaining memory.

"*My son...*" Dagrun grunted, his voice heavy with exhaustion, his pride and strength whittled down to nothing as he knelt, making a spectacle before Ezekiel.

“I am NO ONE’S SON!” Vincent shouted, his voice breaking as he looked between Dagrun and Ezekiel. “I belong...to *none*. No longer...”

Adalja’s breath hitched, her hand reflexively reaching out—but for what?

There was no one to stop this.
Not Ezekiel.
Not even Elias.

“Why turn your hand against me...?” Dagrun choked against the blade, barely audible across the stone path.

Vincent let out a soft, broken sob. A sprinkle of remorse at the Norseman’s desperation.

“*Because...*” the prince paused as he lowered his head to Dagrun, mumbling something so quiet, so soft, that only Persephone could hear him.

Dagrun’s amber eyes widened...then darted towards Ezekiel—a flicker of raw emotion crossing his face at whatever the prince had told him.

The Jarl jerked with the might of all his Gods towards the King, but Vincent held him firm. His broken, conniving smile grew in tandem with the fears of the watchers. But his gaze was only pointed at Ezekiel, standing tall besides his silent smiling jester.

Vincent’s face was a prediction of what he would bring.
The bruising, the swelling, the pain—
It was but a spark to the man’s burning, sinister potential.

The tension was suffocating, choking her like a noose. The pounding pulse in her throat ached, her chest tightened with every second that Dagrun remained beneath the blade.

Please, Vincent! Her thoughts screamed, and as though tethered by more than oath, her husband spoke up for her.

“Vincent, please. Think of Olivja,” Elias choked, his voice desperate, but powerless. “Release him. This is not the time—”

“I *AM* THINKING OF OLIVJA!” Vincent’s shout was frayed at the edges; an accumulation of pain built for far too long.

With the movement of his shout, the blade jerked, and a thin line of blood spilled brightly down the Jarl's neck.

"No." Vincent's voice lowered, cracked, and his grip did not falter.
"This is the perfect time."

Adalja's hand flew to her mouth. She wanted to scream, to plead with Vincent, but her voice was caught in her throat.

He turned tear-filled eyes to the small, stunned gathering, drawing a deep breath.

"Let her gods bear witness to this..."

His smile dropped, his lips coming up in a snarl. Not of anger.
Of *disgust.*

"There are no lengths I would not go..." His voice trembled.
"For *love.*"

Time slowed.
So did sound.
So did sight.
Even her heartbeat faltered. All at the vision of Vincent's vengeance.

His blade, powered by past, sliced clean across Dagrun Ragnarvik's throat.

Blood splattered like hands, grasping for forgiveness, for a second chance.
But it would not come.

All that came were cries.

With a throat-wrenching scream, Adalja's voice cut through the stillness like waking from some horrid nightmare. Elias' cry was guttural, horror threaded through his despair. The king's roar was not only anger—but pain. His fury erupted, his alliance *shattered*.

But another cry rose behind them—louder than all.
Edith, Olivja's maid. Dagrun's mother-in-law.

The loyal Norsewoman broke from the maidens, her screams splintering like her soul had cracked in two.

But no cry could soften the weight of Dagrun's body collapsing, heavy at Vincent's feet.

Blood spilled onto the sacred stones beneath the gods' gaze, bright and crimson, staining the sanctity of the space forever.

Edith dropped to her knees beside his lifeless body, her sobs raw and broken as they filled the air. Her hands trembled as she wove them through his blood-matted hair, pulling him close, cradling his head in her lap.

The sight of his blood-soaked form barely registered in their minds; all that mattered was that the Jarl of Ragnarvik was dead, his warmth slipping from her grasp as she clung to him.

"You watched him die!" Edith screamed to the sky, voice hoarse, hands bloody. She buried her face in his hair, muffling her cries. "*My precious boy...*"

Adalja's knees buckled.
"No..." she cried, a part of her splintering with every drop of blood.

Her mind clawed for something—anything—to hold onto, but all she could see was Olivja...slipping away from her, *again.*

Her whimpered "*Olivja...*" went unnoticed, lost in the stunned silence.

The weight of grief and betrayal crushed her chest as she watched the man she had once seen as a father depart their realm so violently, so ruinously.

The violence of it, the destruction he left behind, carved something deep within her—something she feared would never heal.

Vincent stood frozen, the blade trembling in his hand as he lifted it towards his father, blood staining its edge like a grim testament.

"I am the bitter fruit sown from the seeds of your lies, father!" the prince spat, voice hoarse and broken—yet somehow proud. "Now...you shall reap the harvest."

"*Seize him!*" Ezekiel's command cracked through the heavy air, startling the knights into action.

They surged forward, grabbing Vincent by the arms and dragging him back. He didn't resist, his blade falling from his hand, clattering onto the stones.

Adalja barely registered the commotion. Her eyes were fixed on Dagrun's lifeless form, his blood pooling beneath him.

"No...no, no, no..." she panicked, her feet moving of their own accord as she staggered towards him.

"Adalja!" Elias' voice was distant, a dull echo in her ears.

She didn't care. She had to reach him. She had to do *something*.
She couldn't lose another father—another piece of Olivja.

Her knees struck the blood-slick stone, but before she could reach Dagrun's body, Elias' arms wrapped around her, pulling her back.

She caught the sight of a small red ribbon, frayed and tattered, and the white flower, a lily, broken in three, splattered in Dagrun's blood.

"Let me go!" she sobbed, struggling against him. "Please, Elias, please! I cannot bear to lose her again!"

Elias held her firmly, his voice breaking as he strained, "Adalja...you can't. It is done!"

"No!" she cried, her voice cracking. "*Runey*!"

He didn't answer. He wouldn't answer ever again.

Elias scooped her up, cradling the grieving queen as he carried her towards the castle. Her sobs grew louder, raw and unrelenting, as she pounded weakly against his chest.

By the time they crossed the ballroom threshold, her strength had abandoned her entirely.

What had begun as a day of renewal, of hope and new beginnings, now lay shattered—twisted into the heart of a treacherous end.

She collapsed against him, her cries muffled against his shoulder.

Elias pressed her against the nearest wall, holding her tightly, his face buried in her hair as his own grief streamed hot and silent.

"*Shh...shh..*"
He tried to quiet her cries, petting her hair with all the strength he could manage as his hands and chest trembled.

Behind them, the gods stood cold and unyielding, forever standing as silent witnesses to love, betrayal, and bloodshed.

THREAD LVIII

IT TOOK HOURS TO SETTLE ADALJA.

Their marriage, already doomed from the start, was now eternally tainted by the Jarl's death.

It took a lot of strength to get her back to her room, and even more so to ease her into his arms. It was the least he could do after she had so carefully taken care of him the night prior. He would have held her forever if he could.

The image of Dagrun, the man he loved and admired—broken and deceased, now etched on his eyes, and into their marriage.

He squeezed her tighter—whispering soft promises, assuring her that everything would be well—but somehow he knew this was only the beginning of something far worse.

After settling Adalja, King Elias was summoned to the main room to speak with his father. He knew what was coming, and it tore at his heart.

Elias couldn't say goodbye to his Queen—not after all they'd been through. He knew telling her would risk crumbling her all over again, so he didn't.

He pressed his lips to her forehead, a whisper of a kiss, and then another; his touch lingering. He whispered a promise of his return against her skin and left her to rest in her bed.

But he knew that wasn't the full truth.

Now that the wedding was over, he was bound to face what was inevitable: War.

As Ezekiel's rightful heir, he would be leading the charge as the General.

His father's war was not a cause he believed in, nor a bloodshed he wished to lead. But perhaps, if he played his part—if he took command as General—he could steer it towards something better. Perhaps he could end it. Not for glory. Not for his father. But to spare the realm from further ruin.

King Elias stood tall in the foyer, the silence pressing in around him as he waited for Ezekiel's orders. The weight of his new attire seemed heavier than ever.

He had changed out of his wedding cords and into his general's garb. His black breastplate gleamed with his family's sigil, a stark contrast to the blood-red sash that draped across his chest. His black and grey cloak trailed behind him like the burden of past and future, while his sword gleamed at his side—an icy promise of swift retribution. His mask was gone, tossed aside with the remnants of his father's control.

For years, it had been his cage—the barrier his father used to hide behind, to silence the voice inside him that yearned for something more. But now, for the first time, he stood before the world unguarded, exposed.

Elias would never wear it again. It was no longer his to claim.

Yet beneath the armour and regalia, a sick emptiness curled inside him. His mind drifted to his brother—who should have been riding to battle beside him. He was nowhere to be seen after the wedding.

Footsteps echoed from the top of the stairs, and then Ezekiel appeared. His dark cloak billowed behind him like a gale, his expression hardened by the events Vincent had set in motion. All sense of warmth, of fatherly familiarity, had vanished, replaced by a coldness that Ezekiel had rarely set upon Elias.

Behind him, trailing like his lanky shadow, was Nimble, their bells jingling quietly as the braids dragged across on the stone. They descended the stairs in silent, unnatural grace—moving not with steps, but with slow, fluid contortions.

A backbend first, palms brushing the stairwell like a dancer lowered by invisible strings. Then a slow, deliberate handstand—limbs weightless, liquid, wrong—their pointed toes stretching high above Ezekiel's head—before curling into a slow bend again. Up and down, again and again.

Until they landed upright at the bottom of the stairs—with eerie poise—one step behind Ezekiel, perfectly still.

Their drawn smile remained, but it smudged in all the wrong ways, black paint streaked over the white. Their blue eyes found Elias, and for a moment, Elias wondered if Ezekiel had harmed Nimble in a release of anger.

Ezekiel's jaw was clenched, his hands fisted at his sides, trembling with fury.

The King was fractured at the hands of his own son.

Elias couldn't help but feel a twisted sense of pride.

Vincent had shattered Ezekiel's resolve, his empire, and now, for the first time, Elias could see his father as the broken man he truly was.

As awful as it had been to watch Dagrun's demise, Elias was proud of Vincent for breaking free, for making their father bleed. He only wished he could tell him.

A heavy sigh broke the stillness. Ezekiel's voice was low, almost bitter. "*Ahh*, Elias...I am sorry your brother has brought such ruin upon yet another joyous evening of yours—"

"He has ruined *nothing*, Lord Father," Elias interjected quickly, his words sharper than he intended. "My union is forged. The Ragnarviks shall not learn of Dagrun's death until we command it, thus we still hold their trust."

Ezekiel's eyes softened for a moment, as though pride flickered behind his gaze.

"That's my boy." The chuckle that followed was hollow. He landed a heavy hand on Elias' shoulder, a touch that was both familiar and unsettling.

Elias felt it twist through his bones, the pressure of everything his father had done to him—but more so, to Vincent.

Ezekiel's hand lingered for a moment, but Elias stiffened, rage rising. All he could think about were the same hands that had driven his brother to madness.

"The rest of the knights shall be sent to the frontlines with you, save for a few to guard your bride and your maddened brother of course. That, or I'll have him sent to The Mercy House..." Ezekiel's voice was low, insistent. His hand clamped tighter on Elias' shoulder.

Elias shuddered. His brow lowered.

The Mercy House... Worthyn's prison for the mad. He had never seen it, but he knew it well. A place his father favoured—where he sent dissenters, questioners, anyone who dared pull back the veil on his lies. The thought of Vincent confined there made Elias sick.

"Now, when this war is over, Elias, I swear it—I will yield my crown to you. You will be the King of Midhelm."

Elias' eyes went cold. He wrenched his shoulder free from Ezekiel's grasp.

"Unlike you, Lord Father," he said with a firm and resolute tone, "it is not power I desire, but *peace.*"

Ezekiel's eyes narrowed, his face momentarily contorting with what almost looked like heartbreak.

"My son," he said softly. "Hear me—when this war ends, these lands will know a peace greater than you could ever imagine."

"I will see to that myself," Elias snapped, voice sharp. "But hear *me* now: should so much as a single hair be harmed upon my brother—or my queen—I shall place the crown in Perdyr's hands, and *your* head with it."

The words hung between them like poison in the air. Because Elias was no longer his son—but a king. A general. A man forced to bear the wounds of Ezekiel's mistakes—and he was determined to fix every last one.

"I trust the meaning is clear, *Ezekiel.*"

Nimble's head snapped sideways, birdlike. But Eli did not falter. He stood his ground, eyes burning with a fury he'd never dared show before—daring his father to retaliate. It was the first time he'd ever dared speak to him with such open disdain. All the suffering—the deaths, the lies—had been the price of silence. The cost of years of blind obedience.

But he had power now. As a general. As a King of Pembrook.
And he would wield it for good.

Behind Ezekiel, Nimble watched Elias as if the words had been aimed at them instead. But against the pain in their eyes, the painted smile remained. Their hands were uneased—twisting together at their stomach.

Then, without a word, they slowly crouched at the king's heels—knees and arms cradling his calf. It was something between reverence and defence.

Ezekiel's hand moved—slow, practised—and settled atop Nimble's head. Like some pet of his.
Not a push. Not a grip. A flat palm, a swipe of a thumb along the braidline.
Gentle.

Elias flinched at the gentleness—an otherworldly thing, a kind of touch he had never known from his father. Even now—on the eve of sending his own son to war. King Worthyn stood silent, face set in stone.

Only now did he understand: Elias was no longer within his grasp...nor his heart.

THE WINTER AIR BIT AT HIM as he fled from the foyer and stepped outside, cold sharp enough to steal his breath. His pace quickened as the chill settled deep in his bones, urging him towards the stables.

He deliberately avoided the gardens—their dark aura pressing on him like a suffocating weight.

As he descended the hill, his breath visible in the frigid air, he spotted a geared horse waiting beyond the stables. Elias brushed its side in a fleeting gesture of comfort before he ducked inside to find his own mount.

Within, a figure stood, hooded and shadowed by the dim light filtering through the slats of the stable roof. They were bent over, securing something to *his* horse's saddle.

Elias approached, curious, tilting his head to catch a better glimpse of the figure.

"I'm well equipped to ready my own horse, sir," he called out, his voice steady despite the tension coiling in his chest.

The cloaked figure turned, slow and deliberate, and as the hood fell back, Elias' breath hitched.

Standing before him was Brahms, battered and broken, his face a grim testament to violence.

His lip was split, both cheeks bruised and swollen, and his left eye bore the ugly bloom of a wound barely beginning to heal. But it was his gaze that struck Elias the hardest: cold, distant, and void of recognition. The warmth he once knew, the comfort of those dark eyes, was replaced by a raw, unrelenting anger.

Elias' chest tightened, his heart lurching at the sight. His feet moved before his mind could catch up. His cloak billowed behind him as he reached out, fingers twitching.

"Brahms," he whispered, voice strained over everything unsaid. His hands cupped the knight's bruised face, gripping it gently yet firmly, as if grounding himself in the bruises, the proof of what had been done.

The king's voice was low with restrained anger. "Look at me—I will not let this go unpunished, I swear it—"

Brahms' hands flew to Elias' wrists, his grip iron-strong, but Elias held fast. Their eyes locked, the air between them crackling with tension. Behind Brahms' fury, Elias saw it—the hurt, raw and unhidden.

His gaze flickered to the bruises trailing down Brahms' neck, peeking out from beneath his collar, and his blood boiled. He knew who had done it...and he had been powerless to stop it.

And Brahms was *furious.*

"Don't play the hero," he growled, his voice laced with venom. "You will do *nothing*. Your loyal knights—*Jori, Kai.* I should have seen it sooner—why the Worthyn men hold such hatred for me."

Elias' stomach dropped, his grip faltering for a fraction of a second. "No—"

"They told me—all of it!" Brahms cut him off, his voice bitter. "How you used to *bed* them. How easy it was for them to please you. And I believed—" His voice cracked, raw emotion slipping through before he steeled himself.

"Forget it. I deserved it, did I not? For failing to protect Adalja. For losing Olivja. For daring to stand in the path of their *precious prince...*"

Elias' face paled. The words hit him like a blade to the gut.

Those relationships had been destroyed—the same as everything else—by his father.

He had been young, reckless, and desperate to understand himself, his body, and the desires he'd been taught to suppress. But being with his knights was a risk he couldn't hold—wouldn't take lightly. And perhaps that was part of the reason he had shied away from Brahms.

"It was not as you may think," Elias said hastily, a note of desperation creeping into his voice. "Allow me to explain..."

"I daresay, I know the answer—because 'I'm not like the others'?" Brahms scoffed, his lip curling in a pained smirk, his tone sharp and cutting—laced with jealousy that struck Elias like a dagger.

"You would be correct, My Lord." He tossed his palms up, like it was humorous. "You could barely share a breath with me, but you welcomed them into your bed."

Elias bit his cheek. He'd never meant to pull away that night at the inn. But he was afraid...

With Brahms, it felt different—something he couldn't understand but didn't have the time to. And when he wanted to, when he drunkenly wished to find out what about Brahms pulled him so, they were interrupted, and he panicked.

Just like before—with Kai. With Jori.

He'd convinced himself it was the right thing to do—pulling away—that it would protect them all.

But now, seeing the pain in Brahms' eyes, he realised he had failed. He had done it *again.* He'd broken another heart.

"Enough," Elias' voice broke, raw and pleading.

"Or what? Am I to be returned to Jori? Let your ex-lovers continue to pummel me in the name of Worthyn—I no longer care!"

"I tried to stop them, Brahms—I begged them to release you!" Elias shouted the truth, but it fell on deaf ears.

"It matters not. I care not," Brahms hissed. "*Such was beaten out of me.*"

Elias shuddered. The guilt was the final weight that fell on his shoulders that day—he wasn't sure he could bear any more. His hands trembled at his sides, aching to reach out—to touch him, to reassure him, to make Brahms feel wanted.

"Brahms, I—" Elias bit his bottom lip. "I feel more for you than all others—"

"If this is the cost of your feelings," Brahms' laugh was hollow, biting. He stepped back, his expression darkening. "Then I want nothing of it."

His chest cinched tight, crushing in on itself as Brahms' words lodged like thorns in his lungs. Elias reached for him again, but the knight tore away from his touch, his shoulders rigid, his body recoiling as if Elias had burned him.

"Please, grant me a moment to explain, Brahms..." Elias said, his voice cracking.

"I've heard enough," Brahms hissed, the words echoing through the stables. "*I've felt enough.*" His entire frame was taut with barely restrained anguish, muscles drawn tight beneath his armour.

"From you...from them," he muttered, eyes narrowing.
"No love of yours will make me willing to suffer ruin."

There was a pause—brief, breathless—where Brahms looked as though he might break apart. In tears. Or in flames.

"I will not let ruin befall you, Brahms, *forgive me...*" Elias' voice was barely a whisper. "I'll carry all the blame, all the shame for what was done to you," the king said, stepping closer, his voice quaking with emotion. "Each bruise upon your flesh feels as if it were struck upon mine!"

For a moment, Brahms' eyes softened—but the anger returned, swift and sharp. He laughed, "easy to declare when you are not the one bleeding, Elias."

He stood there, chest caving with each word, frozen in the fear of what he'd ruined before it could even bloom. The guilt gnawed at him, the heartache clawing its way free.

Elias trembled as he tried to rectify whatever was left between them—to mend what had been shattered.

"Tell me—please—tell me how I can make this right," Elias begged, his voice cracking. "I cannot bear this between us. Not after everything we've endured. Jori—Kai—they mean nothing to me!"

Brahms turned away, raking a hand through his messy curls, breath coming fast and shallow.

"We have a war to fight," Brahms said—voice calm now, resigned. "*Your* war. And a kingdom that waits for your rule. You need not trouble yourself with courting the favour of one so lowly as a knight."

Elias closed the last step between them. Fear of losing his truest ally stung his eyes. He reached for him.

"No," he breathed, fingers sliding up to cup Brahms' jaw and the nape of his neck in one firm span. Warm skin met his own. The rough edge of Brahms' stubble rasped against Elias' palm; his pulse throbbed beneath his thumb.

"The war can wait an hour," the king insisted. "Let me set this right." His voice quivered with need, and his gaze dipped—once—down to Brahms' lips. Heat pooled in the inch of air between them, every breath shared, every heartbeat a drum.

He could do it—close that sliver of distance and lay bare how desperately he meant to keep this man, to burn away every doubt that lingered.

Yet he held still, because the knight was right.

And the look in Brahms' eyes—equal parts betrayal and sorrow—rooted Elias where he stood, envying the very air that brushed the knight's mouth. And the man caught it, the way Elias hesitated *even now.*

Brahms' throat worked, his skin burning beneath his touch. When he spoke, his voice was lowered, trembling—like he didn't want to say it: "I shall not become your distraction again. Forgive me for losing sight of myself..."

Elias whimpered at the resolve.
The words chipped at his remaining hope—a quiet confession, full of shame.

He shook his head, already knowing he was losing this battle. The war hadn't even begun, and already, he was *bleeding.* But he wouldn't give up, not yet.

"Brahms, do not choose this. Not now, I beg you, I—" *need you*. He would have finished, but the words caught in his throat.

Brahms was his last tether, the last person he could rely on, could trust. He wouldn't have Adalja or Vincent now, Olivja was dead, Dagrun was dead. The last remaining light in his heart belonged to the hope that he still had Brahms.

The both were headed to the unknowns of war, and Elias was clinging to, *at least*, going through it *together*.

"I know my place, Your Highness," he said, the title bitter on his tongue. His voice was heavy with finality. "And it is not with you...I've learned that. *I've accepted that.*"

And just like that his hope crumbled.

Elias stood frozen as Brahms pulled away, shoulder plates colliding—a fleeting, electric moment that left him reeling. Be it real or imagined, a spark flew between the metal plates, only to be diminished by the coldness between them.

For a moment, the king thought he might say something more, but instead, Brahms shouldered his leather bag and moved towards the exit. He paused, his silhouette framed by the pale moonlight.

"*I hope the stirrups are to your liking, my King.*"

Then he was gone.

Brahms mounted his horse, the leather creaking as he settled into the saddle. With a soft whistle, he urged the animal forward. The sound of hoofbeats faded into the distance.

Elias stood alone in the stables, his heart aching, his vision blurring with unshed tears. The air felt colder now. *Emptier.*

And when the last echo of Brahms' departure faded, Elias clutched at the stirrup of his horse—the only thing keeping him from breaking completely.

Elias drew a deep, shuddering breath. His hands tightened—anchoring himself to something solid. His mind churned, a tempest of grief, regret, and resolve.

He had been crowned a king, married a woman he couldn't love in the way she deserved, and lost a father whose death left an unfillable void. And now

Brahms—the one he couldn't bear to lose—had ridden away with words between them that cut deeper than any blade.

But there was no time for mourning. *Not yet. Not in the night.*

He released the stirrup and straightened, the raw edges of his emotions forging themselves into something sharper, more focussed.

This wasn't about him anymore—not his pain, not his failures, not the love he hadn't been brave enough to claim. This was about a kingdom drowning in bloodshed and despair, about a future that could still be saved if only he had the strength to seize it.

Elias turned towards his mare, his movements purposeful now. As he swung into the saddle, the weight on his chest didn't lift, but it hardened—becoming a mantle he would carry into battle.

If war was the only path to end the suffering, then he would carve it himself.

The moon-lit sky stretched before him, vast and uncertain, but he would meet it head-on. And when the sun rose again, it would rise over a man who had made his choice—a prince no longer, but a general, shaped by loss, driven by duty, and ready to claim whatever future lay beyond.

He nudged his steed forward, Juniper's hooves striking the earth with steady resolve. Elias didn't look back.

Midhelm's fate had fallen into his hands—cold, trembling, unwilling.

And his war?
It had only just begun.

Thread LIX

ᚦᛖ ᛒᚢᚱᛞᛖᚾᛋ ᛟᚠ ᚺᛖᛁᚱᛋ ᚦᛖ ᛒᚢᚱᛞᛖᚾᛋ ᛟᚠ ᚺᛖᛁᚱᛋ ᚦᛖ ᛒᚢᚱᛞᛖᚾᛋ

ᚨᛞᚨᛚᛃᚨ

ADALJA STOOD IN HER CHAMBERS, the hearth's flames casting flickering shadows across the stone walls, her face as hard and still as the stones themselves. The Queen stared blankly, exhaustion faintly glowing beneath her eyes—the silent toll of grief lodged deep in her chest.

She was still in her wedding gown and cloak. She hadn't moved to change. *Couldn't.*

The pristine white fabric was sullied, no longer untouched—or beautiful. Crimson stains bloomed across the bodice and sleeves—a mockery of innocence. Of new beginnings.

The splattered symbol sneered at the very idea of purity, marking her not as a bride, but as a witness.

Her curls, once a wondrous testament to her vibrancy, now hung in a loose braid—Elias' handiwork from earlier. A few stubborn strands slipped free to frame her face. The memory of his hands in her hair washed over her in a wave—gentle, steady, soft. She wished he were still here.

She wished the fire felt warm.

But it didn't. Not anymore.
Because her heart, though beating, had forgotten how to warm itself. The flame was gone. All that remained for kindling was *parchment.*

Olivja's letters—every one she could carry—were clutched tightly in her hands, as if sheer strength could pull her back.

She had begged Sapphire to retrieve them; now they lay sprawled in a small chest, their words known only to the gods.

She shook her head slowly, rogue tears slipping free. Dagrun's name was scrawled across too many endings—the letters fanned across the desk like wilting petals. A sob broke loose.

Jarl Ragnarvik...the first man she had ever watched die. She hoped it would be the last.

The image clung to her mind like blood to her gown—impossible to scrub clean. The memory replayed again and again, vivid as the moment itself.

The letters she clutched felt like a gateway, each one an echoing voice that no longer lived. They haunted her, spectral reminders of what was lost and what could never be regained. So she hadn't dared to read them. Words carried voices, memories, feelings...and Adalja feared what they might summon.

Tears broke loose like a summer storm.

The weight of her failure—her unspoken love for the woman she hadn't dared to claim, and now never could—gnawed at her with every breath. She was desperate to feel *her*...but the words were as dead as Olivja.

The Norsewoman was gone, and all that remained were these pieces of paper—testaments to a love that had never fully bloomed, now suffocated by the violence inside the castle walls.

Walls that now bore her name. She was reminded of it each time the firelight caught the polished edge of her wedding band.

The parchment in her grip crinkled softly, the sound too loud against the oppressive silence. Her fingers trembled.

Then slowly, as if surrendering a burden too great to carry—Adalja set the letters down on the table, one by one. Each one heavier than the last.

Her hand hovered over the final page, reluctant to let it go. But she did. It fell with a soft whisper atop the rest. Adalja exhaled, chest tight.

Then the door swung open.

She barely had time to register the motion before it clicked shut behind the intruder.

Adalja turned her head over her shoulder, expecting Elias—his steady presence the only thing that still made sense. The only thing she desired.

But what met her gaze was not him.
It was a twisted silhouette, and it unsettled her to her core.

"*Vincent.*"
Adalja breathed his name, her voice barely a whisper as her heart stilled at the sight of the weary man before her.

He had changed since the wedding.

A loose cream tunic hung from his frame, the deep V-neck exposing the sharp line of his collarbone. The shirt hung untucked and wrinkled as if he had dressed in haste.

The soft fabric draped over dark, fitted trousers tucked into black boots. He looked almost unreal—like an exhausted, broken angel had fallen into her chamber.

She wanted to scream, to run, to move—*anything*—but all she could do was stand frozen.

He yanked off his hood and cowl, tossing them near the door, his eyes wide with tears.

Her gaze swept over his bruised, bloodied face, catching the haunted intensity in his eyes as they scanned her room—trying to absorb every trace of life it held.

She took a tentative step back as he came closer, her focus faltering. His bloodshot eyes were robbed of their light, a stark reminder of the tears he'd shed.

Regardless of all he had done...Adalja knew Vincent was a victim—a pawn of his father's cruelty, a prisoner of his own choices. A man already dead long before she ever met him.

Her hands trembled as she watched him, eyes wide. He took a hesitant step forward, his gaze piercing yet filled with something unfamiliar. The dark glint in his eyes sent a chill through her. In it, she saw echoes of his brother from the night before—the same brokenness, the same desperation...the same pain.

Except there was no consoling him.
She was not the one he wanted to hold.

Vincent opened his mouth, his voice cracking as he spoke. "Adalja..."
Her name hung in the air, fragile like glass, almost too painful to say.

Adalja wiped the tears streaming down her cheeks, her heart aching at the sight of him—a man who once radiated confidence and light, now reduced to a hollow, shattered figure.

"What—why are you here?" she exhaled, afraid of what he might do after all she'd seen him capable of.

"I..." His voice faltered as he took two slow steps towards her. "I had to see that you were safe." His voice trembled, and his eyes flickered over her, as if struggling to believe what he was seeing.

"Safe...?" she repeated. He was the one she feared most.

When their eyes met, her breath was stolen. For a fleeting moment, she saw a frightened child in him—until the brutal memory of Dagrun surged up, crushing any pity that stirred. The room closed in around her, sharp and isolating.

How was Vincent free? Ezekiel's rage had been plain at the wedding, yet his son had gone unpunished?

"Because I—I thought she was safe. But she wasn't..." His voice broke to a whisper. "Olivja...*Li-iv.*" A sob ripped from his chest as he tried to say her name again, tears streaking his face.

Adalja's voice wavered as she shuddered, trying to steady herself. "Vincent..." she managed, her hands slowly lowering as firelight cast dangerous shadows over his beaten face.

He stepped closer until he was in the centre of the room. His gaze lingered on the fire crackling in the hearth, a frown branded into his expression.

"I couldn't save her," he growled, more to himself than to her. "*I couldn't save any of them...*"

He began pacing, breath shallow and ragged, scrubbing at his face as if he could wipe away the guilt etched deep into his skin. The cuts from Vincent's last confrontation with his father no longer bled, but their pain lingered, carving scars too deep to heal.

"You're hurt…" Adalja said, her hand trembling as she cautiously reached for him, desperate to ground him. Though she feared him, she couldn't ignore the broken man before her. "Think not on it—you must rest now—"

"I do not long for rest!" he spat, his voice cracking. "I long for *Olivja*! But I cannot have her," he said, voice breaking, eyes shining with tears.

"He stole her from me—killed her…" The words spilled from him like blood from an open wound.

"*What*?" she whimpered, brows furrowing as he confessed the opposite of what she believed.

"She…she was meant to be my *salvation*," he cried, his voice raw. "My way out of all this…but he took her from me. STOLE her from me! Same as all the rest…and—and I could not stop him. I could not shield her!" His voice sank into a guttural growl, thick with pain carved deep into his soul.

Adalja's thoughts spun as she tried to process his words.

Vincent didn't kill Olivja?

The certainty she had clung to splintered beneath the depth of his raw, desperate grief. Her heart clenched, caught in a vice of colliding emotions. She wanted to scream at him, to accuse him, to demand the truth—but the anguish in his eyes gave her pause.

Could someone so broken, so consumed by guilt and rage, truly be capable of lying in this moment? Or was he simply unravelling, unable to face the depths of what he'd done?

Her gaze flicked to his shaking hands, then back to his face, searching for some sign, some clue. What stood before her now was only a hollowed shell, a man crushed beneath the weight of his own sins.

"But I can protect *you*, Adalja," Vincent rushed, not giving her a chance to respond. "I-I *know* I can—this time I *will*…and I know what I did to your parents is beyond forgiveness."

The prince's voice quieted suddenly, as if something inside him broke. "*I had no choice...*" he trailed off before muttering, "*None of us did.*"

His wide, fevered eyes held the ghosts of his past—a mother long dead, a father who had torn apart everything he loved, and a lover they both shared, in one capacity or another—ripped away too soon.

"I know you must despise me, princess. I know it well," Vincent said, each word strained, like grief and rage were pulling his throat in opposite directions. "I brought poison to their blood. I spilled Dagrun's. I did not wish it—but I did it all the same." His words turned to a growl, his voice a beast he could no longer control.

He was unravelling before her, utterly alone.

Whether for her safety or his sanity, she responded in a fragile murmur. "Why, Vincent...?"

"WHY ELSE, ADALJA!?" he shouted, as though the question itself were unthinkable.

But as quickly as his anger spiked, it crumbled back into sorrowful whimpers.

"I-I could no longer let him command me...command *us*," he cried at the mention of his brother.

He was an image of grief—rage and anguish warring with all else.

"I did it all to make him feel what I've borne all my life...the pain, the emptiness, the *rot*—" he scoffed bitterly, eyes blazing with fury at the thought of his father. "The very rot that's festered within me since my mother's death. I wanted to tear him asunder, and I thought—no—I *knew* this would bring it to pass."

His voice dropped to a hoarse whisper, the words laden with deep despair. "Forgive me, Adalja. *I beg you*. I only sought to hurt *him*...and in doing so, I've ruined all. And now you...you are here—alone—just as I am, and it is all my doing..."

"You are not alone, Vince..." Adalja whimpered, reaching for something to pull him back from the edge of insanity. "You...you have Elias, yo—"

"He's GONE!" Vincent roared, flinging one hand towards the door.

"He's gone?" she asked, worry flashing through her.

Adalja didn't understand. He *promised* to come back to her.

"He—" Vincent laughed, tired and bitter. "He *left* you—*me*—*here* in this—this *coffin*—with Ezekiel! All for a meaningless war!"

His eyes flashed with rage, the rawness of his grief exposed.

Adalja flinched but stayed silent, breath shallow as her gaze flicked between his broad frame and the door.
Fear gripped her—tight, inescapable.

He stopped, hand shooting up—not to rake, but to claw at his hair—as if relief might be buried there. His fingers gripped hard, tugging at the strands—jagged and ruined, like him— and his breath came in sharp, uneven bursts.

"I am near undone," he muttered, a short, bitter laugh escaping him—foreign, hollow.

"I cannot undo what I've wrought...I've lost *all*...I am losing myself now. I've lost my grip, Adalja, I know it, but I also know how to set it right."

"You haven't lost all," she murmured reassuringly. It was more a desperate prayer than a fact.

Adalja took a daring step forward, swallowing fear to smother the wildfire burning through Vince.

His hands curled into fists, then dropped limp, as if every ghost of his failures dragged at his bones. His shoulders sagged, and his voice dropped to a whisper.

"You're right...because you're still here, Adalja. *Alive*." His eyes lifted to hers again, voice softening to a near plea. "I can still make things right. I still have a choice—to protect you and *still* make him pay. And then, finally, I'll make it up to her."

Suddenly, he covered his face with both palms and turned to the fire, his broad shoulders heaving with each breath. She didn't dare move—barely even breathed—afraid that the slightest motion might shatter whatever fragile barrier kept his unravelling rage from consuming them both.

"I loved her..." he mumbled. She wasn't sure he even meant her to hear it.

His confession made her heart ache in ways she didn't understand. She was slowly seeing a broken man for what he was—a hurt child.
A soul adrift.

"I loved her as well," Adalja murmured, tears tracing her lips as she spoke.

His head lifted slowly, green eyes gleaming with envy that sent a chill down her spine.

In a fit of anguish, Vincent's composure snapped. He surged towards her, swift and sharp, until his chest pinned hers. His hands seized her cheeks, forcing her head upwards so she could not look away.

"No. You did not love her—not as I did," he whimpered, voice catching as he leaned into her, eyes digging into hers, drowning in the sorrows beneath them.

His grip tightened, curling against her cheeks, pulling a soft whimper from her throat. "You *had* her." His breath faltered. "You—you felt Olivja's love, *knew* what it meant to be loved *by* her. You—you were *enough* for her..."

Adalja's breath caught on a sharp lump rising in her throat. It was shaped like his voice and cut like guilt. She had no answer—not while her heart sagged from the loss, her soul splintered beneath his grief.

"Somehow," she breathed, barely more than a whisper, her gaze faltering under his piercing stare. "I felt the weight of her love, yes, but...she never knew mine."

Her throat cinched tight; her hands curled, useless at her sides. "I never spoke the truth of what dwelled in my heart to her."

Vincent's expression contorted—grief, anger, and something hollow, something bitter.

"Tell me she knew," he rasped, though his voice trembled with doubt. "She *had to* have known..."

His jaw tightened. A dry, broken laugh slipped from his lips as he shook his head. His thumbs brushed her cheeks, rough and trembling.

"Swear to me Liv died knowing she was loved."

Her breath shuddered, chest tightening—she didn't know how to respond without breaking him further. Her eyes squeezed shut. Fresh tears slipped down her cheeks, dampening his hands.

"I...I know not," she whispered, voice fragile and torn. "I know not if she ever knew."

Vincent's eyes darkened, a flicker of something dangerous cutting through the grief—sharp, hollow rage beneath the devastation. His thumbs pressed harder into her cheeks. His breath quickened.

"You do not *know*?" he breathed, sharp and ragged. His brows twisted, as if her words had struck bone.

"How—how could you not tell her?" His breath hitched, eyes wide and wild. "How could you let her die not knowing?"

Adalja's throat closed so tight it hurt to breathe. Fresh tears blurred her vision.

"I was scared..." Her voice buckled. "I...I always ran from her. I thought I'd have time—I thought—"

"There is never enough time," Vincent growled, his voice ragged and venomous. He pressed his forehead to hers, breath sharp and uneven. His hands slid from her face to her neck, fingers curling beneath her jaw with just enough pressure to keep her still—to force her to face him.

"*I* loved her," Vincent growled, low and dangerously steady. "I loved her more than a poet loves his quill, more than the knife loves the heart!"

His hands tightened, just enough to steal her breath. "And still...*she chose you*."

A single tear slid down his cheek, cutting through the sharpness of his words, though his expression didn't soften. His eyes burned with a bitterness Adalja had never seen.

"And..." Vincent's voice cracked. "In chasing you...she was running from *me*."

Adalja shook her head, tears slipping down her cheeks as her shaking hands lifted to his wrists. "'Tis not true—"

"Isn't it?" His fingers curled into the back of her neck, just shy of cruel. "She died...and you were the last person she loved."

Her throat clenched. A sob escaped.
"I didn't deserve her," Adalja choked out. "I was but a coward—"

"As was I," Vincent hissed. His forehead pressed harder against hers. "But I would've *burned the world* to make her love me the way she loved you...And *I have*."

Adalja's chest tightened, his confession blooming like ruin beneath her ribs. "Vincent..."

His eyes closed briefly, breath hot and trembling against her skin.

"You were enough for her," Vincent whispered.
His hands fell away from her neck, but his face lingered. His eyes glistened, his breath thin and unsteady.
"*I was not*."

Adalja's heart broke for him—for the sheer emptiness in his voice.

"She's gone," he breathed, almost to himself. "*Gone*...and I...I must set things right."

Her fingers lifted to his cheek before she even realised. Her thumb brushed a stray tear from his bruised cheek—delicate and slow. Vincent's eyes fluttered shut beneath her touch. A ragged breath escaped his lips.

Slowly, his hands dropped to her waist, curling loosely around the fabric of her dress. He slumped forward, resting his head atop hers, like a branch bowed by winter.

"I must save you," Vincent rasped into her hair. "I must keep you safe...from my father, from war, from *pain*."

The lost prince's fingers tightened at her hips, seeking redemption in her.

"So run away with me." His voice quieted, the softness of his plea curling into desperation.

Adalja stiffened under his touch, heart pounding with panic as she tried to gather herself.

"*Please*, Adalja." His voice cracked—raw, jagged—but beneath the plea was a dangerous edge that made her chest fold in on itself. "Come with me. We will go to Ragnarvik."

Adalja pressed her hands to his chest, trying to regain some control in the moment, to pull him out of this fragile dream of escape.

"Solvig will take us in," he said, voice quivering like a flame in the wind. "We can stay with her. We can be close to Olivja." His eyes darkened, gaze sharpening beneath the tears.
"We'll have each other."

Adalja's breath came quicker now. She tried to step back, but his hands tightened. Her heart hammered against her ribs, skin burning beneath his iron grip.

"Vincent—"

"You think we are meant to linger here?" His voice hardened, his teeth flashing beneath the twist of his mouth. "You think I can *remain* here...knowing what he did to her? Knowing I cannot bring her back?" His hands clenched in the fabric of her skirt, breath faltering as he looked down at her.

"I am left with naught but emptiness here. You—" His voice cracked, desperate and fragile. "You are all that remains of her."

Adalja opened her mouth to speak, but the words died on her tongue as Vincent's hands slid up to her ribs—firm, possessive.

"I will not lose you," Vincent hissed. His grip tightened, his knuckles white.
"So you'll come with me. You *must* come with me. *Dammit, Adalja, I need you*! I need you to."

Adalja trembled, unsure, hesitant to touch him. She knew denying him would only deepen the spiral—and she wanted to help, to steady him, to feel Olivja through him. So she nodded, carefully resting a hand on his cheek.

"Very well..." Her voice quivered as she forced a small, sad smile onto her lips.
"Yes, we—we can go. I will leave with you."

Vincent's breath hitched, but there was no peace in his expression. His green eyes trailed over her face, searching—frantic and desperate.

"Say it again," he demanded. His eyes were wide, as though she had shocked him, breath shallow as his hands curled further around her. "Say it again...as though it be true..."

Adalja's chest squeezed. "I will leave with you," she whispered, though her voice wavered. "I will run with you to Ragnarvik."

Vincent's jaw twitched, and for a moment, it seemed as though the silence between them was a god pressing on his ribs. He pulled her closer, hugging her; a hand sliding up through her curls, his breath hot against the side of her head.

"We shall go now," he choked out, his voice breathy and ragged. Then he pulled back, as though they had no time, and turned for the door. His hand seized her wrist, his grip harsh enough to make her flinch. "We must leave at once, Princess."

Her feet stumbled beneath her as he pulled her towards the door. His breath was sharp; his jaw clenched so tightly the tendons in his neck strained beneath his skin.

"What of our things?" she asked, voice thin and wavering as she tried to stall—anything to slow him down.

Because the letters sat on the desk.
She couldn't leave them behind...the only thing she had left of all their love.
She wouldn't dare.

But Vincent's grip tightened painfully. His other hand curled into a fist at his side.

"I will get you whatever you desire once we are safe," he said in haste, his gaze burning as he turned towards her. "There is no time, Adalja!"

She pressed her palm against her stomach, the muscles knotting tight like its own clenched fist. Her chest rose and fell erratically. She yanked her hand back, a sharp, instinctive motion fuelled by her growing fear.

"Vincent—I-I only need one thing!" she stammered, reaching for the desk, fingers extended.

She needed to grab the chest, that was all—then they could leave.
Her foot caught on the edge of the rug, and she stumbled forward, colliding with the desk.

The impact sent the small chest and a vase tumbling to the floor.

The sharp crack of shattering ceramic sliced through the room, shards scattering across the stone like fractured stars. The scent of crushed petals and spilled water curled through the air. The chest burst open as it hit the floor, spilling its contents in a flurry of papers—old, worn letters with edges curled and yellowed, dampened where the water had touched them.

Vincent froze, eyes snapping to the scattered letters.

For a moment, all the air seemed to leave the room. His breathing hitched, sharp and uneven, and his gaze locked onto the parchment as though it were a living thing that might lash out at him.

"What...are these?" he rasped, his voice low and dangerous.

Her heart pounded so loudly she was certain he could hear it. She dropped, her shaking hands darting to gather the letters, but Vincent was faster. His hands trembled as he snatched a crumpled page that had fallen at his boots. Blood drained from his face—his lips parted, eyes darting across the paper.

"*Olivja...*"
Her name fell from his lips like a whispered prayer.

The prince's hands curled around the letter. His face was a mask of anguish and fury, disbelief etched deep as if he could not fathom Adalja possessing something so sacred.

Suddenly, he scrambled, breath ragged, rifling through the fallen pages, snatching up anything bearing Olivja's name. Vincent's dark eyes raced over the words faster than his mind could grasp them. His body shook, fingers trembled violently.

Adalja pressed herself back against the desk, watching the storm in his eyes gather, threatening to swallow him whole. He stumbled to his feet, hands shaking as he read through the letters haphazardly.

"Th-those are mine, Vincent," she said, her voice faltering under the gravity of his anguish. She swallowed hard, fear crawling up her throat.

"*They're from her...?*" His words hung in the air, heavy and unfinished, as though speaking them aloud might shatter what little ground he stood on.

The letters tore in his grasp, knuckles blanching with the strength of it.

Adalja went still—prey before a predator.
Whatever momentary trust she'd held that he wouldn't hurt her—shattered.

Vincent's fingers trembled over the ink, his chest rising and falling in shallow, erratic breaths. His eyes glistened, unshed tears catching the dim light. The letters were tearing open wounds he was desperately trying to stitch shut.

It was why she had never dared read them herself.
But the prince knew no such restraint.

"*No...you've no right to these...*" The words came as a whimper, barely audible.

"Olivja is *dead*! She's GONE, Adalja!" he screamed.

Her breath caught as his rage, his jealousy, overtook him. Tears streamed down his face, faster than hers had ever fallen, his head shaking with force.

Olivja's words sliced the final thread of his sanity, unravelling him completely. He turned—and as he paused before the hearth, his silhouette burned into her eyes—shoulders rising and falling as if every choice leading to this point carved deeper into his spine.

Adalja whimpered, "*...Vincent?*"

She knew what he was thinking...
But he gave her no time to stop him.

In a single motion, he hurled the papers into the low-burning fire. They swirled through the air before catching flame, casting the room in a sudden, brighter glow. The fire roared hotter with the remnants of Ragnarvik love.

Adalja's heart shattered, eyes wide with terror as the final pieces of her love burned before her. Each letter that curled into ash was love lost.
Devotion turned smoke.

"NO!" she screamed. "Vincent, *STOP!*" She lunged forward, desperate to save any remnants of the letters—even if they were charred, even if they burned her.

But Vincent was quicker, engulfing her in his strong arms before she could reach a single word she never got to read. He hurled her back, their steps unsteady across the paper covered, tear slicked stone.

"She is no longer in this world; her love is not some gift for you to hoard!" Vincent's voice cracked, guttural, as the words echoed against her hair.

But she wasn't listening.

Olivja was dying all over again. Only this time, in front of her eyes.
Adalja clawed at his tense forearm as it barred across her chest, scoring red marks into his already wounded vessel.

"*I NEED THEM*! *I need her*!" She sobbed the words, voice raw.

Unable to battle her frantic thrashing, and desperate to keep her from the flames, Vincent shoved her aside—she slipped from his arms. Adalja stumbled forward, a sob caught in her throat as she flung out her arms to brace her fall.

Another scream tore through the room—this time, not from heartbreak.

Pain burst through her limbs as she hit the ground, shards of ceramic driving deep beneath her skin under the full weight of the fall.

A cry ripped from her throat as she rolled onto her back, clutching her thigh. Her dress bloomed with crimson beneath trembling hands, spreading like fire. Several shards of broken pottery protruded from her skin like a clutch of quills driven in by the stone itself—inked not with words, but blood.

Her breaths came fast and shallow, gaze flicking to Vincent in both fear and need. But his expression was frozen, chest heaving as he stared at the blood like it was the first time he'd ever seen it.

The distraught prince's lips parted soundlessly, his head shaking rapidly—denial.

Vincent's hand flew to his hair, fingers clawing through white strands as panic twisted his features. His gaze darted between her wound, the broken pottery, and the spreading blood.

She knew it had been an accident. He hadn't meant for her to fall.
For a moment, rage and grief had turned him into a monster—but now, in the face of her pain, perhaps a crumb of the man he once was had returned.

"Adalja—"
He dropped to his knees beside her, uncaring of the dangerous ground, and seized her shoulders with trembling hands. His grip was too hard, too frantic,

as he pulled her into his lap. His body curled protectively over her as his breath scraped against her ear.

"Please...I beg you. I did not mean to—truly, forgive me, Adalja," his voice shook—uneven, almost breaking. "Let me help you. Let me see, I'll stop the bleeding." His hands were already grasping at her leg.

"No! Pl-please, Vincent," she breathed, voice thin and sputtering. She tried to push him off, but even the slightest movement drove the shards deeper.

He held her tighter. Closer.
The splinters shifted—and she cried out a sharp sob.
He was too strong. Too much. Too blind to the damage he'd caused...and was still causing.

"It-it *hurts*!"

His green eyes snapped to hers, pupils blown wide, feverish from everything unravelling.

Her heart hammered as he gripped her leg; rough yet grounding. Vincent seized the jagged shard buried in her thigh. Pain surged—sharp, blinding—and she screamed, legs thrashing beneath him.

But he only held her tighter, pressing her face into his chest, her cries muffled against linen.

"I have you...forgive me...I-I would never hurt you," he rasped, his voice raw and broken, a sob breaking through. His eyes burned with frantic intensity as they locked onto hers. "I made an oath to Elias—I vowed you'd come to no harm by my side. I need but a moment, princess..."

He didn't wait for permission.

His fingers curled around the shard—then, with one sharp yank, he tore it free. Pain exploded through her leg, and she screamed, her body lurching beneath him.

Her hands flew to his chest, shoving on instinct—but his grip was iron. He clamped his palm over the bleeding wound, stanching the flow.

"V-Vince! *You mustn't*!"
She writhed in his grip, thick tears soaking through his shirt.

But his presence stunned her.

"*Stop.*" The warning came low and steady, his voice cutting through the room like a blade.

He eased her down onto the fur rugs, away from the scattered shards she'd left behind. His hand shot up, seizing her wrists, pinning them to still her struggle.

Prince Worthyn's breath came hard and fast against her face. He hovered inches above, firelight carving sharp shadows across the hollow planes of his cheeks. His eyes gleamed, dark and unreadable beneath the flickering flame.

"Let me finish," he said, but it was no plea. His voice broke. "I am not asking you."

His free hand moved carefully, plucking splinters from her forearms and palms—each sting almost worse than the ache in her thigh. His breath hitched, rough and uneven. His forehead dropped to hers, suffocating her with his presence and the pain of his aid.

"I must get them out. Then we shall go—we'll ride for Ragnarvik, I swear it."

Her mind scrambled for a thread of trust amidst the chaos. She flinched beneath his touch, limbs burning, pulse a frantic thrum in her throat.

"Enough—*please*!" she whimpered, her body shaking beneath him. "I am in pain—"

"I know, darling, I know it hurts," he cooed, voice cracking. "But I *must* do this...I have to—"

His eyes squeezed shut; his head tilted towards her shoulder. A ragged sound escaped him, somewhere between sob and gasp. His hand moved from her wounds to cradle her face, his thumb dragging roughly along her cheekbone.

"Look at me—I cannot lose you," he whispered harshly. "I *will not* lose you too."

"*Please*, take me from here," Adalja choked, afraid to feel yet another shard torn from her limbs—desperate for anything if it meant the end of this pain. Even if her heart was breaking, even if he was unravelling in front of her—falling apart—while she was *trapped* beneath the wreckage.

He faltered for a moment, eyes tearful—so much like Elias, yet so far. And her own, oceans of pain and panic, stared back up at him—begging. He nodded, throat bobbing.

"We'll go," he murmured, voice a thin, frantic thread. "You know not what this means to me, Adalja. I will protect you—you have my word."

Her breath caught, her muscles easing beneath his hold. She opened her mouth, but no sound came.

Because—
The door creaked open.

A slow, drawn-out groan of iron hinges cut through the frantic rasp of Vincent's breath.

Adalja's wide, tear-filled eyes flicked towards the sound, pulse halting mid-beat.

The dark outline of a figure filled the doorway, haloed by flickering torchlight. The cloak's edges swayed with the draft, casting shifting shadows across the threshold.

Her gaze sharpened, narrowed—waiting for the figure to dissolve, to break apart beneath uneven light and prove it a trick of her failing mind.

A ghost. A hallucination.
But it didn't dissolve.

Her gaze stayed pinned to the figure.

Tall. Silent.
Wrapped in dark silk and shadow.

A hooded cloak fell in elegant folds down her frame, half-veiling her face in soft darkness. Beneath its open edge, her dress shimmered with quiet menace—deep obsidian fabric that slithered across her skin with every breath.

Skin glinted beneath the slashed neckline, marked with charcoal runes trailing down her throat, winding across her collarbone and curling along her hands in jagged, ancient patterns. Her hair was long—too long—falling in dark, wild strands.

But it was her *eyes* that made Adalja's blood run cold.

Gold. Blazing. Staring from beneath the dark hood with a quiet, cutting intensity that burned straight through the room.

Not golden in the way of sunlight or warmth—no, this was the gleam of fire at the edge of a storm, the glint of a blade beneath candlelight. Cold and sharp and endless.

The figure stepped forward. Slow. Measured.
The whisper of her cloak across the stone sent a chill twisting down Adalja's spine.

Adalja's chest folded inward. Her mouth opened, and a sound broke free—a fractured gasp, strangled and trembling beneath disbelief and muscle memory.

"*...Olivja?*"
Her voice splintered, raw and broken.

The figure didn't move. Didn't blink.

But those amber eyes—

They burned.

Thread LX

ᚦᛖ ᛒᚢᚱᛞᛖᚾᛋ ᛟᚠ ᚺᛖᛁᚱᛋ ᚦᛖ ᛒᚢᚱᛞᛖᚾᛋ ᛟᚠ ᚺᛖᛁᚱᛋ ᚦᛖ ᛒᚢᚱᛞᛖᚾᛋ

ᛟᛚᛁᚠᛃᚨ

The door creaked open, slow and deliberate, as though the very room held its breath.

For a moment, the amber light spilled from the corridor, carving a long shadow—like a ghost returning to haunt the living.

Olivja stepped through the threshold, her frame stark against the glow behind her. The quiet shuffle of her black dress and heavy fur cloak brushing the floor was the only sound. Her footsteps were soft—but unyielding.

Her amber gaze swept over the room.

Adalja lay crumpled on the ground, blood and shattered ceramic scattered like relics—forsaken, forgotten. Beside her, a man knelt, his trembling hands pinning her wrists.

Tears streaked her lover's face as their eyes met. A broken sob clawed its way from Adalja's lips, cutting through the icy calm in Olivja's chest like a blade.

"*Olivja*?"

The man turned—ashen, wild-eyed. His hair was unevenly hacked; his face bruised, desperate.

For one flickering moment, the sheer gravity of returning almost brought her to her knees.

She had dreamt of this—returning triumphant, stopping the marriage, exposing the true Pembrook killer. She would take Adalja's hand and escape everything that had tried to destroy them...

But as her gaze settled on Vincent, crouched above Adalja with blood on his face and madness in his eyes, all her plans burned to ash.

He knelt there, frozen.
His breath hitched, lips parting as his glassy eyes traced her face—like his mind couldn't make sense of her.

"*Liv*?" His voice was barely a whisper, disbelieving. "Is it truly you? *Tell me I've gone mad...*"

"W-why...is your hair so short?" was the first thing she asked—because that alone was a horror. A sign of something broken.

A sign that told her he had lost himself.
That she no longer knew this man.

But before he responded, he moved.

He lurched towards her like a drowning man breaking the surface—reaching, grasping, afraid she'd vanish. He stood and his fingers caught her face, his touch frantic and disbelieving.

Her chest seized at the sight of him—his ruined hair, the dark bruises blooming across his cheek, the dried blood at his temple. He looked as if he had been torn apart and barely stitched back together.

Her hands shot up to cup his face, feeling the heat of his battered skin beneath her palms. Her fingers trembled as they brushed over the raw wounds, the swelling along his jaw. Her heart pounded, a sharp, unbearable ache rising in her throat.

"What happened, Vincent?" she whispered, her voice cracking with horror—raw and fragile.

Vincent sucked in a breath, his fingers twitching against her skin. He stared at her—like he couldn't believe she was real. Like grief and madness had conjured her.

Then his grip on her tightened, his forehead pressed against hers, a choked sound escaping his lips.

"Olivja—" he whimpered, almost collapsing into her, his fingers curling into her cheeks. "*I thought you were dead.*"

She swallowed hard, ignoring the sting in her eyes, her hands sliding down his arms, feeling the tension and tremors in his body.

"Who did this to you?" she demanded, low and furious.

His distant eyes told her everything.
She'd seen that look before.

Her entire body went rigid. Her grip on him tightened, nails digging into his arms. "Vincent. Where is he?" she asked, her voice sharper, colder.

Vincent barely shook his head, thumbs brushing her skin, desperate to keep her close. "No...no, that matters not. *You do—*"

"It matters to me!" Her heart hammered. She felt his pulse beneath her fingers, saw the fear flickering in his eyes. *Her Vincent*, her oldest friend, was standing before her in ruin.

She had been gone too long. Too much had happened in her absence. And she was going to kill Ezekiel for it.

But Vincent wouldn't let her go. His hands tightened, his breath hot and unsteady.

"Forget him—I care only for you!" he said, voice trembling. "*My Olivja, you're alive,* " he whispered, his thumbs smearing the charcoal runes on her cheeks.

"How are you alive? What did he do to you? *Did Ezekiel hurt you*?" A broken sob fanned her face as he leaned in, his nose featherlight against hers.

She stiffened under his grasp, absorbing his tear-streaked face.

"I am not the one bleeding," she countered, voice raw and pained.

Her hand pressed to his chest, and the other returned to his cheek, carefully wiping at a bruise his father had given him. His heart was beating wildly against her palm.

Something was wrong—he was a fragment of himself: Happy to see her, and yet he was afraid.

"Ezekiel," he whimpered, tears spilling as he leaned into her touch. "He returned, furious with me, and...I—" Vincent choked, then stopped swiftly.

He slowly pulled back, mouth parting in a silent gasp, eyes stilling as though a thousand thoughts raced past. His hands tightened on her cheeks, throat bobbing before he finally managed to speak again.

"God, Olivja—Forgive me..." he grunted, voice weighed down by guilt. "I had to. Please, hear me, i-it was the only way to hurt him as he hurt me. As he hurt you—" He faltered, shoulders sagging.

"Vincent, what are you saying? S-steady your breath..." She tried to console him, moving a hand to grasp his wrist as his hold grew more painful.
"I know you spilled Pembrook blood—"

"It is not that!" Vincent shook his head, body trembling as though the truth might tear him apart. "I thought you were gone—I thought," he paused, eyes flickering across her face. "I wouldn't have hurt him if I knew—"

"Hurt *who*?" she interrupted, her anxiety mounting with every beat he dodged the truth.

She was already on the precipice of losing him to the deaths of the Pembrooks and the witches...but there was more now? More people he had harmed that she had to forgive?

"*Dagrun.*"

Every part of her recoiled.
Hands left his frame like his skin had scalded her.

No. Impossible. I heard wrong...
But he went on...as if it were true.

His voice cracked, and he sank to his knees before her, face contorted with anguish.

"Forgive me...please..."

"Wh...what? *No...*" she exhaled.
She refused to believe that Vincent would hurt someone she loved...let alone her father.

"*Where is pabbi, Vincent?*" Olivja asked in the quietest of whispers.

"*Olivja...I—*"

She lost her balance, mind spinning. She couldn't hear Vincent's final words over the blood thundering in her ears.

Dagrun. Her father. *Gone.*
And Vincent—the boy she had once trusted more than anyone—had been the one to wield the blade?

Her eyes burned with unshed tears, but her expression remained unreadable, her silence a cold abyss.

"No..." she breathed.
"...*What have you done, Vincent...?*"

For the first time, Vincent had no answer.

He looked up at her, broken and bloodied, and in the space between them, everything they had ever been shattered into pieces too jagged to ever fit together again.

He clutched at her hips, gripping her dress in his hands, his tearful face reduced to that of his younger self, begging for forgiveness.

Olivja's heart was a battlefield, torn between love and fury, loyalty and vengeance.

For so long, her purpose had been clear—avenge the Pembrooks, bring honour to her father, and rise from betrayal's ashes. But now, the lines she had drawn so sharply blurred in the face of Vincent's broken figure before her.

He was her best friend, her only friend for so long, the one she trusted above all, yet also the man who had destroyed everything.

How could she reconcile the boy who once held her hand with the man now drenched in her father's blood?

The weight of his sins crushed her chest, the memory of Dagrun's laugh echoing in her ears like a haunting hymn.

She *wanted* to forgive him, to find some fragment of redemption in his shattered gaze, but forgiveness felt like a betrayal—a knife twisted into the memory of the man who raised her.

Her fingers trembled against the hilt of her blade.

Could she live with herself if she spared him?
Could she breathe if she didn't?

His grip bruised her thighs, a growl of frustration leaving him.

"No! *Don't*—don't look at me like that, Olivja, *please,*" Vincent begged, his voice breaking like splintered glass, the words cutting their way out. "*I-I had to...*"

She froze, the world narrowing to the sound of his sobs, of the man who had murdered her father now begging for absolution at her feet.

Because even in her fury, she didn't hate him...*why?*

Tears spilled down her cheeks, relentless and burning. And her vision blurred with faces of the dead—her father, the Pembrooks, everyone she had sworn to avenge.

She wanted to scream, to rage—but all she could do was stand there, shaking, as grief and fury threatened to swallow her whole.

Vincent looked up at her, his tear-streaked face twisting with pain and anger.

"He took everything from me! He took you!" he shouted, voice cracking. "This was never how it was meant to end...I believed you lost, Olivja. *Gone.* What was I to do? Tell me—*tell me what should I have done!?*"

Her breath hitched, and she staggered back, the blade at her hip trembling as though begging to be removed from its spot.

She couldn't bear to look at him—
Not the pleading in his eyes.
Not the blood on his hands.

Because she *wanted* to forgive him.
And she knew if she kept looking into those eyes, *she would.*

She turned her back to him, her voice breaking—a whisper, a prayer, a plea.
"*Why...?*"
The word not meant for Vincent but for the gods above.

The dagger glinted in her hand as she unsheathed it from her belt, her knuckles whitening with tension.

She wasn't a killer, no matter how much sparring she had done with her father. Not a warrior, no matter what the faith-borns might assume.

She never wanted to kill Vincent—not for the Völur, not for the Pembrooks. Not even now.

Somewhere, deep down, she had already forgiven him for it all. But the thought of her father lying cold in some *Christian grave* filled her with an unrelenting, numbing rage.

A rage she'd never been taught to wield.

A rage she never wanted to use.

"No..." Vincent cried behind her, voice low, dark, and desperate.
"No!" he shouted. "Do not turn away from me, Olivja!"

His footsteps thundered as he surged forward, seizing her bicep with bruising force and yanking her back towards him.

The world seemed to stop.

She didn't think—she couldn't think.
Her body moved before her mind could catch up.

In one trembling, furious motion, she turned and drove the dagger into his chest.

Vincent's breath hitched, a sharp gasp escaping him as his grip faltered.

His wide, glassy eyes dropped to his chest, shock and betrayal flickering deep within them.

Her own breath came in ragged, shuddering bursts as the dagger's hilt pressed against her palm.

The warmth of his blood spread, stark against the icy weight pressing in her chest...In his eyes.

"*L...Li-iv...*?" His voice cracked, barely above a whimper, but the words died in his throat, strangled by the life slipping away.

For a heartbeat, they were frozen in time, tethered only by the blade between them.

Then his knees buckled, his weight sagging against her.

She fell with him, gasping for breath—crushed by the dead weight of what she had done. His head fell into her lap, body growing limp as his strength drained with every fading heartbeat.

"No—" she whimpered, her voice raw, her anger, fear, and love bleeding out in a single, uncontrollable rush.

His once-vibrant eyes held nothing but fear—fear for himself, fear of her, fear of his unfinished quest. His last word came weakly, as if he couldn't comprehend how she had hurt him like this.

"Oli—vja..." His voice trembled, disbelief in every breath. Blood spilled from the corner of his mouth, staining the moment with finality.

"Vincent—*w-wait*—no," she gasped, cupping his blood-slicked face as tears blurred her vision.

Her chest ached with the cold, crushing realisation of her choice. The weight of him in her lap was unbearable—physically, emotionally.

His breath hitched, lips parting as if to speak, but only a wet, gurgling gasp escaped. His hands, weak and shaking, barely clung to her wrists.

He was slipping.
Fading.
Dying.

But then—

"Ek elska thik—Livja," he managed, clearer than anything he'd said that night.

Norse?

I love you.
He had said it—so clearly.

Her already-blurred eyes widened—and shattered. She shook her head, confused, hurt, shocked all in one.

"W—why do you know that?" Her words fractured, lost in the sobs that tore through her. "Stop this, Vincent."

She hadn't wanted this.
She hadn't wanted to *end him*.
Hadn't wanted to hear those words—not like that.

"You—you *can't!*" she shouted, breaths raggedly fanning his paling face.

She pressed her forehead to his, fingers curling into his ruined hair as she rocked him.

"Stay—Forgive me—*please, stay,*" she cried, her tears mingling with his, sliding down his cheeks. "*My hands betrayed me*...I did not mean it. *Th-the Norns*—they twisted fate—*I-I did not mean it!*"

But the cold, unyielding dagger—the evidence of her choice—reminded her of the truth.

His green gaze softened, then slowly dulled as he held her one last time.

Then, as the last vestige of his soul slipped away, his body grew too heavy to hold. He collapsed fully into her arms, and the weight of their shared past—of everything that had led to this moment—pulled her down with him.

Her heart stopped.
His heart stopped.

Her breath caught in her throat as she stared into his vacant, lifeless eyes.

"Vince?"

She wasn't speaking to him anymore.
She was speaking to herself.
To the boy who had once held her hand through the darkest of nights, to the man who had torn her world apart.

She slid her rune-covered hands into his hair, gripping hard at his scalp, appalled by how short it was. He wasn't Vincent anymore...just a shattered boy, held together by the glue of fleeting love.

And now, he was not even that.

"VINCENT!"

Her voice broke, louder than before, shattered by a grief she could no longer hold back.

She pulled him closer, cradling his head against her chest, her tears staining his skin.

"No—why? Why!?"
Why did it have to be him—
The one who killed the Pembrooks. Who killed her father and the witches.
Who was her first kill...
Who loved her.

NO! This cannot be your plan, Odin—please!

Her sobs cracked, splitting her soul in two. Screams tore from her throat—wild, ragged, animalistic gasps that clawed at the silence.

"Forgive me...please! *FREYJA, hear me!*" she howled to the gods.
"Take his soul, not mine! Let him lie in your realm...I'll swallow the darkness when it is my time!"

The words choked out of her, lost in a flood of despair. "Grant him mercy...*merciful Freyja*...take him to your field...*I beg you*!" She sobbed as she pressed her lips to his forehead, hoping—more than anything—that she was heard.

In one day, everything was shattered.

Her father was gone.
Vincent was dead.
And she—she was nothing but ruin.

The blood pooling beneath them was a tidal wave drowning her—smothering her with every piece of what was taken and destroyed.

This was the toll she paid—the curse she carried.
The price of vengeance.

"What have I done?!" Her voice cracked, desperate, shattered.
No answer came, only the hollow echo of fate's cruel design.

She was unravelling, gasping for air as if she had taken her own life along with his.

Her hands trembled as she pulled his cold hand to her cheek.
"*Norns*...why have you cursed me so?" she whispered, pressing her face against his palm, desperate for even a flicker of the love that once was.

Only sorrow answered.
Heavy. Crushing. Relentless.

Tears burned her cheeks, dripping onto his lifeless skin. She cradled his head, a strangled cry ripping from her throat—raw, ragged, beyond reason.

And then—softly, strangely—the iron scent of blood faded.

In its place, she caught the wild breath of summer grass. Sun-warmed clover.

Her sob hitched.

"*Olivj*a...?"

She heard her name, and for the briefest instant, she thought it was Vincent.

But it wasn't.

Slowly, she lifted her tear-streaked face to meet Adalja's wide, weeping eyes.

Adalja sat on the floor too, clutching her bleeding wounds, watching Olivja.

"You...you must go—you need to run," Adalja said, her voice trembling as fresh tears spilled down her cheeks. "They'll come for you—the knights—*Ezekiel*—you are not safe here...!"

Olivja still clung to Vincent, unwilling to let go—despite the anger and hatred tangled in her chest. She couldn't part from him. She couldn't accept that she had killed him.

Perhaps she *should* stay—perhaps she should let justice take her too.
She glanced down at his vacant face...

Footsteps echoed in the hall—

She had no more time to mourn.

Her eyes found Adalja—bleeding, breathless, broken.

She was the *true* reason Olivja had returned.
The reason for all her suffering.
Her reason.

She needed to run. To disappear.

But she needed Adalja more.

Her precious Adalja—she was the fire behind every wound. Every thought.
Olivja's tear-filled gaze clung to her, as if memorizing her face for the last time. For one final, desperate moment.

Their eyes locked.

When Olivja spoke, her voice cracked—thin as a whisper:

"...*Come with me.*"

WHAT THE GODS LEFT UNSAID...

ᚦᛖ ᛒᚢᚱᛞᛖᚾᛋ ᛟᚠ ᚺᛖᛁᚱᛋ ᚦᛖ ᛒᚢᚱᛞᛖᚾᛋ ᛟᚠ ᚺᛖᛁᚱᛋ ᚦᛖ ᛒᚢᚱᛞᛖᚾᛋ

The mountain breeze carried the scent of pine and wildflowers, mingling with the faint aroma of smoke curling from a stone chimney. Solvig, Highwife of Ragnarvik, tilted her face to the sky, letting the warmth of the sun kiss her cheeks as she lingered on the threshold of their cabin and the wild outdoors. Her hands brushed the rough wood of the doorframe.

Below, the field stretched in waves of green and gold, dotted with splashes of violet and white where the wildflowers had claimed their place. Walls of snowcapped mountains encased the clearing as though shielding them from the outside world; a moment of true serenity.

She could hear the children's laughter—a sound so unguarded, so free, that it nearly hurt to listen. Vincent's steady, boyish voice carried on the wind, giving some stern instruction. And then came Olivja's unmistakable giggle, high and full of defiance.

Solvig's lips curved into a small smile, letting the sound settle in her chest like an ember warming her. Here, hidden in the folds of Ragnarvik's rugged mountains, the world fell away.

"They never stop, do they?" Lilli's voice came soft behind her, low and warm like honey.

Solvig turned, her heart catching for a moment, as it always did, at the sight of her.

Lilli had tied back her white hair in a loose braid, though a few strands danced in the breeze, brushing her chestnut skin. Her gown, plain for a queen, was dusted with flour from their earlier baking. She leaned against the doorframe with easy grace, the green of her eyes softer here, away from the heavy halls of her husband's keep.

"They're learning to grow," Solvig murmured, letting her gaze return to the field. "Vincent's teaching her to braid the stems properly this time, though I doubt she'll listen."

Lilli laughed, stepping closer until their shoulders brushed. "That child listens to no one."

Solvig squinted, catching sight of her daughter wrestling with a daisy stem, its delicate flower wilting in her too-small hands.

Elias ran around in circles, running stems and flowers in large batches to Olivja, desperate to help her complete the task. Vincent, standing tall for his age, reached to guide Olivja, his tone patient but firm.

"Hold it *gentle*, Olivja," Vincent instructed, demonstrating the motion. "It's not a sword." He crouched low, his small hands carefully arranging the daisy stems into a circle, "Like *this*."

His voice was steady despite his growing frustration with the toddler heiress. Olivja, still unsteady on her feet, plopped down beside him, her chubby fingers reaching for the flowers, only to crush them in her grasp *again*.

Solvig chuckled softly. "He has your care for detail."

"And they both have your stubbornness," Lilli replied, her voice tinged with affection. "Though they'll grow into it well enough." The words lingered between them, laced with an unspoken knowledge that these moments were fleeting.

Solvig reached for Lilli's hand.
She lifted it to her lips, pressing a warm kiss to her ring finger. Their eyes met—*held*.

And before the moment could steal too much, she let go, her fingers trailing over smooth knuckles one last time.

Some distances could not yet be crossed...even here.

"Do you think they'll remember these moments?" Solvig murmured.

Lilli hesitated, her gaze fixed on the children.

"Even if they forget *everything else*...I pray the gods leave them the feeling."

One burden ends...

Another begins.

Act II:
Perdyr

To Those Who Bore the Burden With Us...

The threads have been woven, yet the weight lingers still...

You have walked beside them, felt the burdens they carried, and now those burdens rest in your hands.

Take care—for the weave does not loosen, and *the next strand has already been tied*.

For every step taken, every page turned, the Norns thank you. Never have we been so bound to a story as this one. It is as if the heirs' lives were gifted to us by the gods themselves. Never once did we doubt, nor grow weary of sharing and shaping their tale.

What began as an outlet for our love blossomed into a desperate need—to share the heirs' story with the world. Though these heirs live only in heart and mind, our tears and laughter have bled onto these pages as surely as the ink itself.

Thank you for enduring the endless, draining nights, the rambling conversations, and the spiralling thoughts this world has stirred in us. We hope you feel it all.

Thank you to the historians, linguists, and mythologists whose wisdom enriched this realm. Thank you to the readers (early and present) who love and ache with the passion of these heirs, who see themselves within, and who eagerly await the next chapter. Thank you to the friends and family who stood steadfast—even as we locked ourselves away to write.

The Norns see you all. *It was never by chance that you found this story.*

The weave continues—another tale brews in the shadow...

The Authors' Note:

From Anais:
Hello! Thank you for coming this far—you must have enjoyed Act I. ;) Gods, what a ride.
This story has been brewing in our minds since we first met, slowly cultivated in our cauldrons until this very moment—and beyond. I remember the first time we talked about writing it together—back then, it was so different—a crumb compared to the cake we ended up with.
These characters, these stories, these lives feel like our children. And as women in-sapphic-love, you can only imagine how important that is for us...*(teasing!)*

I had grown so tired of poor representations of love, queer and neurodivergent voices, diverse identities, and of pagans being marked as barbaric. Tired of books being used as *selling points,* instead of being shared as *art, expression, thought, and love.* I'm tired of love having *labels,* of people forcing themselves—or being forced—into boxes for acceptance or society's sake.

We wrote this to challenge those thoughts. To challenge why the world has to name colours—when we could just enjoy their beauty.
I hope this book challenges you. I hope this story makes you question the boxes you've placed yourself in, or those others have placed you in. Or maybe, I hope it makes you feel more secure in your choices.

Life has no boundaries, no labels, no rules. It just *is.* And so are these characters, and so is this story.

I hope you found yourself yelling, crying, screaming at these pages—and I hope you fell in love with Midhelm. Because it is real. It exists. It is out there. And you are now a witness to it—so we don't have to suffer alone anymore. <3 *(Kidding!)*

Thank you from the bottom of my heart. The rest of the story is complete and on its way. This was only a taste of what's in store for you...
— With Love, Anais

From Alexis:
Thank you for making it this far into the journey!

We know how far these threads have come—and how far they will go. Your dedication does not go unnoticed.

This series began as a quiet whisper, a small spark we once giggled over—before the weight of it truly sank in. It became an anchor we hadn't noticed at first, dragging at our feet, already knotted to our hearts. Humanness has always been at the core of us, and we understood that deeply. With this story came the raw, tragic, desperate telling of lives we felt compelled to share.

Within each heart on these pages, we bleed.

Not a single character walks unscathed, for each carries a piece of us—and the love we have for one another—stitched into the very edges of their being. Every vow, every testament of love and yearning, every desperation and fate, became a love letter we wrote to each other.

Whispers of the love I hold for Anais are woven through every relationship, every confession, every kiss and laugh I had the privilege to write.

I have long carried this truth as a writer, but only now—on this journey, and in loving her—do I understand it fully. A writer is only as good as their experiences. And gods, if love is not the most relentless, transformative teacher in life, I do not know what is.

The fun of it lived in the endless nights of writing, in laughter and tears, in conversations that bled into dawn, in emotional breaks, gasped realizations in the shower or just before sleep, and in the songs we shared along the way.

I hope you've had just as many endless nights, heart flutters, and aching moments with this story as we did while creating it.

But above all—
Who you are, what you do, where you go, who you love, how you love—there are no boundaries. We do not exist to live within boxes, nor do we come into this world defined by anything. If there's one truth we hope stays with you, let it be this:

Love has no boundaries.
—Yours truly *Alexis*

In Appreciation of Some of the Ancients

This story carries within it the echoes of older voices and older loves.

To Sappho of Lesbos, *whose surviving fragments still burn with love, longing, and the delicate ache of touch. Her poetry taught us that desire is sacred, and that women's hearts have always spoken in fire.*

To Homer, and to the bond between Achilles and Patroclus, *whose grief and love endure all. Their love, buried beneath war and retelling, has been unearthed by centuries of readers and queer folk who recognised what the gods did not speak aloud.*

Their words, their silences, and their flames have shaped the hearts of these characters.

We offer this series in quiet thanks—and in loud hope that this story, in some small way, might further immortalise your love.

MEET THE AUTHORS

ANAIS & ALEXIS ARE "*THE NORNS*"

Sapphic co-writers, co-creators, and partners in every sense of the word. Both have been writing for over a decade and fell in love over their shared passion in writing, music, spirituality and life.
This is only the beginning of their saga...

Find them at:
Website: theburdensofheirs.com
Instagram: @anais.and.alexis / @theburdensofheirs
Email: Thenorns@theburdensofheirs.com

Content Warning – Full List

This series includes depictions of mature and potentially triggering content, including:

—Graphic Torture —Coercion and Manipulation
—Substance Abuse —Violence and Death —Parental Abuse
—Physical Trauma —Grief and Loss —Domestic Violence
—Abuse of Power —Complex Sexual and Romantic Relationships
—Mental Health Struggles —Sexual Content

These themes are presented with narrative intent and emotional weight that may be intense for some readers.

Intimate Romantic Chapters:

Chapters including explicit sexual content:

~~Chapter 31, Chapter 55~~

Sexual Themes/Intense Romantic Content:

~~Chapter 25, Chapter 30, Chapter 42~~

While these scenes include sexual themes and/or content, they also contain meaningful character development and emotional turning points. Skipping them is entirely your choice, but doing so may result in missing key elements of the characters' journeys.
Read in the way that feels right for you.

www.ingramcontent.com/pod-product-compliance
Lightning Source LLC
Chambersburg PA
CBHW020920310726
48980CB00011B/966/J

* 9 7 9 8 9 9 3 1 3 7 9 2 6 *